D0596069

'The author's use of the oral-history format, with its shifting voices and points of view, is a stroke of genius: the reader is in a state of near-constant confusion at the beginning, which is slowly replaced by unease and then dread as the various commentators start to see the bigger picture. A very creepy, very effective novel.' *Booklist*

'*The Three* is dark, twisted and unnerving in all the best possible ways, this is one not to miss.' *The Tattooed Book*

'Lotz manages to weave horror, dread, sorrow and satire expertly into what is, no doubt, one of the best books you'll read this year.' *Something Wicked*

'Sarah Lotz has just written the perfect horror story. This will be undoubtedly one of the best horror stories published in 2014.' *The Book Plank*

'Lotz evokes the spirit of John Wyndham's novels – that feeling of humanity under attack from forces which it would find hard to comprehend, and therefore dismisses as non-existent. There are many chilling moments within the story, but she saves the best for last – and it'll give you a whole new perspective when you come to reread the book (which you will definitely want to do).' *The Sci Fi Bulletin*

'One fantastic novel that is gripping, biting and refusing to let go.' *I09*

'*The Three* is a gripping, deeply unsettling thriller that [will] have you reading deep into the night and will stay with you long after the final page.' *Sci Fi Now*

'Imaginative, intelligent, brilliantly written, giving any mind an intense work out of the kind that extends into your dreams (or nightmares) and takes over your life for a while, this is absolutely one NOT to be missed. When you can, grab a copy, find a day that is YOURS, find yourself a corner and enter the world of *The Three*…it may be closer than you think . . .' *Liz Loves Books*

'From Chiselhurst in middle England to rural Texas to Khayelitsha in Cape Town, every character reads as real, their voices effortless and clear and resonating correctly. A stunning piece of work.' *Glen Mehn*

THE
THREE

SARAH LOTZ

HODDER

First published in Great Britain in 2014 by
Hodder & Stoughton
An Hachette UK company

First published in paperback in 2015

7

A CIP catalogue record for this title is available from the British Library

B-format ISBN 978 1 444 77038 4
A-format Paperback ISBN 978 1 444 79911 8

Printed and bound by Clays Ltd, St Ives plc
Typeset in Plantin by Hewer Text UK Ltd, Edinburgh

Hodder & Stoughton policy is to use papers that are natural, renewable
and recyclable products and made from wood grown in sustainable
forests. The logging and manufacturing processes are expected to
conform to the environmental regulations of the country of origin.

Hodder & Stoughton Ltd
338 Euston Road
London NW1 3BH

www.hodder.co.uk

For Uncle Chippy
(1929–2013)

HOW IT BEGINS

Come on, come on, come on . . .

Pam stares up at the seat belt light, willing it to click off. She's not going to be able to hold it in much longer, can almost hear Jim's voice scolding her for not going before she boarded the plane: *You know you got a weak bladder, Pam, what in the heck were you thinking?*

Truth is, she hadn't dared use one of the bathrooms at the airport. What if she found herself face to face with one of those futuristic toilets she'd read about in the guidebook and couldn't figure out how to flush it? What if she accidentally locked herself inside a stall and missed her flight? And to think Joanie suggested that she spend a few days exploring the city before taking the connecting flight to Osaka! Just the thought of navigating Tokyo's alien streets by herself makes Pam's already clammy palms sweat – the airport had been bewildering enough. Rattled and greasy after the flight from Fort Worth, she'd felt like a sluggish giant as she slogged her way towards Terminal 2 and her connecting flight. Everyone around her seemed to crackle with efficiency and confidence; compact bodies swarmed past her, briefcases swinging, eyes hidden behind sunglasses. She was aware of every extra pound she carried as she squeezed onto the shuttle, colouring each time someone shot a look in her direction.

Thankfully there had been plenty of other Americans on the flight to Tokyo (the nice boy sitting next to her had patiently shown her how to work the video system), but on this flight she's painfully aware she's the only . . . what's the word – the one they always use on the detective shows Jim likes? Caucasian, that's it.

And the seats are far smaller; she's squashed in like a canned ham. Still, at least there's an empty space in between her and the business-type fellow sitting in the aisle seat – she won't have to worry about accidentally nudging him. Although she'll have to disturb him when she squeezes out to use the bathroom, won't she? And Lordy, it looks like he's falling asleep, which means she'll have to wake him.

The plane continues to climb and still the sign glows. She peers out of the window into darkness, sees the red blipping light on the wing emerging through cloud, grips the arms of her seat and feels the aircraft's innards thrumming through her.

Jim was right. She hasn't even reached her destination and already this whole enterprise has been too much for her. He'd warned her that she wasn't cut out for long-distance travel, had tried to convince her that the whole thing was a bad idea: *Joanie can fly home anytime she likes, Pam, why bother travelling halfway around the world to see her? Why'd she want to teach Asians anyway? Aren't American kids good enough for her? And besides, Pam, you don't even like Chinese food, how in the heck are you going to cope with eating raw dolphin or whatever it is they eat over there?* But she'd stuck to her guns, chipping away at his disapproval, surprising him when she wouldn't back down. Joanie had been gone for two years and Pam needed to see her, missed her terribly, and from the photos she'd seen on the Internet, Osaka's gleaming skyscrapers didn't look that different from those of normal American cities. Joanie had warned her that she might find the culture perplexing at first, that Japan wasn't all cherry blossoms and geishas smiling coyly from behind fans, but Pam assumed she'd be able to handle it. She'd stupidly thought it would be some sort of fun adventure she'd be able to brag about to Reba for years afterwards.

The plane levels out and finally the seat belt sign pings off. There's a flurry of movement as several passengers jump up from their seats and start rummaging in the overhead compartments. Praying there won't be a queue for the bathroom, she unclicks her belt, steels herself to edge her bulk past the fellow in the aisle seat, when an almighty booming sound rockets through the plane. Pam immediately thinks of a car backfiring, but planes don't backfire, do they? She yelps – a delayed reaction that makes her feel faintly stupid. It's nothing. Thunder, maybe. Yes, that's it. The guidebook said it wasn't unusual for storms to hit—

Another bang – this one more like a gunshot. A chorus of reedy screams drifts from the front of the aircraft. The seat belt light flashes on again and Pam fumbles for the belt; her fingers are numb, she can't remember how to tighten it. The plane drops, giant hands press down on her shoulders, and her stomach feels like it's being forced up into her throat. Uh-uh. No. This can't be happening. Not to her. Things like this don't happen to people like her, ordinary people. *Good* people. A jolt – the overhead lockers rattle, then, mercifully, the aircraft seems to calm itself.

A ping, a babble of Japanese, then: 'Please remain in your seat with your seat belt tightly fastened.' Pam breathes again; the voice is serene, unconcerned. It can't be anything too serious, there's no cause for her to panic. She tries to peer over the backs of the seats to see how everyone else is reacting, can only make out a series of bowed heads.

She grasps the armrests again; the plane's vibration has increased, her hands are actually juddering, a sick throb reverberates up through her feet. An eye half-hidden behind a fringe of jet-black hair appears in the gap between the seats in front of her; it must be the small child she remembers being dragged down the aisle by a stern, lipsticked young woman just before they took off. The little boy had stared at her, clearly fascinated (you can say what you like about Asians, she'd thought, but their children are as cute as buttons). She'd waved and grinned, but he hadn't responded, and then his mother had barked something at him and he'd slid obediently into his seat, out of sight. She tries to smile, but her mouth is dry and her lips catch on her teeth and oh Lordy, the vibration is getting worse.

A white mist floats down the aisle, drifts around her, and Pam finds herself batting uselessly at the screen in front of her, fumbling for her headphones. This isn't happening. This can't be happening right now, uh-uh. No, no, no. If she can just make the screen work, watch a movie, something reassuring – like that romcom she'd seen on the way here, the one with . . . Ryan somebody. The plane lists violently again – it feels as if it's rolling from side to side *and* up and down and her stomach flips again – she swallows convulsively, she won't be sick, uh-uh.

The businessman stands up, arms flailing as the plane heaves – it looks like he's trying to open the overhead locker, but he can't get his balance. *What are you doing?* Pam wants to scream – has the feeling that if he doesn't sit down the situation will get worse – the vibration is getting so bad it makes her think of the time her washing machine's stabiliser broke and the darn thing bucked across the floor. A flight attendant looms out of the mist, gripping the seat backs around her. She gestures at the businessman, who meekly falls back into his seat. He fumbles in his inside jacket pocket, pulls out a phone, rests his forehead against the seat in front of him and starts talking into it.

She should do the same. She should phone Jim, tell him about Snookie, remind him not to feed her that cheap stuff. She should phone Joanie; but tell her what – she almost laughs – that she might be late? No, tell her that she's proud of her, but – can they even get a signal here? Won't using her cellphone mess with the plane's navigational systems? Does she need a credit card to work the handset on the back of her seat?

Where is her phone? Is it in her fanny pack with her money and passport and pills, or did she put it in the bag? Why can't she remember? She reaches down for her purse, her stomach feeling like it's squashed against her spine. She's going to vomit, she just knows she is, but then her fingers touch the strap of her bag – Joanie had given it to her the Christmas before she left two years ago – that had been a good Christmas, even Jim had been in a good mood that day. Another jolt and the strap leaps away from her grip. She doesn't want to die like this – not like this. Not amongst strangers, not looking like this, with her hair greasy – that new perm had been a mistake – her ankles swollen, uh-uh. No way. Quickly – think of something nice, something good. Yes. This is all a dream, she's actually sitting on the couch with a chicken mayo sandwich, Snookie on her lap, Jim dozing off in his La-Z-Boy. She knows she should pray, knows that this is what Pastor Len would tell her to do – if she prays, will it all go away? – but for once in her life she can't think of the words. She manages a 'help me, Jesus', but other thoughts keep intruding. Who'll look after Snookie if something happens to her? Snookie's old, nearly ten, why did she leave her? Dogs don't understand. Oh Lord, there's that pile of ripped pantyhose hidden in the back of her underwear drawer that she keeps meaning to throw away – what will they think of her if they find it?

The mist is thickening, burning bile rises in her throat, her vision blurs. A sharp *crack*, and a yellow plastic cup swings into her eye-line. More Japanese words – her ears are popping, she swallows, realises she can taste the spicy noodle mess she ate on the last flight, has time to feel relief that she no longer needs to pee. Then English: *something help fellow passengers something something*.

The businessman continues to babble into his phone, it's torn out of his hand as the plane bucks once more, but his mouth keeps moving; he doesn't seem to be aware he's no longer holding it. She can't get enough air into her lungs, it tastes tinny, artificial, gritty, makes her gag again. Flashes of bright light blind her momentarily, she reaches for the mask, but it keeps swinging out of her reach and then she smells something burning – like plastic left on a stove top. She'd done that once, left a spatula on the burner – Jim had gone on about it for weeks. *You could have burned the house down, woman.*

Another message . . . *brace, brace, brace for impact.*

An image of an empty chair fills her head and she's flooded with self-pity so acute it hurts – it's her chair, the one she always sits on every Wednesday at Bible group. A sturdy, reliable, *friendly* chair that never complains about her weight, its seat pitted with wear. She always gets to the meeting early to help Kendra put the chairs out, and everyone knows that she always sits to the right of Pastor Len, next to the coffee maker. They'd prayed for her the day before she left – even Reba had wished her well. Her chest had filled with pride and gratitude, her cheeks burning from being the centre of so much attention. *Dear Jesus, please take care of our sister and dear friend, Pamela, as she* . . . The plane shudders – and this time it's joined by a thuck thuck thuck as bags and laptops and other debris spill out of the overhead compartments, but if she keeps concentrating on that empty chair, then everything will be fine. Like that game she sometimes plays when she drives back from the store: if she sees three white cars, then Pastor Len will ask her and not Reba to do the flowers.

A rending sound like giant metal fingernails scoring a blackboard, the floor convulses, a weight pushes her head towards her lap, she feels her teeth knocking against each other, wants to scream at whoever is viciously yanking her hands above her head to stop. Years ago, a pick-up had pulled out in front of her car as she was driving to fetch Joanie from school. At that moment everything had slowed right down – she'd been aware of tiny details, the crack in her windscreen, the rust peppering the other car's bonnet, the shadowy shape of its baseball-capped driver – but this, this is happening too fast! *Make it stop it's going on for too long* – she's whipped and pummelled and beaten; her head, she can't keep her head up and then the seat in front of her rushes up to her face and then white light flares, blinding her and she can't—

A bonfire crackles and spits, but her cheeks are cold; freezing in fact, there's a real bite in the air. Is she outside? Of course she is! Stupid. You can't have bonfires indoors, can you? Where is she though? They always have a get-together at Pastor Len's ranch on Christmas Eve – she must be out in the yard, watching the fireworks. She always brings her famous blue cheese dip. No wonder she's feeling so lost! She's forgotten to bring the dip, must have left it on the counter – Pastor Len will be so disappointed and—

Someone's screaming – *you can't scream at Christmas, why are you screaming at Christmas? It's a happy time.*

She lifts her left hand to wipe her face, but can't seem to . . . that's not right, she's lying on her arm, it's twisted behind her back. Why is she lying down? Has she fallen asleep? Not at Christmas when there's always so much to do . . . she has to get up, apologise for being so rude, Jim's always saying she needs to buck up her ideas, try and be a little bit more . . .

She runs her tongue over her teeth. They don't feel right; one of her incisors is chipped, the edge nips her tongue. She crunches down on grit, swallows – Lordy, her throat feels like she's been swallowing razorblades, is she—

And then the knowledge of what's happened hits her all at once, the force of it making her gasp, and with it comes a white surge of pain, blooming up from her right leg and shooting into her stomach. *Get up, get up, get up.* She tries to lift her head, but when she does, hot needles spike the back of her neck.

Another scream – it sounds fairly close to her. She's never heard anything like it – it's naked, raw, barely human. She needs it to stop, it's making the ache in her gut worse, as if the scream is directly connected to her innards, tugging at them with every wail.

Oh thank you, Jesus, she can move her right arm and she inches it up, probes her belly, touches something soft and wet and just plain *wrong*. She won't think about that now. Oh Jesus, she needs help, she needs someone to come and help her, if only she'd listened to Jim and stayed at home with Snookie and hadn't thought all those bad thoughts about Reba . . .

Stop it. She can't panic. That's what they always say, don't panic. She's alive. She should be grateful. She needs to get up, see where she is. She's no longer in her seat, she knows that for sure, she's lying on some sort of mossy, soft surface. She counts to three, tries to use her good arm to heave herself over onto her side, but she's forced to stop as a flare of agony – as sharp and startling as an electric shock – flashes through her entire body. It's so intense she can't believe the pain actually belongs to her. She keeps absolutely still, and mercifully, it begins to fade, leaving a worrying numbness in its wake (but she won't think about that either, nuh-uh).

She squeezes her eyes shut, opens them. Blinks to clear her vision. Tentatively she tries to turn her head to the right, and this time she's able to do so without that horrible, intrusive pain. *Good.* A bruise of orange light in the background casts everything in silhouette, but she can make out a thick grove of trees – strange twisted trees, ones she can't identify – and there, just in front of them, a curved piece of twisted metal. Oh Lordy, is that the plane? It is . . . she can see the oblong shape of a window. A pop, a hissing sound, a soft boom and the scene is suddenly lit up clear as day. Her eyes water, but she won't look away. She won't. She can see the jagged edge of the fuselage, cruelly sheared from the rest of its body – where is the rest? Was she sitting in that part? Impossible. She couldn't have survived that. It's like a huge broken toy, makes her think of the yards around the trailers where Jim's mother used to live. They were scattered with debris and old car parts and broken tricycles and she hadn't liked to go there, even though Jim's mother had always been kind to her . . . Her vision is limited due to her position, and she ignores the cracking sound she hears as she cranes her head so that her cheek is resting against her shoulder.

The screaming ceases abruptly, mid-howl. *Good.* She doesn't want this time to be muddied with someone else's pain and noise.

Wait . . . Something's moving, just over by the tree line. A dark shape – a person – a small person, a child? The child who was sitting in front of her? She's flooded with shame – she hadn't given him or his mother a moment's thought as the plane dropped. She'd only thought of herself. No wonder she couldn't pray, what sort of Christian is she? The figure flits frustratingly out of her line of sight, but she can't inch her neck any further over.

She tries to open her mouth to shout; can't seem to make her jaw move this time. *Please. I'm here. Hospital. Get help.*

A soft thud behind her head. 'Ack,' she manages. 'Ack.' Something touches her hair, and she feels tears rolling down her cheeks – she's safe. They're here to rescue her.

The shush-pad of running feet. *Don't go. Don't leave me.*

Bare feet suddenly appear in front of her eyes. Small feet, dirty, it's dark, so dark, but they look to be smeared with black goop – mud? blood?

'Help me, help me, help me,' that's it, she's talking now. Good girl. If she's talking she's going to be fine. She's just in shock. Yep. That's all. 'Help me.'

A face looms towards her; it's so close she can feel the whisper of the boy's breath on her cheeks. She tries to focus on his eyes. Are they . . .? Nuh-uh. It's just the poor light. They're white, all white, no pupils *oh Jesus help me*. A scream grows in her chest, lodges in her throat, she can't get it out, it's going to choke her. The face jerks away. Her lungs are heavy, liquid. Now it hurts to breathe.

Something flickers in the far right of her field of vision. Is it that same child? How could he have got all the way over there so quickly? He's pointing at something . . . Shapes, darker than the trees around them. People. Definitely people. The orange glow is fading, but she can see their outlines clearly. Hundreds of them, it looks like, and they're coming towards her. Drifting out of the trees, those strange trees, knobbled and bubbled and twisted like fingers.

Where are their feet? They don't have feet. That's not right.

Uh-uh. They aren't real. They can't be real. She can't see their eyes, their faces are inky black blobs that remain flat and unmoving as the light behind them blooms and dies.

They're coming for her – she knows this.

The fear ebbs away, replaced with a certainty that she doesn't have long. It's as if a cold, confident Pam – a new Pam, the Pam she's always wanted to be – enters and takes over her battered, dying body. Ignoring the mess where her stomach once was, she gropes for her fanny pack. It's still here, although it's shifted around to her side. She closes her eyes and concentrates on opening the zip. Her fingers are wet, slippery, but she's not going to give up now.

The whup-whup sound fills her ears, louder this time, a light floats down from above and dances over and around her and she can make out a row of disembodied seats, the metal struts catching the light; a high-heeled shoe that looks brand new. She waits to see if the light will halt the crowd's approach. They continue to creep forward, and still she can't make out any facial features. And where is the boy? If only she could tell him not to go near them, because she knows what they want, oh yes, she knows exactly what they want. But she can't think about that now, not when she's so close. She digs inside her bag, yips with relief when her fingers graze the smooth back of her phone. Careful not to drop it, she ekes it out of the bag – has time to marvel at the panic she felt earlier when she couldn't remember where she'd put it – and instructs her arm to bring it up to her face. What if it doesn't work? What if it's broken?

It won't be broken, she won't let it be broken, and she caws in triumph when she hears the chiming do-do-do-dah welcome message. Nearly there . . . A tut of exasperation – she's such a messy bunny, there's blood all over the screen. Using the last of her strength to concentrate, she finds her way to the applications box, scrolls to 'voice recorder'. The whup-whupping is deafening now, but Pam shuts it out, just as she ignores the fact that she can no longer see.

She holds the phone to her mouth and starts speaking.

BLACK THURSDAY

FROM CRASH TO CONSPIRACY

Inside the phenomenon of The Three

ELSPETH MARTINS

Jameson & White Publishers

New York ✶ London ✶ Los Angeles

A NOTE FROM THE AUTHOR

There can be few readers who do not feel a frisson of dread when the words Black Thursday are mentioned. That day – January 12, 2012 – when four commuter planes went down within hours of each other, resulting in the deaths of over a thousand people, has joined the annals of the devastating disasters that have changed the way we look at the world.

Predictably, within weeks of the incidents, the market was flooded with non-fiction accounts, blogs, biographies and opinion pieces, all cashing in on the public's morbid fascination with the accidents themselves, and the child plane crash survivors known as The Three. But no one could have predicted the macabre chain of events that would follow or how fast they would unfold.

As I did in *Snapped*, my investigation into gun crime perpetrated by US children under the age of sixteen, I decided that if I was going to add my voice to the mix, the only way forward was to collate an objective account, letting those involved speak in their own words. To this end, I have drawn from a wide variety of sources, including Paul Craddock's unfinished biography, Chiyoko Kamamoto's collected messages, and interviews personally conducted by me during and immediately after the events in question.

I make no apologies for the inclusion of subject matter that some may find upsetting, such as the accounts of those who were first on the scenes of the tragedies; the statements from former and current Pamelists; the *isho* found at the crash site of Sun Air Flight 678; and the never-before-published interview with the exorcist hired by Paul Craddock.

While I freely admit to having included excerpts from newspaper reports and magazine articles as context (and, to some extent, as a narrative device), my main motivation, as it was in *Snapped*, is to provide an unbiased platform for the perspectives of those closest to the main players in the events that occurred from January to July, 2012. With this in mind, I urge readers to remember that these accounts are subjective and to draw their own conclusions.

Elspeth Martins
New York
August 30, 2012

They're here. I'm . . . don't let Snookie eat chocolate, it's poison for dogs, she'll beg you, the boy. The boy watch the boy watch the dead people oh Lordy there's so many . . . They're coming for me now. We're all going soon. All of us. Bye Joanie I love the bag bye Joanie, Pastor Len warn them that the boy he's not to—

The last words of Pamela May Donald (1961–2012)

PART ONE

CRASH

From chapter one of *Guarding JESS: My Life With One of The Three* by Paul Craddock (co-written with Mandi Solomon).

I've always liked airports. Call me an old romantic, but I used to get a kick out of watching families and lovers reuniting – that split second when the weary and sunburned emerge through the sliding glass doors and recognition lights up their eyes. So when Stephen asked me to collect him and the girls from Gatwick, I was more than happy to do it.

I left with a good hour to spare. I wanted to get there early, grab myself a coffee and people-watch for a bit. Odd to think of it now, but I was in a wonderful mood that afternoon. I'd had a call-back for the part of the gay butler in the third series of *Cavendish Hall* (type-casting, of course, but Gerry, my agent, thought it could finally be my big break), and I'd managed to find a parking spot that wasn't a day's hike from the entrance. As it was one of my treat days, I bought myself a latte with extra cream, and wandered over to join the throng waiting for passengers to emerge from baggage reclaim. Next to a Cup 'n' Chow outlet, a team of bickering work-experience kids were doing an execrable job of dismantling a tacky Christmas display that was well-overdue for removal, and I watched their mini drama unfold for a while, oblivious that my own was about to begin.

I hadn't thought to check the flight information board to make sure the plane was on time, so I was taken unawares when a nasal voice droned over the intercom: 'Could all those awaiting the arrival of Go!Go! Airlines Flight 277 from Tenerife please make their way to the information counter, thank you.' *Isn't that Stephen's flight?* I thought, double-checking the details on my BlackBerry. I wasn't too concerned. I suppose I assumed the flight had been delayed. It didn't occur to me to wonder why Stephen hadn't called to let me know he'd be late.

You never think it's going to happen to you, do you?

There was only a small group of us at first – others, like me, who'd arrived early. A pretty girl with dyed red hair holding a heart-shaped balloon on a stick, a dreadlocked fellow with a wrestler's build and a middle-aged couple with smokers' skin who were dressed in identical cerise shell suits. Not the sort of people with whom I'd usually choose to associate. Odd how one's first impressions can be so wrong. I now count them all among my closest friends. Well, this type of thing brings you together, doesn't it?

I should have known from the shell-shocked expressions on the faces of the spotty teenager manning the counter and the whey-faced security woman hovering next to him that something horrific was afoot, but all I was feeling at that stage was irritation.

'What's going on?' I snapped in my best *Cavendish Hall* accent.

The teenager managed to stutter that we were to follow him to where 'more info would be relayed to us'.

We all did as we were told, although I confess I was surprised the shell-suited couple didn't kick up more of a stink, they didn't look the type to take orders. But as they told me weeks later at one of our '277 Together' meetings, at that stage they were in denial. They didn't *want* to know, and if anything untoward had happened to the plane, they didn't want to hear it from a boy who was barely out of puberty. The teenager scurried ahead, presumably so that none of us would have the chance to interrogate him further, and ushered us through an innocuous door next to the customs' offices. We were led down a long corridor, which, judging by its peeling paint and scuffed floor, wasn't in a section of the airport typically encountered by the public gaze. I remember smelling a rogue whiff of cigarette smoke wafting in from somewhere in a flagrant disregard of the smoking ban.

We ended up in a grim windowless lounge, furnished with tired burgundy waiting-room seats. My eye was caught by one of those seventies tubular ashtrays, which was half-hidden behind a plastic hydrangea. Funny what you remember, isn't it?

A guy in a polyester suit clutching a clipboard waddled towards us, his Adam's apple bobbing up and down like a Tourette's sufferer's. Although as pale as a cadaver, his cheeks were alive with a severe shaving rash. His eyes darted all over the place, briefly met mine, then his gaze settled into the far distance.

It hit me then, I think. The sickening knowledge that I was about to hear something that would change my life forever.

'Go on then, mate,' Kelvin – the fellow with the dreads – finally said.

The suit swallowed convulsively. 'I am extremely sorry to relay this to you, but Flight 277 disappeared off the radar approximately an hour ago.'

The world swayed, and I could feel the first wisps of a panic attack. My fingers were tingling and my chest was starting to tighten. Then Kelvin asked the question the rest of us were too afraid to ask: 'Has it crashed?'

'We cannot be certain at this time, but please be assured we will relay the information to you as soon as it comes in. Counsellors will be available for any of you who—'

'What about survivors?'

The suit's hands were trembling and the winking cartoon plane on his plastic Go!Go! badge seemed to mock us with its cheeky insouciance. 'Should have called it Gay!Gay! Air,' Stephen used to quip whenever one of Go!Go!'s dire adverts came on the television. He was always joking that that cartoon plane was camper than a bus-load of drag queens. I didn't take offence; that was the sort of relationship we had. 'Like I say,' the suit flustered, 'we have counsellors at your disposal—'

Mel – the female half of the track-suited couple – spoke up. 'Sod your counsellors, just tell us what's happened!'

The girl holding the balloon started sobbing with the gusto of an *EastEnders* character, and Kelvin put his arm around her. She dropped the balloon and I watched as it bounced sadly across the floor, eventually ending up lodged next to the retro ashtray. Other people were starting to drift into the room, ushered by more Go!Go! staff – most of whom looked as bewildered and unprepared as the spotty teenager.

Mel's face was as pink as her shell-suit top and she was jabbing a finger in the official's face. Everyone seemed to be screaming or crying, but I felt a curious distance from what was going on, as if I was on set, waiting for my cue. And this is a ghastly thing to admit, but I thought, *remember what you're feeling, Paul, you can use it in your acting*. I'm not proud of that. I'm just being honest.

I kept staring at that balloon, and suddenly I could hear Jessica and Polly's voices, clear as a bell: 'But Uncle Paaaaauuuuul, what keeps the plane in the air?' Stephen had asked me round to Sunday lunch the week before they left, and the twins hadn't stopped badgering me about the flight, for some reason assuming I was the font of all knowledge about air travel. It was the kids' first time on a plane, and they were more excited about that than they were about the holiday. I found myself trying to remember the last thing Stephen had said to me, something along the lines of, 'See you when you're older, mate.' We're non-identical, but how could I not have sensed something awful had happened? I dragged my phone out of my pocket, recalling that Stephen had sent me a text the day before: 'Girls say hi. Resort full of twats. We get in at 3.30. Don't be late ;).' I thumbed through my messages, trying to find it. It was suddenly absolutely vital that I save it. It wasn't there – I must have accidentally deleted it.

Even weeks afterwards, I wished I'd kept that text message.

Somehow, I found myself back in the Arrivals area. I don't remember how I even got there, or if anyone tried to stop me leaving that ghastly lounge. I drifted along, sensing that people were staring at me, but right then, they were as insignificant as extras. There was something in the air, like that heavy feeling you get just before a storm hits. I thought, sod it, I need a drink, which, since I'd been on the wagon for a good ten years, wasn't like me. I sleep-walked towards the Irish theme pub on the far side of the area. A group of suited yobs were gathered around the bar staring up at the TV. One of them, a florid-faced prat with a Mockney accent, was talking too loudly, going on about 9/11, and telling everyone that he had to get to Zurich by 5.50 or 'heads would roll'. He stopped, mid-sentence, as I approached, and the others made room for me, drawing back as if I were contagious. Of course, I've learned since then that grief and horror *are* contagious.

The TV's sound was up to full volume and an anchor – one of those botoxed American horrors with Tom Cruise teeth and too much make-up – was yabbering into shot. Behind her was a screen capture of what looked to be some sort of swamp, a helicopter hovering over it. And then I read the strap-line: Maiden Airlines Everglades crash.

They've got it wrong, I thought. *Stephen and the girls were on Go!Go!, not that plane.*

And then it hit me. Another plane had gone down.

At 14.35 (CAT time), an Antonov cargo and passenger plane leased by Nigerian carrier Dalu Air crashed into the heart of Khayelitsha – Cape Town's most populous township. Liam de Villiers was one of the first paramedics on the scene. An Advanced Life Support Paramedic for Cape Medical Response at the time of the incident, Liam now works as a trauma counsellor. This interview was conducted via Skype and email and collated into a single account.

We were dealing with an incident on Baden Powell Drive when it happened. A taxi had clipped a Merc and overturned, but it wasn't too hectic. The taxi was empty at the time, and although the driver had only minor injuries, we'd need to ferry him to Casualty to get stitched up. It was one of those rare still days, the southeaster that had been raging for weeks had blown itself out, and there was only a wisp of cloud trickling over the lip of Table Mountain. A perfect day, I guess you could say, although we were parked a bit too close to the Macassar sewage works for comfort. After smelling that for twenty minutes, I was grateful I hadn't had a chance to scarf down the KFC I'd bought for lunch.

I was on with Cornelius that day, one of our newer guys. He was a cool oke, good sense of humour. While I dealt with the driver, he was gossiping with a couple of traffic cops who were on the scene. The taxi-driver was shouting into his cellphone, lying to his boss while I dressed the wound on his upper arm. You wouldn't have known anything had happened to him; he didn't flinch once. I was just about to ask Cornelius if he'd let False Bay Casualty know we were en route with a patient, when a roaring sound ripped out of the sky, making all of us jump. The taxi-driver's hand went limp and his phone clattered to the ground.

And then we saw it. I know everyone says this, but it was exactly like watching a scene from a movie; you couldn't believe it was actually happening. It was flying so low I could see the chipped paint in its logo – you know, that green swirl curving round a 'D'. Its landing gear was down and the wings were dipping crazily from side to side like a rope-walker trying to get his balance. I remember thinking, airport's the other way, what the fuck is the pilot doing?

Cornelius was shouting something, pointing at it. I couldn't hear what he was saying, but I got the gist. Mitchell's Plain, where his family lived, wasn't that far away from where the plane looked to be headed. It was obvious it was going to crash; it wasn't on fire or anything like that, but it was clear it was in severe trouble.

The plane disappeared out of sight, there was a 'crump', and I swear, the ground shook. Later, Darren, our base controller, said that we were probably too far away to feel any kind of after-shock, but that's how I remember it. Seconds later a black cloud blossomed into the sky. Huge it was, made me think of those pictures of Hiroshima. And I thought, yissus, no way did anyone survive that.

We didn't stop to think. Cornelius jumped in the driver's seat, started radioing the base station, telling them we had a major inci-dent on our hands and to notify the centre for disaster management. I told the taxi-driver he'd have to wait for another ambulance to take him to casualty and shouted, 'Tell them it's a Phase Three, tell them it's a Phase Three!' The cops were already on the road, head-ing straight for the Khayelitsha Harare turn-off. I jumped in the back of the ambulance, the adrenaline shooting through me, wash-ing away all the tiredness I was feeling after being on duty for twelve hours.

While Cornelius drove, following in the wake of the police car, I pulled out the bergen, started rummaging in the lockers for the burn shields, the intravenous bottles, anything I thought we might need, and placed them on the stretcher at the back. We're trained for this of course – for a plane going down, I mean. There's a designated ditch site in Fish Hoek in False Bay, and I wondered if that was where the pilot was heading when he realised he wasn't going to make the airport. But I won't lie, training is one thing, I never thought we'd have to deal with a situation like this.

That drive is etched on my memory like you won't believe. The crackle and pop of the radio as voices conferred, Cornelius's white-knuckled hands on the steering-wheel, the reek of the Streetwise two-piece meal I'd never get to eat. And look, this is going to sound bad, but there are parts of Khayelitsha we usually wouldn't dream of entering, we've had incidents when staff have been held up – all the ambulance services will tell you that – but this was different. It didn't even occur to me to worry about going into Little Brazzaville. Darren was back on the radio, talking Cornelius through the procedure, telling him that we were to wait for the scene to be secured first. In situations like these, there's no place for heroes. You don't want to get yourself injured, end up another casualty for the guys to deal with.

As we got closer to the site, I could hear screams mingling with the sirens that were coming from all directions. Smoke rolled towards us, coating the windscreen in a greasy residue, and Cornelius had to slow down and put on his wipers. The acrid smell of burning fuel filled the ambulance. I couldn't get that stench out of my skin for days. Cornelius slammed on the brakes as a crowd of people flooded towards us. Most were carrying TVs, crying children, furniture – dogs even. They weren't looting, these guys, they knew how quickly a fire could spread in this area. Most of the houses are slapped together, shacks made of wood and corrugated iron, a lot of them little more than kindling, not to mention the amount of paraffin that had to be lying around.

We slowed to a crawl, and I could hear the thunk of hands slapping the side of the ambulance. I actually ducked when I heard the crump of another explosion, and I thought, shit, this is it. Helicopters swarmed overhead and I yelled at Cornelius to stop – it was obvious we couldn't go much further without endangering our safety. I climbed out of the back, tried to steel myself for what we were about to face.

It was chaos. If I hadn't seen it with my own eyes, I wouldn't have known it was a plane gone down – I would've assumed a bloody great bomb had gone off. And the heat that was coming from there. . . I saw the footage afterwards, the helicopter footage, that black gouge in the ground, the shacks that were flattened, that school those Americans built, crushed as if it was made of matchsticks; the church split in half as if it was as insubstantial as a garden shed.

'There's more! There's more! Help us!' people were shouting. 'Over here! Over here!'

It seemed like hundreds of people surged towards us yelling for help, but fortunately the cops who were on the scene of the minor collision pushed most of them back, and we could assess what we were dealing with. Cornelius started organising them into triage groups – sorting out who was most in need of urgent attention. I knew immediately that the first child I saw wasn't going to make it. His distraught mother said they were both sleeping when she heard a deafening roar and chunks of debris rained into their bedroom. We know now that the plane broke up on impact, scattering burning parts like Agent Orange.

A doctor from the Khayelitsha hospital was first on the scene, doing a fantastic job. That oke was on the ball. Even before the disaster management team showed up, he'd already allocated areas for the triage tents, morgue and the ambulance station. There's a system with these things, you can't go in half-cocked. They set up the outer circle in record time, and the airport's fire and rescue service were there minutes after we arrived to secure the area. It was vital they made sure that we weren't going to have any more follow-up explosions on our hands. We were all aware of how much oxygen planes carry, never mind fuel.

We dealt mostly with the peripheral casualties. The majority were burns, limbs hacked by flying metal, quite a few amputations, lot of people with ocular issues – specially the children. Cornelius and I just went into overdrive. The cops kept the people back, but you couldn't blame them for crowding around us. Screaming for lost relatives, parents looking for children who were at that school and crèche, others demanding to know the status of injured loved ones. Quite a few were filming it on their cellphones – I didn't blame them – it provides a distance, doesn't it? And the press were everywhere, swarming around us. I had to stop

Cornelius from punching an oke with a camera slung on his shoulder who kept trying to get right up into his face.

And as the smoke died down, you could see the extent of the devastation, bit by bit. Crumpled metal, scraps of clothing, broken furniture and appliances, discarded shoes, a trampled cellphone. And bodies of course. Most were burned up, but there were others, pieces, you know . . . There were yells going up all around as more and more were discovered, the tent they were using as a makeshift morgue just wasn't going to cut it.

We worked through the day and well into the night. As it got darker, they lit up the site with floodlights, and somehow, that was worse. Even with their protective breathing gear, some of the younger disaster management volunteers couldn't deal with it; you could see them running off to vomit.

Those body bags kept piling up.

Not a day goes by that I don't think about it. I still can't eat fried chicken.

You know what happened to Cornelius, right? His wife says she'll never be able to forgive him, but I do. I know what it feels like when you're anxious all the time, you can't sleep, you start crying for no reason. That's why I got into trauma counselling.

Look, unless you were there, there's no way to adequately describe it, but let me try to put it in context for you. I've been doing this for over twenty years, and I've seen some hectic stuff. I've been at the aftermath of a necklacing, the body still smoking, the face fixed in an expression you don't want to see in your worst nightmares. I was on duty when the municipal workers' strike turned bad and the cops opened fire – thirty dead and not all from bullet wounds. You don't want to see the damage a panga can do. I've been at car pile-ups where the bodies of children, babies still in their car seats, have been flung across three lanes of traffic. I've seen what happens when a Buffel truck loses its brakes and rolls over a Ford Ka. And when I was working in the Botswana bush, I came across the remains of a ranger who'd been bitten in half by a hippo. Nothing can compare with what we saw that day. We all understood what Cornelius went through – the whole crew understood.

He did it in his car, out on the West Coast, where he used to go fishing. Asphyxiation, hose from the exhaust. No mess, no fuss.

I miss him.

Afterwards, we got a lot of flak for taking photos of the scene and putting them up on Facebook. But I'm not going to apologise for that. That's one of the ways we deal with it – we need to talk it through – and if you're not on the job, you won't understand. There's some talk of taking them down now, seeing as those freaks keep using them in their propaganda. Growing up in a country like this, with our history, I'm not a fan of censorship, but I can see why they're clamping down. Just adds fuel to the fire.

But I tell you something, I was there, right at ground fucking zero, and no ways did anyone on that plane survive. No ways. I stand by that, whatever those conspiracy fuckers say (excuse my French).

I still stand by that.

Yomijuri Miyajima, a geologist and volunteer suicide monitor at Japan's notorious Aokigahara forest, a popular spot for the depressed to end their lives, was on duty the night a Boeing 747-400D, operated by the Japanese domestic carrier Sun Air, plummeted into the foot of Mount Fuji.

(Translation by Eric Kushan).

I was expecting to find one body that night. Not hundreds.

Volunteers do not usually patrol at night, but just as it was getting dark, our station received a call from a father deeply concerned about his teenage son. The boy's father had intercepted worrying emails and found a copy of Wataru Tsurumi's suicide manual under his son's mattress. Along with the notorious Matsumoto novel, it's a popular text for those who seek to end their lives in the forest; I have come across more discarded copies than I can count in my years working here.

There are a few cameras set up to monitor suspicious activity at the most popular entrance, but I had received no confirmation that he had been seen, and while I had a description of the teenager's car, I couldn't see any sign of it at the side of the road or in any of the small parking lots close to the forest. This meant nothing. Often people will drive to remote or hidden spots on the edge of the forest to end their lives. Some attempt to kill themselves with exhaust fumes; others by inhaling the toxic smoke from portable charcoal barbecues. But by far the most common method is hanging. Many of the suicidal bring tents and supplies with them, as if they need to spend a night or two contemplating what it is they are about to do before going through with it.

Every year, the local police and many volunteers sweep the forest to find the bodies of those who have chosen to die here. The last time we did this – in late November – we discovered the remains of thirty souls. Most of them were never identified. If I come across someone in the forest who I think may be planning on killing himself, I ask him to consider the pain of the family he will be leaving behind and remind him that there is always hope. I point to the volcanic rock that forms the base of the forest floor, and say that if the trees can grow on such a hard, unforgiving surface, then a new life can be built on the foundation of any hardship.

It is now common practice for the desperate to bring tape to use as a marker to find their way back if they change their minds, or, in most cases, to indicate where their bodies may be found. Others use the tape for more nefarious reasons; ghoulish sight-seers hoping to come across one of the deceased, but not willing to become lost.

I volunteered to venture into the forest on foot, and with this in mind, I first checked to see if there was any indication that fresh tape had been tied around the trees. It was dark, so it was impossible for me to be sure, but I thought I discerned signs that someone had recently made his way past the 'do not pass this point' signs.

I was not concerned about getting lost. I know the forest; I have never once lost my way. Apologies for sounding fanciful, but after doing this for twenty-five years, it has become part of me. And I had a powerful flashlight and my GPS – it is not true that the volcanic rock under the forest floor muddies the signals. But the forest is a magnet for myths and legends, and people will believe what they want to.

Once you are in the forest, it cocoons you. The tops of the trees form a softly undulating roof that shuts out the world beyond. Some may find the forest's stillness and silence forbidding, I do not. The *y rei* do not frighten me. I have nothing to fear from the spirits of the dead. Perhaps you have heard the stories, that this place was a common site for *ubasute*, the practice of abandoning the aged or infirm to die of exposure in times of famine? This is unsubstantiated. Just another of the many stories the forest attracts. There are many who believe that spirits are lonely, and they try to draw people to them. They believe this is why so many come to the forest.

I did not see the plane going down – as I said, the forest's canopy conceals the sky – but I heard it. A series of muffled booms, like giant doors slamming shut. What did I think it was? I suppose I assumed that it might have been thunder, although it wasn't the season for storms or typhoons. I was too absorbed in searching the shadows, dips and ruts in the forest floor for evidence of the teenager's presence to speculate.

I was about to give up when my radio crackled, and Sato-san, one of my fellow monitors, alerted me to the fact that a troubled plane had veered off its flight path and crashed somewhere in the vicinity of the forest – more than likely in the Narusawa area. Of course I realised then that this was the source of the booming sound I heard earlier.

Sato indicated that the authorities were on their way, and said that he was organising a search party. He sounded out of breath, deeply shocked. He knew as well as I did how difficult it was going to be for rescuers to reach the site. The terrain in some parts of the forest is almost impossible to navigate – there are deep hidden crevices in many areas that make traversing through it dangerous.

I decided to head north, in the direction of the sound I had heard.

Within an hour, I could hear the roar of the rescue helicopters sweeping the forest. I knew it would be impossible for them to land, and so I ventured forward with added urgency. If there were survivors, then I knew they had to be reached quickly. Within two hours, I started to smell smoke; the trees had caught alight in several areas, but thankfully the fires hadn't spread and their limbs glowed as the flames refused to catch and began to die. Something made me sweep the beam of my flashlight up into the trees, catching on a small shape hanging in the branches. At first, I assumed it was the charred body of a monkey.

It was not.

There were others, of course. The night was alive with the sound of rescue and press helicopters, and as they swooped above me, their lights illuminated countless forms caught in the branches. Some I could see in great detail; they looked barely injured, almost as if they were sleeping. Others . . . Others were not so fortunate. All were partially clothed or naked.

I struggled to reach what is now known as the main crash site, where the tail and the sheared wing were found. Rescuers were being winched to the site, but it was not possible for the helicopters to land on such uneven and treacherous terrain.

It felt strange nearing the tail of the aircraft. It towered over me, its proud red logo eerily intact. I ran to where a couple of air paramedics were tending to a woman who was moaning on the ground; I couldn't tell how badly injured she was, but I have never heard such a sound coming from a human being. It was then that I caught a flicker of movement in my peripheral vision. Some of the trees were still aflame in this area, and I saw a small hunched shape partially hidden behind an outcropping of twisted volcanic rock. I hurried towards it, and I caught the glint of a pair of eyes in the beam of my flashlight. I dropped my backpack, and ran, moving faster than I have ever done before or since.

As I approached I realised I was looking at a child. A boy.

He was crouching, shivering violently, and I could see that one of his shoulders appeared to be protruding at an unnatural angle. I shouted at the paramedics to come quickly, but they could not hear me over the sound of the helicopters.

What did I say to him? It is hard to remember exactly, but it would have been something like, 'Are you okay? Don't panic, I'm here now to help you.'

So thick was the shroud of blood and mud covering his body that at first I did not realise he was naked – they said later that his clothes were blown off by the force of the impact. I reached out to touch him. His flesh was cold – but what do you expect? The temperature was below freezing.

I am not ashamed to say that I cried.

I wrapped my jacket around him, and as carefully as I could, I picked him up. He placed his head on my shoulder and whispered, 'Three.' Or at least that is what I thought he said. I asked him to repeat what he had said, but by then his eyes were closed, his mouth slack as if he was fast asleep and I was more concerned

about getting him to safety and keeping him warm before hypothermia set in.

Of course now everyone keeps asking me: did you think there
was anything strange about the boy? Of course I did not! He had
just been through a horrific experience and what I saw were signs
of shock.

And I do not agree with what some are saying about him. That
he's possessed by angry spirits, perhaps by those of the dead
passengers who envy his survival. Some say he keeps their furious
souls in his heart.

Nor do I give any credence to the other stories surrounding the
tragedy – that the pilot was suicidal, that the forest was pulling
him towards it – why else crash in Jukei? Stories like these only
cause additional pain and trouble where there is already enough.
It is obvious to me that the captain fought to bring the plane down
in an unpopulated area. He had minutes in which to react; he did
the noble thing.

And how can a Japanese boy be what those Americans are
saying? He is a miracle, that boy. I will remember him for the rest
of my life.

My correspondence with Lillian Small continued until the FBI insisted that she no longer have contact with the outside world for her own safety. Although Lillian lived in Williamsburg, Brooklyn, and I am a resident of Manhattan, we have never met in person. Her accounts are extrapolated from our many phone and email conversations.

Reuben had been restless all morning and I'd settled him in front of CNN; sometimes it calms him down. In the old days, he loved to watch the news updates, especially anything political, really got a kick out of it, used to heckle the spin doctors and political analysts as if they could hear him. I don't think he missed a debate or an interview during the midterms, which was when I first really knew there was a problem. He was having trouble recalling the name of that Texan governor, you know, that damn fool one who couldn't say the word 'homosexual' without screwing his mouth up in disgust. I'll never forget the look on Reuben's face as he floundered to remember that putz's name. He'd been hiding his symptoms from me, you see. He'd been hiding them for months.

On that dreadful day, the anchorwoman was interviewing an analyst of some type about his predictions for the primaries when she cut him off mid-sentence: 'I'm sorry, I have to interrupt you there, we've just heard that a Maiden Airlines plane has gone down in the Florida Everglades . . .'

Of course, the first thought that jumped into my head when I heard the words 'plane crash' was 9/11. Terrorism. A bomb on board. I doubt there's a single person in New York who didn't think that when they heard about the crash. You just do.

And then the images came on screen; an overhead view, from a helicopter. It didn't show much, a swamp with an oily mass in its centre, where the plane had plummeted with such force it had been swallowed up. My fingers were freezing – as if I'd been hold-ing ice – though I always make sure the apartment was warm. I changed the channel to a talk show, trying to shake off that uneasy feeling. Reuben had dozed off, which I hoped would give me enough time to change the sheets, take them down to the laundry room.

I was just finishing up when the phone rang. I hurried to answer it, worrying that it would wake Reuben.

It was Mona, Lori's best friend. And I thought, why is Mona phoning me? We're not close, she knows I've never approved of her, always thought of her as fast, a bad influence. It turned out fine in the end, but unlike my Lori, even in her forties Mona hadn't changed her flighty ways. Divorced twice before she was thirty. Without even saying 'hello' or asking after Reuben, Mona said, 'What flight were Lori and Bobby coming home on?'

That bitter coldness I felt earlier was creeping back. 'What are you talking about?' I said. 'They're not on any damn plane.'

And she said, 'But Lillian, didn't Lori tell you? She was going down to Florida to see about a place for you and Reuben.'

My hand went limp and I dropped the phone – her whiny voice still echoing out of the receiver. My legs buckled and I recall praying that this was just one of those sick pranks Mona had been so fond of playing when she was younger. Then, without saying goodbye, I hung up on her and called Lori, almost screaming when I was put straight through to her voicemail. Lori had told me she was taking Bobby with her to see a client in Boston, and not to worry if she didn't get hold of me for a couple of days.

Oh, how I wished I could have talked to Reuben right then! He'd have known what to do. I suppose what I was feeling right then was pure terror. Not the sort of terror you feel when you watch a horror movie or you get accosted by a homeless man with crazy eyes, but a feeling so intense you barely have control of your body – like you're not really connected to it properly any more. I could hear Reuben stirring, but I left the apartment just the same and went straight next door, didn't know what else to do. Thank God Betsy was in – she took one look at me and swept me inside. I was in such a state, I barely noticed the cloud of cigarette smoke that always hangs in the air in her place; she usually came over to me if we were in the mood for coffee and cookies.

She poured me a brandy, made me knock it back, then offered to return to the apartment with me and sit with Reuben while I tried to contact the airline. Even after all that happened afterwards, I'll never forget how kind she was that day.

I couldn't get through – the line was busy and I kept being put on hold. That's when I really thought I knew what hell was like – waiting to hear the fate of those you hold most dear while listening to a muzak version of *The Girl from Ipanema*. Whenever I hear that tune nowadays, I'm taken right back to that awful time, the taste of cheap brandy on my tongue, Reuben moaning from the living-room, the smell of last night's chicken soup lingering in the kitchen.

I don't know how long I tried that same damn number. And then, just as I was despairing of ever getting through, a voice came on the line. A woman. I gave her Bobby and Lori's names. She sounded strained, although she tried to remain professional. A pause that went on for days while she clacked away at her computer.

And then she told me. Lori and Bobby were listed on that flight.

And I told her there must be a mistake. That no way were Lori and Bobby dead, they couldn't be. I would've known. I would've felt it. I didn't believe it. I wouldn't accept it. When Charmaine – the trauma counsellor the Red Cross assigned to us – first arrived, I was still in such denial I told her . . . and I'm ashamed of this . . . I told her to go to hell.

Despite this, my first impulse was to go straight to the crash site. Just to be closer to them. Just in case. I wasn't thinking clearly, I'll admit. How could I have possibly have done that? No planes were flying and it would have meant leaving Reuben with a stranger for God knows how long, maybe putting him in a care home.

Everywhere I looked I saw Lori and Bobby's faces. We had photos up all over of the two of them. Lori holding a newborn Bobby in her arms, smiling into the camera. Bobby at Coney Island, holding a giant cookie. Lori as a schoolgirl, Lori and Bobby at Reuben's seventieth birthday party at Jujubee's, a year before he started to go downhill – when he still remembered who I was, who Lori was. I couldn't stop thinking about when she first told me she was pregnant. I hadn't taken it well, didn't like the idea of her going to that place, shopping for sperm as if it was as simple as buying a dress and then being . . . artificially inseminated. It seemed so cold to me. 'I'm thirty-nine, Momma' (well into her forties she still called me Momma), she said. 'This could be my last chance, and let's face it, Prince Charming isn't going to rock up any time soon.' All my doubts vanished when I saw her with Bobby for the first time of course. She was such a wonderful mother!

And I couldn't help but blame myself. Lori knew that one day I hoped to relocate to Florida, move into one of those clean, sunny, assisted-living places where Reuben would get the help he needed. That's why they'd taken the trip. She was planning on surprising me for my birthday. That was just like Lori, unselfish and generous to her very core.

Betsy was doing her best to calm Reuben down while I paced. I couldn't sit still. I fidgeted, kept picking up the phone, checking it was working, just in case Lori was going to call me to say that at the last moment she hadn't made the flight. That she and Bobby had decided to take a later one. Or an earlier one. That's what I clung to.

News of the other crashes was starting to break, and I kept turning the damn television on and off, couldn't decide if I wanted to see what was going on or not. Oh, the images! It's strange to think of it now, but when I saw the footage of that Japanese boy being carried out of the forest and air-lifted up into a helicopter, I was jealous. Jealous! Because at that stage we didn't know about Bobby. All we knew was that no survivors had been found in Florida.

I thought we'd had all the bad luck one family could ever need. I thought, why would God do this to me? What had I ever done to deserve this? And on top of the guilt, the agony, the crushing absolute terror, I felt lonely. Because whatever happened, whether they were on that plane or not, I'd never be able to tell Reuben. He wouldn't be able to comfort me, make any of the arrangements, rub my back when I couldn't sleep. Not any more.

He was gone too.

Betsy only left when Charmaine showed up, said she was going to go back to her kitchen to make us something to eat, although I couldn't have swallowed a thing.

The next few hours are hazy. I must have settled Reuben in bed, tried to get him to eat a little soup. I remember scrubbing the kitchen counter until my hands were raw and stinging, though both Charmaine and Betsy tried to get me to stop.

And then the call came in. Charmaine answered it while Betsy and I stood frozen in the kitchen. I'm trying to remember the exact words for you, but each time it shifts in my mind. She's African-American, Charmaine is, with just the most gorgeous skin you've ever seen, they age well, don't they? But when she walked into that kitchen, she looked ten years older.

'Lillian,' she said. 'I think you should sit down.'

I didn't allow myself to feel any hope. I'd seen the footage of the crash. How could anyone have survived that? I looked her straight in the eye and said, 'Just tell me.'

'It's Bobby,' she said. 'They've found him. He's alive.'

And then Reuben started screaming from the bedroom and I had to ask her to repeat herself.

Based in Washington, NTSB (National Transport and Safety Bureau) Officer Ace Kelso will be known to many readers as the star of *Ace Investigates*, which ran for four seasons on the Discovery Channel. This account is a partial transcript of one of our many Skype conversations.

You gotta understand, Elspeth, an incident of this magnitude, we knew it would be a while before we could be absolutely sure what we were dealing with. Think about it. Four different crashes involving three different makes of aircraft on four different continents – it was unprecedented. We knew we'd have to work closely and coordinate with the UK's AAIB, the CAA in South Africa, the JTSB in Japan, not to mention the other parties who had a stake in the incidents – I'm talking about the manufacturers, the FBI, the FAA and others I won't go into now. Our guys and gals were doing all they could, but the pressure was like nothing I ever experienced. Pressure from the families, pressure from the airline execs, pressure from the press, pressure from all sides. I wouldn't say I was expecting a clusterfuck exactly, but you got to expect some misinformation and mistakes. People are human. And as the weeks rolled on, we were lucky if we managed to get more than a couple of hours' sleep a night.

Before I get to what I know you want to hear, I'll give you a brief overview, put it into context for you. Here's how it went down. As the IIC [Investigator-in-Charge] on the Maiden Airlines incident, the second I got the call, I started rounding up my Go Team. A regional investigator was already on site doing the initial stakedown, but at that stage all the footage we were getting was from the news. The local incident commander had briefed me via cellphone on the conditions at the site, so I knew we were facing a bad one. You gotta remember, the place where the plane went down, it was remote. Five miles from the nearest levee, a good fourteen miles from the nearest road. From the air, unless you knew what you were looking for, you couldn't see any sign of it – we flew over it before we landed, so I saw that for myself. Scattered debris, a watery black hole about the size of your average suburban home, and that saw-grass that cuts through your flesh.

Here's what I knew when I was first briefed: A McDonnell Douglas MD-80 had crashed minutes after take-off. The air traffic controller reported that the pilots had indicated an engine failure, but I wasn't about to rule out foul play at this early stage, not with reports trickling in about incidents elsewhere. There were two witnesses, fishermen, who saw the plane behaving erratically and flying too low before plummeting into the Everglades; they said they saw flames coming from the engine as it dropped, but this wasn't unusual. Witnesses almost always report seeing signs of an explosion or fire, even if there's no chance of there being any.

I immediately told my systems, structures and maintenance guys to haul ass to Hangar 6. The FAA had assigned us the G-IV to fly to Miami – I needed a full team on this one and the Lear wasn't going to cut it. Maiden's track record with maintenance had caused us some concern before now, but the aircraft itself was known to be reliable.

We were an hour away when I got the call that they'd found a survivor. Remember, Elspeth, we'd seen the press footage – you wouldn't even know a plane had gone down unless you'd been right there at the site, it was completely submerged. I got to admit I didn't believe them at first.

The boy had been rushed to Miami Children's Hospital, and we were getting reports that he was conscious. No one could believe that a) he'd managed to survive, and b) he wasn't taken by the alligators. There were so many of the goddamned things we had to call in armed guards to keep them away while we were pulling up the debris.

When we landed, we headed straight to the site. DMORT [Disaster Mortuary Operational Response Team] were already there, but it didn't look like they were going to find any intact bodies. With so little to go on, top priority was to find the CVR [cockpit voice recorder] and black box; we'd need to get specialist divers in. It was bad in there. Hot as hell, crawling with flies, the stench . . . We needed full bio-hazard suits, which aren't fun to wear in those sorts of conditions. Right from the get-go I could see that it was going take weeks for us to piece this one together, and we didn't have weeks, not now that we knew other planes had gone down that day.

I needed to talk to that kid. According to the passenger list, the only child of that age group on board was a Bobby Small, travelling back to New York City with a woman we assumed was his mother. I opted to go alone, leaving my team on the scene to do the preliminaries and liaise with the locals and other parties who were en route to the crash site.

The press was swarming around the hospital, dogging me to make a statement, 'Ace! Ace!' they were calling. 'Was it a bomb?' 'What about the other crashes, are they connected?' 'Is it true there's a survivor?' I told them the usual, that a press statement would be issued when we knew more, that investigations were still under way etc. etc. – the last thing I was going to do as IIC was shout my mouth off before we had something concrete.

I'd called ahead to say I was on my way, but I knew it was a long shot that they'd let me talk to him. While I waited for the doctors to give me the go-ahead, one of the nurses hustled out of his room, careened straight into me. She looked like she was on the verge of tears. I caught her eye, said something like, 'He's all right, huh?'

She just nodded, scuttled off to the nurses' station. I tracked her down a week or so later, asked why she'd seemed so disturbed. She couldn't put it into words. Said she had a feeling that something was off; she just didn't like being in that room. She felt guilty for saying it, you could see. Said she must have been more affected by the thought of all those people dying at once than she realised; that Bobby was a living reminder of how many had lost their lives that day.

The child psychologist who was on the case arrived a few minutes later. Nice gal, mid-thirties, but looked younger. I forget her name ... Polanski? Oh right, Pankowski. Thanks. She had only just been assigned, and the last thing she wanted was some gung-ho investigator upsetting the boy. I said, 'Lady, we got an international incident on our hands here, that boy in there may be one of the only witnesses who can help us.'

I don't want you to think I'm insensitive, Elspeth, but at that stage the info on the other incidents was sketchy, and for all I knew, that boy could be a key to the whole thing. Remember, in the Japanese situation, it was a while before they confirmed there were any survivors, and we didn't get word about the girl from the UK incident till hours later. Anyway, this Dr Pankowski said the boy was awake, but hadn't said a word, he didn't know his mother was more than likely dead. Asked me to tread carefully, refused to let me film the interview. I agreed, although it was standard procedure to record all witness statements. Gotta say, afterwards, I couldn't decide if I was glad I hadn't been able to film it or not. I reassured her that I was trained in interviewing witnesses, that one of our specialist guys was on the way to do a follow-up interview. I just needed to know if there was anything specific he remembered that could help point us in the right direction.

They'd given him a private room, bright walls, full of kids' stuff. A *SpongeBob* mural, a stuffed giraffe that looked kind of creepy to me. The boy was lying flat on his back, a drip in his arm, you could see the abrasions where the saw-grass had sliced his skin (we all fell foul of that particular hazard in the days to come, let me tell you), but other than that, he'd suffered no other significant injuries. I still can't get over that. Like everyone said at first, it really did look like a miracle. They were prepping him for a CAT scan, and I knew I only had a few minutes.

The doctors hovering around his bed weren't happy to see me, and Pankowski stuck to my side as I approached his bed. He looked really fragile, specially with all those cuts on his upper arms and face, and sure, I felt bad about questioning him so soon after what he'd been through.

'Hiya, Bobby,' I said. 'My name is Ace. I'm an investigator.'

He didn't move a muscle. Pankowski's phone beeped and she stepped back.

'I sure am glad to see you're okay, Bobby,' I went on. 'If it's all right with you, I'd like to ask you a few questions.'

His eyes flipped open, looked straight into mine. They were empty. I couldn't tell if he was even hearing me.

'Hey,' I said. 'Good to see you're awake.'

He seemed to look right through me. Then . . . and listen, Elspeth, this is going to sound as hokey as hell, but they started to swim, like he was about to cry, only . . . Jesus . . . this is hard . . . they weren't filling with tears but with blood.

I guess I musta cried out, because next thing I know Pankowski's at my elbow and the staff are buzzing round the boy like hornets at a picnic.

And I said: 'What's wrong with his eyes?'

Pankowski looked at me as if I'd just sprouted another head.

I looked back at Bobby, stared right into his eyes, and they were clear – cornflower blue, not a trace of blood. Not a drop.

From chapter two of *Guarding JESS: My Life With One of The Three* by Paul Craddock (co-written with Mandi Solomon).

I'm often asked, 'Paul, why did you take on the full care of Jess? After all, you're a successful actor, an *artiste*, a single man with an erratic schedule, are you really cut out to be a parent?' The simple answer is this: just after the twins were born, Shelly and Stephen sat me down and asked me to be the twins' legal guardian if anything should happen to them. They'd thought long and hard about it – Shelly especially. Their close friends all had young families of their own, so wouldn't be able to give the girls the attention they deserved, and Shelly's family wasn't an option (for reasons I'll go into later). Besides, even when they were tots, Shelly said she could tell the girls doted on me. 'That's all Polly and Jess need, Paul,' she'd say. 'Love. And you've got buckets to spare.'

Stephen and Shelly knew all about my past of course. I'd gone off the rails a bit in my mid-twenties after a severe professional disappointment. I was in the middle of filming the pilot for *Bedside Manner*, which was being dubbed as the UK's next hot hospital drama, when I got the news they were cancelling the series. I'd won the part of the main character, Dr Malakai Bennett, a brilliant surgeon with Asperger's syndrome, a morphine addiction and a tendency towards paranoia, and the cancellation hit me hard. I'd done months of research for the role, really immersed myself in it, and I suppose part of the problem was that I'd internalised the character too much. Like so many artists before me, I turned to alcohol and other substances to blunt the pain. These factors mixed with the stress of an uncertain future caused an acute depression and what I suppose one would call a series of mild paranoid delusions.

But I'd dealt with those particular demons years before the girls were even a twinkle in Stephen's eye, so I can honestly say they really did think I was the best choice. Shelly insisted we make it legal, so off we popped to a solicitor and that was that. Of course, when you're asked to do something like this, you never think it's actually going to happen.

But I'm getting ahead of myself.

After I left that horrible room where we'd been funnelled by the inept Go!Go! staff, I spent the next half-hour in that airport pub just staring up at the screen as Sky's rolling banner repeated the terrible news over and over again. And then came the first footage of the area where they thought Stephen's plane had gone down: a shot of the ocean, grey and rolling, the occasional piece of debris bobbing in the waves. The rescue boats scouring the water for survivors looked like toys in that bleak endless seascape. I remember thinking: *Thank God Stephen and Shelly taught the girls to swim last summer.* Ridiculous, I know. Duncan Goodhew would have struggled in that swell. But in moments of emotional *extremis*, it's incredible what you cling to.

It was Mel who came and found me. She may smoke forty Rothmans a day and buy her clothes at Primark, but she and her partner Geoff have hearts as big as Canada. Like I said before, you can't judge a book by its cover.

'Come on, love,' Mel said to me. 'You can't give up hope.'

The yobs at the bar were giving me a wide berth, but they hadn't taken their eyes off me the entire time I was there. I was in a terrible state, sweating and shaking, and I must have been crying at one point as my cheeks were wet. 'What are you staring at?' Mel barked at them, then took my hand and led me back to the briefing room.

An army of psychologists and trauma counsellors had arrived by then. They were busy passing around tea that tasted like sweetened dishwater, and setting up screened-off counselling areas. Mel sat me protectively between her and Geoff: my own shell-suited bookends. Geoff patted my knee, said something like, 'We're all in this together, mate,' and handed me a fag. I hadn't smoked for years, but I took it gratefully.

No one told us not to smoke.

Kelvin, the fellow with the dreadlocks, and Kylie, the pretty redhead who'd been holding the balloon (now nothing but a

squiggle of rubber on the floor), joined us. The fact that us five were
the first to hear the news gave us a shared intimacy, and we huddled
together, chain-smoking and trying not to implode. A nervy woman
– a counsellor of some type, although she looked too high-strung
for the role – asked us for the names of our relatives who'd been on
the doomed flight. Like all the others, she had the 'we'll update you
as soon as we know' line down pat. I understood, even then, that the
last thing they wanted to do was give us false hope, but you *do* still
hope. You can't help it. You start praying that your loved one missed
the flight, that you've got the flight number or date of arrival wrong,
that everything is just a dream, some loony nightmare scenario. I
fixated on the moment before I first heard about the crash – watching those kids dismantle the long-forgotten Christmas tree (a bad
omen if ever there was one, although I'm not superstitious) – and
found myself longing to go back there, before the sick, empty feeling had taken up permanent residence in my heart.

Another panic attack started poking its icy fingers into my
chest. Mel and Geoff tried to keep me talking while we waited to
be assigned a trauma counsellor, but I couldn't get a word out,
which wasn't like me at all. Geoff showed me the screensaver on
his smart phone – a photograph of a grinning twentyish girl, overweight but attractive in her own way. Told me that she was Danielle,
his daughter, the one they'd been there to collect. 'A bright girl,
went through a rough patch but back on track now,' Geoff said
glumly. Danielle had been in Tenerife on a lavish hen party esca-
pade, had only decided to go along at the last minute when
someone else dropped out. How's that for fate?

I was struggling to breathe by now, cold sweat dribbling down
my sides. I knew if I didn't get out of that room immediately, my
head would explode.

Mel understood. 'Give me your number, love,' she said, squeezing my knee with a hand weighted down with gold jewellery. 'Soon
as we know more, we'll let you know.' We swapped numbers (I
couldn't remember mine at first) and I ran out of there. One of the
counsellors tried to stop me, but Mel shouted, 'Just let him go if
he wants to.'

How I managed to pay for my parking and make it back to Hoxton without sliding under a lorry on the M23 is a mystery. Another complete blank. Later, I saw that I'd parked Stephen's Audi with its front wheels on the kerb as if it was a discarded joyride vehicle.

I only came to when I stumbled into the hallway, sending the table we use for post flying. One of the Polish students who lived in the ground floor flat popped his head around his door and asked me if I was okay. He must've seen that I wasn't because when I asked him if he had any alcohol, he disappeared for a few seconds, then wordlessly handed me a bottle of cheap vodka.

I ran into my flat, knowing full well that I was about to fall off the wagon. And I didn't care.

I didn't bother with a glass, I drank the vodka straight out of the bottle. I couldn't taste it. I was shaking, twitching, my hands were tingling. I dug out my BlackBerry, scrolled through my contacts, but I didn't know who to call.

Because the first person I always called when I was in trouble was Stephen.

I paced.

Downed more alcohol.

Gagged.

Then I sat on the sofa and switched on the flat screen.

Normal programming had been suspended in favour of ongoing reports on the crashes. I was numb – and by that stage, well past half-cut – but I gathered that air traffic had been grounded, and more pundits than you could shake a stick at were being ferried into the Sky studio to be interviewed by a grim-faced Kenneth Porter. I can't even hear Kenneth Porter's voice these days without feeling physically sick.

Sky concentrated on the Go!Go! crash, it being the one that was closest to home. A couple on a cruise liner had caught shaky footage of the plane flying dangerously low above the ocean, and Sky repeated it endlessly. The moment of impact was off camera, thank God, but in the background you could hear a woman's voice shrieking, 'Oh my gawd, Larry! Larry! Look at this!'

There was a number people could call if they were concerned their relatives might have been on the flight, and I vaguely thought about dialling it, before thinking, what's the point? When Kenneth Porter wasn't quizzing air safety officials or grimly introducing another repeat of the cruise ship couple's coup, Sky turned its attention to the other crashes. When I heard about Bobby, the boy who'd been found in the Florida Everglades, and the three survivors of the Japanese disaster, I remember thinking, it *could* happen. It could. They could be alive.

I drained the rest of the bottle in one gulp.

I watched a clip of a naked Japanese boy being lifted into a helicopter; footage of a traumatised African man screaming about his family, while behind him toxic black smoke roiled. I watched that crash investigator – the one who looks a little bit like Captain America – urging people not to panic. I watched a clearly shaken airline exec report that flights had been cancelled until further notice.

I must have passed out. When I came round, Kenneth Porter had been replaced by a slick brunette anchor wearing a ghastly yellow blouse (I'll never forget that blouse). My head was throbbing and nausea was threatening to overwhelm me, so when she said that reports were coming in about a Go!Go! passenger being found alive, at first I thought my mind was playing tricks on me.

Then it hit me. A child. They'd found a child clinging to a piece of wreckage a couple of miles from where they thought Stephen's plane had gone down. You couldn't see much from the helicopter footage at first – a group of guys on a fishing boat waving their arms; a small figure in a bright yellow life jacket.

I tried not to get my hopes up, but there was a close-up as she was lifted into a helicopter and I knew in my gut that it was one of the twins. You know your own.

I called Mel first. Didn't think twice. 'Leave it to me, love,' she said. I didn't stop to think how she must be feeling.

It felt like the family liaison team were there in seconds, as if they'd been hanging around outside my door. The trauma counsellor, Peter (I never did catch his last name), a little grey man with specs and a goatee, sat me down and talked me through everything. Warned me not to get my hopes up, 'We have to be sure it's her, Paul.' Asked me if he could contact my friends and family, 'for added support'. I thought about calling Gerry, but decided against it. Stephen, Shelly and the girls *were* my family. I had friends, but they weren't really the type you can lean on in a crisis, although later they all tried to muscle in, eager to grab their fifteen minutes of fame. That sounds bitter, I know, but you find out who your real friends are when life as you know it falls apart.

I wanted to fly out straight away to be with her, but Peter assured me she would be medivacced to England as soon as she was stabilised. I'd completely forgotten that all European planes had been grounded. For the time being, she was being assessed in a Portuguese hospital.

When he thought I was calm enough to actually hear the details, he told me gently that it looked as if there might have been a fire on board before the pilot was forced to ditch, and Jess (or Polly – we didn't know which twin she was at that stage) had been injured. But it was hypothermia they were most concerned about. They took a DNA swab from me to be sure that she really was one of the twins. There's nothing quite as surreal as having the inside of your cheek rubbed with a giant ear bud while wondering if you're the only surviving member of your family.

Weeks later, at one of our first 277 Together meetings, Mel told me that when they heard Jess had been found, she and Geoff didn't give up hope for weeks, not even after they started finding the bodies. She said that she kept imagining Danielle washed up on an island, waiting to be rescued. When air traffic was back to normal, Go!Go! offered to charter a special plane to fly the relatives out to the Portuguese coast, which was the closest they could get to the scene of the crash. I didn't go – I had my hands full with Jess – but most of 277 Together went. I still hate the thought of Mel and Geoff looking out over that ocean, feeling a sliver of hope that their daughter might still be alive.

There must have been a leak inside Go!Go! as the phone rang off the hook from the moment it was confirmed that one of the twins had survived. Whether the hacks were from the *Sun* or the *Independent*, they all asked the same questions: 'How do you feel?' 'Do you think it's a miracle?' To be honest, dealing with their incessant questions took my mind off my grief, which would come in waves, sparked off by the most innocuous thing – a car advert showing an impossibly groomed mother and child; even those toilet paper commercials with the puppies and multicultural toddlers. When I wasn't fielding calls, I was glued to the news like pretty much the rest of the world. They ruled out terrorism early on, but every channel had experts galore speculating about what the causes might be. And like Mel and Geoff, I suppose I couldn't murder the hope that somewhere, out there, Stephen was still alive.

Two days later, Jess was moved to a private hospital in London where she could get specialist care. Her burns weren't severe, but there was the constant spectre of infection, and although the MRI scan showed zero sign of neurological damage, she still hadn't opened her eyes.

The hospital staff were great, really supportive, and they showed me to a private room where I could wait until the doctor gave me the go-ahead to see her. Still swamped with a feeling of unreality, I sat on a Laura Ashley sofa and flipped through a *Heat* magazine. Everyone says they can't understand how the world can just keep turning after someone you love has died, and that's exactly how I felt as I paged through images of celebrities snapped without their make-up on. I dozed off.

I was awoken by a commotion outside in the corridor, a man's voice shouting, 'Wotcha mean we can't see her?', a woman screeching, 'But we're her family!' My heart sank. I knew immediately who they were: Shelly's mum – Marilyn Adams – and two sons, Jason ('call me Jase') and Keith. Stephen had dubbed them the 'Addams Family' long ago for obvious reasons. Shelly had done her best to cut ties with them when she left home, but she felt obliged to invite them to her and Stephen's wedding, which was the last time I'd had the pleasure of their company. Stephen was as liberal as they come, but he used to joke that it was compulsory for an Adams to spend at least three years in Wormwood Scrubs. I know I'm going to come across as simply the most awful snob, but really, they were a walking chav cliché, right down to the casual benefit fraud, the dodgy fags they sold on the side and the souped-up motor in the council house driveway. Jase and Keith – aka Fester and Gomez – had even named their kids (an army of them, spawned by a coterie of different mothers) after the latest celebrity or footballers' kid trends. I believe there was even one called Brooklyn.

Hearing them screeching in the corridor took me right back to Stephen and Shelly's wedding day, which, thanks to the Addams Family, would be remembered by everyone for all the wrong reasons. Stephen had asked me to be his best man, and I'd brought along my then boyfriend, Prakesh, as my plus one. Shelly's mum had shown up in a pink polyester nightmare of a dress that gave her an uncanny resemblance to Peppa Pig, and Fester and Gomez had eschewed their usual knock-off leather jackets and trainers for ill-fitting off-the-peg suits. Shelly had worked hard to organise that wedding; she and Stephen didn't have a lot of cash to throw around back then, it was before they did well in their respective careers. But she'd saved and scrimped and they'd managed to book a minor country house for the reception. At first the two halves of the family kept to their own territory. Shelly's family on one side, me, Prakesh and Stephen and Shelly's friends on the other. Two different worlds.

Stephen said afterwards he wished he'd put a cap on the bar. After the speeches (Marilyn's was a moribund disaster) Prakesh and I stood up to dance. I can even remember the song: *Careless Whisper.*

'Oy oy,' one of the brothers yelled above the music. 'Bum me a fag.'

'Fucking poufs,' the other one joined in.

Prakesh wasn't one to take an insult lying down. There wasn't even a verbal altercation. One minute we were dancing, the next, he was nutting the closest Adams to hand. The police were called, but no one was arrested. It ruined the wedding, of course, and the relationship; Prakesh and I split up shortly afterwards.

It was almost a blessing that Mum and Dad weren't there to witness it. They died in a car crash when Stephen and I were in our early twenties. They left us enough to see us through the next few years; Dad was good like that.

Still, when the Addamses were shown into the waiting room by an intimidated nurse, one of the brothers, Jase I think it was, had the grace to look shamefaced when he saw me, I'll give him that. 'No hard feelings, mate,' he said. 'We got to stick together at a time like this, innit.'

'My Shelly,' Marilyn was sobbing. She went on and on about only finding out when a tabloid leaked the passenger list. 'I didn't even know they was going on holiday! Who goes on holiday in January?'

Jason and Keith passed the time flicking through their phones while Marilyn blubbered – I knew Shelly would have been horrified knowing they were part of this. But I was determined that for Jess's sake, there wouldn't be a scene.

'Popping out for a fag, Mum,' Jase said, and the other one sloped out after him, leaving me alone with the matriarch herself.

'Well, what do you think about this, then, Paul,' she started in. 'Terrible business. My Shelly just gone.'

I mumbled something about being sorry for her loss, but I'd lost my brother, my twin, my best friend and I was hardly in a state to give her any real sympathy.

'Whichever one of the girls they've found, she'll have to move in with me and the boys,' Marilyn continued. 'She can share Jordan and Paris's room.' A massive sigh. 'Unless we move into their house of course.'

Now wasn't the time to inform Marilyn about Shelly's custody decision, but I found myself blurting: 'What makes you think you're going to look after her?'

'Where else will she go?'

'What about me?'

Her chins quivered in indignation. 'You? But you're a . . . you're an *actor*.'

'She's ready,' the nurse said, appearing at the door and interrupting our delightful tête-à-tête. 'You can see her now. But five minutes only.'

Even Marilyn had the nous to realise that now wasn't the time to have this sort of fraught conversation.

We were given greens and face masks (where they found ones big enough for Marilyn's bulk I'll never know) and then we followed the nurse into a room designed to look like a hotel suite, all flowery sofas and state-of-the-art television, the illusion only partially broken by the fact that Jess was surrounded by heart monitors, drips and various other intimidating pieces of equipment. Her eyes were shut and she barely seemed to be breathing. Dressings covered most of her face.

'Is it Jess or Polly?' Marilyn asked no one in particular.

I knew straight away which twin she was. 'It's Jess,' I said.

'How the fu— how can you be so sure? Her face is covered,' Marilyn whined.

It was her hair, you see. Jess's fringe had a chunk cut out of it. Just before they'd left for the holiday, Shelly had caught Jess hacking away at it, trying to copy Missy K's latest half-shorn style. Plus, Jess had the tiniest scar just above her right eyebrow from when she'd fallen against the mantelpiece when she was learning to walk.

She looked so tiny, so vulnerable, lying there. And I swore, right then, I'd do anything I could to protect her.

Angela Dumiso, who is originally from the Eastern Cape, was living in Khayelitsha township with her sister and two-year-old daughter when Dalu Air Flight 467 went down. She agreed to speak to me in April 2012.

I was in the laundry room doing the ironing when I first heard about it. I was working hard to finish in time so that I could catch my taxi at four, so I was already stressed – the boss is very fussy and liked everything, even his socks, to be ironed. The madam ran into the kitchen and I could see by her expression that there was a problem. She usually only wore that face when one of her cats had brought in a rodent and she needed me to clean it up. 'Angela,' she said. 'I've just heard on *Cape Talk*, something's happened in Khayelitsha. Isn't that where you live?'

I said yes, and asked her what it was – I assumed it must be another shack fire or trouble from a strike. She told me that from what she could gather, a plane had crashed. Together we hurried into the sitting room and switched on the television. It was all over the news and at first it was difficult for me to understand what I was seeing. Most of the clips just showed people running and screaming, balloons of black smoke billowing around them. But then I heard the words that chilled my heart. The reporter, a young white woman with frightened eyes, said that a church near Sector Five had been completely destroyed when the plane hit the ground.

My daughter Susan's crèche was in a church in that area.

Of course, my first thought was that I must contact Busi, my sister, but I was out of airtime. The madam let me use her cell-phone, but there was no answer; it went straight to voicemail. I was starting to feel sick, even light-headed. Busi always answers her phone. Always.

'Madam,' I said, 'I have to leave. I have to get home.' I was praying that Busi had decided to collect Susan, my daughter, from crèche early. It was Busi's day off from the factory, and sometimes she did this so that they could spend the afternoon together. When I left at five that morning to catch the taxi to the Northern suburbs, Busi was still fast asleep, Susan by her side. I tried to keep that image – Busi and Susan safe together – in my mind. That's what I concentrated on. I only started to pray later on.

The madam (her real name is Mrs Clara van der Spuy, but the boss likes me to call her 'madam', which made Busi furious) said straight away that she would take me.

While I collected my bag, I could hear her having a fight with the boss on her cellphone. 'Johannes doesn't want me to take you,' she said to me. 'But he can go jump. I'd never live with myself if I let you catch a taxi.'

She didn't stop talking all the way there, only pausing when I had to interrupt to give her directions. My stress levels were now making me feel physically ill; I could feel the pie that I'd eaten for lunch turning into a stone in my stomach. As we made it onto the N2 highway, I could see black smoke drifting into the air in the distance. Within a few kilometres, I could smell it. 'I'm sure it's going to be fine, Angela,' the madam kept saying. 'Khayelitsha is a big place, isn't it?' She turned on the radio; the newscaster was talking about other plane crashes that had occurred elsewhere in the world. 'Blerrie terrorists,' the madam swore. As we approached the Baden Powell road exit, the traffic thickened. We were surrounded by hooting taxis full of frightened faces, people, like me, desperate to get home. Ambulances and fire trucks screamed past us. The madam was beginning to look nervous; she was far out of her comfort zone. The police had set up roadblocks to try and prevent more vehicles getting into the area and I knew I would have to join the crowd and make my way to my section on foot.

'Go home, madam,' I said, and I could see the relief on her face. I didn't blame her. It was hell. The air was thick with ash and already the smoke was making my eyes sting.

I jumped out of the car and ran towards the crowds fighting to get through the barricade they had set up across the road. The people around me were shouting and screaming, and I joined my voice to theirs. '*Intombiyam*! My daughter is in there!' The police were forced to let us through when an ambulance came racing towards us and needed to get out.

I ran. I have never run so fast in my whole life, but I didn't feel tired – the fear pushed me onwards. People would emerge through the smoke, some of them covered in blood, and I'm ashamed to say I did not stop to help them. I concentrated on moving forward although at times it was difficult to see where I was walking. Sometimes that was almost a blessing as I saw . . . I saw flags stuck into the ground and blue plastic bags covering shapes – shapes that I knew were body parts. Fires raged everywhere and firefighters in masks were busy cordoning off other areas. People were being physically restrained from going in any further. But I was still too far away from the street where I lived – I needed to get closer. The smoke scorched my lungs, made my eyes stream, and every so often there would be a pop as something exploded. My skin was soon bathed in filth. The scene looked completely wrong, and I wondered if I had wandered into an unfamiliar area. I was looking for the top of the church, but it was not there. The smell – like a spit-braai mixed with burning fuel – made me vomit. I dropped to my knees. I knew I couldn't go any closer if I wanted to carry on breathing.

It was one of the paramedics who found me. He looked exhausted, his blue overalls soaked with blood. All I could say to him was: 'My daughter. I need to find my daughter.'

Why he chose to help me, I do not know. There were so many other people who needed help. He led me towards his ambulance and I sat in the front seat while he got on his radio. Within minutes, a Red Cross kombi arrived, and the driver motioned me to squeeze inside. Like me, the people inside it were all filthy, covered in ash; most wore the expressions of the deeply traumatised. A woman at the back stared silently out of the window, a sleeping child in her arms. The old man next to me shook silently; there were tear tracks on his dirty cheeks. '*Molweni*,' I whispered to him, '*kuzolunga*.' I was telling him that everything would be all right, but I didn't believe it myself. All I could do was pray, making deals with God in my head so that Susan and Busi would be spared.

We passed by the tent filled with the dead. I tried not to look at it. I could see people hefting the bodies – more of those shapes covered in blue plastic – inside it. And I prayed even harder that they did not contain the bodies of Busi or Susan.

We were driven to the Mew Way community hall. I was supposed to sign my name at the entrance, but I just pushed past the officials and ran for the doors.

Even from outside, I could hear the sound of crying. It was chaos inside there. The centre was full of people huddled in groups, covered in soot and bandages. Some were crying, others looked deeply shocked, staring ahead sightlessly, like the people in the kombi. I began to push my way through the crowd. How would I ever find Busi and Susan in this mass? I saw Noliswa, one of my neighbours, who sometimes looked after Susan. Her face was thick with blood and black dirt. She was rocking back and forth and when I tried to ask her about Busi and Susan she just looked blank; the light had gone out of her eyes. Later, I found out that two of her grandchildren had been at the crèche when the plane had crashed into it.

And then I heard a voice saying, 'Angie?'

I turned around slowly. And saw Busi standing with Susan in her arms.

I screamed, '*Niphilile*! You are alive!' over and over again.

We stood and held each other – Susan wriggling, I was squeezing her too tight – for the longest time. I hadn't given up hope, but the relief that they were okay . . . I will never feel anything that powerful again in my lifetime. When we both stopped crying, Busi told me what had happened. She said she had collected Susan from crèche early, and instead of going straight home, had decided to walk to the spaza for sugar. She said the sound of the impact was incredible – they thought at first it must be a bomb. She said she just grabbed Susan and ran as fast as she could away from that sound and away from the explosions. If she had gone home, they would have been killed.

Because our home was gone. Everything we owned had been incinerated.

We stayed in the hall while we waited to be allocated to a shelter. Some of us put up partitions, hanging sheets and blankets from the roof to make makeshift rooms. So many people had lost their homes, but it was the children I felt for the most. The ones who had lost their parents or grandparents. There were so many of them, many of them *amagweja* [refugee children] who had already suffered during the xenophobic attacks four years ago. They had already seen too much.

One boy sticks in my mind. On that first night, I couldn't sleep. The adrenaline still hadn't left my body and I suppose I was still dealing with the after-effects of what I had seen that day. I stood up to stretch and I felt the weight of someone staring at me. On a blanket next to where Busi, Susan and I were lying sat a boy. I'd barely noticed him before – I was too caught up in caring for Susan and queuing for food and water. Even in the dark I could see the pain and loneliness shining in his eyes. He was alone on his blanket; I could see no sign of a parent or a grandparent. I wondered why the welfare people had not taken him to the unaccompanied children's section.

I asked him where his mother was. He did not react. I sat next to him and took him in my arms. He leaned against me, but although he didn't cry or sob, his body was like a dead weight. When I thought he was asleep, I laid him down and crept back to my blanket.

The next day, we heard we were to be moved to a hotel that was donating its rooms to those of us who had lost their homes. I looked around for the boy; I had some idea that perhaps he could come with us, but I couldn't find him anywhere. We stayed in the hotel for two weeks, and when my sister was offered a job at a large bakery near to Masiphumele, I went to work with her. Again, I was lucky. It is much better than being a domestic. The bakery has a crèche and I can take Susan to work with me every morning.

Later, when all the Americans came out to South Africa to look for that fourth child, an investigator – a Xhosa man, not one of the bounty hunters from overseas – tracked me and Busi down and asked us if we had seen a particular child in that hall where we were taken. He matched the description of the boy I had seen that first night, but I didn't tell the man that I'd seen him. I'm not sure why. I think in my heart I knew it would be better for him if he wasn't found. I could see that the investigator knew I was hiding something, but I still listened to the voice inside me that told me to keep quiet.

And . . . he may not have even been the boy they were looking for. There were many *intandane* [orphaned children], and the boy did not tell me his name.

Private First Class Samuel 'Sammy' Hockemeier of the III Marine Expeditionary Force, based at Camp Courtney on Okinawa Island, agreed to talk to me via Skype after he returned to the US in June 2012.

I met Jake when we were both deployed to Okinawa in 2011. I'm from Fairfax, Virginia, and it turned out that he grew up in Annandale, so we became buddies straight away. Found out that in high school I'd even played football against his brother a couple of times. Before we went into that forest he was just a regular guy, nothing special, quieter than most, had a sense of humour that could pass right by you unless you were paying attention. He was a smallish guy, five eight, maybe five nine – those photographs that were all over the Internet made him look bigger than he actually was. Bigger *and* meaner. Both of us got into computer games when we were there, they're big on base, kind of got addictive. That's the worst I could say about him – till he flipped the fuck out, I mean.

We'd both signed up for III MEF's Humanitarian Aid corp, and in early January we heard that our battalion was going to be deployed to Fuji Camp for training – a full-on disaster reconstruction. Jake and I were pretty upbeat when we heard about that. A couple of anti-terrorism marines we'd gone up against at one of the game cons had just come back from there. They said Katemba, one of the nearby towns, was a cool place to hang out in; had a joint where you could drink and eat all you liked for 3000 yen. We were also hoping to get a chance to head into Tokyo and check out the culture. You don't see much of it on Okinawa, on account of it being seven hundred clicks from mainland Japan. The view from Courtney is awesome, looks right over the ocean, but you can get sick of looking at that day in day out, and a lot of the natives on the island don't have a high opinion of the marines. Some of this is down to the Girard incident – that marine who accidentally shot a local woman who was collecting scrap metal from the firing range – and that gang rape back in the nineties. I wouldn't say the locals were actively hostile, but you could tell a lot of them didn't want us there.

Fuji Camp itself is okay. Small, but the training area is cool. Got to say it was colder than a witch's tit when we arrived there. Lots of mist, ton of rain; we were lucky it didn't snow. Our CO told us we'd be spending the first few days preparing equipment for the deployment to the North Fuji Manoeuvre area, but we'd barely settled into barracks when the news about Black Thursday started filtering in. First one we heard about was the Florida crash. Couple of the guys were from there and their families and girlfriends emailed them the latest news. When we heard about the UK plane, and the one in Africa, you should have heard the rumours that were flying around. Lot of us assumed it was terrorists, another rag-head reprisal maybe, and we were convinced we'd be deployed straight back to Okinawa. It's kinda ironic, considering where we were, but the last one we heard about was the Sun Air disaster – none of us could believe it had happened so close to where we were based. Like everyone else, Jake and I were glued to the Internet that night. That's how we heard about those survivors, the flight attendant and the kid. The connection was bad for a while, but we managed to download a YouTube clip of that kid being hoisted into a helicopter. We were bummed when we heard that one of the survivors had died en route to the hospital. It's freaky to think about it now, but I remember Jake saying, 'Shit, I hope it wasn't that kid.' This is going to sound bad, but knowing there was also an American on board, and that she didn't make it, made the Sun Air crash seem more real to us. The fact that one of our own had gone down.

On the Friday morning, my CO said they needed volunteers from the Humanitarian Aid div to help secure the area and clear a landing pad for the search and rescue helicopters so they could get closer to the site. In the briefing meeting, he told us that hundreds of distraught family members had flocked to the site and were interfering with the operation. The press were also turning the whole thing into a clusterfuck; some of them even got lost or injured in the forest and had to be rescued. I was surprised the Japanese wanted us involved. Sure, the US and Japan have an understanding, but the locals are big on doing things their way; guess it's a matter of pride. But the CO said they'd been criticised for dropping the ball after that bullet train crash in the late nineties; didn't get their act together fast enough, waited while the wheels of bureaucracy turned, would only act when a superior told them what to do, that kind of thing. Cost lives.

I stepped up right away and Jake did too. We were told we'd be working in tandem with a bunch of guys from the nearby JGSDF camp and Yoji, this GSDF private who was assigned as our translator, started telling us about the forest en route. He said it had a really bad rep because of the number of people who had killed themselves there. Told us that there had been so many suicides that the cops had been forced to set up cameras on the trees and that the place was full of unidentified bodies that had been there for years. He said the locals stayed away from it because they believed it was haunted by the spirits of the angry dead or some shit like that, souls that couldn't rest or whatever. I don't know much about Japanese spirituality, just that they believe the souls of animals are in pretty much anything, from people to chairs or whatever, but that sounded way too hokey to be anything but bullshit. Most of us started cracking jokes, messing around, but Jake didn't say a word.

Got to say, the Search and Rescue and the GSDF guys hadn't done a bad job of securing the scene, considering what they had to deal with, but they were seriously out-manned. No way they could control the number of people who were milling around outside the morgue tents. After we were briefed, Jake, me, some of our squadron and a bunch of GSDF guys were sent straight to the main crash site. The rest of the division were deployed to secure the temporary morgue tents, help ferry the supplies and set up latrines.

Our CO told us that SAR and the JTSB guys had mapped where most of the bodies had fallen on impact and now they were bringing them down to the tents. I know you're mostly interested in Jake, but I'll give you an idea of what it was like. When I was at school, we'd studied this old song, 'Strange Fruit'. About the lynchings that went on in the Deep South. How the bodies hanging from the trees looked like strange fruit. That's what we saw. That's what some of those freaky trees were holding as we got closer to where the body of the plane had landed. Only most of the bodies weren't whole. Couple of the guys puked, but me and Jake maintained.

Kinda worse than this were the civilians who were stumbling around the scene, calling for their parents or families or loved ones. Most of them had brought offerings – food or flowers. Later, Yoji, who was assigned to help round them up and get them away from the site, told me that he came across one couple who were so convinced their son was still alive, they'd brought him a change of clothes.

Jake and I were sent to help the guys clear the trees for the helicopter pad, and although it was tough going, it was away from the wreckage and it took our minds off what we'd seen. The NTSB guys didn't make it till the next day, but by then things were far more organised.

Our CO said we were to stay at the site that night and we were assigned sleeping quarters in one of the GSDF's tents. None of us were happy about that. There wasn't a private there who wasn't feeling spooked about spending a night in that forest. And not just because of what we'd seen that day. We even spoke in whispers; it didn't feel right to raise our voices. A few of the guys tried to crack jokes, but they all fell flat.

Round about three hundred hours, I was woken by a scream. Sounded like it was coming from outside the tent. Bunch of us leaped up and ran out. Shit, my adrenaline was just pumping. Couldn't see much – the air was full of mist.

One of the guys – I think it was Johnny, this black dude from Atlanta, good guy – pulled out his flashlight and shone it around. The light was wobbling 'cause his hand was shaking. It settled on this shape a few yards from where we were standing: a figure, its back to us, kneeling down. It turned to look at us and I saw it was Jake.

I asked him what the fuck was going on. He looked dazed, shook his head. 'I saw them,' he said. 'I saw them. The people with no feet.'

I got him back into the tent and he fell asleep straight away. The next morning he refused to talk about what had happened.

I didn't tell Jakey this, but when I told Yoji about it, he said, 'Japanese ghosts don't have feet.' And he told me that the Japanese witching hour – the *ushi-mitsu*, no way can I forget that word – was 3 a.m. Got to admit, I got spooked again when I heard Pamela May Donald's message. Stuff she said, well, it sounded too similar to what Jake said that night. I guess I assumed he'd been influenced by what Yoji had told us.

The other guys busted Jake's balls about it for weeks afterwards of course. Carried on even when we got back to Camp Courtney. You know the kind of thing: 'You seen any dead people today, Jakey?' Jake just took it. I guess it was around that time that he'd started emailing that pastor down in Texas. Before then, he was never into religion. Never once heard him mention God or Jesus. Guess he must have done some Googling about the forest and the crashes, come across that pastor's website.

Jake didn't deploy with the rest of the unit when we were sent to help with the rescue effort after the floods in the Philippines; he got sick, really sick. Stomach pains, suspected appendicitis. Course, now they think he was faking it. They still don't know how he got off the island. Reckon he must've bribed a fishing boat or whaler to take him, something like that; maybe one of the Taiwanese crews who smuggle eel fry or meth in the area.

I'd give anything to go back in time, ma'am. Stop Jake going into that forest. I know there's nothing I could have done, but for some reason, even now, I feel responsible for what he did to that Japanese kid.

Chiyoko Kamamoto, the eighteen-year-old cousin of Sun Air 678's only surviving passenger, Hiro Yanagida, first met Ryu Takami on the forum of a popular online role-playing game. The majority of the players are *otaku* (slang for geeks or obsessives) in their teens or twenties, and as one of the few female gamers, Chiyoko became extremely popular.

It's a mystery why Chiyoko chose Ryu, an under-achiever and hikikomori (recluse) as her chat buddy, although this has been the subject of endless speculation. Until events overtook them, the pair messaged each other every day, sometimes for hours. The messages were retrieved from Chiyoko's computer and smart phone after her disappearance, and leaked onto the Internet.

The original was written predominantly in 'chat speak', but for ease of reading and consistency, with the exception of Ryu's use of emoji (emoticons), this has been modified. Translation by Eric Kushan.

(Chiyoko refers to her mother, with whom she had a frosty relationship, as 'Mother Creature' or 'MC'. 'Android Uncle' or 'AU' denotes Kenji Yanagida, Chiyoko's uncle and one of Japan's most celebrated robotics experts.)

Message logged @ 15.30, 14/01/2012

CHIYOKO: Ryu, you there?

RYU: (｡･ω･) Where you been?

CHIYOKO: Don't ask. Mother Creature 'needed' me again. Did you hear? The flight attendant. She died in hospital an hour ago. That means Hiro is the only survivor.

RYU: It's all over 2-chan. So sad. How is Hiro?

CHIYOKO: He's okay, I think. A dislocated collarbone, scratches; that's all as far as I know.

RYU: So lucky.

CHIYOKO: That's what Mother Creature keeps saying. 'A miracle.' She's set up a temporary altar for Auntie Hiromi. I don't know where she got the photograph of her from. MC never liked Auntie, but you'd never know that now. 'Such a shame, she was so pretty, so serene, such a good mother.' All lies. She was always saying Auntie was stuck up.

RYU: Did you find out what they were doing in Tokyo? Your aunt and Hiro, I mean.

CHIYOKO: Yeah. MC says Auntie Hiromi and Hiro were visiting an old school friend. I can tell that MC's pissed that Auntie didn't visit when she was here, but she won't say it out loud, it wouldn't be *respectful*.

RYU: Have any reporters tried to talk to you? That footage of them trying to climb over the hospital walls to get pics of the survivors was crazy – you hear about the one that fell off the roof? There's a clip of it on Nico Nico. What a moron!

CHIYOKO: Not yet. But they found out where my father works. Not even something like this, the death of a sister, is enough for him to take a day off work. He refused to speak to them. But it's Android Uncle they're really interested in, of course.

RYU: I still can't believe you're related to Kenji Yanagida! Or that you didn't tell me when we first met – I would have bragged about it to the whole world.

CHIYOKO: How would that have sounded? Hey, I'm Chiyoko,

and guess what? I'm related to the Android Man. It would've sounded like I was trying to impress you.

RYU: You impress *me*? It should be the other way round.

CHIYOKO: You're not going to start all that self-pitying stuff again, are you?

RYU: Don't worry, you've got me out of that bad habit.
So . . . what is he really like? I need details.

CHIYOKO: I told you. I don't really know him. Last time I saw him was when he, Hiro and Auntie Hiromi came for New Year two years ago, just after we got back from the US, but they didn't stay over and I only said about three words to him. Auntie was really pretty, but quite distant. I liked Hiro though, cute kid. MC says Android Uncle might come and stay with us while Hiro is at the hospital. I don't think she's happy about it. I overheard her saying to Father that Android Uncle is as cold as his robot.

RYU: Really? But he comes across as really funny and cool in that documentary.

CHIYOKO: Which one? There's like a thousand.

RYU: Can't remember. You want me to look it up for you?

CHIYOKO: Don't bother. But how you are on camera might be different to how you *really* are. I think it's a genetic thing.

RYU: What is? Being on camera?

CHIYOKO: No! Being cold. Like me. I'm not normal. I'm cold. A sliver of ice in my heart.

RYU: Chiyoko, the ice princess.

CHIYOKO: Chiyoko, the yuki-onna.

CHIYOKO: So we've established I have an ice princess genetic condition that can only be cured by . . . what?

RYU: Fame? Money?

CHIYOKO: That's why I like you, Ryu, you always have the right answer. I thought you were going to say love and then I was going to be sick.

RYU: o(_ _)o What's wrong with love?

CHIYOKO: It doesn't exist outside of bad American movies.

RYU: You are not completely cold. I know you aren't.

CHIYOKO: Then why do I not care more? Listen, I'll prove it. How many people died in the Sun Air crash?

RYU: 525. No, 526.

CHIYOKO: 526. Yes. Including my own aunt. But all I'm feeling is relief.

RYU: ??(·_·*)

CHIYOKO: Okay . . . let me explain. Since the crash, since she heard about Auntie Hiromi and Hiro, MC hasn't been on my back about going back to cram school once. Is that a bad thing to think? That because of someone's tragedy I get some peace in my personal life?

RYU: Hey you have a personal life. That's something. Look at me.

CHIYOKO: Ha! I knew it was too good to last. Never mind, you can be my own personal hikikomori. I like to picture you locked in your small room, the curtains shutting out the light, chain-smoking and messaging me when you get tired of playing Ragnarok.

RYU: I am not a hikikomori. And I don't play Ragnarok.

CHIYOKO: Didn't we say we would always be honest with each other? I told you what I was.

RYU: I just don't like that word.

CHIYOKO: Are you going to sulk now?

RYU: _|7O

CHIYOKO: ORZ????? Neraa! How long have you been saving that one up? Do people even use that any more? You sure you're really 22 and not 38 or something? And when are you going to grow out of posting all that ascii shit?

RYU: <(_ _)> Let's change the subject. Hey . . . when are you going to tell me about your life in the States?

CHIYOKO: Not again. Why do you want to know so badly?

RYU: Just interested. Do you miss it?

CHIYOKO: No. It doesn't matter where you live, the world's messed up. Another subject please.

RYU: Okaaaay . . . The message boards are still going wild about why the plane crashed into Jukai. There's this whole theory that the captain crashed it on purpose. The suicide captain.

CHIYOKO: I know. That's old news, it's everywhere. What do you think?

RYU: I don't know. Some of the things they are saying might be true. The forest does have a history and it's miles off the Osaka route, why crash there?

CHIYOKO: Maybe he didn't want to land in a populated area. Maybe he was trying to save more lives that way. I feel bad for his wife.

RYU: *You* feel bad? I thought you were the ice princess.

CHIYOKO: I can still feel bad for her. Anyway, that Sun Air corporate drone mouthpiece said the captain was one of their best and most reliable, that he would never have done something like that. Also, they said he had no money worries, so he didn't need the insurance and his medical showed he was in good health.

RYU: They could be lying. And anyway, maybe he was possessed. Maybe he was *made* to do it.

CHIYOKO: Ha! Brought down by hungry ghosts.

RYU: But you have to admit . . . Why so many planes on the same day? There has to be a reason.

CHIYOKO: Like what? Don't tell me, a sign that we're facing the end of the world?

RYU: Why not? It is 2012.

CHIYOKO: You've been spending *way* too much time on conspiracy sites, Ryu. And we'd know by now if it was terrorism.

RYU: Can the real Chiyoko come back now please? You are the one who is always saying the government and the press use us like pawns and lie to us.

CHIYOKO: Doesn't mean I have to believe some half-baked conspiracy theory. Life isn't like that. It's dull. The politicians lie to us, of course they do. How else are we going to be their little good soldiers and not step out of line?

RYU: You really think they'd tell us the truth if it was terrorists?

CHIYOKO: I just said they lie to us. But some secrets are too big even for them to hide. Maybe in the US, but not here. The cover-up would have to go through eight levels of bureaucracy first to be approved. People are so lame. Do they not have better things to do than talk all day about conspiracy theories? Malign a dead man who was more than likely trying to save as many people as he could?

RYU: Hey . . . I'm really getting worried now. Could the ice princess be thawing? Is this a sign she really cares after all?

CHIYOKO: I don't care . . . Okay, I half care. But it still makes me mad. The freaks on the conspiracy sites are as bad as the useless girls who witter all day on Mixi. Can you imagine what would happen if they spent as much energy talking about the things that really matter?

RYU: Like what?

CHIYOKO: Changing the system. Stopping the nepotism, stopping people turning into slaves. Stopping people dying, people being bullied . . . all of that stuff.

RYU: Chiyoko the ice princess revolutionary.

CHIYOKO: I'm serious. Go to school, go to cram school, study hard, make your parents proud, get into Keio, go to work every day for eighteen hours straight, don't stray, don't complain, don't be a non-conformist. Too many don'ts.

RYU: You know I agree with you, Chiyoko. Look at me . . . But what can we do?

CHIYOKO: Nothing. There's nothing we can do. Just suck it up or drop out or die. Poor Hiro. He has a lot to look forward to.

RYU: (_ _) ....o

TRANSLATOR'S NOTES:

Ascii: The term for text art (such as that used by Ryu above). It was popularised on forums such as 2-channel.

ORZ: A popular Japanese emoji or emoticon that denotes frustration or despair. The letters resemble a figure banging its head on the ground (O is the head; R the torso and Z the legs).

Yuki-Onna: (Snow woman). In Japanese folklore the Yuki-Onna is the spirit of a woman who died in a snow storm.

Hikikomori: Someone who is socially isolated to the extent that they rarely (or never) leave their room. It is estimated that in Japan there are almost a million socially isolated adolescents or young adults who have chosen to cut themselves off from society in this manner.

Controversial British columnist Pauline Rogers, known for her confessional style of journalism, was the first to coin the term The Three to refer to the children who survived the crashes on Black Thursday.

This article was published in the *Daily Mail* on 15 January 2012.

It's been three days since Black Thursday and I'm sitting in my newly constructed private office, staring at my computer screen in utter disbelief.

Not, as you may think, because I'm still stunned at the horrendous coincidence that resulted in four passenger planes crashing on the same day. Although I am. Who isn't? No. I'm scrolling through the staggering list of conspiracy websites, all of which have a different – and more bizarre than the last – theory on what caused the tragedy. Just a five-minute Google session will reveal several sites dedicated to the belief that Toshinori Seto, the brave, selfless captain who chose to bring down Sun Air Flight 678 in an unpopulated area rather than cause more casualties, was possessed by suicidal spirits. Another insists that all four planes were targeted by malevolent ETs. Crash investigators have pointed out in no uncertain terms that terrorist activity can be ruled out – especially in the case of the Dalu Air crash in Africa where the traffic controllers' reports confirm that this disaster was due to pilot error – but there are anti-Islamic websites being created by the minute. And the religious nuts – it's a sign from God! – are fast catching up with them.

An event of this magnitude is bound to transfix the world's attention, but why are people so fast to think the worst or waste their time believing in frankly bizarre and convoluted theories? Sure, the odds of this happening are infinitesimal, but come on! Are we that bored? Are we all, at heart, just Internet trolls?

By far the most poisonous are the rumours and theories being circulated about the three child survivors, Bobby Small, Hiro

Yanagida and Jessica Craddock, who, for the sake of brevity, I'm
going to call The Three. And I blame the media who are ensuring
that the public's greed for information about these poor mites is fed
on the hour. In Japan, they're climbing over walls for pictures of the
poor boy who, let's not forget, lost his mother in the accident. Others
rushed to the crash site, hampering rescue operations. In the UK
and the US, little Jessica Craddock and Bobby Small are taking up
more front-page space than the Royal Family's latest gaffe.

More than most, I know how stressful that relentless attention
and speculation can be. When I split from my second husband
and chose to write about the intimate details of our separation in
this very column, I found myself in the centre of a media storm.
For two weeks I could barely step outside my front door without
a paparazzo popping up to try and snap me without my make-up
on. I can empathise completely with what The Three are going
through, and so can eighteen-year-old Zainab Farra, who, ten
years ago, was the only survivor of another devastating air accident, when Royale Air 715 crashed on take-off at Addis Ababa
airport. Like The Three, Zainab was the only child survivor. Like
The Three, afterwards she found herself in the centre of a media
circus. Zainab recently published her autobiography, *Wind
Beneath my Wings*, and has publicly called for The Three to be left
alone so that they can come to terms with their miraculous
survival. 'They are not freaks,' she says. 'They are children. Please,
what they need now is space and time to heal and process what
they have been through.'

Amen to that. We should be thanking our lucky stars that they
were saved at all, not wasting our time building bizarre conspiracy
theories around them or making them the subject of front-page
gossip. The Three – I salute you, and I hope from the bottom of
my heart that you all find peace while you deal with the terrible
events that took your parents.

Neville Olson, a Los Angeles-based freelance paparazzi photographer, was found dead in his apartment on 23 January 2012. Although the bizarre manner of his death became front page news, this is the first time his neighbour, Stevie Flanagan, who discovered his remains, has spoken publicly.

You got to be a particular kind of person to do what Neville did for a living. I asked him once if he felt dirty doing it, hiding in bushes waiting to get an up-skirt shot of whichever starlet was flavour of the month, but he said he was just doing what the public *wanted* him to do. He specialised in the dirt, like those shots he got of Corinna Sanchez buying coke in Compton – how he even knew she'd be in that neighbourhood, he never said; least not to me. He was cagey about how he got his info.

It kinda goes without saying that Neville was a little weird. A loner. I guess his work suited his personality. I met him when he was moving into the unit downstairs from me. The place where we lived at the time, it's this split-level complex in El Segundo. Lots of people who lived there worked at LAX, so you got people coming and going at all hours. I was working for One Time Car Rental, so the place suited me. Convenient. I wouldn't say we were close friends or anything like that, but if we ran into each other, we'd shoot the shit. I never saw anyone visiting him and I never saw him with a woman, not once, or a guy. He kinda came across as asexual. A couple of months after he moved in, he asked me if I wanted to come over and 'meet his roommates'. I thought maybe he'd asked someone in to help share the rent, so I said, sure. I was curious to see what type of person would get along with him.

I almost puked when I went into his unit the first time. Shit, man, it stank. Don't know how to describe it, guess you could say it was kinda like a mix of rotten fish and meat. It was hot and dark in there, too – the curtains were drawn and the A.C. wasn't on. I was like, what the fuck? Then I saw something moving in the corner of the room – this large shadow – and it looked like it was heading straight for me. I couldn't take in what I was seeing at first, then I realised it was a massive fucking lizard. I yelled and Neville laughed liked crazy. He was waiting for my reaction. Told me to chill, said, 'Don't worry, that's just George.' All I wanted to do was get the hell out of there, but I was trying not to be a pussy, you know? I asked Neville what the fuck he was doing with a thing like that in the apartment and he just shrugged, said he had three of the fucking things – monitors from Africa or whatever – and that most of the time he let them run around, rather than keep them in their cages or aquariums. He said they were really intelligent, 'Clever as pigs or dogs.' I asked him if they were dangerous and he showed me this jagged scar on his wrist. 'Big flap of skin came off it,' he said, and you could tell he was proud of it. 'But they're usually cool if you treat them right.' I asked him what they ate, and he was like, 'Baby rats. Live ones. Get them from a wholesaler.' Imagine that being your job, huh, baby rat merchant? He went into this whole spiel about how some people were against feeding rodents to monitors, and all that time I just watched that thing. Willing it not to get too close to me. That wasn't all, he kept his snake collection and his spiders in his bedroom. Aquariums everywhere. Went on and on about how tarantulas make the best pets. Later, they said he was an animal hoarder.

Couple of days after Black Thursday, he knocked on my door, told me he was going out of town. Most of his work was LA-based, but occasionally he'd have to go further afield. That was the first time he asked me to check on his 'buddies'. 'I stock 'em up before I go,' he said. He could be gone for as long as three days and they'd be fine. He asked me to check on their water levels and swore the monitors would be locked up tight. He was usually cagey about his assignments, but this time he told me where he was going, as there was a chance he'd get himself in deep shit.

He said he'd called in a favour to get on one of the charter helicopters, planned on heading to Miami, to that hospital where they'd taken Bobby Small, see if he could get a shot of the kid. Said he had to do it fast, the kid was being taken back to NYC soon.

I asked him how in the hell he thought he was going to get anywhere near there – from what I'd seen on the news, security at that hospital was tight – but he just smiled. He said he specialised in this kind of thing.

He was only gone three days, so I didn't need to go into his place after all. I saw him climbing out of a cab just as I was getting home from my shift. He looked like crap. Really shaken, like he was sick or something. I asked him if he was cool, and if he'd managed to get a picture of the kid. He didn't answer me and he looked so bad I asked him in for a drink. He came right over, didn't even go into his own place to check on the reptiles. You could see he wanted to talk, but couldn't get the words out. I poured him a shot and he knocked it back, and then I gave him a beer because I'd run out of hard liquor. He downed his beer and asked me for another. He downed that too.

The liquor helped, and slowly he told me what he'd done. I thought he was going to say that he'd disguised himself as a porter or something to get into that hospital, maybe sneaked in through the morgue, B-movie style. But it was worse. Clever. But worse. He'd moved into a hotel just down from the hospital, had this whole cover story and fake ID and accent that he'd used before – a UK businessman in Miami for a conference. He said he'd done the same thing when Klint Maestro, the lead singer of the Space Cowboys, OD-ed. That's how come he got the shots of Klint looking all wasted in his hospital gown. It was easy. He just took extra insulin to make himself go hypo. I didn't even know he was an insulin-dependent diabetic, well, why would I? He collapsed at the bar and let the barman or whoever know that he needed to be taken to the nearest hospital. Then he passed out.

In Casualty they put him on a drip, and in order to get admitted, he pretended to have an epileptic fit. He could've died, but he said it wasn't the first time he'd done it, and he always kept a couple of little baggies of sugar in his sock to sort him out. It was his modus operandi kind of thing. Said it was a bitch to move around in that condition (they'd given him valium after the fit and he still felt like shit after making himself hypo).

I asked him if he managed to get to where the kid was and he was like, nah, it was a bust. Said he couldn't get anywhere near Bobby's ward, security was too tight.

But when they found his camera later, it showed he'd managed to get into the kid's room after all. There's a shot of Bobby sitting up in bed, and he's smiling straight at the camera, as if he was posing for a family shot or whatever. You must've seen it. Someone from the coroner's office leaked it. Kinda creeped me out.

He turned down a third beer and said, 'There's no point, Stevie. There's no point to any of this.'

I was like, 'Any of what?'

He acted like he hadn't heard me. I didn't know what the fuck he was talking about. Then he left.

I kinda got wrapped up in work after that. That puke virus was going around, and it seemed everyone at work was off sick. I was working double shifts and dead on my feet half the time. It was only later that I realised it had to have been a week since I'd run into Neville.

Then, one of the guys who lived in the section on the other side of Neville's place, Mr Patinkin, asked me for the super's number, said there was a problem with the drains. Said he thought maybe the smell was coming from Neville's place.

I guess I knew right then something was up. I went down, knocked on the door. I could hear the faint sound of the TV, nothing else. I still had the key, but I wish to Christ I'd called the cops straight off. Mr Patinkin came with me. He needed trauma counselling afterwards; I still get nightmares. It was dark in there, but I could see Neville from the front door, sitting slumped against the wall, legs outstretched. His shape didn't look right. That's because there were bits missing.

They said he died of an insulin overdose, but the autopsy showed that he might not have been completely dead when they started to . . . you know.

It was big news, 'Man eaten alive by pet lizards and spiders'. There was this whole story going around that the tarantulas had spun webs all over his body and were nesting inside his chest cavity. Bullshit. Far as I could tell, the spiders were still all in their spiderariums or whatever you call them. It was the monitor lizards who ate him.

Funny that he became the news. What do you call it? Ironic. There were even guys like him sneaking round the apartment trying to get a photo. The story pushed all that stuff about the The Three miracle children off the front page for a day. Later on it all got dredged up again when that preacher guy went on about it being another sign of the apocalypse or whatever – the animals turning on humans.

The only way I can deal with it is to think that maybe that's how Neville would have wanted to go. He loved those fucking lizards.

PART TWO

CONSPIRACY

JANUARY–FEBRUARY

A former follower of Pastor Len Vorhees's Church of the Redeemer, Reba Louise Neilson describes herself as 'Pamela May Donald's closest friend'. She still lives in Sannah County, South Texas, where she is the coordinator of the local Christian Women's Preppers' Centre. She is adamant that she was never a member of Pastor Vorhees's Pamelist sect and agreed to talk to me in order 'to let people know that there are good people living here who never wanted anything bad to happen to those children.' I spoke to Reba on a number of occasions via phone in June and July 2012, and collated our conversations into several accounts.

Stephenie told me about it first. She was crying on the phone, couldn't hardly get her words out. 'It's Pam, Reba,' she said when I finally got her to calm down. 'She was on that plane that crashed.'

I told her not to be silly, that Pam was in Japan visiting her daughter, she wasn't in Florida. 'Not that plane, Reba. The Japanese one. It's on the news now.' Well, my heart just about plummeted into my feet. I'd heard about the crash in Japan of course, as well as the one in that unpronounceable place in Africa, and the plane full of English tourists that crashed into the sea in Europe, but I hadn't for a minute thought Pam was on it. The whole thing was just *terrible*. For a while there, it was as if all the planes in the world were dropping out of the sky. The Fox anchors would be reporting on a crash, then they'd flinch and say: 'And we've just heard another plane has gone down . . .' My husband Lorne said it was like a never-ending punchline.

I asked Stephenie if she'd told Pastor Len, and she said she'd tried the ranch but Kendra had been vague as usual about when he'd be back, and he wasn't answering his cellular phone. I hung up and ran into the den to see the news for myself. Behind Melinda Stewart (she's my favourite Fox anchor, the kind of woman you can imagine getting coffee with, you know?) were two huge photographs, one of Pam and one of that little Jewish boy who survived the Florida crash. I didn't like to think what Pam would have said about her photo, which must've been from her passport and looked for all the world like a mug shot. I hate to say it, but her hair was a mess. Along the bottom of the screen, they kept repeating the words: '526 killed in Japanese Sun Air disaster. Sole American on board named as Texan native Pamela May Donald.'

I just sat there, Elspeth, staring at that photograph, reading those words until it finally hit me that Pam really was gone. That nice investigator man, Ace somebody, from that air crash show Lorne likes, came on the line from Florida and said that it was too early to be sure, but it didn't look like terrorism was involved or anything like that. Melinda asked him if he thought the crashes might have been caused by environmental factors or maybe, 'an act of God'. I didn't like that, I can tell you, Elspeth! Implying that our Lord had nothing better to do than bat planes out of the air. It's the Antichrist who would have had a hand in *that*. I couldn't move for the longest time, then they showed an overhead shot of a house that looked familiar. And then I realised it was Pam's house, only it looked smaller from the air. It was then I remembered Jim, Pam's husband.

I never had much to do with Jim. The way Pam used to speak about him, with a kind of hushed awe, you'd think he was a six-foot giant, but in the flesh he's not much taller than I am. I don't like to say this, but I always suspected him of being free with his fists. We never saw bruises on Pam or anything like that. But it was just strange, her acting so cowed all the time. My Lorne, if he even raised his voice to me . . . Well, I do believe the man is the head of the household of course, but it's a mutual respect thing, y'know? Still, no one deserves to go through what that man went through, and I knew we had to do something to help him.

Lorne was out back, doing the inventory on the canned fruit and reorganising our dried goods. 'You can never be too careful' is what he says, not with those solar flares and globalisation and super storms everyone's talking about, and no way were we going to be caught unawares. Who knows when Jesus will call us up to join him? I told him what had happened, that Pam had been on that Jap plane. Him and Jim worked together at the B&P plant, and I said he should go over and see if Jim needed anything. He was reluctant – they weren't close, they worked in different sections – but he went all the same. I thought I'd better stay home, make sure everyone else knew.

I called Pastor Len on his cellphone first; it went straight to voicemail but I left a message. He called me right back and I could tell by the way his voice was shaking that he'd only just heard the news. Pam and I had been members of what he called his 'inner circle' for the longest time. Before Pastor Len and Kendra came to Sannah County – we're talking, oh, fifteen years ago now – I was a member of the New Revelation church over in Denham. It meant a half-hour drive every Sunday and Wednesday for Bible study too, because no way was I going to worship with the Episcopalians, not with their liberal views on the homosexual element.

So you can imagine how cheered I was when Pastor Len arrived in town and took over the old Lutheran church that had been standing empty for the longest time. Back then, I hadn't heard his radio show. It was his billboards that caught my eye at first. He knew how to attract attention to the Lord's work! Every week he'd put up a banner with a different message: 'Like to gamble? Well, the devil deals in souls'; 'God doesn't believe in atheists, therefore atheists don't exist' were two of my favourites. The only one I didn't care for showed a picture of a Bible with one of those antennas old cellphones used to have coming out of its top and 'App for saving your soul,' which I thought was little too cutesy. Pastor Len's congregation was small at first and that's where I really got to know Pam, although I'd seen her at PTA meetings of course – her Joanie was older than my two. We didn't always see eye to eye on everything, but no one could say she wasn't a good Christian woman.

Pastor Len said he'd organised a prayer circle for Pam's soul the following evening, and, as Kendra was down with one of her headaches, he asked me to call around and tell the Bible study group. Then Lorne came huffing into the house saying that Jim's place was surrounded by TV news trucks and reporters and there was no answer from inside the house. Well, of course, I told all of this to Pastor Len, who said it was our Christian duty to help Jim in his time of need, even though he wasn't a member of the church. Pam had always been a bit tight-lipped about that. My Lorne came with me every Sunday, although he didn't join the Bible study group or the healing prayer circle, and it must have been just terrible for Pam knowing that her husband would be left behind on earth to face the wrath of the Antichrist and burn in hell for all eternity.

Then I set to wondering if Pam's daughter Joanie would be coming home. She hadn't been back for two years; there'd been some trouble between her and Jim a while back when she was still at college. He didn't approve of this boyfriend she had. A Mexican. Or half Mexican, I think he was. Caused a rift right through the family. And I know that hurt Pam. She'd always look wistful when I spoke about my grandchildren. Both of my girls got married straight out of school and settled just minutes away from me. That's why Pam went to Japan. She missed Joanie something awful.

It was getting late, so Pastor Len said we should go and see Jim early the next morning. Oh, he looked smart when he picked me up at eight the next day! I'll never forget that, Elspeth. A suit and a red silk tie. But then he always did care about his appearance before he let the devil in. It feels wrong to say this, but I wish I could say the same about Kendra. She and Pastor Len didn't look like they belonged with each other. She was skinny as a rake and always looked washed-out and dowdy.

I was surprised Kendra came with us that day; she usually has some sort of excuse. I wouldn't say she was snooty . . . she just kept her distance, this vague smile on her face, had trouble with her nerves. Is it true that she ended up in one of them places, those . . . asylums? They don't call them that any more, do they? Institutions, that's the word I was fishing for! I can't help but think that it's a real blessing they never had children. At least they didn't get to witness the pain of their mother giving in to her weak mind. I guess it was the gossip about Pastor Len and his fancy woman that sent her over the edge – but let me make it clear, Elspeth, no way, whatever I may think about what he did later, do I give any credence to *those* rumours.

After a quick prayer, we shot straight over to Pam and Jim's place. It's out on Seven Souls road, and the press was lined all the way along it, reporters and those camera people standing outside the gate, smoking and jabbering. Oh glory, I said to Pastor Len, how are we going to get up into Pam's driveway?

But Pastor Len said we were on Jesus' business and no one was going to stop us doing our Christian duty. When we pulled up next to the gate, a swarm of reporters came rushing up to us, saying things like, 'Are you friends of Pam? How do you feel about what's happened?' They were taking pictures and filming and I knew right then what those poor celebrities must go through all the time.

'How do you think we feel?' I said to a young woman wearing too much mascara who was the pushiest of the bunch. Pastor Len gave me a look as if to say, let me do the talking, but they needed to be put in their place. Pastor Len told them that we were on a mission to help Pam's husband in his time of need, and that he'd come out to give them a statement as soon as we'd ensured Jim was coping. This seemed to appease them, and they drew back to their media vans.

The curtains were drawn and we banged on the front door but there was no answer. Pastor Len went round back to the yard, but he said it was the same story. Then I remembered that Pam kept a spare key under the plant pot next to the back door just in case she ever locked herself out, so that's how we got in.

Oh, the smell! Just about slapped you in the face. Kendra went white, it was so bad. And then Snookie yipped and came running down the passageway towards us. Pam would have near had a heart attack if she'd seen her kitchen like that. She'd only been gone two days, but you'd swear a bomb had hit it. Broken glass all over the counter and a cigarette butt dumped in one of Pam's mother's best china cups. And Jim couldn't have let Snookie out once, there were what my Lorne calls doggy landmines all over Pam's good linoleum. I have to be honest here, Elspeth, as I believe in always speaking the truth, but none of us really liked that dog. Even if Pam bathed her a hundred times a day, she always smelled just awful. And her eyes always had this film over them. But Pam doted on her, and seeing her sniffing at our shoes and looking up at us all hopeful that one of us was Pam . . . well, it near broke my heart.

'Jim?' Pastor Len called. 'You there?' The television was on, so after we'd checked the kitchen, we headed to the den.

I almost screamed when we saw him. Jim was slumped in his La-Z-Boy chair, a shotgun across his lap. The curtains were closed, so it was dark and for a second I thought he might be . . . Then I saw that his mouth was open and he let out a snore. Bottles and beer cans just about near covered the floor and the room stank of alcohol. Sannah County is a dry county, but you can get alcohol if you know where to look. And Jim knew where to look. I don't like to say this, Elspeth, but I wonder what he would have done if he hadn't been passed out. If he'd a tried to shoot at us. Pastor Len opened the curtains, cranked a window, and in the light I could see that the front of Jim's pants was wet.

Pastor Len took charge as I knew he would. He gently took the shotgun off Jim's lap, then shook his shoulder.

Jim jerked and stared up at us, his eyes redder than a bucket of pig's blood.

'Jim,' Pastor Len said. 'We've just heard about Pam. We're here for you, Jim. If there's anything we can do, you know you just have to ask.'

Jim snorted. 'Yeah, you can eff-word off.'

Well, I just about *died*. Kendra let out a sound that could have been a laugh – probably shock.

Pastor Len wasn't at all put out. 'I know you're upset, Jim. But we're here to help you. See you through this.'

And then Jim just started sobbing. His whole body heaved and shook. Whatever they say about Pastor Len now, Elspeth, you should've seen how he handled Jim. With real kindness. Took him into the bathroom to get him cleaned up.

Kendra and I just stood there for a while, and then I nudged her and we got to work. Cleaned the kitchen, scooped up the dog poop and gave that La-Z-Boy a good scrub. And all the time Snookie kept following after us with those eyes.

Pastor Len led Jim back into the lounge, and though the poor man smelled a whole lot better, his tears hadn't dried up none. He was still sobbing and sobbing.

Pastor Len said, 'If it's okay with you, Jim, we'd sure like to pray for Pam with you.'

I was expecting Jim to curse at him again, and for a second, I swear, I could see that so did Pastor Len. But that man was broken, Elspeth. Just about tore in two, and later Pastor Len said that was Jesus' way of showing us that we needed to let him in. But you got to be *ready*. I've seen it a thousand times. Like when we were praying for Stephenie's cousin Lonnie, the one who had that motor neurons disease. It didn't work because he hadn't let the Lord into his heart. Even Jesus can't work with an empty vessel.

So we knelt right there next to the couch, surrounded by empty beer cans, and prayed.

'Let the Lord into your heart, Jim,' Pastor Len said. 'He's there for you. He wants to be your Saviour. Can you feel him?'

It was a beautiful thing to see. Here was a man, so smashed by grief that he was crying fit to break, and here was Jesus, just waiting to take him in His arms and put him back together again!

We sat with Jim for a good hour at least. Pastor Len kept saying, 'You're now part of our flock, Jim, we're here for you, just as Jesus is here for you.' It was so heart-warming, I'm not ashamed to say I cried like a new-born baby.

Pastor Len helped Jim back into his La-Z-Boy and I could see on his face that it was time to get down to practicalities.

'Now, Jim,' Pastor Len said. 'We got to think about the funeral.'

Jim mumbled something about Joanie dealing with that.

'Aren't you going to fly over there and bring Pam back?' Pastor Len asked.

Jim shook his head, and a shifty look came into his eyes. 'She left me. I told her not to go, but she wouldn't listen.'

There was a banging on the door and we all jumped. Darn reporters had come up to the house!

We could hear them shouting: 'Jim! Jim! What do you think about the message?'

Pastor Len looked at me and said, 'What message they talking about, Reba?'

Well, of course, I didn't have an inkling.

Pastor Len straightened his tie. 'I'll go and sort those vultures out, Jim,' he said, and Jim looked up at him, that shifty look replaced with pure gratitude. 'Reba and Kendra will fix you something to eat.'

I was glad to have something to do, Elspeth. Pam, bless her, she'd made a whole lot of meals for Jim, all placed neatly in the freezer, so it was easy just to pull one out and put it into the microwave. Kendra didn't do much to help, she gathered that dog in her arms and started whispering to it. So it was up to me to get to work cleaning up the rest of the mess in the den and convincing Jim to eat the potpie I'd put on a tray for him.

When Pastor Len came back in the house, he had this dazed expression on his face. Before I could ask what was bothering him, he picked up the TV remote and clicked onto Fox. Melinda Stewart was saying that a bunch of Jap journalists had made their way to the crash site in that forest place where Pam's plane had gone down, and they'd taken several of the passengers' cellphones. Some of the passengers – God rest their souls – had recorded messages on their phones when they knew they were going to die, and the reporters had leaked them. Printed them before some of the families knew for sure their loved ones were even gone, if you can credit it.

And one of those messages was from Pam, although I didn't even know she had a cellphone. Pam's message was scrolling along the bottom of the screen, and Pastor Len cried, 'She was trying to tell me something, Reba. Look. My name, right there!'

I guess we'd forgotten about Jim, 'cause we heard him yell, 'Pam!' and then he screamed her name over and over.

Kendra didn't help calm him down. She just stood in the doorway, Snookie in her arms, still cooing at that dog as if it was a baby.

The following are the messages (*Isho*) recorded by Sun Air Flight 678 passengers in their final moments.

(Translation by Eric Kushan, who notes that some of the linguistic nuances may have been lost.)

Hirono. Things are getting bad here. The cabin crew are calm. No one is panicking. I know I'm going to die and I want to tell you that – oh things are falling they're falling everywhere and I must . . . Don't look in my office cupboard. Please, Hirono, I'm begging you. There are other things you can do. I can only hope that
Koushan Oda. Japanese citizen. Age 37.

There is smoke that doesn't feel like smoke. The old woman next to me is crying silently and praying and I wish I was sitting here next to you. There are children on this flight. Um . . . uh . . . Take care of my parents. There should be enough money. Call Motobuchi-san, he'll know what to do about the insurance. The captain is doing everything he can, I have to trust in him. I can sense by his voice that he is a good man. Goodbye, goodbye, goodbye, goodbye, goodbye
Sho Mimura. Japanese citizen. Age 49.

I must think I must think I must think. How it happened . . . okay, a bright light came into the cabin. A bang. No, more than one. Was the light before the bang? I don't know. The woman at the window, the big *gaijin* [foreigner] is wailing it hurts my ears and I need to get my things in case we . . . I'm recording this so that you know what will happen. There is no panic, although I feel as if there should be. For the longest time I wanted to die, and now that it's coming I realise that I was wrong to wish this, that my time was coming too soon. I'm scared and I don't know who will hear this. If you can pass this message onto my father tell him that
Keita Eto. Japanese citizen. Age 42.

Shinji? Please answer! *Shinji!*

There was a light, bright and then . . . and then.

The plane is going down, it's crashing it's going down and the captain is saying that we have to be calm. I don't know why this is happening!

All I ask . . . take care of the children, Shinji. Tell them that I love them and

Noriko Kanai. Japanese citizen. Age 28.

I know that the Lord Jesus Christ will take me into his arms and that this is his plan for me. But oh, how I wish I could see you once more. I love you, Su-jin, and I never told you. I hope that you hear this; somehow I hope it gets back to you. I wanted us to be together one day, but you are so far away now. It's happening

Seojin Lee. South Korean citizen. Age 37.

They're here. I'm . . . don't let Snookie eat chocolate, it's poison for dogs, she'll beg you, the boy. The boy watch the boy watch the dead people oh Lordy there's so many . . . They're coming for me now. We're all going soon. All of us. Bye Joanie I love the bag bye Joanie, Pastor Len warn them that the boy he's not to

Pamela May Donald. American citizen. Age 51.

Lola Cando (not her real name) describes herself as a former sex worker and website entrepreneur. Lola's accounts are extrapolated from our many Skype conversations.

Lenny came to see me once, mebbe twice a month for three years or so. Drove all the way out of Sannah County, gotta be an hour's drive at least, but that was fine for Lenny. Said he liked the drive, gave him time to think about stuff. He was strictly vanilla. Later, people tried to get me to say he was some sort of pervert, but he wasn't. And he wasn't into drugs or funny stuff, neither. Just straight missionary position, a finger of bourbon and a chat, that was all he liked.

I got into this business through my girlfriend Denisha. She's a specialist, provides a service for clients who find it hard to connect with women. Just 'cause you're housebound or in a wheelchair, doesn't mean your sex drive's gone. I don't do much specialist work, you understand. Most of my regulars are just your average Joes, guys who are lonely, or whose wives have gone off sex. I check out all my guys good, and if there isn't a connection there or if they want funny stuff, I say, sorry, my schedule's full.

I'm not into drugs; I didn't start doing this 'cause I was feeding a habit. Girls like me and Denisha, the ones who do this for a living without seeing the dark side, you don't hear much about us in the media. And like Denisha's always saying, it beats stacking shelves at Walmart.

I had an apartment I used for, y'know, business dealings, but Lenny didn't like to go there. He was real cautious about things like that, almost paranoid. He preferred us to meet at one of the motels. There are several that'll give you a good deal on an hourly rate, no questions asked. He always insisted that I check in before him.

Well, that day he came late. A good half hour late, which wasn't like him. I set out the drinks, got the ice from the machine and watched a re-run of *Party-Time* while I waited, the one where Mikey and Shawna-Lee finally get together. Just as I was about to give up on him, he came flying into the room, out of breath and all sweaty.

'Well, hi, stranger,' I said, which was always how I greeted him.

'Never mind that, Lo,' he said. 'I need a goddamn drink.' That gave me a jolt. I'd never heard him take the Lord's name in vain before. Lenny said that the only time he ever took a drink was when he was with me, and I believed him. I asked him if he wanted to, you know, start his usual, but he wasn't interested. 'Just the drink.'

His hands were shaking and I could see he was real agitated about something. I fixed him a double and asked him if he wanted me to rub his shoulders.

'Uh-uh,' he said. 'I need to sit for a moment. Think.'

But he didn't sit, he paced up and down that room like he was fixing to wear out the carpet. I knew better than to ask him what was on his mind. I knew he'd tell me when he was ready. He handed me his glass and I poured him another two fingers.

'Pam was trying to tell me something, Lo.'

Course then I didn't have a clue what he meant. I said, 'Len, you gotta start from the beginning.'

He started telling me all about Pamela May Donald, the woman who was killed on the Japanese plane, about how she was one of his congregation.

'Len,' I said, 'I'm real sorry for your loss. But I'm sure Pam wouldn't want you to get all upset about her.'

He acted like I hadn't spoken. He dug in his bag – he always carried this satchel, like he was a grown-up school kid or something – pulled out a Bible, and slapped it on the table.

I was still trying to keep it light. 'You want me to spank you with that or something?'

Big mistake. His face turned bright red, puffed up like one of those fish. He's got what you call an expressive face, which makes people trust him, I guess, looks like he can't lie. I apologised real fast; that look scared me.

He told me about how Pam had left that message, one of the ... what you call them? Those messages that she and some of the Japs had left on their phones while that plane was going down.

'It means something, Lo,' he said. 'And I think I know what it is.'

'What, Lenny?'

'Pam saw them, Lola.'

'Pam saw who, Lenny?'

'All those who haven't taken the Lord into their hearts. Everyone who is going to be left behind after the Rapture.'

I come from a religious background, you understand, brought up in a good Baptist home. There isn't much that's in the Bible that I don't know about. People may condemn me for what I do, but I know in my heart Jesus wouldn't judge me. Like my girlfriend Denisha is always saying (she's an Episcopalian), some of Jesus' best friends were sex workers.

Anyhow, even before Black Thursday, Len was one of those End Times believers. You know, those guys who saw signs that the tribulation was on us everywhere: 9/11, earthquakes, the Holocaust, globalisation, the War on Terror, all that. He truly believed it was only a matter of time before Jesus would whisk all the saved up into heaven, leaving the rest of the world behind to suffer under the Antichrist. Some of them believed the Antichrist was already on the earth. That he's the head of the UN or president of China or one of those Muslims or Arabs or some such. Later on, course, they were saying pretty much everything in the news was a sign. That foot and mouth outbreak in England, even that norovirus thing that hit all of those cruise ships.

Me, I don't know how I felt about the whole Rapture thing. That one day, whoop, all the saved would just disappear into the sky, leaving their clothes and worldly possessions behind. Seems too much trouble to me. Why would God bother with all that? Lenny gave me the *Gone* books to read – you know what I'm talking about? – that series where the reborn Christians are Raptured all at once and the UK prime minister ends up being the Antichrist. I told him I'd read them, but I never did.

I poured myself a stiff drink. Knew I was in for a good hour at least. Sometimes Lenny ran through his radio show for me. I pretended that I listened to it, but I never did. More of a TV type of girl, you know?

When I first started seeing Lenny, I figured him for one of those money-hungry evangelicals, the guys you see on TV trying to get people to donate to their ministries, going on about why tithing is necessary even if you're on welfare. Thought at first he might be a conman of some sort, and I've met my fair share of that type I can tell you! But I got to thinking, after I'd known him for a while, that he really did start to believe his own ... I don't want to call it bullshit, like I say, I'm a card-carrying Baptist, but I never set much store by all that fire and brimstone stuff. But there's no denying that Lenny wanted to join the big boys, powerful fellows like that Dr Lund – the one President Blake was such buddies with. Lenny was desperate to get on the evangelical speaking circuit. His radio show was supposed to be his way in, but in all the years he'd been doing it, he hadn't gotten very far. And it wasn't just for the money either. Respect, that's what Lenny wanted. He was tired of living off of his wife's money.

'Listen to this, Lola,' he said, then he read out the message. Didn't make much sense to me. Seemed to me that Pam was mostly concerned about that dog of hers.

Then he started talking about how it was a miracle that those three kids survived practically unscathed. 'It's not right,' he said. 'They shoulda died, Lola.'

I admitted it was strange. But then everyone thought it was strange. I guess it was one of those crazy things you can't quite get all the way into your head. Like 9/11. Unless you were there and actually experienced it. But you know, I think people get used to anything in the end. Like recently, my block keeps getting these power outrages and after all the bitching and moaning, it's crazy how quickly we've come to terms with it.

'The boy. The boy ...' he kept muttering. He read out a passage from Zechariah, then flipped through to Revelation. Lenny was big on Revelation, but it gave me the heebies when I was a kid.

And, I gotta say, it was me who put the next bit into his head. Look, I'll admit, sometimes I play dumb, Lenny liked it (hell, they all like it). 'You know what I could never get my head around, Lenny?' I said. 'Those four horsemen. Why horsemen, anyhow? And all those different colours.'

Well, Lenny froze like I'd just blasphemed. 'What you say, Lo?'

I thought I'd said something to make him angry again, and I watched him carefully in case he was going to snap at me. He stood, still as a statue, his eyes darting from side to side. 'Lenny?' I said. 'Lenny, honey, you okay?' Then he just clapped his hands and laughed. First time I ever heard Lenny laugh. He took my face between his hands and kissed me right on the mouth. 'Lola,' he said. 'I think you got it!'

I said, 'What do you mean, Lenny?'

But all he said was, 'Take your clothes off.'

Then we did it, and he left.

The following is a transcript of Pastor Len Vorhees's radio show, *My Mouth, God's Voice,* **aired on 20 January 2012.**

Good listeners, I don't need to tell you that now more than ever, we're living in Godless times. We're living in a time when the Bible is shunned in our schools in favour of scientific evolutionary lies, where many are expelling God from their hearts, where sodomites and baby murderers and heathens and Islamofascists have more rights in our country than good Christian men and women. Where Sodom and Gomorrah cast a pall over every aspect of our daily lives, and our world leaders are trying with all their might to construct the culture of globalisation favoured by the Antichrist.

Good listeners, I have good tidings. I have proof that Jesus is listening to us, that He is heeding our prayers, that it is only a matter of time before He takes us to sit at His side.

Listeners, I want to tell you a story.

There was once a good woman. Pamela May Donald was her name, and she was a good *God*-fearing woman, who had taken Jesus into her heart with every fibre of her being.

This woman decided to take a journey, to visit her daughter in a far-flung area, Asia, to be exact. She didn't know, as she packed her bag, as she kissed her husband and church goodbye, that she was about to be part of God's plan.

That woman got on a plane at . . . she got on a plane in Japan, and that plane went down, struck out of the air by forces we can only guess at.

And as she lay dying, as she was lying on that cold hard foreign ground, her life-blood leaking from her veins, God spoke to her, listeners, and gave her a message. Just like God spoke to the prophet John on the island of Patmos when He showed him the vision of the seven seals in Revelation. And Pam recorded that message, listeners, so that we would have the benefit of understanding God's meaning.

Now, John is told that the first four seals will come in the form of four horsemen. We know, and this is a fact, that the four horsemen are sent to fulfil a divine purpose. And we know from Ezekiel that that purpose is to punish the faithless and the godless. The horsemen will bring plague, famine, war and panic to the earth; they will be the harbingers of the Tribulation.

There are many who believe the seals have already been opened, listeners, and I'll admit, it's hard not to, what with everything that's going on in the world right now. But Pam was being shown that God, in his wisdom, has only *now* opened the seals.

What Pamela May Donald was saying in her message to me, because, good listeners, in her wisdom she directed her message to *me* – me personally – is that the four horsemen are now here. Here on earth. As she lay dying, she said, 'The boy, the boy, Pastor Len, warn them.'

Y'all have seen the news. Y'all will have seen the three child survivors – and maybe four, we don't know for sure that there aren't any other survivors, it's chaos down in Africa, as we all know. Y'all know *for a fact* that there was no way that those three children could have survived such a cataclysmic event virtually unscathed. These three are the only survivors, I'll repeat that, listeners, because it is important, the *only* survivors. Even the crash investigators can't explain it, nor the doctors, nor the medical experts, no one can explain why these children were saved.

Loyal listeners, I believe these children have been inhabited by the spirits of the four horsemen.

'Pastor Len,' Pamela May Donald said. 'The boy. The boy.' What boy could she mean but that Japanese child who survived?

It's clear as a bell. How much clearer could the message be? The Lord is good, listeners, He isn't going to mess around with obfuscation. And in His good grace He showed us further evidence that what I say is the truth. In Revelation six, verses one to two:

I watched as the Lamb opened the first of the seven seals. Then I heard one of the four living creatures say in a voice like thunder, 'Come!' I looked, and there before me was a white horse!

A white horse, listeners. Ask yourselves this . . . what colour was the insignia on that Maiden Airlines plane that went down in Florida? A white dove. *White*.

When the Lamb opened the second seal, I heard the second living creature say, 'Come!' Then another horse came out, a fiery red one.

What colour was the insignia of the Sun Air flight? Red. Y'all seen it, brothers and sisters. Y'all seen that big red sun. Red. The colour of communism. The colour of war. The colour, good listeners, of blood.

When the Lamb opened the third seal, I heard the third living creature say, 'Come!' I looked, and there before me was a black horse!

Now it's true that that British plane, the one that crashed into the sea, has a bright orange insignia. But I ask you this, what colour was the writing on that plane? Black, listeners. *Black*.

When the Lamb opened the fourth seal, I heard the voice of the fourth living creature say, 'Come!' I looked, and there before me was a pale horse! Its rider was named Death. Now we know that the colour of Death's horse is written as *khlōros* in the original Greek, which translates as green. The insignia on that African plane that went down. What colour was it? That's right. *Green*.

I know there will be many nay-sayers who'll say, but Pastor Len, that could all just be a coincidence. But God doesn't work in coincidences. We know this for a fact.

There will be more signs. More signs, brothers and sisters. There will be war, there will be plague, there will be conflict and there will be famine.

The judgement has been unleashed on earth. And when the King of Kings opens up that sixth seal, those who are chosen will be saved and take their rightful place next to Jesus in the Kingdom of Heaven.

Our time is now. The signs are clear. They couldn't be clearer if God had put a great big red ribbon on them, shouted them out from the heavens.

And I'm asking you listeners – *good* listeners. Are you ready?

Space does not permit me to include excerpts from all of the conspiracy theory sites that sprang up after Black Thursday, but among the most vocal of the 'alternative theorists' was author and self-styled UFOlogist Simeon Lancaster, whose self-published books include *Aliens Among Us* and *Lizards in the House of Lords*. Lancaster refused to talk to me, and has subsequently denied that he in any way influenced Paul Craddock's actions. The following is a short extract cached from a blog posted on his website, aliensamongstus.co.uk, on 22 January 2012.

ALIEN INTERVENTION: BLACK THURSDAY, ALL THE PROOF WE NEED

Four plane crashes. Four continents. Events that have transfixed the world's media like none other IN THE HISTORY OF THE WORLD. There can be no other explanation except than that The Others, our alien infiltrators, have decided to WIELD THEIR POWER and FLAUNT it.

It's only a matter of time, mark my words, before the Majestic 12 effect a high-level cover-up. They will deny that there are any 'supernatural' causes in their crash reports, you wait and see. Already they are saying that the pilots were to blame for the African crash. Already they are saying that hydraulic failure is the cause of the Japanese crash.

We know this is not so. THEY WILL LIE. They will lie because they are IN CAHOOTS with our alien overlords. It's a wonder The Three children (if they even are children) haven't already been taken to the labs (see map for possible locations) for protection.

Let's look at the evidence:

FOUR PLANES

FOUR??? We know that the chances of any one person being involved in a plane crash are one in 27 million. So what are the odds of FOUR planes crashing on the same day with only THREE survivors??? The chances of that alone are off the scale. So this was a deliberate event. Terrorists? Then why hasn't anyone come forward to claim that they did it? BECAUSE THE TERRORISTS AREN'T RESPONSIBLE. The Others are responsible.

BRIGHT LIGHTS

Why did at least two of the passengers on board the Sun Air flight report seeing bright lights in their messages? There is NO evidence of an explosion, or of a fire on board. Or of depressurisation. THERE CAN ONLY BE ONE EXPLANATION. We know that some of the Others' V crafts have been seen only AFTER bright lights appear in the sky. BRIGHT LIGHTS are a sure sign that they are here.

WHY CHILDREN?

One thing that we can all agree on is that there is NO WAY The Three could have survived the crashes. So there's that.

But why would The Others choose children? I believe it's because as a species, we nurture our young, but not only that, our gut reaction will be to PROTECT them and care for them.

We know that the Others' preferred method of attack is infiltration and STEALTH. It would be too obvious to put themselves in GOVERNMENT again. They've tried that before and they have been OUTED!!!!! They are here to watch us. We don't know when their next move will be. The Three will be controlled by alien forces working on their minds and bodies and we will see this showing itself in time to come.

The children have been IMPLANTED and they are watching us to see what we will do.

THIS CAN BE THE ONLY EXPLANATION!!!!

PART THREE

SURVIVORS

JANUARY–FEBRUARY

Lillian Small.

Zelna, one of the carers at the Alzheimer's day care centre where I used to take Reuben when he was still mobile, called her husband Carlos's condition 'Al', as if it was a separate entity, an actual person rather than a disease. Most mornings when Reuben and I arrived, Zelna would say to me, 'So what do you think Al did today, Lily?' And then she'd relate one of the funny or disturbing actions that Al had 'made' Carlos do – like when she found him wrapping all her shoes in newspaper so that they wouldn't feel the cold, or the way he called visiting the care centre 'going to work'.

She even wrote a blog about it for a while, 'Al, Carlos and Me Makes Three', which won a couple of awards.

I started getting into the habit of calling Reuben's condition Al, too. I suppose it gave me hope that somewhere, deep inside, the real Reuben was still there, biding his time, fighting to stop Al taking over completely. Although I knew it wasn't rational to think this way, it stopped me blaming Reuben for taking away the last years we'd looked forward to spending together. I could blame Al instead. I could *hate* Al instead.

Zelna was forced to put Carlos in a care facility a couple of years ago, and when she moved to Philadelphia to live with her daughter, we lost touch. I miss her – I miss the care centre – being around other people who knew exactly what I was going through. We'd often laugh about the crazy things our respective spouses or parents did or said. I remember Zelna cracking up when I told her about Reuben insisting on wearing his boxer shorts over his trousers, like he was auditioning for the role of a geriatric Superman. It wasn't funny of course, but laughter can be the best medicine, don't you think? If you don't laugh, you'd cry. So I don't feel guilty about that. Not one bit.

But even when Reuben could no longer make it to the care centre, putting him in a home wasn't an option for me. It wasn't just the expense, I'd been inside those places. I didn't like the smell of them. I thought I'd cope looking after him myself. Lori did what she could, and there was always Betsy and the agency if I needed a break. I didn't use the agency often, there was a high staff turnover, and you never knew who you would get.

I don't want you to think I'm kvetching, we got by, and I was lucky. Reuben was never violent. Some of them get like that – paranoid – think their carers are trying to imprison them, especially when they lose the ability to recognise facial features. And he wasn't a wanderer, didn't try and get out of the apartment as long as I was with him. Reuben's condition progressed quickly, but even on bad days, when Al was in full control, as long as he could see my face when I spoke to him, he mostly kept calm. He suffered from terrible nightmares, though. But then he always was a dreamer.

I managed.

And I had my memories.

We were happy, Reuben and I. How many people can say that honestly? That's what I've got to fall back on. In the magazines Lori used to get, they're always saying how the perfect relation-ship is when you're best friends with your partner (oh, how I hate that word! Partner, it sounds so cold, don't you think?), and that's how we were. And when Lori came along, she slotted perfectly into our lives. A close-knit, regular family. Lived by routine. Reuben was a good husband. A good provider. After Lori left to go to NYU, I felt a bit blue, I suppose I was suffering from that empty nest syndrome, and Reuben surprised me with a road trip to Texas – Texas of all places! He wanted to explore San Antonio, check out the Alamo. Before Al took his sense of humour away, we used to joke that whatever happened, 'We'd always have Paris, Texas.'

Our life before Al came wasn't all plain sailing though. Whose life is? There were issues over the years. Lori going off the rails at college, the lump I found in my breast that we managed to catch just in time, the mess Reuben's mother got herself into with that younger fellow she met down in Florida. We dealt with all that.

It was Reuben who suggested we move to Brooklyn when Lori told us she was pregnant. He could see how worried I was about her bringing up a child alone. Her career was just taking off, and she needed support. I'll never forget when she invited us to her first show at New York Fashion Week. Reuben and I were so proud! A lot of the models were men wearing women's dresses, which made Reuben raise an eyebrow, but we've never been that close-minded. Plus, Reuben loved New York, was a real city person. We'd travelled around a lot in the early days when he was working as a substitute teacher, so we were used to packing up and moving. 'Let's go against the tide, Lily, and move into the city. Why not?' In truth, it didn't matter to Reuben where we lived. He was always a reader. Loved books. All books. Fiction, non-fiction, history of course. Spent most of his spare time stuck in a book, and you can do that anywhere, can't you? That was the other great tragedy about Al showing up – one of the first things to go was Reuben's ability to read, although Reuben hid this from me at first as well. It hurts to think of the months he sat up in bed, turning the pages of a book that he had no way of following, just to spare me the worry. A couple of months after his diagnosis, I discovered the real extent to which he'd been trying to hide his condition from me. In his sock drawer, I found a stack of index cards, where he'd written down reminder notes to himself. 'FLOWERS', he'd written on one. That broke my heart. Every Friday for forty-five years, he'd buy me flowers without fail.

I was a bit nervous about moving to Lori's neighbourhood. Not because I was reluctant to leave Flemington. Reuben and I were never much for being social and the few friends we did have had already left for Florida to get away from the New Jersey winters. The house was paid up, so we had that money, but properties in Flemington had been hit hard when the bottom fell out of the market. Lori was worried that her neighbourhood would be too young and modern for us, said it was 'full of hipsters and wannabe artists', but there's a fairly large Hasidic community there still, and the sight of them reassured Reuben when he first started getting really sick. Maybe it had to do with his childhood; his family were Orthodox.

Lori helped us find a nice apartment block just down from the park, a five-minute walk from the loft where she lived on Berry Street. We got lucky, our immediate neighbours were older, like us, and Betsy and I hit it off straight away. We both loved needlework – Betsy was big into cross-stitching – and we watched the same shows. Reuben found her a bit intrusive at first – plus he didn't like the fact that she was a smoker, he's big against that – but it was Betsy who suggested he volunteer at the adult literacy centre. That, of course, was another of the things Reuben was forced to give up. He hid that from me as well, made some excuse about wanting to be home more to help me with Bobby. And oh, I loved looking after Bobby when he was a baby! We had a good year or so where he became the centre of our lives; Lori dropped him off with us every morning, and Reuben and I always took him to the park when the weather was nice. He had his moments, all kids do, but he was a bright little boy, a ray of sunshine in our lives. And it kept us busy!

Then *wham*. Al came along. Reuben was only seventy-one. I kept it from Lori for as long as I could, but she wasn't stupid, could see that he was becoming increasingly forgetful, saying strange things. I guess she put it down to him becoming a little eccentric in his old age.

I was forced to tell her at Bobby's second birthday party. I'd made a devil's food cake, Lori's favourite, and we were trying to get Bobby to blow out the candles. He was crotchety that day – the terrible twos, you know? Then Reuben said, out of the blue, 'Don't let the baby burn, don't let him burn.' And then he burst into tears.

Lori was horrified, and I had to sit her down, tell her that we'd got the diagnosis six months previously. She was upset, of course she was, but she said, and I'll never forget this, 'We'll get through it together, Momma.'

I felt bad, of course I did, landing this on her. We'd moved to the city to help her with Bobby, and now the tables were turned. Lori had her career and Bobby, but she came to see us whenever she could. Bobby was too young to understand what was happening to his grandfather. I worried it would upset him, but Reuben's funny ways didn't seem to bother him.

Oh, Elspeth, those days after I heard about Bobby! The guilt I felt at not going straight down to Miami to be with him in that hospital. That was when I realised the extent of how much I really hated Al. I wanted to scream at him for stealing Reuben away when I had all this other trouble to deal with. I don't ask for sympathy, others have it far worse than I do, but I still couldn't shift the idea that I was being punished for something. First Reuben, then Lori. What next?

A lot of it is just a blur, there was so much going on. The phone ringing nonstop, the reporters and the TV people hounding me. In the end I had to take the phone off the hook and use that cellphone Lori had given me. And even then somehow they managed to get hold of the number.

I couldn't step outside the door without a camera in my face: 'How do you feel?' 'Did you sense he was alive all along?' They wanted to know how Bobby was feeling, how he was coping, what he was eating, if I was religious, when he was coming home, if I was going to fly down and see him. They offered me money. Lots of money, begged me for photographs of him and Lori. I don't know where they got that one of him on his first day at school; I suspect it was from Mona. I never came out and accused her of it, but where else would they have got it? And don't get me started on the advertising and movie people from Hollywood! They wanted to buy the rights to Bobby's life story. He was only six! But money was the last thing I was thinking about then. We were told there would be insurance even though Maiden Air went bankrupt almost immediately. Lori wasn't badly off, but she wasn't rich. She'd earmarked all her savings for me and Reuben, for a place in Florida. But we wouldn't need that now, would we?

In truth, not all of the attention was poisonous. People left gifts, sent letters. Some were heartbreaking, especially the ones from people who had lost children themselves. I had to stop reading those letters in the end. They really did break my heart, and my heart couldn't take much more.

Reuben's sister, who had never once offered to fly down to help care for him before this, called three or four times a day, asking me what I was going to do about shiva for Lori. But how could I think about that with Bobby down in Miami? I was almost thankful most of the planes were grounded and she couldn't come and poke her nose in. Betsy, bless her, took care of the food in those first days. There were people in and out all the time – Charmaine helped with that, making sure they weren't reporters in disguise. People from the neighbourhood who'd heard about Lori. Reuben's old students from the adult literacy centre. Lori's friends and colleagues. All kinds of people. Blacks and Latinos and Jews, all sorts. All of them offering to help.

Betsy even got in touch with her Rabbi who offered his services for a memorial service, even though he knew we were secular. A funeral was out of the question until they released the body . . . but I don't want to dwell on that. That day . . . when we put her to rest . . . I can't, Elspeth.

One night, it had to be two days after we heard about Bobby, Reuben and I were alone in the apartment. I sat down on the bed, and felt such a wave of despair and loneliness I actually wanted to die. I can't describe it, Elspeth. It was all too much. I had to be strong for Bobby, I knew that, but I wasn't sure if I had it in me. I don't know if somehow, the force of my pain gave Reuben the strength to push Al away for a few seconds, but he reached over and took my hand. He squeezed it. I looked into his eyes, and for a second, I saw Reuben, the old Reuben, my best friend, and it was as if he was saying, 'Come on, Lily, don't give up.' Then that expressionless mask – Al – fell back into place and he was gone.

But it gave me the strength to go on.

Charmaine knew how guilty I felt about not being with Bobby, and she put me in touch with his psychologist down in Miami – Dr Pankowski. She helped a lot, said it wouldn't be long before he could come home. She said his MRI was clear and he'd started talking, wasn't saying much, but seemed to understand what had happened to him.

When we got the news that he could come home, I got a visit from the mayor's aide, a nice young man, African-American. 'Bobby's a miracle child, Mrs Small,' he said. 'And here in New

York we look after our own.' He offered to post a policeman outside my building when the press attention got too much and even sent a limousine to take me to JFK.

Charmaine came with me to the airport while Betsy and one of the carers they'd sent stayed to help with Reuben. I was as nervous as I was on my wedding day!

Bobby was arriving on a special charter plane, in an area of the airport where the politicians and important people usually flew into, which meant that for once, the reporters wouldn't be hounding us. They gave me a seat in the waiting area, and I could feel all the staff trying not to stare at me. I hadn't bothered with my appearance for the last few days, and I was feeling self-conscious. Charmaine held my hand all the while. I don't know what I would have done without her. She still keeps in touch.

The day was cold and crisp, but with one of those clear blue skies, and Charmaine and I stood up to watch the plane landing. It seemed to take forever before they opened the doors. And then I saw him climbing down the stairs, holding tightly to a young woman's hand. Dr Pankowski had travelled with him, bless her. She looked too young to be a doctor, but I'll always be grateful to her for what she did for him. They'd given him new clothes so he was wrapped up all warm, his hood hiding his face.

I took a step towards him. 'Bobby,' I said. 'It's me. It's Bubbe.'

He looked up at me and whispered, 'Bubbe?' Elspeth, I wept. Of course I did. I kept touching him, stroking his face, making sure he really was there.

And when I took him into my arms it was as if the lights flicked back on inside me. I can't explain it better than that, Elspeth. You see, I knew, right then, whatever had happened to my Lori, whatever had happened to Reuben, that now I had Bobby back with me, everything was going to be just fine.

**Lori Small's best friend Mona Gladwell agreed to talk to me via
Skype in late April 2012.**

Look, Lori was my friend, my *best* friend, and I don't want to
sound like I'm trashing her, but I reckon it's important people
know the truth about her and Bobby. Don't get me wrong, Lori
was special, did a lot for me, but she could be . . . she could be a
bit flaky sometimes.

Lori and I met in high school. My folks moved to Flemington,
New Jersey from Queens when I was fifteen, and me and Lori hit
it off straight away. On the surface, Lori was your typical good
girl. Good grades, polite, never got into trouble. But she had this
whole secret life her folks never knew about. Smoked pot, drank,
messed around with boys; usual kids' stuff. Reuben was teaching
American history at the school at the time, and Lori was careful to
protect his rep. Reuben was cool. None of the kids at school ripped
into him. He was just Mr Small, not wildly popular, but he had a
way of telling a story. Quiet. A dignity about him, I guess. He was
smart, too. But if he knew Lori was out drinking and screwing
around behind his back, he never let on.

As for Lillian . . . I know she never liked me, blamed what
happened to Lori at college on me, but she was okay. But then
compared to my folks, pretty much anyone is. Lillian never
worked, seemed happy being a homemaker – kept busy sewing
and cooking or whatever – and Reuben made just enough for
them to live on. Apart from their politics – they were way more
liberal than you'd think, looking at them – it was kind of like they
were still living in the 1950s.

After graduation, Lori and I both decided to apply to NYU –
Lillian wasn't happy about that, although NYC is only an hour or
so from Flemington. Didn't take long for Lori to get into the party
scene, start doing heavy drugs, coke mainly. We had this whole
system for when she knew her folks were coming to visit; we'd

clear up the room we shared, she'd cover up her tattoos, make sure there was no evidence on show, but she got to a point where she couldn't hide it any more. Lillian flipped out, insisted that Lori come home with her and Reuben, so Lori ended up dropping out. After she got clean, she came back to the city and tried a million different careers: yoga instructor, personal stylist, manicurist, bartender. That's where I met my first husband, at one of the bars she worked in. It didn't last. Neither the job nor the husband.

Then, out of nowhere Lori applied for this fashion design course – convinced Reuben and Lillian to pay for it, though I don't know where they found the cash. I thought it was just another flaky move, but turned out she was good at it – hats especially, which became her thing. She started getting commissions, moved to Brooklyn where she could afford to set up her own studio. She designed a hat for my second wedding, refused to charge me for it, even though she was just starting out.

It was just after she did that Galliano show that she found out she was pregnant. 'I'm keeping this one,' she said. 'The big four-oh is coming up and I might not get another chance.' Wouldn't say who the father was, so I suspected she'd done it on purpose. I'm not saying she slept around, but she liked to have a good time. Didn't see the point of being in a relationship.

She concocted this whole crazy story about being artificially inseminated so that Lillian wouldn't freak out. I couldn't believe she was going to go through with it – it didn't seem right. But she said it was easier that way. After that preacher was going on about Bobby not being born of man – that he was unnatural and all that stuff – I could have said something, told the truth, but I thought it would all die down. Who could take that seriously?

When she was pregnant, Lori went through this whole religious stage, talked about sending Bobby to Cheder classes when he was old enough, shul, the whole shebang. Jewish mother syndrome, she said. It didn't last. I'd thought she'd freak when Lillian and Reuben decided to move to Brooklyn, but in actual fact she was pleased. 'It might not be a bad idea, Mona.' And yeah, before Reuben got sick, having Lillian on tap did make it easier. Specially when Bobby was a baby. It all backfired when Reuben got really bad and Lori had to be the supportive one. She was good at it, though. In a way, it made her grow up. I admired her for stepping up to the plate like that. Still . . . sometimes I wonder if she wanted Lillian and Reuben to move down to Florida so that they'd be out of her hair, although that makes me sound like a prize bitch, doesn't it? I wouldn't have blamed her. She had a lot to deal with.

And Bobby . . . I don't like to say it, but I swear to God he was a different kid after the crash. I know, I know, it could've just been PTSD or shock or whatever. But before it happened . . . when he was small . . . look, there's no other way to say it. He was the toddler from hell, threw a tantrum about a million times a day. I called him Damien after that kid in the movie, which made Lori mad. Lillian didn't see the half of it – Bobby behaved like a little angel whenever he was with her, I guess because she let him have his way all the time. And Reuben started getting sick when Bobby was two or so, so she wasn't around him all that much. Lori also spoiled him rotten, gave him whatever he wanted, though I told her the only person she was hurting was him. I'm not saying she was a bad mother. She wasn't. She loved him, and that's all they need, right? Although the truth of it was, I couldn't tell if he was spoiled or just what my mother would call a bad seed.

Lori hoped he'd settle down when he started at school. One of those arty Magnet schools had just opened up in the neighbourhood and she decided to enrol him there. It didn't help. Within days of him starting there she was called in to talk about his 'difficulties integrating', or whatever bullshit way they described it.

This one time, when Bobby was four or so, Lori had this big client she had to see. She was stuck for a babysitter and as Lillian was taking Reuben to be assessed by a new doctor, Lori asked me to babysit. I was living in an apartment in Carroll Gardens at the time, and my then-fiancé had bought me a kitten, cute little thing, we named her Sausage. Anyway, I left Bobby in front of the television while I had a shower, and as I was drying my hair I heard this high-pitched screaming sound coming from the kitchen. I swear, I never knew animals could scream like that. Bobby was holding Sausage by her tail and swinging her from side to side. He had this look on his face that said, 'Jeez, this is fun.' I'm not ashamed to say that I whacked him; he fell and knocked his forehead against the kitchen counter. Bled like anything. I had to rush him to the emergency room to get stitches. But he didn't cry. Didn't even flinch. Lori and I fell out over that for a while, but it didn't last long, we had too much history. Last time she asked me to babysit though.

Then after the crash . . . it was like he was a whole new person.

From chapter three of *Guarding JESS: My Life With One of The Three* by Paul Craddock (co-written with Mandi Solomon).

The press attention after Jess was medivacced to the UK was like nothing I could have imagined. The three 'miracle children' were fast becoming the story of the decade, and the UK public's thirst for news on Jess's condition was unquenchable. Paparazzi and tabloid hacks had taken up permanent residence on the steps of my apartment building, and the hospital was practically under siege. Gerry warned me not to say anything too personal on my cellphone, just in case it was being hacked.

I will say that the public support Jess received was overwhelming. The gifts from well-wishers soon filled Jess's room; others left messages, flowers, cards and legions of soft toys outside the hospital – there were so many that you could barely see the railings that ringed the grounds. People were kind. It was their way of showing they cared.

Meanwhile, my relationship with Marilyn and the rest of the Addams Family was deteriorating daily. I couldn't avoid encountering them in the waiting room, and side-stepping Marilyn's demands for me to hand over the keys to Stephen and Shelly's house was becoming unendurable. But the real cold war didn't start in earnest until January 22nd when I overheard Jase haranguing one of Jess's specialists outside her room. She still hadn't woken up at that stage, but her doctors had assured us that there was no sign of impaired cognitive functioning.

'Why the fuck can't you wake her up?' Jase was saying, while jabbing a nicotine-stained finger into the poor doctor's chest. The doctor assured him they were doing everything they could.

'Yeah?' Jase sneered. 'Well, if she ends up being a fucking vegetable, you lot can fucking well look after her then.'

That was the last straw. As far as I was concerned the Addamses had shown their true colours. I couldn't stop them visiting Jess, but I could let it be known that under no circumstances were they going to take care of her once she was discharged. I contacted Shelly's solicitor straight away and instructed her to inform the Addamses of Shelly and Stephen's custody arrangements.

A day later, there they were on the front page of the *Sun*. 'Jess's Gran Cut Out Of Her Life.'

Fair play to the photographer, he'd caught them in all their thuggish glory, Ma Addams glaring into shot, the brothers and various offspring scowling around her like an advert promoting the benefits of birth control. Marilyn especially wasn't shy about letting her views be known:

'It's not right,' Marilyn (58) says. 'Paul's lifestyle, it's not moral. He's a gay and we're upstanding citizens. A family. Jess would be better off with us.'

The *Sun* didn't miss a trick of course. They'd got their hands on a photograph of me taken during last year's gay pride parade, dressed in a tutu and laughing with my then-partner, Jackson. This was displayed in a full colour spread opposite the Addamses' mug shots.

The story spread like wildfire and it wasn't long before the other tabloids managed to procure similarly compromising photographs of me – no doubt courtesy of my friends or ex-friends. I suppose I couldn't blame them for cashing in. Most were struggling artists themselves.

But the tide really turned against me when Marilyn and I were invited to appear on the Roger Clydesdale show. Gerry warned me not to go on it, but I could hardly let Marilyn have her say unchallenged, could I? I'd met Roger at a media launch a few years before, and on the few occasions I'd caught his morning 'current affairs' show, he'd been rather harsh on what he called benefits scroungers. I suppose I naively assumed he'd be on my side.

The atmosphere inside the studio was electric with anticipation; you could tell that the audience was gagging for a showdown. They weren't disappointed. At first, I'll be honest, I thought it was going my way. Marilyn slumped on the studio couch, mumbling inarticulate answers to Roger's trademark, 'Why aren't you actively looking for a job?' questions. Then he turned his gimlet eye on me.

'Do you have any experience dealing with children, Paul?'

I told him that I'd been looking after Jess and Polly since they were babies and reiterated that Stephen and Shelly had chosen me as Jess's guardian.

'He just wants the house! He's an actor! He doesn't care about that kid!' Marilyn squealed, for some reason getting a round of applause from the audience. Roger paused for several seconds to let the furore die down, and then he dropped his bombshell. 'Paul . . . Is it true you have a history of mental illness?'

The audience erupted again, and even Marilyn looked a bit thrown.

I wasn't prepared for the question. I stuttered and stammered and did an appalling job of explaining that my breakdown was a thing of the past.

Of course, this revelation spawned countless screaming headlines along the lines of: 'Nutter to take care of Jess.'

I was devastated, of course. No one likes to see things like that written about them, and I only had myself to blame for being too open. I've been harshly criticised for how I dealt with the press after that. Among other things I've been called a publicity whore and an 'alleged egomaniac and narcissist'. But whatever the press chose to say about me, I had Jess's best interests at heart. I'd put my career on hold for the foreseeable future in order to devote all my time to her. Quite frankly, if I was interested in exploiting her for monetary gain, I could have made millions. Not that money would be an issue, Shelly and Stephen's life policies were fully paid-up and there was the compensation that I was intending to put into trust for Jess. She would always be looked after. The reason I appeared on the various morning shows was nothing to do with money and everything to do with setting the record straight. Anyone else would have done the same.

As you can see, I had a lot on my plate, but Jess was my priority. She was still unresponsive, but apart from her burn injuries, physically she was doing well. I needed to start thinking about what to do about her living arrangements.

Dr Kasabian, who was pipped to be Jess's psychologist when she eventually woke up and started talking, suggested that it might be best for her to be in familiar surroundings, which meant moving into Stephen's house in Chiselhurst.

Walking in there that first time was one of the hardest things I've ever done. Everything, from the wedding and school photos on the walls, to the dried-up Christmas tree in the driveway that Stephen hadn't got around to throwing away, was a reminder of what Jess and I had lost. When I shut the door behind me, the shouts of the hacks outside filtering through (yes, they even followed me on this painful errand), I felt as bereft as I did when I first got the tragic news.

But I made myself confront the scene. For Jess's sake I had to be strong. I walked slowly through the house, finally breaking down completely when I saw the photos of me and Stephen as kids that he'd put up in his office. There was me, pudgy and gap-toothed; him, svelte and serious. Physically, you would never have known we were twins, and our personalities were similarly diverse. Even at age eight I knew I wanted to be on the stage, whereas Stephen was far more retiring and serious. Still, even though we didn't run in the same circles at school, we were always close, and when he met Shelly, our relationship actually deepened. Shelly and I got on like a house on fire straight away.

Though it broke my heart, I made myself stay the night in the house – I needed to acclimatise for Jess's sake. I barely slept, and when I did, I dreamed of Stephen and Shelly. The dreams were so vivid it was as if they were right in the room with me, their spirits clinging to the house. But I knew I was doing the right thing where Jess was concerned, and I know they gave me their blessing.

To date, their bodies haven't been recovered. Nor has Polly's. In some ways that's a blessing. Rather than a terrible trip to identify them in some soulless Portuguese morgue, my last memories of them are of our final dinner together: Polly and Jess giggling, Stephen and Shelly talking about their last-minute holiday. A happy family.

Through all of this, I don't know what I would have done without Mel, Geoff and the rest of the good people from 277 Together. Remember, these are men and women who had lost their own loved ones in the most horrendous way possible, but they sprang to my defence at every opportunity. Mel and Geoff even accompanied me when I moved my belongings into the house, helped me decide what to do about the family photos displayed everywhere. We decided to put them away until Jess had had time to fully accept her parents and sister's deaths. They were my rocks, and I mean that from the bottom of my heart.

The bile spewed by the Addamses and their tame hacks wasn't all we had to deal with, especially when all the conspiracy stories started going viral. Mel was especially incensed by this – you wouldn't know it to look at her, but she's a staunch Catholic, and she was genuinely offended by the horsemen conspiracy theory in particular.

Around that time, we got the news that a memorial service was being planned. The few bodies that had been recovered wouldn't be released until after the inquest, which could be months away, and all of us felt that we needed some closure. They still didn't know what had caused the Go!Go! crash, although terrorism had been ruled out, as it had in all of the four disasters. I tried not to catch too much of the ongoing investigation on the news – it just made me feel worse – although I'd gathered that they suspected it might have had something to do with an electrical storm that had caused severe turbulence for other flights in the area. Mel told me she'd seen the footage from the Navy sub they'd sent down to try and retrieve the black box from the wreckage on the ocean floor. She said it looked so peaceful down there; the middle section of the aircraft looked barely damaged, settled forever in its watery grave. She said the only thing that kept her going was the thought that it had been quick. She couldn't bear the idea of Danielle and the other passengers knowing they were going to die, like those poor passengers on the Japanese flight, who'd had time to leave messages. I knew exactly what she meant, but you can't think like that, you just can't.

The memorial service was going to be held at St Paul's, with an additional service in Trafalgar Square for the public. I knew the Addams Family would be there, no doubt with their favourite hack from the *Sun* in tow, and I was understandably nervous.

Again, Mel, Geoff and their army of friends and family came to my rescue. They stuck to my side throughout that fraught day. To be honest, they were from the same background as Shelly's family. Geoff had been out of work for years, and they lived on a council estate in Orpington not far from where the Addamses lived. It wouldn't have been unreasonable for them to take Marilyn and co's side, especially as I was being painted as a 'public school snob with artistic aspirations'. But they didn't. When we arrived at the service, coincidentally at the same time as the Addamses (how's that for fate? There were thousands of people there), Mel jabbed a finger in Marilyn's face and hissed, 'You cause any trouble here and you'll be out on your ear, you hear me?' Marilyn was wearing a cheap black fascinator that resembled a giant spider, and although she remained stony-faced, it quivered indignantly. Jase and Keith bristled but they were both stared down by Gavin, Mel and Geoff's oldest son, a shaven-haired fellow with the build and look of a strip-club bouncer. I found out later he was 'connected'. A geezer. Someone you wouldn't want to mess with.

I could have hugged him.

I won't dwell on the service itself, but one part in particular touched me – Kelvin's reading. He'd chosen that W. H. Auden poem, 'Stop all the Clocks', the one most people know from *Four Weddings and A Funeral*. It could have been mawkish, but here was this huge dreadlocked fellow, reading with quiet dignity. When he read the line, 'Let aeroplanes circle moaning overhead' you could have heard a pin drop.

I'd barely made it outside the cathedral when I got the call from Dr Kasabian. Jess had woken up.

I don't know how Marilyn and the Addamses found out that she'd emerged out of her coma – I assume one of the nurses must have called them – but when I arrived at the hospital, my emotions threatening to swamp me, there they were, waiting outside her room.

Dr K knew all about our fraught relationship – he didn't live under a stone – and insisted that the last thing Jess needed right now was a tense atmosphere. Marilyn grumpily agreed to button her lip, told Fester and Gomez to wait outside, and we were ushered in to see her. Marilyn, her fascinator still quivering, made sure she reached Jess's bedside first, practically pushing me out of the way.

'It's me, Jessie,' Marilyn said. 'Nana.'

Jess looked at her blankly. Then she reached out a hand towards me. I wish I could say that she knew who we were, but there was no recognition in her eyes, which was absolutely understandable. But I can't help but think that she looked at both of us, sized us up, and figured out, right then, who would be the lesser of two evils.

Chiyoko and Ryu.

Message logged @ 19.46, 21/01/2012

RYU: You there?????

Message logged @ 22.30, 21/01/2012

CHIYOKO: I'm back.

RYU: When?

CHIYOKO: Like five minutes ago.

RYU: 24 hrs no messaging. No you. It was . . . strange.

CHIYOKO: That's sweet. What did you do while I was gone?

RYU: Usual. Slept. Ate something, watched an ancient episode of *Welcome to the NHK*, but it was just a filler. And hey . . . you lied.

CHIYOKO: What do you mean?

RYU: I saw you on TV. You're pretty. Um . . . you look a bit like Hazuki Hitori.

CHIYOKO: . . .

RYU: Sorry. Didn't mean to make you uncomfortable. Forgive this stupid geek.
  (< ^ _ ^ >) \

CHIYOKO: How did you know it was me? I wasn't wearing a name badge.

RYU: It *had* to be you. You were next to Hiro, standing behind your uncle, am I correct? There was almost as much footage of Hiro and Kenji as there was of what's her name, minister Uri's crazy wife. The one who believes in aliens.

CHIYOKO: Aikao Uri.

RYU: Yes, her. So, was it you?

CHIYOKO: Maybe.

RYU: I knew it! I thought you said you weren't into fashion?

CHIYOKO: I'm not. Enough with the personal stuff.

RYU: Sorry again. So how was it?

CHIYOKO: It was a memorial service, how do you *think* it was?

RYU: Am I making you grumpy?

CHIYOKO: Hey, I'm the ice princess. I'm always grumpy. I'll tell you about it if you want to hear. How much detail do you want me to go into?

RYU: I want to hear all of it. Listen . . . I know this is against the rules, but . . . just gonna say it: You want to Skype?

CHIYOKO: . . .

RYU: You still there?

CHIYOKO: Let's carry on as usual.

RYU: Whatever is cool for you, ice princess. I know what you look like now. You cannot hide from me (wwwwwwwwwwww-www). Sorry, evil laugh over.

CHIYOKO: It feels strange, you knowing my face. Like you have power over me or something.

RYU: Hey! I told you my real identity first. You cannot believe how hard that was.

CHIYOKO: I know. I'm not being paranoid.

RYU: I've told you things I have never told anyone. You don't judge me. You don't stare at me like the old bitches in the neighbourhood.

CHIYOKO: How could I? We live in different prefectures.

RYU: You know what I mean. I trust you.

CHIYOKO: Except you know what I look like and I don't know what you look like.

RYU: You're better looking than me. (^ _ ^)

CHIYOKO: Enough!!!!!!!

RYU: Okay. So tell me, how was it? It looked really emotional. At the shrine . . . all those photographs of the passengers . . . They looked like they went on forever.

CHIYOKO: It was. Emotional, I mean. Even this ice princess could not fail to be affected. 526 people. I don't know where to start . . .

RYU: Start at the beginning.

CHIYOKO: Okay . . . So, I told you we had to leave really early. For once in his life Father took the day off and Mother Creature said I should dress in black, but not to be 'too fashionable'. I'm like, hey, no problem, MC.

RYU: You looked good.

CHIYOKO: Ai!

RYU: Sorry.

CHIYOKO: Because of Android Uncle's status, we'd managed to get accommodation at one of the lodges near to Lake Saiko, so that we didn't have to leave immediately afterwards unlike most of the victims' families, although a lot of them were staying at the Highland Resort or one of the other Mount Fuji tour hotels.

CHIYOKO: Our place was Japanese style, run by this ancient couple who couldn't take their eyes off Android Uncle. The woman went on and on about bringing us tea and how to get to the closest onsen, as if we were there for a holiday.

RYU: Sounds like my neighbours.

CHIYOKO: Yeah. Real old busy-bodies. As we arrived, the morning mist was settling and it was cold. MC didn't stop talking in the car the whole way there, pointing out where Mount Fuji would be if you could actually see it – the cloud hid it from view that whole day. Android Uncle greeted us, he'd arrived the night before from Osaka with Hiro and the sister of one of his lab assistants, who he'd asked to help look after Hiro. I know MC was offended because he went back to Osaka after Hiro left the hospital instead of staying with us, but she put on her polite and respectful face.

CHIYOKO: Android Uncle looked much older than I remembered him.

RYU: Do you think he makes his robot look older as he ages?

CHIYOKO: Ryu! It's not like you to be so dark!!!

RYU: Sorry. And Hiro?

CHIYOKO: He was sleeping when MC, Father and I arrived, it was still really early, remember. The assistant bowed and scraped to the parents, simpering at Android Uncle. You could see that she had her eye on him as a future husband. When MC, Father and Android Uncle went off to another room to talk privately, she was straight on her cellphone, texting away like crazy.

RYU: I think I saw her! Big head. Pasty face. Fat.

CHIYOKO: How do you know that wasn't me?

RYU: Was it? If so, I'm really sorry. I didn't mean to offend you.

CHIYOKO: Of course it wasn't me!

RYU: o(_ _)o Forgive this idiot.

CHIYOKO: You're so gullible. When the parents and Android Uncle finished their private conversation they came back in and we hung around and made really really awkward conversation. 'I must go wake Hiro,' Android Uncle said. 'It is time.' 'Let me go,' the assistant said. I'm going to call her Pasty-Face. Pasty-Face bowed like an asshole and left the room. This bit was funny. We heard this screech and she came running downstairs saying, 'Aiii, Hiro bit me!'

RYU: Hiro bit her? Seriously!!!!

CHIYOKO: She deserved it. Mother Creature said that Hiro was probably having a bad dream and woke up with a fright. I could tell she didn't think much of Pasty-Face either, which made me happy to be around her for once. Android Uncle went upstairs to fetch him. Hiro was dressed in a little black suit, his eyes puffy from sleep. After that, Android Uncle barely glanced at him or spoke to him.

RYU: What do you mean?

CHIYOKO: I think he found it painful to look at him, as if he reminded him too much of Auntie Hiromi. Hiro doesn't look anything like her, but perhaps they had the same mannerisms. Shall I continue?

RYU: Please.

CHIYOKO: Hiro looked at us, one by one, and when he saw me, he came shuffling over and took my hand. I didn't know what to do at first. His fingers were ice cold. MC looked surprised that Hiro had chosen me, and kept trying to entice him over. But he didn't move. He leaned against me, and I heard him sigh.

RYU: You think you reminded him of his mother?

CHIYOKO: Maybe. Maybe he realised the rest of the people in the room were fucking losers.

RYU: !!!!

CHIYOKO: Then we drove to the memorial site and the shrine. We were still early, but already there were thousands of people there, as well as packs of reporters and TV cameras. There was this sudden hush when people saw Hiro – he still refused to let go of my hand – and all you could hear were the click and whir of the reporters' cameras. Several people bowed respectfully, although I didn't know if they were bowing to Android Uncle or Hiro. It was a strange feeling being the centre of attention and I could tell Pasty-Face was lapping it up. Father just kept this empty expression on his face and MC didn't know where to look. The crowd even drew back so that we were able to walk straight up to pay our respects to Auntie's photograph without waiting in line. It was still misty, and the air was thick with incense. Am I boring you? Going into too much detail?

RYU: No! I'm touched. You should be a writer. Your words are beautiful.

CHIYOKO: Are you serious??????

RYU: Yes.

CHIYOKO: Ha! Tell that to the exam board.

RYU: Please continue.

CHIYOKO: As we stood there, a ripple went through the crowd and a small woman approached us. I didn't recognise her straight away. Then I realised it was Captain Seto's wife. She's old, at least forty, but she's much prettier in real life.

RYU: *That* wasn't on TV.

CHIYOKO: It was brave of her to come, especially as so many assholes were still saying the crash was Captain Seto's fault. That makes me so mad, especially as the *isho* proved that he was calm and controlled right up until the last moment. Plus there's the phone footage that businessman filmed when the cabin filled with smoke, so it was obviously a mechanical problem. His wife was so dignified and calm. She bowed at Hiro, but didn't speak. I wish now that I'd said something to her. I wanted to tell her that she should be proud of what her husband had done. Then she left. I didn't see her again.

RYU: That must have been intense.

CHIYOKO: Yeah. You probably saw the rest on TV.

RYU: Did you talk to the prime minister?

CHIYOKO: No. He looks way older and smaller in real life, though. And his bar-code head is far more pronounced in the flesh. The wind lifted some strands and you could see his scalp.

RYU: !!!!!

CHIYOKO: Hey, did you hear Android Uncle's speech about how Auntie Hiromi was valued in life and he would do his best to honour her memory while he brings up Hiro?

RYU: Of course.

CHIYOKO: Even I almost cried. It wasn't just his words, it was the atmosphere. I'm starting to sound like some kind of spiritual freak, huh?

RYU: No. I could sense the atmosphere even here in my crappy room.

CHIYOKO: And all the time, Hiro held onto my hand. I kept looking down at him to make sure he was okay, and MC and Pasty-Face kept vying with each other to fuss around him, but he acted like they weren't there.

RYU: That American who was on the plane. That was her daughter who spoke, right? Her Japanese was good.

CHIYOKO: Yeah. That message her mother left . . . What do you think she was trying to say? 'The boy, the boy . . .' Do you think she saw Hiro before she died?

RYU: I dunno. My English is bad and I only read the translation. There's a load of speculation on 2-chan and Toko Z about it.

CHIYOKO: Why do you waste your time on those sites? Seriously? What are they saying now?

RYU: That thing she said about the dead people. They're saying she must have seen the spirits of the dead.

CHIYOKO: Yeah right. Like she couldn't have meant the most obvious thing – the *real* people who'd died in the crash? People are idiots.

RYU: Did you see the photo of her?

CHIYOKO: Which one?

RYU: The one on that US site – celebautopsy.net. The one that rogue reporter took before journalists were prevented from going to the site. It was horrible.

CHIYOKO: Why did you even look at it?

RYU: Followed a link, got lost . . . Hey . . . sorry to ask this. But did your aunt leave a message?

CHIYOKO: I don't know. My uncle hasn't said. If she did, the press didn't leak it to the magazines.

RYU: So . . . after the blessings and the speeches, what happened next?

CHIYOKO: We went back to the lodge. Pasty-Face insisted that Hiro needed a nap, and this time he went with her quietly. That whole day, he didn't say one word to anyone. Mother Creature says it's because he's still traumatised.

RYU: Of course he is.

CHIYOKO: Later, Pasty-Face tried to gossip with me, but I gave her my best evil cat stare and she got the message and spent the rest of the night on her phone. Android Uncle barely said a word, although MC tried to talk to him about what to do with Auntie's remains after they're released.

RYU: I thought they said there will be a mass cremation?

CHIYOKO: Yeah. But they're having two – one here and one in Osaka. Auntie was born in Tokyo, but lived in Osaka so he'll have to decide what to do. But Mother Creature managed to convince him to stay a few days with us in the city before he leaves for Osaka.

RYU: Seriously? Kenji Yanagida is in your house???? Right now?

CHIYOKO: Yeah. Not only that, but Hiro is fast asleep in my bed, a metre from where I'm sitting.

RYU: And Pasty-Face?

CHIYOKO: MC told her to go back to Osaka – said that she wasn't needed.

RYU: I bet that annoyed Pasty-Face.

CHIYOKO: Yeah. For once I was actually proud to be MC's daughter.

RYU: Another difficult question and one you don't have to answer . . . did you go to the crash site? I heard that some of the families requested to go the next day.

CHIYOKO: No. They'd arranged several coaches to take anyone who wanted to go from the Kawachiko station. I wanted to go, but Mother Creature and Father wanted to get back to the city. I'll go someday, though. Oh! I forgot to tell you. After the service that guy who found Hiro came up to pay his respects.

RYU: The suicide monitor guy?

CHIYOKO: Yeah.

RYU: What was he like?

CHIYOKO: Um . . . quiet, but he looked like the sort of person you could trust. Sad, but not depressed, if that makes sense? Real old school though. Hang on. Mother Creature is calling me. Got to go.

RYU: (ᕗ('・ω・`)

Message logged @ 10.30, 22/01/2012

CHIYOKO: Ryu, you there?

RYU: Always. What's up?

CHIYOKO: Android Uncle has just found out that Pasty-Face has been sending emails to the *Shukan Bunshun*, trying to sell her story. Mother Creature is furious, Android Uncle is seething. Mother Creature has asked if he wants Hiro to stay here when he goes back to Osaka, to avoid all the attention. She's offered my services as his minder.

RYU: What? YOU look after the kid?

CHIYOKO: Yeah. What, you think I'll try to corrupt him?

RYU: Will you? Not corrupt him, I mean, but look after him?

CHIYOKO: You know the scene here. What else can I do? I'm not cut out for the freeter lifestyle.

RYU: You could always join my yakuza gang, baby. We need good people.

CHIYOKO: Cliché. Look, I have to go. MC wants to taaaaaaalk again.

RYU: Well, keep me posted.

CHIYOKO: I will. And thanks for being there.

RYU: Always. •*:¸.。.:*•'(*°▽°*)'•*:¸.。.:*•° °•*

are not so intrusive – but there was still much attention. And the crazy rumours! The whole of Tokyo appeared to be fascinated by Hiro. I heard tales from the hotel staff that some believed the boy would be reincarnated as the new face of Japan, that he would be... so many stories! It was during this period – because the rumours were so disturbing, and because I was worried about Kenji – that I decided that instead of running home, I would stay in Osaka for a while.

Dr Pascal de la Croix, a French robotics professor who is currently based at MIT, was one of the few people Hiro Yanagida's father, renowned robotics expert Kenji Yanagida, agreed to talk to in the weeks following the crash that took his wife's life.

I have known Kenji for years. We met at the 2005 Tokyo World Exposition when he unveiled the Surrabot #1 – his first android doppelgänger. I was immediately captivated – what skill! Although the Surrabot #1 was an early model, even then you could barely tell Kenji and it apart. Many people in our field dismissed his work as narcissistic or fanciful, scoffed at the fact that Kenji's focus was more on human psychology than robotics, but I did not. Others found the Surrabot #1 deeply disturbing, tapping, as it does, into the uncanny valley inside all of us. I have even heard people say that creating machines that look exactly like human beings is unethical. What nonsense! For, if we can understand and unlock human nature, surely that is the highest calling?

Let me move on. We kept in touch over the years, and in 2008, Kenji, his wife Hiromi and their son came to stay with me in Paris. Hiromi did not speak much English, so communication with her was limited, but my wife was enchanted with Hiro. 'Japanese babies, so well behaved!' I think if she could have adopted that child then and there she would have done so!

I happened to be in Tokyo when I heard the news about the plane crash and Kenji's wife's demise. I knew immediately that I must go to see him, that he would need his friends more than ever. I had lost my father, you see, a man to whom I had been very close, to cancer the year before, and Kenji had been very kind with his condolences. But Kenji did not answer his phone, and his assistants at the Osaka University would not reveal to me where he was. In the days that followed there were pictures of him everywhere. There was not the media madness that attended the survival of the American boy and the poor child from Britain – the Japanese are not so intrusive – but there was still much attention. And the crazy rumours! The whole of Tokyo appeared to be fascinated by Hiro. I heard tales from the hotel staff that some believed the boy harboured the spirits of all those who had died in the crash. Such nonsense!

I thought of going to the memorial service, but did not think it would be my place to do so. Then I heard that Kenji had returned to Osaka. I decided that instead of returning home, I would make one last attempt to see him, and I booked myself on the next available flight to Osaka. By then, air traffic was almost back to normal.

I am not ashamed to say that I used my reputation to gain entrance into his laboratory at the university. His assistants, many of whom I had met before, were respectful, but told me that he was unavailable.

And then I saw his android. The Surrabot #3. It was sitting in the corner of the room, and a young assistant appeared to be talking to it. I knew immediately that Kenji was talking through it; I had seen him doing this before on many occasions. In fact, if he was asked to go on the lecture circuit and could not leave the university, he would send his robot instead and talk through it remotely!

You want that I should explain a little how the mechanism works? In the most simple language I can use, it is controlled remotely, through a computer. Kenji uses a camera to capture his face and head movements and these are transmitted to servos – little micro-motors – embedded inside the android's face plate. This is how it mirrors his facial movements – even blinking is replicated. A microphone records Kenji's voice, and this is conveyed via the android's mouthpiece, right down to the slightest intonation. There is also a mechanism inside its chest – not unlike those used by high-end sex doll manufacturers – which simulates breathing. It can be most disconcerting talking to the android. At first glance it certainly does look like Kenji. He even changes its hair whenever he has a haircut!

I insisted on speaking to it and said without hesitation, 'Kenji. I was so sorry to hear about Hiromi. I know what it is you are going through. Please, if there is anything I can do, let me know.'

There was a pause, and then the android said something in Japanese to the assistant. She said to me, 'Come,' and told me to follow her. She led me through a bewildering number of corridors, and down towards a basement area. She politely refused to answer any of my questions about Kenji's well-being, and I could not help but admire her loyalty to him.

She knocked on an unmarked door and it was opened by Kenji himself.

I was shocked when I saw him. After just talking to his android doppelgänger, the fact that he had aged terribly was even more noticeable. His hair was dishevelled and there were dark circles under his eyes. He snapped something at his assistant – which was unlike him, I had never seen him be discourteous before – and she hurried away, leaving us alone.

I gave him my condolences, but he barely seemed to hear them. He kept his features absolutely still; only his eyes showed any sign of life. He thanked me for coming all this way to see him, but said it was not necessary.

I asked him why he was working in the basement and not the lab, and he told me that he was tired of being around people. The press hadn't stopped harassing him since the memorial service. Then he asked me if I wanted to inspect his latest creation and waved me inside the room.

'Oh!' I said, as soon as I stepped inside. 'I see that your son is visiting you.'

But before I finished the sentence I realised my mistake. The child sitting on the small chair next to one of Kenji's computers was not human. It was another of his replicas. A surrabot version of his son. 'Is this your latest project?' I asked, trying to hide my shock.

For the first time he smiled. 'No. I made that last year.' And then he gestured to the far corner of the room where a surrabot dressed in a white kimono was sitting. A female surrabot.

I walked towards her. She was beautiful; perfect, a slight smile on her lips. Her chest rose and fell as if she was breathing in and exhaling deeply.

'Is that . . .?' I could not say it.

'Yes,' he said. 'It is Hiromi, my wife.' Without taking his eyes off her he said, 'It is almost as if her soul is still here.'

I attempted to ask why he had felt the need to build a replica of his deceased wife, but the answer is obvious, is it not? He avoided my questions, but he did tell me that Hiro was living in Tokyo with relatives.

I did not say what I was thinking: 'Kenji, you have a son who is alive. Who needs you. Do not forget this, my friend.'

Not only was this not my business, I knew that his grief ran too deep to listen to what I was saying.

So I did the only thing I could do. I left.

Outside, not even the city's beauty could calm me. I felt unsettled, as if something in the world's axis had shifted.

And as I stood, looking back at the university building, it started snowing.

Mandi Solomon is the ghost/co-writer of Paul Craddock's unfinished memoir, *Guarding JESS: My Life With One of The Three*.

My main objective when I meet the subject for the first time is to win their trust. There's usually a tight deadline on celeb memoirs, so I generally have to work fast. Most of my clients have spent their careers seeing exposés or just plain bullshit written about them (or their PR agencies have collaborated in the bullshit) so they're practised at keeping their true selves under wraps. But readers aren't stupid, they can smell fakery a mile off. It's important to me that we include at least some new material, balance the usual PR buff with some genuine revelations and shockers. I didn't have that problem with Paul of course. He was up front right from the beginning. My publishers and his agent put the deal together in double-quick time. They wanted the inside story of how Jess was coping; they knew the attention on her would be mega, and they weren't wrong. The story grew bigger every day.

Our first meeting was at a coffee bar in Chislehurst, gosh, sometime in early February. Jess was still in hospital and Paul was busy moving his stuff into her house, getting the place ready for her to come home. My first impression of him? He was fairly charming, witty, slightly camp of course, but then he is – or was – an actor. His brother's death had obviously hit him hard, and when I touched on that, there were a few tears, but he didn't seem at all embarrassed about showing emotion in front of me. And he was remarkably candid about his past, the fact that in his twenties he drank too much, experimented with drugs, slept around a bit. He didn't go into detail about his stint in Maudsley Psychiatric Hospital, but he didn't deny it either. Said his breakdown was stress-related after he had a professional disappointment. I never for one second thought he wouldn't be capable of looking after a child. If anyone asked me after that first meeting what I thought of him, I would've said he was a good guy, maybe a bit self-obsessed, but nothing compared to some I've dealt with.

After I've won their trust, I give my clients a Dictaphone – a digital voice recorder actually – and I encourage them to talk into it as often as possible without thinking too much about what they're saying. I always reassure them that I won't put in any information they're uncomfortable with. Most insist on a contract to this effect, which is fine by me. There are always ways to get around that kind of thing, and in any case, most of them like to add an edge to their life story. You'd be amazed at how quickly they get used to the Dictaphone method, some of them using it as their personal therapist. Have you read *Fighting for Glory*? The tell-all biography of Lennie L, the cage fighter? Came out last year. Gosh, the things he used to say. I could only use half of them. Quite often he'd leave the recorder on while he was having sex, which I eventually began to think was deliberate.

Paul took to the Dictaphone method like a duck to water. At the beginning, things appeared to be going well. I had the rough draft of the first three chapters down, and I sent him an email detailing what else I thought we might need. The downloads came as regular as clockwork, and then – about a week or so after Jess got home – they stopped. I rationalised that he had his hands full dealing with Jess, the press attention, and the crazies who wouldn't leave them alone, so I covered for him for a month or so. He kept promising he'd send me more. Out of the blue, he said the book was off. My publishers were furious, threatened to sue. They'd paid the advance, you see.

It was Mel who found it. Paul had left a flash drive for me in an envelope on the dining-room table, with my name and telephone number on it. I gave it to the police of course, but not before I downloaded it and made a copy. I had some idea of transcribing it, maybe publishing it later, but I couldn't listen to it after that first time.

It scared me, Elspeth. It scared the living shit out of me.

The following is a transcript of Paul Craddock's voice recording dated 12 February 2012.

10.15 p.m.

So here we go again, Mandi. God, every time I say your name that Barry Manilow song pops into my head. Was it really about his dog? Sorry, this isn't really the place to be flippant, but you did say to let go and say whatever came into my head, and it takes my mind off, you know, Stephen. The crash. Fucking everything.

(A sob)

Sorry. Sorry. I'm fine. It happens sometimes, I think I'm coping and then . . . So. Day six since Jess came home. It's still like the slate has been wiped clean – her memories about life before Black Thursday are still spotty, and she has no recollection at all of the accident. She still does her morning ritual, as if she's disconnected from the real world and needs to remind herself of who she is: 'I'm Jessica, you're my Uncle Paul, and Mummy and Daddy and my sister are with the angels.' I'm still a bit guilty about the angels thing, Stephen and Shelly were atheists, but you try explaining the concept of death to a six-year-old without bringing heaven into it. I keep reminding myself that Dr Kasabian (God, the other day I slipped up and called him Dr Kevorkian – don't put that in) said that it's going to take some time to adjust, and changes in her behaviour are normal. There's no sign of brain damage as you know, but I did some more Internet research and PTSD can do strange things. But on the bright side, she's far more communicative – more so than she was before the crash, if that makes sense.

A funny thing happened this evening while I was putting her to bed, but I'm not sure we can use it for the book. You remember I told you we were reading *The Lion, the Witch and the Wardrobe?* Jess's choice. Well, out of nowhere, she goes, 'Uncle Paul, does Mr Tumnus like to kiss men like you do?'

I was *floored*, Mandi. Stephen and Shelly had decided that the girls were too young for the birds and the bees conversation, never mind anything more complex, so as far as I know they hadn't discussed the fact that I'm gay with the twins. And I don't let her see the papers or go on the Internet, not with all that crap they're saying in the States about her and the other two kids. Not to mention the bile fucking Marilyn and the Addams family keep spouting to the tabloids about me. I thought about asking who had told her I 'liked to kiss men', but decided against making a big deal out of it. It was possible a hack had got to her and the hospital had covered it up.

She wasn't going to let it go. '*Does* he, Uncle Paul?' she kept asking. You know the book, right, Mandi? Mr Tumnus is the first of the talking animals that Lucy bumps into when she goes through the wardrobe into Narnia – a little goateed fellow with deer's legs, a faun or something. (He actually looks a lot like that trauma counsellor who came over just after I heard the news about Jess.) And to be honest, in the illustration Mr Tumnus does look as camp as fuck with his little scarf tied jauntily around his neck. I suppose it isn't outside the realms of possibility that he'd just been off cottaging with some centaurs in the forest. God. Don't put that in either. I think I said something like, 'Well, if he does, that's his choice, isn't it?' and carried on reading.

We read quite far, and I was a bit nervous when we came to the bit where Aslan, the talking lion, gives himself up to the evil queen to be slaughtered. Stephen told me that when he read this to the girls last year, they'd sobbed and sobbed and Polly had even had nightmares.

But this time around, Jess was dry-eyed. 'Why would Aslan do that? It's just stupid, isn't it, Uncle Paul?'

I decided not to explain that Aslan's death is a Christian allegory, Jesus dying for all our sins and all that bollocks, so I said something like, 'Well, Edmund has betrayed the others, and the evil queen says she's going to kill him. Aslan says that he will take Edmund's place because he's good and kind.'

'It's still stupid. But I'm glad. I like Edmund.'

If you remember, Mandi, Edmund is the selfish spoiled lying bastard child. 'Why?'

And she said: 'He's the only one of the children who isn't a fucking pussy.'

Christ, I didn't know whether to tell her off or laugh. Remember I told you she'd picked up a slew of bad language when she was in hospital? It must've been from the porters or cleaners because I can't imagine Dr K or the nurses effing and blinding around her.

'You shouldn't say things like that, Jess,' I said.

'Like what?' And then she goes: 'It doesn't work like that. A fucking wardrobe. As *if*, Uncle Paul.' This thought seemed to amuse her, and she fell asleep soon after that.

I suppose I should be grateful that she's talking and communicating at all. She doesn't get visibly upset when I mention Stephen and Shelly and Polly, but it's early days. Dr K says I should prepare myself for some emotional fallout, but so far so good. We're still a ways from sending her back to school – the last thing we need is for the kids there to tell her what's being said about her – but we're inching towards making a normal life.

So what else? Oh yeah, tomorrow Darren from Social Services is coming to check 'that I'm coping'. Did I tell you about him? Darren's okay, a bit beardy and sandals and granola, but he's on my side, I can tell. I might need to think about getting an au pair or something like that, although that old busy-body from next door, Mrs Ellington-Burn (how's that for a name!), keeps nagging me to let her look after Jess. Mel and Geoff say they're also happy to babysit. What a pair of troopers. Thinking you could say something like: 'Mel and Geoff continued to be my backbone, while I struggled with my new single father status.' Too arsey? Well, we can work on it. You did a great job with the first chapters, so I'm sure it will be cool.

Hang on, let me get my tea. Fuck! Shit. Spilled it. Ow. That's hot. Okay . . .

No nutters phoned today, thank God. The group who are convinced Jess is an alien stopped after I asked the police to give them a warning, so that just leaves the God squad and the press. Gerry can handle the movie people. He still thinks we should wait a while and auction Jess's story. Seems a bit greedy, specially with the insurance money, but Jess might thank me when she's older if I set her up financially for life. Hard call. Can't imagine how that American kid is coping, the attention must be insane. I really feel for his grandmother, although at least she's in New York and not one of those Bible Belt states. I suppose it will all die down eventually. I told you another chat show in the States is trying to get The Three together, right? One of the big ones this time. They wanted to fly Jess and me to New York, but there's no way she's up to that. Then they suggested a Skype interview, but it all fell through when the father of the Japanese boy and Bobby's gran said no way. There's plenty of time for all that. I wish I could turn the bloody phone off some days, but I need to be available for social services and other important calls. Oh! Did I tell you I'm booked on *Morning Chat with Randy and Margaret* next week? Do watch it and tell me what you think. I only agreed because the booker just would not give up! And Gerry says it's a chance to set the record straight after all that crap about me in the *Mail on Sunday*.

(*The sound of a ring tone – the theme to* Dr Zhivago)

Hold on.

Fucking Marilyn again. At this time of night! Not answering that. Thank you Caller ID. They'll only harangue me about when I'm going to bring Jess round to see them. I can't put them off forever as they'll only run to their favourite *Sun* hack and blab, but I'm still holding out for an apology for that *Chat* magazine exposé about me being a basket-case. I hope you're not taking all that crap seriously, Mandi. Do you think we should say more about it in the book? Gerry says we should play it down. There's not much to tell, to be honest. Had a little slip-up, ten years ago, big deal. And I haven't been tempted to have another drink since the day I got the news.

(yawns)

That should do for now. Nighty night. I'm going to bed.

3.30 a.m.

Okay. Okay. It's cool. Breathe.

Something fucked-up has just happened. Mandi . . . I . . .

Deep breath, Paul. It's just in your head. It's just in your fucking head.

Talk it out. Yeah. Fuck. Why not. I can delete this, can't I? Narrative psychology, Dr K would be proud.

(laughs shakily)

Christ, I'm soaked through with sweat. Sopping. It's fading now, but this is what I remember.

I woke up suddenly, and I could feel there was someone sitting on the end of the bed – the mattress was sagging slightly as if there was a weight on it. I sat up, felt this huge wash of dread. I guess I knew instinctively that whoever it was was too heavy to be Jess.

I think I said something like, 'Who's there?'

My eyes adjusted to the dark and then I saw a shape at the end of the bed.

I froze. I've never felt fear like it. It . . . fuck, *think*, Paul. Jesus. It felt like . . . like a load of cement had been injected into my veins. I stared at it for ages. It was sitting slumped, motionless, looking down at its hands.

And then it spoke. 'What have you done, Paul? How could you let that thing in here?'

It was Stephen. I knew immediately from his voice it was him, but his shape looked different. Warped. More hunched, the head slightly too big. But it was so real, Mandi. Despite the panic, for a second I was absolutely convinced that he was actually there, and I felt a huge surge of joy and relief. 'Stephen!' I think I yelled. I reached out to grab him, but he'd gone.

5.45 a.m.

God. I've just played that back. It's so strange, isn't it, how dreams can seem so real at the time, but fade so quickly? Must be my subconscious telling me something. I wish it would hurry up and get light though. I can't decide if I should send this to you or not. I don't want to come across as a nutter, not with all the stories going around about me as it is.

And what did he mean, 'How could you let that thing in?'

PART FOUR

CONSPIRACY

FEBRUARY–MARCH

This is the second account from Reba Louise Neilson, Pamela May Donald's 'closest friend'.

Stephenie said she almost had a conniption when she heard Pastor Len's show about Pamela's message. He always discussed what he was going to say on his radio show with his inner circle after Bible study, but that time he just flat came out with it. I barely slept after I heard it. Couldn't figure why he wouldn't have shared something so important with his church first. Later he said the truth had come to him just that day and he felt called to spread the news as soon as he was able. Stephenie and I both agreed that those children couldn't have survived something like that without God's guiding hand, and those colours on the planes matching John's vision in Revelation, well, how could that be a coincidence? But when Pastor Len started saying that Pam was a prophet, like Paul and John, well, I found that hard to take, and I wasn't the only one.

Now, I know the Lord has a plan for us all that we can't always make sense of, but Pamela May Donald, a prophet? Plain old Pam who'd get her panties in a knot if she burned the brownies for the Christmas fundraiser? I kept my doubts to myself, and it was only when Stephenie brought it up when she was visiting with me that I even aired my views on the subject. We both had all the respect in the world for Pastor Len back then, we really did, and we decided not to breathe a word about how we felt to him or Kendra.

Not that we saw much of Pastor Len in the days directly after that show aired. I don't know when he found the time to sleep! He wasn't even there for Bible study that Wednesday; in fact he called me up and asked me to head up the meeting. Said he was driving down to San Antonio to meet with a website designer, wanted to start his own Internet forum to discuss what he called 'the truth about Pam', and would only be back late.

I asked him, 'Pastor Len, you sure you should be messing with the Internet, isn't it the devil's work?'

'We need to save as many as possible, Reba,' he said. 'We need to get that message out there however we can.' And then he quoted from Revelation: '"When Christ returns, every eye shall see Him."'

Well, how could I argue with that?

My daughter Dayna showed me the website when it was up a couple of days later: 'pamelaprophet.com' it was called! There was this huge photograph of Pam on the main page. Must have been from years before as she looked a good decade younger and at least thirty pounds lighter. Stephenie said that she'd heard that Pastor Len was even on that Twitter and that he was already getting emails and messages from all over.

Well, a week or so after the website was up and running, the first of what Stephenie and I privately called the 'Lookie-Loos' started showing up. At first, they were mostly from the neighbouring counties, but when Pastor Len's message went 'viral' (which is what Dayna says it's called), Lookie-Loos from as far away as Lubbock arrived. Congregation just about doubled overnight. That should have made my heart sing, so many being called to the Lord! But I will admit, I still felt a sense of doubt, especially when Pastor Len got a banner made up for outside the church, 'Sannah County, Home of Pamela May Donald,' and started calling his flock the Pamelists.

A lot of the Lookie-Loo folks also wanted to see Pamela's house, and Pastor Len was talking to Jim about charging an entrance fee, so that he could use the money to 'advertise the message far and wide'. Not one of us thought that was a good idea, and I felt it was my duty to take Pastor Len aside and air my concerns. Jim may have taken Jesus into his heart, but he was drinking more than ever. Sheriff Beaumont was forced to give him a warning for DUI once or twice, and whenever I drove over to fix him something to eat, he stank like he'd been bathing in whiskey. I knew Jim wouldn't be able to cope with strangers bothering him day and night. I was mightily relieved when Pastor Len agreed with me. 'You're right, Reba,' he said. 'I thank Jesus every day that I can always count on you to be my good right hand.' And then he said we should keep a closer eye on Jim, as 'he was still struggling with his demons.' Me and Stephenie and the rest of the inner circle drew up a rota so we could make sure he was eating and check that the house didn't fall into disrepair while he went through his mourning period. Pastor Len was keen to get Pam's ashes flown back to the US as soon as they'd finished their investigations, so that we could hold a proper memorial service for her, and asked me to find out when Joanie was going to send them. Jim wouldn't even hear me out on this matter. I can't be sure – he wasn't one to tell you anything, even when he wasn't under the influence of alcohol – but I don't think he'd even spoken to his daughter. You could see plain as day that he'd just given up. Folks would bring him meals and fresh milk, but a lot of the time he just left them to rot; didn't bother putting them in the refridgerator.

It truly was a whirlwind couple of weeks, Elspeth!

After he set up that website, Pastor Len would call me or Stephenie up almost every day, saying how the signs he'd predicted were coming thick and fast. 'You see on the news, Reba?' he'd say. 'There's that foot and mouth disease in the UK. That's a sign that the faithless and ungodly are being stricken with famine.' Then there was that virus that hit all the cruise ships – the one that spread to Florida and California – which had to mean that plague was rearing its ugly head. And of course as far as war was concerned, well, there's always plenty of that, what with those Islamofascists our poor brave marines have to contend with and those deranged North Koreans. 'And that's not all, Reba,' Pastor Len said to me, 'I been thinking . . . how about the families those three children are living with? Why would the Lord choose to place his messengers within such households?' I had to admit there was something in what he was saying. Not only was Bobby Small living in a Jewish household (although I know the Jews have their place in God's plan) but Stephenie said she'd read in the *Inquirer* that he was one of those test-tube babies. 'Not born of man,' she said. 'Unnatural.' Then there were those stories about the English girl being made to live with one of those homosexuals in London, and the Jap boy's father making those android abominations. Dayna showed me a clip of one of them on that YouTube; I was shocked to my very core! It looked just like a real person, and what did the Lord say about making false idols? There was also all that ungodly talk about evil spirits living in that forest where Pam's plane crashed. I did feel sorry for Pam, dying in such a horrible place. They do believe strange things in Asia, don't they? Like those Hindus with all those false gods that look like animals with too many arms. Enough to give you nightmares. Pastor Len put all of this up on his website, of course.

I can't quite recall exactly how long it was after Pastor Len's message started going viral that Stephenie and I went over to the ranch to visit with Kendra. She'd taken Snookie home with her, and Stephenie said it was our Christian duty to check that Kendra was coping. We both knew she had problems with her nerves and both of us had discussed at length how she seemed to be getting worse lately, what with all the Lookie-Loos flooding into town. Stephenie took along one of her pies, but to be honest, Kendra didn't look that pleased to see us. She'd just given that dog a bath, so it didn't stink too bad, and she'd even tied a red ribbon round its neck like it was one of those celebrities' pets. All the time we were there, Kendra barely took any notice of us. Just kept fussing with that dog as if it was a baby. Didn't even offer us a Coke.

We were just about to leave when Pastor Len came roaring up in his pick-up. He sprinted into the house, and I've never seen anyone looking as pleased with themselves as he did that day.

He greeted us, then said, 'I've done it, Kendra. I've done it!'

Kendra barely took any notice, so it was up to me and Stephenie to ask him what he meant.

'I just got a call from Dr Lund! He's invited me to talk at his conference in Houston!'

Stephenie and I couldn't believe our ears! We both watched Dr Theodore Lund's show every Sunday, of course, and Pam had been real jealous of me when Lorne bought me a signed copy of Sherry Lund's *Family Favourites* recipe book for my birthday.

'You know what this means, don't you, hon?' Pastor Len said to Kendra.

Kendra stopped fussing with that dog and said, 'What now?'

And Pastor Len grinned fit to burst and said, 'I'll tell you what now – I'm finally gonna be playing with the big boys.'

The following article, by British journalist and documentary filmmaker Malcolm Adelstein, was originally published in *Switch Online* magazine on 21 February 2012.

I'm standing in the gargantuan lobby of the Houston Conference Centre, where the annual End Times Bible Prophecy Convention is taking place, clutching a Bible with a fly-fisherman on the cover, and waiting for a man with the unlikely name of Flexible Sandy to finish publicising his latest novel. Despite an entrance fee of five thousand dollars, the conference attracts thousands of attendees from all over Texas and beyond, and the parking lot is filled with Winnebagos and SUVs sporting number plates from as far afield as Tennessee and Kentucky. I also seem to be the youngest person here by a good couple of decades – a sea of grey hair undulates around me. It's safe to say I'm more than a bit out of my comfort zone.

Felix 'Flexible' Sandy has a colourful background. Before his conversion to evangelical Christianity in the early seventies, he'd enjoyed a successful career as a contortionist, trapeze artist, and circus impresario – a fire and brimstone Southern version of P.T. Barnum. After Flexible's biography, *A High-Wire to Jesus*, was a bestseller in the seventies, the legend is that rising Bible Prophecy star Dr Theodore Lund approached him to write the first in a series of fictional End Times themed books. Written in fast-paced Dan Brown-style prose, the series details what will happen after the Rapture occurs and the world's saved literally disappear in the blink of an eye, leaving the earth-bound non-believers to contend with the Antichrist – a character who has an uncanny resemblance to former UK prime minister Tony Blair. Nine bestselling books later (it is estimated that over 70 million copies have been sold), Flexible Sandy is still going strong. He also recently launched his own website: 'rapturesacoming.com', a site that tracks global and national disasters in order to let members know (for a small fee of course) how close, on any given day, we might be to Armageddon. With his wiry frame and perma-tanned skin, eighty-year-old Flexible exudes the vigour of someone half his age. As he deals with the snaking line of devoted fans that stretches in front of him, his smile doesn't slip one iota. I'm hoping to persuade Flexible to take part in a documentary series I'm producing about the rise of the American End Times Movement. For the last few months I've been emailing his publicist – a brittle, efficient woman who has been eyeing me distrustfully since I arrived – to set up a meeting. Last week she hinted that I might get a chance if I turned up in Houston at the conference where he would be launching his latest book.

For those not in the know, End Times prophecy is basically the conviction that any day now, those who have taken Jesus as their personal saviour (aka born again) will be spirited up to heaven (aka raptured) while the rest us will endure seven years of horrendous suffering under the yoke of the Antichrist. These beliefs, based on the literal interpretation of several biblical prophets (including John in Revelation, Ezekiel and Daniel), are far more widespread than many people realise. In the US alone, it's estimated that over 65 million people believe that the events laid out in Revelation could actually happen in their lifetime.

Many high-level prophecy preachers can be cagey about talking to the non-evangelical press, and I rather naively hoped my English accent would help break the ice with Flexible. Five thousand dollars is a lot of money to shell out if all I'm going to get for it is a themed Bible. (Incidentally, on sale in the lobby are also Bibles for children, 'Christian wives', hunters and gun enthusiasts – but the fly-fisherman version caught my eye. I'm not sure why. I've never even been fishing.) Plus, I'm rather optimistically hoping that if Flexible agrees to talk to me, I might be able to persuade him to introduce me to the big cheese himself – Dr Theodore Lund. (I'm not holding out much hope; I've been told by fellow journalists that I'd have a better chance of being invited to go lap-dancing with Kim Jong-Il.) A mega-star of the evangelical movement, Dr Lund boasts his own TV station, a franchise of True Faith mega-churches that bring in hundreds of millions of dollars a year in 'donations', and the ear of former Republican President 'Billy-Bob' Blake. He also commands a global following on a par with Hollywood A-listers: his three Sunday services are internationally syndicated, and it's estimated that over 100 million people worldwide tune in every week to watch his prophecy-themed chat show. Although not as hard-line as the Dominionists, the fundamentalist sect who are actively campaigning for a US governed by strict Biblical rule (which would entail the death penalty for abortionists, gays and naughty children), Dr Lund is a harsh opponent of gay marriage, is vehemently pro-life, disputes global warming, and is not adverse to using his clout to influence political decisions, especially where Middle Eastern policy is concerned.

The queue of fans waiting to get their books signed by Flexible shuffles forwards. 'These books changed my life,' the woman in front of me tells me unsolicited. She has a shopping trolley piled high with various editions of the *Gone* books. 'They brought me to Jesus.' We chat about her favourite characters (she favours Peter Kean, a helicopter pilot whose languishing faith is restored – too late – when he witnesses his born-again wife, children and co-pilot being raptured before his eyes). I decide that it would be churlish to face Flexible without a copy of his novel, so I grab a couple from a towering dump-bin. Next to the piles of *Gone* books, a glossy cookbook display catches my eye. The cover sports a photograph of a heavily made-up woman with the tight eyes of the newly face-lifted. I recognise her as Dr Lund's wife Sherry, the co-presenter of his weekly after-sermon chat show. Her cookbooks regularly top the New York Times Bestseller lists and the sex manual she co-wrote with Dr Lund, *Intimacy the Christian Way*, was a runaway success in the eighties.

While Flexible gamely interacts with his geriatric fan base, I check out the displays advertising the talks, discussions and prayer groups that are scheduled back to back throughout the weekend, most sporting glossy life-size cut-outs of the celebrity preachers who are the main draw-card to the event. As well as several 'Are You Ready For the Rapture?' talks, there are symposiums on

Creationism and a hastily tacked on addition to the line-up – a 'get-together' with Pastor Len Vorhees, the new kid on the End Times block. Vorhees recently caused a minor Twitter storm with his extraordinary pronouncement that the three children who survived Black Thursday's disasters are actually three of the four horsemen out of Revelation.

Finally, the line dries up and it's my turn. The snippy publicist whispers something in Flexible's ear and he fixes the beam of his smile on me. His small eyes glint like black shiny buttons.

'England, huh?' he says. 'I was in London last year. That's a heathen country that needs saving, am I right, son?'

I assure him that he most certainly is.

'What sort of work you into, son? Patty here says you want to do an interview, something like that?'

I tell him the truth. That I make documentaries for television, that I'd love to chat to him and Dr Lund about their careers.

Flexible's button eyes bore into mine with more intensity. 'You with the BBC?'

I say that I have worked for the BBC, yes. It's not really a lie. I started my career as a runner for BBC Manchester, although I was fired after two months for smoking dope in the greenroom. I decide not to mention this.

Flexible seems to relax. 'Hold on, son, I'll see what I can do.' This is much easier than I was expecting. He waves his publicist over again, who manages to smile at Flexible and scowl at me simultaneously, and they share a terse whispered exchange.

'Son, Teddy's real busy right now. Tell you what, why don't you come up to the penthouse in a couple of hours? I'll see what I can do about getting you two acquainted. He's a big fan of the *Cavendish Hall* show you fellas have over there.'

I'm not sure what *Cavendish Hall*, a saccharine period drama that's making waves around the world, has to do with me, but it turns out that Flexible Sandy is still under the impression that I work for the BBC. I scuttle away before his publicist convinces him to change his mind.

*

Rather than head back to my bijou hotel room (fortunately included in the price tag), I decide to see if I can catch one of the talks. I'm thirty minutes late for Pastor Len Vorhees's 'get-together', but I mention to the usher that I'm a personal friend of Flexible Sandy's and he lets me slip inside.

It's standing room only in the Starlight Auditorium, and all that's visible of Pastor Len Vorhees is the top of his coiffed hair as he strides back and forth in front of the audience. His voice wavers every now and then, but it's clear from the chorus of 'Amen's that he's getting his message across. I'm vaguely aware that Pastor Len's bizarre theory has provoked fierce debate in the world of End Times believers, especially from the Preterist movement, which, unlike most of the other factions, believes that the events laid out in Revelation have already occurred. And I'm learning that Revelation is most certainly the basis of Pastor Len's wild assertions. According to the prophecy of John, the four horsemen will bring with them war, pestilence, famine and death, and Pastor Len starts to list various recent 'signs' that he says prove his theory. Among them are the gruesome account of the lizardy death of a paparazzo who'd allegedly broken into Bobby Small's hospital room (animal attacks are also included in Revelation's list of woes) and the details of the recent norovirus scourge that turned a fleet of cruise liners into vomit-filled hell ships. He manages to conclude with a frankly terrifying proclamation that war will soon ravage the African nations and bird flu will decimate the Asian population.

Longing for a stiff drink, I slip out on the chorus of 'Amen's to wait for my audience with Flexible Sandy and Dr Teddy Lund.

I'm gobsmacked when I'm let into the suite by Dr Lund himself, who greets me with a dazzling grin that shows off his state-of-the-art dental work. 'Good to meet you, son,' he says, gripping my hand between two of his. His skin has a slightly artificial glow, as if he's an irradiated fruit. 'Can I get you a beverage? You Brits like your tea, don't you?' I burble something along the lines of 'Indeed we do,' and allow him to lead me over to where Flexible and a slick-suited man in his early fifties are sitting in extravagantly upholstered armchairs. It takes me a second to realise that the fiftyish man is actually Pastor Len Vorhees. He's clearly not as at ease as the other two men; I get the impression of a child on his best behaviour.

Introductions are made and I allow myself to be swallowed up by the couch opposite. They all beam at me; none of their smiles meet their eyes.

'Flexible tells me you work for the BBC,' Dr Lund begins. 'I tell you, son, I'm not one for television, but I like that *Cavendish Hall* show. They knew how to behave in those days, didn't they? Had their morals straight. And you're out here wanting to do a documentary, something like that?'

Before I can get a word in, he continues, 'We get a lot of fellas wanting to do interviews. From all over the world. But I tell you, now might be the right time to get the message into England.'

I'm about to respond when two women appear through the door that leads to one of the suite's bedrooms. I recognise the taller of the two as Dr Lund's wife, Sherry – she's as coiffed and air-brushed as the photograph on the back of her latest cookbook. The woman hovering behind her couldn't be more of a contrast. She's as thin as a broom, her lined mouth is lipstick-free, and a white miniature poodle of some sort lolls in her arms.

I get to my feet but Dr Lund waves me back down. He introduces Sherry, and the other woman as Pastor Len's wife, Kendra. Kendra barely glances in my direction and Sherry beams at me for a nanosecond before turning to her husband. 'Don't forget that Mitch is on his way to see you, Teddy.' She blasts me with another practised smile. 'We're just going to take Snookie for some air.' Then she sweeps Kendra and the dog out of the suite.

'Let's get down to business,' Dr Lund says to me. 'What exactly do you have in mind, son? What sort of documentary are you planning on doing?'

'Well . . .' I say. And suddenly, for absolutely no reason, my carefully practised pitch dries up and my mind goes blank. In desperation I fix on Pastor Len Vorhees. 'Perhaps I could start . . . I caught your talk, Pastor Vorhees . . . it was, um, interesting. May I ask you about your theory?'

'Ain't a theory, son,' Flexible growls, while managing to keep his smile in place. 'It's the truth.'

I have no idea why these three men are making me feel so nervous. Maybe it's the force of their collective convictions and personalities – you don't get to be a Fortune 500 preacher by being uncharismatic. I manage to get myself under control. 'But . . . if you're saying the first four seals have just been opened, doesn't this contradict what you believe? That the church will be raptured *before* the horsemen bring devastation to the earth?' Eschatology – the study of End Times prophecy – gets complicated very fast. From my research, I've been led to believe that Dr Lund and Flexible are followers of Pre-Tribulation Rapture theory, where the Rapture of the church will take place just before the seven year tribulation period (i.e. before the Antichrist takes over and makes life miserable for the rest of us). Pastor Len's beliefs fall within the Post-Tribulation Rapture theory, whereby reborn Christians will remain on the earth as witnesses during the fire and brimstone stage, which, according to him, has just begun.

Pastor Len's handsome features ripple and he picks at his lapel, but Flexible and Dr Lund chuckle in unison as if I'm a child who's said something inappropriate but amusing. 'There's no contradiction here, son,' Flexible says. 'We know from Matthew twenty-four, "Ethnic group will rise against ethnic group. And government against government. There will be famines and earthquakes in various places. All these are the beginning of birth pains."'

Dr Lund chips in. 'This is happening all over. Right now. And we know that these birth pains signal the opening of the first four seals. We also know from both Revelation and Zechariah that the four harbingers are then sent throughout the world. White to the west, red to the east, black to the north and the pale horse to the south. Now that the seals have been opened, punishment will be exacted upon Asia, America, Europe and Africa.'

I'm struggling to follow this logic, but I manage to pick up on the last bit. 'And Australia? Antarctica?'

Flexible chuckles again and shakes his head at my denseness. 'They aren't part of the global moral decline, son. But they'll get their turn. The world's governments and the UN will all gather together to make the many-horned beast.'

Now that I haven't been taken by the seat of my pants and booted out, I'm feeling slightly more confident. I point out that the NTSB is indicating that the causes of the crashes are down to fully explainable events – pilot error, a possible bird strike, mechanical failure – and not supernatural interference (somehow I manage to phrase this without sounding like I'm talking about aliens or the devil).

Pastor Len opens his mouth to comment but Dr Lund jumps in. 'I'll answer this, Len. You think God wouldn't have the power to make these events look like accidents? He wants to test our faith, root out the believer from the heathen. We have heeded his call. But we're in the business of saving souls, son, and when the fourth horseman is found, even the most reluctant will be called to his fold.'

I feel my mouth lolling open. 'The fourth horseman?'

'That's correct, son.'

'But there were no survivors of the crash in Africa.'

Pastor Len and Dr Lund exchange glances, and Dr Lund gives the tiniest nod.

'We believe there is,' Pastor Len says.

I stutter that according to the NTSB and the agencies in Africa, there is no chance that anyone on the Dalu Air flight could have survived.

Dr Lund smiles humourlessly. 'That's what they said about the other three incidents, and look what the Lord chose to show us.' He pauses. Then he asks the question I know has been coming. 'Have you been saved, son?'

Flexible Sandy's peculiar button eyes bore into mine and I'm suddenly back at school, standing in front of the headmaster. I'm overwhelmed with the desire to lie and claim that yes, I am one of them, among the saved. But it passes and I tell them the truth. 'I'm Jewish.'

Dr Lund nods in approval. Flexible Sandy's grin doesn't falter. 'We need the Jews,' Dr Lund says. 'You're an important part of the coming events.'

I know what he's talking about. After the Rapture and the Antichrist's rule, Jesus will return to vanquish the infidels and power-drive the Antichrist off his throne. This battle is pipped to take place in Israel, and Dr Lund, like many prophecy believers, is vociferously pro-Israel. He believes, as it says in the Bible, that Israel belongs to the Jews and the Jews alone, and he is adamant that land swapping and peace accords with Palestine should be forcefully opposed. It's rumoured that during President 'Billy-Bob' Blake's tenure in the White House, Dr Lund was a regular visitor. I really want to question him about the elephant in the room – why someone who truly believes the end of the world is imminent would bother to meddle in politics – but Dr Lund stands up before I can think how to phrase it.

'Go well, son,' he says. 'Get hold of my publicist, she'll help you out.' With another round of handshakes, I'm dismissed. (A few days later I do as he suggests, but receive only a curt 'Dr Lund is unavailable' response, and a flat silence to my other stabs at communication with Flexible Sandy.)

As I leave the conference, my fly-fisherman's Bible and my *Gone* books tucked under my arm, I pass a phalanx of huge body-guards surrounding a man in an even more expensively cut suit than Dr Lund's. I recognise him immediately. It's Mitch Reynard, former governor of Texas, who announced his intention to run for the Republican presidential nomination just a couple of weeks ago.

**The following is an extract from *rapturesacoming.com*,
Felix 'Flexible' Sandy's website.**

A personal message from me today, believers. Our brothers Dr
Theodore Lund (who needs no introduction!) and Pastor Len
Vorhees of Sannah County have shown us the Truth, irrefutable
proof that the first four seals as laid out in Revelation have
been opened, and the horsemen are set loose upon the world
to punish the ungodly with Famine, Plague, War, Pestilence and
Death. Some of you may be saying, but Flexible, weren't the
seals broken a long time ago? The world has been in moral
decline for generations, hasn't it? I say that may be, but God in
His wisdom has now shown us the truth. And if you think about
it, believers, it's going to play out just like it did in *Thief in the
Night*, the ninth in the *Gone* series, which I don't need to tell
you is available to order from this very site.

And that's not all, you'll see that the signs are hotting up
fast, with major incidents coming thick and fast this week.
Good news for all of us waiting to be taken up to Jesus' side!

Flexible

The full list can be found under the headings if you CLICK on
them, but here are our top choices:

PLAGUE (rapturesacoming probability rating: 74%)
The vomiting bug that started on those cruise liners has taken
hold throughout the US:
www.news-agency.info/2012/february/
norovirus-spreads-to-US-East-Coast
*(Thanks to Isla Smith of North Carolina for sending this one
through! Flexible appreciates your faith, Isla!)*

WAR (rapturesacoming probability rating: 81%)

Well, what can I say? War is always a strong indicator and it's not letting us down today! The holy War on Terror still rages in Afghanistan and check out this link below:
www.atlantic-mag.com/worldnews/
north-korea-nuclear-threat-could-be-a-reality

FAMINE (rapturesacoming probability rating: 81%)

That foot and mouth disease looks like it's finding a foothold in the rest of Europe. Check out this headline: 'New Strain of Foot and Mouth Could Have Massive Impact on Farming, UK govt warns.'
(source: www.euronewscorp.co.uk/footandmouth/)

DEATH (rapturesacoming probability rating: 91%)

And I looked, and behold a pale horse: and his name that sat on him was Death, and Hell followed with him. And power was given to them over the fourth part of the earth, to kill with sword, and with hunger, and with death, and with the beasts of the earth. (Revelation 6:8)

There's been a spate of animal attacks recently, just like it says in verses 6:8. Check out these links:

'American tourist slain in Botswana rogue hyena attack' (www.bizarredeaths.net)

'Inquest on LA photographer eaten alive by pet lizards postponed' (www.latimesweekly.com)

A Flexible note: This one is of particular interest, as the photographer had ties to Bobby Small, which makes this a nine on the scale! Not since 9/11 have we been this close!

Lola Cando.

I hadn't seen Lenny for a while, not since he told me about Pamela May Donald's message. Then he called me up, asked me to meet him at one of our motels. Lucky for him I had a cancellation. One of my regulars, ex-marine – a sweet fella – was feeling blue and wanted to postpone.

Anyhow, that day, Lenny burst into the room, snatched the drink I poured for him and started pacing up and down. Told me he'd just got back from a conference in Houston. He looked just like a little kid who'd been to Disneyland for the first time. He must have talked non-stop for half-an-hour at least. He was saying how he'd been hanging out with Dr Lund, who'd invited him to appear on his Sunday show. Said he'd even had dinner with Flexible Sandy – the fella who wrote those books I never got around to reading. Went on about how the room where he'd given his talk had been packed to the rafters with the faithful.

'And guess who else was there, Lo?' he asked while he pulled off his tie. I didn't know what to say, wouldn't have been surprised if he'd said Jesus himself, way he was talking about those guys with all that awe in his voice. 'Mitch Reynard,' he said. 'Mitch Reynard! Dr Lund has given him his backing.'

I'm not one for politics, but even I knew who this fella was. Caught him on a couple of the news segments Denisha likes to watch. Smooth guy, ex-preacher, looked a bit like Bill Clinton, always had the right answers, used to be a member of that Tea Party contingent. He was never out of the news when it turned out he was running for the Republican presidential nomination. Got a lot of criticism from the liberals for what he was saying about feminism and how gay marriage was an abomination.

Lenny started getting carried away, talking about how this could even be his ticket to getting into politics himself. 'Anything is possible, Lo. Dr Lund says we must do everything in our power to sway the vote, make sure the country gets back to a good moral footing.'

Talking about morals, far as I was aware, Lenny never saw anything hypocritical about paying for my services. Maybe he didn't even see it as adultery. He didn't talk about his wife often, but I got the impression they hadn't been intimate for a while. Course, last couple of times I saw him, there wasn't much adultery going on; he was too busy unloading on me.

Would I say that fame went to his head? Yeah, sure. After he set up the website and got involved with Dr Lund, he was like a kid with a new toy. He said he was in contact with people from all over the world. Fellas right down in Africa even. There was that Monty guy he said he emailed every day, and a marine who was doing his duty somewhere in Japan. Jake somebody. I can't recall his surname even though he was all over the news later on. Lenny told me all about how that marine had been into the Japanese forest where that plane had crashed. 'Where Pam breathed her last breath.' He said that Dr Lund had tried to contact Bobby's grandmother, wanted to invite Bobby onto his show as well, but wasn't getting anywhere. I really felt for the poor woman. Both me and Denisha did. It couldn't have been easy being the focus of all that attention when you were still in mourning.

Lenny went on and on about how he was getting requests to do interviews from all over – talk shows, radio shows, Internet blogs, the whole caboodle, and not just the religious ones either. 'Aren't you worried they'll ridicule you, Lenny?' I asked him. He let slip that Dr Lund's PR team had warned him to be careful about talking to the non-Christian press, and I thought that was wise advice. What he was saying about the children being the horsemen, you could see how lots of folks would think that was just plain nonsense.

'I'm spreading the truth, Lo,' he said. 'If they want to ignore it, that's their business. When the Rapture comes, we'll see who has the last laugh.'

We didn't even do it that day. He just wanted to talk. As he left, he reminded me to catch Dr Lund's *True Faith Togetherness* show that weekend.

I was curious to see how Lenny would come across, so come Sunday, I settled down to watch it. Denisha couldn't figure out what the hell I was doing. I hadn't told her that Lenny was one of my clients. I respect my regulars' privacy, which I know sounds like a lie seeing as here's me talking to you now! But I never asked to be outed, did I? I wasn't the one who went to the reporters. Anyhow, first off, Dr Lund stood at this big gold pulpit, a huge choir behind him. That church of his, the size of a shopping mall, was bursting at the seams. He basically just repeated Lenny's theories about Pamela May Donald's message, stopping every five minutes so that the choir could sing a bit more and the congregation could chime in with their 'Amen's and 'Praise Jesus's. Then he went on about how the time was ripe for God's judgement, what with all the immorality going on, the gays and the women's libbers and the baby killers and the school boards who promote Evolution. Denisha kept clicking her tongue. Her church knows all about what she does for a living, and they have no problem with the gays, either. 'It's all the same to them, Lo,' she said. 'People is people, and rather be upfront about it than hide it. Jesus never judged nobody, did he? 'Cept those money-lenders.' Most of those rich preachers and high-end pastors had skeletons in their closets, and every day there seemed to be a new scandal about one of them. But not Dr Lund. He was known to be squeaky clean. Denisha reckoned he had the right connections to keep his dirty doings out of the media; knew where the bodies were buried.

After his sermon, Dr Lund walked over to an area at the side of the stage, which was decorated like a living room, all expensive rugs and oil paintings and lampshades with gold tassels. On the couch waiting for him were Dr Lund's wife, Sherry, Lenny and a skinny woman who looked like she needed feeding up. That was the first time I saw Pastor Len's wife, Kendra. She couldn't have looked more different to Sherry, who Denisha said had the look of Tammy Faye Bakker about her – all eyelashes and drag queen accessories. But Lenny came across okay. He was a bit agitated, kept fidgeting and his voice wobbled some, but he didn't

embarrass himself. Dr Lund did most of the talking. Kendra
didn't say one word. And the look on her face . . . it was hard to
read. I couldn't tell if she was nervous, thought the whole thing
was just dumb, or if she was bored out of her mind.

Pastor Len Vorhees agreed to be interviewed on DJ Erik Kavanaugh's notorious Talk NYC radio show, *Mouthing Off*. The following is a transcript of the show aired on 8 March 2012.

ERIK KAVANAUGH: On the line with me today, I have Pastor Len Vorhees from Sannah County, Texas. Pastor Len – can I call you that, by the way?

PASTOR LEN VORHEES: Yes, sir, that's absolutely fine.

EK: That's a first, no one's ever called me sir before. Gotta say, you're politer than most of the guests I usually have on here. Pastor Len, you are trending on Twitter right now. Do you think it's right for an evangelical Christian to use social media in this way?

PL: I believe we should use any means possible to spread the good news, sir. And since I got the message out there, there are people flocking into Sannah County, eager to be saved. Why, at my church they're practically spilling out the doors. *(He laughs)*

EK: So it's like that scene in *Jaws*. You're gonna need a bigger church?

PL: *(Pause)* I'm not quite sure what—

EK: Now let's get down to exactly what you're saying. Some people might say that your belief that these children are the horsemen is – and I can find no other way to say this – absolutely batshit crazy.

PL: *(Laughing nervously)* Well now, sir, that kind of language isn't—

EK: Is it true that you came up with this theory after one of your parishioners, Pamela May Donald, the sole American on board the Japanese plane that crashed into that forest, left a message on her phone?

PL: Ah . . . yes, that's correct, sir. Her message was addressed to me and her meaning was clear as day. 'Pastor Len,' she said. 'Warn them about the boy.' The only boy she could mean was the Japanese boy who was the sole survivor of that crash. The *sole* survivor. And then the airplanes' insignias—

EK: In the message she also mentions her dog. If you believe she was saying that the Japanese boy is some sort of end-of-days harbinger, surely this means you also believe we should all go around treating the family pooch like a deity now?

PL: *(Several seconds of dead air)* Well now, I wouldn't go so far as to—

EK: On your website, pamelaprophet.com – you should check it out folks, trust me – you say that there are facts that back up what you're saying. Signs that the misery the horsemen are supposed to bring is already coming to pass. Let me give any listeners who may not have heard the details of your theory an example. You're saying that the foot and mouth outbreak they've just been having in Europe was brought on by the appearance of the horsemen, am I right?

PL: That's correct, sir.

EK: But surely there's always stuff like this going on? The UK experienced exactly the same thing a few years ago.

PL: That's not the only sign though, sir. If you put them all together, you can clearly see that there is a pattern of—

EK: And these signs, you're saying they're all pointing towards the fact that the end of the world is nigh when all the saved will

be raptured. Is it fair to say you evangelical guys are looking
forward to this event?

PL: I wouldn't say that looking forward is the right way to
phrase it, no, sir. It's important to let your listeners know that by
taking the Lord—

EK: So these signs are like God's way of saying, time's up folks,
get saved or burn in hell forever?

PL: Uh . . . I'm not certain that—

EK: Your beliefs have come under radical fire from religious
leaders of, let's say, more traditional persuasions. More than a
few of them have said that what you're saying, and I quote, is
'utter fear-mongering nonsense'.

PL: There will always be doubters, sir, but I would urge your
listeners to—

EK: You've got some heavy hitters behind you. I'm talking
about Dr Theodore Lund of the End Times Movement. Is it
true he used to go shooting with former President 'Billy-Bob'
Blake?

PL: Uh . . . you'll have to ask him about that, sir.

EK: I don't need to ask him about his views on women's rights,
the Israeli peace accords, abortion and gay marriage. He's
radically opposed to them. Do you share his views?

PL: *(another long pause)* I believe we should look to the Bible for
guidance on these matters, sir. In Leviticus it says that—

EK: Doesn't it also say in Leviticus that owning slaves is cool and
that kids who backchat to their parents should be stoned? Why

do you guys take on board, say, the anti-gay stuff and not the
other crap?

PL: *(dead air for several seconds)* Sir . . . I object to your tone. I
came on the show to tell your listeners that time is—

EK: Let's move on. Your theory about The Three isn't the only
one doing the rounds. There are quite a few nutjobs who are
adamant that those kids are possessed by aliens. Why are their
views any crazier than what you believe?

PL: I'm not sure what you—

EK: The Three are just children, surely? Haven't they been
through enough? Wouldn't the Christian thing to do be not to
judge them?

PL: *(another long pause)* I don't . . . I—

EK: So let's say they're possessed, are the real children still inside
their bodies? If so, must be getting crowded in there, am I right?

PL: God . . . Jesus works in ways we can only—

EK: Ah, the 'God works in mysterious ways' defence.

PL: Uh . . . but you can't . . . you can't discount the signs
that . . . How else did those children survive the crashes? It's—

EK: Is it true you believe there is a fourth child who has survived
the crash in Africa? A fourth horseman? You're saying this even
though the NTSB is absolutely adamant that no one could have
survived that tragedy?

PL: *(clears throat)* Uh . . . that crash site . . . there was much
confusion down there. Africa is . . . Africa is a—

EK: So how did these horsemen bring down the planes? On a practical level, it seems like a lot of effort to go to, doesn't it?

PL: Um . . . I can't tell you that for sure, sir. But I will tell you this, when they release the crash reports, there will be signs of . . . of . . .

EK: Supernatural interference? Like the alien people believe?

PL: You're twisting my words, sir. I didn't mean that—

EK: Thank you, Pastor Len Vorhees. We'll be opening the lines for callers after this message.

NTSB investigator Ace Kelso spoke to me again at length after the preliminary crash investigation findings from all four incidents were revealed at a press conference, which was held in Washington, Virginia on 13 March 2012.

As I said at the press conference, it's rare for us to reveal our findings so soon. But this was a special case – people needed to know the incidents weren't down to terrorism or some goddamned supernatural event, and the families of the survivors needed closure. You wouldn't believe the number of calls the Washington office fielded from whackos convinced we were in cahoots with sinister *Men in Black* government agencies. Course, added into the mix was the fact that after Black Thursday the aviation industry was suffering financially, needed to get back on track. You heard that a few of the more unscrupulous airlines are cashing in on the fact that all three survivors were seated towards the rear of the aircraft? Charging a premium for the seats at the back; considering relocating First and Business Class to the rear to recoup lost profits.

It was obvious to us early on that terrorism wasn't a factor. We knew from the bodies and wreckage recovered that none of the aircraft in any of the four instances had broken up significantly mid-air, which would have been the case had an explosive device been triggered. Sure, we had to consider a possible hijacking scenario at first, but no organisation came forward at any time to take responsibility.

As you know, there's still a massive operation underway to locate the CVR and black box from the site of the Go!Go! Air incident, but we're confident we know the sequence of events that led to the disaster. First of all, from the aircraft's flight path and the weather data, we know they found themselves flying into a severe thunderstorm. The last contact from the aircraft, an automated telemetry message to the Go!Go! Air technical centre, indicated that the aircraft had undergone multiple electrical failures, most notably of the static port heating system. This would have resulted in ice crystals forming in the static ports, which in turn would have resulted in inaccurate airspeed readings. Thinking that their airspeed was too low, the pilots would have progressively increased the speed of the aircraft to avoid a stall. We believe they continued doing so until they exceeded the aircraft's capabilities and literally flew the wings off the thing. We're almost certain Jessica Craddock's burn injuries were caused by a fuel fire after the event, or from a malfunctioning flare.

Now, the Dalu Air flight was a different story. The series of factors that added up to *that* crash pointed to an accident waiting to happen. For a start, the design of the Antonov AN-124 dates back to the seventies, light years away from the 'fly by wire' technology used by Airbus. The aircraft was also operated by a small Nigerian outfit that mostly flew freight and which, it must be said, didn't have the best safety record. Won't go into too many technicalities again, but Cape Town International airport's ILS wasn't working that day – apparently it can be hokey. Also, the Antonov wasn't fitted with modern navigation equipment such as LNS [Lateral Navigation System] and wasn't adequately equipped to deal with the alternative approach system. The pilots misjudged the approach, came in approximately one hundred feet too low, the right wing clipped a power line and the Antonov immediately crashed into a densely populated township situated adjacent to the airfield. Gotta say, we were all impressed with how the Dalu Air investigation was handled by the CAA and the Cape Town Disaster Management Team. Those guys and gals know their stuff. You wouldn't think it for a third world country, but they really got their ducks in a row asap. The head investigator – Nomafu Nkatha (don't think I pronounced that correctly, Elspeth!) – gathered eye-witness accounts immediately after the event, and several people had caught the moments before impact on their cellphone cameras.

The investigators have still got a job on their hands identifying the bodies of those killed at the site. Looks like a lot of them were refugees or asylum seekers and it's going to be a near-impossible task tracking down family members for DNA matches. The CVR was recovered eventually. Guys had been collecting the parts, selling them off to tourists – can you *believe* that shit? But like I say, top marks to the team out there.

Next one I'll deal with was the Maiden Air crash – the one I was IIC on, before I was asked to oversee the whole operation. The evidence suggests that the aircraft suffered an almost total power loss on both engines due to ingestion – probably as a result of multiple bird strike. This occurred roughly two minutes after take-off, which is the most vulnerable phase of the climb. The pilots were unable to return to the airport and the aircraft crashed into the Everglades approximately three to four minutes later. We found the black box on this one, but the data was compromised. The N1 Turbines on both engines showed damage consistent with bird strike although there was, curiously, no trace of snarge. In line with my recommendations, the board ruled that engine failure due to multiple bird strike was the most probable cause of the crash.

Then we had the one that I'd say was the most controversial. I'm talking about the Sun Air incident. The rumours that were going around about the cause of that crash were hard to contain – most notably the fallacy that Captain Seto was suicidal and brought the plane down deliberately. On top of this, the Japanese minister of transport's wife said publicly that she believed aliens were involved. There was real pressure on us to sort that out asap. We had the CVR, which indicated a loss of hydraulics, and we know from the black box that the aircraft was effectively brought down by shoddy workmanship. The failure to follow basic repair procedures to the tail section resulted in rivets giving way. The structural integrity of the fuselage was compromised, resulting in explosive decompression some fourteen minutes into the flight. The rudder was damaged and the hydraulics were lost, and when this happens, it's just about impossible to steer the aircraft. Pilots fought with that baby as hard as they could. Gotta admire them for that. We ran comparative test in simulators and no one has been able to keep it in the air as long as they did.

Course, we had to field a ton of questions at the press conference, lots of the reporters wanted to know where the bright lights a couple of the passengers said they'd seen came from. Could have been any number of things. More than likely lightning. That's why we made the transcript of the CVR recording public asap, to stop those rumours in their tracks.

The following transcript, taken from the Sun Air Flight SAJ678 Cockpit Voice Recorder, was first published on the National Transportation and Safety Bureau's website on 20 March 2012.

Capt – Captain
FO – First Officer
ATC – Air Traffic Control

Transcript commences at 21h44 (fourteen minutes after take-off from Narita airport).

FO: Passing flight level three three zero, captain, that's a thousand foot to go. Looks like it should be nice and smooth at three four zero, not much CAT forecast.

CAPT: Good.

FO: Do you have—

[A loud bang. Depressurisation alarm sounds.]

CAPT: Mask! Put on your mask!

FO: Mask on!

CAPT: We're losing the cabin, can you control it?

FO: The cabin is at 14,000 already!

CAPT: Go to manual and close the outflow valve. Looks like we've got a decompression.

FO: Ah, Captain, we need to get down!

CAPT: Try again.

FO: The valve is fully closed, it's no use – I can't control it!

CAPT: Have you closed the outflow valve?

FO: Affirmative!

CAPT: Okay, understood. Tell ATC we are starting an emergency descent.

FO: Mayday, mayday, mayday – SAJ678 commencing emergency descent. We've had an explosive decompression.

ATC: Copy that. Mayday SAJ678, you can descend, there is no other traffic to affect you. Standing by.

CAPT: I have control. What is our grid mora?

FO: Level 140.

CAPT: Disconnecting the auto-throttle, dial in flight level 140.

FO: Flight level 140 set.

[*Captain is on the intercom*]

CAPT: Ladies and gentlemen, this is your captain speaking. We are starting an emergency descent. Please put on your oxygen masks and follow the cabin crew's instructions.

CAPT: Commencing emergency descent. Closing thrust levers, deploying speed brake. Read the emergency descent checklist.

FO: Thrust lever closed, speed brake down, heading selected, lower level selected, start switches to continuous, seat belt signs on, pax oxygen switch on, squawking 7700, ATC notified.

CAPT: Can't control the heading – she's yawing to the right. I can't get the wings level!

FO: [*expletive*] Rudder or aileron?

CAPT: I've got full left aileron, but she's not responding!

FO: Master caution hydraulics. I am cancelling the light. We've lost all hydraulics, we've got system A, and system B low pressure lights on! I'll get the QRH and read the hydraulic checklist.

CAPT: Get me some hydraulics back!

FO: [*expletive*]

CAPT: I'm going to take some more thrust on three and four engines.

FO: It looks like the standby system is gone too. The hydraulic quantities are all empty!

CAPT: Keep trying.

FO: We've got 2000 feet to level off.

FO: 1000 feet to level off!

[*Sound of altitude warning horn.*]

CAPT: I'm stowing the speed brake and taking some more thrust on numbers one and two.

FO: The nose is dropping – pull up!

CAPT: She's not responding! More thrust to slow the descent.

CAPT: Okay. She's levelling off – still can't control the heading. Keeps going to the right.

FO: Try and take more thrust on three and four.

CAPT: Okay. More thrust on three and four . . .

CAPT: It's still not helping – she's still rolling to the right!

ATC: Mayday SAJ678, what is your heading?

FO: Mayday SAJ678 we've lost all hydraulics, we will come back to you.

CAPT: We've got no rudder!

FO: We are going to have to go to manual reversion!

CAPT: [*expletive*] Feels like we're in manual reversion already! I am struggling to control. Let's see if we can get some of the speed off – 300 knots.

FO: The nose is dropping again!

CAPT: Is there an airfield close to us?

FO: The—

CAPT: Give me more thrust on three and four!

[*Sound of GPWS, whoop whoop, pull up, whoop whoop, pull up, too low terrain, too low terrain, whoop whoop, pull up, whoop whoop, pull up, too low terrain.*]

CAPT: Full thrust all four . . . pull up! Pull up!

FO: [*expletive*]

CAPT: Pull up! Pull up!

[*Recording ends.*]

The following article was published in the *Crimson State Echo* on 24 March 2012.

END TIMES PREACHER STARTS HUNT FOR 'FOURTH HORSEMAN'

At a recent press conference in Houston, Dr Theodore Lund, one of the driving forces behind the Evangelical End Times Movement, told a gathering of the world's press that: 'The fourth horseman is out there and it's only a matter of time until he is found.' Dr Lund is referring to the theory, first aired by a backwater Texan preacher, that The Three miracle children who survived Black Thursday's devastating events are possessed by the Riders of the Apocalypse, sent by God to usher in the End Times. The theory is based on the last words of Pamela May Donald, the only American citizen on board the plane that crashed into the notorious Aokigahara 'suicide forest' in Japan. Dr Lund and his followers are adamant that there is no other explanation for The Three's so-called miraculous survival, and believe that various global events, such as unprecedented floods in Europe, a drought in Somalia and the escalating situation in North Korea, are all signs of the impending end of the world.

And now Dr Lund has made the extraordinary statement that there is another child – a fourth horseman – who survived the doomed Dalu Air flight that crashed in Cape Town, South Africa. Citing the recently published Dalu Air passenger list, Dr Lund said that there was only one child on the flight who was close to the same age as the three children who survived the other disasters virtually unscathed – a seven-year-old Nigerian boy named Kenneth Oduah: 'We strongly believe Kenneth will prove to be one of God's harbingers.'

Dr Lund is undeterred by the South African Civil Aviation Authority's definitive statement that there were 'categorically no survivors of Dalu Air Flight 467.'

'We'll find him,' he said. 'It was chaos down there after the crash. Africa is a messy place. The child could easily have got lost or wandered off. And when we do find him, it will be all the proof those who have not yet entered Jesus' fold will need.'

When questioned what he meant by this, Dr Lund replied: 'You don't want to be left behind when the Antichrist comes, you're going to experience suffering worse than you can ever imagine. As it says in Thessalonians, "The day of the Lord will come as a thief in the night," and Jesus could call us to him any day now.'

REWARD 200,000 US Dollars!!!

For the discovery of Kenneth Oduah, a seven-year-old Nigerian passenger travelling on the Antonov cargo and passenger plane that crashed into Khayelitsher [*sic*] Township, Cape Town, South Africa on 12 January 2012. It is believed that Kenneth left the children's home where he was taken after the crash and may currently be living on the streets of Cape Town.

According to his aunt, Veronica Alice Oduah, Kenneth has a large head, very dark skin and a crescent-shaped scar on his scalp. If you think you know of his whereabouts, please contact findingkenneth.net or call +00 789654377646 and leave a message. Normal rates apply.

REWARD 200,000 US Dollars!!!

PART FIVE

SURVIVORS

MARCH

Chiyoko and Ryu.

(Translator Eric Kushan notes that he has chosen to use the Japanese term *izoku* in the transcript below, instead of the rough translation 'families of the bereaved' or the more literal translation, 'families left behind'.)

Message logged @ 16.30, 05/03/2012

RYU: Where have you been all day? I was getting worried about you.

CHIYOKO: Six *izoku* came today.

RYU: All at once?

CHIYOKO: No. Two came together in the morning; the rest came separately. So tiring. Mother Creature is always saying we have to treat the families with respect. I know they're in pain, but how does she think Hiro feels having to listen to them all day?

RYU: How *does* he feel?

CHIYOKO: It must be really boring for him. They all shuffle up to him and bow, and then they all ask the same thing. 'Did Yoshi, or Sakura, or Shinji or whoever suffer? Did they say anything before they died?' Like Hiro would know who these people are! It creeps me out, Ryu.

RYU: That would creep me out, too.

CHIYOKO: If they come when MC is out, I tell them to go away. MC always lets them know that he's still not speaking, not that this seems to make any difference to them. But today, while MC was in the kitchen preparing tea, I did an experiment. I told them that he does actually talk, but he's very shy. I told them that he's always saying that there was no panic or horror as the plane went down and that no one suffered except for the American woman and the two survivors who died in hospital. Was that evil of me?

RYU: You told them what they wanted to hear. If anything, it was kind.

CHIYOKO: Yeah, well . . . I only said it because I wanted to get them out of the house. I can only serve so much tea and wear my 'I'm sorry for your loss' face for so long. Oh, I meant to tell you. You know that most of the *izoku* who come here to see Hiro are ancient. Well today a younger woman came. Younger as in she could walk without a stick and didn't look shocked when I didn't serve the tea in exactly the right way. She said she was the wife of the man who sat next to the American.

RYU: I know who you mean . . . Keita Eto. He left a message, didn't he?

CHIYOKO: Yeah. I re-read it after she left. It basically said that before he got on that plane he was suicidal.

RYU: Do you think his wife knew how he felt before he died?

CHIYOKO: Well she certainly knows now.

RYU: That must hurt. What did she want to know from Hiro?

CHIYOKO: The usual. If her husband had acted bravely when the plane went down, and if he'd said anything else apart from what he'd left on the message. She asked this in a matter-of-fact manner. I got the impression she was really just curious to see Hiro rather than wanting reassurance. Like he's some kind of exhibit. It made me mad.

RYU: They'll stop coming soon.

CHIYOKO: You think? Over five hundred people died in the crash. There are hundreds of families who might still want to see him.

RYU: Don't think like that. At least now they know why the plane did crash for sure. That might help.

CHIYOKO: Yeah. Perhaps you're right. I hope it gives the captain's wife some peace.

RYU: She really got to you.

CHIYOKO: She did. I'll admit that I think about her often.

RYU: Why do you think that is?

CHIYOKO: Because I know what it's like. To be shunned, to have people saying terrible things about you.

RYU: Did that happen to you when you were in the States as well?

CHIYOKO: You really like digging for information, don't you? But to answer your question, no, I was not shunned when I lived in the States.

RYU: Did you make friends there?

CHIYOKO: No. Just acquaintances. You know I find most people dull, Ryu. That includes Americans. Although I know you admire them.

RYU: I do not! Why do you think that?

CHIYOKO: Why else are you so interested in my life there?

RYU: I told you, just curious. I want to know everything about you. Don't get mad. _|7O

CHIYOKO: Ai! The attack of the ORZ again.

RYU: I knew that would cheer you up. And just so you know . . . I am very happy that the anti-social ice princess thinks I am worth talking to.

CHIYOKO: You and Hiro are the only two people I can stand being around.

RYU: Except you've never met one of us and the other one doesn't talk back. Do you prefer that? The silent treatment?

CHIYOKO: Are you jealous of Hiro, Ryu?

RYU: Of course not! That's not what I meant.

CHIYOKO: It is not always necessary to talk to make yourself understood. You'd be amazed how much emotion Hiro can express by just using his eyes and body language. And yes, while I admit it's soothing to talk to someone who can't answer back, it's also frustrating. Don't worry, I am not about to choose the Silent Boy over you. Besides, he's taken a liking to *Waratte Iitomo!* and *Apron of Love*, which I know you would never do. I hope it passes.

RYU: Ha! He is only six.

CHIYOKO: Yeah. But those shows are for moronic adults. I don't know what he sees in them. MC is worried what the authorities will say if he doesn't go back to school soon. I don't think he should go back. I hate the thought of him being with other children.

RYU: I agree. Children are cruel.

CHIYOKO: And how can he defend himself if he can't even speak? He needs protecting.

RYU: But he can't stay away forever, can he?

CHIYOKO: I need to find a way to teach him how to protect himself. I don't want him to go through what we went through. I couldn't bear it.

RYU: I know.

CHIYOKO: Hey. He's right here now, sitting with me, do you want to say hello?

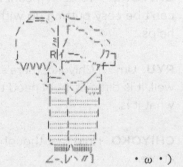

RYU: Hello, Hiro! (/ ・ω・)(/　　　　∠-.レヽ〃)　　　　・ω・)

CHIYOKO: Nice! He just bowed back at you. MC says she also wants to take him back to the hospital to get him checked out again. I keep fighting her on this. What is the point? There's nothing physically wrong with him.

RYU: Maybe he just doesn't have anything to say.

CHIYOKO: Yeah. Maybe that's it.

RYU: You heard what the Americans are saying? About the fourth child? The one in Africa?

CHIYOKO: Of course. It's stupid. MC says an American reporter called here yesterday. A foreigner who works for the *Yomiuri Shimbun*. They are as bad as Aikao Uri and her alien crap. How can a minister's wife be so foolish? I take that back, I shouldn't be surprised. I'm worried that she will ask to come and see Hiro.

RYU: Yeah. 'Take me to your leader, Hiro.'

CHIYOKO: !!! Listen, Ryu. I just want to say, I appreciate you listening to me.

RYU: Where did that come from?

CHIYOKO: I've been meaning to say it for a while. I know it can't be easy putting up with my ice princess ways. But it helps.

RYU: Um . . . Chiyoko, there's something I need to tell you as well. It is difficult, but I need to get it out. I think you can guess what it is.

CHIYOKO: Hold that thought. The MC is screaming something at me.

Message logged @ 17.10, 05/03/2012

CHIYOKO: Android Uncle is here! He didn't say he was coming so MC is freaking out. More soon.

Message logged @ 02.30, 06/03/2012

CHIYOKO: Ryu. Ryu!

Message logged @ 02.40, 06/03/2012

RYU: I'm here! Sorry, sleeping. Your message beep woke me up.

CHIYOKO: Listen . . . got something freaky to tell you. But you have to promise to keep it to yourself.

RYU: You really have to ask?

CHIYOKO: Okay . . . Android Uncle brought Hiro something. A gift.

RYU: What? Don't leave me in suspense!!!

CHIYOKO: An android.

RYU: !!!!!!!!!!!!!!!!!!!!!!!!

CHIYOKO: It gets better. It's an exact copy of Hiro. It looks just like him, although his hair is different. You should have heard MC scream when she saw it.

RYU: Are you serious? A robot version of Hiro?

CHIYOKO: Yes. Android Uncle says he was making it before Auntie Hiromi died. It is really really disturbing. Even freakier than his own surrabot. And that's not all.

RYU: There's more? What could be weirder?

CHIYOKO: Wait. Android Uncle brought it here because of

what MC had told him about Hiro refusing to speak. He thought it might help him. You know how AU's android works, right?

RYU: I think so. He uses a camera to film his facial movements and they get relayed via computer to the android's sensors.

CHIYOKO: Full marks! It took ages for AU to set it all up. While MC and I watched, he focused the motion-capture lens on Hiro's face and told Hiro to try and say a few words. Hiro moved his lips – whispering, really – and then the android said . . . wait for it . . . 'Hello Daddy.'

RYU: !

CHIYOKO: MC almost fainted. It looks so real. There's a mechanism in its chest that makes it look as if it's breathing. It even blinks every so often.

RYU: Can you imagine what would happen if you filmed that and put it up on Nico Nico???

CHIYOKO: Aiiiii!!! The reporters would go insane!!!!

RYU: But if he's talking . . . won't the investigators want to know what he saw during the crash?

CHIYOKO: What does it matter? They have their answers now. You read the transcript of the pilots' last words. The authorities know what caused it. The best thing we can do is wait and see if this is going to help Hiro communicate with us. And it seems to be working. Guess what he said at dinner?

RYU: What????

CHIYOKO: Because of AU showing up, MC decided she was going to make his favourite natto dish.

RYU: Gross.

CHIYOKO: I know. I hate it too. I gave Hiro his bowl, he looked down at it, moved his lips and then his android said, 'I don't like it, please may I have some ramen.' Even MC laughed. MC asked me to put him to bed, and then I sneaked down to listen to what she and AU were saying. Father was out as usual.

RYU: And???

CHIYOKO: MC was saying that she's worried about Hiro not going back to primary school – about what the authorities will say. AU said he would use his status to make sure that Hiro won't have to go back for a while, at least until he is talking normally and won't cause too much attention. AU went on and on about how we must keep what's happening with the android quiet. MC agreed.

RYU: He must be grateful that you are taking such good care of Hiro.

CHIYOKO: I suppose. But listen, Ryu. You mustn't tell anyone about this.

RYU: Who am I going to tell?

CHIYOKO: I dunno. You always seem to be on 2-chan. You and your pet ORZ symbol.

RYU: Very funny. Look, you've called him back: _|7O

CHIYOKO: Ai!!! Put it away!!!! I've got to go, I need to sleep. But hey, what did you want to tell me earlier?

RYU: It can wait. Talk later?

CHIYOKO: Of course. Stay tuned for more exciting updates in the Crazy World of the Ice Princess and the Incredible Talking Boy.

RYU: You're funny.

CHIYOKO: I know.

Lillian Small.

Bobby had been living with us for six weeks when Reuben woke up for the first time. I'd had a carer in that day to watch Reuben so that I could take Bobby to the park. I'd been worrying about Bobby not spending time with other children, but it didn't seem right to send him back to school, not with the constant media attention. I was plagued with nightmares that I'd be late collecting him and one of those fanatical religious types would kidnap him. But we needed to get out of the apartment; we hadn't been able to leave for days. The whole area was teeming with those damn news vans. Still, at least we finally knew why the plane had gone down. The NTSB investigator who came to tell me of their findings before they held the press conference – a woman, which surprised me – said that it would have been instantaneous and Lori wouldn't have felt a thing. Knowing that Lori hadn't suffered gave me some comfort, but it did reopen the wound again, and I had to excuse myself for a few minutes so that I could get my grief out. The investigator couldn't take her eyes off Bobby; I could tell she couldn't believe he'd survived. And the fact that birds brought that plane down . . . *birds*! How can something like that happen?

Then, just after that died down, those damn End Timers started more of their nonsense, saying that a fourth child must have survived the crash in Africa. This brought on a fresh wave of journalists and film crews, and another crowd of those religious types with their wide staring eyes and end-of-the-world placards. Betsy was furious. 'Those *meshugeners*, they should be arrested for spreading those lies!' I'd stopped reading the papers after the poison they spread about Bobby being 'unnatural', never mind what else they were saying about him being possessed. In the end, I had to ask Betsy not to show me the articles or even tell me about them. I couldn't bear to hear it.

It got so bad that I had to devise a special routine before Bobby and I could even leave the apartment. First I'd ask Betsy to look outside and check that there were none of those alien people or the shouty religious types hanging around in the park, and then Bobby would put on his disguise – a baseball cap and a pair of clear-lensed glasses. He treated it like a game, bless him: 'Dress up time again, Bubbe!' I'd taken to dyeing my hair after all those photographs of me and Bobby at Lori's service were published. It was Betsy's idea, we'd spent half-an-hour in Walgreens choosing a colour. We decided on auburn, which I worried made me look a bit brassy. How I wished I could have got Reuben's opinion on that!

Bobby and I had a fine time that day. It was raining, so there were no other children there, but it did both of us good. For an hour, I could almost pretend we were living a normal life.

After we got back from the park, I settled Reuben in bed. He'd been more serene, I suppose you'd call it, since Bobby came to live with us. He slept a lot and his dreams didn't seem to haunt him.

I made a rare roast beef sandwich for both of us, and Bobby and I settled onto the couch to watch a movie on Netflix. I chose something called *Nim's Island*, which I regretted immediately as there was a dead mother right in the opening credits. But Bobby didn't flinch. He still hadn't internalised (I think that's the correct term) what had happened to Lori. He'd settled into life with me and Reuben as if he'd always lived with us. And he never mentioned Lori unless I talked about her first.

I told him over and over again that his mother had loved him more than life itself, and that she'd always be with him in spirit, but this didn't seem to go in. I'd been putting off taking him to another trauma counsellor – he didn't seem to need it – but I still kept in touch with Dr Pankowski, who assured me not to worry. She said children have an inbuilt coping mechanism to help them come to terms with sudden trauma, and not to panic if I noticed some changes in his behaviour. I never liked to say anything to Lori, but a few times when I babysat Bobby, just after Reuben got sick, he'd acted out a little. Thrown a tantrum or two. But after the crash and his mother's . . . after Lori . . . it was as if he'd grown up overnight; as if he knew we all had to work together to get over it. And he was far more affectionate. I tried to hide my grief from him, but whenever he saw me crying, he'd put his arms around me and say, 'Don't be sad, Bubbe.'

As we watched the movie, he snuggled against me, and then he said, 'Can't Po Po watch with us, Bubbe?' Po Po was Bobby's name for Reuben. I can't remember where it came from, but Lori thought it was cute, so she encouraged him to use it.

'Po Po's sleeping, Bobby,' I said.

'Po Po sleeps a lot, doesn't he, Bubbe?'

'He does. It's because . . .' How do you explain Alzheimer's to a child? 'You know Po Po has been sick for a while, don't you, Bobby? You remember that from before you came to live with us.'

'Yes, Bubbe,' he said gravely.

I don't remember falling asleep on the couch, but I must have done. I woke up to the sound of laughter. The movie had finished so it wasn't the television.

It was Reuben.

I sat completely still, Elspeth, barely daring to breathe. Then I heard Bobby saying something – I couldn't catch the words – followed by that laugh again.

I hadn't heard that sound for months.

My neck was aching from the angle in which I'd fallen asleep, but I didn't take any notice of that. I moved faster than I had in years!

They were in the bedroom, Reuben sitting up, his hair all mussed, Bobby perched at the end of the bed.

'Hello, Bubbe,' Bobby said. 'Po Po has woken up.'

That dead expression – the Al mask – was gone. 'Hello,' Reuben said, clear as you please. 'Have you seen my reading glasses?' I had to clap my hand to my mouth to stop myself from screaming. 'Bobby wants me to read him a story.'

'Does he?' I think I said. I'd started shaking. It had been months since Reuben had had a clear period – an anti-Al moment – if you don't count that hand squeeze he gave me just after we found out about Bobby surviving. Word coherence was the first thing Al had stolen from Reuben, and here Reuben was, speaking clearly, all the words in their correct order.

I thought perhaps I was dreaming.

Then Reuben said, 'I've looked in the turvey but I couldn't find them.' I didn't care that he'd used the wrong word then – all I could think was that I was witnessing some kind of miracle.

'I'll look for you, Reuben,' I said. He hadn't needed his glasses for months – well, he wasn't going to be reading, not with Al. My pulse racing like a runaway train, I searched everywhere I could think of, pulling things all over the place. I was terrified that if I didn't find those glasses he'd retreat and Al would take over again. I finally found them at the bottom of his sock drawer.

'Thank you, dear,' Reuben said. I remember thinking that was strange; Reuben had never called me 'dear' before.

'Reuben . . . are you . . . how are you feeling?' I was still finding it a struggle to speak.

'A little bit tired. But otherwise goodness.'

Bobby padded off to the bedroom and brought back one of his old picture books. A strange one that Lori had bought him years ago called *Vegetable Glue*. He handed it to Reuben.

'Hmmmm.' Reuben squinted at the book. 'The words . . . they're not right.'

He was fading again. I could see the shadow of Al reappearing in his eyes.

'Shall I ask Bubbe to read it to us, Po Po?' Bobby asked.

Another look of confusion, then a spark of life. 'Yes. Where's Lily?'

'I'm here, Reuben,' I said.

'You're a redder. My Lily was dark.'

'I dyed my hair. Do you like it?'

He didn't answer – he couldn't. He was gone again.

'Read it to us, Bubbe!' Bobby said.

I sat on the bed and started reading the book, my voice shaking.

Reuben fell asleep almost immediately. When I was tucking Bobby into bed, I asked him what they'd been talking about when I heard Reuben laughing.

'He was telling me about his bad dreams, and I told him that he didn't need to have them anymore if he didn't want them.'

I didn't expect to sleep a wink that night. But I did. I woke to find Reuben gone from his side of the bed. I ran through to the kitchen, my heart thudding in my chest.

Bobby was sitting on the counter, jabbering away to Reuben who was spooning sugar into a cup filled with milk. I didn't care that the counter top was covered in coffee grounds and crumbs and spilled milk, the only thing I could take in right then was the amazing fact that Reuben had dressed himself. His jacket was inside out, but other than that, he looked fine. He'd even tried to shave, and he hadn't done too bad a job of it. He glanced at me and waved. 'I wanted to fetch bagels, but I couldn't find the key.'

I tried to smile. 'How are you feeling today, Reuben?'

'Fine thank you for asking, you're welcome,' he said. He wasn't all back, there was something not quite right about him – something lacking in his eyes still – but he was up and about, he was dressed, and he was talking.

Bobby tugged on Reuben's hand. 'Come on, Po Po. Let's go watch TV. Can we, Bubbe?'

Still feeling dazed, I nodded.

I didn't know what to do with myself. I called the care agency and told them that I didn't need anyone that day, and then I made an appointment with Dr Lomeier. I did all these things automatically.

Getting out of the apartment, even with the miracle, wasn't going to be simple. Reuben hadn't been outside for weeks and I worried about him getting overly tired. I thought about asking Betsy to do her usual sweep of the area to check there weren't any reporters lurking around, but something stopped me from knocking on her door. Instead, I called a taxi even though it was only a few blocks to the Beth Israel clinic, and told Bobby to put on his disguise. We were lucky that day. I couldn't see any of those reporters, and the people passing by the apartment – a Hasidic man and a group of Hispanic teenagers – didn't spare us a glance. The taxi driver managed to park right outside the front door. He gave Bobby a strange look, but didn't say anything. He was one of those immigrant drivers. A Bengali or something like that. I don't think he even spoke English; and I had to direct him to the clinic.

Probably I should tell you a little bit about Dr Lomeier. I didn't like him, Elspeth. There's no doubt that he was a good doctor, but I didn't appreciate the way he used to speak about Reuben as if he wasn't there when I used to take him in for his check-ups: 'And how is Reuben doing today, Mrs Small, are we having any difficulties with him?'

He was the first doctor who'd mentioned the possibility of Alzheimer's as the cause of Reuben's forgetfulness, and Reuben didn't like him either. 'Why'd I have to get news like that from a putz like him?' The specialist we were referred to was far more personable, but that meant a trip into Manhattan, and I wasn't ready to take Reuben all that way. For now, Dr Lomeier would do. I needed answers. I needed to know what we were dealing with.

When we were shown into his room, Dr Lomeier was friendlier than usual. 'Is this Bobby?' he said. 'I've heard all about you, young man.'

'What are you doing on your computer?' Bobby said. 'You have pictures. I want to see!'

Dr Lomeier blinked in surprise, and then turned his computer screen around. It showed a photograph of an alpine scene. 'Not that picture,' Bobby said. 'The ones with the ladies holding their peepees.'

There was an awkward silence and then Reuben said, clear as a bell, 'Well, go on, show him the pictures, doc.' Bobby grinned at him, as pleased as punch.

Dr Lomeier's mouth dropped right open. It sounds like I'm exaggerating, Elspeth, but you should have seen the man.

'Mrs Small,' he said. 'How long has this been going on?'

I told him Reuben had started talking last night.

'He started talking *coherently* last night?'

'Yes,' I said.

'I see.' He shifted in his chair.

I almost expected Reuben to say something like, 'Oy, I am here you know, schmuck.' But he kept silent.

'I have to say, Mrs Small, I am quite astonished if what you say is true. Reuben's deterioration has been ... In fact, I'm quite surprised to see that he is mobile at all. I expected that I would have to refer you to one of the state homes quite some time ago.'

The anger hit like a fist. 'Don't talk about him like that! He's here! He's a person you ... you ...'

'Putz?' Reuben said brightly.

'Bubbe?' Bobby looked at me. 'Can we go now? This man is sicky.'

'It's your grandfather who is sick, Bobby,' Dr Lomeier said.

'Oh no,' Bobby said. 'Po Po isn't sick.' He tugged at my hand. 'Let's go, Bubbe. This is silly.' Reuben was already on his feet, making for the door.

I stood up.

Dr Lomeier was still flustered, and his pale face had turned red. 'Mrs Small ... I urge you, please make another appointment immediately. I can refer you to Dr Allen at Mount Sinai again. If Reuben is showing signs of improved cognitive ability, then it could mean that the Dematine dosage he is on is working with far more efficacy than we could ever have envisaged.'

I didn't say that Reuben had been refusing to take his medication for weeks now. Whatever was causing his transformation, it wasn't the Dematine. I couldn't get him to swallow it.

feeling and that Bobby had tried to bite her. Ana was all for going in to see the principal, but I talked her out of it. Knew it would blow over, or maybe Lori would come to her senses and . . .

Talk about it, what with all that hit the papers, I feel bad saying that because nobody's immortal. William decided to put

Stan Murua-Wilson's daughter, Isobel, is a former classmate of Bobby Small's. Mr Murua-Wilson agreed to talk to me via Skype in May 2012.

Goes without saying that all of us parents at Roberto Hernandes were super-shocked when we heard about Lori. We just couldn't believe something like that could happen to someone we knew. Not that Lori and I were close or anything. My wife, Ana, isn't jealous, but she had an issue with Lori's behaviour at a couple of PTA meetings. Ana said she was flirty, called her a grade-A flake. I wouldn't have gone that far. Lori was okay. Most of the kids at Roberto Hernandes are Hispanic – but it's got this integration and diversity ethos thing going on – and Lori was never like, hey, look at me, sending my kid to a public school so that he can get real with the kids from the neighbourhood. A few of the white parents whose kids go to Magnet schools are like that, you know, smug. And Lori could easily have sent Bobby to one of the good yeshiva schools in the neighbourhood. I reckon part of Ana's problem with Lori was Bobby . . . he wasn't the easiest kid, if you want to know the truth.

I'm an English major, was planning on teaching before Isobel came along, and Bobby's behaviour – pre-crash, I mean – and Lori's attitude to it reminded me of that short story by Shirley Jackson, *Charles*. You know it? About this boy called Laurie who comes home every day from kindergarten with tales about this evil kid called Charles, who's been acting up in class, bullying the other kids and killing the class hamster and stuff. Laurie's parents are full of *schadenfreude*, and say things like, 'Why don't Charles's parents discipline the boy?' Course, when they eventually go to the school for a parent-teacher meeting, they find out that there's no kid in the class called Charles – the bad kid is actually their own son.

A couple of parents tried to speak to Lori about Bobby, but it never seemed to go in. Ana freaked out last year when Isobel came home and said that Bobby had tried to bite her. Ana was all for going in to see the principal, but I talked her out of it. Knew it would blow over, or maybe Lori would come to her senses and dose him up with Ritalin or whatever; that kid had serious ADD.

Can I say he was a different child after the crash? There's a lot of talk about this, what with all that shit the prophecy nut jobs are saying, but because Bobby's grandmother Lillian decided to put him into the home schooling programme – I guess because of all the attention he was getting from the media and those freaks – it's hard for me to say. But there was one time I came across him, round about late March. The weather wasn't great, but Isobel had been on my back about going to the park all day, and in the end I gave in.

When we got there, Isobel was like, 'Look, Daddy, there's Bobby.' And before I could stop her, she ran right over to him. He was wearing a baseball cap and glasses, so I didn't recognise him straight off, but Isobel saw through that straight away. Bobby was with an elderly woman who introduced herself as Betsy, Lillian's neighbour. She said that Lillian's husband, Reuben, was having a bad day, so she'd offered to take Bobby out for a while. Betsy was a real talker!

'You want to play with me, Bobby?' Isobel asked. She's a good little girl. Bobby nodded and held out his hand. Together they went over to the swings. I was watching them closely, giving half an ear to Betsy. You could tell she thought it was weird that I stayed home and looked after Isobel while Ana went out to work. 'Never would have happened in my day,' she kept saying. Lots of my buddies in the area are the same. Doesn't make you less of a man or any of that shit. We don't get bored. We have a jogging club; meet at the rec centre for racquetball, that kind of thing.

Isobel said something to Bobby and he laughed. I started to relax. There they were, heads together, chattering away. They seemed to be having a great time.

'He doesn't see enough of other children,' Betsy was going on. 'I don't blame Lillian, she has her hands full.'

On our way home, I asked Isobel what she and Bobby had talked about. I was worried that maybe Bobby had been telling her about the crash and his mother dying. I hadn't broached the death issue yet with Isobel. She had a hamster that was getting more and more sluggish by the day, but I was planning to just replace it without her knowing. I'm a coward like that. Ana's different. 'Death is a fact of life.' But you don't want kids to grow up too quickly, do you?

'I was telling him about the lady,' she said. I knew exactly what she meant. Since she was three, Isobel had suffered from night terrors. A specific hallucination where she'd see a terrifying image of a hunched old woman whirling in front of her eyes. Part of the problem is that my mother-in-law fills Isobel's head with all kinds of stories, superstitious stuff like El Chupacabra and all kinds of other bullshit. Ana and I used to fight about that a lot.

Isobel's condition had gotten so bad last year that I'd shelled out for a psychologist. She said that Isobel would eventually get over it, and I prayed this would be the case.

'Bobby is like the lady,' Isobel said. I asked her what she meant, but all she said was, 'He just is.' Freaked me out a bit.

This doesn't mean anything, but . . . after she saw Bobby that day, Isobel hasn't woken up screaming once or complained about 'the lady' visiting her. Weeks later I asked her again what she meant – that thing about Bobby being like the lady – but she acted like she didn't have a clue what I was talking about.

Transcript of Paul Craddock's voice recording, March 2012.

12 March, 5.30 a.m.

It was just one drink, Mandi. Just one . . . I had another one of those nights, Stephen came again, but this time he didn't speak, he just . . .

(Sound of a thump, followed by a toilet flushing)

Never again. Never fucking again. Darren – you remember, from social services – is going to be here in a few hours and I can't let him smell the stale booze on me. But it helps. I can't deny that.

Oh God.

12 March, 11.30 a.m.

Think I got away with it. Was careful not to reek of mouthwash, which is a dead giveaway. Found one of those cheap spray-on deodorants at the back of the bathroom cupboard, which made me stink of manufactured musk instead. But it's the last time I'm going to take a chance like that.

Not that I spent much time with Darren in any case. Jess had him wrapped around her little finger as usual. 'Darren, do you want to come and watch *My Little Pony* with me? Uncle Paul bought me the whole series.' She definitely wasn't this outgoing before the crash. I'm certain of that now. She and Polly were never what you'd call precocious. They were always shy around strangers, but I guess a slight change in behaviour is to be expected. Darren says we should think about putting her back in school after the Easter hols. We'll see what Dr K says.

Thanks for being so understanding about me not sending you the recordings for a while. It's just . . . talking it out like this . . . it really does help, you know? I'll get back to the proper stuff soon, I promise. It has to be grief, doesn't it? Denial or whatever. Isn't that one of the stages everyone goes through when they're in mourning? Thank fuck Jess isn't going through any of this. She seems to have accepted everything, hasn't even cried yet – not even when the dressings came off her face that first time and she saw her scars. They're not bad; nothing that a little bit of make-up won't fix when she's older. And her hair is starting to grow back. We had some fun the other day choosing hats on the Internet. She picked out a black trilby that was remarkably stylish. Can't imagine pre-crash Jess going for that kind of thing. It wasn't very Missy K, who has the dress sense of a retarded, colour-blind drag-queen.

But still . . . accepting everything like she has . . . that can't be normal, can it? I'm almost tempted to show her the family photographs I put away before she came home, see if I can jump-start some sort of emotional response, but I'm not ready to look at them yet and I'm careful not to get too upset around her. Now they've released what they call their preliminary crash findings, I hope to Christ this is going to mean I get some closure. And 277 Together is helping. I haven't told them about the nightmares. No way am I going to do that. I trust them, specially Mel and Geoff, but you never know. The fucking papers will print anything, won't they? Did you see that whole sob-story thing in the *Daily Mail* – the *Daily Heil*, Stephen used to call it – about Marilyn? She says she's been diagnosed with emphysema, 'And all I want is to see little Jessie before I die, boo hoo.' Pure emotional blackmail. I keep expecting to see Fester and Gomez skulking outside the house. But I suppose even the Addams Family aren't stupid enough to risk a restraining order. And I can always call Mel's hardcore geezer son Gavin to come over and put the fear of God into them if they do show up, can't I?

Christ, listen to me. Babbling like an idiot. It's the stress. Not getting enough sleep. No wonder those American Gitmo bastards used sleep deprivation as a torture tool.

(The sound of a ring tone – the theme to Dr Zhivago*)*

Hang on. Phone.

11.45 a.m.

Lovely. Well, that was nice. A hack as usual, from the *Independent* this time. Isn't that supposed to be a rational paper? Wanted to know how I was feeling about the rumours that one of those religious pricks is going to start searching for the fourth horseman, if you can believe *that*.

What the fuck has it got to do with me? Jesus. The fourth kid? It's such bollocks. He even had the gall to ask me if I'd noticed any change in Jess's behaviour. Seriously? Is this what the press is up to now? Believing in snake charmers and religious freaks? Are the nutters running the asylum? Oooh, that's not bad. Must remember to keep this in when I delete all the dream stuff.

Right. Coffee, get Jess dressed and then off to Waitrose. Only two paparazzi Neanderthals out there today; should be able to slip out no problem.

15 March, 11.25 p.m.

Hmmm . . . not sure what to say about this. Weird day.

This morning, paparazzi or not, I decided we needed to get some fresh air. I was going stir-crazy and Jess has been watching way too much TV. But we can't go out most of the time, not if we don't want to be papped to death. Thank Christ she has no interest in the news channels, but there's only so many times I can hear the *My Little Pony* theme tune without my brain exploding. We walked down the lane to the stables at the end of the street, trailed by a group of greasy hacks with comb-overs.

'Smile for the camera, Jess!' they were crowing, panting round her like a posse of paedos on a day-trip out of Broadmoor.

It took all my strength not to tell them to go fuck themselves, but I put on my 'good uncle' face and Jess played up to them as usual, posing with the horses and holding my hand while we made our way back home.

As we were due to meet with Dr K the next day, I thought it might be an idea to try again to get Jess to open up about Polly,

Stephen and Shelly. It's worrying me, her being so self-contained and . . . happy, I guess. Because that's what she is. All the fucking time, like a kid from a 1980s cheesy American sitcom. She's even stopped using bad language.

As usual, she listened to me calmly, that slightly patronising expression on her face.

I gestured at the *My Little Pony* episode playing on repeat – I have to admit, despite the godawful theme track, the show is weirdly addictive. By now, I pretty much know every episode off by heart. 'Remember when Applejack refuses to accept any help from her friends and she ends up getting herself into trouble, Jess?' I wittered on in my Cheery Uncle voice. 'In the end Twilight Sparkle and the others help her out and she realises that sometimes the only way to deal with difficult issues is to share them with her friends.'

Jess didn't say anything. She looked at me as if I was completely bonkers.

'I'm saying, you can lean on me whenever you want to, Jess. And it's fine to cry when you're sad. I know you must miss Polly and Mummy and Daddy terribly. I know I can't replace them.'

'I'm not sad,' she said.

Maybe she's blocked them out of her mind. Maybe she's pretending that they never existed.

For the thousandth time I asked her, 'Shall I see if any of your friends want to come over and play tomorrow?'

She yawned, said, 'No thanks,' and went back to watching those bloody ponies.

3.30 a.m.

(Sobbing)

Mandi. Mandi. I can't take it any more. He was here . . . Couldn't see his face. Said that thing again, which is all he says:

'Why did you let that thing in here?'

Oh God, oh fuck.

4.30 a.m.

There's no way I can go back to sleep. No fucking way.

They're so real. The dreams. Incredibly real. And . . . shit. This is beyond mental . . . But this time I was sure I could smell something – a faint odour of decaying fish. As if, over time, Stephen's body is rotting. And I still can't see his face. . .

Right. That's enough.

I have to stop this.

It's absolutely insane.

But . . . I'm thinking maybe all this stems from guilt. Maybe that's what my subconscious needs me to deal with.

I'm doing my best for Jess, of course I am. But I can't help but feel I'm missing something. That I should be doing more.

Like when Mum and Dad died. I left it all up to Stephen. Let him do all the arrangements for the funeral. I was touring at the time, doing an Alan Bennett in Exeter. Thought my career was more important; convinced myself that Mum and Dad wouldn't want me messing up my big break ha ha. Some break. We were lucky if the house was half full most nights. I suppose I was still angry at them. I never came out to them, but they knew. They made it clear that I was the black sheep of the family and Stephen was their golden boy. I know what I told you before, Mandi, but me and Stephen weren't close as kids. We never fought or anything, but . . . Everyone liked him. I wasn't jealous, but it was easy for him. It wasn't easy for me. Thank God for Shelly. If it wasn't for her, we would never have re-connected.

But I knew . . . I've always known . . . He was too good, Stephen was. Better than me.

(a sob)

Even stood up for me when I didn't deserve it.

And I knew in my heart, deep down, that he knew I wasn't good enough to look after Jess.

Him and Shelly . . . they were successful, weren't they? And here's me . . .

(*a loud sniff*)

Listen to me. Poor little miss self-pity.

It's just guilt. That's all it is. Guilt and regret. But I'll do better with Jess. I'll prove to Stephen that he and Shelly were right to give me custody. Then maybe he'll leave me alone.

21 March, 11.30 p.m.

I gave in and asked Mrs Ellington-Burn to look after Jess while I went to the 277 Together meeting tonight. I usually take Jess with me, and she always behaves like a little angel. Mel sets her up with something to do in the community centre foyer, colouring-in or whatever, and I bring Stephen's Mac along so that she can watch Rainbow Dash and the girls on repeat, but a few of the 277s . . . I don't know, I get the impression that it's awkward for them if she comes along. They're all lovely to her of course, it's just . . . well, I can't blame them. It's a blatant reminder that their relatives didn't survive, isn't it? Must feel unfair to some of them. And I know they must want to ask her what those last seconds before the plane went down were like. She says she doesn't remember anything, and why would she? She was knocked unconscious when it happened. The AAIB investigator who came to talk to her before they had that press conference did his best to nudge her memory, but she was adamant that the last thing she remembered was being in the pool at the hotel in Tenerife.

Mrs E-B practically threw me out of the door, couldn't wait to hang out with Jess. Maybe she's lonely. I've never seen anyone apart from the Jehovahs visiting her, but then she is such a miserable old cow most of the time. Thankfully she left her yappy dog at home, so at least I didn't have to worry about its vile poodle hair getting all over the covers. I don't think her sniffiness towards me is personal. Geoff said she looks at him as if he's got shit on his shoe (a typical Geoffism), so I think it's just her monumental snobbishness at play. I was nervous about leaving Jess with her, but Jess just cheerfully waved me off. I haven't said this out loud before, but . . . sometimes I can't tell if she really gives a shit if I'm around or not.

Anyway . . . where was I? . . . Oh yeah. 277 Together. I almost blurted the whole thing out. Told them about Stephen. Told them about the nightmares. Christ. Instead, I rattled on and on about all the press attention, how it was getting me down. I knew I was eating into everyone's time, but I couldn't stop.

Finally Mel had to interrupt me as it was getting late. While we were having tea, Kelvin and Kylie stood up and said they had an announcement. Kylie turned bright red and twisted her hands, and then Kelvin told us that they'd started seeing each other and were planning on getting engaged. We all started crying and clapping. I was a bit jealous, to be honest. It's been months since I've even had a drink with anyone I'd remotely like to shag, and there's not much chance of that now, is there? I can just imagine what the *Sun* would say. 'Jess's Nutty Uncle Turns Home into Perverted Sex Den' or something. I told them I was happy for them, although he's way older than she is, and the whole thing seemed a bit hasty – it's only been a month since they started going out.

Still, he's a good bloke. Kylie's lucky to have him. Really sensitive underneath all those muscles and that 'yeah man, innit' attitude. I started developing a bit of a thing for him myself after I heard him read that poem at the memorial service. Knew it wouldn't go anywhere. Kelvin's as straight as they come. They all are. I'm the only gay in the meeting, ha fucking ha. After everyone had congratulated them, Kelvin said his folks – he lost both of them in the crash – would have loved meeting Kylie; they'd been on at him for decades to get married. That set us all off again. Geoff was practically bawling. We all knew that Kelvin had given his parents the trip to Tenerife for their ruby wedding anniversary. It must be bloody awful to deal with that. It reminded me of Bobby Small's mum. The reason she was in Florida was to look for a place where her parents could settle down, wasn't it? Horrendous. So much for fucking karma.

A group of 277s were going to the pub afterwards for a few drinks to celebrate, but I decided it wasn't a good idea to tag along.

The temptation to have a stiff drink would have been too much. I'm not sure if it was my imagination, but several of them seemed relieved when I turned them down. Probably just my old friend paranoia rearing its ugly head again.

When I got back, Mrs Ellington-Burn was slouched on the couch reading a Patricia Cornwell novel. She didn't seem to be in any hurry to get home, so I decided to ask her if she'd noticed anything different about Jess – appearance aside of course – since the crash. I wanted to see if it was just me who thought Jess's personality had undergone a *Doctor Who*ish transformation.

She thought about the question long and hard, then she shook her head, said she couldn't be sure. Still, she said that Jess had been 'an absolute treasure' that evening, although surprisingly, Jess had asked to watch something other than *My Little Pony*. Mrs E-B rather testily admitted they'd gone through a marathon of reality shows – everything from *Britain's Got Talent* to *America's Next Top Model*. Then Jess had gone to bed without being prompted.

As she still didn't make a move to leave, I rather pointedly thanked her again and smiled expectantly. She got to her feet and stared straight at me, the jowls in her huge bulldog face quivering. 'Bit of advice for you, Paul,' she said. 'Watch what you put in your recycling bins.'

I was hit with another wave of paranoia, for a second I thought maybe she'd found one of my bottles of what I call 'coping booze' and was about to blackmail me. I've made a big deal about being on the wagon, so I can hardly have that coming out. Not on top of everything else. 'The press, you see,' she said. 'I've caught them digging through the bins a couple of times. But don't you worry, I sent them on their way.' Then she patted my arm. 'You're doing a good job. Jess is absolutely fine. She couldn't be in better hands.'

I saw her out, and then I burst into tears. I was limp with relief. Relief that at least one person thought I was doing some good where Jess was concerned. Even if it was that crusty old cow.

And now I'm thinking, I *have* to get the nightmare situation under control. Get my act together, bury the self-pity once and for all.

22 March, 4.00 p.m.

Just back from Dr K.

After he finished with Jess – the usual, she seems to be coping, we can definitely look at getting her back into school soon etc. etc. – I tried to talk to him about some of my concerns. Mentioned that I'd been having bad dreams, but didn't go into detail for obvious reasons. He's easy to talk to, kind, overweight, but in a cuddly bear way that suits him, not in a 'hide the cakes *quick*' way. He says that my nightmares are a sign that my subconscious is working through my grief and anxiety and as soon as the press attention wanes, things will settle down. He says I mustn't underestimate the pressure I'm under from the hacks, the Addams Family and the nut-jobs who still phone occasionally. He says it's fine to take something to help me sleep, and gave me a prescription for some tablets that he says are guaranteed to knock me out.

So . . . let's see if they work.

But I'll be honest. Even with the sleeping tabs, I'm afraid to fall asleep.

23 March, 4.00 a.m.

(a sob)

No dreams. No Stephen. But this . . . this is, uh . . . not worse, but . . .

I woke up – around the time Stephen usually comes, three a.m. – and I could hear voices coming from somewhere. And then a laugh. Shelly's laugh. Clear as day. I jumped out of bed and ran downstairs, heart in my throat. I don't know what I was expecting to find, maybe Shelly and Stephen standing in the hallway saying how they'd . . . fuck, I dunno, been kidnapped by Somalian pirates or something and that was why we hadn't heard from them. I was only half-awake, so I suppose that's why I wasn't thinking straight.

But it was just Jess. She was sitting inches away from the television screen watching the DVD of Shelly and Stephen's wedding.

'Jess?' I said really softly, not wanting to give her a fright. I was thinking, fuck, has she finally decided to face up to their loss?

Without turning around she goes, 'Were you jealous of Stephen, Uncle Paul?'

'Why would I be jealous?' I asked her. Didn't occur to me then to ask why she was calling him Stephen and not Daddy.

'Because they loved each other and you have no one who loves you.' I wish I could get across her tone of voice. Like a scientist interested in a specimen.

'That's not true, Jess,' I said.

Then she said, 'Do you love me?'

I said yes. But it was a lie. I loved the old Jess. The old Paul loved the old Jess.

Fuck me. I can't believe I just said that. What do I mean by the old Jess?

I left her rewatching the DVD, then slipped into the kitchen and found myself unearthing an old bottle of cooking sherry. I'd hidden it away – out of sight, out of mind.

She's still watching the video now. Over and over again. The fourth time now, I can hear the music they played at the ceremony. 'Better Together' by Jack fucking Johnson. And she's laughing. Laughing at something. But what could be funny?

I'm sitting looking at the bottle now, Mandi.

But I won't touch it. I won't.

Geoffrey Moran and his wife, Melanie, were instrumental in setting up 277 Together, the support group for those who lost loved ones in the Go!Go! Air disaster. Geoffrey agreed to speak to me in early July.

I blame the press. They're the ones who should answer for this. You hear about that phone hacking, them getting away with printing lies; I couldn't really blame Paul for getting a bit paranoid. The buggers even tried to get me and Mel to say bad stuff about him a few times, came at us with leading questions. Mel told them to sling their hooks, of course. We're tight at 277 Together; look after our own. Now, I think it's a miracle myself, those three kids surviving like that, it's simply one of those things in life you just can't explain. But try telling that to your alien fanatics or those Yanks with their conspiracy bollocks. And if it wasn't for those bleeding reporters, none of that crap would have seen the light of day. They're the ones who kept it in the public eye. Buggers should be bleeding shot, the lot of 'em.

We knew what Paul was, course we did. And I don't mean about him being gay. What people do behind closed doors is their business. I'm talking about him being a bit of a luvvie, wanting to be the centre of attention. He told us he was an actor straight away. I'd never heard of him, though he said he'd had a few roles on telly in the past, guest ones, you know. Cameos. Must have bruised his ego, not getting where he wanted to in life. Reminded me a bit of my Danielle. She was much younger than him of course, but it took her a while to decide what she wanted to do, tried all sorts until she went in for that beauty therapy. Just takes some people longer to find their way in life, doesn't it?

Before Paul started to behave . . . well . . . before he started becoming a bit more withdrawn than usual, he used to irritate Mel a bit. He would talk for hours at the meetings if you let him. But when we could, we tried to help him out with Jess. It wasn't always easy; we've got our own grandchildren to take care of as well. Our Gavin, he's got three little ones, but Paul was a special case. He needed all the back-up he could get, poor bugger, what with the press at him all the time and the other side of the family – bad seeds, Mel called them – giving him all that grief. Gavin would've stepped in if that family had mucked about at the memorial service. Gavin's applying for the police next year. He'll make a good copper, they always do, them that've seen the other side of the law, so to speak. Not that he ever got himself into real trouble.

That snooty neighbour also did what she could. Right snobbish she was, but her heart was in the right place. She saw off one of those paparazzos by throwing a bucket of cold water over the bugger. Fair play to her for that, poker up her arse or not.

When the Discovery Channel was planning that special programme on Black Thursday, just after the findings were released, the producer approached me and Mel to be talking heads on that show, wanted us to say what we felt when we heard about the plane going down. It's horrible to think about it now, but before we lost our Danielle, me and Mel used to love that air-crash investigation show, the one with that American investigator, Ace Kelso. Wish I'd never seen it now, of course. Mel turned the producers down flat, so did Kylie and Kelvin. They'd got together by then. Kylie had lost her other half in the crash and Kelvin was single, so why not? Sure, he was that much older than her, but May–September relationships can work, can't they? Look at me and Mel. She's seven years my senior and we've been going strong for over twenty years. Kylie and Kelvin were planning an August wedding, but they're talking about postponing it now. I told them, we need some joy in our lives, don't let what happened to little Jess put you off.

That's when I should have realised something wasn't right with Paul for definite. When he said he didn't want to be part of the Discovery show, I mean. I'll say this for him – he didn't try to put Jess in the spotlight. Opposite, really. But in the early days he wasn't shy about appearing in front of the media. First couple of months, it was like he was always on the morning shows, sitting on the couch talking about how Jess was coping. And no, I don't think that gave the press the right to pry into his private life and hound them like they did. You'd have thought after what happened to the People's Princess, they'd have learned their lesson. How much blood needs to be spilled before they'll bleeding well stop? I know, I do go on, but it makes my blood boil.

As for Jess . . . she was a real sweetheart. Absolute treasure. Gave you the impression she was wiser than her years, which wasn't surprising seeing what she'd been through. Never stopped smiling, never complained about the scars on her face. Right sunny disposition; it's amazing how kids can bounce back from things like that, isn't it? I read that biography, the one by that Muslim girl who was the only survivor of a plane crash in Ethiopia, and she said how none of it seemed real to her for years. So maybe that was how Jess was coping. Mel couldn't touch that book. Nor could most of the 277s. Kelvin says that even now he has to get his mates to screen what's on telly before he can watch it. Can't see anything about airplanes or crashes, or even watch any of them police procedurals.

And no, there was nothing bleeding strange about Jess. I'll go on the record about that. Bloody Americans and their lies about those poor kids. Made Mel apoplectic. And it wasn't just us who thought Jess was fine, was it? We would have heard from the school, wouldn't we? Her teacher's a no-nonsense type of woman. And her psychologist and the bloke from the social never saw anything untoward going on, did they?

Last time I saw Jess I was on my own. Mel was off helping Kylie choose a wedding venue and Paul was in a pickle, said he had a meeting with his agent. I fetched her from school and took her to see the horses down the lane. I always asked her how she was doing at school, I was a bit concerned that maybe she'd be facing bullying and that from the other kids. Jess's scars weren't bad, but they were still there and you know what kids can be like. But she said no one ever made fun of her. Tough little cookie. We had a nice time that afternoon. When we got back to the house, she asked me to read her a book, *The Lion, the Witch and the Wardrobe.*

She could read well herself, but she said she liked me to do the voices of the characters. She thought that book was funny, couldn't seem to get enough of it.

When we heard Paul arriving home, she smiled at me, just the most lovely smile, reminded me of my Danielle when she was little. 'You're a good man, Uncle Geoff,' she said. 'I'm sorry your daughter had to die.' I always think about that whenever I think about her now. Brings me to tears.

Chiyoko and Ryu (this exchange took place three months before their disappearance).

Message logged @ 13.10, 25/03/2012

RYU: Are you there?

Message logged @ 13.31, 25/03/2012

RYU: Are you there?

Message logged @ 13.45, 25/03/2012

CHIYOKO: I'm here.

RYU: I was worried. You haven't been silent for this long before.

CHIYOKO: I was with Hiro. We were talking. MC is out so we have the house to ourselves for once.

RYU: Has he spoken about the crash yet?

CHIYOKO: Yeah.

RYU: And??????

CHIYOKO: He says he remembers being hoisted up into the rescue helicopter. He said it was fun. 'Like flying.' He said he was looking forward to doing it again.

RYU: Weird.

CHIYOKO: I know.

RYU: Is that all he remembers about the crash?

CHIYOKO: That's all he'll say so far. If he does know anything else, he's not saying. I don't want to push him too hard.

RYU: Has he spoken about his mother yet?

CHIYOKO: No. Why are you so interested anyway?

RYU: Of course I'm interested! Why wouldn't I be?

CHIYOKO: I'm being too hard on you again, aren't I?

RYU: I'm used to it now.

CHIYOKO: Ice burns from the ice princess.

RYU: Chiyoko . . . when he talks through the android, who do you look at? Hiro or it?

CHIYOKO: Ha! That's a good question. Mostly Hiro, but it's strange . . . I'm so used to it now. It's almost like it's his twin. Yesterday I found myself talking to it as if it was alive when Hiro left the room.

RYU: RYU:!!!

CHIYOKO: I'm glad one of us is laughing. But the way I'm reacting to it, forgetting that it's not actually alive, is exactly why Android Uncle made his surrabot in the first place.

RYU: ???

CHIYOKO: He wanted to find out if people would eventually start treating androids as if they were human once they got over the uncanny valley feeling. Now we know that they *will* start seeing them as human. Or at least ice princesses will.

RYU: Sorry, I was being dense.

RYU: Hey . . . Did you see that interview where he said that sometimes, when people touch the surrabot and he's miles away, working it remotely, he can feel their fingers on his skin? The brain is a strange thing.

CHIYOKO: It is. I wish I knew why Hiro will only talk through it. I know he has a voice, so he's capable of speech. Maybe it gives him an emotional distance, although in this house we are all emotionally distant ha ha.

RYU: Like cameramen who can film horrible scenes without turning away. Yes. I think you are right about the distance.

CHIYOKO: Listen to this: I asked him if he wanted to go back to primary school today.

RYU: And?

CHIYOKO: He said, 'Only if I can bring my soul.'

RYU: His what?

CHIYOKO: It's what he's started calling his surrabot.

RYU: You need to keep that quiet. Especially as Aikao Uri is in the news again with her crazy alien theories. You don't want to give her any ideas.

CHIYOKO: What is she saying now? Did she mention Hiro again?

RYU: Not this time. But she really does believe she was abducted by aliens. There's a cool clip of her talking about being probed on Nico Nico. Whoever made it has intercut it with scenes from *E.T.* It's very funny.

CHIYOKO: She's as bad as those religious Americans with all their fourth child stuff. It stirs it up again. All the attention. The silt settles, and then someone pokes a stick in the water and it becomes cloudy.

RYU: Ha! Very lyrical. You should become a writer. I could illustrate your stories.

CHIYOKO: We could have our own manga factory. Sometimes I think . . . wait. There's someone at the door. Probably just a salesman or whatever trying their luck.

Message logged @ 15.01, 25/03/2012

CHIYOKO: Guess who that was?

RYU: I give up.

CHIYOKO: Just guess.

RYU: Captain Seto's wife.

CHIYOKO: No. Try again.

RYU: Aikao Uri and her alien friends?

CHIYOKO: No!

RYU: Toturo in his cat bus?

CHIYOKO: Ha! I must tell that to Hiro. I told you I let him watch *My Neighbour Totoro*, even though MC said I mustn't in case it upset him, didn't I?

RYU: No! You didn't tell me. And did it upset him? Or his android?

CHIYOKO: No. It made him laugh. He even thought the part where the girls' mother is in the hospital was amusing.

RYU: That kid is seriously weird. So?? If it wasn't the cat bus, who was it?

CHIYOKO: It was the American woman's daughter.

RYU: Σ(O_O ;) ! ! Pamela May Donald's daughter?

CHIYOKO: Yeah.

RYU: How did she find out where you lived?

CHIYOKO: Probably got it from one of the *izuko* support group members. But it's not impossible to find from other sources. The magazines are always saying that the house is near to Yoyogi station, and there are those pictures of it on the *Tokyo Herald* website.

RYU: What is she like?

CHIYOKO: I thought you saw her when you watched the memorial service?

RYU: I mean what sort of person is she?

CHIYOKO: At first I thought she was a typical foreigner. And in some ways she is. But she was very serene, quiet, dressed conservatively. Greeted me as if she knew of my status as Shinjuku's Number One Ice Princess.

RYU: You let her into the house????

CHIYOKO: Why not? She's an *izoku* like all the others. Not only that, I let her talk to Hiro.

RYU: Hiro or Hiro's soul?

CHIYOKO: Hiro's soul.

RYU: You let him talk to her through the surrabot???? I thought you were angry with her?

CHIYOKO: Why would I be angry?

RYU: Because of what her mother has caused.

CHIYOKO: That's not her fault. It's the stupid Americans. And she looked so lost when she arrived. It must have taken courage to come all the way from Osaka to see him.

RYU: Something's not right. The ice princess would never normally behave in such a manner.

CHIYOKO: Maybe I wanted to hear what she was going to say to Hiro. Maybe I was curious.

RYU: How did she react when she saw Hiro's soul and realised she'd have to talk to him through it?

CHIYOKO: She just stared at it and then she gave it one of those self-conscious bows Westerners do when they're trying to be polite. I could hear him giggling through it straightaway. He was hiding behind the screen in my room with the computer and the camera. I was impressed that she didn't scream or freak out.

RYU: And what did she ask?

CHIYOKO: First of all she thanked him for agreeing to talk to her. Then she wanted to know what they always want to know, which is, did her mother suffer.

RYU: And?

CHIYOKO: And Hiro said yes.

RYU: Ouch. What did she say to that?

CHIYOKO: She thanked him for being honest.

RYU: So Hiro admitted that he'd spoken to her mother?

CHIYOKO: Not exactly. He didn't really give her any straight answers. I thought perhaps that she was going to start getting really frustrated, but then Hiro said, 'Don't be sad,' in English!

RYU: Hiro can speak *English*?

CHIYOKO: Auntie Hiromi or Android Uncle must have taught him some phrases before the crash. Then she showed him a photograph of her mother, asked him if he was sure that he'd seen her. And again, he said to her, 'Don't be sad.' She started crying; real weeping. I was worried that this would upset Hiro, so I asked her to leave.

RYU: Chiyoko, it is not my place to say . . . But . . . I don't think you should have done that.

CHIYOKO: Thrown her out?

RYU: No. Let her talk to Hiro's soul.

CHIYOKO: I didn't ask your opinion about that, Ryu. And anyway, I thought you were in love with the Americans?

RYU: Why do you make it so hard for me?

CHIYOKO: It's not fair of you to make me feel guilty.

RYU: I wasn't trying to make you feel guilty. I was trying to be your friend.

CHIYOKO: Friends don't judge each other.

RYU: I was not judging you.

CHIYOKO: Yes you were. I don't need that from you as well. I get it all the fucking time from MC. I'm going.

RYU: Wait! Can't we at least talk about this?

CHIYOKO: There's nothing to say.

Message logged @ 16.34, 25/03/2012

RYU: Are you still mad?

Message logged @ 16.48, 25/03/2012

RYU: _|7O

Message logged @ 03.19, 26/03/2012

CHIYOKO: Ryu. Are you awake?

RYU: I'm sorry about earlier. Did you see I even sent you an ORZ?

CHIYOKO: Yeah.

RYU: Are you okay?

CHIYOKO: No. Mother Creature and Father are fighting. They haven't done that since before Hiro came. I'm worried they'll upset him.

RYU: What are they fighting about?

CHIYOKO: Me. MC says Father has to be stricter on me and make me go back to free school. She says I have to be made to work on my future plans. But then who will look after Hiro?

RYU: You're really attached to that kid now.

CHIYOKO: I am.

RYU: So . . . what do you want to do with your life?

CHIYOKO: I'm like you; I never look further than a day ahead. What are the choices? I don't want to work for a corporation, become a slave for life. I don't want to do some dumb freeter job. I'll probably end up living in a tent in the park with the homeless. MC would be happiest if I got married and had children and made that my life's goal.

RYU: Do you think that will ever happen?

CHIYOKO: Never!!!!!! I love Hiro but the thought of having the responsibility for someone else's life . . . I will live alone and die alone. I've always known that.

RYU: You're not alone, Yoko.

CHIYOKO: Thanks, Ryu.

RYU: Did the ice princess just say thank you????

CHIYOKO: I have to go. Hiro has woken up. I'll talk to you tomorrow.

RYU: ☆・*:.｡.(●≧▽≦)｡.:*・☆

PART SIX

CONSPIRACY

MARCH–APRIL

Lola Cando.

The last time Lenny came to see me, he was spitting mad. Second he got to the motel he drank a double bourbon straight down, then another. Took him a while to calm down enough to tell me what was going on.

Turned out that Lenny had found out Dr Lund had organised a rally for Mitch Reynard in Fort Worth. Some sort of pro-Israel, 'Believers Unite' convention, and it burned Lenny bad that he hadn't been invited to speak at it. And that wasn't all of it. After he did that radio show – the one where that New York DJ ripped him a new one – Dr Lund had sent a publicist down to see Lenny. The publicist (who Lenny described as a 'jumped-up two-bit lackey in a suit') told him that he wasn't to draw too much attention to himself, and to let Dr Lund and Flexible Sandy spread the news about Pamela's message their way. Lenny was also pissed that Dr Lund didn't want him involved in searching for that fourth child.

'I've got to find a way to convince him that he needs me, Lo,' he said. 'Pamela chose me, *me,* to spread the word. He has to see that.'

I wouldn't say I felt sorry for Lenny, but Dr Lund cutting him off, hijacking his message, you could see it made him feel like the unpopular kid at school. And I don't think it had anything to do with money. Lenny said his website was bringing in donations from all over the world. You ask me, it was pride more than anything.

Dr Lund may have cooled towards him, but Lenny's message was catching on like wildfire. People I never thought of as religious were going and getting themselves saved. Couple of my johns even went and did it. Some of them, sure, you could see they were just doing it as insurance – in case it did turn out to be the truth. Didn't matter that the Episcopalians and even those

Muslim leaders were saying there was no reason to panic, people really started believing it, you know? There were just all these signs happening all over the world – signs of plague, famine, war and whatever. That puke virus and the foot and mouth disease were getting worse, and then came that drought in Africa and the big scare when the North Koreans threatened to test their nuclear weapons. That was just the start. Then there were all those rumours about Bobby's grandfather and that robot stuff that was going down with the Japanese kid. It was almost as if every time Lenny's theories were shot down by someone, up would come another sign that backed them up. If you'd asked me back when I first met Lenny if he could have caused such a stir, I wouldn't have credited it.

'I need a stronger platform, Lo,' he kept saying. 'Dr Lund's taking everything. He's acting like it was all his idea.'

'Isn't this all about saving souls though, honey?' I asked.

'Yeah, course it's about saving people.' He got real mad about that, went on about how time might be running out and how he and Dr Lund should be working together. He didn't even want to do his usual that day. Too wound up, couldn't . . . you know. Said he had to go meet with that Monty fellow anyhow, start planning on how he was going to get back into the big boys' good graces. He told me that there were quite a few 'messengers' like Monty already staying at his ranch, and I guess he was thinking about how it would be a good thing to invite more.

After he left, I was getting all my stuff together, ready to head on back to my apartment and my next client, when there was a knock on the door. I figured maybe it was Lenny again, regretting that he'd wasted our hour together just talking. I opened it, saw a woman standing there. I knew who she was straight away. I'd have known her just by the dog, that Snookie. She looked even thinner than when she appeared on Dr Lund's show. Skinny – too skinny, like one of those anorexics. But her expression was different. She didn't look as lost as she did back then. She didn't come across as angry or anything like that, but there was a look in her eyes that said, 'Don't mess with me.'

She looked me up and down and I could tell she was trying to figure out what Lenny saw in me. 'How long have you and him been doing this?' she asked straight off.

I told her the truth. She nodded, and then pushed past me into the room. 'You love him?' she asked.

I almost laughed. I said that all Lenny was to me was one of my regulars. I wasn't his girlfriend or mistress or anything like that. I know quite a few of my clients are married; that's their business.

This seemed to give her some comfort. She sat down on the bed, asked me to fix her a drink. I handed her the same drink Lenny always has. She sniffed it, then drank it in one gulp. It ran down her chin and made her gag, but it didn't seem to bother her. She waved her hand around the room and said, 'All this, what you been doing with him. I paid for it. I paid for everything.'

I didn't know how to answer that. I knew Lenny depended on her for money, didn't know the extent of it though. She put the dog down on the bed next to her. It sniffed the sheets, then slumped on its side as if it was fixing to curl up and die. I knew they didn't allow animals in the motel, but I wasn't about to tell her that.

She asked me what Lenny liked, and I told her the truth. She said that at least he hadn't been hiding some weird sexual fetish from her all those years.

Then she asked me if I believed in what he was saying, about the children being the horsemen. I said I wasn't sure what to believe. She nodded, stood up to leave. Didn't say anything else to me. There was a deep sadness inside her. I could see that straight off. It had to have been her who told the *Inquirer* about me and Lenny. It was only a day or so afterwards that this reporter called me up, pretending he was a regular john. Luckily I had my wits about me that day, but it didn't stop the photographers trying their luck for days afterwards.

I came clean to Denisha after that, told her that Lenny was one of my clients. It didn't surprise her. You can't shock Denisha. She's seen it all. Probably you're wondering how I feel about Lenny now. Like I say, people are always trying to get me to say he was a monster. But he wasn't. He was just a man. I guess when I decide to do that book those publishers are always after me to write, then I might talk about it more, but that's all I've got to say on the subject for now.

The following article, by award-winning blogger and freelance journalist Vuyo Molefe, was first published in the online journal *Umbuzo* on 30 March 2012.

Bringing Home the Bodies:
The Personal Cost of the Dalu Air Crash

It's the day before the Dalu Air crash memorial is to be unveiled in Khayelitsha, and the press photographers are already circling. Teams of council workers have been bussed in to cordon off the area around the hastily constructed memorial sculpture – a sinister black glass pyramid that looks like it would be more at home on the set of a science-fiction B-movie. Why a pyramid? It's a good question, but despite the number of editorials damning the peculiar choice of design, no one I've spoken to, including Ravi Moodley, the Cape Town city councillor who commissioned it, and the sculptor herself, artist Morna van der Merwe, seems to be prepared to give me (or anyone else) a straight answer.

The site is also swarming with conspicuously fit security men and women, all wearing stereotypical black suits and ear pieces, who eye me and the other press representatives with a mixture of contempt and distrust. Among the great and the good lined up to attend tomorrow's ceremony are Andiswa Luso, who's pipped to be the new head of the ANC Youth League, and John Diobi, a Nigerian high level preacher-cum-business-mogul who reportedly has ties with several US mega-churches, including those under the sway of Dr Theodore Lund, who hit the headlines worldwide with his theory that The Three are the harbingers of the apocalypse. It's rumoured that Diobi and his associates are putting up the reward money for the discovery of Kenneth Oduah, the Dalu Air passenger deemed most likely to be the fourth horseman. Although the South African Civil Aviation Authority and the National Transportation Safety Board have insisted that no one on board Dalu Air Flight 467 could have survived, the reward has already ignited a hysterical man-hunt, with locals and tourists alike eager to get in on the action. And the fact that Kenneth's name is etched on the memorial, despite the absence of his remains or DNA being discovered in the wreckage, has angered several Nigerian evangelical Christian groups – another reason for the high security presence.

But I'm not here to antagonise the security staff or petition the VIPs for an interview. Today, it's not their stories I'm interested in.

Levi Bandah (21), who hails from Blantyre, Malawi, meets me at the entrance to the Mew Way community hall. Three weeks ago, he travelled to Cape Town in order to search for the remains of his brother Elias, who he believes is one of the casualties killed on the ground when the fuselage cut a deadly swathe through the township. Elias was working as a gardener in Cape Town in order to support his extended family back in Malawi, and Levi suspected something was wrong when Elias did not contact the family for over a week.

'He sent us a text every day, and money came to us every week. My only choice was to travel here and see if I could find him.'

Elias is not listed among the deceased, but with so many unidentified remains – most believed to belong to illegal immigrants – still awaiting DNA matches for formal identification purposes, this isn't a guarantee of anything.

In many African cultures, including that of my own – Xhosa – it is vital that the bodies of the deceased be returned to their ancestral homeland to be reunited with the spirits of the ancestors. If this is not done, it is believed that the spirit of the deceased will be restless and will cause grief to the living. And bringing home the body can be an expensive business. It can cost up to 14,000 rand to transport a body back to Malawi or Zimbabwe by air freight; without help, a sum way beyond the reach of the average citizen. For the families of refugees, transporting a body over two thousand kilometres by road is a daunting and gruesome prospect. I've heard stories of funeral directors colluding with families to disguise bodies as dried goods in order to cut the air-freight costs.

In the days following the crash, Khayelitsha rang with the sound of loudspeakers, as families of the victims petitioned the community to donate whatever they could so that bodies could be returned to their homelands. It is not unusual for the bereaved to receive double the amount they need; with many people from the Eastern Cape migrating to Cape Town for work, no one knows when they will be the one in need of help. And the refugee communities and societies are no different.

'The community here has been generous,' says David Amai (52), a soft-spoken and dapper Zimbabwean from Chipinge, who has also agreed to talk to me. Like Levi, he is in Cape Town waiting for the authorities to give him the go-ahead to bring the remains of his cousin, Lovemore – also a victim of the crash devastation – home. But before he left Zimbabwe, David had something Levi's family didn't have – the certainty that their loved one was dead. And they didn't hear it from the pathologists working the scene. 'When we did not hear from Lovemore, at first we did not know for sure if he had died,' David told me. 'My family consulted with a herbalist (sangoma) who performed the ritual and spoke to my cousin's ancestors. They confirmed that he had connected with them and we knew then that he was gone.' Lovemore's body was eventually identified by DNA and David is hopeful that he can soon bring his remains back home.

But what if there is no body to be buried?

With no remains to bring back to his family, Levi's only option was to collect some of the ashes and earth at the site, which would be immediately buried when he returned home. This is where his story veers into the stuff of nightmares (or farce). As he attempted to gather a small bag of earth, an over-zealous cop swooped down on him, accusing him of stealing souvenirs to sell to unscrupulous tourists and 'Kenneth Oduah hunters'. Despite his protestations, Levi was arrested and thrown in a holding cell, where he languished, in fear of his life, for the weekend. Thankfully, hearing of his plight, several NGOs and the Malawian Embassy stepped in, and Levi was released relatively unscathed. His DNA has been taken and he's waiting for confirmation that Elias is among the victims. 'They say it won't take long,' he says. 'And the people here have been good to me. But I cannot return home without some part of my brother to restore to my family.'

As I leave the site, I receive a text from my editor saying that Veronica Oduah, the aunt of the elusive Kenneth, has landed in Cape Town for tomorrow's ceremony, but has refused to speak to the press. I can't help wondering how she must be feeling. Like Levi, she is living in a cruel limbo of uncertainty, hoping against hope that somehow, her nephew hasn't joined the ranks of the dead.

Superintendent Randall Arendse is the controller of the Site C Police Station, Khayelitsha, Cape Town. He spoke to me in April 2012.

Fourth horseman, my arse. Every bloody day we'd get a new 'Kenneth Oduah' being brought into the station. Usually it was just some street kid who'd been bribed with a couple of bucks to say he was Kenneth. And it wasn't just us. They were rocking up at every station in the Cape. Those US arseholes didn't know what they'd started. Two hundred K USD? That's nearly two million rand, which is more than what most South Africans will see in a lifetime. We had a photograph of the boy, but we couldn't see the point of comparing it with the chancers that came in. Most of my guys, they'd been there that day, seen the wreckage. No ways anyone on that plane made it out alive, even if they were a *bliksem* rider of the apocalypse.

At first it was just the locals who were trying their luck but then the foreigners started arriving. There weren't that many at first, but the next thing you know, they were rolling in. It didn't take long for our local crooks to get in on the action. Some of the sharper ones even offered their services online. Soon there were syndicates organising these tours in just about all of the townships. None of them had accreditation permits. But that didn't stop the punters falling for the scams. *Jis*, man, some of them even paid up front. It was like shooting fish in a barrel, and I can tell you off the record, I wouldn't be surprised if some of the cops were in on the action.

I can't tell you how many punters got stranded at the airport waiting for their 'all inclusive package' to come and pick them up. We got professional bounty hunters coming out here, ex-cops, even a few of those blerrie big game hunters! Some of them were after the cash and didn't give a shit if it was true or not, but quite a few who came really believed the kak that preacher was saying. But Cape Town is a complex place. You don't just waltz into Gugs or the Cape Flats or Khayelitsha in your fancy hire car and start asking questions, no matter how many lions or cheetahs you've shot in the bush. Quite a few of them found that out the hard way when they were relieved of their valuables one way or another.

I'll never forget these two big American guys who came into the station one evening. Shaven heads, muscles on their muscles. Both of them were ex US Marshals, used to be marines. Thought they were tough, told us afterwards they'd been instrumental in bringing some of America's Most Wanted to justice. But when I first met them they were shaking like little girls. They'd hooked up with their so-called 'guide' at the airport and he'd taken them where they wanted to go – into the middle of Khayelitsha. When they arrived at their destination, their guide relieved them of their Glocks, cash, credit cards, passports, shoes and clothes, leaving them with nothing but their boxers. Toyed with them as well. Made them walk barefoot into an old outhouse that stank to high heaven, tied them up and told them that if they shouted for help, he'd shoot them. When they finally got free it was dark, they reeked of shit and the *skelm* was long gone. Couple of locals took pity on them and brought them to the station. My guys laughed for days about those two. Had to drop them off at the US embassy in just their undies. None of the spare clothes we had at the station fitted them.

Fact is, people here are tough, most of them fight just to get by every day, and they'll take a chance if they can. Not everyone, of course – but it's hard here. You got to be streetwise. You got to respect the people or they'll *naai* you big time. What, you think I'm going to breeze into downtown LA or wherever, act like I own the place? I swear, these *moegoes* who came here might just as well have handed over their valuables to the guys at immigration, cut out the middle man. Eventually we had to put up signs at the airport to warn people. Reminded me of that movie, *Charlie and the Chocolate Factory*. The hunt for that golden ticket with everyone going *befok*.

I mean, it was a major headache for us guys, the police and that, but it was *lekker* for the tourism industry. Hotels were full, tour buses were packed, everyone from the street kids to the hoteliers were coining it. Especially the street kids. See, at one stage, the rumour spread that Kenneth was living on the streets somewhere. People will believe anything given half a chance.

It was Kenneth's aunt I felt sorry for. She seemed like a nice lady. My cousin Jamie was on the security detail for her when they unveiled the Dalu Air memorial statue and she flew down from Lagos. He said she was bewildered, kept saying that as those other kids had survived miraculously, why shouldn't Kenneth be alive?

Those fundamentalist fuckers gave her unrealistic expectations. Ja, that's what it was. False hope.

Didn't even stop to think that what they was doing was cruel.

Reba Neilson.

It was all becoming too much for me. It felt like Pastor Len was turning his back on his real inner circle in favour of people like that Monty. Did I mention Monty to you, Elspeth? Can't quite recall if I did. Well, he was one of the first Lookie-Loos who elected to stay – came to Sannah County soon after Pastor Len got back from that conference at Houston. Within days of showing up he was padding along at Pastor Len's side, loyal as a stray dog that'd just been fed. I didn't take to him right from the start, and I'm not just saying that because of what he did to that poor Bobby. There was something about him, something shifty, and I wasn't the only one of that opinion. 'That fella looks like he could do with a good scrubbing,' Stephenie was always saying. He had these tattoos all up his arms – some of which didn't look very Christian to me – and his hair needed a pair of shears taken to it. Looked like one of them Satanists they sometimes feature in the *Inquirer*.

And since Monty arrived, Jim seemed to have dropped out of Pastor Len's favour. Sure, Pastor Len dragged him out to church on Sundays sometimes, and I know he hadn't given up the idea of doing those tours of Pam's house, but most of the time Jim just sat at home and drank himself stupid.

Pastor Len asked Stephenie's cousin Billy to quote on some construction work he wanted done at the ranch, so it was Billy who told us that those people looked to be moving there permanently. If you didn't know better, he said, you'd a thought it was one of those hippy communes.

I had so many sleepless nights during those weeks, Elspeth. I can't tell you how I suffered. What Pastor Len was saying about the signs . . . it made so much sense and yet . . . I just couldn't get over Pamela, dowdy old Pam, being a prophet.

I all but wore out Lorne's ear talking about it.

'Reba,' he said to me. 'You know that you're a good Christian woman and Jesus will save you whatever happens. If you don't want to follow Pastor Len's church no more, then maybe Jesus is telling you not to.'

Stephenie also felt the same as I did, but it wasn't that easy to break away. Not in a community like ours. I guess you could say I was biding my time.

Stephenie and I were worried that Kendra wouldn't be able to cope with all those new Lookie-Loos arriving, and we decided that even though we didn't agree with all that Pastor Len was doing lately, it was only right that we should go over there and see how she was coping. We planned on doing it at the weekend, but that Friday, the story about Pastor Len's fancy woman broke. Stephenie came straight over soon as she heard about it, brought me a copy of the *Inquirer*. It was all over the front page: *End Times Preacher's Sordid Love Tryst*. The photographs showed a big woman wearing purple pants and a tight top, but the pictures were so grainy you couldn't tell if she was tanned, black or one of those Hispanics. I didn't believe that story for one second. Even after he let the devil in, I firmly believe the real Pastor Len, the good man who had been the head of our church for fifteen years, was still in there somewhere. I refuse to believe that all of us could have been fooled for so many years. Besides, as I said to Stephenie, where would Pastor Len find the time to mess around with fallen women? He barely had time to sleep, what with all he was doing.

Well, just as me and Stephenie were finishing up talking, who should come up the driveway but Pastor Len himself. My heart plummeted when I saw he had that Monty with him.

'Reba,' Pastor Len said, the second he came through the screen door. 'Is Kendra here?'

I told him I hadn't seen her.

Monty sat himself right down at the table, helped himself to a glass of iced tea without even asking. Stephenie's eyes narrowed, but he didn't pay any mind to her.

'All Kendra's clothes are gone,' Pastor Len said. 'The dog too.

She say anything to you, Reba? 'Bout where she might be going? I tried her brother in Austin and he says he hasn't seen her.'

I told him I didn't have an inkling where she might've gone, and Stephenie said the same. Didn't mention that I didn't blame her for getting out of there, what with all those strangers taking over her home.

'It's probably for the best,' he said. 'Me and Kendra . . . we had certain disagreements about the role of Jesus in our lives.'

'Amen,' Monty said, although I couldn't see any reason for it.

Stephenie was trying to hide the *Inquirer* with her arms, but Pastor Len saw what she was doing.

'Don't you listen to those lies about me,' he said. 'I ain't never done nothing immoral. Jesus is all I need in my life.'

I believed him, Elspeth. That man had real conviction, and I could see that he wasn't lying.

I made a fresh pitcher of iced tea and then I decided to air what was on my mind. 'How are you planning on feeding all the new folks who have shown up, Pastor Len?' I'm not ashamed to say I looked right at Monty when I said it.

'The Lord will provide. Those good folks will be well taken care of.'

Well, they didn't look like good folks to me. Specially the ones like Monty. I said something about people taking advantage of his good nature, and Pastor Len got real irritated with me. 'Reba,' he said. 'What did Jesus say about judging people? As a good Christian, you should know better than that.'

Then he and that Monty took off.

I was upset by the altercation, I really was, and for the first time in years when Sunday came around I didn't go to church. Stephenie told me later it was full of the new Lookie-Loos, and quite a few of the inner circle had stayed away.

Well, it had to be two days later, something like that. I was keeping myself busy, wanted to get the canning done that week (by then we had a good two years' worth of canned fruit, Elspeth, but there was still plenty to do). Lorne and I were talking about ordering in some wood, storing it out back in case the power gave out, when I heard a pick-up shuddering to a stop outside the porch. I looked out and saw Jim slumped behind the wheel. I hadn't seen him since the week before when I'd gone over to take him a pie. He'd refused to answer the door and it pains me to say it, but I left it on the front step.

He just about fell out of the car, and when me and Lorne ran up to steady him he said, 'Got a call from Joanie, Reba.' He stank real bad, of booze and sweat. It looked like he hadn't shaved for weeks.

I wondered if his daughter had called to tell him that Pam's ashes were finally going to be coming home, and that's why he was so upset.

I sat him in the kitchen and he said, 'Can you call Pastor Len for me? Get him to come right over?'

'Why didn't you just drive on up to his ranch?' I asked. Fact is, he shouldn't have been driving anywhere. You could smell the alcohol on him from a mile away. It was enough to make my eyes water. If Sheriff Beaumont had seen him in that state he would've locked him up for sure. I fixed him a Coke straight away to take the edge off. After me and Pastor Len had had that altercation, I wasn't keen on calling him, but I did it all the same. Didn't expect him to answer, but he did. Said he'd be right over.

Jim didn't say much while we waited for Pastor Len, though me and Lorne tried to draw him out. And the little he did say didn't make much sense to us. Fifteen minutes later, Pastor Len showed up, his dog Monty in tow as usual.

Jim said straight off, 'Joanie went to see that boy, Len. That boy in Japan.'

Pastor Len just froze. Before they went their separate ways, Pastor Len was always saying how Dr Lund had been trying for the longest time to get to speak to one of those children. Jim's eyes fluttered. 'Joanie said that Jap boy . . . said she talked to the boy, but not *to* him exactly.'

None of us knew what in Jesus' name he was talking about. 'I don't get you, Jim,' Pastor Len said.

'She said he was talking through this android. This robot that looked just like him.'

'A robot?' I said. 'He was talking through a robot? Like the ones on YouTube? What in *heaven*?'

'What does it mean, Pastor Len?' Monty asked.

Pastor Len didn't say anything for at least a minute. 'I guess maybe I should give Teddy a call.' That's what Pastor Len called Dr Lund. Teddy, like they were good friends, although we all knew he and Dr Lund were having issues. Later Lorne said he reckoned Pastor Len was hoping a story like that would make up for the lies about his fancy woman; repair some of the damage done.

Then came the kicker. Jim said he'd already been to the newspapers about the story. Told them the lot, 'bout how Joanie had been round to see that Jap kid and talked to that robot that looked just like him.

Pastor Len turned as red as a canned beet. 'Jim,' he said. 'Why didn't you tell me about this first before you went to the papers?'

Jim got that stubborn look on his face. 'Pam was my wife. They offered me money for the story. I wasn't going to turn that down. I gotta live.'

A ton of money was coming to Jim from Pam's insurance, so that wasn't any excuse. Lorne said he could see plain as day that Pastor Len was ornery because he wanted to use that information for himself.

Jim banged his fist on the table. 'And people gotta know those kids is evil. How could that boy survive and not Pam, Pastor Len? It's not fair. It's not right. Pam was a good woman. A good woman.' Jim started crying, saying how those children were murderers. How they'd killed all those people on the planes, and he couldn't understand why no one could see that.

Pastor Len said he'd drive him home, with Monty following in Jim's pick-up. It took both of them to carry him out to Pastor Len's new SUV. Jim was crying fit to burst, shaking and howling. That man shouldn't have been left alone after that. It was obvious that his mind was broken. But like I said he was stubborn, and I know in my heart that he would have turned me down flat if I'd offered to take him in.

Just before this book was due to go into print, I finally managed to secure an interview with Pastor Len's estranged wife, Kendra Vorhees. I spoke to her at a state-of-the-art psychiatric clinic where she is currently residing (I have agreed not to print the name or exact location).

I'm shown to Kendra's room, an airy, sun-filled space, by an orderly with a perfect manicure. Kendra is sitting at a desk, a book open in front of her (later I see that it's the latest in Flexible Sandy's Gone *series). The dog on her lap – Snookie – wags its tail half-heartedly as I approach, but Kendra barely seems to register my presence. When she finally looks up, her eyes are clear and her expression far shrewder than I'm expecting. She's so slender that I can see every vein beneath her skin. There's a slight Texan drawl to her voice, and she speaks carefully, perhaps as a result of the medication she's taking.*

She waves me into an armchair opposite the desk and does not object when I place my recording device in front of her.

I ask Kendra why she decided to talk to me and not one of the other journalists eager to interview her.

I read your book. The one where you interviewed those children who accidentally shot their siblings with Mommy's .38 Special, or who got it into their heads to murder their classmates with Daddy's semi-automatic toy. Len was spitting mad when he saw me reading it. Course he was, he's big on that second amendment baloney, the right to bear arms and all that.

But you mustn't think I'm after revenge for what Len did with that prostitute. A 'ho' they call them, don't they? I liked her, if you want the truth. She was refreshingly honest, which is rare these days. I hope she takes her fifteen minutes of fame and runs with it. Milks it for all it's worth.

I ask her if she was the one who leaked the story about Pastor Len's indiscretions. She sighs, fusses with Snookie and nods briefly. I ask her why she leaked the story if it wasn't for revenge.

Because, the truth shall set you free! (*she laughs abruptly and humourlessly*). You can say what you darn well please when you write this up, by the way. What you darn well please. But if you want the real truth, I did it to get Len away from Dr Lund forever. Len was broken-hearted when the big boys kicked him out of their club after he made a fool of himself on that radio show, but I knew it wouldn't take much for him to go crawling back if Dr Lund snapped his fingers. I thought I was doing it for Len's own good, anyone could see that Dr Lund was a manipulator. And Dr Lund wouldn't want an acolyte with a sex scandal to his name muddying up his shiny reputation, not now he's got all those political aspirations. Turns out it was the worst thing I could have done. It goes through my head a thousand times a day, what if I hadn't followed Len that day? What if I'd let it be? I keep thinking, if Len had wormed his way back into Dr Lund's good graces, would that have made a difference in the end? Would it have stopped him from listening to that Jim Donald's crazy talk? Everyone's saying how Len 'let the devil in', but it's not as simple as that. Fact is, disappointment pushed Len over the edge. A broken heart will do that to you.

I open my mouth to comment, but she continues.

I'm not mad. I'm not crazy. I'm not a loony tune. It wore me out, all that pretending. You can't play a part all your life, can you? They say I've got depression. Clinical. Might be bipolar, but who knows what that means? This place isn't cheap. I'm making my good-for-nothing brother pick up the bill. He's been working his way through Daddy's money, got the lion's share, so it's about time he shelled out. And who else was I going to ask? I thought of maybe approaching Dr Lund himself. Even when we were at that godawful conference, you could tell he thought I was an embarrassment. I know for a fact he didn't want me to appear with Len on his show that one time. His wife didn't take to me either. It was mutual. You should have seen her face when I declined to join her Christian Women's League. 'We got to put those feminists and baby killers in their place, Kendra.'

She narrows her eyes at me.

I can see you're more than likely one of those feminists, am I right?

I tell her that I am.

That will make Lund even madder when he reads what I have to say. I'm not. A feminist, I mean. I'm not anything. No labels on me, no causes. Oh, I know what those ridiculous women back in that godawful place think of me. Fifteen years I lived there. They thought I was stuck-up, had ideas above my station because of where I'd come from. They also thought I was weak; meek and weak. The meek shall inherit the earth. Len could set their pulses a-flutter, of course. I'm surprised he didn't take up with one of them. But I suppose I should be grateful he chose not to foul in the back yard.

What a life! Stuck in a backwater county with a preacher for a husband. It was not what Daddy had envisaged for me. It was hardly what I had envisaged for myself. I had ambitions, not many. Thought about maybe teaching once. I have a college degree, you know. And those women tried to interest me in all their prepping nonsense. If there is a solar flare or a nuclear war, a thousand cans of pickled turnips aren't going to save you.

Pamela was the best of the bunch. In another life we could have been friends. Well, maybe not friends, but she wasn't as much of a bore as the others. Wasn't as dull or gossipy. I felt for her, living with that husband. Mean as a junkyard dog, that Jim. I liked Joanie, the daughter, too. I was rejoicing inside when she made the break, went off to see the world.

She fusses with Snookie again.

I like to think that at least Pam will have some comfort knowing that Snookie's being taken care of.

I ask her how she met Pastor Len.

Where else? At a Bible rally. A rally in Tennessee, which is where I went to college. We met across a crowded tent. *(she laughs humourlessly)* Love at first sight – for me at least. Took me years to realise that Len only found me attractive because of my other assets. All he wanted was his own church, 'That's what I was put on the earth to do,' he'd say. 'Preach the Lord's word and save souls.'

He was a Baptist back then, so was I. He'd gone to college late, been working his way around the South. All full of fire and Jesus, worked for a time as a deacon for Dr Samuel Keller. Doubt you'll remember him. Low level, but it looked like he was on track to be another Hagee before he got caught with his pants down in the nineties. Shit will stick and ain't that the truth, as my daddy used to say, and after Keller was discovered canoodling with that young boy in a public convenience, Len discovered that finding another position wasn't going to be easy, least not till all the hoo-ha calmed down. His only choice was to start up on his own. We moved around a lot, looking for the right place. Then we came to Sannah County. Daddy had just died, left me my inheritance and we bought the ranch with that. I think Len had some idea of farming on the side, but what did he know about farming?

He was a beautiful man to look at. Still is, I suppose. Knew the benefits of good grooming. Daddy wasn't happy when I brought him home. 'Mark my words, that boy will break your heart,' he said.

Daddy was wrong. Len didn't break my heart, but he sure as hell tried.

Tears start running down her cheeks, but she appears not to notice. I hand her a tissue, and she wipes her eyes absentmindedly.

Don't mind me. I wasn't always like this. I did believe, oh I did. No. I lost my faith when God saw fit not to give me children. That's all I wanted. It might have been different if I could have been given that. It's not much to ask. And Len wouldn't consider adopting. 'Children aren't part of Jesus' plan for us, Kendra.'

But I've got a baby now, haven't I? Oh yes. One that needs me. Who needs to be loved. Who deserves to be loved.

She pets Snookie again, but the dog barely stirs.

Len isn't an evil man. No. I'll never say that. He's a disappointed man, poisoned by thwarted ambition. He wasn't clever enough, or charismatic enough – not till he got fire and brimstone in his eyes – not till that woman mentioned him in that message.

Sound bitter, don't I?

I shouldn't be mad at Pamela. I don't blame her really. Like I say, she was a good woman. Len and I . . . I guess we were stagnating, had been for years, and something had to change. He had his radio show and his Bible and healing groups, he'd spent years trying to get what he called 'the big boys' to take notice of him. And I've never seen him so excited as when he got invited to that goshdarn conference. There was a part of me – the part that hadn't died by then – that thought it might really be the making of us. But he let it all go to his head. And he really did believe in that message. He *does* believe in that message. People are saying he's a charlatan, no better than those alien people or those crazy cult leaders, but that part at least isn't an act.

I couldn't stand it when all those people started coming to the ranch. They upset Snookie. I reckon Len thought he'd make a fortune from all the tithes they'd bring. Did it to prove to Dr Lund that he could get a loyal following, too. But none of the ones who came had any money. That Monty, for starters. I could sense him watching me sometimes. There was something wrong with the way that man's mind was wired. I spent a lot of time in my room, watching my shows. Len tried to get me out to church on Sundays, but by then I couldn't face it. Other times me and Snookie would just get in the car and drive and drive, not caring where we ended up.

It was bound to go sour. I told Len not to do that radio show with that smart-mouth New York man. But Len wasn't one to listen. He didn't like it if you contradicted him.

I knew Dr Lund was out to pull one over him eventually, and that's what he did. Took Len's words and used them for his own ends. Len would rage up and down, trying to get Dr Lund or that Flexible Sandy on the phone, but eventually he couldn't even get their publicists to speak to him. It was all over the news that more and more people were getting themselves saved, and Dr Lund was taking the lion's share of the credit. He had the contacts, you see. And when he got behind that Mitch Reynard and didn't invite Len to speak at that pro-Israel rally, well, I have never seen Len so upset. I didn't stick around to see his face after the story in the *Inquirer* came out; I left the day it was published. He denied it, just like I knew he would. But being ousted out of the big boys' club did more damage to his self-esteem than any news story – however sensationalist – could do. In fact, I don't doubt that Lund's dismissal hurt Len far more than me leaving him.

It was cruel. Dr Lund opened the door a crack, let Len see into the palace, and then slammed the door on him.

She sighs.

Snookie needs his nap now. It's time for you to go. I've said my piece.

Before I leave, I ask her how she feels about Len now, and a spark of anger flares in her eyes.

I haven't got room in my heart for Len any more. I haven't got room for anyone.

She kisses the top of Snookie's head and I get the impression she's forgotten I'm still here.

You'd never hurt me, would you, Snookie? No. No, you *wouldn't*.

SURVIVORS

APRIL

Lillian Small.

I was living a strange half-life. Some days Reuben could communicate as clearly as I'm talking to you now, but whenever I brought something up about our old house, or one of our old friends, or a book he'd particularly enjoyed, a worried expression would fill his eyes, and they'd dart about as if he was desperately trying to access the information and coming up empty. It was as if the time before he woke up was a blank. I decided not to push him. This is hard to talk about . . . but the fact that he didn't seem to recall our past together or even get our 'Paris Texas' joke any more – that was almost as painful as the days when Al was back.

Because some days Al *would* be back. I knew immediately when he woke up if it would be a Reuben or an Al day; I could see it in his eyes when I brought him his morning coffee. Bobby took the whole thing in his stride, acted the same towards Reuben whether he was himself or Al, but it took its toll on me. That uncertainty; not knowing what I was going to be facing each morning. I only asked Betsy or called the care agency in to help when I was sure it was going to be an Al day. It wasn't that I didn't trust Betsy, but I couldn't forget the way Dr Lomeier had reacted when Reuben spoke to him. I couldn't bear the thought of what those lunatics would say if they found out about Reuben. They still wouldn't leave us in peace. I can't count how many times I had to hang up the phone when I realised it was one of those religious putzes, begging me to let them talk to Bobby.

And . . . even when it was a Reuben day, he still wasn't quite himself. For some reason he'd developed an addiction to *The View*, a show he loathed before he got sick, and he and Bobby would spend hours watching old movies, though Reuben was never much of a film buff. He'd also lost interest in the news channels, even though there were all those political debates going on.

One morning, I was in the kitchen, making Bobby's breakfast

and steeling myself to wake Reuben, when Bobby came rushing in. 'Bubbe,' he said. 'Po Po wants to go for a walk today. He wants to go out.'

Bobby took my hand and led me into the bedroom. Reuben was sitting on the bed, attempting to pull on his socks. 'Are you all right, Reuben?' I said.

'Can we go into the city, Rita?'

That's what he'd started calling me: Rita. After Rita Hayworth! The red hair, you see.

'Where would you like to go?'

Bobby and Reuben exchanged glances. 'The museum, Bubbe!' Bobby said.

The movie *Night at the Museum* had been on the night before, and Bobby had been fascinated by the scenes where all the exhibits came to life. It had been an AI day, so I doubted anything about the film had seeped into Reuben's consciousness, which was a relief as halfway through it, Bobby said, 'The dinosaur is like you, Po Po. It's come to life just like you did!'

'Reuben?' I said. 'You think you're up to going out today?'

He nodded, as eager as a little child. 'Yes please, Rita. Let's go and see the dinosaurs.'

'Yeah! Dinosaurs!' Bobby joined in. 'Bubbe? Do you think they really existed?'

'Of course, Bobby,' I said.

'I like their teeth. One day I'll bring *them* back to life.'

Bobby's enthusiasm was infectious, and if anyone deserved a treat, it was him. Poor little boy had been inside for days, although he never complained, not once. But the more time we spent out and about, the more likely it was that something might happen. What if we were recognised? What if one of those religious fanatics followed us and tried to kidnap Bobby? And I worried that Reuben's strength wouldn't hold out. His mental faculties may have been improving, but physically he tired easily.

But I put all those fears aside, and before I could change my mind, I called a taxi.

We ran into Betsy as we were leaving, and I prayed that Reuben wouldn't say anything. Of course I'd had a million close encounters of this type, and part of me longed to talk to someone about it – I hadn't told a soul, other than the sterile Dr Lomeier, that is. I mouthed 'doctor' at Betsy and she nodded, but Betsy's smart, and I could see she knew I was hiding something.

The taxi managed to find a spot right outside our door, a blessing as I could see a few of those *meshugeners* with their offensive billboards gathered around the park, even at nine in the morning.

Mercifully, the taxi driver – another one of those Indian immigrants – didn't recognise us, or if he did, he didn't let on. I asked the driver to take us over the Williamsburg Bridge so that Reuben could see the view and oh Elspeth, I did enjoy the journey! It was a lovely clear day, so the skyline looked like it was posing for a postcard and the sun bounced off the water. I pointed out all the sights to Bobby as we zipped through Manhattan, the Chrysler building, Rockefeller Plaza, the Trump Tower, and he sat glued to the window asking me question after question. That trip cost a fortune, almost forty dollars with the tip, but it was worth it. Before we went into the museum, I asked Bobby and Reuben if they wanted a hot dog each for breakfast, and we sat and ate them in Central Park like regular tourists. Lori had brought me and Bobby here once – not to the museum, but to the park. Bobby had been grumpy that day, and the weather was freezing, but I still remember it fondly. She hadn't stopped talking about all the commissions she was getting; she was so excited about her future back then!

Even though it was a week day, the museum was full and we had to queue for quite a while. I started feeling anxious that we'd be recognised, but most of the people around us were tourists – a lot of Chinese and Europeans. And Reuben was starting to look tired; beads of sweat were popping on his brow. Bobby was full of energy; he couldn't keep his eyes off the dinosaur skeleton in the foyer.

The man at the ticket counter, a chatty African American fellow, did one of those double-takes when I approached him. 'Don't I know you, ma'am?'

'No,' I said, probably a bit rudely. After I paid and turned away, I heard him call, 'Wait!'

I hesitated; worried that he was going to point out who Bobby was to the whole museum. But instead he said, 'Could I offer you a wheelchair for your husband, ma'am?'

I could have kissed him. Everyone always says that New Yorkers are brash and self-involved, but that's just not true.

Bobby was tugging on my hand. 'Bubbe! The dinosaurs.'

The vendor disappeared and came back with a wheelchair. Reuben sank into it immediately. By now I was really getting worried about him. He was beginning to look confused, and I was concerned that Al might have decided to sneak back to cause trouble for us.

The ticket man guided us towards the lifts. 'Go on, son,' he said to Bobby. 'You show your grandparents the dinosaurs.'

'Do you believe that the dinosaurs come to life at night, Mr Man?' Bobby asked him.

'Why not? Miracles do happen, don't they?' And then he winked at me, and I knew for sure that he knew who we were. 'Don't worry, ma'am,' he said. 'I'll keep quiet. You go on and enjoy yourselves.'

We went straight up to the floor that housed the dinosaur exhibits. I had it in my mind that we'd take a quick look for Bobby's sake, and then head straight home.

I told Bobby to stick close to me, there were crowds everywhere, and it was quite a struggle pushing our way into the first room.

Reuben looked up at me and said, 'What am I? I'm scared.' And then he started crying, something that he hadn't done since he 'came to life', as Bobby put it.

I did my best to settle him. A few people were staring at him and the last thing I wanted was to draw attention to us. And when I looked up, Bobby was gone.

'Bobby?' I called. 'Bobby?'

I looked for his Yankees baseball cap, but couldn't see it anywhere.

The panic hit like a tidal wave. I left Reuben where he was and just ran.

I pushed past people, ignoring the grunts of 'Hey, lady, watch it,' icy sweat pouring down my sides. 'Bobby!' I shouted at the top of my lungs. Images kept flashing through my head. Bobby being taken away by one of those religious types, kidnapped and made to do all kinds of terrible things. Bobby lost in New York, wandering around and . . .

A woman guard came rushing up to me. 'Calm down, ma'am,' she said. 'You can't shout in here.' I could tell she thought I was deranged, and I didn't blame her. I felt like I was losing my mind.

'My grandson! I can't find my grandson.'

'Okay, ma'am,' she said. 'What does he look like?'

It didn't occur to me to tell her who Bobby actually was – that he was *the* Bobby Small, one of The Three, the miracle child, or any of that nonsense. All of that just went out of my head and I'm glad I didn't – the cops would have been called immediately and no doubt the whole thing would have been front-page news the next day. The guard said that she would alert the staff at the entrances and exits, just in case, but then I heard the most beautiful word in the whole world. 'Bubbe?'

I almost fainted with relief when I saw him skipping up to me. 'Where you been, Bobby? You frightened me half to death.'

'I was with the big one. He's got huge teeth like a wolf! But come on, Bubbe, Po Po needs us.'

Can you believe it, I had forgotten about Reuben, and we hurried back to the exhibit hall where I'd left him. Mercifully, he'd fallen asleep in the chair.

I didn't feel safe again until we were heading home in a taxi. Thankfully Reuben was calm when he woke from his nap, and while he wasn't himself, at least I didn't have to deal with a full-on AI panic on top of everything else.

'They didn't come to life, Bubbe,' Bobby said. 'The dinosaurs didn't come to life.'

'That's because they only come alive at night,' Reuben said. He was back. He took my hand and squeezed it. 'You did good, Lily,' he said. Lily – he'd called me Lily, and not Rita.

'What do you mean?' I asked him.

'You didn't give up. You didn't give up on me.'

Then I did cry. I couldn't help it, the tears just flowed.

'Are you okay, Bubbe?' Bobby asked. 'Are you sad?'

'I'm fine. I was just worried about you,' I said. 'I thought I'd lost you back in that museum.'

'You can't lose me,' Bobby said. 'You really can't, Bubbe. It's impossible.'

This is the last recorded IM conversation between Ryu and Chiyoko.

Message logged @ 20.46, 03/04/2012

CHIYOKO: I THOUGHT YOU WERE MY FRIEND!!!!! How could you do this to me?????????? www.hirotalksthroughandroid/tokyoherald I hope they paid you well. I hope it was worth it.

RYU: Chiyoko! I swear, I swear it wasn't me.

CHIYOKO: MC is furious. Android Uncle is threatening to take Hiro back to Osaka. There are reporters everywhere. I will die if I lose him. How could you do it????

RYU: It wasn't me!

CHIYOKO: You have ruined my life, NEVER CONTACT ME AGAIN.

RYU: Yoko? Yoko? Please. Please! IT WASN'T ME.

Devastated after Chiyoko blocked him from messaging her, Ryu went on the 2-chan Single Men's 'Broken Hearted' message forum under the avatar Orz Man, starting the thread: 'Loser Geek Needs Help.' Almost immediately, his story went viral, catching the imaginations of the board's inhabitants, and eventually attracting millions of hits.

Translation by Eric Kushan, who notes that American shortcuts and slang have been used to approximate the Japanese net slang used on the boards.

NAME: ORZ MAN POST DATE: 2012/04/05 01:32:39.32
Need some advice from u Netizens please!!! I need to reconnect with a girl who is blocking me from contacting her.

NAME: ANONYMOUS111
Why'd she dump u Orz?

NAME: ORZ MAN
She thinks I betrayed a confidence, but it wasn't me. _|7O

NAME: ANONYMOUS275
Been there dude but need more info.

NAME: ORZ MAN
Okay . . . this may take a while. I've been talking to this girl online, who I'll call the ice princess. She's way above my level, so u can imagine how amazed I was that someone like her would spend time with a loser like me. We were getting on well, talking every day and sharing stuff, u know? Then . . . something happened. A . . . let's call it a story was leaked that made her family look bad and she thought it was me and now she has blocked me from messaging her.

I don't want you guys to think I'm a loser. But it hurts. When she stopped taking my messages, it was like my stomach was made of glass and then it shattered.

NAME: ANONYMOUS111

'Like my stomach was made of glass.' That's beautiful, Orz.

NAME: ANONYMOUS28

I'm cryin here.

NAME: ORZ MAN

Thanks. I'm in a bad way. It hurts like a physical pain. I can't eat or sleep. I keep reading our messages over and over again. I spent hours today analysing every single word we've ever shared.

NAME: ANONYMOUS23

Ouch!!!! U gotta learn that women are only there to cause u pain, Orz dude. Fuck them.

NAME: ANONYMOUS111

Ignore 23.
Been where u r Orz. Is there any hope you can reconnect?

NAME: ORZ MAN

I don't know. I can't live without her.

NAME: ANONYMOUS23:

What does she look like? Is she hot????

NAME: ANONYMOUS99

<SIGH> U r such a noob 23.

NAME: ORZ MAN

I've only seen her once. And not in person. She looks a little like Hazuki Hitori.

NAME: ANONYMOUS678
Hazuki Hitori from the Sunny Juniors? Ba-doom! Orz, yr taste is good, dude. I'm in love with her too.

NAME: ANONYMOUS709
Hazuki???? Arrrrrr-oooooooooooooooooooooooooooooooooooo oooooooooooooooo

NAME: ANONYMOUS111
Keep your lust in check, Netizens.
Orz, u need to go and talk to her in person. Tell her how u feel.

NAME: ORZ MAN
It's not as easy as that. This is embarrassing. U guys . . . I still live with my parents and I'm kinda housebound.

NAME: ANONYMOUS 987
It's cool. I also live at home.

NAME: ANONYMOUS55
Me too. Big deal.

NAME: ORZ MAN
Not what I meant. I haven't left the house in um . . . a while. I haven't even left my room.

NAME: ANONYMOUS111
How long is a while, Orz?

NAME: ORZ MAN
U guys r going to judge me!!!!
Over a year. _|7O

NAME: ANONYMOUS87
Meatspace can be a fucker. Here's a tip, Orz. If u don't want to go to the bathroom then keep old plastic water bottles under

yr desk for emergencies. What I do when I'm on a gaming binge.

NAME: ANONYMOUS786
LOL!!!
Good advice, 87!

NAME: ANONYMOUS23
Netizens. Orz here is a hikikomori.

NAME: ANONYMOUS111
Orz socialises on the net, which means he is capable of human contact. He's just a recluse not a proper hikikomori.
[The thread is briefly disrupted by an argument about the true nature of a hikikomori]

NAME: ANONYMOUS111
Orz, you still there?

NAME: ORZ MAN
I'm here. Listen . . . sorry for wasting yr time. Writing that makes me realise . . . What would she see in me anyway? Why would she even look at such a loser?
Look at me . . . No job, no cash, no hope.

NAME: ANONYMOUS111
Is yr princess dead? No. Then there is always hope. Netizens, this man needs our help. Time to suit up.

NAME: ANONYMOUS85
Get the weapons loaded.

NAME: ANONYMOUS337
Train that princess in your sights.

NAME: ANONYMOUS23
Locked and loaded, SIR!

NAME: ANONYMOUS111
First, we gotta help Orz get out of his room.

NAME: ANONYMOUS47
Orz. Some good advice:

1. Clean yrself up so that u look as presentable as possible. No bed hair or pimples.
2. Go to Uniqlo and get some good clothes nothing flashy.
3. Go and see The Princess.
4. Offer to buy her dinner.
5. At dinner, tell her how you feel.

That way, even if she cuts you off, you will have no regrets.

NAME: ANONYMOUS23
Orz might not know where she lives if they've only been talking online. He said he has no money so how can he buy new clothes?

NAME: ORZ MAN
Thanks for the advice. I don't have her address but I know she lives near the Yoyogi station.

NAME: ANONYMOUS414
There is a good pasta place near there.

NAME: ANONYMOUS23
Pasta for a first date? Go Yakitori, French or ethnic then u have a talking point.
[The thread diverts into a discussion about the best place to take a first date]

NAME: ANONYMOUS111
It's not a first date. Orz and his princess are cyber soul mates. Netizens, yr missing the point. First Orz has to clean up and get out of his room.

NAME: ORZ MAN
You really think I should try and see her in person?
[A chorus of 'yes', 'do it dude', 'what have you got to lose' etc., follows]

NAME: ORZ MAN
Okay. You have almost convinced me! Now the practicalities . . . I think I can get some money but not much. The princess lives in a different prefecture so I need somewhere to stay while I search for her house. Can't afford a hotel. Any suggestions? Any of u stayed over in a net cafe? Is it an option?

NAME: ANONYMOUS89
Not ideal, but I have done it once on the outskirts of Shinjuku. Cheap and u can get vending food there.
[The netizens bombard Orz with advice, arguing about where he should stay and how best to attract the princess's attention]

NAME: ORZ MAN
I got to sleep. Been up for 20 hours. Thanks guys. U really helped me. Don't feel so alone any more.

NAME: ANONYMOUS789
U can do it, Orz.

NAME: ANONYMOUS122
Do it for the geeks.

NAME: ANONYMOUS20
Good luck!!!! We are all there with you, Orz. C'mon dude, u can dooooooooooooooooo it.

NAME: ANONYMOUS23
Fuckin do it man.

NAME: ANONYMOUS111
Keep us posted!!!!!
[Two days later, Ryu, aka Orz Man, reappears on the thread, during which time, much speculation has gone on]

NAME: ORZ MAN POST DATE: 2012/04/07 01:37:19.30
Don't know if any of you here on the thread I started the other day are listening. Been reading through what all of u have been saying. So blown away by the amount of support I have on this site!
    Just wanted to let u guys know I took your advice. I left the house.

NAME: ANONYMOUS111
Orz! Where are u now?

NAME: ORZ MAN
I'm staying in a net cafe cubicle.

NAME: ANONYMOUS111
What is it like being out in the big bad world? We need details. Start from the beginning.

NAME: ORZ MAN
Ah. Like I said, I followed all your advice. First, I cleaned myself up. Brushed my teeth, which were yellow from too much smoking. Next, the hair. Didn't have cash for a haircut, so did it myself. Don't think I did too bad a job!
    Now the hard part. U guys are seriously gonna judge me for this. My parents were at work when I left and I took the savings my mother keeps in the kitchen. Not much but enough to keep me going for a couple of weeks if I'm careful. I left a note, but I still feel bad about it. I said I'd decided to leave to find a job so that I would no longer be a burden on the family.

NAME: ANONYMOUS111

U did the right thing, Orz. U can pay them back when u are on yr feet.

NAME: ANONYMOUS28

Yeah, Orz. U did the only thing u could do in that situation. Keep going and tell us the full deets.

NAME: ORZ MAN

Thanks guys. More details . . . okay.

My shoes were still in the cupboard next to the front door where I'd left them a year ago. They were covered in dust.

Leaving the house was one of the hardest things I've ever done. Trying to think of how to explain it . . . when I stepped outside, I felt like I was a matchstick in an ocean. Everything looked too bright, too big. The curtain twitchers were out in force. I know they have been gossiping about me for months, something that has caused my mother a lot of distress.

It was early afternoon when I left, but even my district seemed to be unbearably busy. Kept feeling the tug of my room. It was like I was being pulled back, but I fought against it and made myself jog to the station. I bought a ticket to Shinjuku before I could change my mind. It felt like everyone I saw was pointing and laughing at me.

Won't go into the constant panic attacks I had to fend off when I arrived at Shinjuku. Not knowing what to do, I went into a Yoshinoya outlet although I didn't feel like eating. I made myself ask the counter guy if he knew of somewhere cheap I could stay. He was cool, gave me directions to this net cafe.

Going to be honest here . . . kinda freaking out . . .

NAME: ANONYMOUS179

Don't freak out dude. We're here 4 u. So what's next? How will you find her house?

NAME: ORZ MAN

I've done some research. Her family . . . let's just say they are not unknown, and I have managed to source the address.

NAME: ANONYMOUS179

U mean she's famous???

[The next few hours are spent dispensing more words of wisdom and speculating on who the princess's family could be]

NAME: ORZ MAN

I'm thinking that if I get up the nerve to see her, the best thing to do would be to wait for her parents to leave the house.

NAME: ANONYMOUS902

U thought what u r going to say?

NAME: ANONYMOUS865

Orz's broken glass stomach is tinkling. He lights a cigarette and stands beneath a streetlight watching the princess's house. He crushes the cigarette under his boot, walks up to the front door, and knocks.

She opens it. He can't breathe. She is even more beautiful than he remembers.

'It's me, Orz,' he says, taking off his shades.

'Take me away from all of this,' she pleads, dropping to her knees in front of him. 'Do me, do me now!'

NAME: ANONYMOUS761

Nice work 865, made me LOL!!!

NAME: ORZ MAN

Been thinking . . . I might know how to get her attention . . .

NAME: ANONYMOUS111

Don't leave us in suspense.

NAME: ANONYMOUS2
Yeah, Orz. We're on yr team, dude!!!!

NAME: ORZ MAN
I'll tell u tomorrow if it works. If it doesn't I will be curled in a ball, slitting my wrists and sobbing.

NAME: ANONYMOUS286
Victory is yr only option Orz! You can do iiiiit!!!!
[After Ryu left the message board, the following exchange occurred]

NAME: ANONYMOUS111
Netizens . . . I think I know who the princess is.

NAME: ANONYMOUS874
Who?

NAME: ANONYMOUS111
Orz said that the princess's family is well known. He also said that she lives near the Yoyogi station.
Hiro lives in Yoyogi.

NAME: ANONYMOUS23
Hiro????????? Miracle child Hiro? Android boy?

NAME: ANONYMOUS111
Yeah. Hiro is staying with his aunt and uncle. They've got a daughter. Checked through the footage of the memorial service. Spotted a girl who looks like Hazuki in the crowd standing near the family, and another one who is not as hot.

NAME: ANONYMOUS23
Our humble Orz is in love with Android Boy's cousin??? GO ORZ!

17 April, 12.30 p.m.

God. It's been a while . . . How are you, Mandi? Do you know, even though I've been rambling into this fucking thing as if you're my closest friend or Dr K substitute, it struck me the other day that I couldn't remember your face. I even went on Facebook to check out your profile pic to remind me what you look like. I told you how much I hate Facebook, didn't I? My own fault. I stupidly accepted friend requests from a shed-load of people without checking them out properly first. Bastards hate-bombed my wall and Twitter account because of the Marilyn thing.

Mandi, I'd like to apologise for ignoring your calls. I just didn't . . . I had a few bad days, okay? More than a few, let's be honest. A few weeks ha ha. I couldn't see an end to them. Stephen . . . well, you know. I don't want to go there. And I haven't done much about sorting out what we can keep in amongst all this drivel. I haven't done much of anything, to be honest.

It was too soon. All this. It was too soon after the accident. I can see that now. But I'm thinking maybe we can rework it later after I'm . . . after I'm feeling more like myself. Not in a good place at the moment, you see.

Some days I find myself looking at photographs of Jess, trying to spot the difference. She caught me at it the other day. 'What are you doing, Uncle Paul?' she asked, all sweet and cheery, damn her. She has this way of creeping up on me.

'Nothing,' I snapped at her.

I felt so guilty that the next day I went to Toys R Us and spent the equivalent of a down payment on a car on product-placement toys and other crap. She now has the entire set of extortionately expensive My Little Ponies, as well as a bushel-load of themed

Barbies, which I know would make feminist Shelly turn over in her grave.

But I'm trying. God, am I trying. It's just . . . she isn't herself. Jess and Polly used to love the stories Stephen made up for them – silly takes on *Aesop's Fables*. I tried making one up the other day – a version of 'The Boy Who Cried Wolf' – but she looked at me as if I'd gone mad.

Ha! Maybe I have.

'Cause there's this other thing. Last night I did a Google marathon again, trying to get to the bottom of how I'm feeling about Jess. There's this medical condition. It's called Capgras Delusion. It's really rare, but people who suffer from it are convinced that the people they live with have been replaced by proxies. Like changelings. I know it's mental even to think like this. Dangerous even . . . But at the same time, it's actually reassuring knowing there is a particular syndrome that would explain it all. But it could just be stress. That's what I'm clinging to right now.

(Clears throat)

And Christ. It's been busy. What with Jess's first day back at school. This we could use, I think. It's just the kind of thing readers want, isn't it? I think I told you Dr K and Darren decided that it would do her good to get back after the Easter hols. It wasn't ideal, her doing home schooling. I'm not much of a teacher and . . . it meant interacting with her for hours.

The press were out in their droves as usual, so I put on the performance of my life, all smiles, could have got a BAFTA for my role as 'Concerned Guardian'. While the hacks howled outside the gates, I walked her into the classroom. The teacher, Mrs Wallbank, had got the kids to decorate it; there was a big 'Welcome Back Jess!' banner hanging across the blackboard. Mrs Wallbank is a strapping too-jolly woman who looks like she's fallen out of an Enid Blyton novel. The sort of person who spends her weekends visiting heritage sites, hiking hairy-legged up wind-swept hills. Just the sight of her made me want to get rat-arsed and smoke a pack of Rothmans (yes, yes, Mandi, twenty a day now, though never in the house. Another bad habit to hide, ha ha, although I've discovered that Mrs E-B isn't averse to a sneaky ciggie).

I soon found out that Mrs Wallbank speaks to the children like adults, but treats grown-ups like retards. 'Hello, Jess's uncle! Now don't you worry about a thing. Jess and I will be just fine, won't we?'

'Are you sure you're ready for this, Jess?' I simpered.

'Of course, Uncle Paul,' she said, with that complacent smile I've come to loathe. 'You go back home and have a fag and a vodka.'

Mrs Wallbank blinked at me, and I tried to make a joke of it.

Feeling that sense of relief I always feel whenever I'm not around her, I ran out of there.

Outside, I tried to ignore the hacks' usual questions: 'When are you going to let Marilyn see her granddaughter?' I muttered the usual bollocks about 'when Jess is feeling up to it', etc. etc. Then I jumped in Stephen's Audi and just drove around a bit. Found myself in the heart of Bromley. I parked and went to Marks & Spencer to buy something special for Jess's first-day-back-at-school supper. And all along I knew I was just playing a part. Pretending to be the caring uncle. But I can't . . . I can't stop thinking about Stephen and Shelly – the real Stephen and Shelly, not the Stephen who comes to me at night – and it's only the thought of not letting them down that keeps me going. I keep thinking that if I throw myself into the part, eventually it will become reality. Eventually I'll get back onto an even keel.

Anyway, I was standing in the queue, clutching a basket full of those ghastly pasta ready-meals Jess likes so much, when I found my eyes drifting over to the Wines of the World section. Pictured myself sitting down, right there, and gulping bottle after bottle of Chilean red until my stomach exploded. 'Come on, love,' the old woman behind me said, 'there's a till open,' and that snapped me out of it. The cashier recognised me straight away. Gave me what I've come to call a standard 'supportive smile'. 'How's she doing?' she whispered conspiratorially.

'Why's it always about her?' I almost snapped. I forced out something along the lines of, 'she's doing wonderfully, thanks so much for caring,' and somehow managed to leave without punching her in the face or buying the whole of the alcohol aisle.

24 April, 11.28 p.m.

I'm doing okay this week, Mandi. It's better now that she's at school. We even spent an evening together watching a *The Only Way is Essex* marathon. She loves that appalling reality programme, can't seem to get enough of spray-tanned morons talking utter shit to each other in nightclubs, which should worry me slightly. But I suppose all her friends at school are into that kind of rubbish, so I should look at it as reassuringly normal behaviour. She's still relentlessly cheerful and well-behaved (just once I wish she'd throw a tantrum or refuse to go to bed). I keep convincing myself that Dr K's right, that of course her behaviour is going to change after going through all that trauma. It'll just take time for us to adjust. 'Jess,' I asked, during a commercial break – a relief from all the banality on screen. 'You and me . . . we're okay, right?'

'Of course we are, Uncle Paul.' And for the first time in ages I thought, it's going to be fine. I'll get over this.

I even phoned Gerry to let him know I was ready to get back to work. He asked about the recordings of course, said your publishers were on his back, desperate for me to send through more material, and I made my usual excuses. They'd have an orgasm if I sent this through unedited.

But I'll sort it out. Yeah.

25 April, 4.00 p.m.

Phew. Big big day, Mandi. Darren's just left (God, he can be an anal twat, went through the cupboards and the fridge to check what Jess was eating, which I'm fairly sure isn't standard procedure), when the phone rang. As you know, it's usually either the press or a tenacious religious freak who's somehow managed to scalp or bribe someone to get my new number. But today, surprise, surprise, it was one of the alien abduction people. They've been keeping schtum since I sicced the cops onto them just after Jess got out of hospital. I almost hung up straight away, but something stopped me. The guy calling – Simon somebody – sounded fairly reasonable. Said he was phoning to see how I was doing. Not Jess, but *me*. I had to be careful; ten to one the phones being hacked, so I let him do most of the talking. I didn't really have to say much to be fair. As I listened, I almost felt like I was watching myself from across the room. I knew it was mental to give him the time of day. He says that what the aliens do – he called them 'the others', like in a lazily scripted B-movie – is abduct people, place a microchip inside their body and use 'alien technology' to control them. He says they're in cahoots with the government. It made me ... why not be honest? No one else is going to hear this. Shit, okay ... Look, on some level it made a weird kind of sense.

I mean ... what if Black Thursday is a government experiment thingy after all? There are an awful lot of people who believe there's no way those kids could have survived those crashes. And I don't mean the obvious nutters like those bible bashers. Or the freaks who think the kids are possessed by the devil. Even that investigator who came to ask Jess if she remembered anything about the crash stared at her as if he couldn't believe she was alive. Sure, in the Japanese crash there were other people who initially survived the impact, but they didn't last long. And how exactly *did* Jess survive? Most of the other bodies ... well, they were in pieces, weren't they? And that Maiden Airlines plane looked like it had been through a blender when they started dredging it up from the Everglades.

Okay ... deep breath, Paul. Calm the fuck down. Lack of sleep, it can screw with your mind, can't it?

29 April, 3.37 a.m.

He's back. Three nights in a row now.

It sounds crazy, but I'm getting used to it. I no longer get a fright when I wake up and see him sitting there.

Last night I tried to talk to him again. 'What are you trying to tell me, Stephen?'

But he just said the same thing he always says, then disappeared. The smell is getting worse. I can still smell it on the sheets, even now. Rotten fish. Rotten . . . flesh. Fuck. I can't be imagining that, can I? *Can I?*

And . . . I have an admission. I'm not proud of it.

I couldn't take it last night. I left the house at four a.m. – yeah, that's right, leaving Jess alone – and drove to the all-night Tesco's in Orpington. Bought myself a half-jack of Bells.

By the time I got home it was empty.

Hid the bottle under the bed with the others. Mrs E-B may be my new sneaky fag ally, but she'd be horrified at the number of empties I'm collecting. I'm getting out of control; got to cut back again. Got to stop this shit.

30 April

So much for my resolution to get my act together.

I've just been through Jess's bedroom. I don't know what I was expecting to find. A 'To Serve Man' manual maybe, like in that old *Twilight Zone* episode, ha ha.

(*Paul's laughter makes way to sobbing*)

It's okay. I'm okay.

But she *is* different. She is. There's no getting away from that. She's even taken down all her old Missy K posters. Maybe aliens have good taste.

(*Another laugh that turns into a sob*)

But . . . how can she not be Jess?

It has to be me.

But . . .

It's getting harder to hide all this from Darren. I can't allow myself to crack. Not now. I need to cover all bases. Get to the bottom of this. I've even considered giving in and taking her to see

Marilyn. But would the fat cow even be able to tell if there's something different about Jess? Shelly hated going round there, so Marilyn saw the girls less than I did. I suppose it's worth a shot. She is Jess's flesh and blood, isn't she?

But in the meantime, I asked Petra, one of the yummy mummies at Jess's school, to bring her daughter Summer over to play this afternoon. Petra's always emailing and calling and asking if there's anything she can do to help, so she jumped at the chance. She even offered to collect the girls from school and bring them here.

So . . . I'm leaving the recorder in Jess's bedroom. Just to check. Just to be sure. See what Jess talks about when I'm not around. It's what a good uncle would do, isn't it? Maybe Jess is in pain and will open up to Summer and then I'll know that the way she's behaving is because she has what Dr K calls 'unexplored trauma'. They'll be here in five minutes.

(*Sound of approaching children's voices, which get gradually louder*)

'. . . So you can be Rainbow Dash and I'll be Princess Luna. Unless you want to be Rarity?'

'Have you got *all* of the ponies, Jess?'

'Yeah. Paul bought them for me. He also bought me Pageant Gown Barbie. Here.'

'Oh cool! She's so beautiful. But it's not even your birthday.'

'I know. You can have her if you like. Paul can get me a new one.'

'Really? You're the bestest! Jess . . . what are you going to do with all of Polly's toys?'

'Nothing.'

'And, Jess . . . did it hurt? When you got burned?'

'Yes.'

'Will the scars go away?'

'It doesn't matter.'

'What doesn't?'

'If they go away or not.'

'Mummy says it's a miracle you got out of that plane. She says I'm not to ask you questions about it in case it makes you cry.'

'I'm not going to cry!'

'Mummy says you can cover the scars with make-up later on so that people won't stare.'

'C'mon! Let's play!'

(*For the next fifteen minutes the girls play 'My Little Pony meets Barbie in Essex'.*)

(*Distant sound of Paul's voice calling them to come downstairs for a snack.*)

'Aren't you coming, Jess?'

'You go first. I'll get the ponies. They can eat with us.'

''Kay. Can I really have Pageant Gown Barbie?'

'Yes.'

'You're my bestest friend ever, Jess.'

'I know. Now you go first.'

''Kay.'

(*The Dictaphone captures the sound of Summer leaving the room. There's a pause of several seconds, followed by the sounds of approaching footsteps and breathing. Then, a second later:* 'Hello, Uncle Paul.')

When I flew to London to meet with my UK publishers a few days after Jess's funeral in July, Marilyn Adams invited me to interview her at her residence, a well-maintained, three-bedroomed council house, filled with mod-cons.

Marilyn is waiting for me on the couch, her oxygen tank close to hand. As I'm about to start the interview, she digs out a box of cigarettes from the side of the couch, lights up and takes a deep drag.

Don't tell the boys, will you, love? I know I shouldn't, but after all this business . . . How can it hurt? A ciggy is my only bit of comfort these days.

I know what you've read in the papers, love, but we didn't really have bad feelings towards Paul back then, other than him wanting to keep Jess away from us. I had a cousin who was like that, a gay, I mean. We're not bigoted, honest to God. Lots of them about aren't there, and I love that Graham Norton. But the press . . . well, they twist your words around, don't they? Do I blame Shelly for giving Paul custody? Not really. She just wanted a better life for herself and the girls, and who can blame her? Never had much growing up. I know people think we're scroungers, but we have every right to live how we want to live, don't we? You try getting a sodding job these days.

Some people think we only wanted Jess because we were after Stephen and Shelly's house and all that insurance money. I'd be lying if I said it wouldn't have come in handy, but that was the furthest thought from our minds, honest to God. We really just wanted to spend time with little Jess. It dragged on and on, and some days the stress would just get so much I could barely sleep. 'You're going to give yourself a heart attack with all that worrying, Mum,' the boys kept saying. So in the end, when I got really ill, I backed off, decided not to get the lawyers involved. Thought it would be for the best. Jessie could always come and find us when she was older, couldn't she?

So when Paul rang and asked if we wanted to see Jess, well, you could have knocked me over with a feather. The social had been promising for ages that they would do what they could, but I didn't put any store in what they said. We were all dead excited. We thought it would be best not to overwhelm her, it can be right chaos here sometimes when we all get together, so I decided that it would be just me, the boys and her cousin Jordan, who was closest to her age. I told little Jordan that his cousin was coming for a visit and he said, 'But isn't she an alien, Nana?' His dad went to cuff him round the ear, but Jordie was only repeating something he'd heard at school. 'How could anyone believe any of that bollocks?' Keith would always say whenever one of those bloody Americans started up about The Three being out of the Bible or whatever it was they was saying. He said the buggers should be sued for defamation, but that wasn't up to us, was it?

I got a right shock when the social worker dropped her off. She'd shot up like a tree since I'd last seen her. All those photographs in the press didn't do her justice. The scars on her face weren't too bad, made her skin look a bit tighter and shinier, that was all.

I nudged Jordan and told him to go up and give her a hug. He did as he was told, although I could see he wasn't too keen.

Jase went out and got us all a McDonald's, and I asked Jessie all about school and her friends and that. She was a right little chatter-box. Bright as a button. Didn't seem at all out of her depth around us. I was a bit surprised, to be honest. The last time I'd seen her, she was dead shy, her and her sister Polly. Hung around their mother's skirts whenever Shelly brought them over. A pair of little princesses, me and the boys used to joke. Not rough and tumble like the others. Not that we saw the twins often, mind. Shelly only really brought them round on Christmas and birthdays, and there was a right set-to one year when Brooklyn bit Polly. But Brooklyn was only a toddler back then; she didn't know what she was doing.

'Why don't you go show Jessie your room, Jordan? Maybe she wants to play on the Wii?' I said.

'She looks funny,' Jordan said. 'Her face is funny.'

I gave him a smack and told Jess not to take any notice.

'It's okay,' she said. 'My face is funny. It wasn't supposed to happen. It was a mistake.' She shook her head as if she was a thousand years old. 'Sometimes we get it wrong.'

'Who gets it wrong, love?' I asked.

'Oh, just us,' she said. 'Come on, Jordan. I'll tell you a story. I have lots of stories.'

Off they went, the two of them, Jess and Jordan. It warmed my heart seeing them together like that. Family's important, isn't it?

I find it hard to get up the stairs these days, what with my lungs like they are, so I asked Jase to pop up and keep an eye on them. He said they were getting on like a house on fire, Jessie talking ten to the dozen. Before you knew it, it was time to send her home.

'Would you like to come again, Jess?' I asked her. 'Spend more time with your cousins?'

'Yes please, Nana,' she said. 'That was interesting.'

After the bloke from the social had collected her, I asked Jordan what he thought of Jess, if he thought she'd changed and that, but he shook his head. Wouldn't say much about her at all. I asked him what they'd been talking about all afternoon, but he said he couldn't remember. I didn't press him on it.

Paul phoned me that evening, and I got a right shock again when I heard his voice! Civil he was, as well. Asked me if I'd noticed anything strange about Jess. His words. Said he was a bit concerned about her.

I told him what I'm telling you now, that she was a lovely little girl, a real joy to be around.

He seemed to find this funny, laughed like a ruddy drain, but before I could ask him what was amusing, he hung up.

Course, it wasn't that long afterwards that we heard what he'd done.

Lillian Small.

The call came in at six that morning, and I rushed to answer it before it woke Reuben. I hadn't been sleeping well since that day at the museum, and I'd got into the habit of slipping out of bed at around five, in order to spend a few minutes alone and settle my nerves before I discovered which husband I would be facing.

'Who is this?' I snapped into the phone. If it was one of the papers or a *meshugener* taking a chance by calling so early, I wasn't in a mood to treat them lightly.

There was a pause, and then the caller introduced himself as Paul Craddock, Jessica's uncle. His clipped English accent reminded me of one of those characters on that *Cavendish Hall* show Betsy never stopped talking about. It was a strange conversation, full of long, uncomfortable pauses, although you'd think we'd have lots to talk about. I remember thinking how strange it was that neither of us had thought to be in contact before. The children were always being linked together in the news articles, and every so often, the producers of one of the big talk shows would get it into their heads to try to get all three children to appear together, but I always turned them down. I could immediately pick up that there was something not right with Paul; I suppose I put it down to the time difference or maybe a distortion on the line. He finally managed to make himself clear. He wanted to know if I'd noticed anything different about Bobby, if his personality or behaviour had changed after the crash.

It was the same sort of question those damn reporters were always asking and I was short with him. He apologised for disturbing me and hung up without saying goodbye.

I was agitated after the call, couldn't settle down. Why would he ask me something like that? I knew that Paul, like me and the family of that little Japanese boy, must be suffering under the pressure of all the press attention. I suppose I also felt guilty that

I'd been so short with him. He'd sounded troubled, like he needed to talk.

And I was tired of feeling guilty. Guilty about not sending Bobby back to school; for not taking Reuben back to Dr Lomeier so he could be seen by the specialist; for hiding his condition from Betsy. Like Charmaine, who still called to check up on us every week, Betsy had been there for me from the beginning, but I couldn't shift the feeling that what was happening to Reuben was my private miracle. *And* my private burden. I knew what would happen if the story got out. The ridiculous story about the little Japanese boy interacting with that robot his father made him was all over the news for days.

I made myself a cup of coffee, sat in the kitchen and stared out of the window. It was a lovely spring day, and I remember thinking how nice it would be to just go out for a walk, sit in a cafe somewhere. Have some time to myself.

Reuben was awake by then, and it was Reuben, and not Al, who was there that day. I thought, I could just pop out for ten minutes, sit in the park in the sun. Breathe.

I made Bobby his breakfast, cleaned the kitchen, and asked Reuben if he'd mind if I slipped out for a few minutes.

'You go, Rita,' he said. 'Go and have a nice time.'

I made Bobby promise that he wouldn't leave the apartment, and then I left. I walked down to the park, sat on the bench opposite the sports centre, and raised my face to the sun. I kept telling myself, just five minutes more, and then I'll get back and change the sheets on the bed, take Bobby to the store with me to buy milk. A group of young men pushing baby buggies strolled past me, and we exchanged smiles. I glanced at my watch, realised I'd been sitting there for over forty minutes – where had the time gone? I was less than five minutes from my building, but accidents can happen in seconds. The sudden rush of panic made me feel nauseous, and I hurried home.

And I was right to be worried. I screamed out loud when I ran into the apartment and saw the two of them standing there in my kitchen in their identical suits. One of them had his eyes closed and was holding Bobby's hand to his chest. The other one had his hand raised above his head, and was muttering something under his breath.

'Get away from him!' I yelled at the top of my voice. I could see right away what they were. The fanaticism radiated out of them. 'Get the hell out of my apartment!'

'Is that you, Rita?' Reuben called from the other room.

'The men asked to come in and watch *The View* with us, Bubbe,' Bobby said. 'Are they the ones Betsy calls *bupkes*?'

'Go to your room, Bobby,' I said.

I turned on the two men again, fury sparking through every vein. They looked like twins, their blond hair identically parted to the side, that same smug, self-righteous expression on their faces, which made the situation all the more disturbing. Bobby told me later they'd only been there for five minutes before I got home and that they hadn't done anything other than what I'd seen in the kitchen. They must have watched me leaving and decided to take a chance. 'All we ask is that you let Bobby's spirit wash over us,' one of them said. 'You owe it to us, Mrs Small.'

'She owes you nothing,' Betsy said from behind me – thank God she'd heard me yell. 'I've called the cops, so you get your Bible-thumping tushes out of here.'

The two men glanced at each other and made for the door. They looked like they were thinking about spouting more of their nonsense, but the look on Betsy's face shut them up.

Betsy said she'd take care of Bobby while I made a statement. I knew it was too late to worry about her finding out about Reuben. The police commissioner himself came to see me later that day. He said I should consider round-the-clock protection, maybe hire private security, but I didn't want a stranger in my home.

When I'd finished with the police, I could see immediately that Betsy knew and wanted to talk about Reuben's transformation. What choice did I have then but to come clean? And who did I have to blame but myself?

Lillian Small's neighbour, Betsy Katz, agreed to speak to me in late June.

What pains me most of all was that I'd been careful around those reporters. Those newspaper people, they could be smart. So clever with their sneaking around. Calling me up and asking leading questions as if I was born yesterday and wouldn't see right through what they were doing. 'Mrs Katz,' they'd say, 'isn't it true that Bobby is acting a little strange?' 'You can keep your acting strange,' I'd tell them. 'Does it hurt to be so stupid?'

If it wasn't for Bobby, I don't know if Lily would have found the strength to go on after Lori died. Lori was a nice girl, arty sure, but she was a good daughter. Me, I don't know if I would have been able to go on after a stab in the heart like that. And that Bobby! What a lovely child! It was never a burden taking him off Lily's hands. He'd come into my kitchen and help me make cookies, used to let himself in as if he was one of the family. Sometimes we'd sit down and watch *Jeopardy* together. He was good company, a good boy, always happy, always with a smile on his face. I worried that he wasn't spending enough time with other children – what kid wants to spend all his free time with old ladies? – but it didn't seem to worry him. I'd told Lily many times that Rabbi Toba's family ran a good yeshiva in Bedford-Stuyvesant, but she wouldn't hear of it. But could I blame her for wanting to keep him so close? I was never blessed with children, but when my husband Ben fell to cancer ten years ago this September, I felt the loss like a knife in my heart. Lily had lost too much already. First Reuben, then her daughter.

I knew that Lily was trying to hide something from me, but not in my whole life could I have guessed what it was. Lily wasn't a good liar, she was an open book. I didn't nag her to tell me. I figured that eventually she would come to me and tell me herself.

I was cleaning my kitchen when I heard Lily shouting that day. My first thought was that something must have happened to

Reuben. I ran straight to her apartment. When I saw those two strange men in their suits, and their fanatical eyes, I called the cops right away. I knew what they were. Me? I could spot one of those fanatics a mile off after they started crawling around the neighbourhood. Even when they thought they were being so clever by dressing up like business people. They were smart, ran out of there before the cops arrived. While Lily made a statement, I went into the apartment to watch Bobby and Reuben.

'Hello, Betsy,' Bobby said. 'Po Po and I are watching *From Here to Eternity*. It's an old movie where everyone is coloured black and white.'

And then Reuben said, clear as day. 'The oldies are the goodies.'

And how do you think I reacted? I almost jumped out of my skin. 'What you say, Reuben?'

'I said, they don't make films like they used to. Are you having trouble with your hearing, Betsy?'

I had to sit down. I'd been helping Lily care for Reuben since Bobby came out of hospital, and I hadn't heard him speak a word that made any sense in all that time.

Lily came back in and she saw right off that I knew. We went into the kitchen and she poured us both a brandy. She explained it all to me. How he'd started talking out of nowhere one evening. 'It's a miracle,' I said.

When I got back to my place, I couldn't settle down to anything. I had to talk to someone. I tried calling Rabbi Toba, but he wasn't in and I needed to get it off my chest. So I called my sister-in-law. Her best friend's nephew Eliott, a good boy – or so I thought then – was a doctor and she told me I should talk to him. I was just trying to help. I thought maybe I could get a second opinion for Lily.

Saying it now, it sounds like I was a real fool, I know this.

I don't know if they paid him, or what they did, but I know it was him who talked to those reporters. The next day, when I left the house to go to the store – just to buy myself some bread as I was having soup that evening – I saw all the reporters hanging around the apartment, but that wasn't new. They tried to talk to me but I gave them the brush-off.

I saw the headline on a placard outside the bakery: 'It's a miracle! Bobby's Senile Grandfather Starts to Speak.' I almost threw up right there. May God forgive me, but it did cross my mind that I could blame it on those religious putzes who had conned their way into the apartment. But the article made it clear that the news had come from a 'source close to Lillian Small'.

I was so worried. I knew what this could mean for Lily. All those crazies, led by that real dangerous one, I knew they would jump on this like flies on a turd.

I ran back home and I said to Lily, 'I never meant to let it out.'

She turned white, and could I blame her? 'Not again,' she said. 'Why won't they leave us alone?'

Lily never forgave me. She didn't cut me out of her life, but there was a watchfulness when she was around me after that.

I wonder, I really do, if this wasn't part of what caused everything else afterwards. May God forgive me.

PART EIGHT

CONSPIRACY

APRIL–JUNE

The following article appeared on makimashup.com on 19 April 2012 – a website dedicated to reporting 'the weird and the wonderful from around the world'.

Japan's Queen of Weird

The first video clip shows a beautiful Japanese woman kneeling on a tatami mat in the centre of an elegant, dimly lit room. She adjusts her bright red kimono, blinks and then starts reciting from *Stolen*, a Japanese best-selling memoir written by Aki Kimura, who was sexually assaulted by three US marines on Okinawa Island in the 1990s. In the second clip, she spends twenty minutes talking in explicit detail about an alien abduction. In the third, she lectures on why Sun Air crash survivor Hiro Yanagida is a national treasure, a symbol of Japan's endurance and identity.

These clips, which first appeared on the Japanese video-sharing platform Nico Nico Douga, have gone viral, attracting more hits than any clip in the history of the site. What makes them so compelling has little to do with the eclectic subject matter of the woman's monologues, and everything to do with the woman herself. You see, the woman isn't human. She's a surrabot – the android doppelgänger of Aikao Uri, a former pop idol who hit it big in the 1990s before retiring to marry politician Masamara Uri. Aikao is no slouch when it comes to notoriety. Rarely out of the news, she started a fashion craze for shaved eyebrows in the early 2000s, is fervently anti-American (this is rumoured to stem from her failure to make it in Hollywood in the mid-nineties), always wears traditional Japanese dress as a rejection of western fashion ideals and most controversially of all, recently shared her belief that she has been abducted by aliens several times since her childhood.

Watching Aikao Uri's surrabot talk is disconcerting. It takes several seconds before your brain adjusts and you realise there's something just . . . wrong about the otherwise eloquent woman. Her cadence is unemotional, her mannerisms just a split second too slow to be convincing. And her eyes are dead.

Aikao freely admits that she commissioned her own surrabot after the news broke that Sun Air crash survivor Hiro Yanagida will only communicate via the android doppelgänger made by his father, a renowned robotics expert. Aikao believes that speaking through surrabots, which are controlled remotely, using state-of-the art camera and voice-capturing equipment, 'will bring us closer to a pure way of being'.

And Aikao isn't the only one who has embraced this 'pure way of being'. Known worldwide for their 'out there' fashion sense, young Japanese trend-setters are also jumping on the surrabot bandwagon. Those who can't afford their own surrabot (the cheapest android doppelgängers can cost up to 45,000 US dollars) have taken to purchasing realistic mannequins and sex dolls and modifying them. The streets around Harajuku – where cosplayers traditionally congregate to show off their style – is buzzing with fashionistas, both male and female, eager to flaunt their own versions of the surrabot craze, which has been dubbed 'The Cult of Hiro'.

There's even talk that girl bands, such as the wildly successful AKB 48 ensemble and the Sunny Juniors, are creating their own all dancing, all lip-synching surrabot line.

In mid-April I flew out to Cape Town, South Africa to meet with Vincent Xhati, a private investigator who was on a full-time retainer to discover the whereabouts of the elusive Kenneth Oduah – the so-called 'fourth horseman'.

The Arrivals area at the Cape Town International Airport is teeming with wannabe tour guides, all shouting, 'Taxi, lady?' and waving fliers for 'all-inclusive Khayelitsha tours' in my face. Despite the chaos, it's easy to spot Vincent Xhati, the private investigator who's agreed to escort me around Cape Town for a couple of days. At six foot four and weighing in at three hundred pounds, he towers over the taxi drivers and tour operators. He greets me with a wide grin, and immediately takes charge of my luggage. We make small talk as we push through the throng towards the parking lot. A couple of jaded male cops in blue uniforms saunter around, eyeing everyone with suspicion, but neither they, nor the signs warning new arrivals not to 'go off with strangers', appear to be deterring the tour hawkers. Vincent bats a couple of the more tenacious away with a snapped '*Voetsek.*'

Exhausted after the sixteen-hour flight, I'm dying for a coffee and a shower, but when Vincent asks me if I'd like to go straight to the Dalu Air crash site before checking into my hotel, I say yes. He nods in approval and ushers me towards his car, a slick black BMW with tinted windows. 'No one will mess with us in this,' he says. 'We will look like a politician.' He pauses, glances at me, and then roars with laughter.

I sink into the passenger seat, noting that there's a copy of the grainy photograph of Kenneth Oduah – taken when he was four years old – mounted on the dashboard.

As we leave the airport behind and glide onto a slip road, I spot Table Mountain in the far distance, cloud dribbling over its edge. It's heading into winter, but the sky is a perfect, eggshell blue. Vincent sweeps onto the highway, and I'm immediately struck by the obvious signs of poverty around us. The airport facilities may have been state-of-the-art, but the road is flanked by sagging shacks and Vincent is forced to brake sharply as a small child dragging a dog on a rope lead zigzags through the traffic.

'It is not far,' Vincent says, clicking his tongue as he's forced to undertake a rusty mini-bus packed full of commuters that's hogging the fast lane.

I ask him who has hired him to search for Kenneth and he smiles and shakes his head. The journalist who gave me Vincent's details assured me that Vincent could be trusted, but I can't help feeling a stab of unease. I ask him about the reports of the Kenneth hunters who have been mugged.

He sighs. 'The press have exaggerated this. Only the ones who behaved in a stupid manner have had trouble.'

I ask him if he believes Kenneth is actually out there somewhere.

'It doesn't matter what I believe. Maybe the child is here somewhere, maybe he isn't. If he can be found, I will find him.'

We pull off the highway, and on our right I make out the edges of a vast area crammed with small brick houses, tin and wood shacks, and row after row of outhouses that look like sentry boxes.

'Is that Khayelitsha?'

'Ja.'

'How long have you been looking for him?'

'Since the beginning. It has not been an easy ride. There was some trouble at first from the Muslim community who tried to stop people talking to those of us who were searching for him.'

'Why?'

'You did not have that in America? Ah. The troublemakers assumed that Kenneth was a Muslim boy, and they objected to the Americans coming here and claiming that he was one of their messengers. Then it was made public that he is from a Christian family, and now they don't care!' Another roar of laughter.

'I take it you are not religious?'

He sobers up. 'No. I have seen too much.'

He turns right, and within minutes we're in the heart of the township. The dirt roads that weave through the endless rows of shacks are unmarked. There's a proliferation of Coke signs, most attached to old shipping containers that I realise are makeshift shops. A group of small children dressed in dirty shorts wave and grin at the car, then whoop and chase after it. Vincent pulls to the side of the road, hands one of the children ten rand and instructs him to watch the BMW. The kid puffs out his chest and nods.

A few hundred metres from us, a tour bus is parked alongside a row of hawkers selling their wares. I watch as an American couple pick up a wirework sculpture of a plane and start haggling with a vendor.

'We'll walk from here,' Vincent says. 'Stay close to me and don't make eye contact with any of the locals.'

'Okay.'

Another laugh. 'Don't worry, you're fine here.'

'Do you live here?'

'No. I live in Gugs. Gugulethu.'

I've seen the aerial footage of the place where the plane went down, tearing a jagged passage through the landscape, but the people here are clearly tenacious, and already there is little sign of the devastation. Construction is starting on a new church and shacks have already grown up all over the sites where the fires raged. A gleaming black glass pyramid, engraved with the names of those who lost their lives (including that of Kenneth Oduah), sits incongruously in the centre.

Vincent sinks to his haunches and runs his fingers through the soil. 'They still find bits. Bones and pieces of metal. They worm their way up out of the earth. You know like when you have a wound? A splinter? The earth is rejecting them.'

The mood is subdued as we retrace our steps and head back onto the highway. More mini-buses whiz past, packed full of people heading into the city. Table Mountain races towards us, the cloud now obscuring its trademark flat top.

'I will take you to your hotel and then we will go hunting tonight, okay?'

Cape Town's Waterfront area, where my glass and steel-skeletoned hotel sits, couldn't be more of a contrast to where I've just been. It's almost like being in a different country. Hard to believe that the designer stores and five-star restaurants are just a short taxi ride away from the poverty of the township.

I shower, then head down to the bar and make some calls while I wait for Vincent. There are several middle-aged men hanging around in small groups, and I do my best to eavesdrop. Many are American.

I've been trying to secure an interview with the South African Civil Aviation Authority's head investigator, but her office has declined to talk to the press. I dial the number anyway. The secretary I speak to sounds weary. 'It is all in the report. There were no survivors.' I am also stonewalled in my efforts to talk to the aid workers who were first on the scene after the crash.

Vincent breezes into the hotel as if he owns the place; equally at home in this extravagant luxury as he is in the heart of Khayelitsha.

I tell him about my strike-outs with the CAA.

'You can forget them. But I will see what I can do about getting others to talk to you.'

He gets a call on his cell. The conversation is brief and in Xhosa.

'My associate has rounded up tonight's boys.' He sighs. 'It will come to nothing. But I must follow them up. My boss wants a full report every day.'

We head down towards the docks, slowing when we reach an underpass. The area is gloomy and ill-lit and I feel another stirring of unease.

Vincent's associate, a small wiry man called Eric Malenga, is waiting for us under a partially completed flyover. He's surrounded by three scruffy boys, all of whom appear to be unsteady on their feet. I learn later that many street kids are addicted to sniffing glue, and the solvent they inhale makes them uncoordinated. Vincent tells me that these children scratch a living begging and hustling in the town centre. 'Sometimes they get tourists to buy them cereal and milk, and then they sell it to the backpackers,' he says. 'Others sell their bodies.'

As we approach, I notice a fourth child sitting apart from them on an overturned crate. He's shivering, but I can't tell if this is from fear or the bite in the air.

The tallest of the kids – a skinny boy with a runny nose – perks up when he sees us approach and points to the child on the crate. 'There he is, boss. That's Kenneth. Do I get my reward now, boss?'

Vincent tells me that the latest 'Kenneth' isn't even Nigerian. He's the racial classification known as 'coloured', a word that makes me wince.

Vincent nods wearily at Eric, who ushers the small child towards his car.

'Where is Eric taking him?' I ask.

'One of the shelters,' Vincent says. 'Away from this bunch of skebengas.'

'But he said he was Kenneth, boss,' the boy with the runny nose whines. 'He told us, I swear.'

'You know why everyone is looking for Kenneth?' I ask.

'Ja, lady. They think he is the devil.'

'That's not true,' says another boy. 'He needs to go to a sangoma; he's possessed by the spirit of a witch. If you meet him, then you don't have long to live.'

'He only comes out at night,' the third one chimes in. 'If he touches you, the part of the body he touches will die. He can spread Aids even.'

'Ja. I heard that too,' the tall boy – clearly the ringleader – says. 'I know someone who has seen him, lady. If you give me a hundred, I'll take you.'

'These boys don't know anything,' Vincent says, but he hands them each twenty rand, and sends them on their way. They whoop and run off unsteadily into the night. 'This is what it is like all the time. But I have to be thorough, make my report every day. Most days I check the morgue in case he shows up there, but I won't take you there.'

The next day Vincent meets me at my hotel to say that he's heading out to the West Coast to 'follow a lead'. He puts me in touch with a cop at a Khayelitsha police station who he says will talk to me, gives me the name of a paramedic who arrived at the scene minutes after the crash, and passes on the cellphone number of a woman who had lost her home in the devastation. 'She knows something,' he says. 'Maybe she will talk to you. A foreigner.' Then, with another wide grin and a complicated handshake, he leaves.

(*Ten days later, I'm at home in Manhattan, when I receive a text message from Vincent. All it says is: <they got him>*)

The following statement was taken at the Buitenkant Police Station in Cape Town on 2 May 2012.

SOUTH AFRICAN POLICE SERVICE

EK / I: Brian van der Merwe

OUDERDOM / AGE: 37

WOONAGTIG / RESIDING: 16 Eucalyptus Street, Bellville, Cape Town

TELEPHONE: 021 911 6789

WERKSAAM TE / EMPLOYED AT: Kugel Insurance Brokers, Pinelands

TELEPHONE 021 531 8976

VERKLAAR IN AFRIKAANS ONDER EED:

STATES IN ENGLISH UNDER OATH:

On the night of 2 May 2012 at approximately 10.30 p.m., I was aprehended (*sic*) at the bottom of Long Street, Cape Town CBD outside the Beares Furniture Store. I had stopped to give a child a lift in my car when I realised that police officers had pulled up in their vehicle next to me.

I told the officers that the reason I stopped was because I was worried for the child's safety. The boy, who was aged eight or nine, shouldn't have been out there at that time of night and I had pulled over to offer him a lift.

I deny that I solicited the boy for sex, and when officers found me in the car, I deny that my jeans were undone and that the boy was performing a sexual act on my person.

Sergeant Manjit Kumar pulled me out of the car and gave me a smack across my face, which I insist be recorded here. Then he asked the boy his name. The boy did not answer. One of the other officers, Constable Lucy Pistorius, said to the boy, Are you Kenneth? The boy said yes.

I did not resist arrest.

BvdMerwe
_____
HANDTEKENING / SIGNATURE

Andiswa Matebele (not her real name) is the head carer at a place of safety for abandoned and abused children in Cape Town (the exact location cannot be disclosed for obvious reasons). Andiswa agreed to talk to me via phone on the condition that I not reveal her name or the location of the place of safety.

Shame, when the boy was first brought to us he was very under-nourished, and even before I gave him a bath, I made sure that he had a large bowl of putu and lamb stew. I was very worried about him, and not just because the sores on his legs and arms were infected. He had seen a doctor, who prescribed antibiotics, and he was given a course of ARVs as there were signs that he may have been working as a sex worker. This is not uncommon for street children. Many of them have been abused by their parents, and they know of no other way to survive.

What can I tell you about the boy? He did not have a Nigerian accent as far as I could tell, but it was difficult to be sure as he so rarely spoke. He seemed to be older than seven years, which is the age of Kenneth Oduah. As he ate, I asked him, 'Is your name Kenneth?'

'Yes, my name is Kenneth,' he said. But then, later on, I found that I could ask him anything and he would agree with me.

The next day, a forensics team came to the shelter and took a saliva swab from him so that they could run a DNA test. I was informed that the boy would be staying here until they could be sure that he was indeed Kenneth. I felt very strongly that if the boy did in fact turn out to be this child, then he should be reunited with his aunt and family as soon as possible.

I am not from Khayelitsha, but I have been to the memorial site and seen where that plane went down. I do find it hard to believe that anyone could have survived such a thing, but it was the same with the crash in America and the ones in Asia and Europe, so I did not know what to think. Little by little, by asking him direct questions, I managed to extract the boy's story. He said that he had lived for a while on the beach in Blouberg, then in Kalk Bay and then he had decided to make his way back to the CBD.

I kept a close eye on him to ensure that the other children did not bully him – this can happen – but most of them gave him a wide berth. I did not tell them who he might be. I was the only person who had that knowledge. Some of the other staff are superstitious and already there was talk that if a boy had survived the crashes, then it was certain he was a witch of some type.

Two weeks later we heard that the DNA did indeed match Kenneth Oduah's aunt, and it wasn't long before the authorities organised a big press conference. I assumed that Kenneth would be taken away almost immediately after that, but then the police called to say that Kenneth's aunt had fallen sick (perhaps from the shock of hearing about her nephew) and so could not travel from Lagos to formally identify and collect the boy. They told me another family member, a distant one, was en route instead.

He arrived the next day, and said he was the cousin of Kenneth's father. I asked him if he was sure that the boy was his relative and he was adamant that he was.

'Do you know this man, Kenneth?' I asked the boy.

'I know this man,' the boy said.

'Do you want to go with him or stay here with us?'

The boy did not know what to say to that. If you asked him, 'Do you want to stay?' he would say, 'I want to stay,' but then, if I asked him, 'Do you want to go with this man?' he would say, 'I want to go.'

He did not seem to know what was going on.

He was taken away that night.

The following article was published in the UK's *Evening Standard* online edition on 18 May 2012.

Rapture Fever Sweeps the US

An enterprising pastor has opened the first drive-through baptism centre in San Antonio, Texas, where, for the price of a Happy Meal, you can secure your place in heaven.

'You can get saved on your lunch hour!' Pastor Vincent Galbraith (48) beams. 'Just drive on in, take Jesus into your heart and drive back to work in the knowledge that when the Rapture comes, you'll be one of God's chosen.'

Pastor Galbraith, a follower of Dr Theodore Lund's End Times movement, came up with the idea after his church was overrun by panicked wannabe Christians who had taken on board the bizarre theory that The Three, and now Kenneth Oduah, are the harbingers of the apocalypse. And so far, even though it's been open for less than a week, the lines snake around the block. 'People are getting desperate and rightly so,' the former insurance salesman turned pastor says. 'Those signs can't be ignored and I knew someone had to come up with a solution. We're not picky. I don't care what your religious affiliation was before. Muslim, Jew, atheist, all are welcome. You never know when the Lord is gonna call us to Him.' He chuckles. 'And at this rate I'm thinking about franchising it.'

Pastor Galbraith's new enterprise is only one of the many indications that thousands of people in the US's Bible Belt and beyond are taking the Riders of the Apocalypse theory seriously. In a recent poll undertaken by CNN in conjunction with *Time* magazine, a whopping 69% of Americans believe that the events of Black Thursday could be a sign that the end of the world is imminent.

In Kentucky, Hannigan Lewis (52) is proselytising the 'Down Tools' movement. 'The Rapture could happen at any time,' says the ex fork-lift driver. 'If you are flying a plane, driving a bus, and you're one of the saved, well hell, when you're taken up to Heaven all of a sudden, think of the carnage.' Borrowing a phrase from an unpopular UK Conservative Party campaign, he's encouraging Rapture believers to get 'back to basics' and divorce themselves from any technology that could potentially harm those left behind when the faithful are raptured.

But not all American believers are buying into the theory. Pastor Kennedy Olax, the head of the Austin-based Christians for Change organisation, says: 'We would counsel people not to give in to the hysteria sweeping the country at this time. There is no reason to panic. The ridiculous and unproven horseman theory is nothing but fear-mongering, stemming from a desire to whip up the religious right and get Reynard into the White House now that we're in an election year.'

Other groups are worried about the political and social changes this religious hysteria could bring. And now that Dr Lund and his rapidly growing End Times movement have publicly backed hard-line Republican presidential hopeful Mitch Reynard, their concerns appear to be increasingly legitimate. 'We're worried,' said Gay and Lesbian League spokesperson Poppy Abrams (37). 'We know that Dr Lund is working hard to draw together all the disparate evangelical and fundamentalist groups that make up the religious right, and Mitch Reynard is running on anti gay marriage and pro-life platforms. He may not be ahead in the polls yet, but his support is growing daily.'

Iman Arif Hamid of the US Islamic Coalition is more philosophical. 'We are not worried that there will be a backlash against Muslims like we saw after 9/11. Most of the vitriol appears to be targeted at the abortion clinics and the homosexual community. So far there have been no reports about Muslim citizens being marginalised.'

Although the horseman theory hasn't yet caused the same level of panic in the UK, many British clerics of all denominations, from Catholic to Church of England, have seen an increase in church attendance. And now that the so-called fourth horseman has been found, maybe it's only a matter of time before we're super-sizing our own baptisms on this side of the Atlantic.

Reba Louise Neilson.

It pains me to talk about this, Elspeth. But I feel I need to tell my side. People out there need to know that there are good Christian folk in Sannah County who never wanted any harm to come to those children.

I reckon Pastor Len really started letting the devil into his heart just after Kendra upped and left, and Dr Lund broke away from him for good. Then there were all those reporters making fun of him (Stephenie said they even did a skit about him on *Saturday Night Live*, though she doesn't usually watch that kind of programming). And all those folks, the Lookie-Loos, they didn't help any. A whole new wave of them came after they found Kenneth Oduah out in Africa and people started saying that Bobby Small's grandfather had started talking again even though he had that Alzheimer's. There were so many I heard he had to hire in some of those chemical toilets and you could barely see Pastor Len's ranch from the road for the number of Winnebagos and pick-ups that were parked on his property. I'm not saying some of them weren't good Christian folk, but I'd see them around town sometimes and some of them had a lost look in their eyes, as if their souls were broken. People like that Monty.

But in my opinion, the real tipping point was Jim.

Glory, that was a terrible day. I can recall it right down to the last detail. I was in the kitchen, fixing Lorne a sandwich – bologna and cheese, his favourite. I had the TV on in the kitchen, and Mitch Reynard was being interviewed by Miranda Stewart, talking about how the US had been going to hell in a hand basket, and that the time was ripe to get the country back onto a good moral footing (Stephenie thinks he looks a little bit like that George Clooney, but I'm not so sure). He and Dr Lund were always on the news around that time. They were being lambasted left, right and centre by the liberal element, but they stuck to their guns, and rightly so. The phone rang just as I was about to take Lorne his lunch. When I heard Pastor Len's voice on the other end of the line, I don't mind admitting that I felt uncomfortable. I thought maybe he was going to ask me why I hadn't been at church or Bible study for a while, but all he wanted to know was if I'd seen Jim. Pastor Len said he was planning one of his special early-morning prayer meetings, and Jim had agreed to come over to the ranch and talk to the new Lookie-Loos about what a good woman Pamela had been. I said that I hadn't seen Jim for a week or so, but I was fixing to take him a lasagne that evening. Pastor Len asked me if I wouldn't mind going over there early to check on him as he wasn't answering his phone. He said he hoped to see me at church that Sunday, then hung up.

I couldn't settle for a good half-an-hour after that – part of me still felt guilty for turning my back on the church like that – and then I called around the Inner Circle to see if anyone had any news about Jim. Fact is, by then, most people had stopped taking him food and checking up on him. Stephenie, Lena and I were the only ones left who still went by occasionally, though he never seemed grateful. Next, I tried Jim's number three or four times, but there was no answer. Lorne was out back, and I asked him if he'd drive me over to Jim's place to make sure he hadn't passed out drunk and maybe hit his head.

I thank the Lord every day that Lorne had the day off; I could never have faced it on my own. I knew that something untoward had happened the second we pulled up. I could see it by the number of flies that were crawling on the inside of the screen door. It was black with them.

Lorne called Manny Beaumont straight away, and we stayed in the truck while he and his deputy went inside. Sheriff Beaumont said it was obvious it was suicide; Jim had put his shotgun in his mouth and blown his head clean off his shoulders. And he'd left a note addressed to Pastor Len. We didn't know what it said until Pastor Len read it out at Jim's funeral. That's when things really took a turn.

Jim may have committed a sin against God by taking his own life, but me, Stephenie and a few of the other Inner Circle folk agreed to do the flowers for his service. The church was packed to the rafters with Pastor Len's Lookie-Loos, strangers who'd never even known Jim. Lorne said that Pastor Len was playing up to the TV cameras that were there, no doubt hoping that Dr Lund would see him on the news.

'Jim is a martyr,' Pastor Len said. 'One of the witnesses, like his wife, Pamela. Time is running out. There are still thousands that need to be saved before it is too late. We need more time and Jesus, He ain't gonna wait forever.'

Lorne says the authorities should have stopped him right then and there. But what could Sheriff Beaumont do? This is America, people have a right to do what they want on their own land, and Pastor Len wasn't breaking any laws. Not then he wasn't. He didn't come right out and say that those children should be killed.

Pastor Len had been my guiding light for the longest time. I'd trusted in his words, heeded his sermons, looked up to him. But what he was saying, about Pamela being a prophet, and that Jim killing himself wasn't a sin but his way of showing us that the fifth seal had been opened, didn't sit right with me, and that's a fact. I believe that Jesus spoke to me and said, Reba, break away. Break away now. For good. So that's what I did. And I know in my heart that I did the right thing.

Although Private First Class Jake Wallace attempted to destroy his laptop's hard drive after he disappeared from his base on Okinawa Island, the following correspondence was recovered by an anonymous hacker and posted on the popular debunking blog, VigilanteHacks, as alleged proof that Pastor Len Vorhees played a part in Jake Wallace's subsequent actions.

To: **bearingthecross@yahoo.com**
From: **messenger778@moxy.com**
Date: 25/04/2012

Dear Sir,

Thank you for the last link to your latest sermon on YouTube. It was awesome to hear your voice and know that you are thinking of your Messengers all over the world. But it made me mad to read the disrespectful comments below it. I did what you said and didn't respond to them altho I wanted to with all of my heart!!!!! I also set up another email address under another name like you said to do as you can see!!!!!

I have lots to tell you Sir. You said to tell you if I had another one of my dreams about Mrs Pamela May Donald. I had one last night. This time I came out of my tent and into the forest clearing where the crash happened. Mrs Donald was lying on her back, and her face was covered with a thin white shroud. When she breathed in the shroud fell into her open mouth and I had to try to pull it out so that she would not suffacate [*sic*]. The shroud felt greasy and slipped in my hands and then she was gone and my sister Cassie was there and she also had a shroud and she said to me Jake I can't breathe either and then I woke up. I was as cold as I was in the forest and I had to bite my fist to stop from screaming again.

Sir, without your messages I would feel so alone. Even the Christian marines here make jokes about the boy and the robot that he speaks thru and they just don't see that it is no joking matter. There is a group who are copying what the kid is doing and talking only thru robots and False Idols and I am afraid that the Antichrist's influence is spreading even to this island. I am keeping a low profile like you said and just doing my duty and my training, but it is hard. If we can save one person, isn't that what we must do? There are American families and children here and innocents. Isn't it my duty as a Messenger to save others before it is too late?

Yours Faithfully,

J

To: **messenger778@moxy.com**
From: **bearingthecross@aol.com**
Date: 26/04/2012

True Messenger,

It is our lot and our Burden to be surrounded by those who refuse to see the truth. Be careful that they do not worm their way into your heart with their lies and their charm causing Doubt. Doubt is the demon you must be on your guard against. This is why I am saying to you to keep a low profile. I see your point about the innocents and I myself also struggle with this, but the time will come when we will stage the final battle and then those who have taken the Truth into their hearts will be saved.

How I rejoiced to hear of your dream! It is another SIGN! Like our prophet Pamela May Donald, you were shown proof in that forest when you saw those who will be taken up and Saved. Pamela May Donald is showing you the true way. She is showing you that like the bile spewed forth by the false prophets Flexible Sandy and Dr Theodore Lund, words are empty and only ACTIONS matter when the time comes to be tested.

You are being tested, Jake. You are being tested by the Lord our God to see if you will stray from the path. YOU and YOU alone are our voice and heart in that heathen nation. I know it is lonely, but you will receive your reward. The signs are building, Jake. The signs are BUILDING. My Messengers are growing, as more and more of the chosen have flocked to join me. But you, you who are out on his own, in a land of the Heathen, are the bravest of us all.

He which soweth sparingly shall reap also sparingly; and he which soweth bountifully shall reap also bountifully.

Remember the Ears and Eyes of the many-headed AntiChrist are watching all of our Messengers so be vigilant.

To: **bearingthecross@aol.com**
From: **messenger778@moxy.com**
Date: 07/05/2012

Dear Sir,

It is good of you to write to me so often as I know that you must be very busy now that your true Messengers are joining you in person as well as in spirit. I wish with all my HEART that I could be with them but I know this is not part of God's plan for me!!!!

You're [*sic*] words bring me True Comfort but your meaning is clear, do not worry Sir I am being careful and always delete them as you said I should.

There was another anti-US base protest in Urima yesterday. I felt a strong urge to go and speak to the Heathens to tell them that they must turn to Jesus before it is too late. In Luke it says that we must love our enemies, do good to them, and lend to them without expecting to get anything back, but I knew that for the Greater Good I shouldn't do that.

Yours faithfully,

J

To: **bearingthecross@aol.com**
From: **messenger778@moxy.com**
Date: 20/05/2012

Dear Sir,

I have been checking my email everyday now and I have run thru my mind everything I have said in case I have offended you as I haven't got an email from you for a while and then I saw the news about the death of Pamela May Donald's husband.

It says that he committed the sin of suicide. Can this be right?

I know you must be very busy with your Mourning but please try and write to me even if it is only one line as reading your words gives me strength. I have tried to find your website but I can't get on to it any more which makes me worry that you and the other True Believers have been overtaken by those who are working for the Antichrist.

Sir, I need your Help. There are floods in the Philippines, which has to be another sign of the evil overtaking the world. Some of the guys say that my unit is going to be shipped out to help with the rescue efforts. Can I still be your Voice and Heart and Ears and Eyes if I leave here?

I feel very alone.

J

To: **bearingthecross@aol.com**
From: **messenger778@moxy.com**
Date: 21/05/2012

Sir? Are you there? My unit leaves in 3 days what should I do?

To: **messenger778@moxy.com**
From: **bearingthecross@aol.com**
Date: 21/05/2012

True Messenger,

You are not alone. You must have faith that even in my Silence I am by your side. We are being persecuted and belittled by the False Prophets and their Flatterers but we will not break.

I have sent you a copy of my last blog post, which explains Jim Donald's actions.

Jim Donald like his Beloved Wife has sacrificed himself to tell us the Real Truth, the Truth that I have suspected since the beginning when Pamela May Donald paid the ultimate price to personally send her prophecy.

You are one of the chosen. You are special. We are facing a Holy War and time is running out. It is time for God's Soldiers to step forward. Are you prepared to be one of God's Soldiers?

We need to talk but not where the eyes and ears of the Antichrist and his Flatterers can hear. Let me know of a time I can call you where we will be undisturbed.

To: **bearingthecross@aol.com**
From: **messenger778@moxy.com**
Date: 27/05/2012

Dear Sir,

I am sorry to go against your wishes but this is agony to me! I keep thinking about my family and my sister especially who haven't been saved and what will happen to them if they do not see the Truth before it is too late.

I have received your donation. I have made contact with a group who I think can help me leave but I am not sure.

I am in the sick bay like you said I should so I cannot write for long. My unit has left. Can we talk again? I need to hear your voice as I am having Doubts.
J

To: **messenger778@moxy.com**
From: **bearingthecross@aol.com**
Date: 27/05/2012

DO NOT contact me again. I will contact you.

My heart has been truly warmed by the messages I've been receiving following our Brother Jim Donald's Martyrdom.

For that's what he was, Loyal Messengers. Jim Donald was a martyr. He was a martyr who gave up his life for all of us just like his dear wife Pamela did. I urge you not to take any credence of Dr Lund's words that by taking his own life Jim Donald was committing a sin. Jim is a martyr who died so that we would know the truth. A prophet who sacrificed himself to bring us the Good News that God in His Glory has chosen to open the fifth seal.

As it says in Revelation 6:9, *And when he had opened the fifth seal, I saw under the altar the souls of them that were slain for the word of God, and for the testimony which they held.*

Loyal Messengers, Jim Donald, like Pamela May Donald, was a martyr to his beliefs. I was there when he was saved, after he mourned the death of his beloved wife, and at the moment of his death, God chose to send him a vision.

I'm choosing to put his last words here for you all to see:

Why were they saved and not her? She was a good person and a good wife and I don't want to do this any more they are not rite in the head they are evil. They brought on the deaths of thousands and will bring on the deaths of more UNLESS THEY ARE STOPPED.

Jim's meaning, just like Pamela's, is clear. Time is running out for all of us and we must do what we can to bring as many people to the Pamelist flock as soon as we can. Is there a higher calling than saving as many as we can before that sixth seal is opened?

Pamela May Donald was the Lord's conduit. She was the vessel through which His message was conveyed. Dr Lund and those other charlatans have tried to hijack her message and Jim has proved this. Dr Lund does not believe that the fifth seal has yet been opened, but he is wrong.

'The boy, warn them,' Pamela May Donald told me.

And they cried with a loud voice, saying, How long, O Lord, holy and true, dost thou not judge and avenge our blood on they that dwell on the earth?

I'm gonna come right out and say it: I never trusted Len Vorhees. Not from the first day he arrived in Sannah County. Could talk the talk, all right, but far as I was concerned, that man was all hat and no cattle.

But Reba took to him right away and I guess it saved us driving over to Denham County every Sunday for church. None of us knew what to think when he started saying that those kids were the four horsemen. Reba was loyal to that church, and I wasn't going to push her. Way I saw it, it was plain that Len was using a dead woman's last words for his own ends, as a means to get in with those big-time preachers up in Houston. Then he went and mixed Jim Donald up in that. Jim could be as mean as a box of snakes, but Pam's death hit him hard. Stopped coming into work, wouldn't talk to his buddies. Len shoulda let him be, let him drink himself to death if that's what he wanted.

You know who I blame for it all going bad? Not Jim and not even those reporters who spread it all over the newspapers and TV. I blame Dr Lund and that writer guy, Flexible Sandy. They encouraged Len right from the beginning. No one can say they're not guilty, no matter what slick language they use to deny it.

A week after Jim's funeral, Stephenie's cousin Billy had to deliver some lumber to Len's ranch, and he asked me to ride along with him. Said he didn't want to go up there on his own, and his regular man was down with that puke virus that was hitting the county. Reba asked me to take along some of her canned peaches. 'For the children out there.'

It'd been a while since I'd last been to Len's ranch, must have been near Christmas or thereabouts. I'd seen all those new people of course, driving around in their pick-ups and SUVs with dented sides, and part of me was curious to see what was going on up

there. Billy said it made him uneasy being around them. Most
were from the state, but others had driven up from as far away as
New Orleans.

We got up to the gate, saw that there were a couple of men
standing there. One of them was that Monty guy, the one Reba
took against. They waved us down, asked us what we wanted, like
they were sentries. Billy told them and they stood back, let us go
through, but they stared at us real suspicious.

There weren't as many trailers or tents as I expected, but there
were enough. Kids were running everywhere; women huddled in
groups. As we drove up, I could sense them watching us. I said to
Billy that Grayson Thatcher, who used to work the place before
Len came, would've near had a heart attack if he'd seen what had
happened to his ranch.

Soon as we drew up, Pastor Len came striding out of the ranch-
house, this big grin on his face, and a couple of guys appeared
from the barn, started unloading the wood.

I greeted him as polite as I could, handed over the peaches
Reba had sent.

'Thank her for me, Lorne,' he said. 'She's a good woman. Tell
her I'd be mightily glad to see her out here on Sunday. I was sorry
to close the church in town, but God has shown me that my path
leads here.'

Course, I had no intention of telling Reba any such thing.

Then, coming from the pasture out back, I heard gunfire.
Sounded like automatic weapons, too. 'What you doing out there,
Len? Hunting season's closed.'

'We gotta keep sharp, Lorne. God's work isn't only about
prayers.'

It's everyone's God-given right to protect himself. I taught my
girls how to shoot, same as me and Reba have been encouraging
them to be prepared for any of those solar flares they're predicting
will occur. But this sounded like a whole nother rodeo – like they
were fixing for some sort of battle. The more I looked around, the
worse I got to feeling. It was clear they were fixing to set up some
kind of secure compound. Rolls of barbed wire stacked up next to

the old feed barn, and Billy said they were more than likely going to be using that wood to build some kind of fence.

Billy and I got out of there as fast as we could. 'You think we should tell Sheriff Beaumont 'bout what they're doing out here?' Billy asked.

You could see it was going to go bad, you could smell it as if it was two-day-old roadkill.

So we went and saw Manny Beaumont. Asked him if he knew what was going on up at that ranch. Manny said that until the Pamelists broke any laws, there wasn't nothing he could do about them. Lots of questions were asked later. Why weren't the FBI monitoring his emails, things like that, like they do with those Islamofascists? Guess they didn't reckon on a backwater preacher being able to reach out into the wider world and cause the trouble that he did. Or maybe they were worried they'd have another Waco on their hands if they tried to shut him down.

Before Private First Class Jake Wallace left Okinawa Island, he sent the following email to his parents in Virginia on 11 June 2012. It was released to the press after his body was formally identified.

Mom, Dad,

I'm doing this for you and Cassie.

Someone has to become God's Soldier in the Fight for Souls and I have stepped up to do my duty. The signs are getting clearer. Those floods in the Philippines, the war that's going to happen in North Korea. The fourth Horseman they found down in Africa.

I got to work fast now as time is running out.

I am writing this to beg you to go and get Saved and take Jesus into your hearts before it is too late.

Dad, I know you don't believe, and I am begging you as your son to please look at the evidence. God would not lie to us. You used to tell me that 9/11 was a government conspiracy and you would get pissed when none of us agreed with you. Please, Dad. Take Mom and Cassie to church and take the Lord into your heart. TIME IS RUNNING OUT.

I will see you in heaven when Jesus takes us up to his bosom.

Your Son,

Jake

Monty Sullivan, the only Pamelist who agreed to speak to me, is currently incarcerated in the North Infirmary Command Protective Custody section at Rikers Island, where he is awaiting trial. We spoke via phone.

EM: *When did you first hear about Pastor Len Vorhees and his theory about the horsemen?*

MONTY SULLIVAN: I guess it was right at the beginning. I was a truck driver back then, delivering chickens from Shelby County to all over the state. The CB was quieter than usual, and I'd started playing the radio dials, looking for a rock station. Back then, I wasn't into those religious shows at all. Heck, I didn't even like country that much. When I was crossing into Sannah County, I came across Pastor Len's show. Something about his voice got my attention.

EM: *Can you be more specific?*

MS: He sounded like he truly believed what he was saying. A lot of pastors and preachers you hear on the radio and TV, you get the idea that all they're after is poor folks' hard-earned cash. I was never much into religion back then, got turned off it when I was younger because of my ma. She was a real believer, sent off a monthly tithe to one of those super-church preachers down in Houston even when we didn't have food in the house. I could tell Pastor Len was different, he didn't once ask folks to send him any cash. And what he was saying, it caught my attention straight off. Course, Black Thursday was all over the news, and lots of preachers, specially the evangelicals, were saying it was another sign that we were all heading for Armageddon. Said the same thing after 9/11, so that wasn't new. But Pastor Len's point of view hit home. What he said about Pamela May Donald's last words . . . The evidence was just too strong. All those colours on the planes matching up with the colours of the horsemen that John saw in Revelation; the facts that those kids shouldn't have got away unhurt. When I finished my run a couple of days later, I went straight on the Internet, found Pastor Len's site, pamela-prophet.com. He'd put all the evidence right there, in black and white. I read it all, then dug out my ma's Bible which was the only thing of hers I still had. I'd sold the rest, though she didn't leave me much. Guess you could say I was pretty wild in those days. I wasn't into drugs or anything heavy, but I liked a drink back then, so that's where the money went.

After I heard Pastor Len's show and read that website, I don't think I slept for three days. I could feel something growing inside me. Course, Pastor Len told me later it was the Holy Spirit.

I sent him an email, saying how I'd been real impressed by what he was saying. I didn't think there was much of a chance I'd hear back from him. But I'm damned if he didn't send me a message within the hour. And a personal one, not one of those automated messages lots of people use. I know it off by heart. Must've read it a million times: 'Monty, I sure appreciate you contacting me. Your faith and honesty proves that I am on the right path, the path to saving more good folks just like yourself.'

I waited till my day off, then I drove through the night, straight to Sannah County and Pastor Len's church. Waited in line to get saved. Had to have been fifty people that day and there was a real festive atmosphere. We all knew we were doing the right thing. When I introduced myself to Pastor Len as he came along the line, thanking us for coming to his church, I never thought he would recall who I was, but he knew me straight off. 'You're the fella who wrote me from Kendrick!' he said.

The way he explained things so clear, I realised that I'd been blind for years. It broke my ma's heart that I turned my back on the church when I was younger, and I wished that she could have lived long enough to see that I went back to Jesus' fold. How can I not have seen we were heading for the End of Days? How can the Lord not have been priming to bring down His judgement on us after what was going on in the world? The more I looked into it, the more it made my head spin. Do you know that children in America are made, *made* to read the Koran in schools? But not the Bible, no ma'am. Intelligent Design is banned, but not the handbook of the infidels? Then there's the gays and the baby murderers and the liberals conspiring to turn America into a godless nation. Dr Theodore Lund was right about that, even if he did turn his back on Pastor Len's truth afterwards. Turned out that Dr Lund just wanted all the glory that came from Pamela's message for himself. He wasn't dedicated to saving souls; not like Pastor Len was.

EM: *When did you decide to move to Sannah County?*

MS: After I was saved, I came home and wrote Pastor Len almost every day for a few weeks. I felt a calling to move closer to his church round about early March and become one of his Messengers. It wasn't a hard decision, the Lord was nudging me in that direction. When Pastor Len invited me to move to the ranch, I didn't think twice. Jacked in my job, sold my truck and hitched all the way to Sannah County. He needed me as his good right hand.

EM: *Do you have a history of violence?*

MS: Not really, ma'am. Just the odd schoolyard fight, couple of bust-ups back when I used to drink. Not saying I was squeaky clean, but I was never a violent individual. Never ran into any trouble with the law.

EM: *Where did the weapon you used to shoot Bobby Small come from?*

MS: That particular gun belonged to Jim Donald. Wasn't the one he used on himself, but one he'd given to us for safe-keeping. But I knew how to shoot. My father taught me how to use a gun before he cut out and left me and my ma, back when I was twelve.

EM: *Did you know Jim Donald?*

MS: Not well, ma'am. I met him once or twice. Pastor Len said he was struggling to come to terms with the death of his wife. Pastor Len did what he could to help him, but you could see Jim was real cut up about that. He was a real martyr, just like Pamela. He saw the truth about the destruction the horsemen had wrought on the world, and how they'd murdered those innocents on the planes.

EM: *Did Pastor Len instruct you to travel to New York to kill Bobby Small?*

MS: I did what anyone who cares about saving souls would have done. I was acting as God's soldier, doing what I could to eradicate the threat and give people more time to be saved before the Rapture. If we can stop the signs in their tracks, halt the horsemen's work, then we have more time to spread Jesus' message and bring more people into the fold. Now that they've found that fourth horseman, now that fire and brimstone is falling upon the earth with all those natural disasters – the floods in the Philippines and Europe, and those tsunami warnings in Asia – we don't have long.

EM: *But if you believe that the four horsemen are God's messengers, weren't you concerned that by attempting to murder Bobby Small you would be punished by God?*

MS: Now wait just one minute, ma'am. No one's talking about murder. When the Antichrist comes, when that sixth seal is broken, there's no going back. There's no guarantee that you'll get a second chance during the Tribulation. I am on God's side; He knows that Pastor Len and the Pamelists are working hard to bring more people into his fold. And those children were unnatural. Everyone could see that. After a while they started using their power and flaunting it. They may have started off as God's messengers, but I firmly believe what Jim told us – that they became tools of the Antichrist in the end.

EM: *Did Pastor Len Vorhees instruct you to shoot Bobby?*

MS: I can't answer that, ma'am.

EM: *Many people believe that you acted under Pastor Len Vorhees's influence and that he should be as accountable as you.*

MS: Jesus was punished for spreading God's truth. It doesn't matter to me what they say. I'll be in Jesus' arms soon. They can lock me up, they can put me in the chair, it's all the same to me. And maybe it's all part of Jesus' plan. I'm locked in here with sinners, and here's my chance to save as many of them as I can.

PART NINE

SURVIVORS

MAY–JUNE

In the weeks since Ryu first appeared on the 2-chan forum, the speculation over whether his princess was actually Hiro Yanagida's cousin grew to fever pitch. Ryu eventually returned to the forum under his Orz Man avatar.

NAME: ORZ MAN POST DATE: 2012/05/01 21:22:22.30
Hi guys. Don't know if any of u who were on the thread I started a while back are online. Blown away by the way u guys have jumped on my story.

Just wanted to say thanks again.

NAME: ANONYMOUS23
Orz! Cool to have u back. So????? Did it work??? Did u get yr princess? (^人^)

NAME: ORZ MAN
Simple answer: Yes. We r now together.
[This is followed by at least a hundred variations on 'w00t', and 'u r such a Bad Ass Mutherfucker/Boss/Man/The Dude' etc. Ryu goes on to explain how he sprayed an ORZ symbol outside Chiyoko's house to get her attention, much to the Netizens' glee.]

NAME: ANONYMOUS557
Orz. Got to know. Is the princess Android Boy's cousin?

NAME: ORZ MAN
I was waiting for you to ask me that . . . I've been following some of the threads. I can't confirm for obvious reasons.

NAME: ANONYMOUS890
Orz, u met Android Boy yet?

NAME: ORZ MAN
See above. _|7O

NAME: ANONYMOUS330
How hot is the princess, dude?

NAME: ORZ MAN
How to answer this and be honest . . .
When I first saw her . . . She wasn't the person I thought she was. But somehow, that didn't matter.

NAME: ANONYMOUS765
So she's the fat chick who was at the memorial service and not the one who looks like Hazuki? Bummer, dude.

NAME: ANONYMOUS111
Welcome back, Orz. Ignore 765

NAME: ANONYMOUS762
Dude, get to the good bits. Have you done her yet????

NAME: ANONYMOUS111
Don't be crude. Let Orz Man speak

NAME: ORZ MAN
I'm going to sound soppy here, but guys, being with her has changed my life.
Even though she is a princess, we have more in common than I thought possible. She has also had a hard time in the past like me. We have the same views on everything: society, music, gaming, even politics. Yeah, we have heavy conversations sometimes!
Even started telling her stuff I haven't told anyone before.
She helped me find a job at a Lawsons outlet, so I now have some money coming in (not much, but enough to keep me from starving).

This is going to sound lame ... but sometimes I have this dream that we are married and living together in an apartment and we never have to go out.

NAME: ANONYMOUS200
Aw. Yr making me jealous here, Orz.

NAME: ANONYMOUS201
Sounds like lurve.

NAME: ANONYMOUS7889
Come on, Orz Man, tell us about Hiro. Have you met his surrabot yet?

NAME: ANONYMOUS1211
What does he think about the Cult of Hiro?

NAME: ORZ MAN
Guys, no offence, but this is a public message board and I can't talk about this in detail. The princess will freak out if anything I said got into the magazines.

NAME: ANONYMOUS111
U can trust us, Orz, but see yr point.

NAME: ORZ MAN
Let's just say that a certain person is soothing to be around. Not like anyone I have ever met.

That is all I am going to say.

NAME: ANONYMOUS764
How often do you see the princess?

NAME: ORZ MAN
Almost every night. Her parents are kind of strict, and they wouldn't approve of her seeing someone like me so we have to sneak around.

There's a small children's playground opposite her house and I wait there for her. There's an apartment block next to it, so sometimes I feel like I'm being watched, but I can stand it.

NAME: ANONYMOUS665
Orz smokes another cigarette, waiting for his princess to come out and join him. He knows he looks cool. Maybe tonight will be the night. Some of the neighbours look out of their windows at him but he knows they won't mess with him. He flexes his muscles and they disappear.

NAME: ANONYMOUS9883
The ice princess runs out of the door wearing nothing but a short dress that is see thru . . .

NAME: ANONYMOUS210
The princess falls into his arms and she doesn't care who is watching her . . .
[The thread is disrupted by graphic descriptions of a sexual nature]

NAME: ORZ MAN
blushes
Can u imagine if she ever read that?

NAME: ANONYMOUS45
Dude, tell us that you did it with her for reals.

NAME: ORZ MAN
I got to go. She's waiting for me.

NAME: ANONYMOUS887
Orz, don't leave us out of it. We're there with u every step of the way. A geek getting a princess? How often does that happen outside of galge?

NAME: ANONYMOUS2008
Yeah Orz u owe it to us to let us know how the story goes.

NAME: ORZ MAN
I know. Knowing u guys are there for us makes all the difference even if you are deranged sex fiends.

It's good to know we r not alone.

I spoke to graphic artist and Greenpoint resident Neil Mellancamp via Skype in June 2012.

After all those whackos started showing up, no one in the neighbourhood came right out and said they wished Lillian and Bobby would move somewhere else, but you could see most of us were thinking it.

I live a few blocks from Lillian's place, on the other side of McCarren Park, and the neighbourhood became a circus pretty much day one after they found out where Bobby lived. Whole area was buzzing. First there were the reporters and the guys who wanted a soundbite for one of their blogs or tweets or whatever: 'What's it like living so close to the miracle child?' etc., etc. I always told them to go fuck themselves, although there were lots of guys in the neighbourhood who saw this as a chance for their fifteen minutes. Assholes. Then came the UFO crowd. They were totally mondo bizarro, but you could tell most of them were harmless. They'd hang out outside Bobby's building shouting shit like, 'I wanna go with you, Bobby!' but the cops cleared them out. They weren't as tenacious as the religious whack-jobs. Those ones came in waves. There were freaking scores of the fuckers when the news broke about Lillian's husband, a whole contingent who wanted Bobby to heal them – looked to me like they'd hired themselves a bus and driven down especially from Nutsville Carolina or wherever. 'Bobby! Bobby!' you could hear them shout, even after it got dark. 'I got cancer, touch me and heal me.' Those weren't anywhere near as bad as the nasty ones, who'd hang around the park and harass people. 'God hates fags,' they'd shout, but what that had to do with a six-year-old is anyone's guess. There were others that looked like they'd fallen straight out of a comic strip: 'The End is Near,' and 'Have YOU been saved?' on their T-shirts and placards. Soon it felt like I couldn't step outside the apartment without running into one of them. You know the neighbourhood, right? It's a mix, like a lot of Brooklyn, you got your arty crowd, hipsters, Hasidics, lots of guys from the Dominican Republic, but the nut-jobs stood out a mile.

Don't get me wrong, much as it all got old really quickly, I felt sorry for Lillian. Most of us did. My girlfriend reported a couple of the nastier ones for hate speech, but what could the cops do? Those freaks didn't care if they were arrested. They wanted to be martyrs.

That morning, I was heading to work, and for some reason, I decided to take the L train rather than the bus, which meant I had to walk through the park and on past Lillian's building. In the early mornings, a lot of what my girlfriend calls the 'hipster dad gang' jog through the park while pushing their baby buggies, but the guy I saw hanging around the benches near the sports centre was definitely not a stay-at-home dad who dabbled in pop-up restauranteuring or whatever in his spare time. This dude was just sitting there, but I could tell something was off with him, and not just because of how he was dressed. It was a warm morning – not hot and humid like it sometimes gets – but muggy, and this guy was dressed for winter, long black army-style trenchcoat, a black beanie hat. I nodded at him as I passed by, but he looked straight through me. I tried to shrug it off, but when I reached Lorimer I just got this feeling that I should hang around, check what he was doing in the neighbourhood. For all I knew, he could just be some poor homeless guy or whatever, but something told me to be sure. I looked around for the cops that were sometimes parked outside Lillian's building, but I couldn't see them. I'm not a spiritual person or anything, but this voice inside me said, Neil, go get yourself a coffee, check the dude out, and then head to work. So that's what I did. I grabbed a large black Americano from Orgasmic Organic and started on back to the park.

When I got back to Lillian's street, I could see the creepy dude heading towards me, walking really slowly. That feeling came back, and I knew there was something seriously wrong with him. The street wasn't empty, there were lots of people heading out to work, but I focussed on him and sped up my pace. The door to

Lillian's apartment opened, and an old woman with dyed red hair and a kid in a baseball cap stepped out onto the pavement. I knew it was them straight away. Whoever thought up that disguise didn't use their imagination.

'Watch out!' I screamed. The next bit happened fast, but also like in slow motion, if that makes sense. The creepy guy pulled out a gun – I don't know guns so I couldn't have told you what it was – and just started crossing the road, ignoring the traffic. I didn't think twice. I ran straight for him, flipped the lid off the top of my coffee, and threw it right at the fucker. Right in his face. He still got a shot off, but it went wide, hit a Chevrolet that was parked in the street.

Everyone was screaming and yelling, 'Get down, get the fuck down!'

Next thing I know, this dude came out of nowhere – found out later he was an off-duty cop who'd just gotten off work – and shouted at the gunman to 'drop his fucking weapon'. The freaky dude did as he said, but by then you could see he wasn't a threat. He was blubbering and rubbing at his eyes and face. That coffee was hot and his skin was bright red. He dropped to his knees in the middle of the road and the cop kicked his gun away and got straight on his radio.

I ran over to Lillian and Bobby. Lillian's face was ashen, and I was scared she was going to have a heart attack or a stroke or something. But Bobby, I don't know if it was the shock or whatever, but he'd started giggling. Lillian grabbed his hand and pulled him inside. Seemed like seconds later the street was full of police cars. That freaky dude was hauled to his feet and taken away. I hope the fucker rots in hell.

That cop called me later, said I was a hero. Mayor's office said I was looking at a civilian medal for bravery. But I did what anyone would've done, you know?

I didn't see Lillian and Bobby around the neighbourhood after that. They went to that safe house, right? That's what the old lady who lived in their building said. Lillian sent me this really cool email, saying as how she'll never forget what I did that day. I teared up when I read it. The next time I saw them was on the news.

This is the last email I received from Lillian Small, dated 29 May.

We're doing the best we can, Elspeth. I'm still shaken, who wouldn't be after something like that? But I'm trying to be strong for Reuben and Bobby. Bobby is fine – I don't think he was really aware of what was going on.

I think I've given you all you wanted to know. If, in your book, you could please say that we don't know why Reuben started talking again, but it isn't anything to do with Bobby. I thought about denying it, after those evil men started saying it was another sign, but Betsy knows the truth and so does Bobby. I don't want him to read this book and the news reports when he's old enough and see that his Bubbe is a liar. I believe in my heart that Reuben made one last effort to kick Al out of his consciousness so that he could spend time with his grandson. It was the force of his love that made this possible.

They're insisting that we move to a safe house now. There isn't much choice if I want to keep Bobby safe. There's talk of putting Reuben in a care facility in a different state, but I won't have that.

No. We're a family and we're going to stick together whatever happens.

14 May, 5.30 a.m.

I can't get rid of the smell. That fishy smell. The one Stephen leaves when he comes. I've tried everything; even resorted to scrubbing the walls with Domestos. The bleach made my eyes burn, but I couldn't stop.

Jess didn't take any notice as usual. She sat in the lounge watching *The X Factor* while her mad uncle flitted through the house with a bucket of toilet cleaner. Couldn't give a toss, as Geoff would say. I invited Mrs E-B around; I was hoping maybe she had some old-lady wisdom about getting rid of lingering odours (I lied and said that I'd burned Jess's fish fingers). But she said she couldn't smell anything, apart from the eye-watering sting of bleach. She took me outside into the garden for a cigarette, patted my hand again, and said that maybe I was trying to do too much, especially with all the pressure from the media. She said I should try to cry more, get my grief out that way instead of bottling it up. Went on and on about how cut up she was when her husband died ten years ago. She said she didn't think she'd be able to go on, but God helped her find a way.

Hello, God, it's me, Paul. Why the fuck aren't you listening?

It's like I'm split in two. Rational Paul and Going Mental Paul. It's not like it was before. That was just a depressive episode. More than once I've picked up the phone to call Dr K or Darren to beg them to take Jess away from me. But then Shelly's voice pops into my head, 'All they need is love, and you've got buckets to spare, Paul.'

I can't let them down.

Could it be Capgras Syndrome? Could it?

I've even . . . God. I even made an excuse to take Jess over to Mrs E-B's place so that I could see how Mrs E-B's dog reacted to her. In the movies, animals can always sense if there's something wrong with someone. If they're possessed or whatever. But that dog didn't do anything. It just lay there. Got to take it a day at a time.

Got to.

But the pressure of acting normal when I'm screaming inside . . . Jesus. The Discovery Channel wants me to do some kind of interview about how I felt when I heard the news about the crash. I can't. Turned them down flat. And I completely forgot about a *Sunday Times* photo shoot that Gerry organised weeks ago. When the photographers showed up I slammed the door on them.

Gerry's tearing his hair out, and he's no longer buying my 'I'm still grief-stricken' card. He says your publishers are going to sue, Mandi. Let them. Fuck, what do I care? It's all falling apart.

And the pills don't work.

How the fuck did she know the Dictaphone was in her room?

21 *May,* 2.30 *p.m.*

While Jess was at school I did some more Internet research. Googled the crap out of the Pamelists, the alien theorists, even the ones who believe the kids are possessed by demons (there are a lot of these).

Because the kids. The other kids. Bobby Small and Hiro whatshisname. They're not normal, either, are they? I could tell Lillian was hiding something when I phoned her, and now I know what it was. There's no cure for Alzheimer's. Everyone knows that. No. There's something up with Bobby. And the other one, talking through an android. What the fuck is that all about?

Couldn't find much on Kenneth Oduah apart from what I was expecting – a shedload of hysterical religious sites (The Final Proof We Need!), several satirical articles, and some bumf about him being kept at a safe house in Lagos 'for his own safety'.

What if they are the horsemen? I know, I know. Mel especially would freak if she heard me talking like this. But just hear me out. Sane Paul won't even take this on board, but I think we need to keep an open mind. There's definitely something wrong with Jess. And weird shit is happening around the other two. Or three. Who the fuck knows what gubbins the other one is up to?

Aliens, horsemen or demons – oh my!

(starts sobbing)

Should I call Lillian again? I just don't know.

28 May, 10.30 p.m.

I know I should feel sorry for Bobby after being attacked like that, but I only feel sorry for Lillian.

It's all over the news of course. Every bloody channel. In the old days I'd try to stop Jess watching it. Keep her away from it, but why bother? It doesn't seem to affect her either way.

On the Sky report they had a collage of photographs of the crashes and giant blown up pics of The Three. I found Jess sitting inches from the screen, her My Little Ponies littered around her, watching as Sky did a 'timeline' of events and brought pundits in to discuss it ad nauseam.

I made myself approach her. 'Do you want to talk about this, Jess?'

'Talk about what, Uncle Paul?'

'Why that little boy is on the news. Why your photograph is on the news.'

'No thanks.'

I hovered around for a few more seconds, then ran outside for a fag.

Darren says it's likely that the police will be keeping a close eye on the house, just in case the religious nutters decide to jump across the Atlantic and target Jess.

Tonight after she has gone to bed, I'm going to try one last time to get Stephen to talk to me. 'How could you let that thing in here?' He has to mean Jess, right?

I should have done it ages ago.

I'm going to stay up all night, drink enough coffee to fell a horse, and when Stephen comes I'm going to *make* him talk to me.

30 May, 4.00 a.m.

I must've dropped off. Because when I woke up, there he was. All the lights were on, but he looked like he was in the dark. Sitting in shadow. Couldn't see his face.

He shifted his position, and the smell was so strong I gagged.

'What do you want? Please tell me,' I begged him. 'Please!'

I reached out to grab him, but there was nothing there.

I ran into Jess's room, shook her, thrust a photo of Polly in her face. 'This is your sister! Why don't you fucking care?'

She turned over, stretched, and smiled at me. 'Uncle Paul, I need to sleep. I've got school in the morning.'

Jesus. Could it be that she's the rational one?

God help me.

1 June, 6.30 p.m.

A couple of cops came to see me today, showed up this morning before I was even dressed. Actually, they're not police, but Special Branch. Sane Paul, the me before all this fucked-up shit happened, was squeeing inside. Calvin and Mason, they're called. Calvin and Mason! Like the title of a butch cop show. Calvin's black, speaks with a public school accent, and has shoulders like a prop forward. Totally Sane Paul's type. Mason is older, a silver fox.

I made them tea, apologised for the lingering bleach smell (after Mrs E-B's reaction I've learned not to mention the fishy rotten stench). They wanted to know if I'd had any threatening phone calls lately, like the ones we got right at the beginning when Jess first came home. I said no. Told them the truth. That the only hassle we were getting these days was from the press.

Jess was on its best behaviour of course. Smiling and laughing and acting like a charming little celebrity. Hot they may be, but I don't think much of Mason and Calvin's detection skills. They fell for it, of course. Hook, line and sinker. Mason even had the gall to ask if he could have a photo with her to show to his daughter.

They said they'd be keeping an eye on the house, and to give them a call if I was worried about anything. I almost said, 'Would you mind giving my brother a warning, and telling him to leave me the fuck alone?' My dead brother! And IT, of course. Imagine how that would have gone down.

Must stop calling Jess 'it'. Not right, just feeds the monster.

When they left, I tried to call Lillian again. No answer.

2 *June, 4.00 a.m.*

(*sobbing*)

Okay.

Woke up. Felt that familiar weight on the bed. But it wasn't Stephen. It was Jess, although she's not heavy enough to make a dent in the mattress, is she?

'Do you like your dreams?' she said. 'I've given them to you, Uncle Paul. So that you can see Stephen whenever you like.'

'What are you?' It was the first time I'd come out and said it.

'I'm Jess,' she said. 'Who do you think I am? You're such a silly billy, Uncle Paul.'

'Get out!' I screamed at her. 'Get out get out get out.' My throat is still sore.

She laughed and skipped away. I locked the door behind her.

I'm running out of options. They'll take Jess away from me if they find out what I'm thinking. Some days I think that would be a good thing. But what if the real Jess is still in there, trying to get out, trying to get help? What if she needs me?

It's time to be proactive. Explore my options. Keep an open mind. Do more research. Cover all bases.

I don't have any other choice.

Gerhard Friedmann, a 'secular exorcist' who works throughout Europe, agreed to talk to me via Skype in late June after I made a donation to his organisation.

Before I begin to answer your questions, I would like to make something clear. Exorcism is not a word I like to use. It has too many connotations. No, I exact 'inner healing and spirit deliverance'. That is the service I offer. I also want to make it clear that I do not charge a fee for this service, but merely ask for a donation, of whatever amount the subject or client chooses to provide. I am also not affiliated with any particular church or religious institution. I just go about my practice in a slightly different manner. And business is very good at the moment. Let us just say that it is rare that I do not fly first class. At around the time I was contacted by Mr Craddock, I would say that I was doing up to three spirit deliverances and cleanses a day, all around Europe and the UK.

I ask Gerhard how Paul Craddock contacted him.

I have a number of ways in which prospective clients can get in touch with me. Mr Craddock contacted me through one of my Facebook accounts. I have several. I am also on Twitter, of course, and have a website. As his circumstances did not allow me to come to his residence, we agreed to meet at a location that I sometimes use for spirit deliverance.

(*He refuses to reveal this location*)

I ask him if he was aware who Paul Craddock was before they met.

Yes. Mr Craddock was very candid about this, but I assured him that our relationship would be confidential – akin to that of a doctor/patient agreement. I was aware of the theories about Jessica Craddock and the other children, but did not let these influence my diagnosis. I am only talking to you now because the news that

Mr Craddock contracted my services was leaked by his defence team.

I tell him that I have been on his website where he states that there is a spirit that manifests itself as homosexuality. I ask if he was aware that Paul Craddock was gay.

Yes, I knew of this. But I knew that in his case this wasn't the root of the problem.

He was concerned that he or his niece was infested with bad energy, possessed, if you like. When we met, he was agitated, but not overly so. He kept saying, over and over again, that he had contacted me in order to 'rule out this option', and asked me to investigate this possibility. Mr Craddock told me that he was having extremely disturbing dreams, in which his dead brother would come to him, and that he was having difficulty relating to his niece. These are both symptoms of spirit possession and/or sickness induced by overexposure to negative energy.

I ask him if he was aware of Paul Craddock's mental health issues.

Yes. He was very upfront about this. I am always careful not to confuse, for example, a schizophrenic episode with possession, but I knew immediately that this was not what I was dealing with. I am extremely intuitive when it comes to this.

I ask him how he usually goes about his spirit deliverance.

The first thing I do is settle the subject, make sure they're comfortable. Then I anoint their forehead with oil. Any oil will do, but I prefer to use extra-virgin olive oil, as this seems to get the best results.

Next, I must decipher if I am dealing with bad energy poisoning or entity possession. If it is possession, the next step is to discover what kind of entity has attached itself to the client and call it out by name. Entities are disturbing and powerful phenomena that have made their way to earth from a different plane. They attach themselves to someone who is already weakened, perhaps because of abuse or because they have been poisoned by someone else's bad energy, which has allowed their defences to be compromised. There are many many types of entities; the ones that I specialise in are those that have found doorways into this realm through sites where much negativity has taken place.

I also do object cleansing, as objects can also harbour negative energy. This is why I always encourage people to be careful when handling antiques and artefacts from museums.

I ask him why, if Paul Craddock believed Jessica was also possessed, he didn't request that she also be cleansed.

That was not possible because of his current situation. He said he was under surveillance from the press, who followed him and Jess everywhere.

But when he went into more detail about his symptoms, which included being plagued by the sense that Jess wasn't the real Jess but a facsimile, I was certain that if it was an entity that was causing the problem, then it had attached itself to him, and not to his niece. The grief and anguish he would have suffered after his family was killed in the plane crash would have weakened his defences enough for him to be a prime candidate for possession. He also expressed concern that Jess could be an alien being, but I assured him that aliens don't exist and he was more than likely dealing with a bad energy influx.

And, as soon as I tuned into him, I did indeed find that he was suffering from severe malaise caused by an over-toxification of bad energy. I assured him that once we had gone through the cleansing ritual – which involves anointing with oil and transference of bad energy via touch – he would no longer be plagued by the dreams he was experiencing or the belief that his niece was a changeling.

Afterwards, I warned him that although he had been cleansed, he was still compromised, and there would still be traces of bad energy inside him that could eventually attract an entity. I encouraged him to avoid stressful situations at all costs.

He thanked me, and as he left, he said, 'There can only be one explanation now.'

I ask him if he knew what Paul Craddock meant by this.

Not at the time.

PART TEN

END GAMES

END GAMES

Joe DeLesseps, a salesman who regularly travels through Maryland, Pennsylvania and Virginia, agreed to talk to me via Skype in late June.

I operate in three states, selling just about anything that you can care to think of in the hardware line; there are still people out there who prefer to deal with a human being rather than a computer. I keep off the turnpike when I can. I prefer the back roads. Like my grandson Piper would say, that's just how I roll. Over the years I've carved out several routes for myself, got my favourite places to stop off for coffee and pie, some of which I've been visiting for years, though more and more mom and pop outlets have been hit by the recession. I'm not a fan of those chain motels either, prefer the family-run joints. You may not get cable and Taco Bell on tap, but the company and the coffee's always better and the rates are competitive.

I was running behind schedule that day. Wholesaler I'd seen in Baltimore liked to talk, and I'd lost track of time. Almost decided to take the interstate, but there's this little roadhouse just before Mile Creek Road – one of my favourite routes which takes you near Green Ridge Forest – where the coffee's good and the pancakes even better, so I decided to take the long way instead. My wife Tammy is always nagging me to watch my cholesterol, but I figured that what she didn't know wouldn't hurt her.

I made it there round about five, half-an-hour before closing time. Pulled up next to a new Chevy SUV with tinted windows. Soon as I walked in, I figured it had to belong to the small group sitting drinking coffee in one of the booths by the window. At first glance I thought they were just an ordinary family: a couple with their child, on a road-trip with grandma and grandpa. But when I looked closer, I could see they didn't seem to fit together. There wasn't that companionable ease you see with most families or holidaymakers; the younger couple especially looked on edge.

Could practically see the creases on the younger fellow's shirt where he'd just pulled it out of its packaging.

I knew Suze, the short-order cook, would be wanting to head home, so I ordered my pancakes real quick and put extra cream in my coffee so that I could chug it down faster.

'Po Po wants to go to the bathroom,' the little kid said, pointing to grandpa. But the old fella hadn't said a word. I could see there was something not right with him. Had a vacant look in his eyes, like my pa got right at the end.

The older woman helped the old fella shuffle his way to the bathroom. I greeted her as she passed my table, and she gave me a weary smile. Red hair you could see was dyed, an inch of grey roots. Tammy would have said that there goes a woman who hadn't found the time to take care of herself in quite a while. I could feel eyes on me; the younger fella was checking me out. I nodded at him, said something about how we could do with some rain, but he didn't respond.

They left a few minutes before I did, but they were still helping that old-timer into the SUV when I made my way outside.

'Where you headed?' I asked, trying to be friendly.

The younger fella gave me a look. 'Pennsylvania,' he said. I could tell he'd just pulled that answer out of his ass.

'Uh-huh. Well, drive safe.'

The older, red-haired woman gave me a tentative smile.

'Come on, Mom,' the younger woman said to her, and the red-head jumped as if she'd just been pinched.

The little kid waved at me and I winked back at him. Cute little guy.

They took off at a clip, heading in the wrong direction for Pennsylvania. That SUV would've been equipped with GPS, and I could see the young fella knew what he was doing. Guess I thought, none of my business.

I didn't see it happen. I came around the bend; saw the broken glass. The Chevy was on its roof on the wrong side of the road.

I pulled over, dug in the back for my first-aid kit. Driving as much as I do, you're apt to encounter a lot of accidents, and I'd been keeping a kit in the car for years. Even did a course a couple a years ago.

They'd hit a deer. I figure the young fella musta yanked too hard on the wheel and flipped the car. Could see straight off that the two at the front – the driver, that young fella, and the young woman with the hard eyes – were gone, and it would have been quick. You couldn't tell which parts was deer, which parts was human.

The old fella in the back was gone, too. No blood, but his eyes were open. Looked like he was at peace.

The woman with the red hair was a different story. There wasn't much blood on her, but I could see her legs were trapped. Her eyes were open, and they were dazed.

'Bobby,' she whispered.

I knew she must mean the boy. 'I'll look for him, ma'am,' I said.

Couldn't find him anywhere at first. Figured he must have been flung out of the back window. Found his body two hundred yards from the vehicle. He was in the culvert, lying face up, as if he was watching the sky. You can tell when the soul is gone. There's an emptiness. Looked like there wasn't a scratch on him.

There was no way I could get the woman out of there – needed the Jaws of Life to do that – and I was worried she might have spinal injuries. She'd stopped crying by then and I held her hand as she drifted away. I listened to the sound of the engine ticking and waited for the cops.

I only found out who they were the next day. Tammy couldn't believe I hadn't figured it out sooner; that boy's face was always plastered over the magazines she gets.

Didn't seem right. What are the chances of that poor kid being in two fatal accidents? I'd been planning to keep on going right till Tammy forced me to retire, but maybe this whole thing is a sign that it's time to quit. A sign that enough is enough.

I thought long and hard about whether or not to include Bobby Small's autopsy report in this book. I decided to include an extract after various conspiracy sites insisted that his death was faked. It should be noted that according to pathologist Alison Blackburn, the State of Maryland's Chief Medical Examiner, no anomalies were found when she conducted a thorough internal examination.

Bobby Small was formally identified by Mona Gladwell, who declined to talk to me again.

(Sensitive readers may wish to skip over this. It can, however, be found in its entirety at *http://pathologicallyfamous.com/*)

OFFICE OF THE CHIEF MEDICAL EXAMINER
STATE OF MARYLAND

Decedent: Bobby Reuben Small   Autopsy number: SM 2012 –001346
Age: 6 years   Date: 11/06/2012
Sex: Male   TiME: 9.30 a.m

Examination and summary analysis performed by: **Alison Blackburn, MD, Chief Medical Examiner**
Initial examination: **Gary Lee Swartz, MD, Deputy Chief Medical Examiner**
Osteological examination: **Pauline May Swanson, Ph.D., ABFA**
Toxicology examination: **Michael Greenberg, Ph.D., DABFT**

ANATOMIC FINDINGS
Young, male boy with superficial abrasions of forehead, nose and chin. Complete dislocation between C6,C7 and C7,T1. Severing of inter-vertebral disc and anterior ligament C6,C7. Fractured spinal process C6. Partial tearing of posterior root filaments and multiple bleeding points observed.

CAUSE OF DEATH
Traumatic disruption of cervical cord.

MANNER OF DEATH
Accidental death consistent with ejection from a motor vehicle.

CIRCUMSTANTIAL SUMMARY
Bobby Small, a 6-year-old male, was the sole survivor of a plane crash 6 months ago, in which his mother was killed. He suffered minor injuries in the crash from which he made a full recovery. He was being targeted by a religious group and a decision was made to move him to a place of safety with his grandparents. All three were being transported in a Chevrolet Suburban SUV by two FBI agents. Bobby was seated between his grandparents in the rear of the vehicle where he was secured by a lap seat belt. At approximately 5 p.m. they stopped at Duke's Roadside Diner in Maryland. The group were observed there by Mr Joseph DeLesseps, a travelling salesman. They stirred his interest as he thought them a strange group. The adults had coffee and Bobby had a strawberry milkshake and a plate of fries. The group left around 5.30 p.m. followed soon after by Mr DeLesseps, who saw the Suburban drive off at speed. At approximately 5.50 p.m. Mr DeLesseps rounded a bend in a wooded section of the road and spotted the Suburban crashed at the side of the road. He found the vehicle against a large tree with a dead deer partially on the hood of the car and partially through the shattered windshield. In the vehicle were two dead people in the front seats and a dead elderly man in a rear seat. There was a severely injured elderly woman in the other rear seat. There was no sign of the little boy he had seen in the diner, so Mr DeLesseps searched around the vehicle. He found the body of the boy in a small culvert two hundred metres from the SUV. There was no sign of life. He called 911 immediately.

DOCUMENTS AND EVIDENCE EXAMINED
1. Report from vehicle examination centre re Chevrolet Suburban. Evidence of damage to hood and front windshield

consistent with impact from a deer. Crumpling of rear of vehicle consistent with impact with a tree trunk. Shattered rear window and damaged central lap belt. No evidence of any pre-accident damage or faults to the vehicle.

2. Report from RTA examination team. Skid marks indicate likelihood of sudden braking secondary to impacting with deer at moderate to high speed with resultant spinning off the road of vehicle and rear off-side impact with tree. Adult seat belts remained in place, but central, rear lap belt open and partially damaged, resulting in the ejection of the male child casualty through the shattered rear window.

IDENTIFICATION

On 11/06/2012 at 9.45 a.m. a complete post mortem examination was performed on the body of Bobby Small, who was identified by the Norfolk County Chief Medical Examiner's Office. David Michaels was present as autopsy assistant.

CLOTHING AND VALUABLES

Bobby Small was wearing a bright red baseball cap (retrieved at the scene), blue jeans, a red *Night at the Museum* T-shirt, a pale grey hooded sweatshirt, and a pair of red Converse sneakers.

EXTERNAL EXAMINATION

The body is that of a well-nourished white young male consistent with a stated age of 6 years.

Body length 45 inches Weight 46lbs.

Light blonde, medium length slightly curly scalp hair. No nevi or tattoos. A small scar on the forehead. Superficial abrasions to forehead, nose and chin. Pupils equal and regular. Light blue irides. Healthy milk teeth with absent two upper front incisors.

Although Paul Craddock attempted to destroy his computer's hard drive, several documents and some email correspondence were recovered, including the following, which was leaked to the press:

(The spelling errors have been left uncorrected to illustrate his frame of mind)

List of Weird Shit Jess said today (8 June)

(more on the new obsession with boredom). Uncle Paul, do you get bored being you? I'm bored being me. (goes back to watching her new favourite show, fucking *TOWIE*). These people are bored being them. (I ask her wtf that means). Being bored is like being a cup that can't be filled (v fucking zen, where'd she hear that??????? Certainly not on Celeb Big Brother).

(10 June)

I hand her her supper she says, Uncle Paul, does Stephen smell as bad as these fish fingers now? (I scream, she laughs). I leave she turns channel to the news. I hear her laughing at something else. Almost throw up when I see it's a report that Bobby Small has been killed in a car accident. I ask whats funny she says, he's not dead he's just playing silly-billy. Like mummy and daddy and polly.

(I'm in the kitchen, thinking about the pills again ie how many would it take to be sure). She glides in without me seeing her. Moves too close to my face. She says, am I special paul? They say I am at school. It's so easy.

(14 June)

It finds me crying. Do you want to come play my little pony with me? You can be princess luna again and stephen can be princess celestia (laughs).

1) POSESSION: FOR: she alwaqsy seems to know what I'm thinking, knows things she couldn't know like about sexual ortienattion, knows aboput the stephen dreams ssays she sent them

2) POSSESSION AGAINST: NOT RATIONAL I KNOW THIS WHAT AM I THINKING and she doesn't have fits or anything like on the checklist on the inetrnet or speak in funny voices and that prick gerhard said it was unlikely although i don;t trust his opinion

3) HORSEMAN THEORY FOR: colours of the planes, signs lots of no way thwy could have survived, other children acting weird too there's Bobby's seniles granddad talking and Hiro talking through a fucking robot and how can so many be wrong because so many believe this is the truth and nw they have found the fourth child altho that could all be more bullshit

4) HORSEMAN THEORY AGAINST: batshit crazy, even archbishop of canturbury and that top iman say it is utter bullshit and they also believe in sky fairies and if there is a horseman inside her wehere is the real jess and why does she look like hersefl. Signs they have put on the website could have happend anyway and the foot and mouth thing blown over now anyway and aniomals bite people all the time anyway same as floods etc etc

5) CAPGRAS SYNDROME FOR: my history of mental illness although that was stress related only and would be nice as is a medical cpondition that woould explain why i don't think shes jess evben though she looks just like jess amnd sometimes talks like her. I wish it is this

6) CAPGRAS SYNDROME AGAINST: never had it before, no head injury (unless I was drunk and hit my head and didn't realise it) its very very very fcking rare

7) ALIENS FOR: same as possession and would explain how sometiems she seems to be watching me like i'm an expriment

8) ALKIENS AGAINST: because it s not rationla altho the eveidence can be persuasive and this is the only one I haVen't discounted yet needto look into moerew okay paul

To: **actorpc99@gmail.com**
From **openyreyes.com**
Subject: **RE: Advice in confidence**
Date: 14/06/2012

Paul, thanks for your email, happy to help in any way I can.

As I said when we spoke telephonically, the commonest way in which they work is by implanting a MICROCHIP inside the subject. I believe that at the moment of the crashes, the children were put into stasis, which is why they were not injured. Then they were implanted. Through 'voice to skull' manipulation, the Others (ALIENS) are able to control and influence those they have chosen. This is a new type of technology that is LIGHT YEARS away from what we can yet do in our realm.

You say you have checked out all the options and have proved this is NOT a case of demonic possession. I applaud you for being so thorough.

I'm not at all surprised that Jess is showing disturbing symptoms, or out of character behaviour – this is to be expected. Remember, a change in PERSONALITY is NOT actually a symptom of PTSD. As you say, look at what's happening with the boy in Japan (talking through a mechanism, a ROBOT) and the boy in America, who was no doubt experimenting with his grandfather's cognative [*sic*] functioning. It is very unlikely he is dead. This is a government ruse as they are in cahoots with the OTHERS. They receive immunity from experimentation and have made a treaty with the aliens so that they can have free rein to feed off our energies.

Your questions about the Pamelist theory are very interesting. I believe that there are a LOT of similarities with the truth. Very close to what WE believe. They are wrong, but MORE RIGHT THAN THEY KNOW.

And what you are feeling mustn't be confused with Capgras syndrome. That is a psychological anomoly [*sic*].

How to proceed? I would be cautious around Jess, it's unlikely she will do anything to harm you. The dreams and visions you are having are probably interference from the chip. I would advise you to watch her carefully, and be careful what you let on to her.

Let me know if there's anything else I can help you with.

Best,

Si

I usually wake very early, at around five, and as I wait for daylight to come, I often watch the clock next to my bed. This is how I knew the exact time of the first gunshot. Although my block is situated only two hundred metres from the busy Hatsudai expressway, it's well insulated from noise, but that sound made its way into my room. A muffled bang, which made me flinch, then another, then two more. I had never heard a gunshot before, except on television, so I did not know what to think. Perhaps that it was fireworks? And I couldn't be sure where it was coming from.

It took me several minutes to climb into my wheelchair, but gradually I made it over to the window where I spend most of each day. I don't go out very often. There is a lift in the apartment building, but it's hard to get through the door without help, and my sister can only find the time to visit me once a week, when she brings me groceries. I lived here for many years with my husband, and when he died I decided I would stay. This is my home.

It was not yet light, the sun was still struggling into the sky, but because of the streetlights I could see from my position that the Kamamoto family's front door was open. It was too early for Kamamoto-san to leave for work; he left every day at six, so that did give me some cause for concern. No one else in the neighbourhood had stirred. When I was questioned by the police later that day, they said that my neighbours who'd heard the gunshots assumed they were hearing a car back-firing.

I opened my window to let in some fresh air, then waited to see if the sound would come again or if anyone would emerge from the house. Then, I saw two figures walking towards the house from the direction of the Hatsudai. When they passed beneath my window, I recognised the girl as Chiyoko Kamamoto and I could tell by his long hair that her companion was the boy I'd seen hanging around in the children's playground many times before. Once, I'd seen him spray-painting a message on the pavement, but he'd cleaned it off, so I did not complain. Those two were very different types of people. Chiyoko walked upright as if she owned the streets; he would hunch over as if he was trying to appear smaller than he was. I had seen Chiyoko slipping out of the house many times at night to meet him, but this was the first time I had seen her returning. They were talking quietly, so I could not hear the details of their conversation. Chiyoko laughed and nudged the boy with her elbow and he bent down to kiss her. Then she playfully pushed him away and turned to walk into her house.

She hesitated when she saw the door was open and turned back to say something to her companion. She went inside and thirty seconds later I heard a scream. Not just a scream, a howl. The anguish in that sound was terrible to hear.

The man, who was still waiting outside, jerked as if he had been slapped, then ran into the house.

Several neighbours started emerging from their doorways, disturbed by the screams, which sounded as if they would never stop.

Chiyoko staggered out into the street, the boy in her arms. I thought at first she was covered in black paint, but as she stumbled into the light beneath my window, it became red. The little boy, Hiro, was limp in her arms, and . . . and . . . I couldn't see his face. Just blood and bone where it should be. The tall boy tried to help her, as did the neighbours, but she screamed at them to leave her alone. She was yelling at Hiro to wake up, to stop pretending.

He was such a dear little boy. Whenever he left the apartment, he would always look up at me and wave. My sister didn't believe me at first when I told her that the miracle child was living in the house across the street from me. The whole of Japan took that boy into their hearts. Sometimes there were photographers waiting in the street; once, one knocked on the door and asked if he could film the house from my apartment, but I refused.

It couldn't have been more than five minutes later that I heard the ambulance arriving. It took three paramedics to take Hiro's body away from Chiyoko; she fought and hit and bit them. The police attempted to drag her towards one of their vehicles, but she twisted out of their grasp, and before they could stop her, she started running away, still drenched in blood. The long-haired boy sprinted after her.

The crowd of onlookers and reporters grew as the news spread. There was a hush as the bodies, encased in their black plastic shrouds, were removed from the house. That was when I turned away from the window.

I didn't sleep at all that night. I thought that I would never sleep again.

The 2-chan message board erupted minutes after the news of Hiro's murder was released.

NAME: ANONYMOUS111 POST DATE: 2012/22/06 11:19:29.15
Fuck! U guys hear about Hiro?

NAME: ANONYMOUS356
Can't believe it.

The Android Boy is dead. Fucking bastard American marine broke into their house. Shot the princess's parents as well as Hiro.

NAME: ANONYMOUS23
U seen the stuff on Reddit? Marine was one of those religious freaks. Like the dude who tried to shoot the kid in the US.

NAME: ANONYMOUS885
Orz was there. Orz and the princess found the body. I'm cryin inside for Orz. U see the pictures of him? He was fighting to get to the Princess while the cops were tryin to keep him away.

I was cheering him on.

NAME: ANONYMOUS987
We all were, dude. So happy they got away in the end. Go Orz!

NAME: ANONYMOUS899
The princess isn't as hot as I thought she'd be. Orz looks like a typical otaku, just like I imagined him.

NAME: ANONYMOUS23
That's cold. Fuck u 899.

NAME: ANONYMOUS555
Where do u think Orz and the princess have gone? Cops will
want to talk to them.

NAME: ANONYMOUS6543
You think Orz is ok?

NAME: ANONYMOUS23
Don't be such a fucking noob 6543! Of course he's not ok!!!!
*[Much speculation followed about what this could mean for Orz
and the princess's future. Then, three hours later, Ryu appeared
on the board.]*

NAME: ORZ MAN POST DATE: 2012/22/06 14:10:19.25
Hi guys.

NAME: ANONYMOUS111
Orz??? That really u?

NAME: ORZ MAN
It's me.

NAME: ANONYMOUS23
Orz, u ok? How is the princess? Where are u?

NAME: ORZ MAN
I don't have long. The princess is waiting for me.
   I showed her yr messages and she says it doesn't matter now
that u know who we really are. She says that u should never
forget what they did.
   She is broken.
   I am broken.
   But wanted to say thanx for giving us all that support.

This isn't easy . . .
   Wanted to let u know that u won't hear from me again.

We're going to be together forever going somewhere where they can't hurt us any more.

I wish I could meet every one of u. Wouldn't have had the balls to leave my room without all yr encouragement.

Goodbye.

Your friend, Ryu (aka Orz Man)

NAME: ANONYMOUS23
Orz??????

NAME: ANONYMOUS288
Orz!!!! Come back, man.

NAME: ANONYMOUS90
He's gone.

NAME: ANONYMOUS111
Netizens, this isn't good. That sounded like a suicide note to me.

NAME: ANONYMOUS23
Orz would never do something like that . . . would he?

NAME: ANONYMOUS57890
If u think about it, if Orz and the princess hadn't been out together that night then the marine might have shot her too.

NAME: ANONYMOUS896
Orz saved her life.

NAME: ANONYMOUS235
Yeah. And if 111 is right, they're going to kill themselves together. A suicide pact.

NAME: ANONYMOUS7689
There's no proof this is what they're gonna do.

NAME: ANONYMOUS111
Those US fuckers. They were behind this. They murdered Hiro and destroyed Orz's happiness. They can't be allowed to get away with it.

NAME: ANONYMOUS23
Agreed. Orz is one of us. They need to pay.

NAME: ANONYMOUS111
Netizens, for once in yr lives it's time to do something that counts.

Melanie Moran agreed to talk to me via Skype shortly after Jessica Craddock's funeral in mid-July.

I blame myself. Geoff says I mustn't but some days I can't help it. 'You've got enough on your plate, petal,' he keeps saying. 'What could you have done in any case?'

Looking back now, with the benefit of hindsight and that, I can't help feeling that I should have seen it coming. Paul had been acting strange for a while, so much so that even Kelvin and some of the others had picked up on it. He'd missed the last three 277 Together meetings, and he hadn't asked me or Geoff to fetch Jess from school or babysit for a good couple of weeks before it happened. To be honest, me and Geoff were relieved to get a bit of a break. We had a lot on our plate, what with our own grand-children to look after, especially after Gavin went for the police exams early. And Paul did have the tendency to take over, make himself the centre of attention. He could be quite needy, self-obsessed. But that said, I should have done more. I should have made more of an effort to go and check up on him.

I heard that social worker of his being interviewed on the radio, trying to explain himself. He was saying how it was no wonder everyone was fooled, Paul was an actor, played different personas for a living. But that's just an excuse. Fact is, the social weren't doing their job. They dropped the ball on that one. So did that psychologist. As Geoff keeps saying, Paul wasn't *that* good an actor, was he?

When we first started 277 Together, a few of the others – not many mind – felt that because Paul was the only one of us who had a relative who'd survived the crash, that he should take a back seat, let the others talk. Me and Geoff, we didn't go along with that. Paul had lost his brother, hadn't he? And his niece and sister-in-law. The first time Paul brought Jess to a meeting, it was hard for most of them to look at her; how do you behave towards a miracle child? Because that's what she was. A miracle, only not in the way those fundies say. You should hear Father Jeremy go off about them, 'Putting Christianity into disrepute'.

We babysat Jess quite a few times while Paul was out doing what he needed to do. Lovely little girl, really bright. I was relieved when Paul decided to send her back to school. Get her right back into a normal way of life. The primary school where she went, it looked like a good supportive place, they had that lovely memorial service for Polly, didn't they? I suppose in some ways it was harder for Paul than it was for us. He had a member of his family who was still alive, but then again, he had a constant reminder that the others were gone, didn't he?

You can tell I'm putting off getting to the next bit. The only people I've told in detail are Geoff and Father Jeremy. It's what my Danielle would have called a total mind-fuck. She had a right mouth on her. Took after me.

Don't mind me; tears are always close to the surface. I know people think of me as a coper, as a tough old bitch, and I am . . . but it gets to you. All this misery, all this death. It's all needless. Jess didn't need to die and Danielle didn't need to die.

I'd turned my phone off that day. Just for a couple of hours. We were coming up for Danielle's birthday, and I was feeling down. Decided to treat myself and have a long soak in the bath. When I switched my mobile back on, I saw I had a message from Paul. First up he apologised for keeping his distance, said he'd had a lot to think about and deal with over the last few days. His voice sounded flat. Lifeless. In retrospect I suppose I should have felt a sense of foreboding then. He asked me if I could come over to his place for a chat. Said he'd be in all day.

I tried calling him back, but it went straight to voicemail. The last thing I felt like doing was going over to Paul's, but I was feeling guilty that I hadn't called to see why he hadn't been at the 277s lately. Geoff was over at Gavin's, watching the little ones, so I went on my own.

When I got there, I rang the bell, but there was no answer. I tried again, and then I realised that the front door was slightly open. I knew something was wrong, but I went inside anyway.

I found her in the kitchen. She was lying sprawled, face up, next to the fridge. There was red everywhere. Spattered on the walls, on the fridge and the other white goods. I didn't want to believe it was blood at first. But the smell. They don't tell you that on the shows, the crime shows. How bad blood can smell. I knew straight away that she was dead. It was hot outside and already a few big bluebottles were buzzing around her, crawling on her face and that. The places where . . . oh Lord . . . the places where he'd cut into her . . . deep gashes, right to the bone in places. A pool of blood was spreading out beneath her. Her eyes were open, staring up, and they were full of blood, too.

I was sick. Just straight away. All down my front. I started praying and my legs felt like they were weighed down with cement blocks. I assumed that a lunatic must have broken in and attacked her. I pulled out my phone, called 999. I still can't believe I managed to make myself understood.

I'd just hung up when I heard a thump coming from upstairs. It wasn't me who made my body move. I know that doesn't make sense. It was like I was being pushed forward. For all I knew, whoever had attacked Jess could still be in the house.

I walked up those stairs like I was some kind of robot, stubbed my toe on the top step, but hardly felt it.

He was lying on the bed, white as a sheet. Empty booze bottles scattered all over the carpet.

I thought he was dead at first. Then he groaned, making me jump, and I saw the packet of sleeping pills clutched in his hand; the empty bottle of Bells next to him.

He'd left a message on the side table, written in large angry letters. I'll never be able to get those words out of my head: 'I had to do it. It is the ONLY WAY. I had to cut the chip out of her so that she would be FREE.'

I didn't pass out, but the time until the police arrived is a blank. That neighbour, the snobbish one, she took me straight inside her house. You could tell she was also beside herself with shock. She was kind to me that day. Made a cup of tea, helped me get cleaned up, called Geoff for me.

They said that it must have taken a long time for Jessie to bleed out on that floor. It goes through your head, all the time. If only I'd visited Paul earlier. If only, if only, if only.

And now . . . it's not anger I feel towards Paul, but pity. Father Jeremy says that forgiveness is the only way forward. But I can't help thinking that it might have been better if he'd died. Locked up like that, in one of those places, what sort of future is he going to face?

The following article, written by journalist Daniel Mimura, was published in the *Tokyo Herald Online* on 7 July 2012

Western Tourists targeted by Orz Movement

Yesterday afternoon, a tour bus packed full of American tourists was pelted with buckets of red paint and eggs when it pulled into the parking lot of the Meiji Shrine in Shibuya. The perpetrators fled before police arrived, but were heard shouting, 'This is for Orz,' as they left the scene. No one was injured in the attack, although several of the elderly tourists were reportedly deeply shaken.

There are also unconfirmed reports of several American language students being harassed in an electronics store yesterday evening in Akihabara and another unconfirmed verbal assault on a British tourist in Inokashira Park.

It is believed that these incidents were perpetrated by the Orz Movement, a group protesting the murder of Hiro Yanagida, which is responsible for defacing several Western outlets and religious institutions with graffiti. On 24 June, two days after the murder of Hiro Yanagida, cleaning staff arrived at the Tokyo Union Church in Ometsando, located next to the iconic Louis Vuitton store, to discover a painting of a blood-soaked handbag daubed next to the entrance. That evening, a stencil of a man spewing vomit appeared on the walls of Toyko's two Wendy's outlets and a McDonald's in Shinjuku, causing both disgust and hilarity. A week later, a masked man was caught on CCTV defacing the sign outside the American Embassy.

The tag signature ORZ is left at every scene. ORZ – an emoticon or emoji – which resembles a figure bashing its head on the ground, signifies depression or despair and was popularised on chat-forums such as 2-channel.

So far, police have been frustrated in their efforts to curb the increasingly radical behaviour, and with copycat ORZ stencils beginning to pop up in cities all over Japan – including as far away as Osaka – all indications are that it spreading fast.

A spokesperson from the Japanese National Tourism Organisation has stressed that Japan is not a nation known for 'violent protests', and that it should not be judged on the actions of a 'misguided minority'.

The Orz Movement has now attracted a vocal and high-profile supporter. Aikao Uri, the head of the rapidly growing and controversial Cult of Hiro, issued the following statement: 'Hiro's unforgivable murder, and the fact that the US government is unconcerned about bringing those behind it to justice, is a clear sign that we need to break ties immediately. Japan is not a child who needs its American nanny watching over it. I applaud what the Orz Movement is doing. It is a shame that our government is too afraid to follow their example.' Unlike many hardline Nationalists, Aikao Uri has called for ties to be strengthened with Korea and the People's Republic of China, going so far as to insist that reparations be made for Japanese World War II war crimes against these nations. She is at the forefront of the campaign for the historic Treaty of Mutual Cooperation and Security between the United States and Japan to be overthrown, and all US troops based on Okinawa Island to be removed. She is married to politician Masamara Uri, who is widely tipped to be the next prime minister.

The following article was published in the *Tokyo Herald* on 28 July 2012.

'Orz Man's' Remains Found in Jukei

Every year, volunteers from the Yamanashi Prefecture police and the Fujisan Rangers undertake a thorough sweep of the notorious Aokigahara forest, searching for the bodies of those who have chosen to end their lives in this 'sea of trees'. This year, over forty bodies were discovered, including the remains of a man who police suspect could be Ryu Takami (22), who achieved notoriety after his story of heartbreak captured the imagination of the 2-chan message board. Takami, who used the avatar Orz Man, was believed to be in a relationship with Chiyoko Kamamoto (18), the cousin of Sun Air Flight 678 survivor, Hiro Yanagida. Chiyoko and Ryu disappeared on 22 June 2012, the same day that Hiro and Chiyoko's parents were shot to death by Private Jake Wallace, an American soldier based at Camp Courtney on Okinawa Island. Private Wallace shot himself at the scene. Shoes, mobile phone and wallet belonging to Chiyoko Kamamoto were found next to the decomposed body. Chiyoko Kamamoto is also believed to have ended her life in the forest, although her body has not yet been discovered.

In a strange twist of fate, the remains were discovered by Yomijuri Miyajima (68), the volunteer suicide monitor who rescued Hiro Yanagida from the scene of the crash on 12 January

2012. Miyajima, who says he was devastated when he heard about Hiro's untimely death, came across the partially decomposed body during a search of the area near to the ice cave.

Takami's disappearance sparked off the ongoing and increasingly violent anti-US protests spear-headed by the Orz Movement and the Cult of Hiro, and authorities are worried that the discovery of his remains could inflame an already volatile situation.

Journalist Vuyo Molefe attended the press conference called by the South African branch of the Rationalist League on 30 July 2012 in Johannesburg. Follow him at @VMtruthhurts.

Vuyo Molefe @VMtruthhurts
Credentials checked again at joburg convention centre entrance. 3rd time now. #chilloutwerenotterrorists

Vuyo Molefe @VMtruthhurts
Lots of speculation going on. Rumours flying that Veronica Oduah is going to pitch.

Vuyo Molefe @VMtruthhurts
@melanichampa Don't know. Been here for an hour. If yr coming bring coffee and doughnuts plis sisi

Vuyo Molefe @VMtruthhurts
FINALLY. SA Rational League spokesperson Kelly Engels appears. Goes on about upcoming US election

Vuyo Molefe @VMtruthhurts
KE: worried bout growing int. support for religious right – could have global implications

Vuyo Molefe @VMtruthhurts
Rumours on point. Veronica Oduah is here! Looks older than 57. Has to be helped to front of room

Vuyo Molefe @VMtruthhurts
VO v nervous. Voice wobbles. Says shes here to come clean. Room gasps. Only one meaning to this

Vuyo Molefe @VMtruthhurts
VO: 'he is not my nephew. They've been keeping him a safehouse
away from me for weeks. I told them that when i 1st saw him.'

Vuyo Molefe @VMtruthhurts
VO: 'They offered me money to keep quiet but i did not want
to take it.' Says K's dad's cousin did take cash tho

Vuyo Molefe @VMtruthhurts
BBC journo: 'who offered money?' VO: 'The Americans. I don't
know their names.'

Vuyo Molefe @VMtruthhurts
Room seriously buzzing. Kelly Engels: 'also have proof from
Jozi lab whistleblower that Ken's mitrochondrial DNA not a
match.'

Vuyo Molefe @VMtruthhurts
Whistleblower also bribed to keep quiet. Says SA g'ment and
religious right faction in cahoots
#surprisesurprisecorruptionagain

Vuyo Molefe @VMtruthhurts
And another surprise guest! Zimbo journo next to me says this
is better than Transport Minister Mzobe's corruption trial.

Vuyo Molefe @VMtruthhurts
New person woman from eastern cape – Lucy Inkatha. Says
'Kenneth' is her grandson Mandla

Vuyo Molefe @VMtruthhurts
LI: 'Mandla ran away from home to find father in cape town.
8-yrs-old has severe learning difficulties'

Vuyo Molefe @VMtruthhurts
Kelly Engels: 'we're all working to get Mandla home asap.'

Vuyo Molefe @VMtruthhurts
Veronica Oduah: 'It is hard, but I have to accept that Kenneth is dead.' Some reporters getting upset.

Vuyo Molefe @VMtruthhurts
KE: 'Now that the truth is out there, people will see exactly how self-serving politicians can be.'

Vuyo Molefe @VMtruthhurts
KE: 'Would like to thank everyone who has been brave enough to come forward and speak up for the truth.'

Vuyo Molefe @VMtruthhurts
RT @kellytankgrl FINALLY some sanity in this mess #dontletthebastardswin

Vuyo Molefe @VMtruthhurts
RT@brodiemermaid Rel.R PR team gonna need another miracle to get out of this #dontletthebastardswin

Vuyo Molefe @VMtruthhurts
Place now in uproar. Waitin for reaction from end timers. Could this influence their majority? #dontletthebastardswin

EDITOR'S NOTE:
AFTERWORD TO THE SPECIAL ANNIVERSARY EDITION

When Elspeth Martins' agent first sent me the proposal for *From Crash to Conspiracy* in early 2012, I was immediately intrigued. I had read and admired Elspeth's first book *Snapped*, and I knew that if anyone could come up with a fresh perspective on the events surrounding Black Thursday and The Three, it was Elspeth. As the book started taking shape, it was clear we had something very special on our hands. We decided to rush it into production, choosing to publish in early October before the landmark 2012 election.

Within a week it went into a second, then a third printing. To date, despite the worldwide recession and a massive drop in book sales overall, more than 15 million print and digital editions have been sold. And no one – least of all Elspeth herself – could have foreseen the furore the book would cause.

So why an anniversary edition? Why republish the book that the Rationalist League has dubbed 'inflammatory and dangerous' in these deeply troubled times?

Apart from the most obvious reason – that the book itself has cultural and historical significance as it undoubtedly influenced the 2012 US presidential election – we were granted the rights to some exciting new material that forms the appendix to this edition. Many readers will be aware that on the second anniversary of Black Thursday, Elspeth Martins disappeared. The facts are these: after travelling to Japan, Elspeth left her hotel in Roppongi, Tokyo on the morning of 12 January 2014. We can only speculate what transpired afterwards, as later attempts to trace her last movements have been hampered by the escalating tension in the area.

It does not appear that her credit cards or phone were used after this date, although a self-published book, *Untold Stories from Black Thursday and Beyond*, by 'E. Martins', appeared on Amazon in October 2014. Speculation is rife as to whether the author is actually Elspeth herself or an impostor eager to cash in on *FCTC*'s notoriety.

For this anniversary edition, we have permission from Elspeth's former partner, Samantha Himmelman, to publish her last known correspondence, which is included below.

Elspeth, if you are reading this, please get in touch.

Jared Arthur
Editorial Director
Jameson & White
New York
(January 2015)

TO: **<Samantha Himmelman> samh56@ajbrooksideagency. com**
FROM: **<Elspeth Martins>elliemartini@fctc.com**
SUBJECT: **Please read**
12 January 2014, 7.14 a.m.

Sam,
    I know you asked me not to contact you again, but it seems fitting to send this to you on the second anniversary of Black Thursday, especially as tomorrow I'm going to the Aokigahara Forest. Daniel – my contact in Tokyo – is desperately trying to dissuade me, but I've come this far, may as well go all the way. I don't want to sound melodramatic, but people do have a habit of going into that forest and not coming out again, don't they? Don't worry – this isn't a suicide note. Not sure what it is. Guess I thought I deserved a chance to make things right, and someone needs to know why I'm here.

No doubt you think I'm crazy travelling to Japan right now, specially with the spectre of the tri-Asian alliance on the horizon, but the situation here isn't as dire as you might have heard. I didn't pick up any hostility from the customs officials or from the people milling around the airport Arrivals area; if anything, they were indifferent. That said, my hotel in the 'Westerners' Sector', which used to be a mega-star Hyatt – gargantuan marble lobby, designer staircases – has seriously gone to seed. According to a Danish guy I spoke to in the immigration queue, the hotels assigned to Westerners are now being run by Brazilian immigrants on limited visas and minimum wage – i.e., zero initiative to give a crap about standards. Only one of the elevators is working, several of the light bulbs in the corridors are dead (I was seriously spooked walking to my room) and I don't think anyone's bothered to vacuum the carpets for months. My room stinks of stale cigarette smoke and there's black mould on the shower tiles. On the upside, the toilet – a sci-fi style thing with a heated seat – works like a dream (thank you, Japanese engineering).

Anyway – I'm not writing to you to whine about my hotel room – see attached. I can't make you read it, for all I know you'll scan the subject line and delete it. I know you won't believe me, but despite all the cut n pasted stuff and transcripts in it (you know me, old habits die hard), I swear I'm not planning on using the content in another book – or at least I'm not now. I'm done with all that.

xx

Letter to Sam

11 January. 6 p.m. Roppongi Hills, Tokyo
Sam – I have so much to tell you, I'm not sure where to start.
But seeing as there's no way I'm getting any sleep tonight, I
guess I'll take it from the top, see how far I get before I flag.

Look, I know you think I 'ran away' to London last year to
escape the flak I was getting after the book was published, and
that was part of it, sure. The Haters and Rationalists still send
emails accusing me of being solely responsible for putting a
Dominionist in the White House, and no doubt you still think
I'm getting everything I deserve. Don't worry – I'm not going to
try to defend myself or trot out my tired justification that there
was nothing in *From Crash to Conspiracy* (or, as you insisted on
calling it, *From Crap to Conservatism*) that wasn't a matter of
public record. Just so you know, I still feel guilty for not showing
you the final manuscript; the fact that it was rushed into
production as soon as I'd signed off on the final interviews with
Kendra Vorhees and Geoffrey and Mel Moran is no excuse.

Incidentally, in August there was a new flurry of one-star
reviews on Amazon. You should check them out – I know how
much of a kick you get out of them. This one caught my eye,
probably because it's unusually restrained and grammatically
correct:

Customer Review

1.0 out of 5 stars Who does Elspeth Martins think she is???
22 August 2013
By zizekstears (London, UK) – See all my reviews

This review is from: From Crash to Conspiracy (Kindle Edition)

I'd heard about the controversy that this so-called 'non-fiction' book caused last year but assumed it was exaggerated. Apparently the Religious Right quoted parts of it in their campaign during the run-up to the election as 'proof' that The Three were not just normal children suffering from PTSD.

I am not surprised the US Rationalist League came down so hard on the author. Ms Martins has framed and edited each interview or extract in a deliberately manipulative and sensationalist manner ('eye-bleeding' ?????? and that awful mawkish stuff about the old man with dementia). She shows no respect for the families of the children or the passengers who died so tragically on Black Thursday.

IMHO Ms Martins is nothing but a lame Studs Terkel wannabe. She should be ashamed for publishing such trash. I will not be buying any more of her work.

Ouch.

But the backlash from the book wasn't the only reason I left. I made the actual decision to get the hell out of the States on the day of the Sannah County Massacre – two days after you'd kicked me out and told me never to contact you again. I first saw those aerial shots of the ranch – the bodies strewn everywhere, black with flies, the gore in the dust – in the anonymity of a Comfort Inn, which seemed as good a place as any to hole up and lick my wounds. I'd been working my way through the bar fridge miniatures and channel surfing when the news broke. I was drunk, couldn't quite make sense of what I was seeing on CNN at first. I actually threw up when I read the strap line: 'Mass suicide in Sannah County. Thirty-three dead, including five children.'

I sat frozen for hours, watching as reporters jostled for position outside the compound gate, spouting variations on the theme: 'Out on bail while he awaited trial for incitement to induce violence, Pastor Len Vorhees and his followers turned their stockpiled weapons on themselves . . .' Did you see the interview with Reba, Pamela May Donald's frenemy? As you know, we'd never met in person, and from her voice, I'd always pictured her as overweight and permed (felt a weird disconnect when I realised she was actually skinny with a grey braid snaking over her shoulder). Reba had been a nightmare to interview – always off on a tangent about the 'Islamofascists' and her prepping activities – but I felt sorry for her then. Like most of Pastor Len's ex Inner Circle, she was of the opinion that Pastor Len and his Pamelists thought that by following in Jim Donald's footsteps they'd be martyred: 'I pray for their souls every day.' You could see in her eyes that she'd be haunted by their deaths for the rest of her life.

This isn't fun to admit, but empathy for Reba aside, it didn't take me long to start fretting about the consequences the Sannah County Massacre would have on me personally. I knew that the Pamelists' mass suicide would result in another wave of requests for comments and begging letters from hacks pleading with me to put them in touch with Kendra Vorhees. It was never going to be over. I guess what finally tipped me over the edge was Reynard's address to the nation, his movie-star features carefully arranged for optimum piety: 'Suicide is a sin, but we must pray for those who have fallen. Let us use this as a sign that we must work together, grieve together, strive together for a moral America.'

There was nothing keeping me in the US any more. Reynard, Lund, the End Timers, and the corporate fuckers who'd backed them could have it. Sam, do you blame me? Our relationship was shattered, our friends were pissed at me (either for publishing *FCTC* in the first place, or for wallowing in self-pity after I was called out for it) and my career had imploded. I thought about the summers I spent staying with Dad in London. Decided that England was as good a place as any.

But Sam, you have to believe me – I'd convinced myself that Reynard's wet dream of a nation governed by biblical law was just that: a dream. Sure, I knew that Reynard and Lund's Make America Moral campaign would unite the disparate fundamentalist factions, but I swear I underestimated how quickly the movement would spread (guess that was partly down to the Gansu Province Earthquake – another SIGN of God's wrath). If I'd known that Reynard's fear-mongering would infect the purple as well as the red states, and how bad it would get, I wouldn't have left without you.

Enough excuses.

So.

I exchanged my Lower East Side hotel room for a flat in Notting Hill. The neighbourhood reminded me of Brooklyn Heights: a mix of brisk professionals with shiny hair, rich hipsters, and the occasional bum rooting through the trash. But I'd given no thought to what I'd actually *do* in London. Writing a sequel to *FCTC* was out, of course. I still can't believe I'm the same woman who was so fired up about writing *Untold Stories from Black Thursday*. Interviews with the crash victims' families (Captain Seto's wife, and Kelvin from 277 Together, for

example); profiles on the Malawian refugees still searching for
their missing relatives in Khayelitsha; an exposé on the new wave
of fake 'Kenneths' who popped up after the Mandla Inkatha
debacle.

I moped around for the first few weeks, living on a diet of
Stoli and take-out Thai. Barely spoke to anyone except the
cashier in the off-licence and the To Thai For delivery guy. Did
my best to turn into a hikikomori like Ryu. And whenever I did
venture out I tried to disguise my accent. The Brits were still
incredulous that Reynard could have won the election after the
Kenneth Oduah scandal – and the last thing I wanted was to be
dragged into political discussions about the 'failure of
democracy'. I guess the Brits thought we'd learned our lesson
after Blake's tenure. I guess we all did.

I tried to avoid the news, but I caught a clip about the anti-
Biblical Law protests in Austin on my Mindspark feed. Jesus,
that scared me. Scores of arrests. Tear gas. Riot police. I knew
from stalking you on Twitter (I'm not proud of this, okay?) that
you'd gone to Texas with Sisters Together Against Conservatism
to join up with the Rationalist League's contingent, and I didn't
sleep for two days. In the end I called Kayla – I needed to know
you were safe. Did she ever tell you that?

Anyway, I'll spare you more details about my self-inflicted London
isolation and get down to what you would call 'the juicy bits'.

A few weeks after the Austin riots, I was en route to
Sainsbury's when the headline on a *Daily Mail* placard caught
my eye: 'Murder House Memorial Plans.' According to the story,
a council employee was pushing for Stephen and Shelly
Craddock's house – the place where Paul had stabbed Jess to
death – to be turned into another Black Thursday memorial.
When I flew to the UK to meet with my British publishers and
interview Marilyn Adams, I'd avoided visiting it. Didn't want
that picture in my head. But the day after that story came out, I
found myself waiting on a freezing platform for a delayed train
bound for Chislehurst. I told myself it was my last chance to see
it before it got the National Trust treatment. But it wasn't just

that. Remember when Mel Moran said she couldn't stop herself from going upstairs to Paul's bedroom, even though she knew it was a bad idea? That's how I felt – as if I *had* to go. (Sounds hokey and Paulo Coehlo-esque, I know – but it's the truth.)

It lurked in a street full of pristine mini-mansions, its windows boarded up; the walls smeared with blood-red paint and graffiti ('beware the DEVIL lives here'). The driveway was choked with weeds and a 'for sale' sign leaned mournfully next to the garage. Most disturbing of all was the mini-shrine of mildewed soft toys piled outside the front door. I spotted several My Little Ponies – some still in their packaging – littered on the steps.

I was thinking about climbing over the locked garden gate to check out the backyard, when I heard a voice shouting: 'Oy!'

I turned to see a stout woman with stern grey hair striding up the driveway towards me, dragging a small elderly dog on a lead. 'You are trespassing, young woman! This is private property.'

I recognised her immediately from the photographs taken at Jess's funeral. She hadn't changed a bit. 'Mrs Ellington-Burn?'

She hesitated, then straightened her shoulders. Despite the military stance, there was something melancholy about her. A general who'd been decommissioned before her time. 'Who wants to know? Are you another journalist? Can't you people stay away?'

'I'm not a journalist. Not any more, at any rate.'

'You're American.'

'I am.' I walked up to her and the small dog collapsed at my feet. I scratched its ears and it looked up at me through smoky, cataracted eyes. It resembled Snookie (both in appearance and smell), which made me think of Kendra Vorhees (the last time I heard from her – just after the Sannah County Massacre – she said she'd changed her name and was planning to move to Colorado to join a vegan commune).

Mrs Ellington-Burn's eyes narrowed. 'Wait . . . Don't I know you?'

I cursed the giant photo the marketing people had slapped on the back of *FCTC*. 'I don't think so.'

'Yes I do. You wrote that book. That ghoulish book. What do you want here?'

'I was just curious to see the house.'

'Prurience, is it? You should be ashamed of yourself.'

I couldn't stop myself from asking: 'Do you still see Paul?'

'What if I do? What's it to you? Now leave, before I call the police.'

A year ago I would've waited until she'd returned to her house and poked around a bit more, but instead, I got out of there.

A week later the phone rang, which was something of an event – the only people who had my new number were my soon-to-be-ex-agent Madeleine and the spammers. I was completely thrown when the guy on the other end of the line introduced himself as Paul Craddock (I later discovered that Madeleine's new PA had been taken by his British accent and given him my number). He said that Mrs E-B had mentioned I was in London, and told me matter-of-factly that in a rather controversial move, one of his consultant psychiatrists had encouraged him to read *FCTC*, in order to help him 'come to terms with what he'd done'. And Sam, this man – who let's not forget had stabbed his niece to death – sounded completely sane: coherent and even witty. He brought me up to speed on Mel and Geoff Moran (who'd moved to Portugal to be closer to their daughter Danielle's resting place) and Mandi Solomon, his ghost writer, who'd joined a splinter End Times sect in the Cotswolds.

He asked me to apply for a visitation order, so that 'we could have a little chat face to face'.

I agreed to visit him. Of course I did. I may have been in the midst of a self-pitying, depressive funk, I may have moved to London to get away from the fallout of the goddamned book, but how could I pass up that opportunity? Do I need to explain why I jumped at the chance, Sam? You know me better than that.

That night I listened to his voice recordings again (I'll admit I got spooked – had to leave the bedroom light on). I replayed Jess saying, 'Hello, Uncle Paul,' over and over again, trying to detect something other than playfulness in her tone. I couldn't.

According to Google Images, Kent House – the high security psychiatric facility where Paul was incarcerated – was a dour, grey-stone monolith. I couldn't help but think that insane asylums (okay, I know this isn't the PC term) shouldn't be allowed to look so stereotypical and Dickensian.

I had to sign a waiver saying that I wouldn't publish the details about my meeting with Paul, and my police clearance and visitation order came through on the last day of October – Halloween. Coincidentally the same day that Reddit first aired the rumour that Reynard was planning to repeal the First Amendment. I was still avoiding Sky and CNN, but I couldn't avoid the newspaper billboards. I remember thinking, how could it be unravelling so fast? But even then, I didn't allow myself to believe that Reynard would manage to secure Congress and the two thirds majority he'd need. I assumed we'd just have to ride out his presidency, deal with the fallout after the next election. Stupid, I know. By then the Catholic church and the Mormons had pledged their support to the Make America Moral campaign – even a moron could have seen where it was heading.

I decided to shell out for a taxi rather than play Russian Roulette with the train service, and I was right on time for my meeting with Paul. Kent House was as forbidding in real life as it looked on Google Images. A recent addition – a brick and glass carbuncle tacked onto the building's exterior – somehow made the whole place look more intimidating. After being searched and scanned by a couple of incongruously cheerful security staff, I was escorted to the carbuncle by a jovial male nurse with skin as grey as his hair. I'd been picturing meeting Paul in a stark cell, bars on the doors, a couple of grim-faced jailors and several psychiatrists watching our every move. Instead, I was buzzed through a glass door and into a large airy room furnished with chairs so brightly coloured they looked insane. The nurse told me that there would be no other visitors that day – apparently the bus service to the institution had been cancelled that afternoon. That wasn't unusual. The UK wasn't immune to the recession caused by Reynard's meddling in the Middle East. But

I have to say, there was an admirable lack of grumbling when the electricity and fuel rationing was proposed; maybe the end of the world is Prozac for the Brits.

[Sam – I couldn't record our conversation as I'd had to leave my iPhone at security, so this is all from memory. I know you don't care about these sorts of details, but I do.]

The door on the opposite side of the room clicked open and a morbidly obese man dressed in a tent-sized T-shirt and carrying a Tesco's bag waddled in. The nurse called out, 'All right, Paul? Your visitor's here.'

I immediately assumed there must have been a mix-up. 'That's Paul? Paul Craddock?'

'Hello, Miss Martins,' Paul said in the voice I recognised from the recordings. 'It's a pleasure to meet you.'

I'd checked out the YouTube clips of Paul's acting roles just before I left, and I searched in vain for any sign of his conventionally handsome features in the sagging jowls and doughy cheeks. Only the eyes were the same. 'Please, call me Elspeth.'

'Elspeth, then.' We shook hands. His palm was clammy and I resisted the urge to wipe mine on my trousers.

The nurse clapped Paul on the shoulder and nodded to a glass-fronted cubicle a few yards from our table. 'I'll be over there, Paul.'

'Cheers, Duncan.' Paul's chair squeaked as he sat down. 'Ah! Before I forget.' He rummaged in the plastic bag and pulled out a copy of *FCTC* and a red sharpie pen. 'Will you sign it?'

Sam – it was going from the bizarre to the surreal. 'Um . . . sure. What do you want me to put?'

'To Paul. I couldn't have done it without you.' I flinched, and he laughed. 'Don't mind me. Put what you like.'

I scribbled, 'Best Wishes, Elspeth,' and pushed the book back across the table to him. 'Please excuse my appearance,' he said. 'I'm turning into a pudding. There's not much to do in here except eat. Are you shocked that I've let myself go like this?'

I murmured something about a few extra pounds not being the end of the world. My nerves were on edge. Paul certainly didn't look or act like a raving lunatic – (not entirely sure what I'd been expecting, maybe some kind of strait-jacketed madman with rolling eyes) – but if he suddenly lost it, lunged across the table and tried to throttle me, there was only one weedy nurse to stop him.

Paul read my mind: 'Are you surprised at the lack of supervision? Staff cut-backs. But don't worry, Duncan's a black belt in karate. Aren't you, Duncan?' Paul waved at the nurse who chuckled and shook his head. 'What are you doing in London, Elspeth? Your agent said you'd moved here. Did you leave the States because of the unfortunate political climate?'

I said that that was one of the reasons.

'I can't say I blame you. If that prick in the White House gets his way, soon you'll all be Living with Leviticus. Where the gays and naughty children are stoned to death and the acned and menstrual are shunned. Lovely. Almost makes me grateful to be in here.'

'Why did you want to see me, Paul?'

'Like I said on the phone, I heard you were in England. I thought it would be nice to meet face to face. Dr Atkinson was in agreement that it might do me good to meet one of my biographers.' He belched behind his hand. 'He's the one who gave me your book to read. And it's lovely to see a fresh face in here. Mrs E-B comes once a month, but she can get a bit much. Not that I'm short of requests for visitation.' He glanced at the nurse in the booth. 'Sometimes I get as many as fifty a week – mostly from the conspiracy nuts, of course, but I've had a fair few marriage proposals. Not as many as Jurgen has, but close.'

'Jurgen?'

'Oh! You must have heard of Jurgen Williams. He's in here too. He murdered five school children, but you'd never know it to look at him. He's actually rather dull.' I had no clue how to respond to that. 'Elspeth, when you put my story in the book . . . Did you listen to the original recordings, or just read the transcripts?'

'Both.'

'And?'

'They scared me.'

'Psychosis isn't pretty. You must have lots of questions for me. You can ask me anything.'

I took him at his word. 'Please let me know if I'm crossing the line here . . . but what happened in the last few days before Jess died? Did she say anything to you that made you . . . made you . . .'

'Stab her to death? You can say it. Those are the facts. But no. She didn't. What I did was unforgivable. She was put in my care, and I killed her.'

'In your recordings . . . you said she taunted you.'

'Paranoid delusions.' He frowned. 'All in my head. There was nothing strange about Jess. It was all me. Dr Atkinson has made that very clear.' He glanced at the nurse again. 'I had a psychotic break, brought on by alcohol abuse and stress. End of. You can put that in your next book. May I ask you a favour, Elspeth?'

'Of course.'

He rummaged in the plastic packet again, this time extracting a slim exercise pad. He handed it to me. 'I've been doing some writing. It's not much . . . some poetry. Would you mind reading it and letting me know what you think? Maybe your publishers would be interested.'

I decided not to mention that I didn't have a publisher any more, although I suspected they would jump at the opportunity to publish poetry written by a notorious child murderer. Instead I said I'd be happy to and shook his hand again.

'Make sure you read all of it.'

'I will.'

I watched him waddling away, and the grey-skinned nurse escorted me back to the security entrance. I started reading the book on the taxi ride home. The first three pages were filled with short, appalling verse with titles like: *Cavendish Dreams* (Reading a line/For the twentieth time/Makes me reflect/We are all actors) and *Flesh Prison* (I eat to forget/Yet it makes my soul sweat/I think . . . will I yet/Ever say no?).

The other pages were blank, but on the inside of the cardboard back cover were the words:

Jess wanted me to do it. She MADE ME do it. Before she went she said that they've been before and sometimes she decides not to die. She said that sometimes they give people what they want, sometimes they don't. Ask the others, THEY KNOW.

Sam, what would you have done with this? Knowing you, you would have contacted Paul's psychiatrist immediately, let him know that Paul was still in the midst of some sort of psychotic break.

That would have been the right thing to do.

But I'm not you.

After *FCTC* came out, I thought maybe I was the only person in the world who didn't think there was something supernatural (for want of a better word) about The Three. I've lost count of the number of whack-jobs who pleaded with me to puff their self-published books on how The Three were still alive and living with a Maori woman in New Zealand/being experimented on in a secret Cape Town military base/hanging out with aliens in Dulce Air Force Base New Mexico (I have proof, miss martins!!!! Why else is the world still going to hell!!!!!). And then there are the countless conspiracy sites that use quotes or extracts from *FCTC* to 'prove' their theories that The Three were possessed by aliens or were multi-dimensional time-travellers. (The following are the ones they tend to fixate on:)

BOBBY: 'One day *I'll* bring [the dinosaurs] back to life.'

JESS: 'It doesn't work like that. A fucking wardrobe. As if, Uncle Paul.'
'It was a mistake. Sometimes we get it wrong.'

CHIYOKO: [Hiro] says he remembers being hoisted up into the rescue helicopter. He said it was fun. 'Like flying.' He said he was looking forward to doing it again.

There are even several websites dedicated to discussing the implications of Jess's obsession with *The Lion, the Witch and the Wardrobe*.

But the rest of us have to admit that there's a rational explanation for all of it: the kids survived the crashes because they got lucky; Paul Craddock's version of events re Jess's behaviour was just the ramblings of a lunatic; Reuben Small could easily have been in remission; and Hiro was simply aping his father's obsession with androids. The kids' changes in behaviour could all have been a result of the trauma they'd suffered. And let's not forget the hours of material I chose *not* to include in the book – Paul Craddock's lengthy complaints about not getting laid; the minutiae of Lillian Small's daily life – where absolutely nothing happened. That Amazon reviewer was spot on when he accused me of being manipulative and sensationalist.

But . . . but . . . '*She said that they've been before and sometimes she decides not to die. She said that sometimes they give people what they want, sometimes they don't.*'

I had a number of options. I could visit Paul again, ask him why he'd chosen to give me this information; I could ignore it as the ramblings of someone who was mentally ill; or I could throw rationality out of the window and look into what the words could possibly mean. I tried the first option, but I was told that Paul wasn't interested in having any further contact with me (no doubt because he was concerned I might reveal what he'd given me to his psychiatrist). The second option was tempting, but presumably Paul had passed this onto me for a reason: *Ask the others, THEY KNOW.* I guess I thought that looking into it wouldn't hurt – what else did I have to do with my time apart from delete abusive emails and wander around Notting Hill in a vodka-fuelled haze?

So I threw reason out of the window and decided to play devil's advocate. Say that Paul was repeating something Jess had told him just before he'd killed her, what *did* it mean? The conspiracy nuts would have a trillion theories about *they've been before and sometimes she decides not to die*, but I wasn't about to

contact any of them. And what about: *sometimes they give people
what they want, sometimes they don't.* After all, The Three *had*
given people – or at least the End Timers – what they wanted:
apparent 'proof' that the end of the world was nigh. Then again,
Jess had given Paul what he thought he wanted – fame; Hiro
gave Chiyoko a reason to live, and Bobby . . . Bobby had given
Lillian her husband back.

I decided it was time to break a promise.

Sam, I know it used to drive you crazy when I kept things
from you (like the entire first draft of *FCTC*, for example), but
I gave Lillian Small my word that I wouldn't reveal that she'd
survived the car crash that killed Reuben and Bobby. Out of all
the people I'd interviewed for the book, her story affected me
the most – and I'd been touched that she trusted me enough to
contact me when she was in hospital. The FBI had offered to
relocate her, and we decided after that it would be best to
break contact – she didn't need any further reminders of what
she'd lost.

I doubted the FBI would simply pass on her phone number,
so I decided to give Betsy – her neighbour – a shot.

The phone was answered with a '*Ja?*'

'I'm looking for Mrs Katz?'

'She no live here no more.' (I couldn't place the accent – it
might have been Eastern European.)

'Do you have a forwarding address? It's really important.'

'Wait.'

I heard the thunk of the handset being dropped; the thump of
bass in the background. Then: 'I have a number.'

I Googled the area code – Toronto, Canada. Somehow I
couldn't imagine Betsy in Canada.

[Sam – the following is the transcript of the call – yeah, I
know, why would I have recorded it and transcribed it if I
wasn't planning on using it in a book or article? Please, trust
me on this – I swear you will not be seeing *Elspeth Martins'
Truth about The Three* on sale in a store near you anytime
soon:]

ME: Hi . . . is that Betsy? Betsy Katz?

BETSY: Who is this calling me?

ME: Elspeth Martins. I interviewed you for my book.

[long pause]

BETSY: Ah! The writer! Elspeth! You are well?

ME: I'm fine. How are you?

BETSY: If I complain, who will listen? What do you think about what is happening in New York? Those riots on the news and the fuel shortages. Are you safe? Are you keeping warm? You have enough food?

ME: I'm fine, thanks. I was wondering . . . do you know how I can get hold of Lillian?

[longer pause]

BETSY: You don't know? Well, of course how would you know? I'm sorry to tell you this, but Lillian has passed. A month ago, now. She went in her sleep – a good way to go. She didn't suffer.

ME: [after several seconds of silence while I fought not to lose control – Sam, I was a fucking mess] I'm so sorry.

BETSY: She was such a good woman, you know she invited me to stay with her? When the first of the blackouts hit New York. Out of nowhere she called me and said, 'Betsy, you can't live there on your own, come to Canada.' Canada! Me! I miss her, I won't lie. But there's a good community here, a nice Rabbi who takes care of me. Lily said she appreciated how you made her sound in your book – smarter than she was. But what Mona said – what poison! Lily found that hard to read. And what do you think about what is happening in Israel? That schmuck in the White House, what does he think he is doing? Does he want all the Muslims down on our heads?

ME: Betsy . . . before she passed, did Lillian mention anything . . . um . . . particular about Bobby?

BETSY: About Bobby? What would she say? Only that her life has been a tragedy. Everyone she ever loved taken away from her. God can be cruel.

I hung up. Cried for two hours straight. For once they weren't tears of self-pity.

But say that I had spoken to Lillian, what *would* she have said anyway? That the Bobby who came home after the crash wasn't her grandson? When I interviewed her all those months ago, whenever she spoke about him I could hear the love in her voice. *Ask the others, THEY KNOW.*

So who else was there? I knew Lori Small's best friend Mona was out (after the *FCTC* furore she denied ever having spoken to me), but there was someone else who'd encountered Bobby and hadn't come away unscathed.

Ace Kelso.

Sam, I can just picture your face as you read this: a mixture of exasperation and fury. You were right when you said I should have put his reputation first. You were right when you accused me of not fighting hard enough to have his admission that he saw blood in Bobby Small's eyes taken out of the later editions (another nail in the coffin of our relationship). And yeah, I should have destroyed the recording refuting Ace's claim that he'd said it off the record. Why the fuck didn't I listen to you?

The last time I'd seen him was in that soulless boardroom in the publishers' lawyers' offices, when he was told he didn't have a case. His flesh hung loose on his face, his eyes were bloodshot, he hadn't shaved in days. His threadbare jeans sagged at the knees; his tatty leather jacket stank of stale sweat. The Ace I'd interviewed for the book and seen on TV was square-jawed, blue-eyed – a real Captain America type (as Paul Craddock once described him).

I had no clue if Ace would even talk to me, but what did I have to lose? I Skyped him, fully expecting that he wouldn't answer. When he did, his voice was blurry, as if he'd just woken up.

ACE: Yeah?

ME: Ace . . . Hi. It's Elspeth Martins. Um . . . how are you?

[*a pause of several seconds*]

ACE: I'm still on extended sick leave. A euphemism for permanent suspension. What the hell do you want, Elspeth?

ME: I thought you should know . . . I've been to see Paul Craddock.

ACE: So?

ME: When I met with him, he was adamant that what he'd done to Jess was the result of a psychotic break. But as I was leaving he handed me a note. Look, this is going to sound crazy, but in it he said that – among other things – Jess told him she'd 'been here before' and 'sometimes she decides not to die'.

[*another long pause*]

ACE: Why are you telling me this?

ME: I thought . . . I dunno. I guess . . . what you said about Bobby . . . Like I say, it's crazy to even think like this, but Paul said, 'ask the others' and I—

ACE: You know something, Elspeth? I know you got a lot of criticism for what you included in that book, but far as I'm concerned you were lambasted for the wrong reasons. You published all that inflammatory stuff about the kids' personalities changing, dropped the bomb and just walked away. You didn't take it further; you assumed everything had a rational explanation and naively thought everyone who read it would also see it like that.

ME: My intention wasn't to—

ACE: I know what your intentions were. And now you're sniffing around to see if there really *was* something up with those kids, am I right?

ME: I'm just looking into things.

ACE: [a sigh] Tell you what. I'm gonna email you something.

ME: What?

ACE: Read it first, then we'll talk.

[The email came through immediately and I clicked on an attachment entitled: SA678ORG

At first glance I thought it was an exact copy of the Sun Air Cockpit Voice Recording transcript that I'd included in *FCTC*. And it was exactly the same, apart from this exchange that occurred a second before the plane ran into trouble:

Captain: [expletive] You see that?

First Officer: Hai! Lightning?

Captain: Negative. Never seen a flash like that. There's nothing on TCAS, ask ATC if there's another aircraft up here with us—]

ME: What the fuck is this?

ACE: You gotta understand, we didn't want to fuel the panic. People needed to know that the causes of those crashes were explainable. The grounded planes had to get back in the air.

ME: The NTSB faked the Sun Air transcript? You're telling me that you guys seriously believed you were dealing with an alien encounter?

ACE: What I'm telling you is that we were confronted by facts that we couldn't explain. Sun Air aside, the only disaster that had a definite cause was the Dalu Air crash.

ME: What the hell are you talking about? What about the Maiden Air disaster?

ACE: We had a multiple bird strike with no snarge. Sure, possibly explainable if the engines had been consumed by fire – but they weren't. How in the hell do two jet engines get imploded by birds – without a trace of matter? And look at the Go!Go! incident. We were grasping at straws with that one – but one thing's for sure – it's pretty damn unusual for pilots to fly into a storm of that magnitude in this day and age. And answer me this, how in the fuck did those three kids survive?

ME: Look at Zainab Farra, the little girl who survived that crash in Ethiopia. The Three were like her, they got lucky—

ACE: Bullshit. And you know it.

ME: This transcript . . . why did you send it to me? Do you actually want me to publish it?

ACE: [a bitter laugh] What's the worst that can happen now? Reynard will give me a medal – more proof that The Three weren't just normal kids. Do what you want with it. The NTSB and JTSB will deny it anyway.

ME: So you're seriously saying you think there's something . . . I don't know . . . otherworldly about The Three? You're an investigator – a scientist.

ACE: All I know is what I saw when I went to see Bobby. It wasn't an hallucination, Elspeth. And that photographer, the one who ended up being dinner for his goddamned reptiles, he saw something as well.

[*another sigh*]

Listen, you were just doing your job. I shouldn't have gone after you for publishing what I said about Bobby. Maybe I said it was off the record, maybe I didn't. But it was the truth. Fact is, you gotta be blind not to see that there was something wrong with those kids.

ME: So what do you suggest I do now?

ACE: Up to you, Elspeth. But whatever you do, I suggest you make it quick. The End Timers are hell-bent on fulfilling their own prophecies. How in the hell do you negotiate with a president who's convinced that the end of the world is nigh and that the only way to save people from eternal damnation is to turn the US into a theocracy? Simple. You can't.

Of course I struggled to believe that the NTSB would actually doctor the record – even if it was concerned about people panicking about the causes of the disasters. Could the transcript be Ace's revenge for the eye-bleeding debacle? If I made something like this public, the Rationalist League would have another reason to string me up.

But you know where this is going, right? I had Paul's note, Ace's (possibly faked) transcript, and his assurances that he really had seen blood in Bobby's eyes.

It could all be bullshit – probably was. But there was one child left.

I spent the next few days researching Chiyoko and Hiro. Most of the links led to new material on Ryu and Chiyoko's tragic love story, among them a recent article on a spate of copycat suicides, but there was surprisingly little on Hiro. I contacted Eric

Kushan, the guy who'd translated the Japanese extracts in
FCTC, to see if he could give me any leads, but he'd left Japan a
few months earlier after the Treaty of Mutual Cooperation
between the States and Japan was overturned, and all he could
suggest was that I look into the Cult of Hiro.

I thought it might have morphed into something
approximating the Moonies or Aum Shrinrikyo, but rather than
becoming a hardcore nationalist cult, it had fizzled into little
more than a bizarre celebrity trend. Now that her husband had
won the election, Aikao Uri appeared to have dumped her alien
theories and surrabot, focusing her energies on campaigning for
the tri-Asian alliance. The Orz Movement had gone completely
underground

Do you remember Daniel Mimura? He was one of the *Tokyo
Herald* journalists who'd given me permission to use a couple of
his articles for *FCTC*. He was one of the few contributors
(along with Lola – Pastor Len's 'fancy woman' – and the
documentary filmmaker Malcolm Adelstein) who'd sent me a
supportive note after the shit hit the fan. He sounded delighted
to hear from me, and we chatted for a while about how the
Japanese people were coping with the spectre of a possible
alliance with China and Korea.

I transcribed the rest of our conversation:

ME: You think Chiyoko and Ryu really did die in Aokigahara?

DANIEL: Reckon Ryu did for sure, they did an autopsy, which is
quite unusual for Tokyo – they aren't done automatically in every
suspicious death. Chiyoko's body was never found, so who
knows?

ME: You think she could be alive?

DANIEL: Possibly. You heard the rumours about Hiro? They've
been circulating for a while.

ME: You mean the usual 'The Three are still alive' bullshit?

DANIEL: Yeah. You want me to go into it?

ME: Sure.

DANIEL: This is crazy conspiricist stuff but . . . Look, to start with, the cops shut down that scene really fast. The paramedics and forensics guys were instructed not to talk to the press. Even the police agency guys couldn't get much of a story out of them, except for the official statement.

ME: Okay . . . but why would they fake his death?

DANIEL: The New Nationalists could have planned it, maybe. I mean, what better way to turn the public against the US? S'pose at a push, if you were that way inclined, you could say they set the whole thing up, staged the scene, killed the Kamamotos and that soldier, made it look like Hiro was dead.

ME: That doesn't make sense. Private Jake Wallace was a Pamelist – he had a motive to kill Hiro. How would they get him involved in a scheme like that?

DANIEL: Hey, don't shoot the messenger. I'm just telling you about the rumours. Hell, I dunno, maybe they got wind about what he was gonna do, set him up. Hacked into his emails like those other guys did.

ME: But the witnesses said that they saw Chiyoko carrying Hiro's body.

DANIEL: Yeah. But have you seen those surrabots Kenji Yanagida makes? They're eerie. Unless you're close up to them, they look seriously convincing.

ME: Hang on . . . wouldn't that mean that Chiyoko would've been in on it?

DANIEL: Yeah.

ME: So let's say what you're saying did happen. Chiyoko sat back and allowed her parents to be murdered . . . why?

DANIEL: Who knows? Money? So that she and Hiro could go off to some unknown country and live out their lives in luxury? And poor old Ryu got caught up in it and ended up another casualty.

ME: You any idea how often I've heard these kinds of theories?

DANIEL: Sure. Like I say, all bullshit.

ME: You ever looked into it?

DANIEL: Dug around a bit, nothing major. You know how these things go. If there was anything to it, someone would have leaked it by now.

ME: Didn't Kenji Yanagida identify Hiro's body?

DANIEL: So?

ME: If anyone knows the truth, it's him. Would he talk to me?

DANIEL: [a laugh] No fucking way. It's all bullshit, Ellie. The kid is dead.

ME: Is Kenji Yanagida still in Osaka?

DANIEL: Last I heard he left the university after being hounded by the Cult of Hiro – they were desperate for him to be one of their high-profile mascots. Apparently he moved to Tokyo, changed his name.

ME: Can you track him down for me?

DANIEL: You have any idea how many people have tried to talk to Kenji Yanagida and been stonewalled?

ME: But I have something they don't have.

DANIEL: What?

I didn't tell Daniel about Ace's transcript. It might be my way into speaking to Kenji Yanagida, it might not.

I know what you're thinking: that I didn't tell Daniel about it because it was my exclusive and I wanted to use it for my own ends – maybe shove it in another book. But again, I'm done with all that, Sam, I swear.

I didn't do anything for the next few weeks. The world was holding its breath after that group of renegade End Timers tried to set fire to the al-Aqsa Mosque at the Temple Mount in another effort to step up the race to the Rapture. Not even I was stupid enough to fly to Asia on what could be the cusp of World War III.

And the news we were getting in from the States was just as depressing. I may have been sticking my head in the sand, but the reports of escalating attacks on gay teenagers; the mass closure of reproductive health clinics; the Internet blackouts; the GLAAD and Rationalist League leaders being apprehended under so-called state security laws, filtered through. There were anti-US protests in the UK, too. The UK was cutting its ties with Reynard's regime, and MigrantWatch were campaigning to stem the tide of US émigrés. And I don't want you to think I wasn't worried about you. That's all I thought about over the holiday season (I'm not going to whine about spending Thanksgiving alone in my freezing flat eating take-out jalfrezi). Thought of you

when those UK celebs joined the US A-listers in their 'Save Our
Bill of Rights' campaign – it would have brought out your
cynical side. All the YouTube clips and supergroup iTunes songs
in the world weren't going to change the convictions of people
who honestly believe that by wiping out 'immorality', they'll be
saving others from burning in hell for all eternity.

But I couldn't let it go.

Remembering what Ace said about not dragging my feet, I
called Daniel in early December and told him I needed help
getting into Tokyo. He thought I was crazy, of course – his
contract had just been cancelled (he said it was happening to
Westerners all over Japan, 'their way of saying we're no longer
welcome'). Even with my British passport, thanks to new
regulations, I'd need a visa, a valid reason for travel and a Japanese
citizen willing to stand as my sponsor and representative. He
reluctantly said he'd ask one of his friends to help.

I tracked down Pascal de la Croix – Kenji's old buddy – and
begged him to ask Kenji to see me. I told him the truth – that I
had new information regarding the Sun Air crash that Kenji
needed to know. I told him I was flying into Tokyo especially to
see him. Pascal was reluctant of course, but he finally agreed to
email Kenji for me on the proviso that if I did get to see him, I
wouldn't publish anything about our meeting.

I reckon I checked my inbox about fifty times a day after
that – filtering through the hate mail and spam – for a response.

It came through on the same day as my visa. An address,
nothing more.

Sam, I'll be honest. Before I left I took a long, hard look at
myself. What the hell did I think I was doing? Didn't following
this up make me as crazy as the End Timers and the conspiracy
freaks? And let's say my batshit insane Kenji Yanagida wild-
goose chase did lead me to Hiro. Say he was still alive and I
managed to talk to him. And he told me that The Three were all
possessed by the horsemen out of Revelation, or were all psycho
aliens, or were three of the Four fucking Tops, what then? Did I
have a duty to 'let the truth be known'? And if I did, would it

make any difference? Look what happened with the Kenneth Oduah scandal. Solid proof that his DNA results were faked, but still millions bought into Dr Lund's bullshit that 'it is God's will that the fourth horseman may never be found'.

The flight was a nightmare. I got the total Pamela May Donald heebies before we even took off. Kept imagining how she must have felt in the minutes before her plane went down. I even found myself composing an *isho* in my head just in case. (I won't embarrass you with it.) It didn't help that half-an-hour into the flight, 90% of the other passengers (all Westerners, mostly Brits and Scandinavians) were already drunk. The guy next to me, some kind of IT specialist who was heading to Tokyo to help disband IBM's Roppongi branch, filled me in on what to expect when we arrived. 'See, it's not that they're openly hostile or anything like that, but it's best to stay in the "Westerners' section" – Roppongi and Roppongi hills. It's not bad, lot of pubs.' He downed his double JD and breathed bourbon fumes over me. 'And who wants to hang out with the Japs anyway? I can show you around if you like.' I declined, and thankfully he passed out shortly afterwards.

When we landed at Narita, we were funnelled to a special holding area where our passports and visas were scrutinised with forensic precision. Next, we were herded onto coaches. At first, I couldn't see any signs that Japan was heading, like the rest of the world, towards economic collapse. It was only as we cruised over the bridge that led into the heart of the city, that I realised the trademark billboards, signage, and even the Tokyo Tower were only half-illuminated.

Daniel met me at the hotel the next day, and painstakingly wrote down step-by-step directions describing how to get to Kenji's address in Kanda. As it's in the old part of the city and outside the Westerners' Approved areas he suggested that I hide my hair, wear glasses and cover my face with a surgical flu mask. It seemed a bit over-the-top, but while he assured me that he doubted I'd run into trouble, he said it was best not to draw too much attention to myself.

*

Sam, I'm exhausted, and I have a big day ahead of me. It's getting light now, but I have one last scene to relate. I haven't had time to transcribe my conversation with Kenji Yanagida – I only saw him yesterday – so you're getting it in Proper Writing.

Without Daniel's detailed directions, I would have been lost within seconds. Kanda – a labyrinth of criss-crossing streets lined with tiny restaurants, minuscule book stores and smoke-filled coffee shops packed with black-suited salarymen – was bewildering after Roppongi's comparatively soulless Western-style architecture. I followed the directions to a narrow alley teeming with overcoated people, their faces hidden behind scarves or flu masks. I paused outside a door set between a tiny shop selling plastic baskets of dried fish and one displaying several framed paintings of children's hands, and checked the kanji on the sign outside it against the lettering Daniel had written out for me. Heart in my mouth, I pressed the intercom button.

'*Hai*?' a man's voice barked.

'Kenji Yanagida?'

'Yes?'

'My name is Elspeth Martins. Pascal de la Croix put me in touch with you.'

After a beat, the door clicked open.

I stepped into a corridor that stank of mildew, and with no other option, started down a short stairway. It ended at an anonymous, half-open door. I pushed through it and into a large cluttered workshop. A small group of people were hanging around in the centre of the room. Then my brain hitched (Sam – I can't think of another way to put it) and it hit me that these weren't people after all, but surrabots.

I counted six of them – three women, two men and (horribly) a child, propped up on stands, the halogen lights bouncing off their waxy skin and too-shiny eyes. There were several more sitting on plastic chairs and frayed armchairs in a gloomy corner – one even had its legs crossed in an obscenely human pose.

Kenji stepped out from behind a worktop covered in wires, computer screens and soldering equipment. He looked a decade older and twenty kilos lighter than on his YouTube clips – the skin around his eyes was creased; his high cheekbones looked as prominent as a skull's.

Without greeting me, he said: 'What information do you have for me?'

I told him about Ace's confession and handed him a copy of the transcript. He scanned it without any change in expression, then folded it and slid it into his pocket. 'Why did you bring this to me?'

'I thought you had a right to know the truth. Your wife and son were on that plane.'

'Thank you.'

He stared at me for several seconds, and I got the impression he could see straight through me.

I gestured at the surrabots. 'What are you doing here? Are these for the Cult of Hiro?'

He grimaced. 'No. I am making replicas for people. Mostly Koreans. Replicas of the loved ones they have lost.' His eyes strayed to a pile of wax masks lying on the bench. Death masks.

'Like the one you made of Hiro?' He flinched (who can blame him? It was hardly a sensitive thing to say). 'Yanagida-san . . . your son, Hiro . . . when he was killed, was it you who identified him?'

I steeled myself for a barrage of invective. But instead he said: 'Yes.'

'I'm sorry to ask this . . . it's just there are rumours that maybe he isn't . . . maybe he . . .'

'My son is dead. I saw his body. Is that what you wanted to know?'

'And Chiyoko?'

'Is this why you came? To ask me about Hiro and Chiyoko?'

'Yes. But the transcript – that's the truth. You have my word on that.'

'Why do you want to know about Chiyoko?'

I decided to tell him the truth. I suspected he would see straight through bullshit. 'I'm following a series of leads regarding The Three. They led me to you.'

'I cannot help you. Please leave.'

'Yanagida-san, I have come a long way—'

'Why can you not leave this be?'

I could see the grief in his eyes. I'd pushed him too far, and to be honest, I was disgusted with myself. I turned to leave, but as I did, I spied a surrabot in a darkened corner, half-hidden behind the facsimile of a corpulent man. She sat in her own private area, a serene figure dressed in a white kimono. She was the only one who appeared to be breathing. 'Yanagida-san . . . is that the copy of your wife? Hiromi?'

A long pause, then: 'Yes.'

'She was beautiful.'

'Yes.'

'Yanagida-san, did she . . . did she leave a message? An *isho*, like some of the other passengers?' I couldn't stop myself. I needed to know.

'Jukei. She's there.'

For a second I thought he meant his wife. Then it clicked. 'She? You mean Chiyoko?'

'*Hai.*'

'The forest? Aokigahara?'

A minuscule nod.

'Where in the forest?'

'I don't know.'

I wasn't going to press my luck any further. 'Thank you, Yanagida-san.'

As I made my way back to the staircase, he said: 'Wait.' I turned to face him. His expression remained as unreadable as the surrabot next to him. Then he said: 'Hiromi. In her message, she said, "Hiro is gone."'

So that's it. That's all I've got. I have no idea why Kenji told me the content of his wife's *isho*. Maybe he really was grateful for the transcript; maybe, like Ace, he thinks that there's no point keeping it to himself any more.

Maybe he was lying.

I'd better send this now. The wifi here is crap – got to go down to the lobby to do it. The forest is going to be cold – it's starting to snow.

Sam – I'm aware that the chances you've actually read this are slim, but just so you know, I've decided I'm coming back home after this. Back to NYC – if the governor isn't bullshitting about holding a referendum for secession, I want to be there. I'm not going to run away any more. I hope you'll be there, Sam.

I love you,

Ellie

HOW IT ENDS

Elspeth's disguise of sunglasses and the now slightly soggy flu mask is just as effective in the suburbs as it was in the city – so far, none of her fellow passengers have spared her a second glance. But as she alights at Ōtsuki – a rickety station that looks like it's stuck in the 1950s – a uniformed man barks something at her. She feels a momentary panic, then realises he's only asking for her ticket. Stupid. She bobs her head, hands it over and he waves her towards an elderly locomotive waiting at an adjacent platform. A whistle blows and she scrambles on board, relieved that the carriage is empty. She sinks onto the bench seat and tries to relax. As the train jolts, shudders, then finds its stride, she looks through grimed windows onto snow-dusted fields, slope-roofed wooden houses and a series of small frozen allotments, barren but for a crop of ice-rotten cabbages. Icy air seeps through cracks in the train's sides; a light drift of snow brushes against the windows. She reminds herself that there are fourteen stops to Kawaguchiko – the end of the line.

She concentrates on the clack of the wheels; tries not to think too deeply about where she's headed. At the third stop, a man with a face as rumpled as his clothes climbs into her carriage, and she stiffens as he chooses the seat opposite hers. She prays that he won't try to engage her in conversation. He grunts, digs in a large shopping bag, and hauls out a packet of what look to be giant nori rolls. He stuffs one in his mouth, then offers her the bag. Deciding that it would be rude to refuse, she murmurs '*Arigato*,' and takes one. Instead of rice encased in seaweed, she bites into some sort of light crispy candy that tastes of Splenda. She takes her time eating it in case he offers her another (she's already nauseous) then drops her head as if she's taking a nap. It's only partly an act; she's exhausted after a sleepless night.

When she next looks up, she's stunned to see a giant roller-coaster filling the window, its rusting frame shaggy with icicle teeth. It must be attached to one of the now-defunct Mount Fuji resorts Daniel told her about; an incongruous dinosaur stuck in the middle of nowhere.

Last stop.

Giving her an enormous smile that makes her feel guilty for pretending to sleep, the old man departs. She hangs back, then follows him across the tracks and into the deserted station, a wooden structure clad in shiny pine that looks as if it would be more at home in an Alpine ski resort. Hurdy-gurdy music plays from somewhere, loud enough to follow her when she exits into the station forecourt. The tourist booth to her right has the aura of a mausoleum, but she spies a single taxi parked next to a bus stop, smoke pouring out of its exhaust.

She digs out the scrap of paper on which Daniel had (reluctantly) written her destination, folds it around a ten thousand yen note and approaches the car. She hands it to the driver, who shows no emotion as he glances at it. He nods, tucks the money into his jacket and stares straight ahead. The taxi's interior reeks of stale cigarette smoke and despair. How many people has this man ferried to the forest, knowing that more than likely they wouldn't be returning? The driver guns the engine before she's even managed to secure her seat belt, and whips through the deserted village. Most of the stores are boarded up; the gas station pumps are padlocked. They pass a single vehicle – an empty school bus.

Within minutes they're skirting a wide glassy lake, and Elspeth has to cling to the door handle as the driver throws the car around the narrow road's curves; clearly he's as keen to be done with the journey as she is. She takes in the sagging skeleton of a large shrine, a forest of neglected grave markers in front of it; a row of rotting kayaks and the burned limbs of several holiday shacks peeking gamely through the snow. Mount Fuji looms in the background, mist cloaking its top.

They leave the lake behind, and the driver swings onto a deserted highway before turning sharply and speeding down a narrower road, lumped with snow and slick with ice. The forest creeps up around them. She knows it has to be Aokigahara – she recognises the bulbous roots that sit above the forest floor's volcanic base. They pass several snow-shrouded cars abandoned by the side of the road. In one, she's almost certain she can discern the shape of a slumped figure behind the wheel.

The taxi driver spins the car into a parking lot and jerks to a stop next to a low shuttered building that screams neglect. He points to a wooden sign strung across a pathway that leads into the forest.

There are several vehicle-shaped humps here, too.

How in the hell is she going to get back to the station? There's a bus stop on the other side of the road, but who knows if they're even running?

The driver taps the steering-wheel impatiently.

Elspeth has no choice but to try to communicate with him. 'Um . . . do you know where I might find Chiyoko Kamamoto? She lives around here.'

He shakes his head. Points at the forest again.

What now? What the fuck did she expect to find? Chiyoko waiting for her in a limousine? She should have listened to Daniel. This was a mistake. But she's here now – what would be the point of going back to Tokyo without exploring all her options? She knows there are villages around here. She'll have to make her way to one of them if the buses aren't running. She murmurs, '*Arigato*,' but the driver doesn't respond. He accelerates away the second she closes the back door.

She stands still for several seconds, letting the silence settle around her. Glances at the pathway's dark mouth. Shouldn't the hungry spirits who lurk in the forest be attempting to lure her into the trees by now? After all, she thinks, they target the vulnerable and damaged, don't they? And what is she if not vulnerable and damaged?

Ridiculous.

Trying not to look too closely at the abandoned vehicles, she picks her way through several deep drifts, and heads towards the snow-covered mounds, which are arranged in a circle in front of the building. She's read that there are several memorials to the crash victims in the area, and she brushes ice crystals from the top of one of them, revealing a wooden marker. Behind it, partially hidden behind another drift, she spots the shape of a Western-style cross. Elspeth wipes away the snow, the melting ice starting to seep through her gloves, and reads the words, 'Pamela May Donald. Never Forget.' She wonders if Captain Seto has a marker here; she's heard that despite the evidence, some of the passengers' families still blamed him for what happened. Perhaps that really would have been a story worth pursuing. *Untold Stories from Black Thursday*. Sam was right: she is *so* full of shit.

A voice behind her makes her jump. She whirls, sees a stooped figure in a bright red windbreaker trudging towards her from behind the building. He snarls something at her.

There's no point hiding. She whips off her sunglasses, the light making her blink.

He hesitates. 'What are you doing here?' His English is tinged with a slight Californian accent.

'I came to see the memorial,' she finds herself lying – she's not sure why.

'Why?'

'I was curious.'

'We do not get Westerners coming here any more.'

'I'm sure. Um . . . your English is very good.'

He smiles suddenly and fiercely. His teeth are ill-fitting and there's a gap between them and his gums. He sucks them back into his mouth. 'I learned it many years ago. From the radio.'

'Are you the custodian?'

He frowns. 'I do not understand.'

She gestures at the dilapidated building. 'Do you live here? Take care of the place?'

'Ah!' Another teeth-snapping smile. 'Yes, I live here.' She

wonders if he could possibly be Yomijuri Miyajima, the suicide monitor who rescued Hiro and came across the remains of Ryu. But that would be too serendipitous, wouldn't it? 'I go into the forest to collect the things that people leave behind. I can trade them.'

Elspeth shivers violently as the cold bites into her cheeks, making her eyes water. She stamps her feet. It doesn't help. 'You get a lot of people coming here?' She nods at the cars.

'Yes. You want to go in?'

'To the forest?'

'It is a long walk to the site where the plane crashed. But I can take you there. You have money?'

'How much?'

'Five thousand.'

She digs in her pocket, hands him a note. Does she really want to do this? She finds that she does. But this isn't why she's here. What she *should* be doing is asking him if he knows the whereabouts of Chiyoko, but . . . she's come this far, why not go into the forest?

The man turns and strides towards the pathway and Elspeth scrambles to catch up. His legs are bowed and he's at least three decades her senior, but he appears to have the vigour of a twenty-year-old.

He unclicks a chain strung across the pathway and skirts a wooden sign, the writing on it peeling and faded. The trees shower her with snow blossoms, the flakes finding their way into her neck where her scarf has slipped. She can hear her own breath, ragged in her ears. The old man cuts across the main path, heading into the depths of the forest. Elspeth hesitates. No one, except for Daniel, knows she's here (Sam might not even read the email she sent her this morning) and he'll be leaving Japan in a few days. If she runs into trouble, she's screwed. She checks her phone. No signal. Of course. She tries to take note of her surroundings, searching for landmarks that might help her find her way back to the parking lot, but within minutes the trees swallow her whole. She's surprised when she doesn't feel the sense of foreboding she was expecting. It's actually, she thinks, quite beautiful. There are brown pockets of earth where the forest's canopy blocks out the sky, and there's something charming about the trees' knobby roots. Samuel Hockemeier – the marine who'd been on the scene a couple of days after the crash – had said they were otherworldly and forbidding.

Still, as she crumps her way through the snow, following in the old man's footsteps, she can't forget that this is where it all started. A sequence of events that was kicked off, not by three children surviving plane crashes, but by a seemingly innocuous message left by a Texan housewife as she died.

The man stops suddenly, then veers off to the right. Elspeth hangs back, not quite sure what to do. He doesn't go far. She steals forward cautiously, stopping dead when she sees a flash of dark blue in the snow. There's a figure curled in a foetal position at the foot of a tree. The remains of a rope snakes into the branches above the body, its frayed end crisp with ice crystals.

The man sinks to his haunches next to it, and starts rooting through the pockets of its dark blue windbreaker. Its head is bowed, so she can't tell if it's male or female. The backpack next to it is half-unzipped, revealing a cellphone and what looks to be some kind of diary. Its hands are blue and furled, the nails white. The sweet roll the old man on the train gave her lumps in her gut.

Elspeth stares at the body with a kind of morbid fascination, her brain unable to process what she's seeing. With no warning, a hot rush of bile floods into her mouth and she turns away, gripping a tree trunk as she dry heaves. She drags air into her lungs, wipes her eyes.

'You see?' the man says matter-of-factly. 'This man died two days ago, I think. Last week I found five. Two couples. We get many who choose to die together.'

Elspeth realises she's shaking. 'What will you do with the body?'

He shrugs. 'They will only come to collect it when the weather is warmer.'

'What about his family? They might be looking for him.'

'It is possible.'

He pockets the cellphone and straightens. Then he turns and walks on.

Elspeth has seen all she wants to see of this place. How could she have found it beautiful?

'Wait.' She calls after him. 'I'm looking for someone. A young woman who lives around here. Chiyoko Kamamoto.' The man stops in his tracks, but doesn't turn around. 'Do you know where she lives?'

'Yes.'

'Will you take me to her? I can pay you.'

'How much?'

'How much will it take?'

His shoulders slump. 'Come.'

She steps back to allow him to pass, then follows him towards the parking lot.

She doesn't look back at the corpse.

Jogging to catch up to him, she flails as she hits a patch of ice, managing to catch her balance at the last moment.

He hauls open a pair of double doors at the side of the building, disappears inside and seconds later Elspeth hears the stutter of an engine trying to start.

A car backs out, its engine chugging asthmatically.

'Get in,' he snaps through the window. It's clear that she's offended him in some way – because she didn't want to go up to the crash site, or because she mentioned Chiyoko?

She climbs in before he can change his mind. He pulls out of the parking lot and onto the road, as heedless of the snow and ice on the road as the taxi driver. He appears to be keeping to the edges of the forest, and as they round a bend, she makes out the snow-dusted roofs of several wooden houses.

The old man slows the car to a crawl, and they creep past a series of draughty-looking single-storey residences. She notes a rusting vending machine, a child's tricycle half-hidden in the snow next to the side of the road, a pile of icicled wood slumped against the side of one of the houses. As they reach the outskirts of the village, he doubles back towards the forest's edge. The road here is hidden beneath untouched snow – not a footstep or animal print marring it.

'Does anyone live here?'

The man ignores her, revs the accelerator and the car lurches awkwardly up a slight incline, and stops a hundred yards from a small structure constructed out of peeling boards that lurks in its own gloomy pocket adjacent to the forest. If not for the sagging veranda huddled around it and the shuttered windows, it would resemble a shed. 'This is the place you want.'

'Chiyoko lives here?'

The old man sucks his teeth, stares straight ahead. Elspeth pulls off a sodden glove and scrabbles in her pocket for the money. '*Arigato*,' she says, handing it over. 'If I need a ride back can I—'

'Go.'

'Have I offended you?'

'You have not offended me. I don't like this place.'

This from a man who strips corpses for a living. Elspeth shivers again. He takes the money and she climbs out. She waits while he backs away, the car farting a black cloud of exhaust smoke. She resists the urge to scream 'wait!' after him. The engine's whine fades quickly; too quickly, as if the atmosphere is greedily absorbing every sound. In some ways the forest was more hospitable. And she's getting that crawly sensation at the back of her neck, as if eyes are on her.

She climbs up onto the wooden porch in front of the house, noting with relief that the floor is littered with cigarette butts. A sign of life. She knocks on the door. Her breath condenses, and for the first time in years she finds herself wishing for a cigarette. She knocks again. Elspeth decides that if no one answers this time, she'll get the hell out of here.

But a second later, the door is opened by an overweight woman dressed in a grubby pink yukata. Elspeth tries to dredge up a memory of the photographs she's seen of Chiyoko. She recalls a pudgy, hard-eyed teenager, her expression defiant. Elspeth thinks the eyes might be the same. 'Are you Chiyoko? Chiyoko Kamamoto?'

The woman's broad face splits into a grin and she gives a small bow. 'Come in, please,' she says. Her English is flawless, and like the old man's, holds a trace of an American accent.

Elspeth steps into a narrow entrance room – the frigid air is no less forgiving in here – and kicks off her sodden boots, wincing as the cold wood bites through her tights. She places her boots on a shelf next to a pair of blood-red high heels and several grimy slippers.

Chiyoko (if it is Chiyoko – Elspeth still isn't sure) waves her through a door and into an equally chilly interior, which appears to be far smaller than it looked from the outside. A short corridor bisects two areas partially hidden behind screens; at the far end, Elspeth can make out what looks to be a small kitchen.

She follows Chiyoko through the screen to her left and into a dimly lit square room, the floor covered in tattered tatami mats. A low stained table squats in the middle of it, several faded grey cushions scattered around it.

'Sit.' Chiyoko gestures to one of the cushions. 'I will bring you some tea.'

Elspeth does as she is told, her knees popping as she kneels. It's only slightly warmer in here, and the air smells faintly of fish. The coffee table is smeared with sauce and wormed with dried noodles.

She hears the murmur of voices, followed by a giggle. A child's giggle?

The woman returns, carrying a tray containing a teapot and two round cups. She places it on the table, then sinks to her knees with more grace than her bulk should allow. She pours the tea, hands Elspeth a cup.

'You *are* Chiyoko, aren't you?'

A smirk. 'Yes.'

'You and Ryu . . . What happened? They found your shoes in the forest.'

'Do you know why you must remove your shoes before you die?'

'No.'

'So you don't track mud in the afterlife. That's why there are so many ghosts without feet.' A giggle.

Elspeth takes a sip of the tea. It's cold, tastes bitter. She makes herself take another, barely stops herself from gagging. 'Why did you move here?'

'I like it here. I get visitors. Some of them come before they go into the forest to die. Lovers who think they are being noble and will never be forgotten. As if anyone cares! They always ask me if they should do it. And do you know what I tell them?' Chiyoko gives Elspeth a sly sidelong smile. 'I tell them do it. Most of them bring me an offering – food, wood sometimes. As if I am a shrine! They have written books about me, songs about me. There's even a fucking manga series. Have you seen it?'

'I've seen it.'

She nods, grimaces. 'Oh yes. You mentioned it in your book.'

'You know who I am?'

'Yes.'

Elspeth jumps as a high-pitched yell sounds from behind the screen door. 'What was that?'

Chiyoko sighs. 'That is Hiro. It is almost time to feed him.'

'*What?*'

'Ryu's child. We only did it once.' Another giggle. 'It wasn't very good. He was a virgin.'

Elspeth waits for Chiyoko to get up and go to the child, but it appears she has no intention of doing so. 'Did Ryu know he was going to be a father?'

'No.'

'*Was* that his body they found in the forest?'

'Yes. Poor Ryu. An otaku without a cause. I helped him get what he wanted. You want me to tell you how it went? It's a good story. You can put it in a book.'

'Yes.'

'He said he would follow me anywhere. And when I said I wanted to die, he said he would follow me to the afterlife, too. He joined an online suicide group before we met, did you know that?'

'No.'

'Nobody knew. It was just before we started talking. He couldn't go through with it. He needed to be pushed.'

'And I'm guessing you pushed him?'

A shrug. 'It didn't take much.'

'And you? You tried too, didn't you?'

Chiyoko laughs and pushes up her sleeves. There are no scars on her wrists or forearms. 'No. Fanciful stories. Have you ever felt like that? Like you wanted to die?'

'Yes.'

'Everyone has. It is fear that stops people in the end. The fear of the unknown. Of what we might find in the next world. But there is no reason to be afraid. It just keeps on going and going.'

'What does?'

'Life. Death. Hiro and I have spent many hours talking about this very thing.'

'You mean your son?'

Chiyoko laughs in derision. 'Don't be ridiculous. He is just a baby. I mean the other Hiro, of course.'

'Hiro Yanagida?'

'Yes. Would you like to talk to him?'

'*Hiro* is here? How can Hiro be here? He was killed by that marine. Shot.'

'Was he?' Chiyoko gets smoothly to her feet. 'Come. You must have many questions for him.'

Elspeth stands, her thigh muscles aching from crouching on the floor. Her vision wavers, her stomach cramps, and for a horrible moment she wonders if Chiyoko has drugged her. The woman is definitely unhinged and if what she's saying about Ryu and the suicidal people who visit her is the truth, she's dangerous. And she can't forget the old man's reaction to the place. Her mouth fills with saliva and she pinches her left arm, refusing to give into her faintness. It passes. She's light-headed from exhaustion. Worn out.

She follows Chiyoko to the other screened-off room across the passageway.

'Come,' Chiyoko says, opening the screen wide enough for Elspeth to slip through. It's dark in here; the wooden shutters are closed. Elspeth squints, and as her eyes adjust, she can make out a crib on the left side of the room, and a futon piled with pillows beneath the windows. The fishy odour is stronger in here. She shudders, remembering Paul Craddock's delusion about his dead brother. Chiyoko plucks a toddler out of the crib, and the child wraps his arms around her neck.

'I thought you said Hiro was here?'

'He is.'

Slinging the toddler on her hip, Chiyoko opens one of the shutters, letting in a shaft of light.

Elspeth was wrong – the pillows on the futon aren't pillows at all, but a figure slumped against the wall, its legs outstretched.

'I will leave you two alone,' Chiyoko says.

Elspeth doesn't respond. As she stares at the surrabot of Hiro Yanagida, it blinks, a fraction too slowly to be convincingly human. Its skin is nicked in places; its clothes are frayed.

'Hello.' The voice – unmistakably that of a child's – makes Elspeth jump. 'Hello,' the android says again.

'Is that you, Hiro?' Elspeth says. The sheer insanity of her situation finally hits her. She's in Japan. Talking to a robot. She's talking to a fucking robot.

'It's me.'

'Can I . . . can I talk to you?'

'You are talking to me.'

Elspeth steps closer to it. There are small brown droplets on the dull skin of its face – dried blood? 'What are you?'

The android yawns. 'I'm me.'

Elspeth's feeling that same kind of disconnect she felt when she was in Kenji Yanagida's workshop. Her mind goes blank. She has no idea what to ask first. 'How did you survive the crash?'

'We chose to. But sometimes we get it wrong.'

'And Jessica? And Bobby? Where are they? Are they actually dead?'

'They got bored. They usually do. They knew how it would end.'

'And how does it end?' It blinks at her again. After several seconds of silence, Elspeth asks: 'Is there. . . is there a fourth child?'

'No.'

'What about the fourth plane crash?'

The robot's head jerks slightly to the side. 'We knew that would be the day to do it.'

'Do what?'

'Arrive.'

'So . . . why children?'

'We're not always children.'

'What does that mean?'

The thing's head twitches and it yawns again. Elspeth gets the impression it's intimating: *figure it out, bitch*. Then it makes a sound that could be a laugh, its jaw opening just a fraction too wide. There's something familiar about the way it's been framing its words. Elspeth knows how it works. She's seen the footage of the camera capturing Kenji Yanagida's facial movements. But there's no sign of a computer in the room. And wouldn't that require some kind of signal? There's no signal here, is there? She checks her phone again to be sure. But Chiyoko could be operating the android from another room, couldn't she?

'Chiyoko? Is that you? It is, isn't it?'

The surrabot's chest rises and falls, then stills.

Elspeth runs from the room, her feet slipping on the tatami mats. She hauls open the door next to the empty kitchen, revealing a tiny bathroom, the small tub swimming with filthy cloth nappies. She backtracks and rips back the screen to the only other room. Chiyoko's son looks up at her from where he's lying on the floor, playing with a dirty stuffed animal, and laughs.

She opens the front door and sees Chiyoko standing on the porch, cigarette smoke coiling around her head. Could she have made it out here while Elspeth was searching the house? She's not sure. She pulls on her boots and joins her.

'Was that you, Chiyoko? Talking through the android?'

Chiyoko stubs her cigarette out on the balustrade; lights another one. 'Did you think it was me?'

'Yes. No. I don't know.'

The cold air isn't helping to clear her head and Elspeth is sick of all this talking in riddles. 'Okay . . . If it wasn't you, what were – are – they? The Three, I mean?'

'You've seen what Hiro is.'

'All I've seen is a fucking android.'

A shrug. 'All things have souls.'

'So is that what he is? A soul?'

'In a sense.'

Jesus. 'Can you please just give me a straight answer?'

Another infuriating smile. 'Ask me a straight question.'

'Okay . . . Did Hiro – the real Hiro – tell you why The Three, whatever the fuck they are, came here and took over the bodies of the kids?'

'Why would they need a reason? Why do we hunt when we have enough to eat? Why do we kill each other over trifles? What makes you think they needed any more motivation other than to simply see *what might happen*?'

'Hiro implied that they've been here before. I've also heard that from Jessica Craddock's uncle.'

A shrug. 'All religions have prophecies about the end of the world.'

'So? What does that have to do with The Three being here before?'

Chiyoko makes a sound somewhere between a sigh and a snort. 'For a journalist, you are very bad at thinking things through. What if they came here before in order to plant the seed?'

Elspeth starts. 'No way. Are you trying to say that they came here thousands of years ago and set this whole thing up – just so that they could return years later and see if the so-called *seed* they planted causes the goddamned end of the world? That's insane.'

'Of course it is.'

Elspeth has had enough. She's so tired the marrow in her bones aches. 'Now what?'

Chiyoko yawns; several of her back teeth are missing. She wipes her mouth with her sleeve. 'Do your job. You're a journalist. You have found what you were looking for. Go back and tell them what you've seen. Write an article.'

'You really think anyone's going to believe me if I say that I've spoken to a goddamned android harbouring the . . . soul or whatever of one of The Three?'

'People will believe what they want to believe.'

'And if they do believe it . . . They'll think . . . they'll say . . .'

'They'll say Hiro is a god.'

'And *is* he?'

Chiyoko shrugs. '*Shikata ga nai*,' she says. 'What does it matter?' She stubs her cigarette out on the top of the balustrade and walks into the house.

Elspeth stands stock still for several minutes, and with no other option, she zips up her jacket and starts walking away.

HOW IT BEGINS

Pamela May Donald lies on her side, watching the boy as he flits with the others in the trees.

'Help me,' she croaks.

She fumbles for her phone. It's somewhere in her fanny pack, she's certain of that. *C'mon, c'mon, c'mon.* Her fingers stroke it, she almost has it . . . *so close, you can do it* . . . but she can't quite seem to . . . There's something wrong with her fingers. They won't work, they're numb, dead, no longer belong to her.

'Snookie,' she whispers, or maybe she only thinks she says it aloud. Either way, it's the only word that comes into her mind before she dies.

The boy skips over to her, tiptoeing around the roots and wreckage. He looks down at Pamela May Donald's body. She's gone. Snuffed out before she could record the message. He's disappointed, but it's happened before and he was starting to get bored with this game anyway. They all were. It doesn't matter. Even without the message, it always ends in the same way.

He sinks to his haunches, wraps his arms around his knees, and shivers. He can hear the distant thwupping sound of the rescue helicopters approaching. He always enjoys being hoisted up into the helicopter's belly. This will be fun, no matter what.

But next time, he'll do it differently. And he thinks he knows how.

ACKNOWLEDGMENTS

Huge appreciation goes to Agent Extraordinaire Oli Munson of A.M Heath, who took one look at the synopsis, said 'go for it', and basically changed my life.

The novel would be far weaker without the outstanding editorial guidance of my super-hero editor Anne Perry who took a chance on me, made me a stronger writer, and taught me how to accessorise – all without losing her sense of humour. Many thanks are also due to Oliver Johnson, Jason Bartholomew and the fantastic team at Hodder; Reagan Arthur and her excellent team at Little, Brown; and Conrad Williams and all at Blake Friedmann.

The following folk kindly shared their expertise, personal experiences, dealt with my endless questions or opened their homes to me: Captain Chris Zurinskas, Eri Uri, Atsuko Takahashi, Hiroshi Hayakawa, Atsushi Hayakawa, Akira Yamaguchi, David France Mundo, Paige and Ahnika at the House of Collections, Darrell Zimmerman at Cape Medical Response, Eric Begala and Wongani Bandah. Thank you all for being so patient and generous. The responsibility for mistakes made and liberties taken (both geographical and factual) is mine and mine alone.

Christopher Hood's superb academic text, *Dealing with Disaster in Japan: Responses to the Flight JL 123 Crash* was an invaluable resource and introduced me to the terms isho and izoku. I'm also indebted to the authors of the following non-fiction books, blogs, articles and novels which helped shed light on the issues I chose to deal with in the novel: *Welcome to Our Doomsday* by Nicholas Guyatt; *God's Own Country* by Stephen Bates; *Shutting out the Sun* by Michael Zielenziger; *The Otaku Handbook* by Patrick W Galbraith; *Quantum: A Guide for the Perplexed* by Jim Al-Khalili;

Train Man by Nakano Hitori; *Are we Living in the End Times?* by Tim LaHaye and Jerry B Jenkins; *Understanding End Times Prophecy,* by Paul Benware; *Below Luck Level* by Barbara Erasmus; Alzheimer's *From the Inside Out* by Richard Taylor; sherizeee.blogspot.com; www.dannychoo.com; www.tofugu.com; Apocalypse Now, Nancy Gibbs (time.com 2002). Many thanks go to the anonymous artists of asciiart.en.com for inspiring Ryu's ascii.

The following generous people read the manuscript and gave insightful and honest feedback: Alan and Carol Walters, Andrew Solomon, Bronwyn Harris, Nick Wood, Michael Grant, Sam Wilson, Kerry Gordon, Tiah Beautement, Joe Vaz, Vienne Venter, Nechama Brodie, Si, and Sally Partridge. Eric Begala, Thembani Ndzandza, Siseko Sodela, Walter Ntsele, Lwando Sibinge and Thando Makubalo kindly weeded out the majority of my stupidity in the South African sections. Jared Shurin, Alex Smith, Karina Brink, ace photographer Pagan Wicks and Nomes helped keep me sane. You all rock.

Lauren Beukes, Alan Kelly (thank you for the naughty bits!), Nigel Walters, Louis Greenberg and my fellow porn elf Paige Nick went above and beyond with their support and feedback. I owe you guys big time. As usual, my friend and editor Helen Moffett pulled my arse out of the fire again and again (may your life be forever rich in artisanal baked goods).

And last but not least, my husband Charlie and daughter Savannah put up with hours of brain-storming, neuroses and plot-solving, and brought me coffee at 3 a.m. I couldn't have written word one without you – thank you for always having my back.

Black Thursday seemed like the end of the world.

It wasn't, but *this* just might be . . .

Look out for the extraordinary follow-up to THE THREE,

DAY FOUR

HODDER &
STOUGHTON

Contents

KEY TO SYMBOLS

- ✚ Map reference
- ✉ Address
- ☎ Telephone number
- 🕐 Opening times
- ✋ Admission prices
- 🚌 Bus number
- 🚆 Train station
- ⛴ Ferry/boat
- 🔀 Driving directions
- ℹ Tourist office
- 👆 Tours
- 📖 Guidebook
- 🍴 Restaurant
- ☕ Café
- 🏬 Shop
- 🚻 Toilets
- ① Number of rooms
- 🚭 No smoking
- ❄ Air conditioning
- 🏊 Swimming pool
- 🏋 Gym
- ❓ Other useful information
- 🏢 Shopping
- 🎭 Entertainment
- 🍸 Nightlife
- 🏃 Sports
- ⭐ Activities
- ❤ Health and beauty
- 👶 For children
- ▷ Cross reference
- ★ Walk/drive start point

HOW TO USE THIS BOOK

Understanding New Zealand is an introduction to the country, its geography, economy and people. **Living New Zealand** gives an insight into the country today, while the **Story of New Zealand** takes you through its past.

For detailed advice on getting to New Zealand—and getting around once you are there—turn to **On the Move**. For useful practical information, from weather forecasts to emergency services, turn to **Planning.**

Out and About gives you the chance to explore New Zealand through walks and drives.

The **Sights, What to Do** and **Eating and Staying** sections are divided geographically into six regions, which are shown on the map on the inside front cover. These regions always appear in the same order. Towns and places of interest are listed alphabetically within each region.

Map references for the **Sights** refer to the atlas section at the end of this book or to the individual town plans. For example, Wellington has the reference ➕ 318 J11, indicating the page on which the map is found (318) and the grid square in which Wellington sits (J11).

UNDERSTANDING NEW ZEALAND

New Zealand took its place on the tourist map in 1880, when modish travellers included it on their route around the world. Although facilities were distinctly basic, visitors managed to fill several letters with enthusiastic reports of the countryside and its varied populations. These days, tourists can opt out of 'tent hotels' for world-class luxury, but New Zealand's beauty remains sublime. There are dozens of ways to experience it, too, from the high-adrenalin of jet-boats and bungy jumps to the serenity of walks, drives or alfresco dining. It is an easy country to enjoy—attractions, transport and Kiwi attitudes welcome more than 2 million visitors a year.

THE LANDSCAPE

New Zealand consists of three main islands—the North Island, the South Island and Stewart Island—with a handful of small, far-flung islands completing the family. The total land area is 270,500sq km (104,795 square miles).

Although compact in size, New Zealand's landscape is rich and varied, with glaciers, braided rivers, lakes, fiords, sounds (flooded riverbeds, found predominantly in the South Island), lowlands, alluvial plains, wetlands, large natural coastal harbours and a rash of offshore islands.

Because New Zealand is located at the meeting point of the Pacific and Indo-Australian tectonic plates, it also experiences frequent earthquakes. A string of volcanoes stretches from the currently active Whakaari/White Island in the Bay of Plenty to Mount Ruapehu in the heart of the North Island. The area also has numerous thermal features, including geysers, mineral springs, blowholes and mud pools, most of which can be found around Rotorua and Taupo.

The South Island is far more mountainous than the North and boasts the country's highest peak, Mount Cook/Aoraki (▷ 131). The country's longest river is the Waikato, which stretches 425km (264 miles) from Lake Taupo to the Tasman Sea.

Great stretches of these wonderful landscapes are unmarked by humans—no roads, no houses, no telegraph poles. Within an hour's drive from most main towns you can find the edge of habitation. Another hour or two in a chosen mode of transport—such as walking, horse-riding or kayaking—and you can be totally remote. While some outdoor areas are deservedly popular, like the tramping tracks of Fiordland, in plenty of other spots you can explore for miles without seeing another soul. Where else in the world can you do that without threat of a poisonous snake or spider?

PEOPLE AND POPULATION

The population of New Zealand currently stands at about 4 million: with just under 3 million in the

Milford Sound is one of the great sights of New Zealand, and the Milford Track is famous worldwide

North Island and just under 1 million in the South Island. Greater Auckland is home to just over 1 million people.

New Zealand is essentially a bicultural society made up of Maori and Europeans, with many other nationalities also present. Maori make up about 14 per cent of New Zealand's total population, with the vast majority living in the North Island. There are around 231,000 Pacific Islanders, with many living in greater Auckland. Asians make up three per cent of New Zealand's total population and are the fastest-growing minority group, again settled mainly in the greater Auckland area.

A number of distinctive personalities have made it big in national and local politics— Georgina Beyer, the world's first transsexual MP; Nandor Tanczos, the Rastafarian Green with waist-length dreadlocks; Tim Shadbolt, the flower-power activist turned mayor of Invercargill; and Dick Hubbard, breakfast cereal magnate and mayor of Auckland.

RELIGION
The dominant religion is Christianity, with Anglican, Presbyterian and Roman Catholic denominations being the most prominent. Minority religions include Hinduism, Islam,

Left, morning mist hangs above Lake Rotoaira; middle, ferns thrive in the wetlands of the southwest; right, natural steam-clouds at Wai-O-Tapu; below, traditional Maori moko (face decoration)

New Zealanders are famous for being the world's greatest travellers, and at any one time a large proportion of citizens are absent or living abroad. More than 400,000 live and work in Australia alone. Through their close trans-Tasman ties, Australian and New Zealand citizens are free to live and work in both countries.

MAORI CULTURE

A big draw for visitors is the vibrant culture of New Zealand's first inhabitants, the Maori. After being threatened with extinction at the turn of the last century, Maori society enjoyed a renaissance towards the end of the 1970s. Language, art and *kapa haka* (performance arts) are thriving. The most popular place for visitors to experience these is Rotorua.

POLITICS
Things change quickly in New Zealand. With its small population and triennial elections, it's sometimes seen as a social laboratory. Currently under the microscope is Mixed Member Proportional representation (MMP), an electoral system that has helped a wider range of MPs into parliament since it was introduced in 1996. As well as the two long-established parties, Labour and National, significant political stakes are held by the environmentally friendly Green Party, family-values oriented United Future and migrant-watching New Zealand First.

Judaism and Buddhism. The Maori developed two of their own minority Christian-based faiths, Ratana and Ringatu, both of which were formed in the late 19th to early 20th centuries. At least a quarter of the total population are atheists or have no religion, and this number is growing.

VISITING NEW ZEALAND
Many visitors from Asia experience New Zealand in three days flat—Auckland, Rotorua, Queenstown. These are great spots, but to get a feel for the country, its people and culture, you really need two weeks minimum. If your flight takes more than 12 hours, three weeks is preferable, simply because jet lag can spoil the first few days.

The easiest way to travel is by road. Coaches are inexpensive, reliable and connect most visitor areas, while campervans have become incredibly popular, providing flexible access to remote quarters with no worry of finding a bed for the night. Rail is limited, with some notable exceptions—the TranzAlpine trip from Christchurch to Greymouth is an attraction in its own right. If time is limited, a good way to see the highlights of both islands is to fly. If you have a contact, it's less expensive to book from within the country, and the earlier the better.

There are ample opportunities to try outdoor activities such as hiking, fishing, hunting and mountain biking. Just be aware that if you bring your own equipment, it must be scrupulously cleaned before you try to get it through customs. Most gear can be easily hired anyway, and the results are all but guaranteed if you use the services of an experienced guide.

LANGUAGE
See pages 308–309.

NORTHLAND

AUCKLAND

WAIKATO

BAY OF PLENTY

GISBORNE

TARANAKI

HAWKE'S BAY

MANAWATU-WANGANUI

NELSON CITY

WELLINGTON

TASMAN

MARLBOROUGH

WEST COAST

CANTERBURY

OTAGO

SOUTHLAND

DUCKS CROSSING

Top, resting by the Emerald Lakes in Tongariro National Park
Middle, a family gathers mussels on the Coromandel shore
Bottom, trekking in the Abel Tasman National Park

Below left, sheep are still a mainstay of New Zealand's agricultural economy
Middle, punting on the River Avon in Christchurch
Right, mountain biking on the Queen Charlotte Track
Opposite, carved figure at the Nga Hau E Wha National Marae, near Christchurch

AUCKLAND, NORTHLAND AND COROMANDEL

Auckland: New Zealand's commercial hub and largest city, with 1.2 million residents. Ferries give access to prettier areas such as Devonport and Waiheke Island, while the Sky Tower gives a 360-degree view of the city and its harbours.

Northland: Warm, humid and sparsely populated, with impressive coastal landscapes. North of Ninety Mile Beach is sacred Cape Reinga. The Waipoua Forest Sanctuary is home to New Zealand's largest kauri tree. The Bay of Islands, known for big-game fishing, has historic sites, including Waitangi National Reserve.

Coromandel: Conservationists and artisans now fiercely defend the sunny peninsula, once exploited for gold, coal and kauri.

CENTRAL NORTH ISLAND

Rotorua: Spectacular geothermal activity includes bubbling mud pools, geysers, steaming lakes and a welcoming spa complex. The tourist capital of Maori culture.

Lake Taupo: New Zealand's biggest lake. Its crystal waters are famed for trout fishing.

The Volcanic Plateau: Three volcanoes rise from an austere plain, including Mount Ruapehu, whose crater still simmers.

New Plymouth: Wedged between Mount Taranaki (Mount Egmont) and the Tasman Sea, the city gains an artistic edge from its cosmopolitan oil industry.

Napier: Destroyed by an earthquake in 1931, the city was rebuilt as an art deco delight.

SOUTHERN NORTH ISLAND

Wellington: The capital city looks a gem from the Botanic Garden's lookout, accessed by cable car. Home to national museum Te Papa, the Beehive parliament building and hundreds of excellent cafés

The Wairarapa: Wine-making has brought boutique shopping and dining to villages like Martinborough and Greytown.

Kapiti Coast: Long white-sand beaches and a pleasant climate. Kapiti Island, 6km (4 miles) off the coast, is one of New Zealand's most important nature reserves.

Wanganui: The serene Whanganui River is rich in Maori history and legend. It is popular for jet-boating and kayaking.

NELSON AND MARLBOROUGH

Nelson: Warm, sandy beaches rival the best of the North Island's, while craggy mountains and rough rivers are distinctly South Island. Its many attractions include the vast stretch of Golden Bay and the easy-to-stroll Abel Tasman National Park.

Nelson City: The quality of local clay has attracted successful potters and other established artists. The town's creativity pulses through The World of Wearable Art and Classic Cars museum.

Marlborough: The first Marlborough wineries were instrumental in putting New Zealand on the world wine map. Now there are 44 within 15km (9 miles) of Blenheim, many also offering world-class cuisine.

CANTERBURY AND THE WEST COAST

Christchurch: Called the Garden City, the South Island's largest city has vast areas of parkland. Visitors can punt on the Avon, visit the landmark Anglican cathedral on Cathedral Square and explore the lively Arts Centre. The Port Hills and beaches make a delightful change to the city's flatness.

Canterbury: From the farms of the Canterbury Plains, the region suddenly rears up into the Southern Alps. Star of these great mountains is Aoraki (Mount Cook). Azure Lake Tekapo has a memorial to sheepdogs of the harsh McKenzie Country.

The West Coast: A thin strip of land between the Southern Alps and the ocean. Narrow State Highway 6 winds through dense rainforest, near Fox and Franz Josef Glaciers, and past Punakaiki Pancake Rocks. Evocative scenery is guaranteed, unlike the weather.

OTAGO AND THE FAR SOUTH

Dunedin: Victorian and Edwardian architecture beckon in Larnach Castle, Olveston and the railway station. The Otago Peninsula is home to the distinguished Royal Albatross Centre, plus many penguins and seals.

Otago: Queenstown is New Zealand's adventure capital, with world-renowned bungy jumping and jet-boating. Quieter but equally scenic towns include Wanaka and Arrowtown, with incredible mountains, lakes, rivers and autumn colour.

Fiordland: The wettest, wildest corner of New Zealand, consisting of mountains and water. Milford Sound is the most accessible of the fiords. Its photographic gems are Mitre Peak and the immense Bowen Falls.

THE BEST OF NEW ZEALAND

BEST PLACES TO STAY

Pukematu Lodge, Russell (▷ 275), a modern B&B with great hospitality and fabulous views.
Huka Lodge, Taupo (▷ 278), the luxury lodge where the stars go to be pampered.
The Lighthouse, Wellington (▷ 281), for unusual accommodation in the capital.
Collingwood Homestead, Collingwood (▷ 282) where Colonial comfort is the tops.
Corstorphine House, Dunedin (▷ 288), a private hotel in a historic, stylish setting.

Above, Collingwood Homestead
Left, Milford Sound, in Fiordland National Park

BEST ADRENALINE RUSHES

Bungy jump from Auckland's Sky Tower (▷ 65, 167)—even watching it from the viewing platform makes your stomach lurch!
Zorb at Rotorua (▷ 177)—but when you've finished rolling downhill in an inflated ball you may not recall which part of Down Under is down under!
Luge down a steep hill on little more than a tray, with Skyline Skyrides near Rotorua (▷ 87)—take the gondola up and the luge down.
Jet-boat on the Shotover River through Skippers Canyon (▷ 147), with tours from Queenstown (▷ 148)—after all, New Zealanders developed the craft specially.
White-water raft on the Buller Gorge from Murchison (▷ 117) or Westport (▷ 202), or join a black-water rafting trip in the Waitomo cave system (▷ 90, 179) if you're fearless.

Above, bungy-jump from the Sky Tower if you dare…
Left, enjoy the thrills of a jet-boat
Below, famed Moeraki Beach

BEST BEACHES

Ninety Mile Beach is an unequalled stretch of soft white sands on the Aupouri Peninsula (▷ 57), near the northern tip of the country, but don't be tempted to drive on it yourself (for tours, ▷ 168).
Kaiteriteri, on the Abel Tasman coast of the South Island (▷ 110), offers golden sands on a stunningly lovely bay.
Wharariki, on Farewell Spit (▷ 111), is a patch of golden sands on a curving spit that harbours wading birds and fur seals.
Rabbit Island, by Nelson (▷ 114), offers seemingly endless miles of volcanic grey sands backed by pine forest.
Moeraki beach (▷ 145) comes with the bonus of a bizarre clutch of rounded boulders, a natural phenomenon well worth seeing.

Above, surfing beaches abound, but beware of rip-tides along the coastline
Below, select your preferred tipple or try new wines

BEST PLACES FOR WINE TASTING

Martinborough's chief advantage (▷ 94, 181) is that there are around 20 vineyards within strolling distance of its Wine Centre—so no danger of drinking and driving as you sample your way around.
Hawke's Bay is famous in international wine circles, and you can compare some of the best at its annual wine festival (▷ 179).
Waiheke Island has a number of excellent vineyards—try Stonyridge for its Cabernet Sauvignon (▷ 170), or join in the annual winefest (▷ 171).
Napier is surrounded by extensive vineyards, including the venerable Church Road winery (▷ 175), where you can also explore the country's only wine museum.
Blenheim (▷ 111) is an otherwise unremarkable town at the heart of the Marlborough/Wairau Valley wineries (▷ 119); for some of the best wine in the South Island, head to Cloudy Bay (▷ 189).

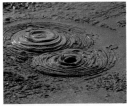

*Above, a thermal mud pool
Right, the stylish White
restaurant*

BEST PLACES TO EAT

White, Auckland (▷ 253) for high-class dining in the City of Sails.
Chocolate Fish Café, Wellington (▷ 260), a relaxed waterfront hang-out frequented by the *Lord of the Rings* cast and crew.
Smokehouse Restaurant, Mapua (▷ 262) is the place for top-notch fish, close by Nelson.
C'est la Vie, Akaroa (▷ 264) for unusually intimate dining and French cuisine in this pretty settlement.
Saffron, Arrowtown (▷ 267) offers wild local ingredients perfectly combined, in a historic setting.

BEST LANDSCAPES

The Bay of Islands (▷ 68) offers some of the most outstanding coastal scenery in the North Island, and doubles as a popular watersports venue.
Rotorua's extensive geothermal landscape (▷ 84) is unrivalled, with stinking, steaming sulphur mud pools, spouting geysers of boiling water, and multi-hued lakes
Abel Tasman National Park (▷ 109), with its sandy bays and azure sea, lush coastal vegetation and famous tramping trail, is a popular holiday destination for Kiwis.
Westland Tai Poutini National Park (▷ 134) boasts two of the great sights of New Zealand—the Franz Josef and Fox glaciers.
Fiordland National Park (▷ 141) takes in a spectacular landscape of steep forested peaks and drowned glaciated valleys, seen to advantage from the Milford Track (▷ 143).

Above, volcanic White Island, a nature reserve; left, penguins get right of way in Oamaru; below, fun at the Antarctic Centre; bottom, Te Papa and part of a modern marae decoration in the museum

BEST PLACES TO SEE WILDLIFE

Tiritiri Matangi Island (▷ 71) is an accessible haven in the Hauraki Gulf, just 35 minutes from Auckland, where endangered native birds such as takahe and little spotted kiwi thrive.
Pukaha Mount Bruce Wildlife Centre (▷ 95) is the Department of Conservation's flagship breeding centre, where you can see stitchbirds, wild eels and kaka parrots.
Kaikoura (▷ 113, 190) is known around the world for the success of its whale- and dolphin-watching tours, and you can also get up close (within smelling distance) to fur seals along this coast.
Oamaru (▷ 145) is the chosen home of little blue and yellow-eyed penguins, with opportunities to see both rare species.
The Otago Peninsula (▷ 147) stretches northeastwards from Dunedin and is home to the only mainland-based royal albatross colony in the world.

BEST BIG MUSEUMS AND GALLERIES

Auckland Museum Tamaki Paenga Hira (▷ 62), set in the Auckland Domain (park), has some of the finest collections of Maori and Pacific Island artefacts in the country.
Auckland Art Gallery (▷ 59) has what is probably the biggest and best collections of New Zealand art, including famous paintings by Goldie and Lindauer.
Te Papa Tongarewa-Museum of New Zealand (▷ 96), the national museum, set in an architecturally intriguing building on Wellington's harbourfront, opened in 1998 with highlights of a vast collection.
The International Antarctic Centre in Christchurch (▷ 128) is the public face of a lively, working campus, giving a great introduction to the science and history of south polar exploration.

BEST LOCAL MUSEUMS

The Matakohe Kauri Museum (▷ 69) celebrates a native New Zealand tree with creative displays about its value to early settlers, from ships' masts to the uses of its valuable gum resin.

The Museum of Caves at Waitomo (▷ 91) is a world-class introduction to the formation of limestone caves and the creatures and people who have used them.

The Museum of Wellington City and Sea (▷ 104) marks the maritime heritage of the 'windy city', with excellent displays of local exhibits.

The World of Wearable Art and Classic Cars (▷ 115) put Nelson firmly on the fashion map, with its wacky and outrageous costume designs and its light-hearted presentation—and the cars are pretty special, too.

Coaltown Museum at Westport (▷ 133) gives an insight into the heyday of mining on the west coast—both for coal and gold—with evocative items including the massive brake drum from the Denniston Incline.

TOP 10 EXPERIENCES

Go for a walk. The Kiwis call it tramping, and there's a huge choice of longer trails (▷ 246) and short strolls to get you closer to nature.

Eat a top-class meal of local delicacies (▷ 248–269). New Zealand lamb is hard to beat for taste and tenderness, the seafood is superb and the modern Pacific-influenced style of cooking is refreshing.

Learn about Maori culture. There are lots of opportunities in major towns to enjoy a Maori cultural event, partake of a *hangi* (▷ 251) or visit a *marae*—Rotorua offers some of the best (▷ 84–87).

Take to the water, even if it's only the Interislander ferry (▷ 52), and look for dolphins and seabirds. Sailing, kayaking and wildlife watching are just some of the options (▷ 151–212).

Ride on the TranzAlpine, the fabulous scenic rail route through the Southern Alps that links Christchurch and Greymouth (▷ 199).

Shop 'til you drop. There's much more to modern New Zealand fashion than the hard-working Swanndri (▷ 197), and the lively markets are a great way to source original souvenirs—try Aotea Square in Auckland (▷ 164), or Nelson (▷ 191), or Dunedin (▷ 205).

Watch sport and talk about it. It's probably the best way to blend in with the locals, whether you pick Ellerslie for racing (▷ 166), the Basin Reserve for cricket (▷ 185), Addington for trotting (▷ 198), or just about anywhere for rugby.

Sit in an outdoor thermal pool and experience natural reinvigoration. Rotorua (▷ 84–87) or Hanmer Springs (▷ 123) are the most obvious venues, but smaller places include Maruia Springs (▷ 130).

Fly over a glacier to experience a bird's-eye view of a moving snow-field—or better still, land on one and see it close up (▷ 200, 202).

Do something that sets your heart racing. New Zealand is becoming the world capital of adventure and adrenaline sports, and Queenstown (▷ 148–149) and Rotorua (▷ 84–87) are the main places, but you'll find opportunities everywhere. Go on—have a try!

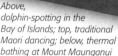

Above, dolphin-spotting in the Bay of Islands; top, traditional Maori dancing; below, thermal bathing at Mount Maunganui

Above, tramping on the scenic Abel Tasman Coast Track Left, Maori carving, Waitangi

Helicopter flights give thrilling access to remote landscapes

Living
New Zealand

Left, *Lord of the Rings* was the making of New Zealand tourism

Left, rainbow kiwi, Otorohanga; right, look smart with the Urban Stroller

New Zealand's
People

It's barely 200 years since European settlers moved into Aotearoa, the land they called New Zealand. In this short time, each city has developed an identity as distinctive as its new residents. Auckland's cosmopolitan citizens are known for their laptops, mobile phones and boating obsessions. Wellington is home to politicians, civil servants and cultured café society. Christchurch people, with their good manners and manicured gardens, are more English than the English. Dunedinites celebrate their Scottish heritage and the untamed freedoms of their wildlife and students. Beyond the cities, the farming folk are characterised by their bush-shirts, gumboots and staunched emotion.

The Maori maintain their cultural stronghold in places such as Rotorua and Gisborne, but their influence touches all parts of the country. Against all odds, Maori culture survived colonisation and continues to gain strength and standing. It is a highly regarded element of the national identity, for despite minor regional differences, the overriding belief is that New Zealanders—Kiwis—are one. They value a practical, down-to-earth approach, with nothing too frilly. They are great travellers who are unencumbered by tradition, and relish new ideas. They see themselves as 'laid back' but stand firm on issues they hold dear.

Retro chic: a restored Christchurch tram

Kiwi Ingenuity
New Zealanders reckon they can make just about anything with a good whack of No. 8 fencing wire. Their flair for lateral thinking has led to a disproportionate number of successful inventions—for example, the three-wheeled Mountain Buggy, developed by Allan Croad in his family garage from an old golf trundler bought for NZ$5 at a school gala in 1992. The company now exports to 16 countries and makes blokes proud to push the pram.

Classic Kiwi inventions include the tranquilliser dart gun, now exported from Timaru to zoologists, farmers and gamekeepers worldwide, and the electric fence, brainchild of a Waikato farmer. Then there's the Hamilton jet-boat—which thrills visitors by speeding through mere centimetres of water—eartags for livestock, the electronic petrol pump, childproof bottle tops, spring-free trampolines and spreadable butter...

Top left, the national flag gives way to black and white in sport, above

Above left, Dame Silvia Cartwright, Governor-General until 2006; above right, a *haka*

Left, an ice-tunnel photo-stop for visitors to the Franz Josef glacier

Prime Minister Helen Clark

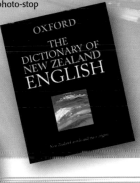

Scruffy Icon

New Zealand's devotion to Oscar-winning film-maker Peter Jackson is absolute.

Jackson has ticked every box on the Kiwi Hero scorecard. He was a DIY self-starter who made war films on his parents' back lawn, aged eight. His breakthrough movie, cult gorefest *Bad Taste*, was created with home-made equipment and a bunch of mates. He stuck by New Zealand when Hollywood offers flowed in, and insisted the *Lord of the Rings* trilogy should be made in his own backyard. New Zealanders love him just as he is…although there was a murmur of approval when, for a *King Kong* press launch, he was rumoured to have trimmed his hair.

The New Immigrants

The New Zealand government has worked hard to attract migrants with investment capital or much-needed job skills—such as trades people and medical specialists. The impact showed clearly in the 2001 census. The Asian population had doubled in 10 years, so for the first time their numbers (240,000) exceeded those of Pacific peoples (231,000). Those of European heritage decreased by 3 per cent to 80 per cent. Just over 14 per cent were Maori. The melting-pot effect is particularly noticeable in Auckland, which is home to two-thirds of Asian and Pacific peoples.

The total population tipped 4 million for the first time in 2003. This figure is always slightly skewed as at any one time an estimated half a million Kiwis are overseas. The majority live in Australia, thanks to the mutual absence of work restrictions.

Women's World

Despite New Zealand's macho history of farming and rugby, women have played a significant role in the nation's development. New Zealand was the first country in the world to give women the vote, in 1893; the first country where two women leaders fought in a general election, in 1999; and the first country to elect a transsexual MP. In the early 21st century women occupied all the top roles in the government—Head of State (Queen Elizabeth II), the Governor-General (Dame Silvia Cartwright, whose term finished in 2006), the Prime Minister (Helen Clark), the Chief Justice (Dame Sian Elias) and the Speaker of the House of Representatives (Margaret Wilson). In Parliament, 37 of the 121 MPs are women, including another party leader—Jeanette Fitzsimons, co-leader of the Green Party.

Local Lingo

The Dictionary of New Zealand English (OUP, 1997) contains 6,000 main entries and 9,300 sub-entries, proving that although the country's official language is English, a visitor should not expect to understand it all. Phrases like 'rattle your dags' (hurry up) reflect a farming background, while 'half pie' (not great) stems from the Maori word *pai* (good). *Jandals* (flip flops), *jaffas* (chocolate balls with an orange coating) and *pikelets* (hotcakes) are part of everyday life and language.

A strong New Zealand accent can be difficult to penetrate—it is similar to Australian, but the 'i' sound gives it away. Kiwis tend to turn it into a 'u' sound, as in 'fush and chups', while Australians say 'feesh and cheeps'. The accent is more-or-less consistent across the country except for Southland, where a rolled 'r' is common.

Above and left, the Coast to Coast endurance race; top right, river surfing; right, the calmer pursuits of mussel gathering and sea fishing

The Great
Outdoors

When Canadian country-pop star Shania Twain visited Central Otago, New Zealand was thrilled. When she decided to buy a slice of it in 2004, the reception was rather cooler. New Zealanders are strongly connected with their land and love to share it with visitors. But they became wary around 1998, when the world's super-rich started snapping up beauty spots at bargain prices. Land values shot up. Young farmers now struggle to get started and traditional *baches* (holiday cottages) are vanishing.

The most sensitive issue is public access to the land on the coast, under threat from developers, and the foreshore, where Maori customary rights and recently enacted Crown ownership don't always sit comfortably. In Twain's case, her company, Soho Properties, took out pastoral leases for Motatapu and Mount Soho Stations near Wanaka that were approved with stringent conservation and access conditions, some being suggested by Soho. Part of the agreement was the establishment of a walking track through both properties and the building of two new huts, funded by Soho Properties. Her land also hosts a walk/bicycle event, The Motatapu Icebreaker. So it's positive outcomes for all, as New Zealanders love being able to use and enjoy their countryside.

A Beautiful Game

Kiwi rugby fans were genuinely shocked that the All Blacks didn't make the final of the Rugby World Cup in 2003. After all, rugby is the national game. Since their victory at the inaugural World Cup in 1987 disappointment has dogged the All Blacks—in subsequent competitions they have made just one final and three semis. But the loyal fans are hoping that will change in the 2007 Rugby World Cup, in France. The All Blacks have led the International Rugby Board's world rankings continuously for nearly four years, so Kiwis are hopeful. What's more, New Zealand is the reigning champion in the under-21s and the under-19s, and the Black Ferns, the women's team, are three-time world champions.

Left, Doug Howlett takes the ball from French defenders at the 2003 Rugby World Cup

Bungy jumping—not a sport for the faint-hearted

Top, unwinding in Auckland; left, thrills and spills; below, not crazy golf but GolfCross, with inventor Burton Silver

Left, popular activities include sailing and mountain biking

Sailing Hopes

New Zealand is a nation of yachties—it's not for nothing that Auckland is known as the City of Sails, and at the Anniversary Day Regatta at the end of January the whole population seems to be out on the water. The whole country was swept up in the enthusiasm in 2000, when Team New Zealand became the first non-US syndicate to retain the America's Cup in 2000. This all fell to pieces in the next defence, in 2003, after star skipper Russell Coutts was lured to the Swiss Alinghi team, and the Kiwi team suffered a series of major equipment failures—the boat was swamped in one race, and the mast snapped in half in another. But hopes were riding high for the 2007 regatta in Valencia, Spain, with fans hopeful that Kiwi ingenuity and know-how would again prevail.

Crazy, But Smart

When A.J. Hackett jumped off the Eiffel Tower in a dinner suit in 1987, attached only to his prototype bungy cord, the world declared Kiwis crazy. Perhaps—but Hackett and co-founder Henry van Asch were on to something. Some 450,000 tourist jumps later, in 2004 a multi-million dollar Bungy Centre was opened at Kawarau Bridge in Queenstown by Prime Minister Helen Clark.

New buzzes are invented every year to enhance New Zealand's reputation as the adventure capital of the world, but bungy remains queen bee. There are now four A.J. Hackett bungy sites (and many non-Hacketts), offering something for everyone, including the original Kawarau site (43m/141ft) for history buffs, Auckland Harbour Bridge (40m/131ft) for those who like smart technology, or Nevis Highwire, near Queenstown (134m/440ft), for the truly brave.

Mountain Madness

Normal people take three hours to drive west-to-east across the South Island. But once a year, hardy souls do it the hard way, in the Speight's Coast to Coast multisport race from Kumara Beach, near Greymouth, to Sumner Beach, near Christchurch. The 243km (151-mile) course consists of 140km (87 miles) cycling, 67km (42 miles) kayaking and 36km (22 miles) running, including a 33km (20-mile) mountain stage across the Southern Alps. Competitors take anything from 10 hours 45 minutes (the course record) to 24 hours. The race's hero is Christchurch man Steve Gurney, who has competed 19 times and won 9 times since it began in 1983. More than 900 competitors from 18 countries vied for a place in the 2007 event, attracted by the promise of personal achievement and a free beer at the finishing line.

Don't Get Mad, Get Cross

It's not for purists, but anyone looking for a unique—yet sedate—outdoor experience in New Zealand couldn't do better than GolfCross. The game is much like golf but uses an oval ball and a large rubber tee. Players use regular clubs but the putter isn't required—instead of holes and greens, the ball is pitched into a triangular goal with a two-sided net.

Surprisingly, the oval ball is easier to control than a round one. How the ball is set on the tee determines whether it will fly straight, hook or slice. The game's creator, Wellington inventor and writer Burton Silver, says this encourages players to take greater risks. The four GolfCross courses are in beautiful farmland (complete with sheep) near Rotorua, Wanaka, Martinborough and Mount Cook/Aoraki.

Left, traditionally carved greenstone (*pounamu*) pendant

Above and below, inventive and quirky modern sculptures abound

Whale Rider threw young Keisha Castle-Hughes into the limelight

The Arts

The Next Precioussss

After starring as Middle Earth, New Zealand's next major film role was Narnia, under Kiwi director Andrew (*Shrek*) Adamson. Work on *The Lion, the Witch and the Wardrobe* began in Auckland in early 2004, the production's budget of over NZ$150 million nicely helping to fill the economic void left by the America's Cup. Later that year, filming moved to locations in the South Island, including high country, coast, alpine plateau, forests and mock English countryside. The only major hiccup was the Ministry for Agriculture and Forestry (MAF)'s refusal to let 14 American reindeer into the country in case they carried potentially deadly Q fever. It took six months to create a replacement team out of fibreglass and motors.

After suffering years of 'cultural cringe', New Zealanders are finding their own confident voice. Through the 1970s and 80s there was a perception that homegrown meant awful. Only accolades from abroad could guarantee artistic acceptance locally. High expectations perhaps had benefits—per head of population, New Zealand has a remarkable success rate. Literature had a good start with Katherine Mansfield (▷ 33) and the murder mysteries of Dame Ngaio Marsh (▷ 307). These days, children's fiction stands out, with Margaret Mahy, Joy Cowley and Lynley Dodd's *Hairy Maclary* selling millions of books worldwide.

Split Enz and Kiri Te Kanawa led the way into the international music scene in the 1980s; performers like Hayley Westenra and opera star Jonathan Lemalu now follow on. In the 1990s, a strong film industry emerged with *An Angel at my Table*, *Once Were Warriors*, *The Piano* and *Heavenly Creatures*. They laid the foundations for the proudest moment in the history of Kiwi arts: Peter Jackson, director of *The Lord of the Rings* trilogy, and Keisha Castle-Hughes, star of *Whale Rider*, together on the red carpet at the 2003 Academy Awards. Fabulous locations and tax breaks should keep the filmmakers coming, but the greatest benefit is New Zealand's new pride in its cultural identity.

Mail boxes are an expression of folk art fun

Maori carvings, above and below right

Singer Hayley
Westenra,
left; WOW,
below

Singing Belles

New Zealand's latest music export is Hayley Westenra (b.1987), young, gorgeous and acclaimed the world over. In 2004, 17-year-old Hayley's album *Pure* stormed into the UK pop chart at No. 8 and the classical chart at No. 1. In New Zealand, the album's 18-week stay at No. 1 made her the country's biggest-selling artist ever. Soon after, she was dovetailing exams at her Christchurch high school with international appearances alongside Pavarotti, José Carreras and Bryn Terfel. She has performed for the Queen, Tony Blair and President Bush.

For those who like something a little more Norah Jones, New Zealand offers Brooke Fraser. She was just 20 when she won 'Tuis' at the 2004 Vodafone New Zealand Music Awards for best female and breakthrough artist of the year.

Wow-wee!

The Montana World of Wearable Art (WOW) awards show is big and getting bigger. Sculptor Suzie Moncrieff started it in 1987 to promote her Nelson art gallery, and it quickly boomed into a two-hour theatrical extravaganza. The televised awards are held each September before an audience of thousands. Entrants, from overseas designers to first-time locals, submit fantastical costume creations in any materials: stained glass, wood panelling, flax, car parts and dried sausage skins have featured. 2004 saw the awards' last night in Nelson; the show then moved to Wellington as part of an expansion plan. The ultimate vision is to stage events in different parts of the world and bring the winners to a grand final in New Zealand. The World of Wearable Art museum remains in Nelson (▷ 114–115).

Eeyore meets Michelangelo

What do you get when you cross a Portaloo with sounds of a braying donkey and a volcano? Some say ground-breaking art, others a shocking waste of tax-payers' money. For sure, it's an animated fracas when the work's creator is to represent New Zealand at the most important contemporary arts event in the world.

The 'Donkey Toilet' (real title *Rapture 2004*), created by a collective known as et al, caused a stink when exhibited at Wellington's City Gallery. But the stuff really hit the fan when CreativeNZ revealed that it provided NZ$500,000 to send et al's work to the 2005 Venice Biennale. It turned out the 'collective' was established artist Merilyn Tweedie, and her Venice installation would feature computer hardware rather than a noisy toilet—but Joe Kiwi remained staunchly unimpressed.

Frame and Mirror

One of New Zealand's literary giants was Janet Frame, and since her death in 2004 her life has been commemorated in a Heritage Trail in Oamaru (▷ 145). Born in 1924 in Dunedin, Frame grew up shy, poor and marked by a head of frizzy orange hair. A misdiagnosed schizophrenic, she passed most of her 20s in psychiatric institutions. Despite the fact she was intensely reclusive, readers knew her through her novels (especially *Owls Do Cry*) and her three-part autobiography: *To the Is-land*, *An Angel at My Table* and *The Envoy from Mirror City*. She became widely recognised in New Zealand after 1983, when her autobiographies brought international acclaim, and she was tipped for the Nobel Prize in 2003. The Janet Frame Heritage Trail in Oamaru includes the railway worker's house where she grew up, and places featured in her books.

Top, dairy farming is widespread; top middle, hops are grown for brewing; top right, kiwi fruit; right, top-grade sheepskins are a by-product of the lamb industry

Income and
Industry

New Zealand is riding a wave of economic stability. The country's seventh successive year of growth was 2006, making this the strongest and longest period since the 1960s. The unemployment rate of 3.7 per cent is the lowest in 20 years. As ever, the country's largest industry is agriculture. It brings in over 60 per cent of export earnings, but national survival no longer depends on the population of 40 million sheep: the 5.2 million (and increasing) dairy and 4.4 million beef cattle are slowly changing the face of agriculture, creating wealth in regions such as Southland. Other industries such as forestry, fishing and deer farming have grown, each nurturing their niche products—such as mussels for the US and ice cream for Japan.

New Zealand's 'clean, green' image is ruthlessly exploited to market agriculture and the other big earner—tourism. More than 2 million visitors spend an estimated NZ$6 billion a year on unique Kiwi experiences. It's estimated that tourism accounts for one in ten jobs in New Zealand.

As prosperity has increased, so has the share price of Kiwi retail icon The Warehouse. The red sheds are 'where everyone gets a bargain', bulk discounting everything from sofas to face cream.

Roadside stalls are a regular sight in the major fruit-growing areas

Spreading the Web

The *Rings* trilogy shone the spotlight on New Zealand's IT industry, highlighting Kiwis' ability to combine creativity with computer genius. Gollum's parents at Weta Workshop continue to lead the way; aside from *King Kong*, their digital experts have been developing cost-effective animation for children's TV since 2003. Kiwis' other successful projects tend to be niche, such as web and email security, e-health systems, farming software, and the technology behind new-wave mobile phone services. It's hard going, though. Despite proven potential, the industry suffers from remoteness and lack of local investment capital. The story is all too common: Small development company is nurtured to world-class standing, then sold to US heavyweight who regrettably shuts the New Zealand office and makes the original staff redundant.

ORGANIC KIWIFRUIT. READY TO EAT. $2 Per bag

Sophisticated wine-making has become a top earner in New Zealand

Above, sheep outnumber citizens by 10 to 1; below, paua shell, used for souvenirs

Engineering feats: the Otira Viaduct (top right); Clyde hydro-electric dam (above); Tararua Wind Farm (right)

Deer Me!

France has Champagne; New Zealand has Cervena. This is top grade, trademarked venison—mild, tender, low in fat, and heavy on the clean, green imagery. With a national herd of 1.6 million, the industry is small fry compared to sheep and dairy. Nevertheless, it holds international significance as the world's number one source of farmed venison, exporting particularly to the US, Europe, Australia and Japan. Some 85 per cent of venison served in American restaurants comes from New Zealand. Deer velvet, known for its medicinal properties, is also in demand and earns around NZ$38 million a year. The deer population has grown 34 per cent since 1994, and the South Island herd by 70 per cent. The name Cervena comes from *cervidae*—Latin for deer— and venison.

Musseling In

What's so special about New Zealand mussels that makes them worth counterfeiting? The green-lipped mussel (*Perna canaliculus*) is native and unique to New Zealand. Its green-and gold shell contains plump meat that is creamy white when male or apricot when female. Their size and taste give them a top reputation among mussel-buffs the world over, especially in the US, where inferior Chinese mussels (*Perna viridis*) have been sold in fake New Zealand packaging. The big concern— other than economic, as the industry is worth NZ$200 million a year— is that Chinese imposters are a potential health hazard. Mussels farmed under the New Zealand Greenshell trademark are grown under such stringent conditions they are safe to eat raw, but Chinese mussels are not. New Zealand's biggest mussel farms are in the Marlborough Sounds.

A Powerful Wind

New Zealand's geographical quirks aren't just for looks—they keep the country running. Mighty rivers like the Clutha and Waikato are dammed for hydro-electricity, which is the main source of power (61.4 per cent). Geothermal activity provides another 6.9 per cent, while gas, sourced particularly from the Taranaki offshore field, Maui, provides 24.4 per cent. But crisis looms. Drought in 2003 lowered lake levels so severely that the country was threatened with blackouts; and Maui reserves are expected to run out around 2015. The government aims to develop renewable energy to take up the slack. In 2004, Te Apiti wind farm was opened in the Manawatu. The country's fifth wind farm, it is expected to become the biggest in the southern hemisphere, with 55 turbines, each able to power 700 homes.

Top Tipple

Accessible and elegant, wine is perhaps the Kiwis' best-loved export. The industry burgeoned from a historical fondness for beer and sherry, surprising the world in 1988 when it was highly featured at the London Wine Trade Fair. Export earnings have rocketed from NZ$18 million in 1990 to NZ$600 million in 2006: more New Zealand wine is drunk overseas than domestically. New Zealand Sauvignon blanc is a reliable award-winner and has become the world's benchmark. Chardonnay, Pinot noir and Cabernet/Merlot blends are also gaining recognition.

New Zealand has 10 main wine-growing areas from Northland to Central Otago, the most established being Gisborne, Hawke's Bay and Marlborough. Many vineyards rate highly on the tourist trail, offering exceptional cuisine to complement tastings.

Right, the problematic possum

Right, a seahorse farm at Napier; below, autumn colour on the Kapiti Coast

Left, a frosty fern; right, cuddling a tuatara

Nature and Wildlife

Even as they step off the plane, visitors discover how serious New Zealand is about protecting its environment. No foreign plant or animal matter slips easily across the border; and a forgotten apple earns a NZ$250 spot fine.

Vigilance has been learned the hard way. Before man's arrival the country's only mammals were bats. The bush was thick with birds, many of which safely evolved as ground-dwellers—including the moa, kakapo and kiwi. The meaty moa was hunted to extinction by the Maori, and with the arrival of Europeans, hundreds more species vanished as their habitats were destroyed. Introduced animals compounded the disaster. With no natural predators, possums, cats, dogs, stoats, ferrets and rats ran rampant and are still a severe menace to native birds.

What's truly remarkable is that in spite of all the losses, wildlife remains one of New Zealand's greatest marvels. Native flora and fauna flourish in wilderness pockets all over the country, as well as a few inner-city areas such as Karori Wildlife Sanctuary in Wellington, where populations of rare kiwis, saddlebacks and kereru thrive. Much can be attributed to the expertise of local conservationists, who are in hot demand as far away as Indonesia and Madagascar.

The emblematic ponga, or black tree fern (*cyathea medullaris*)

Super Bugs

The giant weta is a heavyweight of the insect world. It can grow 9cm (3.5 inches) long, excluding antennae, and weigh up to 80g (3oz)—the same as four average mice. Even so, it is the sweetest-looking of New Zealand's five types of weta and by far the rarest. These nocturnal super-bugs evolved good defences against their natural enemies—birds—but are poor jumpers and no match for hungry stoats, rats or weasels. However, weta breed well in captivity and their track record for survival is good—in evolutionary terms they are older than dinosaurs. The mountain rock weta of the Southern Alps is the largest insect known to tolerate being frozen solid in winter. Most weta eat foliage or animal remains, but will try a human finger if threatened.

Right, bottlenose dolphins off the Nelson coast; left, flora in Wellington Zoo

Below, yellow-eyed penguin; right, a basking New Zealand fur seal

Below, familiar New Zealand birds include the kiwi, the kea (a parrot), the flightless weka, the New Zealand robin and the royal albatross

Keeping the Balance

When Penguin Place on the Otago Peninsula opened to visitors in 1984, there were eight pairs of rare yellow-eyed penguins on the reserve. By 2004 that number had tripled. The attraction now runs programmes for scientific research, native reforestation, predator control and an ornithological hospital. It's cost thousands, but every project was funded with tourist dollars. Eco-tourism creates a win-win situation—if the operators create the best environment possible, wildlife thrives, creating an even more attractive tourist destination. In exchange for their dollars, tourists access a unique, hands-on experience. Top eco-friendly activities include spotting endangered Hector's dolphins near Christchurch, the Waimangu valley near Taupo, and guided nature walks around Queenstown.

Threatened Identity

Human Kiwis were shocked in the 1980s to realise their feathered namesake was in serious trouble. Despite urgent action, the numbers continued to decline by up to five per cent a year. The current total population across six varieties is estimated at 70,000.

However, the Bank of New Zealand Kiwi Recovery Trust is striking back. Operation Nest Egg (ONE) increases chicks' chances of reaching adulthood from five per cent to forty, at which point they can defend themselves. The enormous egg is taken from the sitting adult, and the chick is hatched and reared in captivity. Kiwi chicks fend for themselves once hatched, so in some situations the parents can be left undisturbed and the newly hatched chick removed to a predator proof 'kiwi crèche' within its wild habitat.

The Problem with Possums

One feature of every New Zealand highway is the squashed possum. Never mind, there's plenty more. An estimated 70 million Australian brushtail possums (introduced in 1837) are stripping native forests in 98 per cent of the country, often decimating prized trees such as rata for miles around. Their main food is young tree foliage, but they tuck into flowers, fruit, berries and insects if available. It was originally thought their impact on native birdlife was indirect, but time-lapse video has caught them eating eggs, chicks and adult birds. The NZ$60 million spent each year on possum control is not working. Current hopes lie in a contraceptive vaccine. A fur trade makes a tiny dint in the population, with luxury products like Merinomink (possum/fine wool) clothing, bedspreads, gloves and…nipple warmers.

Treasure or Traitor?

A unique conservation debate was highlighted in June 2004, when the Department of Conservation (DoC) dropped 55 tonnes of rat poison on Little Barrier Island in the Hauraki Gulf. It was the first stage of a NZ$700,000 operation to wipe out the kiore, or Polynesian rat, from New Zealand's oldest nature reserve. The issue was sensitive because some Maori tribes consider the kiore a *taonga*, or treasure. It has probably been in New Zealand as long as the Maori, having arrived with the early canoes, and was once important for food and cloak-making. However, it's a predatory rodent and considered a threat to native weta, frogs, skinks, birds and other wildlife. Although kiore are common in the south-western Pacific and on some of New Zealand's offshore islands, they are rare on the mainland.

Above, carving greenstone (*pounamu*); below, cooking a traditional *hangi*

Above and right, preparing traditional foods; left, the Challenge Pose

The Maori

The Big Issue

Does the Crown own New Zealand's foreshore and seabed? In 1997 the Ngati Apa tribe of Marlborough asked the court. In 2003 the Court of Appeal ruled it was Maori customary land. As no laws had been made to change this, the foreshore and seabed did not belong to the Crown absolutely. Kiwis prize nothing more than a day at the beach, so the Government leaped to legislate in 2004, giving ownership of the foreshore and seabed to the state. Their principles were that these areas should be public domain, with open access for all New Zealanders, but the customary interests of Maori would be protected. Maori—and the Waitangi Tribunal—called the ruling discriminatory because it abolished Maori property rights while apparently protecting everyone else's.

Far from dying out, as predicted by colonists, Maori culture is an integrated component of everyday New Zealand. Te Reo (Maori language) is taught in schools and culturally specific words like *iwi* (tribe), *taonga* (treasure), *whanau* (family) and *tapu* (sacred) are commonly used without elaboration. A Maori television channel was launched in 2003, the same year as the Maori Party in politics. Understanding and value of New Zealand's Maori heritage continues to grow; it's part of what makes the country unique. Indeed, when cyclist Sarah Ulmer won gold at the 2004 Athens Olympics, it was her supporters' spontaneous *haka*, not the medal ceremony, that touched her most.

Ka mate, Ka mate!

Haka were around long before the All Blacks, but the rugby team certainly helped to cement the dance in Kiwi culture. Traditionally *haka* could refer to all Maori dance, but now it implies a vigorous posture dance. Men and women both perform *haka* but the men have the more spirited role, slapping thighs and chests, enlarging their eyes and sticking out their tongues. Haka can intimidate first-time spectators but they are not necessarily war dances—they are also performed at times of welcome, success or strong emotion.

Unfurling Economy

The emerging phrase 'Maori economy' describes enterprises run in line with Maori cultural values, such as *whanaugatanga* (kinship), *kotahitanga* (unity), *kaitiakitanga* (guardianship) and *mana whenua* (control of land). The end product doesn't need a particularly Maori flavour to qualify—Maori exports largely consist of fisheries, beef cattle, sheep meat, wool and forest products. But in some cases the Maori-ness is the product's selling point. Entrepreneurial chef Charles Royal has developed a demand for *pikopiko* (delicately unfurling fern fronds), a traditional Maori food that can be poached, grilled, barbecued or stir-fried. Under the label Kinaki Wild Herbs, he also produces medicinal body rubs containing *horopito* (bush pepper), a traditional aid to skin repair, and *kawakawa*, considered a blood purifier.

The Story of New Zealand

New Land, New People

New Zealand was 680 million years in the making. Humans arrived on its shores perhaps a thousand years ago—hardly a tick on the geological clock—but their effect was profound and irreversible. The first settlers from East Polynesia probably numbered between one and two hundred, but within a century several species of bird were extinct, seals and other seabirds were all but eradicated from the main islands and large tracts of land were destroyed by fire. The easy pickings from New Zealand's great natural store cupboard had gone and the settlers were forced into more considered methods of survival. This marked the transition from the 'archaic' era of Maori settlement to the 'classic'.

Groups became more settled as they developed sustainable food production such as gardening. The tubers of their kumara (sweet potato) became more valuable and had to be protected, giving rise to *pa* (fortified villages). By the 16th century a tribal system had developed. Now fully adjusted to the challenges of their environment, settlers could keep warm, build appropriate shelters and grow food. The focus moved to building social and cultural systems based on the old ways, but suited to their new country. They were no longer immigrants from Polynesia, but Maori.

In the Beginning

There are two quite different Maori myths about New Zealand's origins. One concerns Maui, the heroic trickster, who hauled up the North Island while he was out fishing.

The other is of Papatuanuku (the Earth Mother) and Ranginui (the Sky Father), who embraced each other so tightly their 70 sons were squashed between them. After much discussion, all the sons except one agreed their parents should be prized apart. Tanemahuta stood on his shoulders and pushed up the sky with his feet. He then clothed Papa with the green of the forest and adorned Rangi with the sun and stars, but still they wept for each other, creating rain and mist. Tawhiri-matea, the son who objected to his parents' separation, angrily followed Rangi into the sky and created wind and storms.

The myth of fisherman Maui, whose anchor formed Stewart Island (Rakiura), is celebrated with a massive chain sculpture in Lee Bay

1000

Above, Maori canoes at Wanganui
Right, settlers brought the art of tattooing

Man Becomes Myth

Until recently, Maori arrival in New Zealand was neatly tied up: in AD950, a Polynesian navigator, Kupe, left Hawaiki (Tahiti) with his family and crew. Eventually, he sighted a white cloud (*aotea*), which revealed a bush-covered land. He called it Aotearoa—Land of the Long White Cloud. In 1350, a 'Great Fleet' of seven canoes followed in his wake.

However, 1970s research found these 'truths' were not authenticated by Maori sources but had been cobbled together by a European scholar.

What we do know for sure is the Maori came from East Polynesia, a race of seafarers with the sophisticated navigation needed to complete the 3,000km (1,860-mile) journey and return home. It seems likely that after initial voyages of discovery, men and women came in several canoes, equipped for settlement, during the 13th century.

Hunted Down

Maori settlers walked into a teeming store cupboard. The moa was not the only ground-dwelling bird with little fear of predators, but it remains the most distinctive. It looked like a chunky ostrich, or an enormous kiwi with a long neck. At around 3m (10ft), the giant moa was the world's tallest bird, with drumsticks equivalent to a leg of beef. Even the smaller bush moa were as big as turkeys. They were zealously rounded up and killed in their thousands until, in little more than 100 years, they were gone. Archaeologists have found traces of massive fires that destroyed forests, especially in Hawke's Bay and on the east coast of the South Island—these may have been started as a last-ditch effort to flush out the last of the species.

Codes of Conduct

As Maori culture developed into the tribally organised 'classic' phase, common values emerged. Links between tribes were strong enough for these values to be shared by all, just like the language. For example, it was accepted that people were either *rangatira* (aristocrats) or *tutua* (commoners). *Rangatira* had more *mana* (honour), but anyone could gain or lose *mana* according to their skills and achievements. Another common concept was *utu*. This idea of reciprocation could be positive or destructive, in response to a favour or an insult. It could sweeten relationships between tribes or families—one could gift basalt while the other returned with fish, raising the *mana* of both parties. Or it could mean war, as one tribe rectified another tribe's misdeed, which could have occurred days or decades before.

The first settlers soon hunted the flightless moa to extinction

A Race Wronged

The Moriori came from East Polynesia and settled in the Chatham Islands (Rekohu). They shared the same genes as the Maori and travelled at around the same time, but away from the mainland they developed cultural differences: a society without hierarchy, their own dialect and a covenant to settle disputes by one-on-one combat, rather than warfare. During the 20th century historians portrayed Moriori as an inferior race exterminated by the Maori—a useful justification for European colonisation. Moriori numbers were indeed decimated by the 1835 invasion of two Maori tribes, but descendants survived. However, most kept their heritage quiet until these presumptions were challenged in the late 20th century. In 2004, three Moriori groups signed terms with the Government under the Treaty of Waitangi, and three more were expected to follow suit.

1769

Early settlers (above, below) challenged and saw off Abel Tasman's curious crew in 1642 at Murderers' Bay (left)

NEW LAND, NEW PEOPLE 25

Trading
Goods and Lives

New Zealand's appearance on the world map did not suddenly change life for the Maori. English navigator Captain James Cook came and went in 1769, and the next 70 years brought an odd assortment of Europeans who settled around the edges of Maoridom. Many coastal tribes happily adopted individual missionaries or traders—it was a boost to *mana*, having one's own white man. Similarly, they adopted the goods that suited them best and discarded the rest. Maori bred pigs and grew flax, fruit and vegetables—especially the new white potatoes—specifically to barter with the Europeans. Europeans depended on this trade for survival; Maori came to depend on it for muskets.

By the 1830s the entire country was consumed by a bloody carnage known as the Musket Wars. Trade intensified as the acquisition of guns became obsessive. Traditional power balances were abolished as tribes such as Ngapuhi and Ngati Toa swept across vast sections of the country, annihilating rival tribes on the way. Men, women and children were all game. During 3,000 or so battles that took place from 1818 to 1840, an estimated 30,000 of the total 100,000 Maori population was killed by warfare, disease, starvation, slavery or in the cannibal feasts of victory.

A Floating Laboratory

The first map of New Zealand represented disappointment. Captain James Cook's 1769 circumnavigation proved the country was not the hoped-for corner of a Southern Continent, as suggested by Dutch explorer Abel Tasman in 1642. But Cook's scientific expedition had many successes. He observed the transit of Venus across the sun from Tahiti as directed by London's Royal Society, providing vital data to map the solar system. He proved that regular doses of sauerkraut (rich in vitamin C) prevented sailors from dying of scurvy. And with naturalists headed by Joseph Banks, hundreds of plant and animal specimens were collected.

Deadly muskets replaced traditional Maori weapons carved from wood or stone

James Cook (1728–79)

1769

Above, the first Europeans were keen to map the coastline and exploit whaling resources, right; left, portrait of Te Pehi Kupe in Western dress, c.1826; far right, signing the Treaty of Waitangi

Pakeha Maori

New Zealand's early Europeans were a diverse group. Among the sealers, whalers and missionaries was a small group known as Pakeha Maori—people like Barnet Burns, a trader who came in 1830 and went native. He lived in Mahia, south of Gisborne, under the protectorate of a chief he called 'Awhawee'. He married the chief's daughter, Amotawa, with whom he had three children. Over three intensive years he was abducted by rival tribesmen, escaped, led two major battles and claimed to have been made chief of a tribe of 600. He sailed to England on business in 1835 and gave a series of lectures—resplendent in full Maori dress and *moko* (facial and body tattoos). He never returned to New Zealand, but numerous descendants still live on the East Coast.

Men of influence: right, Samuel Marsden and far right, William Hobson

God and Grammar

Christianity came to the Maori in 1814. Anglican chaplain Samuel Marsden planted three lay workers at Rangihoua, in the Bay of Islands. One, Thomas Kendall, approached his task by immersing himself in Maori culture and language. To his dismay, he nearly converted himself to heathen ways long before any Maori turned Christian. Marsden eventually dismissed him for misdemeanors including adultery, but not before Kendall could accompany his friend chief Hongi Hika and a younger chief, Waikato, to England in 1820. There, Hongi Hika (a fearsome figure of the Musket Wars) had an audience with George IV. The threesome worked with a Cambridge linguist to produce the foundations of written Maori. The conversion rate stayed on zero until the late 1820s, when Christian peace gave an alternative to the bloodshed of the Musket Wars.

The Treaty of Waitangi

In 1839, naval officer William Hobson was sent from London to formally establish New Zealand as a British colony. He invited chiefs from the North Island to sign a treaty at Waitangi on 5 February 1840. The government provided no draft document, so, with no legal training, Hobson and his officials hurriedly prepared the treaty in the four days preceding. Most inter-racial communication occurred in Maori, so it was also translated the night before. Forty-five chiefs signed after extended deliberations on 6 February; by September over 500 had signed. The question was—and still is—what did they agree to? Discrepancies between British and Maori understandings were quickly realised but not easily rectified. Despite good intentions, the Treaty of Waitangi became the most contentious issue in New Zealand's history.

Names for Faces

The word Maori means ordinary. It was widely used by Maori to describe themselves by the 1830s, although to most Europeans they were simply 'New Zealanders'. The Maori version of the Treaty of Waitangi uses the phrase *tangata maori*— ordinary people. As for Europeans, Maori had used the word *Pakeha* since at least 1814, when missionary William Hall recorded he had been referred to as a 'rungateeda pakehaa' (*rangatira pakeha*), meaning a European gentleman. By the 1830s the word's usage among Maori was widespread. Europeans still described themselves according to their home countries, such as British. Pakeha probably originates from *pakepakeha*, an imaginary light-skinned being. The word's use was purely descriptive rather than derogatory, although it was also used for turnip (because of its white flesh) and flea.

1840

A botanical illustration from Cook's first voyage, 1768–71

A *Surge of* Settlers

The year 1840 marked the start of mass migration to New Zealand. The imminent tide of settlers was one reason Hobson needed to push through the Treaty of Waitangi—the Crown's right to purchase land had to be secured before private enterprise companies (notably the New Zealand Company) could steal the march. The next 20 years passed in relative peace, as Maori and Pakeha traded goods and land, but shady deals sowed seeds for future discontent. Maori land was communally owned, and wide consultation was required for a valid sale. New Zealand Company agents in Wellington, Nelson and Wanganui often found it easier to skip difficult owners and close a quick deal, while some Maori found their land had been 'sold' from under them by rivals.

In 1840 there were just over 2,000 Pakeha settlers. By 1858 there were 59,000—3,000 more than there were Maori. As the numbers changed, so did the countryside; settlers made it more homely. Hundreds of plants, birds and animals were introduced, including 1.5 million sheep. The land was surveyed and mapped. Mountains, lakes and rivers known by the Maori for generations were 'discovered' and given European names. New Zealand was becoming 'the Britain of the South'.

Primitive settlers' houses with tin chimneys were replaced by cob, brick and weatherboard

End of an Empire

The most powerful man in 1840 was Te Rauparaha—warrior chief, strategist and entrepreneur. Kicked out of his Kawhia homeland by Waikato relatives, Te Rauparaha and his Ngati Toa tribe conquered Horowhenua with guns in 1823. From his stronghold on Kapiti Island he led murderous raids as far south as Banks Peninsula, and soon dominated the lower North Island and upper South Island. Wellington and Nelson were established only with his permission in the 1840s, but disputes later arose over which areas he actually sold. In 1843 a confrontation over land on the Wairau Plains, north of Blenheim, ended violently and settlers became nervous. Governor George Grey decided Te Rauparaha could not be trusted and arrested him in 1846. During 10 months in prison his *mana* waned. Te Rauparaha died in 1849.

Powerful rivals: Te Ruaparaha and Governor George Grey

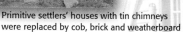

1840

Above, Maori chief Hone Heke defied authorities, sparking the Northern War, in 1845; right, Auckland's Queen Street c.1853

Maori Monarchy

As Maori felt their land and culture slipping away, they looked for strength in unity. Tribes around Waikato, Taranaki and the central North Island acted by selecting the first Maori king: the Waikato chief Te Wherowhero. In 1858, he took his seat at Ngaruawahia, north of Hamilton, in the district now known as the King Country. Maori intended their monarchy to complement the British Crown—the Maori king and Queen Victoria would be joined in accord. They hoped this unity would give Maori a chance against the confident and cohesive settlers. Instead, it aggravated the colonists, who thought it showed disloyalty to the Queen. It was also seen as a stumbling block to further land sales, and fuelled the idea that Maori were getting too big for their boots.

Dreams for Sale

For the equivalent of NZ$101, the New Zealand Company sold investors one town acre (0.4ha) and 100 country acres (40ha). Not that the company had any land to sell—the ships containing buyers and surveyors scooted into Port Nicholson (Wellington) just 18 days before 1,000 unsuspecting migrants. They found no sign of the undulating plains promised in company propaganda, described as perfect for grapevines, wheat, olives and bananas—only swamp, forest, steep hills and sand hummocks. The plan of 1,100 one-acre sections simply wouldn't fit into the proposed Hutt Valley site. Migrants camped on the Petone foreshore, with possessions from beds to pianos heaped around them. At least they wouldn't starve: From the moment they stepped off the boat, they started shooting birds.

Great Shakes

As if the Wellington settlers hadn't enough to contend with, their fledgling town was struck by the country's biggest recorded earthquake in January 1855. It measured 8 on the Richter scale—the 1999 Taiwan quake that claimed 2,330 lives was 7.6. In this case, one person died in Wellington and three in Wairarapa. But it wasn't all bad. The shoreline rose 1m (3ft) on average, leaving Lambton Quay high and dry—it is now a main shopping street. Plans for a new dock had to be shelved (the area is now Basin Reserve cricket ground, ▷ 104), but there was suddenly space for a road to link Wellington with the Hutt Valley, reclaimable land around the harbour and another 100m (110 yards) of beach at Petone. Wooden buildings were proved safer than brick, and carpenters rejoiced.

Heaven or Hell?

The primitive conditions of New Zealand shocked new arrival Georgiana Bowen. She wrote to her sister in 1851: 'It is only Colonists who can have any idea of what roughing it is, and it is ill suited for any but the young, strong and active…We are now in wooden shanties or tents of which perhaps you can form no idea.' Maria Richmond, on the other hand, was smitten after just six months. In 1853 she wrote: 'I have never felt so wide awake as I have done since I landed in New Zealand…the feeling of coming home, as it were, to a country wanting you, asking for people to enjoy and use it, with a climate to suit you, a beauty to satisfy and delight, and with such possibilities for the future.'

Land was cleared of spear grass and matagouri to make way for sheep

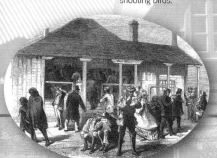

1860

Below, the *Randolph* was one of four ships that brought colonists to the Canterbury settlement in 1850; above left, mail home encouraged more to follow

The Colony Gains Confidence

The colony entered an unsettled time of change. Rapid growth put pressure on towns like Auckland and New Plymouth, which in turn put pressure on Maori to sell more land. Discontent on both sides sparked a series of land wars, which ripped through the North Island from 1860 to 1872. Colonial forces fought Maori and Maori fought each other. By the turn of the century, Maori were considered a dying race. Many tribes had lost their livelihoods and their morale with the confiscation of millions of hectares of land. They were also ravaged by influenza, measles, whooping cough and dysentery.

Meanwhile, the European population boomed. Premier Julius Vogel borrowed a staggering amount of money on the London capital market during the 1870s to put in thousands of kilometres of roads, railways and telegraph lines, and to assist another 100,000 settlers into the country. It was not enough to protect New Zealand from worldwide recession, which lasted into the 1890s, but the advent of refrigeration brought new hope. The first successful shipment of frozen lamb and mutton to England in 1882 granted the country a major new export earner.

Out of enforced bachelor life emerged the Kiwi spirit of self-reliance and mateship

The Bachelor Life

In 1871, men outnumbered women two to one. With no prospect of marrying, many vanished into a men's world of shearing, farm work, timber milling, mining or public works. Once in the back blocks, they would live in shanty camps for years. It was the start of New Zealand's 'bloke' culture, where hard work, honesty, camaraderie, sense of humour and mateship were highly valued. The government aimed to boost the population by offering free passage to single British women. Many obliged; domestic servants could earn more than in England. Even so, mistresses had to bargain hard to keep their staff, and domestics with an apparent impediment to matrimony—such as Gaelic speakers—were preferred. Twenty years later, the sex ratios were nearly balanced.

1860

Above, Gottfried Lindauer's portrait of Ana Rupene and child, c.1880; above right, fighting in the land wars

Chinatown

Gold in Otago and Westland brought a new wave of immigrants—the Chinese. They made up 6 per cent of the Otago population in 1871, virtually all men who lived on the breadline to send money back to their wives and families. Isolated by appearance and culture, they stuck together and were treated with suspicion by Europeans. Their greatest success story was Choie Sew Hoy, whose pioneer gold dredge enabled miners to winkle sand out of river flats as well as the river bed. Hoy established a store in Dunedin importing Chinese goods and became a mentor for other Chinese in the area. Unlike his companions, he opted to stay in New Zealand and married locally. By 1880 he was the best-known Chinese figure in Dunedin. Sew Hoy's Dunedin store still trades on Stafford Street.

A Great Explosion

On 10 June 1886, the ground south of Rotorua shook violently as Mount Tarawera split open, sending a column of fire into the night sky. Tourists staying at the Rotomahana Hotel fled to the *whare* of Sophia, a Maori guide. Her small house sheltered 60 people through the night and was one of only two buildings in Wairoa village to survive the eruption. The rest were buried under tonnes of mud, rock and ash. An estimated 153 people were killed, including the school teacher and five of his children. His wife was later pulled from the mud alive. Lake Rotomahana is now 30m (98ft) higher than before the eruption. The blasted face of Mount Tarawera still tells a tale, and destroyed the famous pink-and-white terraces (▷ 87).

Taking the Lead

Two remarkable world firsts passed into law under Richard ('King Dick') Seddon's Liberal government: old-age pensions (1898) and universal suffrage. Winning the world's first national votes for women took a good deal of hard graft by Kate Sheppard, temperance supporter, writer, speaker and early feminist. She liked women to be 'hearty and hale', and rode a bike around Christchurch when women were considered too fragile for such activity. But she also had the tact, intellect and determination to win allies and advance her battle. Her first petition in 1891 contained 9,000 signatures. Her second, a year later, had 19,000. Her final petition was signed by nearly 32,000 women—around a third of the female population. The Women's Suffrage Bill passed by two votes in 1893.

Blowing the Whistle

New Zealand stamped its first mark on rugby in 1884, when referee W.H. Atack of Canterbury got sick of shouting himself hoarse at two marauding teams. According to the official historian of the NZ Rugby Football Union, Atack was mulling over the problem when his fingers strayed to a waistcoat pocket. There, they encountered a dog whistle. With a flash of inspiration, he realised it would be a perfect way to stop the game. The next time he refereed, he called the teams together and they agreed to play to the whistle. It was a great success and was adopted all over the country. New Zealand's first national rugby team toured the UK in 1888–89 as the New Zealand Native Team—they weren't called the All Blacks until 1905.

Left, gold miners take a break at Monteith's Brewery, Greymouth
Below, Cardrona started as a gold-rush town and retains a frontier feel

Richard 'King Dick' Seddon (1845–1906)

1900

Below, some gold hunters joined the coal mines
Left, Mount Tarawera, 1886

A Nation Goes Forth

There was no doubt New Zealand would fight alongside Mother England when World War I broke out. After a period of relative peace and prosperity, young men jumped at the chance to take part—both Pakeha and Maori. It was exciting, patriotic, a chance for blokes to get together and see the world. They would fight alongside Australians as the Australia and New Zealand Army Corps—ANZACs.

But euphoria vanished when 3,000 New Zealanders landed at Gallipoli on the Turkish Coast on 25 April 1915. The campaign was a disaster from the outset—troops were landed 3km (2 miles) from the intended beach and faced a wall of cliffs. One soldier in five was mown down on the first day. For eight months, they existed in trenches metres away from the Turkish troops, prey to disease, heat, blizzards, snipers and the stench of irretrievable bodies.

Despite valiant attempts to claim the peninsula, the attack was an utter failure. When the troops were finally pulled out in mid-December, the casualty rate stood at 88 per cent. New Zealanders went on to fight at the Western Front and in the Middle East but Gallipoli is still the campaign most remembered. April 25 is ANZAC Day, a national day of commemoration.

Recruiting poster for World War II—New Zealand regiments fought with distinction in Crete and the Middle East

Welfare For All

Few prime ministers have their photos hung over the mantelpiece, but Michael Joseph Savage was different. He was the benign face of the Labour government that stormed to victory in 1935, just as the Great Depression was tailing off. Their mission to look after New Zealanders 'from the cradle to the grave' had a positive effect—a free hospital system, universal super-annuation at 65, a 40-hour working week and a basic wage considered enough to keep a man, wife and three children comfortably. In three years, 3,500 state houses were built with modern kitchens and the luxury of an indoor toilet.

Michael Joseph Savage (1872–1940)

TOGETHER

1900

the IBYSTANDER

Above, pioneer aviator Jean Batten (1909–82); right, Gallipoli; far right, war memorials are a familiar sight

32

Taking Off

When does 'powered flight' become 'controlled'? If you can land in a river and still be 'controlled', then Richard Pearse was a world-class achiever. And even if you can't, his 1902 aircraft still flew 21 months before the Wright brothers'. The South Canterbury farmer created a plane with a two-cylinder engine, vertical rudder, tricycle undercarriage and propeller. Eyewitnesses say that on 31 March 1902 this craft took off from a farm paddock, climbed slowly, turned right and flew 1,200m (3,963ft) before landing in a river. A modified version flew 50m (164ft) one year later before colliding with a gorse bush. Pearse patented ailerons—flaps that give planes vertical control—in 1906, but he let the patent lapse in 1910 because he didn't see much prospect of selling planes in New Zealand.

Deadly Virus

On 11 October 1918, the passenger liner *Niagara* was permitted to dock in Auckland harbour, despite radioed warnings that Spanish influenza was on board. Why wasn't the ship quarantined? Among the passengers were Prime Minister William Massey and his Minister of Finance, anxious to return to work after meetings in Britain and Europe. It's not known if they influenced the decision to let passengers disembark, but by 3 November, 120 cases of flu were admitted to Auckland Public Hospital. There was no cure. The disease quickly spread south, shutting schools, shops and pubs and disrupting industry. More than 6,700 New Zealanders died, including an estimated 2,160 Maori.

Architectural confidence in Dunedin's railway station, 1906

Literary Talent

Katherine Mansfield is New Zealand's best-known writer. Even though she was 'ashamed' of her young country's stifling lack of creativity, her childhood memories gave richness to her masterful short stories. She was born in 1888 to a socialite Wellington family. At the age of 14 she went to England for three years of schooling, and on returning home found she couldn't wait to get back to London. 'It is Life,' she wrote. Her avid pursuit of 'Life' took her back to London in 1908, where she mingled with the intellectual Bloomsbury group of writers. After passionate affairs, an inexplicable marriage and a last-ditch hunt for inner peace, she died of tuberculosis near Paris in 1923, aged 34. She was the first New Zealand-born writer to earn international recognition.

Maoris Enter Politics

By the start of the 20th century, a group of well-educated leaders emerged to fight the Maori cause through politics: Maui Pomare, James Carroll and Apirana Ngata.

Less conventional was Tahupotiki Wiremu Ratana. The ploughman's journey began in 1918, when he heard the voice of God telling him that Maori were God's chosen people, and that he should unite Maori and turn them towards God. Ratana began faith healing and was so successful that a settlement grew around his house, south of Wanganui (it is now called Ratana). Ratana MPs held all four Maori parliamentary seats by 1943 and provided Labour with a vital alliance during 1946 to 1949. Attention to Maori land development, schooling, housing and unemployment brought a marked improvement to Maori conditions. The Ratana church now has over 49,000 members.

Katherine Mansfield (1888–1923)

1945

A replica of Richard Pearse's aeroplane at MOTAT

Age of Assertion

Mother England gently loosened the apron strings in 1931 by proclaiming her Dominions autonomous. New Zealand remained in denial, even as she backed out of their stifling economic relationship in preference for Europe.

In 1984, a new Labour government showed the first signs of the rebellious teenager. It was led by quick-witted barrister David Lange, who soon had to grasp the prickly end of Labour's anti-nuclear stance. When the US ship *Buchanan* refused to confirm or deny its nuclear capabilities, Lange denied it entry. This signalled the effective end of ANZUS, a key defence treaty with Australia and America. The US's subsequent bullying did not impress the public, but on 10 July 1985 the Kiwis' nuke-free stance turned absolute. That night, the Greenpeace ship *Rainbow Warrior* was blown up in Auckland harbour, killing one crew member. The ship was about to sail to Mururoa atoll in the Pacific to protest against French nuclear tests. In a matter of days the New Zealand police caught those responsible—two French agents. The leaders of the US, Britain and Australia barely said a word against it. New Zealanders were outraged, and determined to stand by their principles. The agents were later decorated by the French government.

Then and now: the *Rainbow Warrior* (bottom) is now a dive site (right)

1945

Land Rights to the Fore

The government continued to take Maori land in the 1970s but there was a difference—Maori numbers, awareness and anger had grown. In 1975, a march from Northland ended in Wellington with 50,000 supporters asking the government to guarantee that not one more hectare of Maori land would be lost. The government did not commit. Rather, in 1976, it decided to sell land at Bastion Point, which originally belonged to Ngati Whatua. The tribe had reserved it nearly 100 years before, after selling thousands of hectares for Auckland development. Over time, pockets were lost—much of it to compulsory Crown acquisition. Maori patience ran out when the government tried to sell the land for high-priced housing—protesters occupied the site for 17 months before being arrested in May 1978.

Top, anti-nuclear Prime Minister David Lange, 1986
Right, Waitangi protesters

The Open Market

The Labour government created the welfare state in 1935; in 1984 they took most of it away. With the over-protected economy verging on bankruptcy, finance minister Roger Douglas opened New Zealand to the ravages of the free market. The changes were abrupt, unexpected and painful. Agriculture subsidies were phased out; farmers walked off the land. The dollar was devalued and later floated on the international market. Government enterprises such as the Post Office and New Zealand Steel became State Owned Enterprises and were expected to turn a profit. Thousands of public servants were made redundant and unions reeled as their power base was chipped away. 'Rogernomics' changed New Zealand's fundamental economic values forever.

Divided Fans

Could any other country be so divided by rugby? In 1981, the New Zealand Rugby Union invited the South African Springboks to play three test matches against the All Blacks. Prime Minister Rob Muldoon refused to intervene even though he had signed the Gleneagles Agreement, discouraging sporting contact with apartheid South Africa. It sparked an unofficial civil war—barbed-wire fences, street blockades and riot police became as common as street marches. The first match in Hamilton was abandoned when 300 protestors sat on the pitch, tempting the wrath of 27,000 fans. The violence peaked at the final match in Auckland. Protesters made 362 complaints against the police; 75 were eventually upheld. In all, 2,000 arrests were made and tour defence cost the country NZ$7.2 million.

Running the Race

Ever been for a jog? Thank Aucklander Arthur Lydiard, who formed the world's first jogging group. In 1944, at the age of 27, he struggled to run 10km (6 miles) with a friend. The training method of the day—speeding round a track to point of collapse—didn't work for him. Instead, he devised a programme of gradual build-up. By his early 30s he was New Zealand's top marathon runner, and his times over shorter distances had also improved. A group of younger runners started training under his guidance. Two became stars of the 1960 Rome Olympics—Murray Halberg, who won the 5,000m gold, and Peter Snell, who won the 800m and smashed the Olympic record by 1.4 seconds. Lydiard later applied his principles to fitness for the general public and invented 'jogging'.

Homegrown Supermodel

When everyone was talking about the super-models of Britain, the US and Europe, New Zealand was surprised to realise it had one too. Rachel Hunter (born in Auckland in 1969) started modelling at the age of 17. After starring as 'the Trumpet girl' in an ice cream advertisement on TV, she leapt to the pages of *Sports Illustrated*—the magazine famed for making models famous. She appeared on thousands of covers worldwide, including *Cosmopolitan* and *Vogue*. Not only that, but by 1990 Hunter had married Rockin' Rod Stewart—the British crooner 24 years her senior. For a while she was the ultimate home girl made good—she even brought Rod and her two children home for holidays. In 1999 the pair split but Rachel continued to dominate magazine headlines. She now lives in the US.

Jogging owes its origins to Aucklander Arthur Lydiard

Rugby became a political issue in 1981

1999

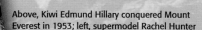

Above, Kiwi Edmund Hillary conquered Mount Everest in 1953; left, supermodel Rachel Hunter

Into the New Millennium

New Zealand's taste for independence has grown to a hearty appetite and the country has bravely adopted its new position as a Pacific nation, closer to Asia than Europe. In trade, the country gradually recovered to establish healthy relationships with countries other than Britain, particularly Australia, the US, Europe, Japan and China. Agricultural products like meat and dairy remained substantial export earners, but tourism, forestry and fisheries widened the economic base. The surprise boon of the new century was film-making. By 2004, nine big-budget Hollywood films had been released or were in production, including the Oscar-sweeping *Lord of the Rings*.

Competitive Spirit

Kiwis were devastated to lose the America's Cup in 2003, and appalled to see England crowned rugby world champions in the same year. The Athens Olympics of 2004 gave them a much-needed boost, as cyclist Sarah Ulmer ripped six seconds off her own world record, and triathletes Hamish Carter and Bevan Docherty won gold and silver. Gold was also won by sculling twins Caroline and Georgina Evers-Swindell.

Race Relations

The Waitangi Tribunal was created in 1975 to inquire into Maori grievances against the Crown but grew teeth only in 1985, when it was able to consider claims dating back to 1840. In October 2000, 870 claims had been registered with the Tribunal. Claims could be historical, such as compensation for confiscated land, or contemporary, if current government actions were thought to breach treaty principles. Apart from tribal land, claims have been made about sharing resources as diverse as the airwaves, oil, fisheries, airspace and, in 2004–5, the foreshore and seabed. Successful claimants, such as Ngai Tahu in the South Island, who settled on a NZ$170 million compensation package, have generated business success and morale. The Tribunal expects to report on all claims by 2012.

Governor-general Anand Satyanand

War Against Terror

After September 11, New Zealand joined the United Nations in disagreeing with the need to invade Iraq. Prime Minister Helen Clark clearly believed the US was wrong to proceed without UN backing. After the invasion, nearly 70 per cent of New Zealanders approved of her Labour government's opposition to the war. The stand was principled but it wasn't easy, especially as New Zealand had high hopes of jumping on Australia's free trade deal with the US. Clark's widely reported comment that the war would never have happened if Al Gore was president was considered by some a major gaffe. In 2003, 61 army engineers and support staff were sent to contribute to reconstruction and humanitarian tasks in southern Iraq. Their deployment ended in October 2004.

After 2000

Above, the elusive America's Cup; right, Sarah Ulmer cycling for gold at Athens

On the Move

ARRIVING

Arriving By Air

The vast majority of visitors to New Zealand arrive by air. The three main international airports are Auckland, Christchurch and Wellington, with Auckland being the principal entry point. Palmerston North and Hamilton in North Island and Christchurch, Dunedin and Queenstown in South Island all offer regular air services to eastern Australia.

Auckland International Airport

Auckland airport, a relatively small, modern gateway to the nation, is 21km (13 miles) south of the city's central business district. The airport has two terminals—international and domestic. A free transit shuttle operates between them every 20 minutes from 6am to 10.30pm, and there is a connecting walkway.

● At the i-SITE visitor information office on the ground floor of the Arrivals hall you can book hotels, check transport details and store luggage. Hospitality ambassadors, dressed in bright blue jackets, or customer service officers, dressed in red jackets, are available for assistance.

● Shops, food outlets, mail boxes, internet access, crêche, free showers (towels are rented out from the florist on the ground floor for a small fee plus deposit) and phones are all available at the airport.

● Additional services include dayrooms containing a bed, desk, TV, coffee, tea and shower, which can be rented from NZ$30 for four hours. There are banks with currency exchange facilities

AIRPORT CONTACTS		
North Island		
Auckland	tel 09-276 8899	www.auckland-airport.co.nz
Wellington	tel 04-388 9900	www.wellington-airport.co.nz
Palmerston North	tel 06-351 4415	www.pnairport.co.nz
Hamilton	tel 07-848 9027	www.hamiltonairport.co.nz
South Island		
Christchurch	tel 03-358 5029	www.christchurch-airport.co.nz
Dunedin	tel 03-486 2879	www.dnairport.co.nz
Queenstown	tel 03-442 3505	www.queenstownairport.co.nz

throughout Departures and Arrivals in the International Terminal. ATMs can be found in various locations in the International Terminal. A medical facility operates just outside the International Terminal.

● All the well-known rental car operators (▷ 41) are represented at both terminals on the ground floor.

Wellington International Airport

Wellington airport, in the suburb of Rongotai, 6km (3 miles) south of the heart of the city, handles both international and domestic flights from one terminal. Take-offs and landings along its short runway are particularly memorable.

● Although there are dozens of Trans-Tasman and Pacific Island flights per week, Wellington primarily operates a busy domestic schedule, with regular daily flights to most principal cities. Air New Zealand and Qantas are the main carriers, but a number of smaller operators fly to upper South Island destinations. These include Sounds Air, who offer flights to Picton, Nelson and Blenheim for relatively low fares.

● The terminal has all the usual facilities, including food outlets, shops, luggage deposit and an information office.

● All the major car rental companies (▷ 41) are represented at the airport. Both shuttles and taxis depart from directly outside the baggage claim area.

Christchurch International Airport

Christchurch airport is 12km (7 miles) northwest of the city. The international and domestic terminals are housed in one building; domestic transfer check-in counters are in the international arrivals hall. The terminal is open for all flight

Air pockets and strong winds enliven flights into Wellington

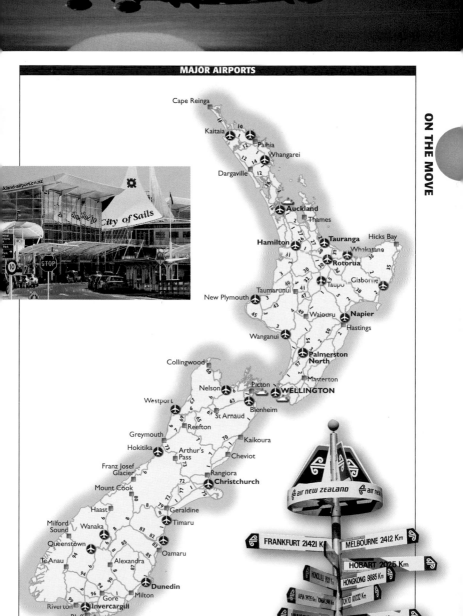

Top, *Auckland International Airport*

Right, *at Christchurch Airport a signpost enables you to calculate just how far you are from home*

arrivals and departures, while the domestic terminal is open from 7.30am to 8pm.

• The international terminal has direct links with Australia, Singapore and Japan.

• There are bars and restaurants in both terminals. The International Atrium has duty-free shopping and other shops, including clothes stores in the departures hall. A smaller variety of shops is available in the domestic terminal. ATMs are found in both terminals.

• Information desks in both the domestic terminal and international arrivals hall can make reservations for local hotels and tours, provide full travel agency services and arrange any further international or domestic travel plans.

Top, Air New Zealand is the national airline; below, many visitors use minivans to get to top locations

NEW ZEALAND INTERNATIONAL AIRLINES

Air New Zealand tel 0800-352 266 www.airnz.co.nz
Freedom Air International tel 0800-600 500 www.freedomair.com

Foreign Airlines Operating to New Zealand
Aerolineas Argentinas tel 0800 0969 747 (UK), 800-333 0276 (US) www.aerolineas.com.ar
Air Pacific tel 0845-774 7767 (UK), 800-227 4446 (US) www.airpacific.com
British Airways tel 0870-850 9850 (UK), 800-AIRWAYS (US) www.british-airways.com
Cathay Pacific tel 020-8834 8888 (UK), 800-233 2742 (US) www.cathaypacific.com
Emirates tel 0870 243 2222 (UK), 800-777 3999 (US) www.emirates.com
Garuda Indonesia tel 020-7467 8600 (UK), 800-3 GARUDA (US) www.garuda-indonesia.com
Japan Airlines tel 0845 774 7700 (UK), 800-525 3663 (US) www.jal.com
Jetstar tel 866-397 8170 (US) www.jetstar.com
Korean Air tel 0800 413 000 (UK), 800-438 5000 (US) www.koreanair.com
Malaysia Airlines tel 0870 607 9090 (UK), 800-552 9264 (US) www.malaysiaairlines.com
Pacific Blue tel 13 1645 (Australia) www.flypacificblue.com
Qantas Airways tel 0845 774 7767 (UK), 800-227 4500 (US) www.qantas.com.au
Singapore Airlines tel 0844 800 2380 (UK), 800-742 3333 (US) www.singaporeair.com
Thai Airways International tel 0870 606 0911 (UK), 800-426 5204 (US) www.thaiair.com

GETTING AROUND

Vehicle Rental

Car

All the major car rental firms have offices at the airports and in cities and provincial towns. There are also many local operators. Shop around, and always read the small print before you sign. Some of the less expensive companies have an insurance excess of NZ$700 even on minor repairs.

● Always go over the car with a company representative and ask for a list of any dents or scratches that you see on the vehicle.

● If you have a digital camera take a few pictures of your own.

● If you do not have a credit card you may have to leave a substantial cash deposit of between NZ$500 and NZ$1,000.

● You must be over 21 and have a valid driver's licence to rent a vehicle; insurance premiums for the under-25s can be high.

● Small, older and, typically, Japanese cars (1,600cc) start at about NZ$80 per day but rates vary depending on season, kilometres covered and the length of time you have the car. A medium-size new car costs around NZ$100 per day with unlimited kilometres. Without unlimited kilometres the cost is about NZ$0.30 per kilometre.

● You can rent a vehicle in one city and drop it off at another. This will almost certainly involve a drop-off fee of around NZ$120–NZ$150. In the summer, if you are returning to Auckland, it is worth shopping around and trying to strike a bargain, since many operators have a glut of cars needing to be driven back north.

● Insurance is not compulsory but highly recommended. Note that you may not be covered on certain roads. You will certainly not be covered if you venture onto any of the 'sand highways' on the coast, such as Ninety Mile Beach (▷ 57), and many companies do not provide cover in the Catlins (▷ 137).

Motorcycle

Motorcycle rental is not an inexpensive option, but it can be a superb way to see the country.

● Depending on the model and package, renting a motorcycle for a week can cost anything between NZ$80 and NZ$1,000. To ride a Harley Davidson expect to pay around NZ$250 a day.

● Website links to motorcycle rental companies are listed on www.piperpat.co.nz.

Campervan (RV)

Campsites are readily available even in the more remote places. Parking in a powered site costs around NZ$10–NZ$15 per night. Note that lay-by (turnout) parking is illegal.

● Like car rental rates, campervan rates vary and are seasonal. Costs are rated on a sliding scale according to model, season and number of days of use. The average daily charge for a basic two-berth/six-berth for rent over 28 days, including insurance, is around NZ$195/NZ$295 in the high season and NZ$90/NZ$140 in the low season.

● The same general rules apply as with car rental. For estimating costs, fuel usage for the average campervan works out at around 14–16L (4gal) per 100km (62 miles).

● Website links to campervan/RV rental companies are listed on www.piperpat.co.nz.

RENTAL CONTACTS

Car Rental Contacts

About New Zealand tel 0800-455 565 www.rentalcar.co.nz

Ace Rental Cars tel 09-303 3112 www.acerentals.co.nz

Avis tel 0800-655 111 www.avis.com

Budget tel 0800-283 438 www.budget.co.nz

Car Rental Centre (cooperative group of rental companies) tel 0800-746 378 www.carhire.co.nz

Hertz tel 0800-654 321 www.hertz.com

Motorcycle Rental Contacts

Adventure Motorcycles tel 0508 RIDE BMW www.adventuremotorcycles.co.nz

Adventure Trailrides tel 0274 510 584 www.adventureride.co.nz

New Zealand Motorcycle Rentals & Tours tel 0800-917 3941 (UK), 866-490 7940 (US) www.nzbike.com

South Pacific Motorcycle Tours tel 03 312 0444 www.motorcycletours.co.nz

Te Waipounamu Motorcycle Hire and Tours tel 03-372 3537 www.motorcycle-hire.co.nz

Bicycle Rental Contacts

Bicycle Rentals tel 0800 444 144 www.bicyclerentals.co.nz (throughout New Zealand)

City Cycle Hire (Christchurch) tel 03-339 4020 www.cyclehire-tours.co.nz

Hedgehog Bikes (Auckland) tel 09 486 6559 www.hedgehog.co.nz

Campervan Rental Contacts

Britz tel 0800-831 900 www.britz.co.nz

Kea Campers tel 09-441 7833 www.kea.co.nz

Kiwi Campers tel 0800 549 44, www.nzcampers.com

Maui tel 09-275 3013/0800 651 080 www.maui.co.nz

Getting Around in Auckland

Auckland's public transportation system has been overhauled to provide a more consistent service between buses, ferries and trains. Information on all types of transport is available from MAXX (see Useful Contacts, below).

The handiest way to travel in the city is by bus. Several travel pass schemes are available: the Auckland Discovery Day Pass gives unlimited travel on the five major bus companies, suburban trains and inner port ferries between 5am on the day of purchase and 4.59am the following morning. Auckland Pass gives one day's unlimited travel on North Star and Stagecoach Auckland buses (including the Link; see below) and includes travel on ferry services to the North Shore. A similar deal is offered by the Three-Day Rover, but for three consecutive days.

BUS

● Most central and suburban buses stop at the Britomart Transport Centre, between Customs and Quay streets, near the waterfront.
● An Auckland Busabout Guide is available from the bus terminal and all major tourist information offices, showing routes and departure points for the main attractions. Fares are on a staged system, 1–8 (NZ$1.60–NZ$9.70).
● City Circuit is a red bus providing a free service around the city's heart every 10 minutes, daily 8–6.
● The Link bus has a flat fare of $1.60 and runs every 10 minutes 6am–7pm weekdays, 7am–6pm Saturdays, every 15 minutes evenings and Sundays. The route is Britomart–Quay Park–Parnell–Museum–Domain–Newmarket–Hospital–University–AUT–Library–Karangahape Road–Ponsonby–Victoria Park–SKYCITY–Queen Street–Britomart.
● The double-decker Auckland Explorer bus has all-day sightseeing with commentary (NZ$30 day pass).

The Britomart Transport Centre, a hub for travel information

GREEN TRAVEL

Walking is a good way of getting to know the cities. Wellington and Christchurch are compact enough to walk to most central attractions, while Auckland's Link and City Circuit buses connect the main areas. Wellington's electric trolleybuses, Auckland's free hybrid electric City Circuit and Christchurch's City Shuttle buses all help minimise effects on the environment.

TRAIN

● Local and intercity trains arrive and depart from the Britomart Transport Centre, near the waterfront.
● Two main commuter lines run west to Waitakere and south to Papakura. Contact MAXX.

FERRY AND WATER TAXI

● Almost all ferries depart from around the Ferry Buildings on the waterfront, at Quay Street. Commuter service is expanding.
● The main ferry company is Fullers, with an information office on the ground floor of the Ferry Building, tel 09-367 9111, www.fullers.co.nz.
● Water taxis sail from the North Shore, tel 0800 111 616, www.watertaxi.co.nz.

TAXI

● Taxis are generally widely available and can be flagged down, ordered by phone or picked up at ranks.
● All Auckland taxi drivers are required to belong to a registered taxi company. Meters are usually based on time, not distance, so it often pays to get an estimate first.

USEFUL CONTACTS

Auckland
Auckland Explorer tel 0800 4 EXPLORER www.explorerbus.co.nz
Britomart Transport Centre tel 09-374 3873 www.britomart.co.nz
MAXX tel 09-366 6400 www.maxx.co.nx

Christchurch
Metro tel 03-366 8855 www.metroinfo.org.nz
Trams tel 03-366 7830 www.tram.co.nz
Tram dining tour tel 03-366 7511 www.tram.co.nz

Wellington
Metlink tel 04-801 7000 www.metlink.org.nz

Getting Around in Christchurch

Christchurch is a walkers' city but it does have a tramline and a good bus network with a new terminal, the Bus Exchange, on the corner of Lichfield and Colombo streets.

BUS
• Nearly all Christchurch buses serve the central Bus Exchange. An exception is the Orbiter, which provides a useful link between suburban hubs and shopping malls.
• Bus fares use a three-zone system, with all the central city in zone 1 (NZ$2.50). Buy your ticket from the driver, or get a Metrocard smart card from the Bus Exchange.
• The hybrid electric free yellow City Shuttle takes in a north south route from the Casino through Cathedral Square and down Colombo Street and back, and operates every 10–15 minutes, Mon–Fri 7.30am–10.30pm, Sat 8am–10.30pm and Sun 10–8.
• The Best Attractions Express Shuttle links the Christchurch

Travel on the vintage tram

Gondola, Christchurch Tramway, International Antarctic Centre and Willowbank Wildlife Reserve and departs regularly from Cathedral Square, directly opposite the tram stop. An all-day pass (with

bonus second day free) allows you to visit each venue as often as you wish (adult NZ$15, child NZ$10).

TRAM
Between 1905 and 1954 Christchurch had a thriving tram system. Since 1995 the restored trams have followed a 2.5km (1.5-mile) loop around the heart of the city, passing various sights of interest on the way (commentary provided).
• Trams operate Apr–end Oct daily 9–6 and Nov–end Mar daily 9–9. A restaurant car offers a daily dining tour at 7.30pm.
• The trams stop at or near many of the main attractions, including the Botanic Gardens and Cathedral Square.
• For more information tel 03-366 6943, **www.tram.co.nz**.

Getting Around in Wellington

Wellington's transportation system is efficient and extensive, with buses, trolley buses, trains, ferries and a vintage cable car. Information on all services is available from Ridewell, tel 04-801 7000.

BUS
• GOWellington buses operate daily 7am–11pm. City and suburban coverage is good and there is a 10-trip ticket system available. Services depart from the main city bus stop at the Railway Station and Courtenay Place.
• The yellow City Circular bus runs every 15 minutes daily 10–4.45 (adult NZ$3, child NZ$1; free with a NZ$6 Daytripper or NZ$9 Starpass ticket), taking in major sights, including Te Papa, Cuba Mall, the cable car on Lambton Quay and the Parliament Buildings.
• A free shuttle service runs to the Interislander ferry terminal from the rail station.
• If you intend to visit the Kapiti Coast or Hutt Valley it's worth considering the Capital

Explorer Pass, which allows a day of unlimited travel on regional buses and trains (NZ$15).
• Cityline runs regular daily services to the Hutt Valley. The Stagecoach Flyer offers express services from Lower Hutt to Wellington and Wellington Airport. The Wellington–Airport fare is NZ$5.50 adult, NZ$3 child.
• The Daytripper ticket (adult NZ$6) is valid on all GOWellington buses, including the City Circular. The STARPass (adult NZ$10) is valid on GOWellington buses and also on Cityline Hutt Valley and Stagecoach Flyer buses.

CABLE CAR
The cable car terminus is on Lambton Quay, and the car runs

every ten minutes (Mon–Fri 7am–10pm, Sat 8.30am–10pm, Sun 9am–10pm) to the Botanic Garden at Kelburn, via Victoria University. One-way journey NZ$2.50 (child NZ$1), both ways NZ$4.50 (child NZ$2, family NZ$12).

FERRY
• The Dominion Post ferry sails from Queens Wharf to Matiu (Somes) Island and Days Bay, and to Petone and Seatoun on weekends.
• For information tel 04-499 1282, **www.eastbywest.co.nz**.

TRAIN
• Tranz Metro operates suburban trains to Johnsonville, Melling, Paraparaumu and Upper Hutt, as well as trains to Masterton and Palmerston North.

Driving

Although it is possible to negotiate the country by train or bus, for sheer convenience driving is the best choice. Many of the country's attractions are off the beaten track and a long walk from the nearest bus stop. You will also free yourself of organised schedules.

Beyond the cities, parking and traffic congestion are rarely problematic. In some remote areas of the country, especially in the South Island, the roads are single track and unpaved, so a little more driving skill is required. Keep the speeds and gears low on these roads. There may well be sheep or cattle along the verges in rural areas, so take extra care. There are very few wild mammals in New Zealand, but you might well encounter the cat-sized, brush-tailed possum, of which there are 70 million or so (▷ 21).

Insurance is generally offered by the car rental companies. If you are planning to visit for several months, many car rental companies offer temporary purchase or long-term rental (▷ 41).

Rules and regulations
● Traffic in New Zealand drives on the left.
● Speed limits are generally 100kph (62mph) on the open road (although they may be lower in some places) and 50kph (31mph) in built-up areas. Be aware that police patrol cars and speed cameras are omnipresent.
● Police operate random breath and blood tests. The alcohol limit for drivers is 80mg (0.003oz) in 100ml (0.2 pints) of blood; for drivers under 21 no alcohol at all is allowed.
● When you are turning, always give way to the right—the oncoming car has right of way. Always check your way is clear in all directions before turning.
● If you are turning left, give way to vehicles coming towards you that are turning right.
● If you are turning right, you

Above, busy Lambton Quay, Wellington

NORTH ISLAND DRIVING DISTANCES (IN KM)										
	Auckland	Cape Reinga	Gisborne	Hamilton	Napier	New Plymouth	Palmerston North	Rotorua	Tauranga	Wellington
Auckland		440	507	127	422	366	530	235	208	656
Cape Reinga	440		943	566	861	805	967	672	645	1100
Dargaville	185	285	685	312	605	554	713	420	390	845
Gisborne	507	943		394	215	600	390	292	300	540
Hamilton	127	566	394		295	242	402	109	108	533
Hicks Bay	508	945	180	398	396	600	574	289	302	730
Kaitaia	325	114	827	450	748	692	853	560	535	982
Masterton	638	1077	448	511	233	343	109	444	530	100
Napier	422	861	215	295		412	178	227	312	320
New Plymouth	366	805	600	242	412		234	315	308	355
Paihia	241	220	745	368	664	610	773	476	447	900
Palmerston North	530	967	390	402	178	234		340	420	145
Rotorua	235	672	292	109	227	315	340		86	460
Taupo	280	720	335	153	143	296	259	84	165	378
Taumarunui	295	726	450	162	264	183	240	172	230	360
Tauranga	208	645	300	108	312	308	420	86		545
Thames	115	554	413	106	360	348	470	200	114	586
Waiouru	423	819	446	267	261	288	145	195	279	264
Wanganui	454	893	466	328	252	160	74	305	439	195
Wellington	656	1100	540	533	320	355	145	460	545	
Whangarei	170	270	680	295	597	540	700	405	381	818

Fuel stops often supply coffee, snacks and basic supplies, too

should give way to vehicles on your right that are turning right.

● Seatbelts must be worn in front seats at all times, and in rear seats where fitted.

● Turn on your headlights from dusk until dawn, or at any other time when you can't see vehicles clearly at a distance of 100m (110 yards) away.

● Dip your headlights when other vehicles are coming towards you, when following other vehicles, when police are directing traffic and when you stop.

Documents

You need a valid driver's licence from your own country or an international driving permit. This must be produced if you rent a vehicle (▷ 41).

Fuel

● Petrol (gas) comes in 91, 95 or 98 octane (all unleaded). LPG (liquified petroleum gas) and diesel are also available. CNG (compressed natural gas) is available only in the North Island.

● Challenge is New Zealand's own brand of fuel, with a network of service stations throughout the country. For a list of locations go to www.challenge.net.nz.

Car breakdown

Most rental companies include a free breakdown service within the deal.

● Members of the the AA in the UK, AAA in the US or driving organisations affiliated to the AIT receive six months' free reciprocal membership of the New Zealand Automobile Association (AA), including breakdown assistance (tel 0800-500 222).

At the scene of an accident

● If you are involved in an accident in which someone is hurt, you must inform a police officer as soon as possible, and no later than 24 hours afterwards.

● If no one is hurt, you must give the owner or driver of any damaged vehicle or property your name and address (and the name and address of your vehicle's owner) as soon as possible and no later than 48 hours after the accident.

● If this isn't possible, report the incident to the police as soon as you can and no later than 60 hours afterwards.

● If your vehicle is insured, tell your insurance company as soon as possible.

● If you injure an animal, tell its owner; if this isn't possible, tell the police or the SPCA (Royal New Zealand Society for the

SOUTH ISLAND DRIVING DISTANCES (IN KM)									
	Blenheim	Christchurch	Dunedin	Greymouth	Invercargill	Kaikoura	Mount Cook	Nelson	Queenstown	Timaru
Alexandra	775	455	190	661	202	641	242	870	93	307
Arthur's Pass	440	150	451	100	668	308	408	385	645	250
Blenheim		318	675	324	900	132	645	116	798	475
Christchurch	318		362	255	579	186	331	425	487	163
Collingwood	251	509	871	384	1088	383	840	135	961	672
Dunedin	675	362		565	217	548	331	790	283	199
Franz Josef Glacier	502	410	563	179	575	518	498	469	404	493
Gore	825	513	151	705	66	699	378	941	169	350
Greymouth	324	255	565		760	339	510	290	583	352
Haast	645	554	421	321	433	660	356	611	262	418
Hokitika	370	270	570	41	700	380	520	337	530	360
Invercargill	900	579	217	760		765	444	1007	187	416
Kaikoura	132	186	548	339	765		517	248	673	349
Milford Sound	1085	773	411	860	278	959	550	1145	291	610
Mount Cook	645	331	331	510	444	517		756	271	211
Nelson	116	425	790	290	1007	248	756		910	590
Oamaru	560	247	115	445	332	433	216	675	319	84
Queenstown	798	407	283	583	187	673	271	910		335
Te Anau	964	652	290	739	158	838	434	1025	170	489
St Arnaud	100	352	710	222	932	232	682	119	839	514
Timaru	475	163	199	352	416	349	211	590	335	

TRAVELLING TIMES AND DISTANCES FROM AUCKLAND					
	DISTANCE	CAR	BUS	TRAIN	AIR
WELLINGTON	647km	9hrs 15mins	10hrs 30mins	12hrs	1hr
CHRISTCHURCH	1,000km	2 days	2 days	2 days	1 1/2hrs
DUNEDIN	1,358km	2–4 days	3 days	Not available	2 1/2hrs
QUEENSTOWN	1,484km	2–4 days	3 days	Not available	2hrs 35mins
BAY OF ISLANDS	241km	4hrs 15mins	4hrs 30mins	Not available	50mins
ROTORUA	235km	3hrs 30mins	4hrs	Not available	45mins

Prevention of Cruelty to Animals, tel 09-827 6094) no later than 48 hours after the accident.

Parking
● Parking in the cities can be very expensive. Do not risk parking in restricted areas or exceeding your time allotment on meters.
● Note that you must park with the flow of traffic, never against it.
● At night, a car parked on the road must show two tail

Right, pay-and-display parking machines are in most cities. Below, prepare to give way on narrow rural bridges—very few have traffic lights

lights and one front light on the side of the car nearest the middle of the road, unless it's

under a street light and visible to other vehicles at a distance of 50m (55 yards) in a 50kph area or 100m (110 yards) in an area with a higher limit.

Buying a car
Although by no means essential, buying a car is a cost-effective option for long stays. Second-hand cars are inexpensive and readily available.

Buying procedure and legalities
● A current international or accepted driver's licence is essential.
● All cars need a safety certificate to be legally on the

road and to obtain registration. Most garages and specialist 'drive in, drive out' Vehicle Testing Stations do a Warrant of Fitness (WOF) test for about NZ$35. If passed, this is valid for six months. If you buy a car with a WOF make sure it is not more than 28 days old.

• Registration can be gained (for a fee) with legal ownership and a valid WOF certificate for six months (about NZ$100) or twelve months (NZ$200).

• The buyer and seller must fill in an MR13A form, which can be bought and submitted at any Post Shop (NZ$10).

• Insurance is not compulsory but a minimum of third party coverage is highly recommended.

• The New Zealand AA offers good insurance rates, emergency breakdown help, free maps and information (tel 09-377 4660, www.nzaa.co.nz).

• To have the car's credentials checked before you purchase, contact AA Auto Report on the New Zealand AA's website (NZ$25) or tel 0800-500 333 and quote the chassis and licence plate number of the vehicle.

• The New Zealand AA provides vehicle inspections, as do other companies found in the *Yellow Pages* (www.yellowpages.co.nz).

Where to buy a car

• There are several auto magazines available at newsagents. The major daily newspapers (such as the *New*

SELECTED ROAD SIGNS

Speed limit on major roads, in kph	Hazard (penguins crossing) ahead	Slow down–sharp bends ahead
Main route sign, with distance to the destination given in km		Unmade road ahead

Zealand Herald, on Wednesday and Saturday) and auctions are also recommended sources of information.

• Car fairs are held at: Ellerslie Racecourse, Greenlane (Sun 9–noon), tel 09-529 2233, www.carfair.co.nz; Manukau Car Market, Manukau City Centre Car Park (Sun 9–1), tel 09-358 5000; Sell It Yourself, 1106 Great South Road, Otahuhu (daily 8–6.30), tel 09-270 3666; 60 Wairau Road, Glenfield (daily 7–7), tel 09-443 3800.

• Car auctions are held at: Turners Car Auctions, corner of Penrose and Leonard roads,

Penrose (Thursday, Saturday), tel 09-525 1920, www.turnersauctions.co.nz; Hammer Auctions, corner of Neilson and Alfred streets, Onehunga (Monday, Thursday, Saturday), tel 09-579 2344, www.hammerauctions.co.nz.

• Sale and guaranteed buy-backs are offered by: Budget Car Sales, 12 Mount Eden Road, Mount Eden, tel 09-379 4120; Downtown Rentals, 31 Neilson Street, Onehunga, Auckland, tel 09-625 6469; Rex Swinburne, 825 Dominion Road, Mount Roskill, tel 09-620 6587.

HOW TO NAVIGATE A ROUNDABOUT (TRAFFIC CIRCLE)

Slow down on the approach to a roundabout and give way to all vehicles that will cross your path from your right. Most multi-laned roundabouts are marked with lanes and arrows, to guide you into the correct lane—but note that not all are marked the same way. If you need to cross lanes near an exit, give way to any vehicles in the lane that you want to enter.

If you're continuing straight ahead (across the roundabout) don't signal on the approach, but signal left before your exit.

ON THE MOVE

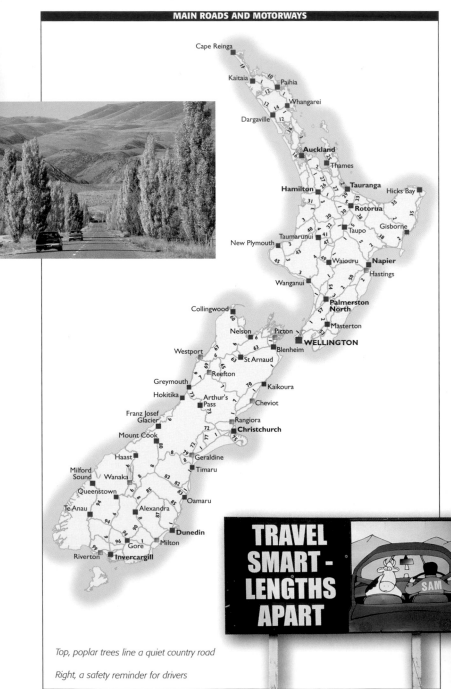

Cape Reinga

Kaitaia
Paihia
Whangarei
Dargaville

Auckland
Thames
Hamilton
Tauranga
Hicks Bay
Rotorua
Gisborne
Taupo
Taumarunui
New Plymouth
Waiouru
Napier
Hastings
Wanganui
Palmerston North
Masterton

Collingwood
Nelson
Picton
Westport
Blenheim
St Arnaud
Reefton
WELLINGTON
Greymouth
Kaikoura
Hokitika
Arthur's Pass
Cheviot
Franz Josef Glacier
Rangiora
Mount Cook
Christchurch
Haast
Geraldine
Milford Sound
Timaru
Wanaka
Queenstown
Oamaru
Te Anau
Alexandra
Dunedin
Gore
Milton
Riverton
Invercargill

Top, poplar trees line a quiet country road

Right, a safety reminder for drivers

TRAVEL SMART – LENGTHS APART

SAM

Buses and Taxis

National bus travel in New Zealand is generally well organised, with high standards of comfort, efficient networks and reliable daily schedules. Several shuttle companies serve the South Island. There are also many local operators and independent companies providing shuttles to accommodation establishments, attractions and activities.

Bus stops are clearly signed

● The two main long-distance bus brands, Intercity (www.intercitycoach.co.nz) and Newmans (www.newmanscoach.co.nz), are operated by the same organisation.

● For information and reservations about bus travel call the following regional offices: Auckland tel 09 623 1503 Wellington tel 04-385 0520 Christchurch tel 03-365 1113 Dunedin tel 03 471 7143.

● In Northland, Northliner Express (tel 09-307 5873, www.northliner.co.nz) runs in cooperation with Intercity.

● Other companies in North Island include White Star (tel 06-758 3338, www.yellow.co.nz/site/whitestar/), which serves the route between New Plymouth and Wellington, taking in Wanganui and Palmerston North; and the Pavlovich Express (tel 0800-759 999, www.pavlovichexpress.co.nz), operating between Auckland, Rotorua, Tauranga and Taupo via Hamilton. Coromandel Explorer Tours (tel 07-866 3506, www.coromandeltours.co.nz) operates around Coromandel.

● The principal backpacker bus companies (▷ 50) are: Kiwi Experience, tel 09-366 9830, www.kiwiexperience.com; Magic Travellers, tel 09-358 5600, www.magicbus.co.nz; Stray, tel 09-309 8772, www.straytravel.co.nz; and Flying Kiwi, tel 0800-693 296, www.flyingkiwi.com.

● Bottom Bus (tel 03-434 7370, www.bottombus.co.nz) runs around the Southern Scenic Route between Dunedin and Milford Sound, via Queenstown.

Concession fares

All bus companies offer a variety of concession fares.

● Infants younger than three travel free and children younger than twelve travel at 33 per cent discount on Intercity and Newmans.

● Passengers over the age of 60 travel at 20 per cent discount, backpackers (YHA, VIP, BBH, Nomads cardholders) and students at 15 per cent.

● Saver fares of 25 per cent discount and supersaver fares of 50 per cent discount are available, but these must be reserved in advance.

● Intercity and Newmans also operate a Club Free-Way Card. This accrues points that can later be redeemed for discounts or free tickets.

Bus passes

Intercity/Newmans Countrywide bus passes can be bought for a choice of four 'hop on–hop off' routes throughout the North and South islands, ranging from an Auckland-to-Christchurch trip from NZ$565 to an Auckland-and-back deal from NZ$729, both driving the length of the South Island.

Intercity/Newmans North Island bus passes

● The Pacific Coast Highway goes from Auckland to Thames (via the Coromandel Peninsula), through Tauranga and Rotorua, and then rejoins the coast at Whakatane before continuing to Gisborne and Napier to Wellington; adult NZ$204, child NZ$140.

● The North Island Value Pass is a flexi-plan ticket between Auckland and Wellington, taking in either Coromandel or Waitomo; adult NZ$155, child NZ$105.

Intercity/Newmans South Island bus passes

● The West Coast Passport operates between Nelson and Queenstown (optional start in Picton or Greymouth); adult NZ$175, child NZ$117.

● The Milford Bound Adventurer is available on services from Christchurch via Mount Cook to Queenstown and then onto Milford Sound; adult NZ$235, child NZ$157.

● The Southern Discovery departs from either Christchurch or Greymouth, taking in Mount Cook, Queenstown and Milford Sound; adult NZ$238. This trip is best combined with the famous TranzAlpine rail journey between Greymouth and Christchurch (▷ 199).

● The West Coast Passport covers the whole of the West Coast, from Picton through Nelson and Greymouth to

Queenstown; adult NZ$175, child NZ$117. Shorter options are available from Nelson (adult NZ$145, child NZ$97) and from Greymouth (adult NZ$125, child NZ$84).

BACKPACKERS AND NO-FRILLS TRAVEL

● An increasingly popular way to get round the country is to use services provided primarily for backpackers by companies like Stray (tel 09-309 8772, www.straytravel.com) and Kiwi Experience (tel 09-366 9830, www.kiwiexperience.com). This travel option is a cross between a bus service and backpacker-oriented coach tour.

● Different passes are offered: Stray's prices start with a NZ$35 Auckland day tour, or a tour round the bottom of the South Island from Dunedin for $330, and go up to a 22-day nationwide tour for NZ$1,200; Kiwi Experience passes range from NZ$89 for a one- or two-day Auckland–Paihia (Bay of Islands) trip or NZ$165 for Queenstown–Milford Sound, to NZ$1,850 for a 38-day comprehensive tour round the whole country.

● No-frills buses have also hit New Zealand roads, with fares on Nakedbus starting from just NZ$1.70, including booking fee (tel 0900-NAKED—calls cost at least $1.80 per minute—www.nakedbus.co.nz). This company doesn't have the comprehensive network of the more established operators, but its services are expanding in both main islands. Bookings must be made on the internet.

TAXIS

● You can take taxi cabs from ranks or hail one in the street.
● If there are three or more of you, taking a taxi can be less expensive than taking the bus, and no tip is expected.
● Long-distance fares should be negotiated in advance of the journey.
● Combined Taxis New Zealand runs a central service putting callers in touch with registered and approved taxi firms in different towns and cities. Call 0800-505555 and when prompted add:

    11 for Auckland
    13 for Christchurch
    14 for Dunedin
    36 for Greymouth
    15 for Hamilton
    31 for Nelson
    34 for Queenstown
    16 for Rotorua
    18 for Tauranga
    12 for Wellington or
    21 for Whangarei.

Other destination numbers are listed in the phone prompts.
● Information on special needs, meet-and-greet packages and taxi tours is available from the New Zealand Taxi Federation (tel 04-499 0611, www.taxinet. org.nz).

Taxis in New Zealand generally offer good value and are a comfortable option for shorter trips

Bicycling

● For information on bicycle rental ▷ 41.
● In towns, some bicycle lanes are coloured to mark them out from the road—for instance, some Christchurch and Hamilton lanes are red; Auckland's bicycle lanes are green.
● Helmets are compulsory for all bicyclists.
● All bicyclists must have a rear reflector (preferably red) on the back of the bicycle; yellow pedal reflectors or reflective leg-straps, and good brakes on the front and back wheels.
● You must have lights (white in front, red behind) to cycle after dark.
● Bicyclists must follow the same rules as drivers, including giving way at intersections (▷ 44).
● Bicyclists can only ride beside another cyclist or a moped—not alongside a car or truck.
● Bicyclists passing another vehicle must ride in single file.
● For more information: Land Transport New Zealand, tel 0800 699 000, www.landtransport. govt.nz; Cycling Advocates' Network (CAN), tel 04-472 2552, www.can.org.nz.

Trains

The rail network throughout the country is disappointing and in a seemingly incessant state of flux. New Zealand has struggled for years to maintain even a core network between its main hubs of population and provincial towns.

● Apart from commuter services in Auckland and Wellington, in the North Island Tranz Scenic (tel 0800 TRAINS, www.tranzscenic.co.nz) operates the Overlander between Auckland and Wellington daily in summer, Friday–Sunday in winter.
● In the South Island are Tranz Scenic's daily TranzCoastal services between Christchurch and Picton, connecting with the Interislander ferry to Wellington, and the daily TranzAlpine between Christchurch and Greymouth.

● The trains themselves are quite comfortable. Service is usually good and most trains have a viewing car at the rear, great for taking in the scenery.
● The tourist Taieri Gorge Limited (tel 03-477 4449, www.taieri.co.nz) runs daily between Dunedin and Pukerangi or Middlemarch, and weekly to Palmerston.

Fares
Tranz Scenic fares range widely from Standard to Super Saver; check your entitlements and any available deals.

● All trains are single class.
● Reservations and timetables are available from Wellington and Christchurch rail stations, i-SITES and travel agents throughout New Zealand.
● Several specialist travel packages are on offer, including Great Train Escapes and Day Escapes, comprising a range of one- to six-day excursions, most of which include accommodation. Prices range from NZ$79 for a day excursion to NZ$545 for six days. Children travel for around 40 per cent of the adult fare.

The TranzAlpine Railway travels through the scenic countryside of the South Island

Domestic Flights and Ferries

In addition to the principal international airports of Auckland, Wellington and Christchurch, New Zealand has many well-served provincial town airports. Air New Zealand Link is by far the dominant carrier. Qantas also flies from Auckland to Wellington and Christchurch. Services are highly professional and efficient, so you will rarely have problems with delays.

DOMESTIC FLIGHTS

Apart from the major domestic operators, there are many smaller companies with scheduled services. These include: Great Barrier Airlines (Great Barrier, Coromandel and Northland), Sounds Air (offering an alternative to the ferry between the North and South islands) and Stewart Island Flights (between Invercargill and Stewart Island). Air2there (tel 04-904 5130, 0800 777 000, www.air2there.co.nz), based at Paraparaumu just north of Wellington, offers services to Nelson, Blenheim and Wellington, bypassing the capital for people on the Kapiti Coast. Mountain Air (tel 09-256 7025, www.mountainair.co.nz,) operates flights between Auckland, Whangarei and Great Barrier Island. Flying anywhere in New Zealand is, on a clear day, a scenic delight.

Domestic discount fares

If you can, reserve domestic flights well in advance via the internet or through a travel agent. Most discounted fares can be bought only in New Zealand.

There are many available deals that can make considerable savings, depending on season and availability. Air New Zealand offers the South Pacific Airpass, which works on a zone and coupon system and must be ticketed prior to arrival. For more information ask your travel agent or see www.airnewzealand.co.nz.

DOMESTIC FERRIES

Other than a few small vehicle ferries and the short trip to Stewart Island from Bluff in Southland, the main focus of ferry travel is the inter-island route across Cook Strait. The two ports are Wellington, at the southern tip of the North Island,

Above, a Sounds Air plane
Below left, Wellington Airport

and Picton, in the Marlborough Sounds, northern South Island.

Linking South and North

The scenic 85km (53-mile) journey across the Cook Strait takes up to three-and-a-half hours, depending on which vessel you take.

● In rough weather the crossing can be something of an ordeal. Sailings are stopped if considered too dangerous, but this does not happen often.

● Reserve tickets well in advance, especially in December and January. Most major visitor information centres and travel agents can organise reservations and tickets.

● On board the Interislander's *Arahua*, *Kaitaki* and *Aratere* ferries there are bars, food courts, cafés, movies, visitor information points, children's play areas and nurseries, and private work desks. The slightly higher-priced Club Class ticket gives access to a private lounge and complimentary tea, coffee, magazines and newspapers.

● A free shuttle bus to the terminal (2km/1 mile) runs from

DOMESTIC AIRLINES
Air New Zealand tel 0800-737 000 www.airnewzealand.co.nz
Great Barrier Airlines tel 0800-900 600 www.greatbarrier.co.nz
Qantas tel 0800-900 600 www.qantas.co.nz
Sounds Air tel 0800-505 005 www.soundsair.co.nz
Stewart Island Flights tel 03-218 9129 www.stewartislandflights.co.nz

Wellington Rail Station 35 minutes before each scheduled ferry departure.

● Fares for passengers range from the standard NZ$65 (child NZ$33) to the saver NZ$45 (child NZ$31). Cars cost NZ$99–NZ$160. The vehicle fare does not include the driver. Motorcycles cost NZ$36–NZ$55, bicycles NZ$10. Best of New Zealand Pass and Travelpass New Zealand are accepted, and children under the age of four travel free.

● Various day/limited-excursion, family and group fares and standard discounted fares are available but must be reserved in advance and are subject to availability. At peak periods (particularly December/January) discounts are rarely available.

● The latest operator making the crossing is the independent Bluebridge, with the ex-Mediterranean vessels *Monte Stello* and *Santa Regina*. Facilities are more basic, but adequate; the service is efficient and the staff friendly. The standard fare is NZ$49 for a passenger (child NZ$25), and NZ$120 for a vehicle.

Getting to Stewart Island

● Stewart Island Experience sails October to May 9.30, 11.30 and 5, and May to September 9.30 and 4.30, from the port of Bluff. The crossing by fast catamaran takes about an hour and costs NZ$51 (child NZ$25.50) one way.

● Secure parking is available in Bluff for NZ$5 per day.

FERRY CONTACTS

Bluebridge tel 0800-844 844 www.bluebridge.co.nz

Campbelltown Passenger Services tel 03-212 7404

Interisland Line tel 0800-802 802 www.interislander.co.nz

Stewart Island Experience tel 0800-000 511 www.stewartislandexperience.co.nz

● Campbelltown Passenger Services offer a regular daily shuttle to and from Invercargill to coincide with the Stewart Island ferries (NZ$12 one way) Reservations are advised.

Northland

● A car ferry operates across the Hokianga from Rawene (tel 09-405 2602, **www**.fndc.govt.nz), providing a useful link up the west coast of Northland. Fullers Bay of Islands (tel 09-402 7421, **http://**fboi.co.nz) operates car ferries linking the Russell area to Opua and passenger-only ferries to Paihia.

Hauraki Gulf

● Passenger ferries operated by Fullers (tel 09-367 9111,

Above, small ferries provide a shuttle service across Auckland's Waitemata harbour
Below, an Interislander ferry passing Pencarrow lighthouse entering Wellington harbour

www.fullers.co.nz) and Kawau Kat (**www**.360discovery.co.nz) criss-cross the Waitemata Harbour and the Hauraki Gulf, serving the North Shore and out to Great Barrier Island.

● Sealink (tel 09-300 5900, 0800 732 546, **www**.sealink. co.nz) operates frequent vehicle ferries to Waiheke Island from Half Moon Bay near Pakuranga, and from central Auckland, and daily (except Saturdays) from central Auckland to Great Barrier Island.

VISITORS WITH A DISABILITY

For visitors with disabilities, New Zealand can be frustrating. While the majority of public facilities are accessible to wheelchairs, older lodgings and some public transportation systems (especially rural buses) are not as well organised. However, the good news is that the situation is improving slowly, and it is now a legal requirement for new buildings to include facilities for people with disabilities.

• Air New Zealand's International Boeing 747, 767 and 737-300 and Airbus A320 planes have onboard skychairs, which are designed to fit within narrow aisles. These are not available on domestic flights, but airports will provide skychairs for wheelchair-users for arrivals and departures.

• Facilities for people with disabilities at Auckland and Christchurch airports include automatic doors, elevators, wheelchair access, accessible toilets and showers, and ATMs with Braille keys. There are also parking spaces for card-holders in front of the terminals and in the airport parking areas.

• A useful sign to look for is the International Symbol of Access. It is awarded by local authorities to inspected properties that meet the needs of the mobility impaired.

• The Youth Hostels Association (YHA) runs 27 hostels in New Zealand, of which 11 are suitable for people with restricted mobility: Auckland International, Christchurch City Central, Franz Josef, Greymouth, Kaikoura, Lake Tekapo, Nelson, Queenstown, Te Anau, Tauranga and Wellington City.

• Visitors with disabilities often receive discounts on travel and some admission charges.

• Parking concessions are available and temporary cards can be issued on receipt of a mobility card or medical certificate.

• *Accessible New Zealand*, by Alexia Pickering, is a guide for visitors with restricted mobility. It covers a range of topics, including attractions, accommodation, shopping and parking, toilets, restaurants, transport and activities.

SPECIALIST TOUR COMPANIES

Accessible Kiwi Tours Ltd
PO Box 550, Opotiki,
Bay of Plenty
Tel 07-315 6988
Fax 07-315 5144
www.tours-nz.com,
Email info@accessible-tours.co.nz
Themed tours for individuals and groups, plus information for independent travel.

Galaxy Motors
PO Box 22114, Otahuhu,
Tel 0800 GALAXY
www.galaxyautos.co.nz
Email: f.hall@xtra.co.nz
Specially equipped cars and vans; tour guides and companions are also available.

Physical Freedom and Manawatu Jet Tours
PO Box 53, Ashhurst,
Tel/fax 06-329 4060
Email man-jet-tours@inspire.net.nz
Range of activities, including jet-boat river rides, drift-rafting, four-wheel driving, clay-bird shooting. Bus accommodates five wheelchairs. Personalised tours available.

USEFUL CONTACTS

Disability Persons Assembly (DPA)
Tel 04-801 9100
Fax 04-801 9565
www.dpa.org.nz
Email gen@dpa.org.nz
Umbrella organisation for people with disabilities, covering the whole country from its offices in Wellington.

Enable New Zealand
69 Malden Street, PO Box 4547, Palmerston North
Tel 0800 ENABLE
www.enable.co.nz
This organisation aims to help people with disabilities, as well as their families, employers and health professionals.

New Zealand Federation of Disability Information Centres
PO Box 24-042, Royal Oak, Auckland
Tel 0800 NZFDIC
www.nzfdic.org.nz
Provides information for people with disabilities via local (independent) information centres.

Weka
Tel 0800 171 981
www.weka.net.nz
New Zealand's disability information website, for people with disabilities, as well as their families and caregivers, health professionals and disability information providers.

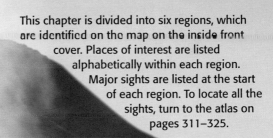

This chapter is divided into six regions, which are identified on the map on the inside front cover. Places of interest are listed alphabetically within each region. Major sights are listed at the start of each region. To locate all the sights, turn to the atlas on pages 311–325.

The Sights

AUCKLAND, NORTHLAND AND COROMANDEL

The northern stretch of New Zealand is warm, humid and sparsely populated, with impressive coastal landscapes and the sunny Coromandel Peninsula. Auckland is the country's biggest city—ferries give access to prettier areas such as Devonport and Waiheke Island.

MAJOR SIGHTS

THE SIGHTS

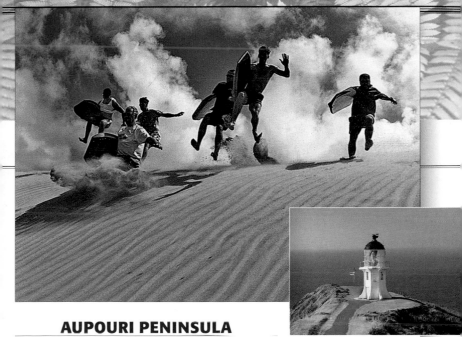

AUPOURI PENINSULA

A stretch of windswept beaches and remote villages in the far north.

New Zealand's most northerly finger of land is bounded by Ninety Mile Beach to the west, and Great Exhibition Bay and Rangaunu Bay and Harbour to the east. At its tip are Cape Reinga and the North Cape—the northernmost point of the North Island. The whole peninsula was once covered in kauri forest; now it consists mainly of extensive dune systems and swamps, interspersed with commercial forestry such as Aupouri Forest.

BEYOND KAITAIA

First stop after Kaitaia (▷ 68) is the Ancient Kauri Kingdom in Awanui, 8km (5 miles) north (daily 9–5), which sells kauri furniture and crafts and displays an imposing, 50-tonne (55-ton) log sculpture. About 17km (10 miles) farther north at Gumdiggers Park (daily 9–5), a reconstructed gumdiggers' village illustrates workers' lives, digging for fossilised kauri gum, around 1900. The route north passes Ninety Mile Beach, an uninterrupted sweep of empty white sand backed by impressive dunes. Join a tour—soft sands and quicksands make driving along it inadvisable, and forbidden by car rental companies.

In the small fishing village of Houhora there are guided tours of the Subritzky/Wagener Homestead, a 19th-century Polish settler's residence little changed since 1900 (11.30, 1.30 and 3.30).

THE FARTHEST POINTS

From Te Kao the road leads north to the vast Te Paki Station and Recreation Reserve, covering 23,000ha (56,830 acres) in all and giving access to the two capes, about 21km (13 miles) away. Local Maori own almost a quarter of the land here, and regard areas around North Cape as sacred. The tip of North Cape is a scientific reserve and has limited public access.

Most visitors head for Cape Reinga and its lighthouse. Views from the hill above extend as far as the Three Kings Islands, 57km (35 miles) offshore. They were named by Abel Tasman, who first spotted them at Epiphany in 1643. The Northland coastline has claimed more than 140 ships since 1808, most foundering around the Cape. The lighthouse contains the lens of an older structure which stood on Motuopao Island, to the south.

Top, enjoying the sand dunes at Te Paki
Above, the lighthouse at Cape Reinga dates from 1941

RATINGS			
Historic interest	● ●		
Photo stops	● ● ● ●		
Walkability	● ● ● ●		

BASICS

🔲 514 G1

ℹ️ Information Far North, Jaycee Park, South Road, Kaitaia, tel 09-408 0879; daily 8.30–5

🚌 Daily tours from Kaitaia, Paihia and Mangonui

www.fndc.govt.nz/infocentre
Information on travel, climate, events, car rental and places to stay.

TIPS

● Pukenui is the last major settlement on the way to the Cape, so it pays to buy fuel and provisions at the café and general store.
● The drive to the Cape from Kaitaia takes about an hour and a half. The road is sealed to Te Paki Station; beyond this point it is metalled and speeds should be kept low.

Auckland

**New Zealand's largest city and the arrival point for most visitors.
A cosmopolitan city on a narrow strip of land between two attractive harbours.**

RATINGS	
Historic interest	●●
Photo stops	●●●●●
Shopping	●●●
Walkability	●●●

*Above, looking across the
Waitemata Harbour to
Devonport and the volcanic
cone of Rangitoto
Above right, the Sky Tower is
illuminated in changing colours
at night
Right, the French-style Art Gallery*

SEEING AUCKLAND

Auckland sits between two natural harbours: the Waitemata, to
the east, and the Manukau, to the southwest. At its heart is the
CBD (Central Business District) and the main thoroughfare of
Queen Street. To either side, the jungle of high-rises occasionally
gives way to older buildings such as the Auckland Art Gallery and
the green sanctuaries of Albert Park and the Domain, with its
crowning glory, the Auckland Museum. Immediately north, the
sails and ferries of Waitemata Harbour herald the end of the
concrete sprawl, and the 1912 Ferry Building is a sharp contrast
to the modern tower blocks behind it.

Viaduct Basin, along the waterfront, was formerly the America's
Cup Village and is the home of the New Zealand National
Maritime Museum. The Harbour Bridge (1959) leads to the huge
expanse of the North Shore, an area of modern suburbs and
relatively calm beaches stretching along to the Whangaparaoa
Peninsula and the edge of the city, 40km (25 miles) away. The

small suburb of Devonport, across the Waitemata Harbour, has a more intimate, affluent atmosphere, with a marina, a lively beach culture and smart villas. Two volcanic cones at Devonport—Mount Victoria and North Head—give excellent city views.

Dominating the southern horizon are Mount Eden and One Tree Hill. South of these landmarks, the low-income suburbs of South Auckland spread to the southern edge of the built-up area at the Bombay Hills, and encompass the Botanic Gardens. In the inner western suburbs, the zoo and the Museum of Transport and Technology (MOTAT) border the lakeside park of Western Springs. Auckland's westward expansion is restricted by the Waitakere Ranges, a hilly recreational area which takes in Auckland Centennial Park.

HIGHLIGHTS

AUCKLAND ART GALLERY (TOI-O-TAMAKI)

➕ 61 C2 ✉ Corner of Wellesley and Kitchener streets ☎ 09-307 7700 🕐 Daily 10–5. Free guided tours 2pm 💲 Adult Collection displays free; special exhibitions NZ$7 day pass, child (under 12) free 💻 ♿
www.aucklandartgallery.govt.nz

The Auckland Art Gallery occupies two buildings in the middle of the city: one in Kitchener Street and the other on the corner of Wellesley and Lorne streets. Together they form the country's largest and most comprehensive collection of national and international art.

The original gallery in Kitchener Street is more than 100 years old and, although it has undergone major reconstruction over the years, it retains its handsome French Renaissance style, with steeply pitched roofs. Works from the permanent collections include international masters, focusing on the 17th century, but the most interesting are those by Charles Goldie (1870–1947) and Gottfried Lindauer (1839–1926), two early European settlers who specialised in oil landscapes and portraits of Maori elders.

The New Gallery, opened in 1995, is across the road. It houses temporary exhibitions and contemporary artists' installations, with a permanent exhibit by modern artist Colin McCahon (1919–1987).

➕ 313 J4

ℹ SKYCITY, corner of Victoria and Federal streets, tel 09-367 6008/0800 AUCKLAND; daily 8–8

🚉 Britomart Transport Centre

www.aucklandnz.com
Comprehensive visitor information including history, places to stay, events and section on other regions.

TIPS
● Get your bearings from the observation decks of the Sky Tower.
● The best time to visit Mount Eden is at dawn, especially on a misty winter morning, before the crowds arrive.

THE SIGHTS

Westhaven Marina

St Marys Bay

NORTHERN MOTORWAY

London
Dunedin

ST MARYS BAY

Gas Works

New

St Marys College

Dublin

COLLEGE HILL

BEAUMONT

Costley

Wood

Ryle

England

Gunson

Ireland

Franklin

Napier

Freemans Bay School

Arthur

FRANKLIN

WELLINGTON

FREEMANS B.

Collingwood

Heke

Anglesea

Beresford

Paget

Picton

Hepburn

Western Park

Auckland Girls' Grammar School

PONSONBY

Salvation Army

NEWT

WILLIAMSON AV

Pollen

Maidstone

HOPETO

Crummer

Mackelvie

NORTH

NEWTO

Sussex

Scanlan

Waima

Turakina

GREAT

Port Dean

Potatau

Home

Keppell

SH16

Haslett

Bright

ARCH HILL

Auckland Zoo, MOTAT

NORTH WESTERN MOTORWAY

Union

Mostyn

Buchanan

Alexander

Aitken

Terrace

IAN

BOND

New Bond

King

NEW

ED

Charles

KINGSLAND

George

Tawari

Kowhai Intermediate School

Onslow

View

DOMINION

Alderley

Kowhai

Walters

Raleigh

Bellwood Ave

Cromwell

Leamington

Valley

A

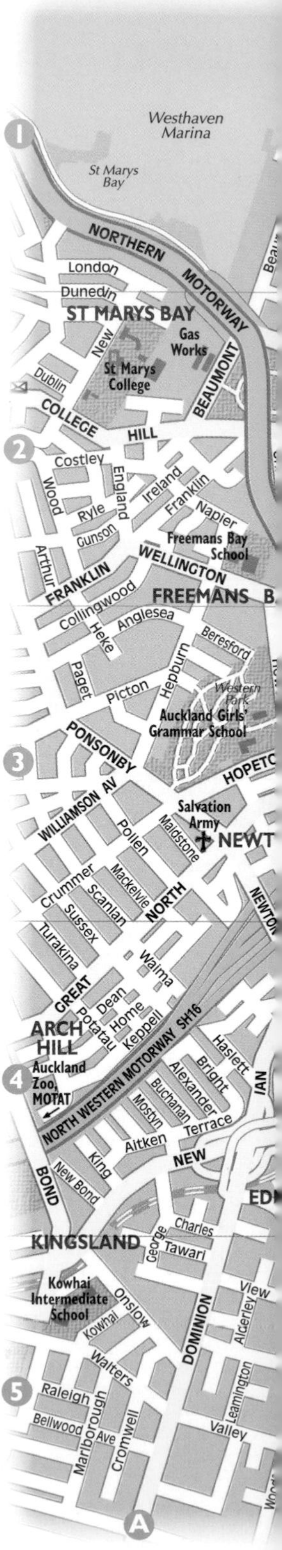

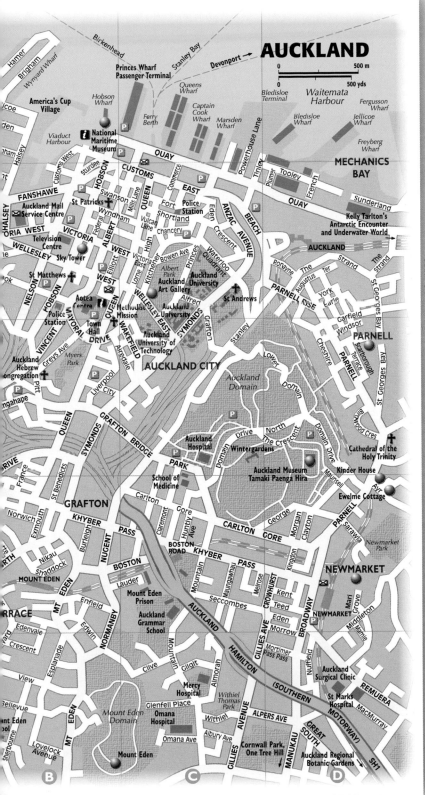

AUCKLAND

0 — 500 m
0 — 500 yds

Waitemata Harbour

MECHANICS BAY

THE SIGHTS

Birkenhead

Stanley Bay

Devonport →

Hamer
Brigham
Wynyard Wharf

Princes Wharf
Passenger Terminal

Queens Wharf

Captain Cook Wharf

Marsden Wharf

Bledisloe Terminal

Bledisloe Wharf

Fergusson Wharf

Jellicoe Wharf

Freyberg Wharf

America's Cup Village

Hobson Wharf

Viaduct Harbour

Ferry Berth

i National Maritime Museum

Customs West

Sturdee

Halsey

QUAY

Powerhouse Lane

Tinley

Tooley

Plumer

French

QUAY

sunderland

FANSHAWE

Auckland Mail Service Centre

CUSTOMS

EAST

Commerce

Eden

Police Station

Fort

Ronayne

The Strand

The Strand

St Patricks

Swanson

Mills Lane

Fort

Shortland

Vulcan Lane

Alfred

ANZAC AVENUE

BEACH

Augustus

The Ter

York

Earle

St Georges Bay

AUCKLAND

Kelly Tarlton's Antarctic Encounter and Underwater World

VICTORIA WEST

Television Centre

Sky Tower

Federal

ALBERT WEST

QUEEN WEST

Victoria East

High

Bowen Ave

Kitchener

Princes

Waterloo Quadrant

Alfred

PARNELL RISE

Garfield

Windsor

PARNELL

Scarborough

Big Wood Cres

WELLESLEY WEST

St Matthews

NELSON

HOBSON

Aotea Centre

Police Station

QUEEN

Methodist Mission

Albert Park

Auckland Art Gallery

Auckland University

WELLESLEY EAST

Elliott

Lorne

SYMONDS

Auckland University

St Andrews

Stanley

Cheshire

PARNELL

Terrace

St Georges Bay

Cathedral of the Holy Trinity

Town Hall

MAYORAL DRIVE

WAKEFIELD

Auckland University of Technology

AUCKLAND CITY

Alfred

Grafton

Lower

Domain

North

Kinder House

Avr

Auckland Hebrew Congregation

Creys Ave

Myers Park

Pitt

Liverpool

City

Auckland Domain

Drive

The Crescent

Domain Drive

Ewelme Cottage

Maunsell

PARNELL

ngahape

QUEEN

SYMONDS

GRAFTON BRIDGE

France

St Benedicts

Auckland Hospital

Wintergardens

Auckland Museum Tamaki Paenga Hira

George

sarawia

Newmarket Park

PARK

School of Medicine

Domain

Morgan

Clayton

Kingdon

GRAFTON

KHYBER

Norwich

Exmouth

Nikau

Spraddock

NUGENT

PASS

Burleigh

BOSTON

Carlton

Claremont

Gore

Huntly Ave

CARLTON GORE

BOSTON ROAD

KHYBER PASS

Melrose

CROWHURST

Kent

Teed

NEWMARKET

Mari

Grove

Middleton

MOUNT EDEN

EDEN

Lauder

Mount Eden Prison

Auckland Grammar School

AUCKLAND

HAMILTON

seccombes

Eden

Morrow

Mortimer Pass Pass

BROADWAY

NEWMARKET

Nuffield

Mamie

RRACE

MT EDEN

Normanby

Edwin

Edenvale

Enfield

Mountain

Clive

Gilgit

Almorah

(SOUTHERN

Auckland Surgical Clinic

St Marks Hospital

MacMurray

REMUERA

View

Bellevue

Mount Eden ool

Sherbourne

Lovelock Avenue

MT EDEN

Mount Eden Domain

Esplanade

Mercy Hospital

Glenfell Place

Omana Hospital

Omana Ave

Withiel Thomas Park

Withiel

Albury Ave

GILLIES AVENUE

ALPERS AVE

MANUKAU

Cornwall Park, One Tree Hill

Mortimer Pass

(SOUTHERN MOTORWAY)

GREAT SOUTH

Auckland Regional Botanic Gardens

SH1

Mount Eden

B
C
D

AUCKLAND MUSEUM TAMAKI PAENGA HIRA

✚ 61 D3 ✉ Domain Drive ☎ 09-304 0443 ◷ Summer daily 9–5.30; winter daily 9–4.30 🖐 Adult NZ$5 donation, child (under 18) free. Maori Concert NZ$15, child NZ$7.50 🎁 Excellent gift shop with jewellery, knitwear, ceramics and books
www.aucklandmuseum.com

Rising above New Zealand's oldest and biggest park, the Domain, the museum is a neoclassical building of 1929 housing the outstanding collections of the Auckland Museum. Among its displays are the Pacific and Maori Taonga (treasures), which combine to form the largest such collection in existence. Other attractions include a children's discovery centre with computers, games and interactive displays; social and settlement history sections; natural history galleries; and Scars on the Heart, the story of New Zealanders at war,

Below, Auckland's famous Harbour Bridge spans Waitemata Harbour
Below middle, Viaduct Basin
Below right, floral display in the Botanic Gardens

Right, jumping from the Sky Tower; far right, Mount Eden

MORE TO SEE

PARNELL

✚ 61 D3

Parnell is a fashionably restored suburb 2km (1 mile) east of downtown, full of craft shops, galleries and restaurants. At the top of Parnell Rise is the modern Auckland Cathedral of the Holy Trinity (Mon–Sat 10–4, Sun 11–4); just behind it, the older St. Mary's (1888) is one of the world's largest wooden churches. Parnell Rose Gardens (daylight hours) bloom from November to March. Nearby St. Stephen's Chapel (1857) is a fine example of the Gothic style that evolved under Bishop Selwyn (1809–78).

NEWMARKET

✚ 61 D2

A modern commercial suburb best known for its shopping, quality restaurants, cafés and entertainment. The grand Highwic House at 40 Gillies Avenue (Wed–Sun 10.30–12, 1–4.30, enter from Mortimer Pass) was the 1860s home of 'colonial gentleman of property' Alfred Buckland (1825–1903). Lion Breweries give tours of their facilities (Mon, Wed–Sat 9.30, 12.15, 3), with samplings included.

from the New Zealand Wars of the 19th century to the campaigns in Gallipoli and Crete in the two world wars (▷ 32).

The highlight of the collection is Maori Gallery, He Taonga Maori, housing a variety of craftwork ranging from woven baskets to lethal hand weapons carved from bone and greenstone. Its focal points are the 25m (82ft) *Te Toki a Tapiri* (Tapiri's Battleaxe), last of the Maori war canoes (*waka*), carved from a single tree trunk in 1836; and Hotunui, a beautifully carved meeting house of 1878. A Maori concert is staged daily at 11am, noon and 1.30 (additional performance Jan–Mar 2.30) by Manaia, the museum's cultural performance group.

The museum was built in tribute to the fallen of World War I; it houses a War Memorial Hall, and veterans gather on the forecourt at dawn every year on 25 April–Anzac (Remembrance) Day. Spread around the museum are the Domain's 80ha (198 acres) of fields, gardens and woods, protected as a reserve by Governor Hobson in 1840. Look for the Wintergarden, and the regular orchestral and operatic outdoor events in summer.

AUCKLAND ZOO

✚ 60 A4 ✉ Motions Road, Western Springs ☎ 09-360 3800 ◷ Sep–end May daily 9.30–5.30; Jun–end Aug daily 9.30–5 🖐 Adult NZ$18, child (4–14) NZ$8 ☐ 🎁
www.aucklandzoo.co.nz

New Zealand's premier wild animal collection is set in parkland near Western Springs, 4km (2.5 miles) west of the city's hub. The zoo has an active programme of conservation and captive breeding of native species including kiwi and tuatara, both of which are on display. Elephants are also on view, and are sometimes taken for walks around the zoo. Imaginative themed exhibits include a huge walk-through aviary, and a rainforest where primates swing freely through the trees. Recent additions include Pridelands—a spacious home for the giraffes, lions and zebras; the adjoining Hippo River; and a state-of-the-art Sealion and Penguin Shores.

CORNWALL PARK

✚ 61 C5 ✉ Greenlane Road, Manukau Road, Campbell Road ☎ 09-630 8485 ◷ Daily 7–dusk 🖐 Free
www.cornwallpark.co.nz

Just south of Mount Eden and 5km (3 miles) south of the Sky Tower, Cornwall Park offers a great escape from city life. Its main claim to fame is One Tree Hill, an extinct volcanic cone with well-preserved

MOUNT EDEN
🟥 61 B5
At 196m (643ft), the closest volcano to downtown Auckland (15 minutes' drive, or bus 274/275 from Customs Street East) provides a terrific view. At its southern base Eden Garden (daily 9–4.30) contains flowering shrubs and native New Zealand plants. Mount Eden village has a fine delicatessen, interesting shops and a number of good cafés and restaurants.

remains of Maori fortified settlements around the summit (the lone pine tree which gives the hill its name was cut down in 2000). Kiwi Tamaki, chief of the Wai O Hua tribe, lived here in the 18th century with thousands of his family and followers, and you can still see the ditches and ramparts that marked their dwellings. Scottish settler and Auckland mayor Sir John Logan Campbell bought the hill and surrounding land, and Huia Lodge, now the visitor office, was his gatekeeper's house. Directly across the road is restored Acacia Cottage (Dec–end Mar 7–dusk, Apr–end Nov 7–4), in which Campbell lived; the oldest house in Auckland, from 1841, it was relocated here from the city in the 1920s.

DEVONPORT
🟥 61 C1 ⛴ Every half hour from Ferry Building, Quay Street; 10-minute crossing
A bronze sculpture on King Edward Parade marks the spot where the first Polynesians landed in their canoe, *Tainui*, in the 14th century. Devonport was later a European settlement and still has many splendid 19th-century buildings, including the restored Esplanade Hotel. Ferries dock at Devonport Wharf, at the end of the main street, Victoria Road, which is lined with cafés and shops selling books, crafts, souvenirs and antiques. A footpath from its far end leads up Mount Victoria, an extinct volcanic cone with traces of a Maori *pa* around the summit. The views of the Hauraki Gulf and offshore islands are magnificent. At the tip of the peninsula, North Head Historic Reserve is another volcanic cone, pocked with 19th-century gun emplacements and tunnels, evidence of a Russian invasion scare. Spring Street leads from the waterfront to the Royal New Zealand Navy Museum (daily 10–4.30).

KELLY TARLTON'S ANTARCTIC ENCOUNTER AND UNDERWATER WORLD
🟥 61 D2 ✉ 23 Tamaki Drive, 6km (4 miles) from downtown ☎ 09-528 0603/ 0800 805050 🕐 Daily 9–6 (last entry 5) 🎟 Adult NZ$28, child (4–14) NZ$14, under 4 free 🚻 🍴
www.kellytarltons.co.nz
This hugely popular attraction, the brainchild of diver Kelly Tarlton, was set up in subterranean storage tanks behind Orakei Wharf. Visits are

KINDER HOUSE
🟥 61 D4 ✉ 2 Ayr Street, Parnell ☎ 09-379 0202 🕐 Tue–Sun 11–3 🎟 Adult NZ$2, child 50c
This two-floor building was built in 1856 as the home of pioneer churchman and artist John Kinder (1819–1903). It now displays some of his art works.

EWELME COTTAGE
🟥 61 D4 ✉ 14 Ayr Street, Parnell ☎ 09-379 0202 🕐 Fri–Sun 10.30–12, 1–4.30 🎟 Adult NZ$3, child free
Not far from Kinder House is Ewelme Cottage, built in 1863 as the Auckland home of the family of Archdeacon Vicesimus Lush (1817–82). It was altered in 1882 but has since remained largely unchanged, and contains colonial furniture and household effects.

AUCKLAND REGIONAL BOTANIC GARDENS
🟥 61 D5 ✉ 102 Hill Road, Manurewa ☎ 09-267 1457 🕐 Summer daily 8–8; winter daily 8–6; visitor office hours vary 🎟 Free
www.aucklandbotanicgardens.co.nz
A 64ha (158-acre), 10,000-plant collection is laid out 20 minutes south of downtown Auckland. Planting began in 1974 and consists mostly of New Zealand natives. There is also an ornamental lake, a nature trail and a fragrant display of New Zealand-bred roses.

divided into two main parts. The Antarctic Encounter displays relate the story of early Antarctic exploration. Before entering a replica of Captain Scott's 1911 South Pole expedition hut, you are primed by a weather update from the modern base, citing barely imaginable sub-zero temperatures and wind speeds. From here a snow cat carries you through Penguin Encounter, where king and gentoo penguins breed in carefully maintained natural conditions.

Through Stingray Bay is the original Underwater World, where Tarlton pioneered the concept of viewing sea life through fibreglass tunnels. Stingrays and sharks glide directly above your head, and smaller tanks contain a host of species including beautiful

ONE TREE HILL

✚ 61 D5

A single totara tree once stood on One Tree Hill and gave the area its original name: Te-Totara-a-Ahua (the totara that stands alone). Settlers cut this tree down in 1852, and to make amends a new totara and several Monterey pines were planted in its place. Most failed to flourish and by 1960 only one pine was left, providing Auckland's greatest landmark before the advent of the Sky Tower. In 1994 this tree was damaged by a pro-Maori activist, and after a further attack in 1999 it was decided that the pine must be removed for safety's sake. On the day of its felling hundreds of people gathered to say goodbye, and a Maori *karakia* (prayer service) was said at dawn.

seahorses, moray eels and the poisonous scorpion fish. Open rock pools and a separate education facility provide a learning experience for children.

MUSEUM OF TRANSPORT, TECHNOLOGY AND SOCIAL HISTORY (MOTAT)

✚ 60 A4 ✉ Great North Road, Western Springs, 4km (2.5 miles) west of downtown ☎ 09-815 5800/0800 668 2869 ⏰ Daily 10–5 🎫 Adult NZ$14, child (5–16) NZ$7, under 5s free, family NZ$30 ▢ ⊞
www.motat.org.nz

MOTAT is near Auckland Zoo, on a site that once pumped water from Western Springs Lake to the city's houses. The original pumphouse and beam engine are part of a complex ranged over two sites and housing an eclectic 30,000-item collection that includes vintage cars, fire engines and motorcycles, telephone boxes and printing presses. MOTAT 2, on Motions Road, occupies the Sir Keith Park Memorial Site (named after New Zealand's most famous wartime aviator) and concentrates on aviation, rail and the military. Prize exhibits include the only Solent Mark IV flying boat in the world, and a World War II Avro Lancaster bomber. The two sites are connected by a vintage tram (NZ$2 round trip), which also stops at the zoo.

NEW ZEALAND NATIONAL MARITIME MUSEUM

✚ 61 B1 ✉ Corner of Quay and Hobson streets ☎ 0800-725897/09-373 0800 ⏰ Oct–end Apr daily 9–6; May–end Sep daily 9–5 🎫 Adult NZ$16, child (5–17) NZ$7, family NZ$36. Cruises NZ$15, child NZ$7, family NZ$35 (*Ted Ashby*)
www.nzmaritime.org

Ranged around the waterfront on Hobson Wharf, the New Zealand National Maritime Museum is as diverse and interesting as you might expect in the City of Sails. The layout is chronological, beginning with a video presentation of early Polynesian arrivals and replicas of their vessels, before moving on to European maritime history. The living quarters of an early immigrant ship are replicated, complete with moving floor and sound effects.

Next come the galleries of New Zealand's yachting history, tracing the nation's participation and triumphs in the Louis Vuitton Cup, the Whitbread Round the World Yacht Race and the America's Cup.

Harbour cruises include a trip aboard the 17m (56ft), traditionally built scow *Ted Ashby*, and excursions aboard the *Pride of Auckland*.

SKY TOWER

🔹 61 B2 ✉ Corner of Victoria and Federal streets ☎ 09-363 6000 🕐 Daily 8.30–11 (observation deck) 👤 Adult NZ$22, child (5–14) NZ$8, under 5s free, family NZ$44; extra NZ$3 for Sky Deck 🍴 Orbit revolves to give 360-degree views of the city; the Observatory gives diners access to the main deck www.skycity.co.nz

In 1997 Auckland's skyline gained a dramatic addition in the concrete needle-shape of the Sky Tower, the southern hemisphere's tallest

Below, the Sky Tower, likened to a hypodermic needle, dominates the city skyline
Bottom, glass floor panels in the Sky Tower's observation platform give vertiginous views

building, at 328m (1,076ft) high, and part of the SKYCITY casino, hotel and shopping complex. It takes a mere 40 seconds for the elevator to reach the main observation deck, and there are even more stunning views from the Sky Deck.

If admiring the view isn't quite exciting enough you can opt for Vertigo Climb—a two-hour guided tour up the interior of the tower's mast, culminating in an internal climb from the upper observation deck to the first crow's nest. For an even bigger adrenalin boost there's Sky Jump, the world's highest land based bungy jump, leaping from 192m (630ft).

BACKGROUND

The first Maori to settle in this area were thought to be hunters of the now extinct moa bird, who arrived before AD1000. From the 12th to the 14th century Maori tribes migrated here, and in the early 18th century Kiwi Tamaki's tribe rose to power, establishing *pa* (fortified Maori settlements) on almost every volcano in the district. A series of brutal conflicts with rival tribes, along with an epidemic of smallpox brought here by the early Europeans, subsequently decimated the area's Maori population.

In 1820 missionaries Samuel Marsden and John Gare Butler were the first white Europeans to pay an 'official' visit. Low-key European settlement followed, and 20 years later Lieutenant-Governor Captain William Hobson bought a triangular section of the isthmus from the Ngati Whatua for £55 and a few blankets. He called this area Auckland in tribute to George Eden, First Earl of Auckland, then Governor General of India.

As a result of the New Zealand Wars (▷ 30) and the discovery of gold in Otago and the nearby Coromandel Peninsula, Auckland entered a period of decline and, in 1865, lost its status as capital to Wellington. By the end of the 19th century its fortunes had revived, thanks to its fertile soils, good climate and a booming kauri industry. Growth continued during the 20th century and a combination of geography, climate, industry, agriculture, and sporting and business opportunities have encouraged its development as a vibrant, cosmopolitan city.

Coromandel Peninsula

**Spectacular coastal scenery, rugged mountain bush
and a relaxed way of life.**

Cathedral Cove, where a natural arch links two beaches

Riding the waves at Whangamata

Visitors on the Driving Creek Railway

RATINGS	
Historic interest	● ● ●
Photo stops	● ● ● ● ●
Shopping	● ●
Walkability	● ● ● ●

BASICS
✚ 315 K4
ℹ 206 Pollen Street, Thames, tel 07-868 7284; Mon–Fri 8.30–5, Sat, Sun, pub hols 9–4
✈ Coromandel–Auckland flights Fri, Sun
⛴ Coromandel–Auckland ferries Tue, Thu, Fri, Sat

www.thamesinfo.co.nz

Gathering mussels on the seashore

SEEING THE COROMANDEL PENINSULA

The Coromandel Peninsula's varied landscapes and laidback style make it the main attraction on the Pacific Coast Highway. The west coast, bounded by the Firth of Thames, is the least developed side, with a ragged coastline of islands and pebble beaches lined with pohutukawa trees. In contrast, the east coast is a stretch of beautiful bays, resort development and some of New Zealand's most popular beaches. Between the two coasts, a spine of bush-covered mountains makes up the Coromandel Forest Park, with historic logging and mining remains.

HIGHLIGHTS

COLVILLE AND THE CAPE ROAD
✚ 315 K4

North of Coromandel town the Colville Road enters the most remote and scenic area of the peninsula. From the beach at Waitete Bay it climbs a hill and drops to the tiny village of Colville, with just a general store-cum-café and a fuel station. Beyond Colville the interior is dominated by 893m (2,930ft) Moehau. The road eventually climbs around the northern tip of the cape and descends to Port Jackson, where there are superb views of Great Barrier Island. Fletcher Bay marks the beginning of the three-hour Coromandel Walkway to Stony Bay, and thence the east coast road and all points south.

COROMANDEL
✚ 315 K4 ℹ 355 Kapanga Road, tel 07-866 8598
www.coromandeltown.co.nz

The township of Coromandel is 56km (35 miles) north of Thames (▷ 73), on the peninsula's west coast. It was built to serve the kauri timber trade, but boomed when gold was discovered at nearby Driving Creek. During the peak gold-rush years of the 1860s and 1870s its population reached 12,000. Today its inhabitants number around 1,000, and it has a carefully nurtured village atmosphere.

Most of Coromandel's cafés and shops are on Kapanga Road, which runs at right angles to the port. Two sites give an insight into gold-hunting days. The Coromandel School of Mines and Historical Museum on Rings Road (summer daily 10–4; winter Sat, Sun

1.30–4) is in the original School of Mines (1897) and includes New Zealand's first prison; the Coromandel Gold Stamper Battery on Buffalo Road (summer daily 10–5) lets you pan for gold in its stream.

A short drive north of town is the Driving Creek Railway and Potteries (daily). You can ride up to the ridge-top Eyefull Tower terminus, through tunnels and across viaducts and past potter and railway restorer Barry Brickell's sculptures.

NEW CHUMS BEACH
✚ 315 K4

This is one of the best beaches in the Coromandel, accessible only on foot. To reach it, take the SH25 east from Coromandel town over the

Quiet and magical Opoutere, on the east coast, is one of the Coromandel's best-kept secrets. White-sand Ocean Beach is guarded by Wharekawa Harbour and a narrow tract of forest. At the tip of the sand spit is the Wharekawa Wildlife Refuge, where oystercatchers and rare New Zealand dotterels breed.

Above, panning for gold
Left, Coromandel Harbour

ranges before descending steeply to Te Rerenga and Whangapoua Harbour, then continue 4km (2.5 miles) north to Whangapoua village and take a 30-minute walk north from the road there to negotiate the headland. Even in bad weather, this stunning beach is definitely worth the walk.

WHITIANGA
✚ 315 K4 ℹ 66 Albert Street, tel 07-866 5555
www.whitianga.co.nz

Whitianga is on glorious Mercury Bay, within walking distance of several fine beaches. There are plenty of leisure activities, but Whitianga is most famous as a sea- and big-game-fishing base.

The Mercury Bay Museum (Dec–Easter daily 10–4), which traces the area's social history, faces the main wharf, where a passenger ferry shuttles across the narrows to Ferry Landing. This was the township's original site, and the stone wharf (built in 1837) is said to be the oldest in the country.

The main waterfront beach is named after a timber ship, HMS *Buffalo*, wrecked here in 1840. Two smaller resorts lie within reach of Whitianga: Cooks Beach, on its southern edge (where Captain James Cook planted the British flag on 5 November 1769 and claimed the country for George III), and Hahei (▷ 220), 35km (22 miles) farther by road and accessible by ferry. Both have wonderful beaches. A track north of Hahei on Grange Road leads in half an hour to Cathedral Cove, a fabulous beach guarding the Te Whanganui-A-Hei Marine Reserve (▷ 228). Strictly speaking, there are two beaches here, connected by a natural rock arch negotiable at low tide.

BACKGROUND

First to set foot here was the Maori explorer Kupe, 1,000 years ago. Captain Cook paid a brief visit in 1769, and from 1795 ships landed regularly to load timber for the British navy. Nearly three quarters of the kauri forests were felled, leaving just 5,000ha (12,355 acres). Coromandel is named after the timber ship HMS *Coromandel*, which called here in 1820. Charles Ring discovered gold in 1852; at the peak of the boom, around 1880, the peninsula's population topped 12,000.

WAIHI
✚ 316 K5 ℹ Seddon Street, tel 07-863 6715
www.waihi.org.nz

Waihi once had 1,200 gold mines, producing half the country's gold. The Martha Mine (free guided tours most weekdays), which sits like a huge bomb crater right in the middle of town, was one of the first, and reopened after a brief redundancy in the mid-1900s. Today, from a lookout behind the information office, you can watch earthmoving trucks winding in and out of the massive, terraced hole.

WHANGAMATA
✚ 316 L5 ℹ 616 Port Road, tel 07-865 8340

The Coromandel's main surfing venue is well served with places to stay and eat, and with water-based activities. There are several good short coastal walks, and south of town the Wentworth and Parakiwai valleys offer longer trails, taking in waterfalls and remnants of the gold-mining industry. The beach at Whangamata is more than 4km (2.5 miles) long.

A natural rock hole by Piercey Island, in the Bay of Islands

The scenic Kai Iwi lakes are a focus for summer activities

Decorative pillars in the unusual public toilets at Kawakawa

THE SIGHTS

BAY OF ISLANDS

✚ 314 J2 **i** Marsden Road, Paihia, tel 09-402 7345 🚢 Maritime Building, Paihia 🚢 Ferry between Russell and Paihia; car ferry to Opua, 9km (5.5 miles) south of Paihia ✈ Bay of Islands airport, between Paihia and Kerikeri www.northland.org.nz

A group of 150 islands huddled in their large bay on the east Northland coast has become a major draw for holidaymakers, who come for watersports and superb coastal scenery. This area is also of huge historic significance, as the site of the signing of the 1840 Treaty of Waitangi—the document that set in train New Zealand's bicultural society (▷ 27). You can explore the islands—now designated a Historic and Maritime Park—by kayak, yacht or sailing ship; you can also go fishing for marlin or shark, dive among shoals of blue maomao, swim with dolphins, bask on the beaches or jump out of a plane.

Most facilities are based in Paihia (▷ 72). From here a ferry crosses the bay to the small village of Russell (▷ 72). State Highway 11 runs to the bay, though a more interesting route

is via the Old Russell Road, which leaves SH1 for the coast at Whakapara, about 26km (16 miles) north of Whangarei (▷ 75). You reach the coast at Helena Bay, which, along with Whananaki and Mimiwhangata to the south and the Whangaruru Peninsula to the north, offers remote and beautiful coastal scenery. From Whangaruru the road passes the neck of the beautiful Cape Brett Peninsula before turning inland and slowly negotiating its way to Russell.

COROMANDEL PENINSULA

See pages 66–67.

HAURAKI GULF ISLANDS

See pages 70–71.

KAI IWI LAKES

✚ 314 H3 **i** Normanby Street, Dargaville, tel 09-439 8360 www.kauricoast.co.nz

Located about 30km (19 miles) south of the Waipoua Kauri Forest (▷ 75), and only 10km (6 miles) from the coast, three freshwater lakes—Kaiiwi, Taharoa and Waikere—form part of the Taharoa recreation reserve. On

their crystal clear waters you can enjoy sailing, windsurfing, water-skiing, jet-skiing and fishing, and you can explore the area along an extensive walking track. Note that, lacking cover and so close to the western coast, the lakes can be exposed to the elements.

KAITAIA

✚ 314 H2 **i** Jaycee Park, South Road, tel 09-408 0879 🚌 Kaitaia Travel Bureau, 170 Commerce Street ✈ Airport 6km (4 miles) north

Kaitaia is the last significant outpost of the Far North, and a good start point for exploring Ninety Mile Beach (▷ 57). It frequently registers the hottest temperatures in the country. Its population is mainly Maori but includes a Croatian minority, whose forebears arrived during the kauri gum boom years of the late 19th century. The Far North Regional Museum (Mon–Fri 10–5, Sat, Sun 1–4) has a number of Maori treasures, including the Kaitaia Carving, one of the earliest Maori carvings in existence, and a 1,500kg (1.5-ton) anchor left by French navigator Jean-François de Surville in 1769. Other collections include moa remains and remnants from the Greenpeace ship *Rainbow Warrior* (▷ 34). The Okahu Estate Winery, on the corner of Okahu Road and the Ahipara/Kaitaia highway, 3.5km (2 miles) from Kaitaia (daily 10–5, closed winter weekends), is New Zealand's northernmost winery and offers free tastings.

KARIKARI PENINSULA

✚ 314 H1

This peaceful, beautiful T-shaped spur juts out on the northeastern coast, before it extends into the long, straight run of the Aupouri Peninsula (▷ 57). Its remote beaches separate Doubtless Bay from the mangrove swamps of

A sparkling inlet of white sands in the Bay of Islands

The stone-built warehouse at Kerikeri was built up a barely navigable creek and is known as 'Kemp's folly'

The kauri timber industry is explained at Matakohe

Rangaunu Harbour and the broad, empty sweep of Karikari Bay to the north. Whales are frequently stranded here. In 1995 more than 100 pilot whales were refloated by locals and officials, only to beach themselves again the following day. Tokerau Bay is the main settlement on the peninsula.

KAWAKAWA

➕ 314 H2

Bizarre as it might seem, the main attraction in this town 17km (10.5 miles) south of Paihia is the public toilet. The Hundertwasser public toilets are the imaginative creation of Austrian artist Friedensreich Hundertwasser (1928–2000). The interior uses tiles of all sizes and shades and stained glass to produce a cheerfully chaotic effect, and the whole building is topped with a grass roof.

South of Kawakawa, local Maori guides give tours of the Kawiti Caves (daily 8.30–4.30), a series of subterranean passages originally occupied by a Maori woman fleeing from her tribe.

KERIKERI

➕ 314 H2 ✖ Airport between Paihia and Kerikeri
www.kerikeri.co.nz

North of Paihia, rolling hills give way to corridors of windbreaks hiding trees of citrus, grape and kiwifruit, for which the area is famous. *Keri* means 'dig', and it was here that the first plough cut into New Zealand soil in 1820. Kerikeri is rich in Maori and early European history; the Kerikeri Historic Basin, 2km (1 mile) northeast of the present town, was the nucleus of New Zealand's first European colonisation.

Where the road meets the Kerikeri River stands the Stone Store (Nov–end Apr daily 10–5;

May–end Oct daily 10–4), the country's first stone building, completed in 1836 and used by the first Anglican bishop, George Selwyn, as a library in the early 1840s. It later housed ammunition during conflicts with Ngapuhi chief Hone Heke, before assuming its intended purpose as a general mission store. A museum occupies the top floor.

Almost immediately next door is the two-floor Mission Station or Kemp House (Nov–end Apr daily 10–5; May–end Oct daily 10–4), the oldest surviving wooden building in New Zealand. The Reverend John Gare Butler had it built in 1821 on land offered by the great local Maori warlord Hongi Hika, who accepted 48 felling axes in return. In 1832 it became the home of lay missionary and blacksmith James Kemp, whose family lived in the house until 1974, when it was given to the nation. The house now contains Kemp family relics.

Overlooking both buildings is the ancient Kororipo *pa*, which was chief Hongi Hika's territory until the 1820s, when he had a European-style house built near by. A stroll across the river leads to Rewa's Village (Dec–end Mar daily 9–5; Apr–end Nov daily 10–4), a re-created pre-European Maori fishing settlement, or *kainga*, named after Hongi Hika's successor. Its reed-and-thatch huts have beds of bracken and fern; traditional cooking areas occupy separate shelters.

In addition to its fruit, Kerikeri is also famous for its arts and crafts. Among many venues are Origin Art and Craft Co-op on SH10 (daily 9.30–5), which displays and sells pottery, stained glass and other crafts; and the Kauri Workshop, on the approach to town on Kerikeri Road (daily 9–5), where kauri and other native wood products are made.

The Aroha Island Ecological

Centre, on Rangitane Road 12km (7 miles) northeast of town (Tue–Sun 9.30–5.30; also overnight visits), and the nearby Rangitane Scenic Reserve are important remnant habitats of the brown kiwi. The island is kept predator-free and offers a small but valuable sanctuary for a few birds. As the kiwi is nocturnal, daytime visitors can only see interpretive material, but if you stay overnight you may see and hear the birds on a guided tour.

MATAKOHE KAURI MUSEUM

➕ 314 J3 ✉ Church Road, Matakohe ☎ 09-431 7417 🕐 Nov–end Apr daily 8.30–5.30; May–end Oct daily 9–5 💰 Adult NZ$15, child (5–15) NZ$3, family NZ$30 🚌 SH12 at Brynderwyn; all Twin Coast Discovery Highway routes stop here 💻
www.kauri-museum.com

Highly imaginative displays in this museum in the village of Matakohe, 45km (28 miles) south of Dargaville, give a detailed account of the natural history of the kauri tree and its exploitation. The Volunteer Hall contains a 22.5m (74ft) kauri slab, a local specimen which was felled by lightning. On the wall at its base are the circumference outlines of larger recorded trees, the largest having a diameter of 8.5m (28ft). Around the hall are exquisite examples of kauri furniture, and models of kauri scows that used to ply the Kaipara Harbour. Other sections include a working Steam Sawmill, monstrous moving equipment and saws, and a superb kauri gum display, with carvings, busts and ornaments fashioned from the tree's resin or sap, some of it hundreds of thousands of years old. Restored kauri buildings in the museum grounds include the 1867 Pioneer Church and 1909 Post Office.

Hauraki Gulf Islands

Dozens of islands within easy reach of Auckland. Volcanic terrain, beach barbecues, diving sites and wildlife sanctuaries.

Above, Matiatia Bay, Waiheke Top, a takahe

Dining al fresco at the Mudbrick Restaurant, Waiheke (▷ 254)

Pohutukawa trees on the shore of Tiritiri Matangi Island

BASICS

➕ 315 K4

ℹ Department of Conservation office, Ferry Building, Quay Street, Auckland, tel 09-379 6476; Mon–Fri 9–5, Sat 10–3

🚢 Fleet of ferries run by Fullers, Quay Street, Auckland, tel 09-367 9111, www.fullers.co.nz: see individual islands for sailings

✈ Airfields at Waiheke (3km/2 miles east of Ostend) and Great Barrier (Claris, Okiwi)

www.aucklandcity.govt.nz
Information for all the main islands, including history and contact numbers.

Vineyard on Waiheke Island

SEEING THE HAURAKI GULF ISLANDS

The scattering of islands between the Coromandel Peninsula to the east and the mainland to the south and west provide an easy escape from the city for day trips or overnight stays. Most of the Hauraki Gulf lies within Hauraki Gulf Maritime Park, which takes in 47 islands and one mainland reserve (North Head in Devonport). Some are wildlife sanctuaries. The most densely populated island is Waiheke, a 35-minute ferry ride from Auckland.

HIGHLIGHTS

GREAT BARRIER ISLAND

➕ 315 K3 ℹ Tel 09-367 6009, www.greatbarrier.co.nz 🚢 Sailings Apr–end Oct Sun–Tue, Thu, Fri; more frequent in summer; always check ahead, tel 09-300 5900 ✈ Daily flights from Auckland

Rugged Great Barrier (or 'the Barrier') is the largest island in the gulf, with a population of around 1,000. This is the habitat for some rare and endangered species, including brown teal and New Zealand's largest skink (lizard), the cheveron. Over half of the island is conservation land.

Great Barrier earned its name from Captain Cook because it appeared to bar the entrance to the gulf. It was one of the first islands to be colonised by Europeans, who mined for gold and copper and plundered its extensive kauri forests. There are old kauri dams, the remains of whaling stations and tramping tracks to explore.

KAWAU ISLAND

➕ 315 J4 ℹ 1 Baxter Street, Warkworth, tel 09 425 9081 🚢 From Sandspit at 10.30am, 2, 3.30
www.warkworth-information.co.nz

Kawau, 8km (5 miles) off the Mahurangi Peninsula, was once the headquarters of Maori pirates. Europeans took possession in 1837, and the island was mined first for manganese, then for copper. Operations ceased in 1869, but remnants of copper mines can be found near the wharf. In 1862 Sir George Grey, Governor of New Zealand, bought the island for £3,500 and began a 26-year stay in Bon Accord Harbour, where he created the Mansion House (daily 10–3.30). Grey amassed a small collection of exotic animals and plants here, unaware of the environmental damage he was unleashing on native flora and fauna. To this day, Australian wallabies and kookaburras inhabit the bush.

RANGITOTO ISLAND
✚ 315 J4 🛈 Rangitoto Island Heritage Conservation Trust, tel 09-634 1398
🚢 From Ferry Building daily at 9.15, 12.15, 3.15
Rangitoto's comparatively young volcanic cone (about 600 years old) dominates views of the Hauraki Gulf from almost every vantage

point in Auckland. Of the island's many walks, most culminate at the summit (two hours). The island's vegetation is of international importance, with 200 species of native tree and flowering plants, 40 kinds of fern, and orchids and lichens. Underfoot are mounds of loose lava scoria.

TIRITIRI MATANGI ISLAND
✚ 315 J4 🚢 Ferries from Pier 3, Ferry Building Wed–Sun at 9am; or the same ferry from Z Pier, Gulf Harbour on the Whangaparaoa Peninsula, 45 mins later
Visitors can wander freely on a network of walkways on this open bird sanctuary 4km (2.5 miles) off the Whangaparaoa Peninsula. The 220ha (544-acre) island has become a haven for rare and endangered species including the takahe, little spotted kiwi, kokako, whitehead, saddleback, North Island robin, kakariki and stitchbird.

WAIHEKE ISLAND
✚ 315 K4 🛈 Korora Road, Oneroa, tel 09-372 1234 🚢 Auckland Ferry Building, daily
The busiest island has a thriving arts and crafts community. Its main village is Oneroa, at the western end of the island. Behind the visitor information office, in the Artworks Complex, Whittakers Musical Museum (daily 10–4) displays instruments dating back 500 years. Live performances are staged at 1pm (except on Tuesday).

Waiheke enjoys average temperatures 5°C (9°F) warmer than the mainland, and has many vineyards and wineries. The island is fringed with beaches, and inland there are walkways through native bush and farmland. One of the most popular is the track to Stony Batter, where an underground complex is linked by a series of tunnels built in World War II as defence against a possible Japanese invasion.

BACKGROUND
Traces of Maori *pa* sites can still be seen on many hillsides. After the arrival of Europeans in the 19th century some of the islands were sold for gold, arms and ammunition.

RATINGS				
Historic interest	● ●			
Photo stops	● ● ● ● ●			
Shopping	●			
Walkability	● ● ●			

TIPS

● Take your own picnic to Rangitoto and Tiritiri Matangi as the shops there do not sell food.
● There is no mains electricity—or streetlight—on Great Barrier Island, so bring a torch: lights out at 10pm.
● Water, sun block and a hat are essential, as the black scoria (volcanic rock) can emanate a lot of heat.

Top, Governor George Grey's gracious Mansion House on Kawau Island

Above, the familiar shape of Rangitoto Island, viewed from Auckland

Pleasure cruisers moored in the bay at Paihia

Divers make the most of the clear waters around the protected Poor Knights Islands, off the Tutukaka Coast

THE SIGHTS

MATAURI BAY

➕ 314 H2
www.matauribay.co.nz

The views above Matauri Bay, studded with the Cavalli Islands, are sublime. Captain Cook named the islands after buying travally (a species of fish) from local Maori. The Samuel Marsden memorial church in Matauri Bay commemorates the missionary who first preached the gospel in the Bay of Islands, on Christmas Day 1814.

This prime venue for deep-sea fishing and diving is probably more famous as the site of the remains of the *Rainbow Warrior*. This flagship of the environmental movement Greenpeace was bombed by French secret service agents in Auckland in 1985 to prevent her leading a protest flotilla to the French nuclear test grounds on the Pacific atoll of Mururoa. Matauri Bay's local Maori tribe, the Ngati Kura, offered the ship a final resting place, and her sunken hull now lies 3km (2 miles) offshore. A memorial on the hill overlooking the islands near the beach pays tribute to the ship, her crew (one of whom was killed) and the campaign for establishing a nuclear-free region.

The Maori *waka* (war canoe) *Mataatua II*, nearby, was built in 1990 to commemorate the Pacific migration from Polynesia in about AD1100.

MURIWAI BEACH

➕ 315 J4
www.muriwai.com

Muriwai, 45km (28 miles) west of Auckland, is the west coast's most visited beach. During summer weekends, locals and visitors flock to its black sands to soak up the sun, enjoy the surf, fish, or look over the gannet colony. Gannets have taken up residence

on the flat rock outcrops at its southern end to breed, forming a small seabird city. In spring you can witness at close range the fluffy white chicks being fed by their angry-looking parents. Muriwai boasts the only major North Island colony, after Cape Kidnappers (▷ 77).

Muriwai itself is well equipped for visitors and has a fine golf course. If Muriwai beach is too busy, you can try another surf spot, Maori Bay, just south of Muriwai and reached via Waitea Road.

PAIHIA

➕ 314 H2   ℹ️ Maritime Building, Marsden Road, tel 09-402 7345
🚢 Maritime Building
www.paihia.co.nz

Paihia is the most convenient base for cruises or other activities in the Bay of Islands Historic and Maritime Park (▷ 68), and for visiting Russell (see below), Kerikeri (▷ 69) and Waitangi (▷ 74). It has a wide range of motels, hotels and other places to stay, as well as plenty of restaurants, cafés and shops. At the Maritime Building on the quayside there are several booking and information offices, including the visitor office. Behind it, Paihia wharf is busy with charter vessels, dolphin-watch boats and the Russell ferries. Next to the wharf, Aquatic World aquarium (daily 9.30–6; extended hours in summer) provides an insight into marine life in the Bay of Islands.

RUSSELL

➕ 314 J2   ℹ️ www.russell.gen.nz
🚢 Paihia Wharf every 20–30 mins Oct–Mar 7.30–10.30; Apr–Sep 7.30–8.30

About 2km (1 mile) across the water from Paihia is the settlement of Russell, which has a village feel and a rich history.

Soon after the signing of the Treaty of Waitangi (▷ 27), Captain William Hobson purchased a block of land at nearby Okiato—renamed Russell after Lord John Russell, then British Colonial Secretary—with the aim of establishing the country's capital there. Nine months later, in March 1841, the capital was transferred to Auckland, and in 1844 the notoriously rowdy whaling port of Kororareka was given the name Russell.

The economic decline that followed the shift of the capital to Auckland provoked resentment among local Maori, who sacked the town in 1845. It was rebuilt the following year, and by the turn of the century had become a quiet summer resort. In 1930 a road was laid between Whangarei and Russell, allowing access by car for the first time.

The Russell Museum (Jan daily 10–5; rest of year 10–4) has a collection of early settler relics and a lot of information about Captain Cook, including a 1:5 scale model of his ship *Endeavour*.

A short distance south along the shore from the museum is Pompallier (Dec–Apr daily 10–5; May–Nov tours at 10.15, 11.15, 1.15, 2.15, 3.15), a French-style dwelling set up in 1842 by early Roman Catholic missionaries as a printing works. It later served as a tannery and a private home, and became a museum in 1990.

The 1836 Anglican Christ Church on the corner of Church and Robertson streets was one of the few buildings to survive the 1845 sacking and ensuing Maori war (bar a few visible musket ball holes), and is the oldest church in New Zealand.

A steep climb up Flagstaff Hill (Maiki) gives grand views. The flagstaff itself was raised after the signing of the Treaty of Waitangi.

A cannon in Russell dates from the 1847 Maori conflict

The view over historic Thames and the Hauraki Plains from the War Memorial Lookout

It was cut down several times by local Maori chief Hone Heke Pokai (▷ 28) and replaced in the 1850s as a gesture of conciliation.

A farther 1km (0.6 mile) north, the earth terraces of the ancient *pa* on the Tapeka Point Reserve make an interesting walk. Long Beach, 1km (0.5 mile) behind Russell, is a pleasant venue on a hot summer's day.

THAMES

316 K5 📋 206 Pollen Street, tel 07-868 7284 🚌 From Auckland, Tauranga www.thamesinfo.co.nz

The historic town of Thames is at the western base of the Coromandel Peninsula (▷ 66–67), at the mouth of the Waihou River and on the fringe of the Hauraki Plains. Behind the town rise the hills of the Coromandel Forest Park.

The best place to start exploring is the War Memorial Monument Lookout on Waiotahi Creek Road, at the northern end of the town, where the panorama takes in the Hauraki Plains and Firth of Thames. Also

at the northern end of town, on attractively preserved Pollen Street, is the Thames Gold Mine and Stamper Battery (daily 10–4). Regular tours take in the impressive ore-crushing stamper and horizontal tunnels, with a commentary about the process and history of gold mining along the way. On the same theme, the Thames School of Mines and Mineralogical Museum (Wed–Sun 11–4) has a collection of rocks and minerals from around the world.

Other places of interest include the Matatoki Cheese Farm (daily 10–4), and the Piako Ostrich Farm (tours daily 11 and 2; closed Tue, Wed, Oct–end Jun). There are also several notable gardens in the area, including Lyndell and Stony Creek Gardens.

Every Saturday the town's popular market is held in Grahamstown, at the north end of Pollen Street.

TUTUKAKA COAST

315 J2 📋 Otaika Road, Whangarei, tel 09-438 1079 🚌 Coastal shuttle from Walton Street supermarket, Tutukaka www.whangareinz.org.nz

The Tutukaka coastline's ruggedly scenic bays are best known for their safe access to some of the best deep-sea fishing and diving in the world. Tutukaka itself has a large, sheltered marina, and the village of Ngunguru, 5km (3 miles) away, has most of the visitor and resident amenities.

Accessed from Tutukaka, the Poor Knights Islands are a popular diving venue, which lie 25km (15.5 miles) offshore—the remnants of a large volcano which erupted more than 10 million years ago. They provide a predator-free refuge for land animals such as the tuatara (a reptile that has changed little in 60 million years), native lizards, giant weta (the largest insect in the world—around the size of a mouse), flax snails, giant centipedes and a wide variety of rare seabirds. They are also home to several species of plants, including the Poor Knights lily, found only here and on the Hen and Chickens Islands off Whangarei Heads (▷ 75). Landing on the Poor Knights Islands is forbidden without a permit.

Tranquil Russell was once a rowdy whaling port tipped to become the country's first capital

Left, the modest exterior of the Whare Runanga conceals a richly carved interior of native woods, above

WAITANGI

Site where the treaty was signed that would shape European-Maori relationships to the present day. The place where New Zealand's modern history began.

The haunting sound of piped Maori song draws you into the visitor complex of the Waitangi National Reserve, where an audiovisual display outlines the events that led to the signing of the Treaty of Waitangi in 1840 (▷ 27), and highlights the significance of the document to this day. A daily 30-minute Maori *kapa haka* performance takes place in the visitor centre's theatre (10.30, 11.30, 1.30, 2.30).

The main focus of the reserve is the beautifully restored wooden Treaty House, built between 1833 and 1834 and once the home of British resident James Busby, who played a crucial role in the lead-up to the signing. The house is full of detailed and informative displays that help clarify the confusing series of events surrounding the creation of the treaty.

AROUND TREATY HOUSE

Near Treaty House is perhaps the most visited Maori meeting house in the country—Whare Runanga. The word 'house' is misleading; Maori meeting houses are essentially works of art, and this is a magnificent example, erected in 1940 and incorporating carved panels contributed by major tribes.

In front of the Treaty House and Whare Runanga a spacious lawn overlooks the bay to Russell. A flagstaff marks the actual spot where the treaty was signed. From the lawn it is a short walk down to the shore where the war canoe (*waka*) *Ngatokimatawhaorua* is housed. This impressive craft, 35m (115ft) long, is named after the canoe in which Kupe, the great Maori ancestor and navigator, discovered Aotearoa (New Zealand). It was commissioned, along with the Whare Runanga, as a centennial project to commemorate the signing of the treaty. The *Ngatokimatawhaorua* continues to be launched every year as part of the Waitangi Day ceremonies hosted on and around the reserve.

The Huia Creek Walkway, which begins near Treaty House, is an easy two-hour walk through the reserve to the Haruru Falls, taking in a good example of mangrove habitat on the way.

Waipu Caves are famous for their glow-worms

A massive kauri log shows the value of such timber in the 19th and early 20th centuries, Parry Kauri Park

WAIPOUA KAURI FOREST

➕ 314 H2 ℹ️ Off SH12 towards southern end of the park, tel 09-439 3011
www.doc.govt.nz

On the west coast within the 15,000ha (37,065-acre) Waipoua Forest is Waipoua sanctuary, of which 2,639ha (6,521 acres) contain mature kauri trees. Walking tracks at the northern end of the forest, immediately next to the highway, give access to the two largest known kauri specimens: Tane Mahuta, or Lord of the Forest, and Te Matua Ngahere, Father of the Forest. Tane Mahuta is an awesome sight, 51.5m (169ft) high, with a girth of 13.8m (45ft). It is estimated to be more than 1,500 years old.

From a parking area 2km (1 mile) south, a 20-minute walk leads to Te Matua Ngahere; a shorter path reaches the Four Sisters, a stand of trees growing together.

WAIPU

➕ 315 J3 ℹ️ 36a The Centre, tel 09-432 0746 🚌 Whangarei–Auckland routes (reserve in advance)
www.waipu.co.nz

A party of 120 Scottish settlers founded Waipu in 1853, and its ethnic origins are reflected in names such as Braemar Lane, Argyll Street and Caledonian Park. The war memorial in the square is made of Aberdeen granite and was shipped from Scotland in 1914 to commemorate the 60th anniversary of the town's founding. The community's heritage is explored in the Waipu House of Memories (daily 9.30–4), which has cases full of early settlers' personal effects.

Every New Year's Day since 1871 the Waipu Highland Games have been celebrated, with highland dancers, pipe bands and kilted, caber-tossing men (Waipu Caledonian Society, www.highlandgames.co.nz).

At the Waipu Caves, 13km (8 miles) west via Shoemaker Road, you can see glow-worms through a 200m (656ft) passage, part of an extensive limestone cave system. You'll need to take a torch and have sturdy footwear.

WARKWORTH

➕ 315 J3 ℹ️ 1 Baxter Street, tel 09-425 9081 🚌 Outside visitor office, Baxter Street
www.warkworth-information.co.nz

This former kauri-milling town is now a farming and tourism service base on the banks of the Mahurangi River. The Warkworth and District Museum (daily 9–4), in the shadow of two 600- to 800-year-old kauri trees within the Parry Kauri Park, uses reconstructed rooms to illustrate the life of early pioneers.

About 4km (2.5 miles) north of Warkworth is Sheepworld (daily 9–5, show 11–2), where you can feed the lambs and get involved in some shearing. A farther 3km (2 miles) north, at the Dome State Forest, walks range from 40 minutes to 3 hours, the best climbing to the Dome Summit, from where you can spot the Auckland Sky Tower (▷ 65) on a clear day.

WHANGAREI

➕ 314 J3 ℹ️ Tarewa Park, Otaika Road, tel 09-438 1079 🚌 Rose Street and outside visitor office ✈️ Onerahi, 9km (5.5 miles) southeast; shuttle bus
www.whangareinz.org.nz

Whangarei is the Northland district's biggest city. Mount Parahaki, on Memorial Drive (off Riverside Drive), once the site of one of the largest Maori *pa* (fortified site), is a good place for an overall view of the city and the bay. You can also walk up via the Mair Park, which has remains of an old gold mine and of further Maori fortifications.

Town Basin is a lively waterfront development with museums, art galleries and craft shops. Its most unusual attraction is Claphams Clock Museum (daily 9–5), a collection of timepieces gathered from around the world.

In the suburb of Maunu, 6km (4 miles) west of town, the Whangarei Museum, Clarke Homestead and Kiwi House (daily 10–4) is a colonial farming complex with a modern gallery housing Maori treasures, including a musket that belonged to the great warrior Hone Heke.

A Scot, William Carruth, was the first to buy land from the Maori in 1839 and settle at the mouth of the Hatea River. The quest for kauri gum and the building of a shipyard in the 1860s brought prosperity, and in the 1930s road and rail links with Auckland were completed.

WHATIPU

➕ 315 J4

Solitude and wilderness are the attractions of Whatipu, 45km (28 miles) southwest of downtown Auckland, at the southernmost tip of the Waitakere ranges. Its huge expanse of sand forms part of the narrow mouth of Manukau Harbour.

At the terminus of the winding, unpaved road a small cluster of buildings called Whatipu Lodge is the last sign of habitation and last chance of accommodation before the beach stretches 6km (4 miles) north to Karekare. Hidden inland among the dune grasses and cabbage trees are extensive wetlands that are home to paradise shelduck, pied stilts and black swans.

THE SIGHTS

CENTRAL NORTH ISLAND

You can't escape the volcanic nature of this landscape, from the volcanoes around active Mount Ruapehu to the geothermal activity that surrounds Rotorua, the tourist capital of Maori culture. Art deco Napier, rebuilt after a devastating earthquake in 1931, is a highlight.

MAJOR SIGHTS

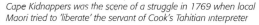
Cape Kidnappers was the scene of a struggle in 1769 when local Maori tried to 'liberate' the servant of Cook's Tahitian interpreter

An Italian Renaissance setting in Hamilton Gardens

CAPE KIDNAPPERS

319 M8 100 Marine Parade, Napier, tel 06-834 1911 Cape Shuttle between Napier and Clifton or Te Awanga; subject to season and tides

This remote and jagged white peninsula marks the southern boundary of Hawke's Bay. Its name recalls the 'rescue' in 1769 of a young Tahitian servant on Captain Cook's ship by local Maori, who mistakenly believed he was being held captive.

In summer up to 15,000 gannets gather here to breed, forming New Zealand's biggest mainland colony (visits Oct–late Apr). An 8km (5-mile) walk leads to the colony from Clifton Motorcamp, but since tides restrict the access times it's best to join one of the many available tours.

EAST CAPE

317 P6 District Council Building, Te Puia, tel 06-864 6853. See also Gisborne, below; Opotiki, page 81 Opotiki and Gisborne; services between Hick's Bay and Whakatane or Gisborne Mon–Sat Gisborne airport 2km (1 mile) west of town

Most of the wild East Cape—the heel of New Zealand's upturned boot—is sparsely populated and mountainous, and much of the Raukumara mountain range, which dominates the interior, remains impenetrable by road. Early European settlers here were few, and the population remains predominantly Maori.

The 343km (213-mile) Pacific Coast Highway (SH35) follows the coast from Opotiki around the mouth of the Motu River and passes near Potala, the northern edge of the East Cape. It continues to Hicks Bay, which has a wild surf beach and is a popular viewing point for the planet's earliest sunrise. Look out here for the Tuwhakairiora Marae (1870),

one of the grandest meeting houses in the area. A beautiful stretch of road passes beaches and rivers on its way to East Cape lighthouse and the North Island's most easterly point.

On the more populous, east side of the cape, a turn-off before the Mata River crossing leads to 1,752m (5,748ft) Mount Hikurangi, the North Island's highest non-volcanic mountain. The mountain is sacred in Maori myth, as the first point of land to appear when Maui fished the North Island from the sea—a statue depicting Maui's canoe faces the rising sun today.

The road continues to Tolaga Bay—a coastal town with a wharf that is 660m (720 yards) long—to Gisborne. At the tiny junction settlement of Nuhaka, south of Gisborne, a scenic coastal road leaves SH2 towards the barren, windswept Mahia Peninsula, which marks the boundary between the Pacific and Hawke's Bay.

GISBORNE

317 N7 209 Grey Street, tel 06-868 6139 Grey Street www.gisbornenz.com

This small city is set in an area of fertile land, with fruit growing and vineyards its main staples— it labels itself the Chardonnay capital of the country. Gisborne was the first place that Captain Cook set foot in on his return to New Zealand in 1769, before retreating from hostile Maori. Cook's Landing Site (marked by a statue of the explorer) and National Historic Reserve are next to the main port and the base of Titirangi (Kaiti Hill). To the west is Te Poho-O-Rawiri Marae (1930), one of the largest carved meeting houses in the country.

A statue on the southern bank of the Turanganui River commemorates Captain Cook's

cabin boy, Young Nick, who was first to sight land in 1769 and gave his name to the promontory Young Nicks Head, which forms the southern edge of Poverty Bay.

The Tairawhiti Museum on Stout Street (Mon–Fri 10–4, Sat, Sun 1.30–4) has regional displays. In the adjacent Te Moana Maritime Museum is the restored wheelhouse of *The Star of Canada*, which foundered at the base of Kaiti Beach in 1912.

HAMILTON

316 K5 Transport Centre, corner of Bryce and Anglesea streets, tel 07-839 3580 Transport Centre Fraser Sreet, Franklin Airport 15km (9 miles) south of city www.hamiltoncity.co.nz www.waikatonz.co.nz

New Zealand's fourth largest city grew out of an 1864 military settlement on the Waikato River. Garden Place lies on Victoria Street, at the heart of the downtown area, which was modernised in the 1990s.

The Waikato Museum (daily 10–4.30) overlooks the river on the corner of Victoria and Grantham streets and contains an impressive collection of Maori treasures, including the exquisitely decorated war canoe *Te Winika*, presented to the museum in 1973 by Te Arikinui Dame Te Atairangikaahu, the late Maori Queen.

South of the city are the 58ha (143-acre) Hamilton Gardens (daily 7.30–sunset), a conglomerate of Japanese, Chinese and English flower gardens. Hamilton Zoo (daily 9–5, extended hours Jan), 8km (5 miles) away on SH23, mixes native New Zealand species with others important to international conservation breeding projects, and has a vast walk-through, free-flight aviary.

Art deco architecture is a feature of the rebuilt town of Hastings

A relic of the Lord of the Rings film-making, strictly for fans

Sunset bathes the hills around Te Mata in scarlet

THE SIGHTS

HASTINGS

🖪 319 L8 🚹 Westerman's Building, corner of Russell and Heretaunga streets, tel 06-873 0080 🚌 Weekday services from Napier www.hastings.co.nz

Hastings is a lively agricultural town 20km (12 miles) south of Napier (▷ 82–83), lined with hanging baskets during the summer flower festival. Like Napier, Hastings was devastated by the earthquake of 1931. In rebuilding the town the architects echoed Napier's art deco and Spanish Mission styles, the best examples of which are the Westerman's Building on Russell Street and the Municipal Theatre on Hastings Street. The art deco clock tower in the middle of town was built in 1935 to house the bells from the Post Office tower, which collapsed in the quake.

HAVELOCK NORTH

🖪 319 M8

Vineyards and orchards surround this prosperous village, which sits in the shadow of the 399m (1,309ft) Te Mata Peak. There are tremendous views from the top of the peak.

Arataki Honey Ltd, on Arataki Road (daily 9–5), is one of the largest beekeeping enterprises in the southern hemisphere, with a staggering 17,000 hives and 40,000 very busy bees.

HAWERA

🖪 318 J8 🚹 55 High Street, tel 06-278 8599 🚌 Daily from Wellington and New Plymouth

Hawera is the largest of the south Taranaki townships, near the coast at the junction of SH45 and SH3. Its most obvious landmark is the water tower, built in 1914 at the request of insurance underwriters who were dismayed at the town's propensity to catch

fire, which it did in 1884, 1895 and 1912. The Historic Hawera heritage trail leaflet, available at the visitor office, details other major buildings.

Realistic life-size wax exhibits and scale models to depict Taranaki's past are made on-site and shown at the privately owned Tawhiti Museum, on Ohangai Road (Boxing Day–end Jan daily 10–4; Feb–end May, Sep–end Dec Fri–Sun 10–4; Jun–end Aug Sun 10–4). A narrow gauge railway runs on the first Sunday of each month, bringing to life the history of logging in the area.

Equally unusual is the Elvis Presley Memorial Record Room, at 51 Argyle Street (call for appointment, tel 06-278 7624), where avid collector and fan Kevin Wasley has amassed memorabilia and around 2,000 of the King's records.

KAWHIA

🖪 316 J6 🚹 Kawhia Regional Museum and Gallery, tel 07-871 0161 www.kawhia.co.nz

Outside the summer, when the population almost trebles, Kawhia (pronounced Kafia) is a sleepy village southwest of Hamilton on the shores of Kawhia Harbour. Most of its points of interest are on the shoreline, extending around to the port entrance and Ocean Beach. This is the most popular beach, best reached through the Tainui Kawhia Forest Track, southwest of central Kawhia.

At the Te Puia Hot Springs on Ocean Beach you can dig your own spa bath, but it's difficult to know exactly where unless you join a local tour.

When the Tainui people first landed here some 750 years ago they tied their canoe to a pohutukawa tree and named it Tangi-te-Korowhiti. The tree

(unmarked) is one of a small grove at the northern end of Kaora Street, and the canoe's burial site is marked with two stones, Hani and Puna, behind the Maketu *marae*, about 500m (545 yards) south of the landing site (ask for viewing permission at the *marae*).

MATAMATA

🖪 316 K6 🚹 45 Broadway, tel 07-888 7260 🚌 Broadway

Large ranches and farmsteads sprawl over this fertile agricultural landscape, which was never a visitor hotspot—until the *Lord of the Rings* movie trilogy came along. A plot of private farmland near Matamata was transformed into the village of Hobbiton (daily tours from visitor office 9.30, 10.45, 12, 1.15, 2.30, 3.45). Director Peter Jackson was obliged to clear away all traces of his sets, including this one, so other than a hobbit hole with a plywood frontage the only real attraction is the view across the Kaimai Ranges.

East of the town on Tower Road, Firth Tower is the main focus of the local history museum (Thu–Mon 10–4).

The Firth Tower, built in 1882 by Yorkshireman Josiah Firth

HAWKE'S BAY

Pretty coastal settlements, wine trails, art deco architecture and Pacific beaches.

Bleached cliffs embrace this scenic bay on the east coast between Havelock North and the Mahia Peninsula. Its fertile soils prompted early European settlers to plant vines, using the wine primarily for religious services; the Catholic Society founded its Mission in Taradale in 1851 and since then the wine industry has boomed, with its capital at Napier (▷ 82–83). Hawke's Bay's diverse 'sub regions'—such as Bay View and the Esk Valley—produce a wide range of wines, and there are more than 25 vineyards in all, most offering sales and tastings. Some have additional attractions—notable architecture, for instance, or fine restaurants and cafés. Chardonnay and Cabernet Sauvignon are two of the region's top wines (for wine tours contact Napier's visitor information office).

ALONG SH2

South of the wine region, SH2 winds its lonely way through the little-visited but stunning region of the Wairarapa (▷ 106), before arriving in Wellington (▷ 101–105). On SH2 there are a number of small towns including Waipawa, Waipukurau, Dannevirke and Norsewood (the last two having strong Scandinavian links). Activities available in the area include ballooning and hiking (▷ 172–179). The wild Kaweka and Ruahine Ranges are good for tramping, but you should plan carefully and go well prepared. The Department of Conservation at 59 Marine Parade, Napier (Mon–Fri 9–4.15) has all the necessary information.

A CURIOSITY

There is one other place worth visiting (if only for the novelty value) on a minor route into the back country. The point of this diversion is to see an unremarkable hill called Taumatawhakatangihangakoauauotamateaturipukakapikimaungahoronukupokaiwhenuakitanatahu, and a sign declares this 85-letter place name the longest in the world. Roughly translated, it means 'the place where Taumata (known as Land Eater), the man with the big knees, who slid, climbed and swallowed mountains, played his flute to his loved one'. To reach the hill from Waipukurau, take the coast road towards Porangahau. After about 40km (25 miles) turn right and follow the AA Historic Place sign.

Top, a stream in the Hawke's Bay area
Above, Mission Estate Winery, one of the oldest in the region

RATINGS	
Historic interest	●
Photo stops	●●●●
Walkability	●●●

BASICS

🔖 319 L8

ℹ️ Central Hawkes Bay Visitor Information Office, Railway Esplanade, Waipukurau, tel 06-858 6488; Mon–Fri 9–5, Sat 9–1

🚌 Services link all main towns and suburbs

www.hawkesbay.com
Well laid-out site with links to local information offices and main attractions.

TIPS

● The Hawke's Bay Wine Trail is outlined in the free leaflet of the same name, and gives details of each vineyard's facilities.

● Tours with exclusive access to the 252m (827ft) summit of Taumata's hill are available through Airlie Mount Farm Walks, tel 06-858 7601.

A walkway spans the steaming silica terraces at Orakei Korako Thermal Reserve

The nocturnal kiwi can be observed at Otorohanga

THE SIGHTS

MOUNT EGMONT NATIONAL PARK

⊞ 318 H8 🚹 16km (10 miles) from North Egmont Village, end of Egmont Road, tel 06-756 0990 🚌 Shuttle services from New Plymouth
www.taranakinz.org.nz

At the heart of Mount Egmont National Park is a 2,518m (8,261ft), beautifully symmetrical dormant volcano with two names: Taranaki, the original Maori name, and Egmont, the name given by Captain Cook in 1770. It was formed by numerous eruptions over 12,000 years—most recently about 350 years ago. Experts believe another may be due any time. The mountain vegetation is called 'goblin forest' due to its diminutive appearance at higher altitudes.

There are 140km (87 miles) of walks in the park, with a duration ranging from 30 minutes to four days. Many people have lost their lives here: in winter the slopes are covered in snow and ice, so climbing boots, crampons and an ice axe are essential. Even in summer crampons are advised on the summit. Visitor offices here and in New Plymouth can advise on routes, hut stays and weather.

Surfers head for the beach at Mount Maunganui

MOUNT MAUNGANUI

⊞ 316 L5 🚹 Salisbury Avenue, tel 07-575 5099 🚌 Services from Tauranga

Dominated by its namesake mountain and graced by golden beaches, the town of Mount Maunganui, 6km (4 miles) north of Tauranga, is inundated with sunbathers every summer. The Hot Salt Water Pools, on Adams Avenue (Mon–Sat 6am–10pm, Sun 8am–10pm), are a popular attraction.

A network of pathways criss-crosses the mountain's wooded slopes, once an important Maori refuge and defensive site. The summit climb, best started south of the motor camp, takes about 45 minutes one-way. From the narrow neck of the Mount, Ocean Beach begins a stretch of sand that sweeps east around the Bay of Plenty. Just offshore are two small islands: Moturiki, noted for fishing, and Motuotau, important for its wildlife.

NAPIER

See pages 82–83.

NEW PLYMOUTH

⊞ 318 H7 🚹 Puke Ariki Museum and Library, tel 06-759 6080 🚌 Corner of Queen and King streets ✈ 10km (6 miles) north of town
www.newplymouthnz.com

Prosperous New Plymouth, the main population hub of the Taranaki region, is a good base for exploring Mount Egmont National Park. It has an excellent modern art gallery, the Govett-Brewster Gallery, at the corner of Queen and King streets (daily 10.30–5). Puke Ariki, on Ariki Street (Mon–Fri 9–4.30, Sat, Sun 1–5), has a collection of Maori items, and includes Richmond Cottage (daily 11–3.30), on Ariki Street, a colonial cottage of 1853.

Other notable sites include the oldest stone church in the country, St. Mary's, on Vivian Street, built in 1846, and the Pou Tutaki (Fitzroy Pole), on the corner of Devon Street East and Smart Road, erected by Maori in 1844 to commemorate Governor Fitzroy's clamp-down on settler acquisitions. The 45m (148ft) Wind Wand, created for the 2000 millennium celebrations on the waterfront by local artist Len Lye, sways gently in the breeze, and lights up at night.

New Plymouth is famous for its parks and gardens, the oldest and finest of which are Pukekura and Brooklands, best reached at Fillis Street, south of the heart of town. Pukekura, opened in 1876, is a well-maintained tract of lakes and gardens, and nearby Brooklands has an outdoor amphitheatre, ponds and gardens, and a historic colonial hospital museum/gallery.

Boats sail from West Quay to the volcanic Sugar Loaf Island's Marine Park, near the port and power station, home to fur seals and seabirds. The shore is part of a 7km (4-mile) Coastal Walkway, culminating in a strenuous climb up Paritutu Rock, which involves pulling yourself up by a cable.

NGARUAWAHIA

⊞ 316 K5 🚌 Pharos Corner

The Maori capital of New Zealand, set at the confluence of the Waipa and the mighty Waikato, 19km (12 miles) north of Hamilton, is home of the Maori King, Tuheitia Paki, and of one of the country's most significant *marae*, Turangawaewae. The *marae*, on River Road, is open just once a year, in March

Raglan is a popular holiday resort for families

Fishing boats moored in the natural harbour at Tauranga

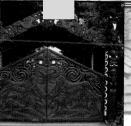

Gates mark the entrance to the Turangawaewae marae

during the annual regatta, when *waka* (war canoes) are raced on the river. The Mahinarangi House, built in 1929, is beautifully carved both inside and out. Next door is the King's official residence.

OPOTIKI

➕ 317 M6 ℹ Corner of St. John and Elliot Streets, tel 07-315 8484 🍴 Hot Bread Shop, 43 St. John Street **www.opotiki.co.nz**

Opotiki, 60km (37 miles) east of Whakatane on the Bay of Plenty, near the mouths of the Waioeka and Otara rivers, is a small town with fine beaches. It was once the base of the Hauhau—a revivalist sect of Maori rebels who were fierce enemies of the early Pakeha.

The Hukutaia Domain, signed about 6km (4 miles) from town, is 1ha (2.5 acres) of bush with many native trees, including a sacred 2,000-year-old puriri tree called Taketakerau, with a girth of about 22m (72ft) and standing over 23m (75ft) high. Its hollow was used by the local *iwi* to store the bones of their dead. The Church of Hinoa (St. Stephen's Anglican Church, 1864), at the north end of Church Street, was built for the Church Missionary Society and the Lutheran missionary Karl Volkner, who was suspected of being a government spy and beheaded by Hauhau emissaries in 1865.

ORAKEI KORAKO THERMAL RESERVE

➕ 316 L6 ✉ 494 Orakei Korako Road, 40km (25 miles) north of Taupo ☎ 07-378 3131 🕐 Daily from 8am; last boat leaves 4.30pm Nov–end Mar, 4pm Apr–end Oct 🎫 Adult NZ$26, child (16 and under) NZ$8 🚌 Shuttle from Taupo **www.orakeikorako.co.nz**

One of the best thermal parks in the country occupies a tranquil

lakeside spot behind the Ohakuri Dam. Jet-boats carry visitors across the Waikato River to the colourful algae-covered silica terraces, boiling pools, geysers and bubbling mud. There's also the subterranean Ruatapu Cave to explore, with the warm Waiwhakaata pool (pool of mirrors) at its 40m (131ft) base, where it's said your wishes will come true if you dip your hand in the water. Look for silver ferns—the national emblem of New Zealand—in the surrounding bush and scrub.

OTOROHANGA

➕ 316 K6 ℹ 57 Maniapoto Street, tel 07-873 8951 🚌 Corner of Maniapoto and Tuhoro streets 🚌 Services from Wellington, Hamilton and Auckland **www.otorohanga.co.nz**

This small town is the main point of access to the Waitomo caves (▷ 90–91) and the site of the Otorohanga Kiwi House and Native Bird Park, on Alex Telfer Drive (daily 9–5). It was established in 1971, and is one of the oldest native bird and reptile parks in the country. More than 50 species are housed here, including three of the four known species of kiwi.

RAGLAN

➕ 316 J6 ℹ 4 Wallis Street, tel 07-825 0556 🚌 Services from Hamilton **www.raglan.org.nz**

Raglan, on the coast west of Hamilton, is the Waikato's main seaside resort and is internationally renowned for its surfing. The most convenient and safest beach for swimming is Te Kopua, reached from the end of Bow Street. Ocean Beach has good views across the bar (port entrance); access is off Wainui Reserve Road. Manu Beach is next, and then Whale Bay—which can only be reached over rocks.

Remote Ruapuke Beach has wild coastal scenery and is reached along the old coast road and Ruapuke Beach Road. Safe and child-friendly beaches near town include Coxs Bay (from the walkway along Government Road) and Puriri Park (Aro Aro Bay) at the end of Wallis Street.

The 756m (2,480ft) summit of Mount Karioi can be climbed from Te Toto Gorge, 12km (7 miles) southwest, in around six hours.

ROTORUA

See pages 84–87.

TAURANGA

➕ 316 L5 ℹ 95 Willow Street, tel 07-578 8103 🚌 Corner of Wharf and Willow streets ⛴ Spirit Harbour Ferry, Coronation Wharf to Mount Maunganui daily 7–5.30 (winter hours vary) ✈ 4km (2.5 miles) east **www.bayofplentynz.com**

Busy Tauranga, on the Bay of Plenty, has enjoyed enormous growth in recent years, and cruise liners as well as merchant ships now negotiate the narrow entrance to its superb natural port. Its proximity to Rotorua (▷ 84–87) and Mount Maunganui (▷ 80) are a significant part of the town's appeal.

The main historical attraction is the Elms Mission House on Mission Street (Wed, Sat, Sun 2–4), site of the original mission, established here in 1834. Nearby, in Robbins Park on Cliff Road, on the eastern side of the peninsula, are the remnants of the Monmouth Redoubt (daily 9–6), built by government forces during the New Zealand Wars of the 1860s. At the base of the hill, on The Strand, is *Te Awanui Waka*, a Maori war canoe carved in 1973.

A series of superb beaches stretches from Mount Maunganui east to Papamoa.

Napier

**The wine capital of the North Island.
Famous for its world-class art deco architecture.**

Busy Marine Parade, and the art deco Sound Shell

Right, a gecko hesitates at the National Aquarium

An underwater tunnel gives a fish's-eye view at the Aquarium

RATINGS				
Historic interest	●	●	●	
Photo stops	●	●	●	●	●
Walkability	●	●	●	

BASICS

✚ 319 M8
ℹ 100 Marine Parade, tel 06-834 1911;
Mon, Tue, Thu, Fri 8.30–5, Wed, Sat,
Sun 9–5
🚌 Travel Centre, Munroe Street
🚉 Munroe Street
✈ Airport north of town; shuttles

www.isitehawkesbaynz.com
Busy site, with visitor information.

The Tom Parker Fountain

SEEING NAPIER

Napier is a bright, dynamic coastal community with a relaxed atmosphere. At first glance it seems to enjoy a perfect relationship with nature; its fertile surroundings and the warm climate have made it the capital of the wine-producing region (▷ 79) of Hawke's Bay. Nature has not always been kind to Napier, however, and on 3 February 1931 an earthquake almost razed the town. The inhabitants set about its rebuilding with a collection of art deco buildings now considered among the finest in the world. Much of the city is negotiable on foot and, given its architectural appeal, is best appreciated from the street. Many of Napier's chief attractions line the long waterfront promenade, Marine Parade.

HIGHLIGHTS

ART DECO ARCHITECTURE

Napier's two central streets, Emerson and Tennyson, have many impressive art deco buildings. The ASB Bank, on Emerson Street, incorporates Maori designs and a fine doorway, while on Tennyson Street the highlights are (from east to west) the *Daily Telegraph* Building, the restored Municipal Theatre and the Desco Centre (art deco heritage society and shop).

Farther afield is perhaps the most attractive building of all, the 1932 Rothmans Pall Mall Building, at the corner of Bridge and Osian streets, in the port area of Ahuriri. The façade and entrance are worth the diversion—especially at night, when they are imaginatively lit. During the day it is possible to have a look at the interior, which shows exquisite attention to detail. A more modern example of art deco is the pharmacy at the southern end of Emerson Street.

MARINE PARADE

Marine Parade creates an impressive perspective, its long promenade lined with Norfolk pines and old wooden houses (the few that survived the earthquake). At its northern end are elegant gardens, including the Centennial Gardens, at the base of Bluff Hill. Farther south the renovated Ocean Spa (Mon–Sat 6am–10pm, Sun 8am–10pm) has hot pools, private spas, health and beauty therapies and a café. More gardens are laid out immediately to the south of the spa complex, dominated by a floral clock, the Tom Parker Fountain (which becomes an aquatic light show after dark) and a statue called *Pania of the Reef*, depicting a Maori maiden.

Heading south you reach the art deco Colonnade and Sound Shell. Once a dancing and skating hall, the Colonnade now houses a bell and memorial dedicated to the crew of HMS *Veronica*, which was in port at the time of the earthquake. Members of the crew were among the first to come to the city's aid and pull victims from the rubble. Every New Year the bell is rung to commemorate their brave efforts. Opposite the Sound Shell, which is occasionally used for open-air concerts, are the Art Deco Tower

TIPS
● The view from Bluff Hill, at the northern tip of town, is worth the climb.
● A good view down Marine Parade and across the city can also be enjoyed from Lighthouse Road, above the Centennial Gardens (reached via Lucy Road, off Coote Road).

(A&B building), which is also lit at night, and the Masonic Hotel.

Past the modern visitor office and Mini Golf Park are the Sunken Gardens, complete with water-lily ponds and a lazy waterwheel. Beyond them, seal and dolphin displays are combined with a project aimed at wild penguin and gannet rehabilitation at Marineland (daily 10–4.30). In daily sessions you can feed and swim with the dolphins. Continuing south you encounter the intriguing Millennium Sculpture, a work using reflective steel discs, by local artist David Trubridge.

Left, stylish architectural detailing on a bank
Above, the modern entrance to the National Aquarium
Below, ornamental fountain at the Mission

HAWKE'S BAY MUSEUM
✉ 9 Herschell Street ☎ 06-835 7781 🕐 Oct–end Apr daily 10–6; May–end Sep daily 9–5 🎟 Adult NZ$7.50, child (under 16) free
www.hawkesbaymuseum.co.nz
A wide range of exhibits set in modern surroundings relates to the history and art of the Hawke's Bay region. Nga Tukemata (The Awakening) presents the art and *taonga* (treasures) of the local Maori and rare evidence that dinosaurs once existed in New Zealand—remains unearthed in the Maungahouanga Valley of northern Hawke's Bay. Special attention is given to the earthquake of 1931, when 100 fires raged over 30 hours after the initial shock, and 258 people lost their lives.

BACKGROUND
When Captain Cook first mapped Hawke's Bay in 1769, Maori were already well established here. In the 1830s seasonal whalers arrived from Australia, and the first significant group of European settlers arrived 20 years later. In 1854 the town was named after British general Charles Napier.

During the New Zealand Wars of the 1860s the residents, with the help of local Maori, defended themselves against aggressive northern tribes. With the development of agriculture, the settlement flourished. The earthquake of 1931 destroyed everything, but the land surrounding Bluff Hill had risen several feet and huge tracts of land, previously underwater or covered in swamp, were now available for use. Earthquake-resistant concrete buildings with art deco designs reflecting the optimism of the jazz era gave the town a new face within a decade, thanks largely to architect Louis Hay (1881–1948).

MORE TO SEE
NATIONAL AQUARIUM OF NEW ZEALAND
✉ Marine Parade ☎ 06-834 1404 🕐 Daily 9–5 (Wed until 4.30) 🎟 Adult NZ$14, child (up to 14) NZ$7.50
www.nationalaquarium.co.nz
The newest of Napier's waterfront attractions hosts an eclectic mix of native and non-native water and land creatures, including seahorses and kiwis. Divers enter the tanks to feed the fish at 10am and 2pm; they also act as guides, conducting tours behind the scenes (extra charge applies).

Rotorua

Boiling lakes, spouting geysers and steaming streets in the volcanic heart of the North Island. A lively place for Maori culture. Hair-raising outdoor pursuits for the adventurous.

Demonstrating the traditions of Maori cooking

A natural steam-cloud engulfs the Rotorua Museum

The crater rim of Tarawera shows geological upheaval

RATINGS	
Outdoor pursuits	● ● ● ●
Photo stops	● ● ● ● ●
Walkability	● ● ●

BASICS

➕ 316 L6
ℹ 1167 Fenton Street, tel 07-348 5179; daily 8–6
🚌 i-SITE, Fenton Street
✈ Eastern shores of Lake Rotorua, about 10km (6 miles) from town; shuttle service

www.rotoruanz.com
Impressive site with interactive maps and community and visitor information.

TIP

● The visitor office has an in-house travel section administering local and national bus, air and rail ticketing.

SEEING ROTORUA

Rotorua—alias Sulphur City—is the thermal and volcanic resort capital of New Zealand, and is often smelt before it's seen. In addition to exploring the geysers, pools and vents of bubbling mud in its immediate vicinity, you can enjoy a Maori *hangi* (feast), throw yourself down a waterfall in a raft, jump out of a plane or shop until you drop—preferably into one of the city's many restorative hot thermal pools. Rotorua sprawls on the southern shores of the lake of the same name, its half-timbered, mock-Tudor buildings recalling its development as a European-style health spa at the start of the 20th century.

HIGHLIGHTS

HELL'S GATE AND WAI ORA SPA

➕ 316 L6 ✉ 15km (9 miles) from Rotorua on SH30 ☎ 07-345 3151 🕐 Daily 8.30–8.30 💲 Adult NZ$20, child (under 16) NZ$8. Spa only NZ$12, child NZ$8 www.hellsgate.co.nz

The aptly named Hell's Gate thermal reserve is one of the most active, with two levels separated by a tract of bush and connected by a warm thermal stream, complete with steaming waterfall. The pools of bubbly mud and water on the lower levels hiss menacingly. The upper level has steaming lakes and tiny steaming vents, scattered with mini mud volcanoes and cauldrons of boiling water. Best of all is the Devil's Cauldron, a pit where a lively, globular mud pool makes wonderfully disgusting noises. Services include massage, sulphur spas, therapeutic mud facials, scrubs and private mud baths.

LAKE ROTORUA

➕ 316 L6

This flooded volcanic crater is the largest of the 17 lakes in the Rotorua thermal region, covering an area of 89sq km (34 square miles) and sitting 279m (915ft) above sea level. Boat trips from the city take in the nature reserve of Mokoia Island. Recreational activities include boating, water-skiing and trout-fishing. On the northern shores are the Hamurana Gardens, at 733 Hamurana Road, where a spring erupts with beautiful clarity and a volume of more than 3,780,000 litres (831,600 gallons) an hour.

OHINEMUTU

Narrow streets lined with steaming drains lead to the former Maori settlement and thermal area of Ohinemutu, on the city's lakefront. The focal point is the Tamatekapua Marae, a beautifully carved meeting house, renovated in 1939 but containing 19th-century carvings. Facing it is St. Faith's Church (daily 8–5), built in 1910. The interior pillars, beams, rafters and pews are carved with Maori designs, and on a window overlooking the lake a Maori Christ is sandblasted, as if walking on the lake, dressed in a *korowai* (chief's cloak). Members of the Arawa tribe are buried in the graveyard, among them the only European to be admitted to full chieftainship: Captain Gilbert Mair (1843–1923), who twice saved the Arawa from inter-tribal attacks.

Above, the fizzing Champagne Pool at Wai-O-Tapu

Inset, fierce carved figures with paua shell eyes guard the Tamatekapua Marae

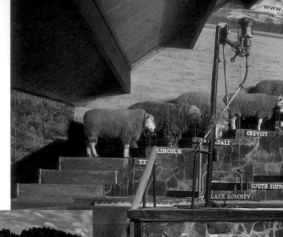

AGRODOME

✚ 316 L6 ✉ 10km (6 miles) north of Rotorua on SH5 ☎ 07-357 1050
🕐 Daily 8.30–5; shows 9.30, 11, 2.30
🎟 Show NZ$22, child (5–15) NZ$11
www.agrodome.co.nz

The Agrodome Complex has a wide array of attractions, from bungy jumping to farm activities. The principal attraction is the Sheep Show, at which you are introduced to 19 different breeds of sheep.

*Above, the Artist's Palette
Right, meeting the sheep at the Agrodome*

BLUE AND GREEN LAKES

✚ 316 L6 ✉ Southeast of city, off SH30

Mount Tarawera Road leads to Blue Lake (Tikitapu), used for boating and swimming, and Green Lake (Rotokakahi), which is sacred and off limits. Beyond them the road enters the Te Wairoa Valley, home of the Buried Village, where the Pink-and-White Terraces, the village and its hotel were laid waste by the 1886 eruption.

BLUE BATHS

✉ Government Gardens ☎ 07-350 2119 🕐 Mon–Fri 10–5 🎟 Adult NZ$9, child (5–14) NZ$6
www.bluebaths.co.nz

Built in the Spanish Mission style during the Great Depression of 1933, the pools flourished as a major social and recreational venue, and were one of the first public baths to have mixed bathing. Restored and reopened in 1999, today they offer hot pools and a museum.

MOUNT TARAWERA

✚ 316 L6

Tarawera is 1,111m (3,645ft) high, with a 6km (4-mile) converging gash of craters. It is a conglomerate of three mountains: Wahanga to the north,

POLYNESIAN SPA

✉ Hinemoa Street ☎ 07-348 1328 🕐 Daily 8am–11pm 🎟 Adult NZ$12, child NZ$8
www.polynesianspa.co.nz

Rain or shine, this luxury spa complex is a delight. Among the treats are hot springs and pools, private spa pools, a family spa—and massage treatments are also available. Outside, in timber-style tubs, therapeutic adult hot springs overlook the lake and range in temperature from 33°C (91.4°F) to 43°C (109.4°F). The best times to go are at lunch and dinner, when the tour buses are elsewhere.

ROTORUA MUSEUM OF ART AND HISTORY

✉ Government Gardens ☎ 07-349 4350 🕐 Oct–end Mar daily 9–8; Apr–end Sep daily 9–5. Guided tours daily 11, 2 🎟 Adult NZ$11, child NZ$5
www.rotoruamuseum.co.nz

People used to come from all over the world to the 1908 red-and-white half-timbered Bath House, which now houses this museum, to take advantage of the thermal water's therapeutic and curative powers. In one wing you can see some of the original baths, changing rooms and equipment used by the early visitors. A superb collection of Te Arawa *taonga* (treasures) contrasts with modern Maori artworks. An excellent audiovisual display, Rotorua Stories, introduces the area's history and legends—complete with shuddering pews during the dramatic account of the 1886 eruption.

WAI-O-TAPU

✚ 316 L6 ✉ 29km (18 miles) south of Rotorua off SH5 ☎ 07-366 6333
🕐 Daily 8.30–5 🎟 Adult NZ$25, child (5–15) NZ$8.50 📷
www.geyserland.co.nz

Wai-O-Tapu is the best thermal park in the region, with an almost surreal range of volcanic features, from mud pools and silica terraces to the beautiful Champagne Pool. If you can, time your arrival with the daily 10.15am eruption of the Lady Knox Geyser, which is signposted on the Wai-O-Tapu Loop Road (off SH5). A self-guided walk around the park takes about two hours, passing the Artist's Palette—a steaming silica field in pastel yellow, green and blue, and the Champagne Pool—an orange-rimmed pool which heats the water to a surface temperature of around 74°C (165°F).

Ruawahia in the middle and Tarawera to the south. Helicopter flights and 4X4 tours give access to the interior. Independent access is discouraged.

SKYLINE SKYRIDES

✉ Fairy Springs Road ☎ 07-347 0027
🕐 Daily 9–late 🎫 Gondola only, adult NZ$22, child (14 and under) NZ$10, gondola and 5 luge rides, NZ$26
www.skylineskyrides.co.nz
Visitors travel up the mountain in gondolas and return on the

infamous luge, which involves riding down a concrete course on a plastic tray with wheels and primitive brakes. A family course provides a gentler version.

TARAWERA FALLS

✚ 316 L6 ✉ 70km (43 miles) from Rotorua on SH30
In the heart of the Tarawera Forest, the Tarawera River flows from the eastern shores of Lake Tarawera and northern slopes of Mount Tarawera. A walkway leads to the point where the river disappears underground before emerging from a sheer cliff face.

Above, the sacred Green Lake
Below, Tarawera Falls

WAIMANGU

✚ 316 L6 ✉ 26km (16 miles) south of Rotorua, off SH5 ☎ 07-366 6137
🕐 Daily 8.30–5 🎫 Adult from NZ$28, child (6–16) NZ$7.50
www.waimangu.com
The volcanic features of the Waimangu volcanic valley were created as a result of the 1886 eruption of Tarawera (▷ 31). Lake Rotomahana is a water-filled crater which, before the eruption, was the site of the famous Pink-and-White Terraces. Both silica terraces were obliterated by the eruption, replaced by the Waimangu Cauldron—the world's largest boiling lake; the Inferno Crater Lake, which rises and falls up to 10m (33ft); steaming cliffs, and boiling springs and steaming fumaroles.

TE PUIA, WHAKAREWAREWA

✉ 3km (2 miles) south of downtown along Fenton Street ☎ Maori Arts and Crafts Institute 07-348 9047 🕐 Oct–end Feb daily 8–6; Mar–end Sep daily 8–5; Maori guided tours hourly 9–5; cultural performances 12.15, 3.15 🎫 Tours NZ$28, child (5–15) NZ$14; evening performance NZ$85, child NZ$50
www.nzmaori.co.nz
This is the most famous of the region's thermal reserves, and includes within its grounds the Rotowhio Marae, the Mai Ora Village (a replica of the former Te Arawa Maori settlement) and the modern Te Puia arts and crafts institute. There are two geysers here: Pohutu, or Big Splash, which goes off 10 to 25 times a day (more recently for days on end), achieving a height of over 30m (98ft), and Prince of Wales Feathers, which is less spectacular. Tracks negotiate other small mud pools and volcanic features and lead back to the Rotowhio Marae, which has a banquet and weaving house, and hosts daily cultural performances. A longer performance in the evening includes a *hangi* (feast).

BACKGROUND

The shores of Lake Rotorua and Whakarewarewa were first settled by Maori from the Arawa canoe in the 14th century. By the 1840s the first missions had been established. When inter-tribal war broke out the Te Arawa sided with the government. After the end of the New Zealand Wars, European settlement began. The population rapidly expanded, drawn by the aesthetic and therapeutic qualities of the thermal waters, and tourism flourished.

Tongariro National Park

**Dramatic and sometimes dangerous volcanic peaks
in New Zealand's oldest national park.
Excellent skiing and walking, as well as stunning scenery.**

*The snow-clad peaks of
Mount Ruapehu*

*A network of tramping trails covers the park, but full preparation is
required before exploring this harsh and exposed terrain*

RATINGS	
Outdoor pursuits	● ● ● ●
Photo stops	● ● ●
Walkability	● ● ● ● ●

BASICS

✚ 316 K8

ℹ Department of Conservation office, Whakapapa Village, SH48, tel 07-892 3729; daily 8–5; www.doc.govt.nz

🚌 All surrounding townships. Local shuttles to Whakapapa Village and walk drop-off/pick-up points

🚆 Services from Auckland and Wellington to Ohakune and National Park

✖ At intersection of SH47 and SH48

www.mtruapehu.com
Information on the whole region, including ski areas, transportation and weather reports.

SEEING TONGARIRO NATIONAL PARK

In 1887 Horonuku Te Heuheu Tukino, the visionary chief of Ngati Tuwharetoa, gave the sacred volcanoes of Ruapehu, Ngauruhoe and Tongariro to the nation to preserve them, creating the heart of Tongariro National Park—the fourth oldest in the world. Since then the park has expanded to cover an area of 75,250ha (185,940 acres), taking in forest, tussock country and volcanic desert. Dominating everything are the majestic volcanic peaks of Tongariro, Ngauruhoe and Ruapehu—all active volcanoes, and quite different in size and appearance. Whakapapa and Turoa offer some of the best skiing in the country (Jul–Oct).

HIGHLIGHTS

MOUNT NGAURUHOE

✚ 316 K7

The youngest of the three volcanoes lies 3km (2 miles) south of Tongariro and reaches 2,287m (7,503ft). Its classic symmetrical cone shape is due to its relative youth and the fact that it has only one vent. In recent years, Ngauruhoe has been the most continuously active, frequently venting steam and gas, and occasionally ash and lava. Its last significant eruption occurred in 1954.

NORTHERN CIRCUIT

ℹ SH48, Whakapapa, tel 06-892 3729; Visitor Centre, SH48, Whakapapa, tel 06-892 3729

The Tongariro Northern Circuit walking trail winds its way over Mount Tongariro and around Mount Ngauruhoe, passing unusual landforms and volcanic features, including lakes, craters and glacial valleys. The walk takes three to four days to complete. The track starts from Whakapapa Village and finishes at the Mangatepopo Road, just off SH47.

MOUNT RUAPEHU

✚ 316 K8 ℹ 54 Clyde Street, Ohakune, tel 06-385 8427
www.mtruapehu.com

About 16km (10 miles) south of Ngauruhoe is the truncated cone of Ruapehu, with its perpetually snow-covered summit peaks and azure crater lakes. This is the North Island's highest mountain, at 2,797m (9,176ft), and in the last century it has seen the most violent activity of the three volcanoes, last errupting in 1995/6. Thousands of visitors come to ski or climb on its slopes, or enjoy its walking tracks—the longest of these, the Round-the-Mountain Track, takes five to six days. Ruapehu has three ski fields: Whakapapa, serviced by Whakapapa and Iwikau villages; Turoa, serviced by Okahune; and Tukino, the smallest of the three, on the eastern slopes.

TONGARIRO CROSSING
🚹 SH48, Whakapapa Village, tel 07-8923729
www.tongarirocrossing.co.nz
When the weather is clear, the views and volcanic features on this one-day hike are unforgettable. The 16km (10-mile) trail involves

steep climbs and the occasional scramble, and can take up to 10 hours. In winter it can be impassable and even in summer it may be dangerous. The walk can be tackled from either north or south.

BACKGROUND
According to local Maori legend, the volcanoes were formed around the 14th century when Ngatoroirangi, navigator and priest of the Arawa canoe, came to New Zealand.

On Christmas Eve of 1953 the wall of Mount Ruapehu's crater collapsed and a mighty lahar (a wash of volcanic rock debris and water) rushed down the Whangaehu River, destroying the rail bridge at Tangiwai. The night train to Auckland arrived moments later, and 151 lives were lost in the disaster. The mountain erupted in September 1995, and again a year later.

Left, Ngauruhoe, from Chateau Tongariro hotel
Above, snowboarding at Whakapapa ski field;
Above right, the Emerald Lakes

MORE TO SEE
OHAKUNE
🚹 318 K8 🚹 Clyde Street, tel 06-385 8427 🚌 Holiday Shoppe
www.ohakune.info
The pretty little ski resort of Ohakune sits near the southern edge of the park. Turoa ski field is 17km (10.5 miles) up the Ohakune Mountain Road. The Department of Conservation field centre, at the base of the road (Mon–Fri 9–12.30, 1–3), shows a video of the 1995/6 Ruapehu eruption.

WHAKAPAPA VILLAGE
🚹 316 K8 🚹 SH48, tel 07-892 3729 🚌 Shuttles to village and ski field
www.mtruapehu.com
Whakapapa is the headquarters and information base for the national park, and gives access to the Whakapapa Skifield and several good shorter walks. Its main landmark is the magnificent Chateau Tongariro Hotel, built in 1929. The Department of Conservation field centre (daily 8–5) has excellent displays and a seismograph monitoring the moods of Ruapehu.

Waitomo

**Bizarre limestone formations in a landscape of caves, gorges, holes and arches.
An astonishing network of more than 360 recorded caves,
the longest over 14km (9 miles).**

Black-water rafting tours of the caves are for the adventurous

A galaxy of glow-worms on the roof of the Waitomo cave

The natural stone arch—once a cave—at Mangapohue

SEEING WAITOMO

Visitors come in droves to the district of Waitomo and its underground world of limestone caves. Above ground, the typical farmland and the resort village itself give no clue to what lies below. Many of the region's features can be enjoyed along the three-hour Waitomo Walkway, which begins opposite the Glow-worm Caves and follows the Waitomo Stream to the Ruakuri Scenic Reserve. A short circular track in the reserve takes in caves and natural limestone bridges, hidden among lush native bush.

HIGHLIGHTS

ARANUI CAVE

✉ 3km (2 miles) west of Glow-worm Caves, in Ruakuri Scenic Reserve ⏰ Hourly tours 10–3 💳 Adult NZ$30, child (5–14) NZ$14; under 5s free. Combined Glow-worm and Aranui ticket NZ$50, child NZ$23
Just 2km (1 mile) away, Aranui is a less frenetic, more sedate experience than the Glow-worm Caves at Waitomo. It was discovered by chance by Maori hunter Ruruku Aranui, in 1910, while he was hunting pigs. Effective lighting brings out the hues and variety of the formations.

GLOW-WORM CAVES

✉ Waitomo Caves Road, off SH3 ☎ 07-878 8227 ⏰ Tours half-hourly 9–5 💳 Adult NZ$30, child (5–14) NZ$14; under 5s free. Combined Glow-worm and Aranui ticket NZ$50, child NZ$23; Glow-worm and museum NZ$33, child NZ$14
🚌 Shuttle from Waitomo and Otorohanga
www.waitomocaves.co.nz
This cave network is Waitomo's biggest attraction, and the most commercial, drawing almost 250,000 visitors annually. The network was first extensively explored in 1887 by a local Maori, Tane Tinorau, and an English surveyor, Fred Mace, and the caves were opened to visitors in 1889. Despite the crowds, the highlight of the 45-minute tour—the silent trip to the glow-worm colony by boat—is still magical. The glow-worm *Arachnocampa luminosa* emits light to attract its prey and is unique to New Zealand. It is the larval stage of a two-winged insect.

MANGAPOHUE NATURAL BRIDGE SCENIC RESERVE

✉ Marokopa Road 🎫 Free

A short streamside walk on the route between Waitomo and Te Anga leads to an impressive natural limestone arch with unusual stalagmites. This was once part of a large cave, and it is hard to imagine that the now rather inconspicuous little stream created it all. About 5km (3 miles) farther on are the Piripiri Caves, reached by a short but stiff climb up a boardwalk. These caves are in stark contrast to the well-lit, visitor-friendly offerings in Waitomo: They are dark and forbidding, and the path into them is steep and quite dangerous. If you are alone do not venture far, and take a torch (flashlight).

MUSEUM OF CAVES

🗺 In the visitor office, Main Street, Waitomo, tel 07-878 7640 🕐 Dec–end Mar daily 8–8, Apr–end Nov daily 8–5 🎫 Adult NZ$5, child (pre-school) free
www.waitomo-museum.co.nz

A thorough introduction to the area is presented at this museum, considered the best of its kind in the world. Displays cover cave formation, the history surrounding the local caves and the natural history, including the spectacular glow-worms. There's a small collection of everyday implements and treasures once belonging to the Tainui Maori, who lived in this valley for 500 years. These include *toki* (adzes), *waka kereru* (bird traps) and an exquisite oyster-shell necklace discovered in a local cave. There are also fascinating exhibits relating to early tourism in the area.

BACKGROUND

The limestone around Waitomo was once a seabed, formed about 30 million years ago. Over the ages its layers have been raised by the action of the earth's plates, bending and buckling and creating a maze of cracks and joints. As rainwater drains into these cracks it mixes with small amounts of carbon dioxide in the air and soil, forming a weak acid. This slowly dissolves the limestone, widening its faults. Over time small streams flow through converging cracks and create underground caves. The caves themselves have a finite lifespan—as is evident at the Lost World, near Waitomo, where part of a cave system has collapsed in on itself.

THE SHEARING SHED

✉ Waitomo Caves Road, Waitomo ☎ 07-878 8371 🕐 Shows daily at 12.45 📅 🎫 Free

Large, fluffy Angora rabbits are cuddled to within an inch of their lives at this unusual venue, and then shorn for their highly prized, fine hair. Angora products—yarn, duvets, underlay and sweaters—are on sale, and there are guided tours to tell you about it all.

WOODLYN PARK

✉ 1177 Waitomo Valley Road, Otorohanga ☎ 07-878 6666 🕐 Shows daily, 1.30; reserve tickets 🎫 Adult NZ$18, child (school age) NZ$9, under 5s NZ$5, family NZ$52
www.woodlynpark.co.nz

This is the main above-ground attraction in Waitomo, if not the whole region—a show hosted by ex-shearer Barry Woods, giving an informative, interactive and very funny interpretation of old and modern-day Kiwi country life. The production is an eccentric affair involving a clever pig, a not-so-clever pig, an axe, an ingenious home-made computer, dogs, sheep, a 'Kiwi bear' and underwear.

THE SIGHTS

Glow-worms hang suspended from the roof on long filaments Left, standing beneath the stalactites in Aranui Cave

Sailing on Lake Taupo, a stretch of water famed for its fishing

A fern uncurls in the sunshine, Te Urewera National Park

The Wairaka Statue guards the entrance to Whakatane harbour

THE SIGHTS

TAUPO

316 L7 ■ Tongariro Street (SH1), tel 07-376 0040 ☐ Gascoigne Street ⊠ 10km (6 miles) south of town
www.laketauponz.co.nz

Massive volcanic eruptions formed the Taupo region's landscape over 250,000 years. The latest occurred in AD186, spewing out ash and debris at up to 900kph (560mph). Its effects were visible from China and Rome, and it was one factor in the creation of the vast and now placid 619sq km (239 square-mile) expanse of Lake Taupo.

The busy resort town of Taupo sits on the northern lakeshore and offers a multitude of activities—principally trout-fishing in the lake, but also bungy jumping, tandem skydiving, mountain biking, golf, sailing and walking. Longer lake cruises take in a remarkable set of Maori carvings, showing a huge tattooed face and covering an entire rockface. These relatively recent creations, can only be seen from the water, at Mine Bay.

The Taupo Museum and Art Gallery at Story Place (daily 10.30–4.30) focuses on the early days of the region. West of the museum, the Waikato River begins its 425km (264-mile) journey to the Tasman Sea, winding north behind the town towards Wairakei Park. Mid-river just before the park is Cherry Island (daily 9–5), a small wildlife attraction.

TE PUKE

316 L6 ■ 130 Jellicoe Street, tel 07-573 9172
www.tepuke.co.nz

Te Puke, 31km (19 miles) south-east of Tauranga, claims to have launched New Zealand's kiwifruit industry. Take a Kiwikart tour at Kiwi360 (daily 9–5), 5km (3 miles) east of the town on SH2.

Next door, at the Vintage Auto Barn (daily 9–5), there are more than 90 classic and vintage vehicles.

TE UREWERA NATIONAL PARK

317 M7 ■ SH38, Aniwaniwa, Lake Waikaremoana, tel 06-837 3900

Te Urewera is a daunting and mysterious place of almost threatening beauty. The national park, northwest of Wairoa, encompasses the largest block of native bush in the North, home to rare kiwis, kakas and kokakos. The focus is Lake Waikaremoana—the Sea of Rippling Waters, created 2,000 years ago, when the Waikaretaheke River was dammed by a huge landslide.

TONGARIRO NATIONAL PARK

See pages 88–89.

TURANGI

316 K7 ■ Ngawaka Place, off SH1, tel 07-386 8999
www.taupodc.govt.nz

This small village on the scenic Tongariro River is famous for trout-fishing, and makes a good base for exploring the Tongariro National Park to the south (▷ 88–89). At the Tongariro National Trout Centre, 3km (2 miles) south of the village on SH1 (daily 9–5), you can see a trout hatchery in operation, with adult fish in a large pool and an underwater viewing area.

WAIRAKEI PARK

316 L7

In the heart of the Wairakei Park, north of Taupo, is one of the country's most spectacular waterfalls. Huka Falls, reached via Huka Falls Road, start as the sedately flowing Waikato River before being forced through a

cleft of solid rock 15m (49ft) wide and 100m (328ft) long. From here they emerge to fall 7m (23ft) into a foaming cauldron. Depending on the flow (regulated at Lake Taupo for electricity generation), the falls vary from 9m to 10m (29ft to 33ft) in height.

Wairakei Terraces, north of Taupo (daily 9–5), are the region's latest thermal attraction. About 1km (0.5 miles) farther on is the Wairakei Thermal Valley.

WAITOMO

See pages 90–91.

WHAKATANE

317 M6 ■ Corner of Quay and Kakahoroa Drive, tel 07-308 6058 ☐ Intercity services and East Cape shuttle ⊠ Northwest of town
www.whakatane.com

The principal town in the eastern Bay of Plenty sits at the mouth of the Whakatane River and has a rich Maori history dating back to 1150, when the Polynesian explorer Toi te Hauatahi landed here. This historic town is a departure point to the active volcano of Whakkaari/White Island, which on a clear day can be seen steaming 50km (31 miles) offshore. Other major activities include swimming with dolphins and fishing. The island closest to shore is Moutohora (or Whale) Island, a wildlife refuge.

Pohaturoa is a large rock outcrop at the corner of The Strand and Commerce Street, used for 600 years as a Maori meeting place. The summit was a sacred place for the bones of early chiefs, and newborns were dedicated to the gods in a stream at its foot. More local history is related in the Whakatane Museum and Gallery on Boon Street (Tue–Fri 10–4.30, Sat, Sun 11–3).

SOUTHERN NORTH ISLAND

The citizens of Wellington take their breaks
on the white-sand beaches of the Kapiti Coast, or
perhaps amid the vineyards of the remote Wairarapa
region. The capital itself boasts the outstanding
Te Papa national museum and dozens
of excellent cafés.

MAJOR SIGHTS

Martinborough's Wine Centre lies at the heart of the town, within walking distance of around 20 small vineyards

A polished act at the Steam Inc Engine Shed, Paekakariki

CAPE PALLISER

✚ 318 K11

The road to the North Island's most southerly point passes the eroded rocky spires and turrets of the Putangirua Pinnacles, and the fishing village of Ngawihi, where tractors and bulldozers wait on the beach to launch the boats. The road ends at the Cape Palliser lighthouse, where a climb up the 250 steps is rewarded with outstanding views towards the South Island. A colony of New Zealand fur seals live on the bluff year-round—keep your distance, especially during the breeding season (Nov–Jan).

Be aware, the drive to Cape Palliser and back takes a day.

CASTLEPOINT

✚ 319 L10 🛈 316 Queen Street, Masterton, tel 06-370 0900
www.wairarapanz.com

Castlepoint is the highlight of the Wairarapa's wild coastline. At the eastern end of the main beach the weather-beaten Castlepoint Lighthouse perches on a stark, rocky headland, that sweeps south to enclose a large lagoon. Just below it is a cave that can be explored at low tide, but take care: a small memorial stone commemorates those who have drowned while exploring the offshore reef.

KAPITI ISLAND

✚ 318 J10 🛈 DoC, Government Buildings, Lambton Quay, Wellington, tel 04-472 7356 ♿ Access by arrangement with DoC, tel 04-472 5821 🚶 Landing permits from DoC NZ$9, child (17 and under) NZ$4.50 🚤 Boats depart from Paraparaumu Beach, 9–9.30, return 3–4 🚂 From Wellington to Paraparaumu

Kapiti Island lies 5km (3 miles) offshore from Paraparaumu, and with its adjunct marine reserve is

administered by the Department of Conservation. The 10km- (6-mile) long, 2km- (1-mile) wide island has been cleared of possums, rats and other predators, and after numerous plant and animal reintroductions is now a haven to native New Zealand species. You can follow tracks through native bush, while inquisitive robins, saddlebacks and stitchbirds flit about your head, and weka and takahe poke about for insects disturbed by your feet. Other occupants include kiwi, little blue penguins and the endangered kokako, which has one of the loveliest bird songs ever to grace the air.

The island has a rich history as the 19th-century stronghold of the Maori warrior Te Ruaparaha, and in the 20th century as a whaling hub. The resorts that line the stretch of mainland between Otaki and Paekakariki, known as the Kapiti Coast, are popular weekend destinations for the people of Wellington.

MARTINBOROUGH

✚ 318 K10 🛈 316 Queen Street, Masterton, tel 06-370 0909 🚌 Services from Featherston

This attractive, busy little town at the hub of the Wairarapa region (▷ 106) was founded in the 1880s by British settler John Martin, who laid out the village square and its radiating streets in the form of the Union Jack flag. Today there are no fewer than 20 vineyards within walking distance of the square, most of which offer tastings, and a wine centre in the heart of the village (daily 10–5) can advise on tours and hours. The Colonial Museum on the square (Sat, Sun, 2–4) occupies the former library, built in 1894.

A limestone gorge, the Patuna Chasm, with stalactites, fossils and waterfalls, can be visited on

Patuna Farm, Ruakokopatuna Road (Oct–Easter, guided tours only). The nearby Ruakokopatuna glow-worm caves can be accessed with permission from Blue Creek Farm (tel 06-306 9797); take a torch and sturdy footwear.

OTAKI

✚ 318 K10 🛈 Centennial Park, SH1, tel 04-364 7620 🚌 Services from Wellington
www.naturecoast.co.nz

Otaki is a small town steeped in Maori history. It has several *marae*, including the finely carved 1910 Te Pou O Tainui Marae on Te Rauparaha Street, as well as the Maori Rangiatea Church, rebuilt after it was destroyed by arsonists in 1995. Otaki is the main eastern base for exploring the Tararua Forest Park: Otaki Gorge Road, 2km (1 mile) south of town, leads to Otaki Forks, where several tracks wind into the mountains.

PAEKAKARIKI

✚ 318 J10 🚌 Services from Wellington

Train enthusiasts flock to this tiny seaside village on the Kapiti Coast to appreciate the restored vintage trains—some still running—at the Steam Inc Engine Shed (Sat 11–3), by the rail station. More vintage transport is shown at the Wellington Tramway Museum (Sat, Sun, 11–5), 5km (3 miles) north of here in Queen Elizabeth Park, where four trams are currently in operation.

PARAPARAUMU

✚ 318 J10 🛈 Coastlands shopping centre, off SH1, tel 04-298 8195 🚌 Services from Wellington
www.naturecoast.co.nz

Paraparaumu is the principal township on the Kapiti Coast and has two main beaches: Raumati

THE SIGHTS

Kaka (bush parrots) are popular feature Pukaha Mount Bruce

Tower blocks mark the heart of modern Palmerston North

PALMERSTON NORTH

A university town, gateway to the south and west, and a place of pilgrimage for rugby fans.

➕ 319 K9

ℹ️ The Square, tel 06-350 1922; daily 9–5

🚌 Corner of Pitt and Main streets

🚆 Services from Auckland and Wellington

✈️ 4km (2.5 miles) northwest of city

www.manawatunz.co.nz
Clearly laid-out guide to events and places to stay in the whole region.

RATINGS	
Cultural interest	🔵🔵🔵⚪
Historic interest	🔵🔵⚪⚪
Walkability	🔵🔵🔵⚪

TIP
● Because it is so flat, you can easily get lost. Don't stray too far from the central square and visible tall buildings without a street map from the tourist office.

This agricultural and university community is set on the Manawatu River, and makes a good base for exploring the southern sector of the North Island. It also gives access through the impressive Manawatu Gorge to the Wairarapa (▷ 106) and Hawke's Bay (▷ 79). The heart of the city is the vast green, tree-lined Square.

Other than Massey University (second in size only to Auckland's university, and named after former prime minister William Massey), the town is perhaps most famous for the New Zealand Rugby Museum at 87 Cuba Street (Mon–Sat 10–12, 1.30–4, Sun 1.30–4). It has a huge collection of memorabilia, and an archive resource of videos with accounts of every All Black game since 1870. The excellent Te Manawa Science Centre, Museum and Art Gallery, at 396 Main Street (daily 10–5), integrates social, cultural and artistic heritage with hands-on science displays. In the museum are Maori *taonga* (treasures) and several significant artworks by contemporary figures such as Colin McCahon and Ralph Hotere. There is also a popular hands-on science section.

AROUND PALMERSTON NORTH
In the Manawatu flatlands north of Palmerston sits Feilding. It is a pretty place on the banks of the Oroua River, relatively prosperous and particularly well known for its gardens. These have played a key role in the town's success in the nation's Most Beautiful Small Town Awards, which it has won a remarkable 12 times. Feilding has a scattering of small museums (traction engines being a local speciality), craft outlets and gardens, and it is a tranquil place to explore on foot, or by horse and cart. It's also fun to watch local farmers bidding at the stock sales on Friday.

Beach, to the south, and Paraparaumu Beach, to the north. The latter is also the base for trips to Kapiti Island (▷ 94).

North of town, off SH1, Southward Car Museum (Nov–Easter daily 10–5; Easter–end Oct daily 10–4.30) has an outstanding collection of 250 vehicles dating from 1895, including cars, traction engines, motorbikes, bicycles and a model railway. Highlights include a Rolls Royce that once belonged to film star Marlene Dietrich.

PUKAHA MOUNT BRUCE WILDLIFE CENTRE

➕ 319 K10 ✉️ 30km (18 miles) north of Masterton on SH2 ☎ 06-375 8004 🕐 Daily 9–4.30 🎫 Adult NZ$8, child (17 and under) free 💻 www.mtbruce.org.nz

Pukaha Mount Bruce is the flagship of the Department of Conservation's endangered species breeding policy, where you can see rare species such as takahe, stitchbird and kokako. Wild indigenous eels live in the stream running through the reserve and gather beneath the bridge at feeding time (1.30pm) in a swirling mass. Cheeky kaka (bush parrots), bred here and now living wild in the area, will happily nibble your ear before cracking open a peanut. They are fed by staff at 3pm.

Vintage style: a Buick at Southward Car Museum

THE SIGHTS

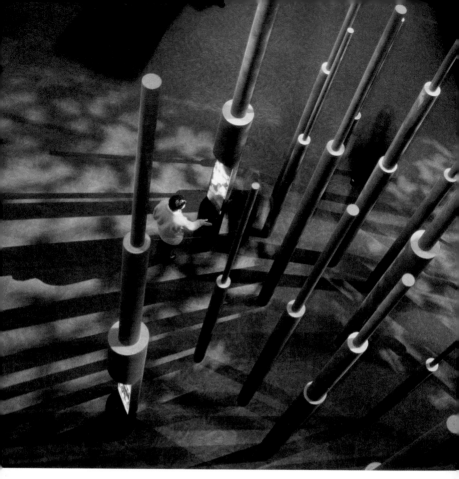

Te Papa Tongarewa-
Museum of New Zealand

One of the largest new museums in the world, covering more than 36,000sq m (387,500sq ft). A museum with an ambitious mission—to explore New Zealand's bicultural heritage and natural history and environment. NZ$317 million has been spent achieving this end since its opening in 1998.

RATINGS	
Cultural interest	● ● ● ● ●
Good for kids	● ● ● ● ○
Historic interest	● ● ● ● ○
Shopping	● ● ● ● ●

SEEING TE PAPA

Te Papa sprawls on the waterfront and uses its setting to great effect, incorporating gardens, waterways, outdoor exhibits and performance areas on the bayside. A vast lobby on ground level gives a wonderful view out over the harbour. From this space, 20m (66ft) high, there is access to the exhibition areas. Te Papa holds a staggering variety of items, including the largest Maori collection held by any museum in the country—almost 16,000

taonga, from woodcarvings, personal ornaments and musical instruments to sections of meeting houses, canoes and storehouses, weapons, woven raincapes and feather and dogskin cloaks, and a contemporary *marae*. European history is represented by 23,500 items, including costume, fine furniture and a major archive of 19th-century photographs (all Level 4).

Among other sections are the world's biggest collection of marine mammal skeletons; the national fish collection; 230,000 dried plant specimens; 65,000 specimens of birds, most from New Zealand (all Level 2); artworks from the late 19th century to the present day by artists including Charles Frederick Goldie, Rita Angus and Colin McCahon (Levels 5–6), and much, much more.

HIGHLIGHTS

MANA WHENUA (LEVEL 4)
This fabulous display of Maori art treasures and artefacts is a great introduction to Maori culture, with personal genealogical histories brought to life on audiovisual screens, and stories and legends told in the carved meeting house. Learn about the myth of the sacred *pounamu* (greenstone), and admire the feathered cloaks and other ornaments.

TIME WARP (LEVEL 2)
The Time Warp section is about information through entertainment. Blastback and Future Rush are two high-tech simulated rides—the former taking you back in time to show the creation of New Zealand from both Maori and geological perspectives (15 minutes), and the latter whisking you to Wellington of 2055, where you'll visit a

BASICS
⊞ 103 C4
✉ Cable Street, Wellington
☎ 04-381 7000
🕐 Fri–Wed 10–6, Thu 10–9
💷 Free; charge for visiting exhibitions; Time Warp rides from NZ$8, child (4–14) from NZ$6, family from NZ$19
🚌 City Circular
🚩 Daily introductory tour Nov–end Mar 10.15, 11.15, 12, 1, 2, 3; NZ$9, child NZ$5
🏛 Level 1: excellent collection of museum merchandise, books, gifts, crafts, jewellery; Level 2 for kids' toys
♿ Wheelchair access on all levels; unisex on levels 1 and 4
☕ Licensed café (level 1) and espresso bar (level 4)
🔊 Te Papa Explorer, NZ$2 (on sale at information desk, Level 2)

www.tepapa.govt.nz
Excellent comprehensive site with information on amenities, exhibitions and research collections.

Signs of a Nation (Level 4) explores the Treaty of Waitangi super-modern house and fly around in a futuristic car (18 minutes). In the Present Zone you can make a virtual bungy jump or shear a virtual sheep.

GOLDEN DAYS (LEVEL 4)

Golden Days re-creates a cluttered junkshop, where the drama of New Zealand's landmark historical events is played out in a 12-minute movie. The absorbing Made in New Zealand, on the same level, showcases the creativity and ingenuity behind 300 years of Kiwi visual arts and culture.

Below, the building stands on the waterfront
Below right, Future Rush, part of the Time Warp

STORYPLACE (LEVEL 2)

Children aged from 18 months to 5 years old can settle down here, an interactive space where carers are at hand to play and tell stories (tickets cost NZ$2 for a 45-minute session). Discovery Centres on Levels 2 and 4 also give children the chance to make their own animated films, read, have a go at weaving or study the world's largest flower.

Don't miss the underground Quake Braker exhibition, which shows how the museum building is designed to reduce the effects of earthquakes.

*Left, the Boulevard Gallery on Level 5
Above, learning in a Discovery Centre*

Below, a lively display including a Holden car, made in New Zealand

HE TANGATA HE TOI

WHERE THERE ARE PEOPLE THERE IS ART

Wellington

**A national capital with a small-town atmosphere.
Well-preserved historical buildings and a
vibrant arts and café culture.**

*Richard 'King Dick' Seddon
watches over the Beehive*

*Catching the cable car down
from the Botanic Garden*

*Admiring the view from the
top of Mount Victoria*

SEEING WELLINGTON

Wellington is New Zealand's capital, and the port for ferries from
the South Island. The city is sandwiched between green hills and
the waterfront, and anyone arriving by road or rail is delivered
right into its high-rise heart. Lambton Quay, the main business
and shopping street, leads to Molesworth Street, Thorndon
and the Parliamentary district. The harbour, with its bordering
main roads of Waterloo Quay, Customhouse Quay, Jervois Quay,
Cable Street and Oriental Parade, sweeps south and east,
encompassing the modern, revitalised watertront. Here the main
landmark is the Te Papa museum (▷ 96–99), the city's top
visitor attraction, which explores New Zealand's bicultural
heritage. Cuba Street leads towards funky Cuba Mall, and
Courtenay Place, lined with restaurants and cafés. Behind the
Central Business District (CBD) are the Botanic Garden and
the hillside suburb of Kelburn. Dominating the view southeast is
Mount Victoria, an ideal place to get your bearings.

HIGHLIGHTS

BOTANIC GARDEN AND CABLE CAR

⊞ 102 A3 ✉ Glenmore Street, Thorndon; cable car 280 Lambton Quay
☎ 04-499 1400; cable car 04-472 2199 ◷ Daily dawn–dusk; cable car Mon–Fri
7am–10pm, Sat, Sun 9am–10pm, every 10 mins 🖾 Free; cable car NZ$2.50, child
(school age) NZ$1, under 5s free 🚌 3, all buses along Lambton Quay ☐ Skyline
Café has great views over the city
www.wbg.co.nz

Wellington's Botanic Garden is magnificent but excruciatingly hilly. The
best way to get there is on the red cable car, an attraction in itself,
which takes about five minutes to climb 121m (440ft). There are
four stations on the way up, and from the summit station there's a
splendid view across the city. Gracing the precarious slopes are 26ha
(64 acres) of specialist gardens, flowerbeds, foreign trees and native
bush. A crowning glory is the Carter Observatory (▷ 186), with static
displays, planetarium shows and audiovisuals. The other highlight is the
Lady Norwood Rose Gardens, a circular display of more than 300
varieties at the northern end of the garden, at the base of the hill,
seen at their best between November and April.

RATINGS

Cultural interest	●●●◐
Shopping	●●●◐
Photo stops	●●◐
Walkability	●●●◐

BASICS

⊞ 318 J11
ℹ 101 Wakefield Street (Civic Square),
tel 04-802 4860; Mon–Wed, Fri 8.30–5,
Thu 9–5, Sat, Sun 9.30–4.30
🚌 Bunny Street
🚉 Bunny Street
🚢 Daily services to Picton, South Island
✈ Rongotai, 6km (4 miles) southeast;
Stagecoach Flyer bus and shuttles to
downtown

www.wellingtonnz.com
Basic visitor information and online
booking service, but limited in detail.

TIP

● Tourism Wellington
promotes a 'four quarters'
map system to help negotiate
the city's streets. The quarters,
mentioned on many maps
and in brochures, run clockwise from Mount Victoria:
Courtenay, Cuba, Willis
and Lambton.

*Native timbers including totara,
matai and kauri were used in the
construction of Old St. Paul's*

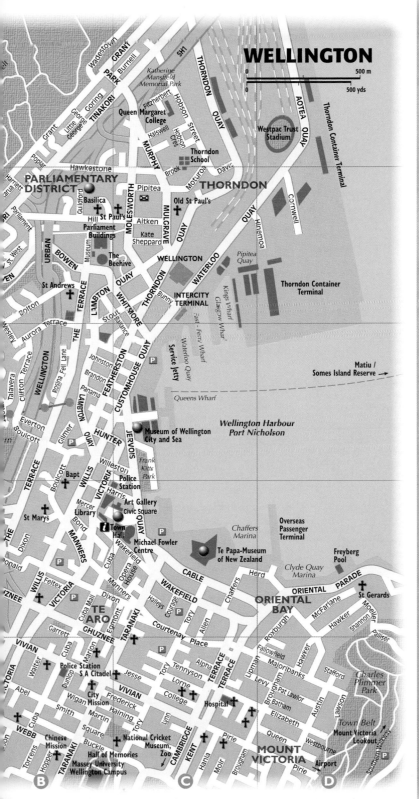

WELLINGTON

0   500 m
0   500 yds

THE SIGHTS

Wadestown
Burnell
GRANT
PARK
Katherine
Mansfield
Memorial Park
TINAKORI
George
Goring
Little
Georges
Grant
Fitzherbert
Hobson Street
Hobson Cres
Halswell
Queen Margaret
College
MURPHY
Brook
Davis
Motorua
THORNDON QUAY
AOTEA QUAY
Thorndon Container Terminal
SH1
Westpac Trust
Stadium
Poplar
Hawkestone
Thorndon
School
PARLIAMENTARY
DISTRICT
Pipitea
Guildford
MOLESWORTH
THORNDON
Hill
Basilica
St Paul's
Old St Paul's
Cornwell
URBAN
BOWEN
Parliament
Buildings
Aitken
Kate
Sheppard
QUAY
Hinemoa
Parliament
Museum
The
Beehive
WELLINGTON
Pipitea
Quay
St Andrews
THE TERRACE
LAMBTON QUAY
WHITMORE
Bunny
WATERLOO
Thorndon Container
Terminal
Bolton
Stout
Balance
INTERCITY
TERMINAL
Kings Wharf
Glasgow Wharf
Aurora Terrace
WELLINGTON
FEATHERSTON
CUSTOMHOUSE QUAY
Johnston
Brandon
Panama
Waterloo Quay
Service Jetty
East-Ferry Wharf
Matiu /
Somes Island Reserve ➞
Clifton Terrace
Rosina Fell Lane
Talavera
Everton
Boulcott
LAMBTON
JERVOIS
HUNTER
Willeston
Queens Wharf
Wellington Harbour
Port Nicholson
TERRACE
Boulcott
Clumet
WILLIS
VICTORIA
Museum of Wellington
City and Sea
Frank
Kitts
Park
Bapt
Harris
Police
Station
St Marys
THE
Dixon
Mercer
Library
Bond
Art Gallery
Civic Square
Chaffers
Marina
Overseas
Passenger
Terminal
Donald
MANNERS
i Town
Hall
QUAY
Wakefield
Michael Fowler
Centre
Te Papa-Museum
of New Zealand
Freyberg
Pool
IZNEE
WILLIS
Feltexa
VICTORIA
Dixon
Opera
House
Manners
CABLE
Herd
Clyde Quay
Marina
PARADE
St Gerards
TE
ARO
Cuba Mall
Marion
Egmont
TARANAKI
WAKEFIELD
Halleys
Courtenay
Chaffers
Tory
Allen
ORIENTAL
BAY
ORIENTAL
McFarlane
Hawker
Shannon
Paliser
Garrett
GHUZNEE
Place
Roxburgh
Moeller
VIVIAN
Walter
Cuba
Police Station
S A Citadel
Jesse
Tennyson
Alpha
TERRACE
Fallowfield
Majoribanks
Lipman
Hawker
Stafford
Austin
Charles
Plimmer
Park
Abel
City
Mission
Dunlop
Frederick
VIVIAN
Lorne
Tory
College
TERRACE
Levy
Pat Lawlor
Batham
Wigan
Haining
Hospital
Lynn
Elizabeth
Smith
Martin
Square
National Cricket
Museum,
Zoo
CAMBRIDGE
KENT
Pirie
Queen
Queen
Westbourne
Town Belt
Mount Victoria
Lookout
WEBB
Chinese
Mission
TARANAKI
Hall of Memories
Massey University
Wellington Campus
Buckle
Hopper
Torrens
Cuba
Hanla
Moir
Brougham
Pirie
MOUNT
VICTORIA
Airport
Southern Walkway

B   C   D

CIVIC SQUARE AND THE WATERFRONT

⊞ 103 C4 🚌 City Circular

A beautiful silver fern orb is suspended above the middle of this public space, which is often used for outdoor events. This is the setting for the excellent City Gallery (daily 10–5), which hosts regular shows of contemporary art in various media and has regular film screenings and performances. Also on the square is Capital E (daily 10–5), where children's events and exhibitions are staged; there's a large toyshop attached.

From Civic Square it's a short walk to the waterfront across the City-to-Sea Bridge, by artist Para Matchitt, which sprouts sculptures celebrating the arrival of the Maori in New Zealand. The waterfront itself is a major focus for the city's museums and recreational activities, and sunny weekends here are abuzz with visitors and locals.

Below, the restored birthplace of writer Katherine Mansfield
Middle, dining out on lively Cuba Street
Right, a view over the city and the harbour from the Botanic Garden

MORE TO SEE

COLONIAL COTTAGE MUSEUM

⊞ 102 A5 ✉ 68 Nairn Street, Brooklyn ☎ 04-384 9122 🕐 Jan–Easter daily 10–4; Easter–end Dec Sat, Sun 12–4 🎟 Adult NZ$5, schoolchild free 🚌 7, 8, 9
www.colonialcottagemuseum.co.nz

A restored and furnished Victorian interior housed in one of the city's oldest buildings (1858), which belonged to the family of carpenter and timber merchant William Wallis for 119 years. Early settler life and Wellington's growth are charted.

KARORI WILDLIFE SANCTUARY

⊞ 102 A3 ✉ Waiapu Road, Karori ☎ 04-920 9200 🕐 Dec–end Mar daily 10–5, plus some evenings 🎟 Adult NZ$10, child (under 14) NZ$4, family NZ$24 🚌 3, 17, 18, 21, 22, 23
www.sanctuary.org.nz

In 1994, 250ha (618 acres) in a valley of regenerating bush in the suburb and hills of Karori was set aside and protected with a predator-proof fence. The benefits are already apparent, as native species are reintroduced and birdsong returns to the bush. The area around the perimeter fence is popular for walking and mountain biking.

MOUNT VICTORIA LOOKOUT

⊞ 103 D5 🚌 20

From a distance, the wooded slopes of 196m (643ft) Mount Victoria hardly seem in character with the movie trilogy the *Lord of the Rings*, but they provided a location for several scenes depicting the Shire in the first film, *Fellowship of the Ring*. Although it is not easy to miss from downtown, reaching the lookout is something of an expedition. The best route is by car, to Thane Road via Majoribanks Street, at the bottom of Courtenay Place. If you lose your way in the web of residential hillside streets, keep heading uphill. On foot, the summit is part of the Southern Walkway. At the top you can watch planes make the tricky landing into Wellington Airport, enjoy the city view and investigate the Byrd Memorial, a tribute to US-born aviator and Antarctic explorer Richard Byrd (1888–1957).

MUSEUM OF WELLINGTON CITY AND SEA

⊞ 103 C3 ✉ Queens Wharf ☎ 04-472 8904 🕐 Daily 10–5 🎟 Free 🚌 City Circular
www.museumofwellington.co.nz

Housed in the former Bond Store, this superb museum competes very successfully with its much bigger neighbour, Te Papa. Its interior, multilevel design combines a modern and rustic feel; its emphasis is on local history, with a particular maritime slant. Of special note is the *Wahine* Disaster Gallery, using original film footage set to a dramatic score to recall the loss of 51 lives on the *Wahine* passenger ferry, which came to grief at the port entrance in 1968.

NEW ZEALAND CRICKET MUSEUM

⊞ 103 C5 ✉ The Old Grandstand, Basin Reserve ☎ 04-385 6602 🕐 Nov–end Apr daily 10.30–3.30; May–end Oct Sat, Sun 10.30–3.30 🎟 Adult NZ$5, child (13–16) NZ$2; 12 and under free if with an adult 🚌 1, 3, 4, 22, 23, 43, 44
www.nzcricket.co.nz

Enthusiasts will love this small but well arranged museum in the old 1924 grandstand of the Basin Reserve cricket ground. It displays national and international memorabilia, dating back to 1743, with emphasis on encounters with arch-enemy Australia. The ground occupies the site of a planned dock, made impractical after the earthquake of 1855. The curious Grecian temple structure inside the eastern boundary fence is a memorial to William Wakefield, leader of the New Zealand Company Wellington settlement from 1840 until 1848.

PARLIAMENTARY DISTRICT

🔢 103 B2 ☎ 04-471 9999 🚌 City Circular, 14

A stroll around this district, focused on Molesworth Street, takes in several of Wellington's most interesting buildings. One is the aptly named Beehive, a city landmark which houses government offices. Designed by British architect Sir Basil Spence and built in 1980, it is hated and loved in equal measure. Tours of Parliament, including the 1922 Parliament House, start here (Mon–Fri 10–4, Sat 10–3, Sun 12–3), and you can watch the House of Representatives in session (times vary). Old Government Buildings on Lambton Quay, built in 1876 to house Crown Ministers, was designed to look like stone, but is actually the world's second largest wooden building (after Japan's Todaji Temple). It was restored in 1994, complete with fibreglass replica chimneys. On Mulgrave Street, Archives New Zealand (Mon–Fri 9–5, Sat 9–1) contains historical documents including the original Treaty of Waitangi (▷ 27). The neo-Gothic Old St. Paul's Cathedral, built in 1866, has impressive interior timberwork and stained-glass windows, and is well worth a look.

The Prime Minister's official residence, Premier House, is a much-enlarged 1843 building on Tinakori Road. Farther north on the same road at No. 25 is the Katherine Mansfield Birthplace (Tue–Sun 10–4), where New Zealand's best-known writer, born in 1888, lived until the age of five (▷ 33). The simple house features in her short stories *Prelude* and *A Birthday*, and has been faithfully restored.

TE PAPA TONGAREWA-MUSEUM OF NEW ZEALAND

See pages 96–99.

BACKGROUND

According to Maori legend Kupe, the great Polynesian explorer, landed here in about AD950. The first European ships to arrive were the *Rosanna* and the *Lambton*, on a preliminary exploration for the first New Zealand Company in 1826, and the first settlers came in 1839 and 1840. The original community was in the area that is now Thorndon. A major earthquake in 1855 created new, flat land suitable for building, and Wellington began to prosper. It became the capital in 1865 and takes its name from Arthur Wellesley, the 1st Duke of Wellington (1769–1852).

The modern Byrd Memorial on top of Mount Victoria

MATIU/SOMES ISLAND RESERVE

🔢 103 D3 ✉ Wellington Harbour
☎ 04-499 1282 🕐 Daily 8.30–5
🚢 Ferry, adult NZ$18.50, child (3–15) NZ$10, under 3s free
www.eastbywest.co.nz

Once a quarantine station, this island now supports a number of protected native birds. Ferries travel here from Queen's Wharf three times a day on the way to Days Bay, near the coastal resort of Eastbourne.

WELLINGTON ZOO

🔢 103 C5 ✉ Daniell Street, Newtown
☎ 04-381 6750 🕐 Daily 9.30–5
🚌 Adult NZ$15, child (3–16) NZ$6
🚌 10, 23 🔲 ▦
www.wellingtonzoo.com

Conservation projects are central to this zoo, whose residents include kiwi, tuatara and a wide variety of non-native species including Sumatran tigers, Malayan sun bears and a troupe of chimps—the second largest in the southern hemisphere.

Castlepoint Lighthouse (▷ 94) stands proud on the rugged eastern seaboard of the Wairarapa region

Modern art displayed at the Sarjeant Gallery, Wanganui

THE SIGHTS

WAIRARAPA

🚩 319 K10 🚹 316 Queen Street, Masterton, tel 06-370 0900 🚍 Services from Wellington to Masterton
www.wairarapanz.com

Wild coastal scenery, relaxed rural towns like Martinborough (▷ 94), vineyards and the North Island's southernmost point (Cape Palliser, ▷ 94) all make this little-visited region worth getting to know.

From Masterton, the chief town, SH2 leads south to Carterton. Here, at the Paua World factory (▷ 180) on Kent Street, you can watch jewels being crafted from exquisite paua (abalone) shells, which are subject to strict quotas and harvesting rules. One of the best views in the Wairarapa can be enjoyed from Mount Dick, 14km (9 miles) along Dalefield Road, at the southern end of the town.

At the Waiohine Gorge, 22km (14 miles) south of Carterton, walks lead high above the river and negotiate the heart-stopping, 40m-high (130ft) swing bridge. Greytown, farther along SH2, is best known for its antiques and craft shops housed in a row of beautifully restored wooden-fronted buildings on Main Street. The Cobblestones Museum on Main Street (daily 9–4.30) is a collection of buildings and memorabilia from early settler days.

Featherston is the Wairarapa's southern point of access, set in the shadow of the Rimutaka Range. In the 1870s this was the base during construction of the Wairarapa–Wellington rail link. Its main attraction now is the Fell Engine Museum on Fitzherbert Street (Mon–Fri 9.30–4, Sat, Sun 10–4), housing the beautifully restored engine that used to climb the 265m (870ft) rise of the Rimutaka Incline. The incline is now part of the Rimutaka Rail Trail, starting at the end of Cross Creek Road, 10km (6 miles) south of Featherston, and leading in a day to Summit and back or to Kaitoke.

WANGANUI

🚩 318 J9 🚹 101 Guyton Street, tel 06-349 0508 🚍 Ridgeway Street, Ingestre Street 🗙
www.wanganuinz.com

Wanganui lies at the mouth of the Whanganui River, once a vital north–south supply route. Formerly a bustling port, Wanganui is now the southern gateway to Whanganui National Park. The area of Queen's Park, east of the central thoroughfare of Victoria Avenue, with its restored Victorian and Edwardian houses, is the city's cultural heart. It's also home to the modern Whanganui Regional Museum (daily 10–4), which contains a fine collection of Maori canoes and illustrates ingenious Maori methods of catching fish and birds. Crowning Queens Park hill is the domed Sarjeant Gallery (daily 10.30–4.30), with more than 4,000 permanent artworks.

Sailings of the restored *Waimarie* paddlesteamer, which worked the river for 50 years before sinking in 1952, leave from Wanganui Riverboat Centre on Taupo Quay (Nov–Apr daily 2pm; May–Oct Sat, Sun 1pm).

Within Cooks Gardens, on St. Hill Street, are the 1899 colonial-style Opera House; a stadium and wooden velodrome; and the Ward Observatory (Fri 8–9.30), built in 1901.

Across the city bridge from Taupo Quay a tunnel takes you 200m (656ft) into the hillside to ride the Durie Hill Elevator (1919) to the top (Mon–Fri 7.30–6, Sat 9–6, Sun 10–5), where you can climb the Durie Hill War Memorial Tower, built of shellrock.

WELLINGTON

See pages 100–105.

WHANGANUI NATIONAL PARK

🚩 318 K8 🚹 74 Ingestre Street, Wanganui, tel 06-348 8475; Cherry Grove, Taumarunui, tel 07-8958201; Owairua Road, Pipiriki, tel 06-385 5022
www.doc.govt.nz

From its source high on the volcanic slopes of Tongariro National Park, the Whanganui River travels 290km (180 miles) to the sea, carving through some of the North Island's least accessible country. At its most remote parts it cuts deep into the soft sand and mudstone and is joined by tracts of forest, which form the heart of the Whanganui National Park. The entire area is difficult to reach, but there are walking tracks and jet-boat and kayak trips along the river itself. Be aware that slips and flooding are real dangers; consult the Department of Conservation before an excursion.

The windy and scenic Whanganui River Road branches off SH4 15km (9 miles) north of Wanganui and follows the river to Pipiriki before turning inland to Raetihi, where it rejoins SH4. The 106km (66-mile) round trip, passes a number of mission settlements that were created in the 1840s by the Reverend Richard Taylor.

Paua shell

NELSON AND MARLBOROUGH

The northern tip of the South Island is known for its gentle, sunny climate, attracting wine-growers to the Marlborough region and artisans to Nelson and its environs. The coastal Abel Tasman is one of the best-loved national parks in the country.

MAJOR SIGHTS

← AWAROA LODGE 17 MINS

Abel Tasman National Park

**The smallest and busiest national park in New Zealand.
Some 23,000ha (56,830 acres) of the best coastal scenery,
beaches and walks in the country.**

*Sparkling sand and sea at
Awaroa Inlet*

*Rich hues glimpsed in a crystal-
clear tidal rockpool*

*Water taxis help visitors access
sections of the Coast Track*

SEEING ABEL TASMAN NATIONAL PARK

More than 170,000 visitors a year come to appreciate the Abel
Tasman's rolling hills of native bush; its granite, limestone and
marble outcrops; its clear, azure waters; and its 91km (56 miles)
of coastline indented with more than 50 sandy beaches. Birds
such as tui and bellbirds inhabit lush pockets of forest, and
pukeko feed in the wetlands—outside the park's boundaries,
these are protected as the Tonga Island Marine Reserve.

Walkers come to enjoy the world-famous Coast Track, sea
kayakers to make the most of an internationally renowned
venue. On an average summer's day the park attracts up to
4,000 people, and you must reserve well in advance for
all places to stay and most activities.

HIGHLIGHTS

AWAROA BAY
✚ 320 G10
A 6km (4-mile), three- to six-hour walk makes the most
of this glorious inlet tucked into a fold of land south of
Totaranui. Its starting point is reached from Takaka along the
Totaranui Road, via Pohara, Wainui Inlet and the Pigeon
Saddle, with tremendous views on the way. From the
Totaranui Road, a right turn takes you on to the Awaroa Road
and the Awaroa parking zone.

To enjoy the walk you need to time your arrival with an
outgoing tide, as it begins on the beach (this stage is best
done barefoot). It ends at Awaroa Lodge, where you can
buy beer, coffee or tea, before retracing your steps to the
Awaroa parking zone, keeping a careful eye on the tide.

COAST TRACK
This world-famous two- to five-day, 51km (32-mile) walk
requires medium fitness; the track itself is well maintained. The
only obstacles and difficult sections are the two estuary crossings at Awaroa Inlet and Torrent Bay—the most scenic beaches
on the route—which must be negotiated at low tide.
There are several ways to tackle the track in whole or in part.

RATINGS	
Outdoor pursuits	● ● ● ● ●
Photo stops	● ● ●
Walkability	● ● ● ● ●

BASICS
✚ 320 G10
🛈 Wallace Street, Motueka, tel 03-528 6543; daily 8–7
🛈 Department of Conservation field centre, corner of King Edward and High streets, Motueka, tel 03-528 1810; Mon–Fri 8–4.30
🚌 Services from Nelson to Kaiteriteri and Marahau via Motueka (southern entrance), and to Totaranui (northern sector)
🚤 Water taxis from Motueka, Kaiteriteri and Marahau; can also be hailed within park
✈ Awaroa Bay (from Nelson or Motueka): Abel Tasman Air (tel 03-528 8290)
www.doc.govt.nz A guide to DoC parks and services, with useful links to other sites and DoC contact details.

*Left, primitive-style wooden
sculpture at Awaroa Lodge
Opposite, marker post on the
Abel Tasman Coast Track*

TIPS

- Visitor information and DoC offices in Motueka can help with reserving places to stay, passes, transportation, activities and tide times.
- General information, hut reservations, maps and leaflets are also available at the DoC office.
- Unmanned DoC information stations and intentions sheets are available at Marahau and Totaranui (seasonal).

MORE TO SEE

KAITERITERI

✚ 320 G10 🚌 Services from Nelson
Scenic launches, water taxis and kayak trips set off from this very pretty village on the dead-end road to the southern boundary of the park. There are two exceptionally good beaches here. At the eastern end of the main beach is the Kaka Pa Point Lookout. Idyllic Breakers Beach, below, looks eastward.

MARAHAU

✚ 320 G10 🚌 Services from Nelson
Marahau is 6km (4 miles) east of Kaiteriteri, on the same southern approach road to the park. It offers a wide range of places to stay and activities, water taxis and a café. Controversy is raging about a NZ$15 million resort development given resource consent on the environmentally sensitive wetlands at the entrance to the park—a project that confirms the worst fears of conservationists about threats to the unspoiled beauty of the Abel Tasman.

*Right, trampers
Below, boardwalk on the trail*

The most popular routes are from the south (Marahau) to the north (Wainui), or from Totaranui in the north (by water taxi from Marahau) to Marahau in the south. There are plenty of campsites and huts along the way and a few independent lodges. The walk involves a lot of bush walking, where views of the sea and beaches are obscured for long periods of time.

INLAND TRACK

The Inland Track is a quieter but more energetic walk than the Coast Track, and leads away from the coast and its hordes of visitors. It provides a link between Marahau and Wainui via the Pigeon Saddle on the Takaka–Totaranui Road, and takes three to five days to cover 37km (23 miles). The main appeals here, other than the fact that the walk is far less popular than the coastal track, are the undisturbed regenerating bush and the occasional sublime views. You may also hear kiwis at night.

TORRENT BAY TO MARAHAU WALK

This 14km (8.5-mile) route takes from three to six hours to complete. From Marahau you can take an early morning water taxi to Torrent Bay (NZ$15; first taxi leaves 8.30), making sure that your arrival at Torrent Bay coincides with low tide. From here the route joins the Coast Track heading south, for which you need to take off your boots and follow the markers across the estuary, and continues via the lovely sands of Anchorage Bay Beach, intimate Watering Cove, and Stillwell and Appletree bays.

BACKGROUND

Maori communities have lived along this coast for at least five centuries, and in 1642 the Ngati Tumatakokiri people saw off the first European visitors—part of Dutch explorer Abel Tasman's crew. From 1855 European settlement got underway, which meant the clearing of forests and quarrying of granite. Fears that logging would strip the coast of its vegetation led to a campaign for the protection of this stretch of shoreline, and in 1942—largely as a consequence of the tireless efforts of conservationist and resident Perrine Moncrieff—the national park was opened. Many place-names within the park are associated with explorations by the French explorer Jules Sébastien César Dumont d'Urville.

Blenheim is at the forefront of South Island wine production

Inside the Te Anaroa cave system, near Collingwood

A gannetry occupies the tip of Farewell Spit

BLENHEIM

321 H11 Rail Station, SH1, Sinclair Street, tel 03-577 8080 Services to Christchurch, Picton and Nelson Grove Road; services from Christchurch and Picton On Middle Renwick Road, 7km (4 miles) west; shuttles **www.destinationmarlborough.com**

The Marlborough region's largest town is a resort known for its wineries—over 50 of them, most clustered off SH6 near the village of Renwick, 10km (6 miles) west of town on the fertile soils of the Wairau Plains. Famous names include Montana, Cloudy Bay and Nautilus Estate, and tours and tastings are widely available (▷ 189). Blenheim's dry climate has its disadvantages: in recent years the whole region has suffered from a severe lack of rain.

The Marlborough Provincial Museum at Brayshaw Park, New Renwick Road, 3km (2 miles) south of town (daily 10–4), is a mainly open-air reconstruction of an early settlers' village. It is at the end of the narrow-gauge Blenheim Riverside Railway (tel 03-578 9442).

COLLINGWOOD

320 G10

This tiny village on Golden Bay was once known as Gibbstown and—unlikely as it now seems—was once a booming gold-mining town promoted as a suitable capital for the nation. That dream turned to dust when the gold reserves ran out and a fire almost destroyed the village. Rebuilt and renamed Collingwood in tribute to Admiral Lord Nelson's second-in-command, the community was struck by fire again in 1904 and yet again in 1967, when the town hall, hotel and two shops

The grey sands of Farewell Spit

were reduced to ashes. Despite its calamitous history, Collingwood retains a few historic buildings, including the courthouse, which is now a café.

South of the village, in the attractive Aorere River Valley, are the privately owned Te Anaroa and Rebecca Caves, on Caves Road, near Rockville (reservations essential, tel 03-525 6044). The Te Anaroa Caves are 350m (1,148ft) long and include stalactites and fossilised shells, and the Rebecca Caves are known for their glow-worms.

If you have time, an exploration of the pretty Aorere River valley (Heaphy Track Road) is recommended, taking in the river gorge at Salisbury Bridge and the Bainham Store, an original store that has changed little in decades and is still open for business.

FAREWELL SPIT AND GOLDEN BAY

320 G9 Freemans Access, Puponga, tel 03-524 8454

Countless tons of sand have been ejected into the northerly ocean currents from river-mouths scattered all the way up the west coast, forming this dynamic though desert-like landscape at the northwest tip of the South Island, with sparse vegetation struggling to take root in the dry and shifting sand. Both Cape Farewell and Farewell Spit were

noted by Abel Tasman in 1642, and named by Cook when he left New Zealand in 1770. The lighthouse at the very tip of the spit was first erected in 1870, and relocated after the sea almost washed it away.

The majority of the spit is a nature reserve, and the mud flats that it creates along its landward edge are one of New Zealand's most important habitats for wading birds. More than 100 species have been recorded around the spit, but it is the sheer numbers of each species that are most notable. Migrating flocks of godwits and knots can run well into the thousands. Black swans are also found here.

The spit is remarkable for its powerful sense of isolation, but from afar and from sea level its extensive dune system appears no more than a coastal mirage. For an impression of its scale, the best viewpoint is around the Pillar Point Light Beacon, accessed from Wharariki Road and Puponga. A marked walk leads from the beacon along the cliffs to Cape Farewell, where you may see or hear (or smell!) fur seals. From here you can descend to Wharariki Beach, one of the most beautiful in the country (you can also reach it from Puponga along Wharariki Road), where golden sands are punctuated with caves, dunes and rock arches.

THE SIGHTS

The famous Mussel Boys restaurant makes the most of Havelock's local produce—green-lipped mussels

A peaceful mooring at Motueka

THE SIGHTS

HAVELOCK

⊞ 321 H10 🏠 65A Main Road, tel 03-574 2114 🚌 Main Road 🚌 Services from Blenheim and Nelson www.rutherfordtravel.co.nz

Travelling west from Blenheim (▷ 111), the SH6 passes through the small village of Renwick before winding through the rolling hills of the Inner Marlborough Sounds to Nelson. About 41km (25 miles) along, at the head of the Pelorus Sound, is the enchanting little fishing settlement of Havelock. The village has a fine café, a famous restaurant (Mussel Boys, ▷ 262), art and craft galleries, a pub and a small but interesting museum on Main Road (daily 9–5). It's also an ideal base for exploring the glorious Pelorus and other outer sounds. Takorika Hill, behind the town, has extensive views.

Havelock was once a thriving gold-mining town and was the boyhood home of one of New Zealand's most famous sons, atomic physicist Ernest Rutherford (1871–1937)—the man who split the atom. His former home is now the youth hostel, and a memorial stands on the main street. These days Havelock's gold is the green-lipped mussel, without doubt the finest-tasting thing in a shell, and a major export industry within the Sounds.

A network of old bridleways makes up the 27km (17-mile) Nydia Track, which begins near Havelock at Kaiuma Bay. The two-day walk takes in an old timber-milling site and magnificent forest on the way to Duncan Bay.

About 18km (11 miles) west of Havelock is the Pelorus Bridge Scenic Reserve, where the Rai and Pelorus rivers flow through bush-clad hills. You can walk in

the area, and there's a great café by the bridge.

KAHURANGI NATIONAL PARK

⊞ 320 G10 ℹ DoC field centres, Millers Acre, 79 Trafalgar Street, Nelson, tel 03-546 9339; corner of King Edward and High streets, Motueka, tel 03-528 1810; Commercial Street, Takaka, tel 03-525 8026 🚌 Services from Nelson, Takaka and Karamea www.doc.govt.nz

Kahurangi, opened as a national park in 1996, is a wide and remote landscape in the northwest of rugged alpine ranges and river valleys. The most notable of these is the Heaphy, which meets, in part, the park's most famous walking route, the 82km (51-mile) Heaphy Track—named for Major Charles Heaphy, the first to traverse the coastal section, in 1846. It takes four to six days to cover the whole route, which reaches its highest point of 915m (3,002ft) at Flannigan's Corner, near Mount Perry. The eastern Heaphy Track trailhead is reached via Collingwood (▷ 111), and Bainham (Aorere River Valley), at the end of the Heaphy Track Road. The route is signposted from Collingwood. The western trailhead starts about 15km (9 miles) north of Karamea. Book hut accommodation ahead in summer.

Some of the country's oldest rock landforms—spectacular

limestone caves, plateaux, arches and outcrops—are contained within the park, and it provides a home for more than half New Zealand's native plant species (over 80 per cent of all alpine species) and more than 18 native bird species, including the New Zealand falcon and the great spotted kiwi, as well as the huge New Zealand land snail.

MOTUEKA

⊞ 320 G10 ℹ Wallace Street, tel 03-528 6543 ✈ Airport on College Street, 2km (1 mile) west www.abeltasmangreenrush.co.nz

Motueka sits among sun-bathed hop farms and orchards, a short distance from several beautiful beaches. Many visitors pass through en route to the Abel Tasman National Park and Golden Bay, making this a bustling resort in summer and a sleepy service town in winter. The best beaches near Motueka (and before the national park) are in Kaiteriteri (▷ 110). For a short walk try the Motueka Quay, reached via the waterfront west of downtown. Motueka has a small museum (Dec–Apr daily 9–4; May–Nov Mon–Fri 10–4).

The route between Motueka and Richmond (SH60), known as Nelson's Coastal Way, is the place to go for arts and crafts and wineries, plus the Touch the Sea Aquarium (daily 9–5) and the Cool Store art gallery next door.

Fruit is grown around Motueka

KAIKOURA

A chance to get close to whales and dolphins, seals and albatrosses on a sparkling azure bay.

The small town of Kaikoura sits on the spectacular northeast coast, in the shadow of the snow-capped Kaikoura mountains. South, a sea trough extends unusually close to the coastline, creating an upsurge of nutritious plankton soup and attracting an extraordinary variety of ocean inhabitants.

Modern Kaikoura was established as a whaling station in the early 19th century. Station manager George Fyffe built Kaikoura's oldest remaining house (Fyffe House) near the Old Wharf in 1860, and gave his name to the mountain immediately behind the township. The whaling industry was replaced by fishing, particularly for crayfish. Today Kaikoura's wildlife is hunted only by the camera, and the resident and migratory whales are the big draw.

WATER-BASED ACTIVITIES

The sea around Kaikoura abounds with dolphins, from the common and bottlenose to the smaller, rare Hector's dolphin. You are most likely to encounter or swim with dusky dolphins; pods running into the hundreds, if not the thousands, are common. Kaikoura is home to its own pod of sperm whales. Whale-watching trips depart from the Whaleway Station off Beach Road, offering a chance to spot dolphins, seals and other wildlife. Other whale species that appear regularly include humpbacks, rights and orcas, and if you are very lucky you may see an enormous blue whale. For details of tours, ▷ 190.

LAND-BASED SIGHTS

Clifftop and shoreline walkways link the northern and southern settlements of Kaikoura, and cross the head of the Kaikoura Peninsula. A good spot to get an overall impression of the town, the peninsula and its mountain backdrop is the lookout just off Scarborough Terrace (off SH1 between the northern and southern settlements). See also the walk, ▷ 234.

There are three historical venues of note: the Kaikoura District Museum, at 14 Ludstone Road (Mon–Fri 12.30–4.30, Sat, Sun 2–4), offering an insight into early Maori and whaling activities; Fyffe House, on Avoca Street near the Old Wharf (Nov–end Apr daily 10–5; May–end Oct Thu–Tue 10–4); and the Maori Leap Cave, 2km (1 mile) south of Kaikoura, a sea-formed limestone cave, discovered only in the 21st century (daily tours).

Top, watching as a sperm whale dives off the Kaikoura coast
Above, fishing from the shingle beach

RATINGS

Historic interest	●●
Outdoor pursuits	●●●
Walkability	●●●●

BASICS

✚ 321 H17

🛈 West End, Kaikoura, tel 03-319 5641; Jan, Feb daily 8–6; Mar–end Dec daily 9–5

🚌 Services from Christchurch, Blenheim, Picton and Hanmer Springs. Shuttles to all main sights

🚆 Clarence Street; services from Christchurch, Blenheim and Picton

www.kaikoura.co.nz
Comprehensive guide to the area's wildlife, environment, activities, art and history, places to stay and eat, and other visitor information.

TIPS

● In midsummer it's advisable to reserve all activities ahead, and essential if you want to go whale-watching or dolphin-swimming.

● Kaikoura is subject to changeable weather. Trips may be cancelled at short notice, so request inclusion on alternative trips.

Nelson

**A vibrant modern town steeped in history, and surrounded
by beaches and national parks.
Claims the title of Sunshine Capital of New Zealand.**

*Dining al fresco at Olivia's, on
the waterfront*

*Right, the Boatshed Restaurant
overhangs the water*

*Far right, South Street's houses are
among the oldest in the country*

SEEING NELSON

Nelson is known as the sunniest place in the country—and this
could apply to its atmosphere, its people and its surroundings, in
addition to its Mediterranean climate. The city's colonial heart is
around Trafalgar Street, and the Saturday market is a highlight
(▷ 191). Within 100km (60 miles) of town are superb beaches
and coastal scenery, as well as three diverse national parks: Abel
Tasman (▷ 108–110), Nelson Lakes (▷ 117) and Kahurangi
(▷ 112). Little wonder that Nelson is considered one of the top
places to visit—and to live—in the country.

HIGHLIGHTS

BEACHES

No visit to Nelson would be complete without a trip to the beach. The
most popular stretch of sand is at the Tahunanui Beach Reserve, just
southwest of downtown. It may not have the same scenic beauty (or
solitude) of more remote beaches in the region, but it is a convenient
place to relax. About 20km (12 miles) farther round Tasman Bay
towards Motueka, off SH60, are the seemingly never-ending sands
and forest swathe of Rabbit Island.

BROADGREEN HISTORIC HOUSE

✉ 276 Nayland Road, Stoke, 6km (4 miles) southwest of downtown ☎ 03-547
0403 🕐 Daily 10.30–4.30 💰 Adult NZ$3, child (school age) NZ$0.50, pre-school
free 🚌 From Travel Centre, 27 Bridge Street
An 11-room cob house of 1855, made of clay, sand and straw,
has been furnished in its original style and opened to the public.
It was built for Englishman Edmund Buxton, following the model of
a Devon farmhouse, and sits amid lawns and rose gardens.

NELSON MUSEUM PUPURI TAONGA O TE TAI AO

✉ Corner of Hardy and Trafalgar streets ☎ 03-548 9588 🕐 Mon–Fri 10–5,
Sat, Sun 10–4.30
www.museumnp.org.nz
The new regional museum covers the natural and human history
of the top of the South Island. Displays include photos of everyday
life from an outstanding collection made in the 1860s, as well as

---

RATINGS

Outdoor pursuits	●●●
Photo stops	●●●●●
Walkability	●●●●●
Shopping	●●●●

BASICS

✚ 321 G10
ℹ Corner of Trafalgar and Halifax
streets, tel 03-548 2304; daily 9–5
🚌 Outside visitor information office;
services from Christchurch, Blenheim,
Picton, Golden Bay, Abel Tasman,
Takaka and West Coast
✈ Airport 6km (4 miles) southwest of
town off SH6

www.nelsonnz.com
Well-designed site with wide-ranging
information on the Nelson region,
including a search database on food
and wine and places to stay.

CENTRE OF NEW ZEALAND
THIS SIGNAL PRESENTED TO THE CITY
TO MARK THE 21ST ANNIVERSARY OF
NELSON JAYCEE. AUGUST 1969.

THIS B.M. IS THE POINT OF ORIGIN
FOR SURVEYS IN THE NELSON DISTRICT

Maori *taonga* (treasures), works of art and a range of domestic and technical objects.

SUTER TE ARATOI O WHAKATU

✉ 208 Bridge Street ☎ 03-548 4699 ⏱ Daily 10.30–4.30 💰 Adult NZ$3, schoolchild NZ$0.50 🍴 🚻 🚌 From Travel Centre, 27 Bridge Street; Double-Decker Express
www.thesuter.org.nz

The Suter, next to Queen's Gardens, is foremost among several major galleries in this city known for its thriving arts and crafts. Four exhibition spaces showcase permanent and temporary historical and contemporary collections. There is also a theatre on the site.

WORLD OF WEARABLE ART AND CLASSIC CARS (WOW)

✉ Quarantine Road, Annesbrook ☎ 03-547 4573 ⏱ Jan–Easter daily 10–6; Easter–end Dec daily 10–5 💰 Adult NZ$18, child (5–14) NZ$7, under 5s free, family from NZ$26 🅿 🚻 🚌 From Travel Centre, 27 Bridge Street; Double-Decker Express
www.wowcars.co.nz

In 1987 Nelson sculptor Suzie Moncrieff created and directed a unique stage show called Wearable Art. Contributors were asked to create a piece of themed artwork in any medium in a form that could be worn in motion. The show became an annual event and has now shifted to Wellington (▷ 187), but the best entries can be seen in this gallery. A fully scripted moving parade of extreme costumes is displayed, reflecting an astonishing array of creative thought and eccentric wit—not to be missed. A second gallery in the same complex houses vintage cars.

BACKGROUND

Maori tribes migrated to this area from the North Island in the 16th century. In the 1840s New Zealand Company agent Colonel William Wakefield negotiated a land purchase at Nelson. Subsequent disagreements about ownership of further land led to the Wairau Affray and the death of his brother, Captain Arthur Wakefield, and 27 others. In 1844 the NZ Company collapsed, leaving many destitute. Recovery began in 1857, when gold was discovered, and by the end of the 19th century Nelson's rich agricultural potential was finally being realised.

Above, strolling on the town's Tahunanui Beach
Below, New Zealand's central point is celebrated

TIPS

● Nelson's vineyards are over-shadowed by the reputation and scale of those in Marlborough, but the wine they produce can be of excellent quality. For more information see www.nelsonwines.co.nz.
● A half-hour's climb to the viewpoint above the Botanical Gardens, off Milton Road or Maitai Road, gives a great view of the town from a site claimed as New Zealand's geographical mid-point.

Above, a coastline indented with appealing little bays characterises Queen Charlotte Sound; left, a fishing boat in the Sounds

MARLBOROUGH SOUNDS

A mosaic of tiny islets, coves and waterways, to be enjoyed along coastal paths or from the water.

The Marlborough Sounds are the South Island's giant entrance foyer. This vast, convoluted system of drowned river valleys, wooded peninsulas and remote green islets has sublime coastal scenery and offers every opportunity for kayaking, wildlife-watching or just relaxation. From its base at Picton (▷ 117) it is only a short journey to Blenheim (▷ 111), the region's capital. On the map, the Sounds take up a relatively small area, but the myriad drowned river valleys create an astonishing 1,500km (932 miles) of coastline, known for seabirds and dolphins. The two main inlets are Queen Charlotte and Pelorus sounds.

EXPLORING THE SOUNDS

There are two popular walking tracks in the sounds: the Nydia Track (Havelock ▷ 112) and the Queen Charlotte Track, a 71km (44-mile), coastal route which leads in three to five days from Ship Cove to Anakiwa. The track is suitable for most people of average fitness, and is open in part to mountain bicycles. It winds its way around sheltered coves, over skyline ridges and through native forest, fringing an extensive network of sunken river valleys.

Boat access in the Sounds is well organised and readily available. Other options include guided and self-guided walks, as well as kayaking trips and a ride on the Magic Mail Run (tel 03-573 6175, www.mailboat.co.nz). There is road access for drivers at Camp Bay (Punga Cove), Torea Bay (The Portage) and Mistletoe Bay (Te Mahia).

EARLY VISITORS

There is evidence of Maori settlement here from as early as the 14th century. Captain Cook visited the Sounds on each of his voyages between 1770 and 1777. He was particularly fond of Ship Cove, near the mouth of Queen Charlotte Sound, which he visited five times: a monument there commemorates the occasions. Less celebrated visits by other early explorers include those of Abel Tasman (before Cook), and French navigator Jules Dumont d'Urville in 1827. In the same year, London whaler John Guard established Marlborough's first European settlement, and the country's first land-based whaling station, at Te Awaiti Bay in Tory Channel, on Arapawa Island.

River at the southern end of Lake Rotoiti, Nelson Lakes

Inside the restored teak hull of the Edwin Fox

MURCHISON

🗺 320 F11 🛈 47 Waller Street, tel 03-523 9350 🚌 Services from Nelson and the West Coast
www.nelsonnz.com

Murchison sits at the head of the Buller Gorge, where the Matakitaki and Buller rivers meet, and gives access to the west coast from the north. Although once an important gold-mining town—and nearly wiped out by a violent earthquake in 1929—it is now a quiet place, primarily of interest for activities such as fishing, white-water rafting, kayaking, caving and mountaineering.

The Murchison Museum, on Fairfax Street (daily 10–4), has exhibits on gold-mining and the town's past.

NELSON

See pages 114–115.

NELSON LAKES NATIONAL PARK

🗺 320 G11 🛈 St. Arnaud, tel 03-521 1806 🚌 Services from Nelson to St. Arnaud

This somewhat underrated national park protects 102,000ha (252,042 acres) of the northernmost Southern Alps range. Dominating the park are two long, scenic and trout-filled lakes, Rotoroa and Rotoiti, which lie cradled in beech-covered alpine ranges, surrounded by beautiful tussock valleys and wildflowerstrewn meadows.

The ranges and river valleys offer superb walking, notably the 80km (50-mile), four- to sevenday Travers-Sabine Circuit and the excellent two- to three-day Robert Ridge/Lake Angelus Track. The principal base for the park is the pretty little hamlet of St. Arnaud, at the northern end of Lake Rotoiti—ask at the visitor information office here about shorter walks in the vicinity.

PICTON

The gateway to South Island and Marlborough Sounds, in summer a buzz of sailing activity, in winter a sleepy port.

🗺 321 H11
🛈 Foreshore, near ferry terminal, tel 03-520 3113; daily 8.30–5
🚌 Services from Christchurch, Nelson and Blenheim
🚆 Service from Christchurch
⛴ Ferries from Wellington
✈ 10km (6 miles) south of town

www.picton.co.nz
Directory information for Picton and Marlborough Sounds.

RATINGS	
Historic interest	● ● ●
Outdoor pursuits	● ● ● ●
Walkability	● ● ● ●

TIP
● For a comprehensive guide to the walks around Picton, get hold of the excellent broadsheet *Picton by Foot*, available free from the visitor information office.

After you have arrived on the modern ferry, with its comfy seats and state-of-the-art radar screens, you will thank your lucky stars for progress when you encounter the old hulk of the 1853 East India trading ship *Edwin Fox*, between the ferry terminal and the heart of town (daily 9–5). Ranked the ninth oldest ship in the world, she carried troops in the Crimean War before being commissioned to bring immigrants to Australia and New Zealand.

MUSEUMS
Next door is the Seashore World (daily 9–6), whose inhabitants include an octopus called Larry, seahorses and rays. Farther towards the town on London Quay is the Picton Community Museum (daily 10–4), which contains a cluttered but interesting range of items focusing mainly on the 1800s whaling operations in the sounds, as well as Maori *taonga* (treasures) and early pioneer settler pieces.

ACROSS THE WATER
A short walk across the footbridge and the inlet leads to the eastern side of the waterfront and Shelley Beach. Here, the Echo Café and Bar (daily 10–late) is based around a scow, built in 1905 and gradually restored after her retirement in 1965. She was the last commercial trader under sail in New Zealand, and served in World War II. During her eventful life, *Echo* was stranded 15 times and damaged 16 times, had two new engines, propellers and shafts, suffered fires in 1911 and 1920, not to mention having seven collisions involving 75 different vessels and being sunk twice. She now has a quieter time as a restaurant.

Tours explore the natural wonders of Rawhiti Cave in Golden Bay, east of Takaka

The Labyrinth Rocks were scoured out by river water

RAWHITI CAVE

➕ 320 G10 ✉ Clifton Road, Golden Bay

This ancient cave 7km (4 miles) east of Takaka has one of the largest cave entrances in the world, laden with thousands of multi-hued tufa stalactites. It can be accessed independently, but the best way to see it is on a three-hour guided walk with Kahurangi Walks (tel 03-525 7177, www.kahurangiwalks. co.nz) through the wonderful gorge of the Dry River. The ground is slippery, so you'll need to wear sturdy shoes.

TAKAKA

➕ 320 G10 ℹ Willow Street, tel 03-525 9136 🚌 Willow Street; services from Abel Tasman and Kahurangi ✈ Airfield 6km (4 miles) west of town on SH60 www.nelsonnz.com

Takaka was founded in 1854 and is the principal business and shopping area for Golden Bay (▷ 111). Particularly busy during summer, it has a life of its own all year as a cosmopolitan art and crafts hub. It is also the main base for visits to the northern sector of the Abel Tasman National Park (▷ 108–110), the vast Kahurangi National Park, and the remote 35km (22-mile) Farewell Spit (▷ 111). The small seaside village of Pohara, about 10km (6 miles) northeast of Takaka on the road to the northern boundary of the Abel Tasman National Park, boasts the best local beach and provides safe swimming.

In the town itself the Golden Bay Museum and Gallery (daily 10–4, closed Sun in winter) displays local treasures and a special feature on explorer Abel Tasman's unfortunate first encounter with the local Maori (when four of his crew were killed). The gallery next door showcases the cream of local arts and crafts talent. There are many other independent studios and galleries in the area, listed in the free *Arts of Golden Bay* leaflet, available at the visitor information office.

The odd and shapely karst features of the Labyrinth Rocks (daily 1–5) form an intriguing sight 3km (2 miles) outside the town on Labyrinth Lane. More interesting land formations can be seen at the Grove Scenic Reserve at Clifton. Here a short 10-minute walk brings you to a spot where massive rata trees grow out of curiously shaped limestone outcrops. There are fine views and a fabulous summer flowering of begonias at nearby Begonia House on Richmond Road (Nov–end May daily 10–5; Jun–end Oct Mon–Fri 10–3).

The Abel Tasman Memorial on the headland just beyond Tarakohe, on Totaranui Road, was erected in 1942 to commemorate the tercentenary of the Dutch explorer's arrival. Drive on towards Totaranui and at the base of Wainui Bay is an easy 40-minute walk to the pretty Wainui Falls. The same road can also take you to the northern beaches and walking access points of the Abel Tasman National Park.

TE WAIKOROPUPU SPRINGS

➕ 320 G10 ✉ North of Takaka, Golden Bay 🕐 Daily 💲 Free

The biggest attraction in the Takaka area is the beautiful, crystal-clear Te Waikoropupu, or Pupu Springs. Turquoise waters bubble out of the ground to create the clearest freshwater lake outside Antarctica, with an extraordinary 62m (203ft) of horizontal visibility. It provides a habitat for a wide range of aquatic plants and fish, including brown trout. The main spring has a basin 40m (131ft) across, and there are several smaller springs, identifiable by the white sand thrown up towards the surface by the action of the water. The spring is a sacred Maori site, and bathing in its chilly waters is not permitted.

The source of the water is the Takaka River and its tributaries, which flow over karstified marble to the south, entering swallow holes and flowing through a massive underground cave system until it reaches this outlet.

To get to this peaceful place follow SH60 north of Takaka, turning left just after the bridge over the Takaka River. Follow Pupu Valley and Pupu Springs Road to the parking zone. There are well-maintained paths and boardwalks through forest and swamp, and the reserve can be explored thoroughly in about 45 minutes (access is free). Nearby the Pupu Walkway, which starts at the end of Pupu Valley Road, retraces an old gold-mining water race.

The clear waters of Pupu Springs give exceptional visibility

Vineyards stretch as far you can see; right, Montana Brancott Winery

WAIRAU VALLEY

**World-class wineries in New Zealand's largest
wine-growing region.**

More than 50 wineries operate in the sunbaked Marlborough region, concentrated in the fertile Wairau Valley and producing highly acclaimed Chardonnay, Riesling, Cabernet Sauvignon, Merlot, Pinot noir, sparkling *méthode champenoise* and some of the best Sauvignon blanc in the world. Montana sowed the first seeds of success in the early 1970s and is now the largest winery in the country, joined by a host of other international names and providing a major national export industry.

Like Hawke's Bay in the North Island, the wineries have been quick to take advantage of the influx of summer visitors. Most offer tours, tastings (free or inexpensive) and good restaurants. The vineyards may lack the architectural splendour or variety of Hawke's Bay (▷ 79), but the wine itself is outstanding.

TOURING THE AREA

Several excellent tours offer full- or half-day overviews of the whole Wairau Valley area, taking in the pick of the crop and the widest variety of wine types. There is always an informative commentary on offer—and often a lunch stop, too. If you have particular tastes, many tour operators will create a personal itinerary; and if you wish to explore by yourself there are plenty of maps and leaflets available at the visitor information office. Most of the wineries are located off SH6, west of Blenheim, and the best time of year to visit them is in April, when the vines are ripe for the picking.

Montana Brancott Winery, at Riverlands on Main South Road (SH1) just south of Blenheim (▷ 111), started it all and is well worth visiting (daily 9–5). It is the central venue for the famous Wine Marlborough festival, held in February (▷ 194), where you can sample more than 150 wines.

In addition to wineries there are distilleries, breweries and orchards in the Wairau Valley, producing everything from liqueurs and fruit wines to olive oil. Prenzel Distillery on Sheffield Street, Riverlands Estate is the country's first commercial fruit distillery, with a whole range of products including fruit liqueurs, schnapps and brandies. The Mud House on Rapaura Road (daily 10–5) has an olive shop, crafts, a coffee house and a restaurant.

RATINGS			
Good for food	●	●	●
Specialist shopping	●	●	● ●
Value for money			● ●

BASICS

⊞ 321 H11

ⓘ Sinclair Street, Blenheim, tel 03-577 8080; summer daily 8.30–6.30; winter Mon–Fri 9–5.30, Sat, Sun 9–4

🚌 Services to Blenheim from Christchurch, Nelson and Picton

🚆 Services to Blenheim from Christchurch and Picton

✈ Airport on Middle Renwick Road, 7km (4 miles) west of Blenheim

www.winemarlborough.net.nz

TIPS

● The visitor information office produces a *Wines and Wineries of Marlborough* wine trail map and a broadsheet called *The Marlborough Wine Region*.

● Detailed information about New Zealand wines can be found in the magazine *Cuisine Wine Country*, available in most bookshops and magazine outlets.

CANTERBURY AND THE WEST COAST

From the expansive farms of the Canterbury Plains the region rears up into the jagged peaks of the Southern Alps. Glaciers are the attraction on the west coast, and the star of these great mountains is Mount Cook/Aoraki. Christchurch—the Garden City—is the South Island's largest settlement.

MAJOR SIGHTS

THE SIGHTS

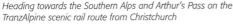

Heading towards the Southern Alps and Arthur's Pass on the TranzAlpine scenic rail route from Christchurch

Lake Brunner, the West Coast's biggest area of fresh water

ARTHUR'S PASS

⊞ 323 F13 ▯ SH73, tel 03-318 9211
▯ Services from Christchurch and Greymouth ▯ TranzAlpine service from Christchurch and Greymouth
www.doc.govt.nz

At the northern edge of Craigieburn Forest Park, road and rail penetrate the vast, open-braided Waimakariri River valley before entering Arthur's Pass National Park. From there it is a short drive to the tiny alpine outpost of Arthur's Pass, 924m (3,031ft) above sea level.

Arthur Dudley Dobson, a pioneer surveyor, first explored the route to the west coast via the east Waimakariri and west Otira river valleys in 1864. A road based on his observations was built within a year; a rail link for the coal and timber trade took another 60 years to complete. To the north, the impressive Otira Viaduct gives a sense of the scale of the engineering challenges.

ARTHUR'S PASS NATIONAL PARK

⊞ 323 F13 ▯ See Arthur's Pass, above

This area of 114,500ha (282,930 acres) extends from Harpers Pass in the northern Southern Alps, to the mountains around the head of the Waimakariri and Otira rivers. Designated a national park in 1929, it embraces mountain ranges, gorges and braided river valleys. One of the highest mountains is 2,270m (7,447ft) Mount Rolleston, southwest of Arthur's Pass. In the eastern part of the park the forests are almost entirely made up of mountain beech, while to the west, on the other side of the Great Divide, the vegetation is more complex, with a variety of podocarp species, beech, kamahi and kaiwakawaka. Many indigenous alpine plant species thrive above

the treeline. The most notable native bird is the green mountain parrot, the kea, which may well fly down to greet you and relieve you of your sandwiches (and your vehicle of anything flexible, from window seals to wipers).

The park has a network of tracks. Braided rivers and their tributaries are notorious for flash floods, so take extra care.

BANKS PENINSULA

See page 122.

CHRISTCHURCH

See pages 124–129.

GERALDINE

⊞ 323 E15 ▯ Corner of Cox and Talbot streets, tel 03-693 1006

Set among the Four Peaks and Peel Forest Mountain ranges, this pleasant country town has a lively arts and crafts community and two museums. The Vintage Car Club and Machinery Museum on Talbot Street (daily 10–4) houses cars and tractors dating back to 1900, and some notable aircraft. A small town museum is on Cox Street (Mon–Sat 10–12, 1.30–3.30, Sun 1.30–3.30) in the 1885 former Town Board office. The town's most unusual attraction is found in the back room of a sweater shop. The shop, called the Giant Jersey, claims to have the biggest sweater in the world: a faithful copy of the Bayeux Tapestry made from a glittering mosaic of more than two million tiny pieces of spring steel, the on-going work of enthusiast Michael Linton. There are good walks in the Talbot Forest Scenic Reserve.

GREYMOUTH

⊞ 320 E12 ▯ Corner of Mackay and Herbert streets, tel 03-768 5101
▯ Mackay Street ▯ TranzAlpine service from Christchurch
www.greydistrict.co.nz

Greymouth is the west coast terminus of the spectacularly scenic TranzAlpine rail journey from Christchurch across the Great Divide and the northern ranges of the Southern Alps. The town was founded during the gold rush, and continued to prosper thanks to the coal and timber industries and its status as the west coast's principal port. The region's mining and nautical past is explored at the History House Museum on Gresson Street (Mon–Fri 10–4).

The Grey River was a famous source of greenstone (*pounamu*), or New Zealand jade, which the Maori sought out. The Jade Boulder Gallery on Guinness Street (Oct–end Apr daily 8.30am–9pm; May–end Sep daily 8.30–5) has a range of crafted greenstone jewels and sculptures, a Jade Discovery Walk, master sculptors at work and a huge, river-polished jade boulder. Also worth a look is the Left Bank Art Gallery on Tainui Street (Nov–end Apr Mon–Fri 10–5, Sat, Sun 10–3; May–end Oct Tue–Sat 10–4), showing the work of west coast artisans in a variety of media.

Shantytown, off SH6 (Rutherglen Road) 11km (7 miles) south of Greymouth (daily 8.30–5), is a re-created 1880s gold-mining settlement complete with shops, bank, saloon, jail, a working sawmill and a steam train which runs daily (9.45–4). You can also try your hand at gold-panning or even tie the knot in the original church.

Lake Brunner (Moana), 37km (23 miles) east of Greymouth, is the west coast's largest lake and one of the prettiest, offering fishing and other water-based activities. Watch for the beautiful white herons (kotuku), which visit outside the summer breeding season.

Top, view from the Akaroa Heritage Path
Above, sheep graze the hill pastures of the peninsula

BANKS PENINSULA

A rugged landscape of hills and flooded harbours formed by two violent volcanic eruptions.

Like the bulb on a jigsaw piece, Banks Peninsula juts out into the Pacific Ocean from Christchurch (▷ 124–129). Its largest harbours are Lyttelton to the north and Akaroa to the south. Akaroa is its main settlement. It has refreshing hill and coastal scenery, historic sites and activities that include cruising and looking for the world's smallest and rarest dolphin, the Hector's dolphin. Captain Cook was the first European to discover the peninsula, but he charted it as an island, naming it after his ship's naturalist, Sir Joseph Banks.

LYTTELTON

Lyttelton, on the opposite side of the volcanic crater of Lyttelton Harbour, is only 12km (7 miles) from Christchurch via the Lyttelton Tunnel. Explorers Robert Falcon Scott and Ernest Shackleton used the port as a base during their Antarctic expeditions, and relics from these heroic times can be seen in the Lyttelton Museum on Gladstone Quay (Tue, Thu, Sat, Sun 2–4). The Lyttelton Timeball Station, high on the hillside off Sumner Road (Wed–Sun 10–5), is the only survivor of three timing contraptions built in New Zealand to aid mariners' calculations of longitude.

Rapapa Island was originally a Maori *pa* and subsequently the base of Fort Jervois, built in 1886 to repel a feared Russian invasion. There are daily sailings (Dec–end Mar 10.20, 12.20; Oct–end Nov, Apr 12.20) to Quail Island, a former leper colony and now a refuge for native birds.

AKAROA

Sprinkled with attractive old colonial wooden houses and picket fences, the pretty village of Akaroa has distinctly French roots. In 1835 Jean Langlois established a whaling station at French Bay and, seeing its potential for settlement, made a down-payment on the land with the local Ngai Tahu Maori. French settlers arrived, knowing nothing of the Treaty of Waitangi (which had placed New Zealand under British sovereignty only 13 days before), and were obliged to sell their claims and integrate. The community's rich history is traced at the Akaroa Museum, on the corner of rue Lavaud and rue Balguerie (Nov–end Apr daily 10.30–4.30; May–end Oct daily 10.30–4). **Don't miss** Barry's Bay Cheese factory tours (Oct–end Apr daily).

The thermal reserve at Hanmer Springs offers the indulgence of naturally heated mineral pools in a landscaped setting

Carving greenstone, or pounamu, at Hokitika

HAAST

322 C14 SH6 beyond Haast River Bridge, tel 03-750 0809 North and southbound services

The Haast region of South Westland contains some of New Zealand's purest ecosystems, taking in mountains, coastal plains and wetlands, dense tracts of forest, swamps, hidden lakes and beaches. From the north, a lush corridor of coastal forest and the 750m (2,460ft) Haast River Bridge brings you to the splintered settlement of Haast, named after German geologist Julius von Haast, who explored the coast in 1863. Several tiny conglomerations make up the community: Haast Junction, Haast Beach, and the remote village of Jacksons Bay. Haast township is inland on SH6.

South of Haast, the unsealed Cascade Road follows the Jackson River valley (a tributary of the Awawata) to tranquil Lake Ellery, then rises to a high point in the valley, where views take in the Cascade Valley and the dramatic glacial sweep of hills to the coast. Inland, the Olivine Range and Red Hills (coloured by magnesium and iron) mark the boundary of Mount Aspiring National Park (▷ 146).

Don't miss at Jackson Bay, the iron-framed grave of Claude Morton Ollivier, who died of pneumonia just weeks after arriving in 1875. The oldest known European grave on the West Coast, it commemorates the first, disastrous attempts at European settlement.

HAAST PASS

322 C15

From Haast township SH6 turns inland and follows the bank of the Haast River before being enveloped by mountains and surmounting the 563m (1,847ft)

Haast Pass, an ancient Maori greenstone trail plagued by floods and landslips. The first of three waterfalls, Roaring Billy, can be viewed on a short loop walk, and about 25km (15.5 miles) farther on, Thunder Creek Falls drop 28m (92ft) into the Haast River. Beyond are the boulders and precipitous rock walls of the Gates of Haast gorge, which foiled road-building attempts until 1960. Above it, Fantail Falls tumble over a series of rocky steps. From here it is a short distance to the Haast Pass and the boundary of Westland and Otago.

Maori greenstone carving, Hokitika

HANMER SPRINGS

320 G12 Amuri Avenue, tel 03-315 7128 Services from Kaikoura and Christchurch

Hanmer's biggest attraction is its Thermal Reserve on Amuri Avenue (daily 10–9). The natural hot springs were first discovered by Europeans in 1859 and became a commercial venture in 1907. Steaming streams connect a series of pools, and the mineral-rich waters range in temperature from a lukewarm 32°C (89.6°F) to a balmy 42°C (107.6°F). The alpine resort is a popular base for mountain bicycling and walking, and in winter for skiing.

HOKITIKA

322 F13 Carnegie Building, corner of Hamilton and Tancred streets, tel 03-755 6166 Tancred Street 1km (0.6 miles) east www.hokitika.org

More gold passed through Hokitika in the 1860s than through any other town on the West Coast. From 1865 to 1867, 37,000 prospectors poured in. Today this is the West Coast's craft capital, attracting crowds to watch glass-blowers and greenstone-carvers and to browse in its galleries, concentrated on Tancred Street. To the south the mountain ranges climb steadily towards the peaks of the Westland Tai Poutini National Park and Mount Cook/Aoraki. Hokitika Gorge, 25km (15.5 miles) east of Hokitika, is crossed via a swinging footbridge—an exciting experience when the river becomes a raging torrent.

KARAMEA

320 F10 Bridge Street, tel 03-782 6652 Services from Westport and Heaphy Track Karamea airstrip

This former frontier settlement, perched on its namesake river-mouth and overshadowed by the peaks of the Kahurangi National Park, is the northernmost town on the West Coast and a base for walkers tackling the Heaphy Track (▷ 112). The limestone caves and arches of the Oparara Basin, 26km (16 miles) north and east of Karamea, are some of the South Island's most remarkable karst scenery. A thick veil of rainforest covers the bizarre formations, creating the eerie mood of a lost world. Bones found in the caves include those of the now extinct New Zealand eagle, with a 3m (10ft) wingspan. Residents include the gradungula spider, the country's biggest, with a leg span of 10cm (4in).

THE SIGHTS

Christchurch

New Zealand's Garden City, where river punts, cricket pitches and parkland serve as reminders of its English roots.

Above, a kea at Willowbank

Stained glass in Christchurch's Anglican cathedral

The snow-capped Southern Alps form the classic city backdrop

RATINGS	
Historic interest	●●●○
Photo stops	●●○
Walkability	●●●○
Shopping	●●●●

BASICS

✚ 323 G14

ℹ Old Chief Post Office, Cathedral Square, tel 03-379 9629; Mon–Fri 8.30–5, Sat, Sun 8.30–4

🚌 Corner of Lichfield and Colombo streets

🚉 Troup Drive, Addington, 3km (2 miles) from downtown. Services to Kaikoura, Blenheim, Picton and TranzAlpine scenic journey to West Coast (▷ 199)

✈ 12km (7.5 miles) northwest of city

www.christchurchnz.net
News, events, visitor information, weather reports, a video introduction to Christchurch, photo gallery and maps.

Opposite, roses flourish in the Botanic Gardens, Hagley Park

Right, a seagull rests on the statue of John Robert Godley (1814–61), founder of Christchurch, outside the cathedral

SEEING CHRISTCHURCH

Christchurch, the largest city in the South Island, has a winning combination of cosmopolitan vivacity, quiet charm and a proud cultural and architectural heritage. Its heart is around Cathedral Square, to the west of the immense, tree-lined Hagley Park, and its borders are known as the Four Avenues: Rolleston Avenue, on the eastern fringe of Hagley Park; Moorhouse Avenue to the south; Fitzgerald Avenue to the east; and Bealey Avenue to the north. One of the most attractive features of the city is the River Avon, which winds its way gently through Hagley Park and downtown from west to east. The city is essentially flat, and has a grid system of streets extending in all directions from Cathedral Square, with most good shopping on the north–south Colombo Street. The central area is easily negotiable on foot.

HIGHLIGHTS

ARTS CENTRE

✚ 127 D3

The lively Arts Centre on Worcester Boulevard occupies the original site of the University of Canterbury. The Gothic-revival buildings now house arts and crafts workshops, galleries, sales outlets, theatres, cinemas, cafés, restaurants and bars. There is a weekend craft market and local entertainment, including buskers. Historical features include the 'den' of physicist Ernest Rutherford (1871–1937), the Great Hall, with its stained-glass windows, and the Townsend Observatory.

AVON RIVER

✚ 126 C3

This pretty river meanders from the northwest tip of the Four Avenues through Hagley Park, the Botanic Gardens and downtown, before continuing through the city's eastern suburbs to the sea. You can feed the ducks, and go punting from the eastern bank, just beyond Cathedral Square and beside the Worcester Street Bridge (summer daily 9–6; winter daily 10–4). Across the bridge and on the right,

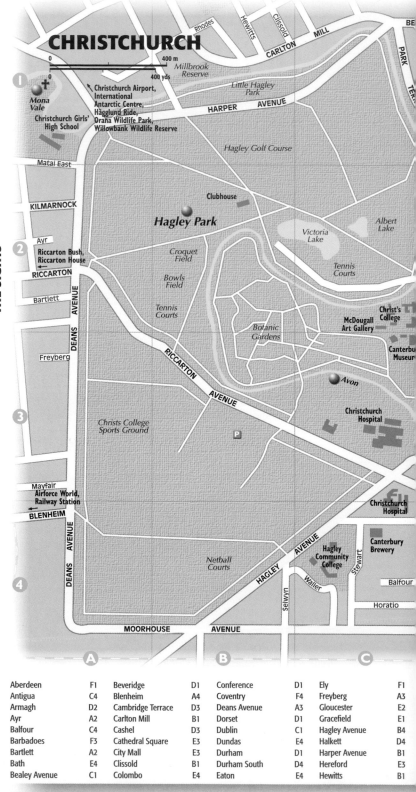

CHRISTCHURCH

0   400 m

0   400 yds

THE SIGHTS

Mona Vale

Christchurch Girls' High School

Christchurch Airport, International Antarctic Centre, Hägglund Ride, Orana Wildlife Park, Willowbank Wildlife Reserve

Millbrook Reserve

Little Hagley Park

HARPER AVENUE

Hagley Golf Course

Matai East

KILMARNOCK

Clubhouse

Hagley Park

Victoria Lake

Albert Lake

Ayr

Riccarton Bush, Riccarton House

RICCARTON

Croquet Field

Tennis Courts

Bartlett

Bowls Field

Tennis Courts

Botanic Gardens

McDougall Art Gallery

Christ's College

Freyberg

RICCARTON AVENUE

Canterbury Museum

Avon

Christs College Sports Ground

P

Christchurch Hospital

Mayfair
Airforce World, Railway Station

BLENHEIM

Christchurch Hospital

Netball Courts

HAGLEY AVENUE

Hagley Community College

Canterbury Brewery

Canterbury Community College

Balfour

Horatio

MOORHOUSE AVENUE

Ⓐ   Ⓑ   Ⓒ

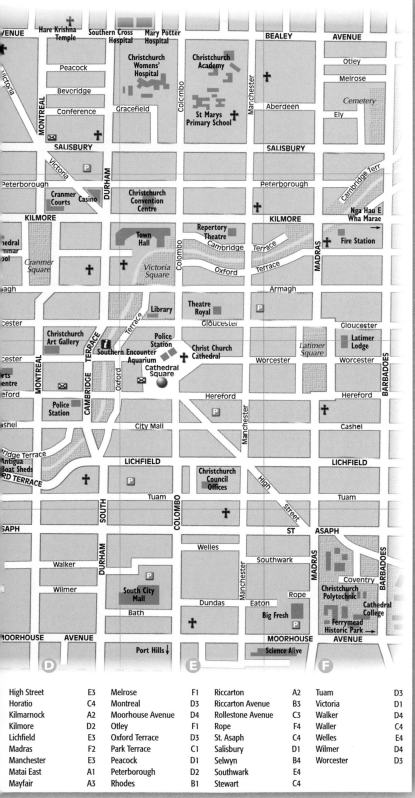

Hare Krishna Temple
Southern Cross Hospital
Mary Potter Hospital
BEALEY
AVENUE
Peacock
Otley
Christchurch Womens' Hospital
Christchurch Academy
Melrose
Bevcridge
Cemetery
Conference
Gracefield
St Marys Primary School
Aberdeen
Ely
Colombo
Manchester
MONTREAL
Victoria
SALISBURY
SALISBURY
Victoria
P
DURHAM
Peterborough
Peterborough
Cranmer Courts
Casino
Christchurch Convention Centre
KILMORE
KILMORE
Cambridge Terr
Nga Hau E Wha Marae
Cranmer Square
Town Hall
Repertory Theatre
Cambridge Terrace
Fire Station
MADRAS
Colombo
Victoria Square
Oxford Terrace
Armagh
Library
Theatre Royal
P
cester
Gloucester
Gloucester
Christchurch Art Gallery
Police Station
Latimer Square
Latimer Lodge
cester
Southern Encounter Aquarium
Christ Church Cathedral
Worcester
Worcester
BARBADOES
MONTREAL
CAMBRIDGE TERRACE
Oxford
Cathedral Square
eford
Police Station
Hereford
Hereford
ashel
City Mall
P
Cashel
Manchester
ridge Terrace
Antigua Boat Sheds
RD TERRACE
LICHFIELD
Christchurch Council Offices
LICHFIELD
P
High Street
SOUTH
Tuam
COLOMBO
Tuam
SAPH
Welles
DURHAM
ST
ASAPH
Walker
Southwark
MADRAS
BARBADOES
Coventry
Wilmer
P
South City Mall
Christchurch Polytechnic
Cathedral College
Bath
Dundas
Eaton
Rope
Ferrymead Historic Park →
MOORHOUSE
AVENUE
Port Hills ↓
Big Fresh
P
MOORHOUSE
AVENUE
D
E
F
Science Alive

farther up Worcester Street, is the Christchurch Art Gallery Te Puna O Waiwhetu (Thu–Tue 10–5, Wed 10–9), designed to evoke the river—but dubbed by locals 'a warehouse in a tutu'. More than 3,000sq m (32,292sq ft) of exhibition space are devoted to New Zealand artists such as Charles Goldie and Ralph Hotere, as well as contemporary artworks and national and international shows.

CATHEDRAL SQUARE

✚ 127 E3 🚌 12, 20, 33

Dominated by its Gothic-revival Anglican cathedral, Christchurch's main square underwent a facelift in the late 1990s, resulting in a profoundly controversial display of sharp angles and steel-and-concrete façades. The cathedral itself (tours Mon–Fri 11, 2, Sat 11, Sun 11.30) has an unusual interior design combining Maori and

Striking modern architecture in the heart of the city

Punting on the Avon reveals the city's English origins

The grand Edwardian mansion of Riccarton House

MORE TO SEE

MONA VALE

✚ 126 A1 ✉ 63 Fendalton Road ☎ 03-348 9660 🕐 Summer daily 9.30–4; winter daily 10–3. Gardens: daily dawn–dusk 🎫 Free 🅿
🚌 Airport bus, 9

In 1905 a beautiful Elizabethan-style homestead was built in 5ha (12 acres) of grounds by Annie Townend, who named it after her mother's birthplace in Australia. The homestead is now a restaurant and café, and the surrounding gardens include a lily pond, rhododendrons, azaleas and exotic trees, all set on the River Avon and accessible by punt.

NGA HAU E WHA NATIONAL MARAE

✚ 127 F2 ✉ 250 Pages Road ☎ 03-388 7685 🕐 Mon–Fri 9–4.30; evening performance and *hangi* 6.45 🎫 Free, or by donation; performance from adult NZ$65 🚌 5, 51

The Marae of the Four Winds is the country's largest *marae*, with a beautifully constructed meeting house complete with green-stone-inlaid steps, which should be rubbed for good luck. Guided tours introduce you to Maori culture, and you can stay to experience the evening performance and *hangi* (feast).

European styles, and its spire can be climbed in part, offering a panoramic view of the city.

Two notable characters inhabit the square, one permanently and the other between November and March. The former is the statue of founding father John Robert Godley; the latter is the Wizard, a local eccentric who wears a pointed hat and has been entertaining the masses with his views on life, the universe and everything for decades. The Four Ships Court, a memorial to the first four immigrant ships, stands outside the 1879 Old Chief Post Office (now the i-SITE visitor information office). The tall cone sculpture was commissioned for the millennium celebrations. Guided walks of the city leave from the southeast corner of the Square (Oct–end Apr 10am, 1pm; May–end Sep 1pm).

HAGLEY PARK

✚ 126 B2 🚌 A, 5, 7, 14, 27, 33

This enormous swath of parkland, covering more than 200ha (495 acres), is divided in two by Riccarton Avenue, and comprises tree-lined walkways, sports fields and, in its central reaches, the well-maintained and varied Botanic Gardens (7–dusk; Conservatory Complex 10.15–4). At the entrance to the Botanic Gardens, on Rolleston Avenue, is the Canterbury Museum (daily 9–5), founded in 1867 and housed in an 1870 neo-Gothic building. The museum's highlights are the impressive Maori collection and the Hall of Antarctic Discovery. Just north of the museum is Christ's College (guided tours Oct–end Apr, tel 03-366 8705), New Zealand's most famous public school, built in 1850. At the southern end of Rolleston Avenue you can hire a punt at the Antigua Boat Sheds, a former boatbuilders' premises dating from 1882.

INTERNATIONAL ANTARCTIC CENTRE AND HÄGGLUND RIDE

✚ 126 A1 ✉ Airport (signposted), Orchard Road ☎ 03-358 9896 🕐 Oct–end Mar daily 9–7; Apr–end Sep daily 9–5.30 🎫 From NZ$30, child (3–15) NZ$20; combination ticket NZ$48, child NZ$36 🏧 🅿 🚌 A, 10 from Bus Exchange

Since the turn of the 20th century and the days of polar explorers Scott and Shackleton, Christchurch has been an important point of access to the Antarctic (Scott is also commemorated with a statue by

ORANA WILDLIFE PARK

126 A1 ✉ 743 McLeans Island Road, near airport ☎ 03-359 7109 ⏰ Daily 10–5 💷 Adult from NZ$19, child (5–14) NZ$7, under 5s free, family NZ$45 🚌 Sunshine Shuttle from Cathedral Square, 10 and 1
www.oranawildlifepark.co.nz
New Zealand's largest captive wildlife reserve is set in 80ha (198 acres) of parkland and has a mix of native and international wildlife, with an emphasis on African animals. Giraffes and rhinos are among the inhabitants, along with the ever-popular inquisitive meerkats, and there is a nocturnal kiwi house.

WILLOWBANK WILDLIFE RESERVE

126 A1 ✉ 60 Hussey Road, off Gardiners Road ☎ 03-359 6226 ⏰ Daily 10–10 💷 Adult NZ$20, child (5–15) NZ$10, under 5s free, family NZ$44 🚌 Best Attractions from Cathedral Square
www.willowbank.co.nz
Native wildlife and farm animals are the focus here, with daily guided tours and night and day kiwi-viewing. The reserve has a very successful kiwi-breeding programme. You can also see the cheeky kea (mountain parrots) being fed.

his widow Kathleen on Worcester Boulevard). The Antarctic Centre is a working campus occupied by Antarctica New Zealand (managers of New Zealand's scientific activities in the Antarctic), the Antarctic Heritage Trust and other official groups. The visitor centre gives an excellent introduction to the great white continent, with displays including the Snow and Ice Experience—a chill-inducing room kept at -15°C (-5°F) and decked with manufactured snow and ice. The Hägglund is a tracked vehicle originally used by the US and New Zealand Antarctic programmes at Scott and McMurdo bases. A 15-minute ride takes you to see some of the centre's main facilities before giving you a taste of the vehicle's all-terrain abilities on an adventure course.

RICCARTON BUSH AND RICCARTON HOUSE (PUTARINGAMOTU)

126 A2 ✉ 3km (2 miles) west of downtown; entrance to reserve 16 Kahu Road ☎ 03-341 1018 ⏰ Deans cottage daily; homestead Mon–Fri 1–4; tours Sun–Fri 💷 Adult NZ$10, child NZ$5, family NZ$25 🚌 24
www.riccartonhouse.co.nz
The Riccarton Estate, set in 12ha (30 acres) of parkland, was the home of Scottish pioneers and brothers William and John Deans, the first European settlers on the Canterbury Plains. You can see the faithfully restored original 1843 Deans cottage, in which they first lived, and the grand Victorian-Edwardian homestead built by the next generation between 1856 and 1874. Riccarton Bush reserve, Canterbury's sole remnant of kahikatea floodplain forest, has survived for 3,000 years.

BACKGROUND

Given Christchurch's strong and obvious English links, it is ironic that the first European settlers on the Canterbury Plains were Scottish. Brothers William and John Deans settled here in 1843, calling it Riccarton. Five years later the government bought this and surrounding land for more concerted settlement.

In 1849 Robert Godley founded the Canterbury Association (mainly worthies from his old university college of Christ Church, Oxford) to establish a new Anglican settlement. In 1850 the first four ships brought 782 colonists to the whaling base of Lyttelton. Despite the collapse of the Association in 1855, the colony flourished and much of its founding English influence prevails.

Above, Christ's College school was built around an open quadrangle

Below, looking for sport in Mona Vale

Lake Kaniere is home to a variety of waterfowl including crested and little grebes, scaup and teal; see also Drive 12 (▷ 236–237)

Glacier-fed Lake Tekapo, milky turquoise from fine rock dust

LAKE KANIERE

⊞ 323 E13 ❚ Carnegie Building, corner of Hamilton and Tancred streets, Hokitika, tel 03-755 6166

Swimming, water sports, picnicking and walking are all popular at this summer haven about 14km (9 miles) inland from Hokitika. The surroundings of the lake, which is the heart of the Lake Kaniere Scenic Reserve, can be explored on foot or by car, boat or bicycle. The two best short walks are the Kahikatea Walk at Sunny Bight (10 minutes) and the Canoe Cove Walk (15 minutes)—both include good beaches. If you are feeling more energetic, the Lake Kaniere Walkway (four hours), which also starts at Sunny Bight, follows the western shore of the lake to Slip Bay at its southern edge. The road on the eastern edge gives access to the hardest walk (seven hours): the ascent of Mount Tuhua.

LAKE OHAU

⊞ 322 D15 ❚ Northern entrance to Market Place, Twizel, tel 03-435 3124 ▣ Twizel: services from Christchurch and Queenstown ✕ Omarama www.twizel.com

Lake Ohau provides a pleasant diversion off SH8 between Omarama and Twizel. In winter it becomes a ski resort, known for its views and quiet atmosphere. Most activity focuses on Lake Ohau Alpine Village, above the southern shores just west of Lake Middleton, a small sub-lake separated from Ohau by a strip of land. In summer the lake and its surroundings are popular for walking, fishing and mountain bicycling. Six forests lie around its shores, with a number of tracks, access points and campsites.

LAKE TEKAPO

⊞ 322 E14 ❚ Kiwi Treasures, Main Street, tel 03-680 6686 ▣ Services from Christchurch and Queenstown

Between Lake Tekapo and Twizel (▷ 133) is the heart of the Mackenzie Country, where lake and mountain ranges give way to the tussock grasslands of the Tekapo River basin. The SH8 delivers you to the southern shores of Lake Tekapo and the settlement of the same name, where the most famous landmark is a solitary stone church overlooking the lake. The Church of the Good Shepherd was built in 1935 in memory of the Mackenzie Country pioneers, who cleared this land of matagouri and speargrass for Merino sheep. Close by is a statue of a sheepdog—a moving tribute to the high-country shepherd's best friend.

If you have time and a robust vehicle it's worth exploring the unpaved roads on either side of Lake Tekapo. The road to the west passes lakes Alexandrina and McGregor before winding its way north to terminate at the Godley Peak Station. On the eastern side the road travels along the lake's edge past the Mount Hay and Richmond

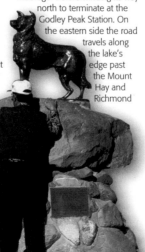

stations before continuing up into the wilds of Macaulay and Godley river basins.

There are plans to open a Mackenzie Heritage Centre in Tekapo.

LEWIS PASS

⊞ 320 G12

From Hanmer Springs, SH7 crosses the northern ranges of the Great Divide (Southern Alps) to the West Coast via the Lewis Pass, Maruia Springs, Springs Junction and Reefton. At the top of the Hope River Valley the road skirts the borders of the Lake Sumner Forest Park and begins to follow the Lewis River to its headwaters and the saddle known as the Lewis Pass, 864m (2,834ft) high.

In pre-European times the Ngai Tahu Maori of Canterbury used this route to access the west coast in search of greenstone. Having negotiated the pass on their return, they are said to have killed their slaves and feasted on their bodily parts. A valley known as Cannibal Gorge immortalises this rather grim tale.

The pass itself was named in 1860 in tribute to pioneer surveyor Henry Lewis. The Lewis Pass offers excellent walks, ranging from one hour to several days, and its lichen-covered beech forests are superb. The five-day St. James Walkway begins near the Lewis Pass summit parking area and is best negotiated in summer or autumn.

Just beyond The Lewis Pass, heading west, is the oasis of Maruia Springs, an attractive Japanese-themed thermal resort.

The bronze statue at Tekapo was sculpted by a farmer's wife in tribute to the dogs that faithfully guarded the remote boundaries of the sheep runs

Icy chunks of the Tasman Glacier float in Terminal Lake

MOUNT COOK/AORAKI NATIONAL PARK

A breathtaking array of mountain peaks crowned by Mount Cook/Aoraki. Training ground of mountaineer Sir Edmund Hillary, who conquered Everest in 1953.

This spectacular 70,696ha (174,690-acre) park backs onto the Westland Tai Poutini National Park (▷ 134–135). The 3,754m (12,316ft) peak of Mount Cook/Aoraki—New Zealand's highest mountain—sits at its heart, towering over lower peaks such as Tasman, at 3,498m (11,476ft), and Mount Sefton, 3,157m (10,361ft), and surrounded by another 19 peaks reaching more than 3,000m (9,840ft). Tipping down from this great chancel are the vast and impressive Hooker and Tasman glaciers. The area is considered sacred by Maori, who see Aoraki as a powerful symbol of being, an ancestor from whom the Ngai Tahu people, the tangata whenua, are descended, and a link between the supernatural and natural world.

MOUNT COOK VILLAGE AND BEYOND

The village is the hub for all activities in the region, including scenic flights and heli-skiing. The only distinctive building is the Hermitage Hotel—the third version to have been built. The original, erected in 1884 farther down the valley, was destroyed by floods in 1913; a second, on the present site, was gutted by fire 44 years later.

In addition to the gargantuan vista of Mount Cook/Aoraki and Mount Sefton, the associate glacier valleys are worthy of investigation. Directly north of the Hermitage is the Hooker Valley. To the east, dwarfing the Wakefield Range, is the vast Tasman Valley, with its own massive glacier—the longest in New Zealand. Both act as watersheds that feed Lake Pukaki, and were once full of ice, hence the incredible expanse of boulder fields that precede the lake waters. Fine glacial moraine (rock flour) gives the glacial lakes their exotic azure shade.

Walks within the park take in every variation, from a strenuous climb to the Muller Hut, 1,768m (5,800ft) up on the ridge of Mount Oliver (the first peak in the region climbed by Edmund Hillary), to the 10-minute Bowen Bush Walk, which starts from behind the Alpine Guides Centre in Mount Cook Village and takes you through classic totara forest. Other tracks lead to the Hooker Valley, Muller Glacier and the Tasman Valley.

RATINGS	
Outdoor pursuits	●●●●●
Photo stops	●●●●●
Walkability	●●●

BASICS

322 D/E14

Bowen Drive, Mount Cook Village, tel 03-435 1818; Oct–end Apr daily 8.30–6; May–end Sep daily 8.30–5

Services to Mount Cook Village from Christchurch and Queenstown

3km (2 miles) south of Mount Cook Village, sightseeing flights

www.mtcooknz.com
Wide-ranging site with information on history, activities and amenities in the region.

TIP

● Always seek up-to-date information on track and weather conditions before embarking on walks in the park, and beware of rock falls.

Above and left, tributes to mountaineer and national hero Sir Edmund Hillary, who trained in this area

131

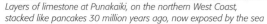

Layers of limestone at Punakaiki, on the northern West Coast, stacked like pancakes 30 million years ago, now exposed by the sea

The Court House, one of many old timber buildings in Reefton

THE SIGHTS

MOUNT SUNDAY

✚ 322 E14

Mount Sunday dominates the Rangitata valley, in stark contrast to the mountainous skyline of the Southern Alps, and was used as the set for Edoras and King Theoden's grand hall in *The Two Towers*, the second of the *Lord of the Rings* movies. From Mount Somers the road leads west through the Ashburton Gorge towards lakes Camp and Clearwater, before opening into a wide tussock valley. A route west towards the end of the valley and the edge of the Mount Harper Range (Harpers Knob) gives a sudden and dramatic view down into the Rangitata valley and, in the far distance, Mount Sunday's prominent outcrop, 611m (2,004ft) high. Direct access to the hill is FORBIDDEN.

PAPAROA NATIONAL PARK

✚ 320 F12 ℹ SH6, Punakaiki, tel 03-731 1895 🚌 Services from Greymouth and Nelson www.doc.govt.nz

Paparoa National Park covers 30,000ha (74,130 acres) on the West Coast, with a predominantly karst (limestone) topography. Its most famous features are the pancake rocks and blowholes of Dolomite Point at the small settlement of Punakaiki. Erosion has produced fluted vertical columns here known as karren, and a 20-minute track loops around lookout points and blowholes. At high tide the spectacle can be amazing, with the ground physically shaking to the thunderous pounding of the waves, and sea spray hissing from the cracks.

Tiromoana, 13km (8 miles) north of Punakaiki, is the northern trailhead for the Inland Pack Track, a 27km (17-mile), two- to three-day route that takes

in the Fox River gorge. This is a system of caves including one 100m (328ft) long, and the 100m-by-30m (328ft by 98ft) Ballroom Overhang, which sits like half an umbrella embedded in the riverbed.

Closer to Punakaiki is the Bullock Creek valley, which leads to Cave Creek—a deeply incised limestone gorge. In 1995 a viewing platform set high above the cavern collapsed, killing 15 students, and as a result there was a complete review of similar structures countrywide.

The area is also home to rare wildlife, such as the Westland black petrel, which nests only on Paparoa's mountains.

PUKEKURA

✚ 322 E13 ✉ 18km (11 miles) south of Ross ☎ 03-755 4144 📠 📧 www.pukekura.co.nz

The population of this tiny west-coast settlement is two: Peter Salter and Justine Giddy. The township was originally a stage-coach stop; a saw mill opened in the 1950s and shut down in the 1980s, and in 1993 Salter and Giddy established the Bushman's Centre here. In later years they bought the pub, houses and heli-pad, which lie within the scenic forest reserve. At the heart is an interactive museum, where you can learn about bushcraft and stroke a pig. Other activities based here include horse trekking, gold-panning and Canadian canoe safaris (▷ 202).

REEFTON

✚ 320 F12 ℹ Broadway, tel 03-732 8391 www.reefton.co.nz

In 1888 this former gold town at the head of the Lewis Pass (▷ 130) became the first town in the southern hemisphere to receive a public electricity supply

and street lighting. Today Reefton has fine fishing in the local rivers and a wealth of walking and mountain bicycling opportunities, mainly within the 180,000ha (444,780-acre) Victoria Conservation Park, the largest forest park in the country.

On the Strand is the Single Fairlie R28 locomotive, the sole survivor of its type. An easy 40-minute walk crosses the river to the former powerhouse that once proudly lit up the town. Blacks Point Museum, just beside SH7 in Blacks Point (summer, Wed–Fri, Sun 9–noon, 1–4, Sat 1–4), has displays about the region's goldfields.

TIMARU

✚ 323 E15 ℹ Landing Service Building, 2 George Street, tel 03-688 6163 🚌 Services from Christchurch and Dunedin

Timaru, halfway between Christchurch and Dunedin, is New Zealand's second biggest fishing port and makes an enjoyable and interesting stop. The South Canterbury Museum, on Perth Street (Tue–Fri 10.30–4.30, Sat, Sun 1.30–4.30), contains exhibits on local maritime history and Maori rock art, of which hundreds of examples can be seen in the area. It also traces the exploits of aviator Richard Pearse (1877–1953), said to have made the first manned flight in 1903, nine months before the Wright brothers of America (▷ 33). A full replica of his impressive flying machine is on display.

The Aigantighe Art Gallery on 49 Wai-iti Road (Tue–Fri 10–4, Sat, Sun 12–4, gardens dawn–dusk), founded in 1956 in a 1908 building surrounded by a sculpture garden, is one of the best art galleries in the country, with works dating back to the seventh century.

Modern Scandinavian chalet-style accommodation at the holiday centre of Twizel

A fur seal basks on the rocks at Cape Foulwind

At Caroline Bay, to the north of the town centre, there's a beach formed in 1877 by land reclamation and harbour development, which provides the focus for the popular Summer Carnival.

TWIZEL

+ 322 D15 | Northern entrance to Market Place, tel 03-435 3124
⊟ Outside information office; services from Christchurch and Queenstown
www.twizel.com

Right in the heart of the Mackenzie Basin stands the rather featureless holiday centre of Twizel, a former hydroelectric-scheme construction town built in the 1970s. Pioneer surveyor John Thompson bestowed the name in tribute to the Twizel Bridge, which crosses the River Tweed on the border between England and Scotland. Twizel's most famous residents are the endangered kaki, or black stilts, which, along with the town's proximity to the Mount Cook National Park, are its biggest draw. Once common in the heartlands and braided-river beds throughout New Zealand, kaki are now one of the rarest wading birds in the world, currently numbering fewer than 100 in the wild. Guided visits to a viewing hide on Lake Ruataniwha, 3km (2 miles) south of Twizel, allow you to view the stalwart survivors and a captive population of 66, bred in enclosed aviaries (late Oct to mid-Apr, daily; winter by prior arrangement only).

WAITAKI VALLEY

+ 325 E16

From Oamaru, SH83 turns through this pretty valley on its way to Omarama, Mackenzie Country and Mount Cook/Aoraki. Its lakes and the Waitaki River are

regulated by an extensive system of hydroelectric dams, and activities include fishing and water sports on lakes Benmore and Aviemore, gliding from Omarama airfield and winter skiing at Lake Ohau (▷ 130). The Clay Cliffs, between Omarama and Twizel, echo the bizarre eroded rock and gravel formations of the Pinnacles in the Wairarapa, North Island (▷ 106).

Travelling from east to west the first settlement of any significance is Duntroon. With the discovery of gold in 1868, the town enjoyed a very brief boom before the diggings proved a failure, earning them the label 'poor man's field'. After a return to relative obscurity, there was more excitement with the discovery of a quartz reef between the Maerewhenua and Otekaike rivers in 1870, but, like the gold, its extraction was short-lived. Duntroon is now a small farming settlement with a number of amenities, activities and scenic attractions. The Elephant Rocks, reached from Livingstone Road, near the Maerewhenua River Bridge, are unusual limestone outcrops, and there are Maori rock drawings at Takiroa, on the other side of the Maerewhenua valley, dating back more than 1,000 years.

West of Duntroon are Lake Aviemore, whose dam has a

1km- (0.6-mile) long fish-spawning race used by up to 3,000 adult trout at a time; and Lake Benmore, with the biggest dam in New Zealand.

WESTLAND TAI POUTINI NATIONAL PARK

See pages 134–135.

WESTPORT

+ 320 F11 | 1 Brougham Street, tel 03-789 6658 ⊟ Services from Greymouth and Nelson ✕
www.westport.org.nz

The West Coast's oldest town has a long main street fed by a flat expanse of orderly blocks and wide roads, and is most often used as an overnight base before heading north to Karamea and the Heaphy Track or south towards Greymouth. The excellent Coaltown Museum on Queen Street South (daily 9–4.30) has a range of displays with an emphasis on coal mining, but also including gold, pioneer and maritime exhibitions. Of note are the simulated walk-through mine and the massive brake drum from the Denniston Incline, with a coal wagon pitched at the incline's 47-degree angle.

Cape Foulwind, 11km (7 miles) south of Westport, is a buttress of land where a fur seal colony thrives on beautiful Tauranga Bay.

Westport's busy main street

Westland Tai Poutini National Park

●

Forested mountains, deep gorges, coastal wetlands and two magnificent glaciers.

*Above, the snout of Fox Glacier
Top, heli-hiking on the ice*

*Sunset reflected in the perfectly
still waters of Lake Matheson*

*Helicopters land visitors on
the glaciers*

RATINGS	
Outdoor pursuits	● ● ● ● ●
Photo stops	● ● ● ● ●
Walkability	● ● ● ●

BASICS

✚ 322 D13–14

ℹ DoC Franz Josef Glacier, southern
end of Franz Josef, tel 03-752 0796;
summer daily 8.30–12, 1–6, winter
8.30–noon, 1–4.45

ℹ DoC Fox Glacier, SH6, northern end
of Fox, tel 03-751 0807; Mon–Fri
9–noon, 1–4.30

🚌 Services to Franz Josef and Fox from
Queenstown and Greymouth

www.doc.govt.nz
Official Department of Conservation
website, covering natural features and
visitor information.

SEEING WESTLAND TAI POUTINI NATIONAL PARK

Westland Tai Poutini National Park is separated from Mount
Cook/Aoraki National Park (▷ 131) by the jagged summits and
peaks of the Southern Alps. To the west of the Alpine Fault the
forests and ravines of the Southern Alps are crowned with permanent snow-fields. Among the glaciers they feed are the two
most famous: Franz Josef (Ka Roimata o Hine Hukatere) and Fox
(Te Moeka o Tuawe), which flow from a height of 3,000m
(9,840ft) at over 1m (3ft) a day, down into forest. Each has its
own access village, offering a variety of walking opportunities
and scenic flights.

HIGHLIGHTS

BRUCE BAY AND LAKE PARINGA

✚ 322 D14 🚌 Atomic Shuttle and Intercity services to Copeland Valley entrance
From Fox Glacier township SH6 winds its scenic way to the most
remote region of the west coast—South Westland. Until 1965 the
road from Fox was rough and petered out at Paringa, and even now
much of South Westland remains unspoiled. South of the heavily
forested Copeland Valley, Bruce Bay is a quiet coastal spot where a
false gold claim was made by three miners during the rush of 1865.
More than 2,000 hopeful prospectors made the long and difficult
journey south, and on realising they had been duped went on the
rampage, destroying the settlement's makeshift stores and shanties.

SH6 continues south, crossing the Paringa River before arriving at
Lake Paringa. The river is the farthest point south that explorer
Thomas Brunner reached in his epic 18-month journey from Nelson
and the Buller Gorge in 1848—a feat marked by a riverside plaque.

FRANZ JOSEF GLACIER

✚ 322 D14 ✉ 5km (3 miles) south of Franz Josef village along Glacier Access Road
New Zealand's steepest and fastest-moving glacier is a dazzling landscape of ice crevasses, pinnacles, caves and ravines descending
almost to sea level through dense rainforest. The juxtaposition of ice
and greenery is unforgettable, and provides an ecosystem found
nowhere else in the world. The glacier access road runs alongside the
cold, grey Waiho River, which appears dramatically from beneath its

● Scenic flights over the
glaciers from above and below
are completely dependent on
good weather conditions,
though guided walks are rarely
cancelled.
● Activities can be reserved
and transportation arranged
at the DoC Information Centre
on Main Road, Franz Josef
(tel 03-752 0288).
● Up-to-date weather forecasts and maps are available at
the DoC information centre.

face. From the parking area you can walk along the wide, rocky
riverbed to within 500m (1,640ft) of the glacier, but to walk on the
glacier itself you must join a guided trip (▷ 200). Perhaps the best
view of the glacier is from the 280m (920ft) viewpoint on Sentinel
Rock, a stubborn remnant of previous glacial erosion, which is easily
reached from the main parking area.

FOX GLACIER

➕ 322 D14 ✉ 5km (3 miles) southeast of Fox Glacier village

Many visitors head for Franz Josef and neglect Fox Glacier, but it is
no less impressive. Fox Glacier valley and the chilly Fox River, which
surges from the glacier terminus, create a significantly different mood,
with precipitous, ice-carved cliffs looming over the village parking
area. Like nearby Franz, Fox can be explored at its terminus independently, or climbed with a guide.

KNIGHTS POINT AND SHIP CREEK

➕ 322 C14 ✉ South of Lake Moeraki

On the coastline south of the National Park, Knights Point gives
spectacular views of sea stacks and virtually inaccessible beaches, and
beyond the viewpoint you may see fur seals dozing on the beach. At
the base of the hill, about 3km (2 miles) south, a small parking area
gives access to Murphys Beach, where, when the tide is out, you can
explore the sweep of sand and the rugged coast.

Farther south is the more popular beach at Ship Creek, where
several excellent short walks explore the beach, the coastal forest and
a small lake between the dunes. In summer it is not unusual to see
Fiordland crested penguins coming ashore to their breeding areas
hidden in the coastal fringe. Ship Creek was named in memory of
a shipwreck on the Australian coast at Cape Otway in Victoria.
The *Schomberg* ran aground on her maiden voyage in 1854, and
several years later pieces of the vessel washed up here, more than
1,500km (930 miles) away.

BACKGROUND

Franz Josef Glacier was sighted and documented by both Abel
Tasman in 1642 and Captain Cook in 1770, but the first thorough
exploration was carried out in 1865 by geologist Julius von Haast,
who named it for the Austrian emperor. Until 1985 the glacier
was receding steadily, but it now seems to be slowing down.
Many are worried that global warming will see the glaciers
recede at an unnatural rate due to a lack of snow at the summits.

LAKE MOERAKI AND MUNROE BEACH

➕ 322 C14 ✉ 18km (11 miles) south
of Lake Paringa

The waters of Lake Moeraki are
popular for swimming, kayaking
and birdwatching, and its outlet
river leads to a wonderful west
coast beach. The parking area
and trailhead to Munroe Beach
are 200m (220 yards) north of
Moeraki River bridge. A path
takes you through forest to the
sands and pounding surf, where,
in the breeding season (Jul–Dec)
or during their late summer moult,
rare Fiordland crested penguins
fight their way through the waves
to waddle into the bush.

*Opposite, waiting for transport
Below, hiking with a guide on
Franz Josef Glacier*

THE SIGHTS

OTAGO AND
THE FAR SOUTH

Queenstown is New Zealand's adventure capital, with world-renowned bungy jumping and jet-boating. The Victorian and Edwardian architecture of Dunedin provides a sedate contrast, with access to the wildlife of the Otago Peninsula. Fiordland, in the far southwest, is the wettest, wildest corner of the country.

MAJOR SIGHTS

Arrowtown's former postmaster's house, now a top-notch B&B

The reservoir of Lake Dunstan generates hydroelectricity

Giant fruit by the town sign indicate Cromwell's claim to fame

ARROWTOWN

⊞ 324 C16 🛈 Lakes District Museum, 49 Buckingham Street, tel 03-442 1824 🚌 Services from Queenstown www.arrowtown.org.nz

This is the best known of New Zealand's former gold-mining settlements, beautifully set beneath the foothills of the Crown mountain range, with pretty tree-lined streets and historic miners' cottages. The Lakes District Museum, on Buckingham Street (daily 8.30–5), depicts the area's chaotic and feverish gold-mining boom (1861–65), and even rents out gold pans for you to try your luck. At the far end of leafy Buckingham Street, reconstructed mud-walled huts illustrate the hardship suffered by Chinese miners.

BLUFF

⊞ 324 C18 🚌 Services from Invercargill

The small port of Bluff heralds the end of the road in the South Island, and is dominated by its aluminium smelter—a jointly run New Zealand-Japanese project. Most visitors come here on their way to or from Stewart Island/ Rakiura (▷ 150), or to photograph the windblasted signpost at the terminus of SH1, which tells them they are several thousand miles from anywhere. En route to the signpost is the quirky Paua Shell House on Marine Parade (daily 9–5), which has become something of a New Zealand legend. Its former owners, Myrtle (who died in 2000) and Fred (who died in 2002) Flutey lined the interior walls with paua shells and amassed a huge collection of other shells.

CATLINS COAST

⊞ 325 C18 🛈 4 Clyde Street, Balclutha, tel 03-418 0388 🚌 Services to Balclutha and Gore from Queenstown, Dunedin and Invercargill www.southland.org.nz

The almost impenetrable coastal forests of the Catlins Coast were thought by the Maori to be the home of a race of hairy giants known as Maeroero. Timbermillers began their relentless destruction of the forest from the 1860s, but a few tracts of podocarp and silver woods have survived and this southeast tip, bordered by the Clutha and Mataura rivers, is still a wonderfully remote area with glorious scenery and rich flora and fauna.

Slope Point, the South Island's southernmost point, can be reached from a roadside parking area and has impressive views of the dramatic headlands. Beautiful Porpoise Bay is a superb place to try and spot Hector's dolphins. At Curio Bay, about 500m (545 yards) west, the petrified stumps and logs of a fossilised forest more than 160 million years old scatter the rock platform.

Both Surat Bay, across the Owaka River 2km (1 mile) south of Owaka, the Catlins' largest town, and Cannibals Bay, north of Owaka, are good places to see Hookers sealions. About 3km (2 miles) east of Owaka is Tunnel Hill Scenic Reserve: the tunnel was dug in 1895 as part of the Catlins River branch railway line, which ran

BLUFF NEW ZEALAND
LATITUDE · LONGITUDE
46°36 min 54 sec SOUTH · 168°21 min 26 sec EAST
AA NEW ZEALAND

EQUATOR
LONDON 18958 km
NEW YORK 15008 km
HOBART 1680 km
CAPE REANGA 1401 km
SYDNEY 2000 km
RUAPUKE ISLAND · WELLINGTON 784 km

between Balclutha and Tahakopa and closed in 1971.

Just beyond the hill is the turn-off to Nugget Point, best visited at sunrise, when the spectacular rock pillars and outcrops take on an orange glow. The islets and rocky, inaccessible coastline are home to seals, yellow-eyed and blue penguins, sooty shearwaters and gannets.

CLYDE

⊞ 325 C16 🚌 Services from Queenstown and Dunedin

The pretty and historic village of Clyde, backed by Clyde Dam and Lake Dunstan (a reservoir), has several notable buildings dating from the 19th century. On Fraser Street, the Clyde Historical Museum and Briar Herb Factory (Dec–end Apr Tue–Sun 2–4), which began processing local thyme in the 1930s, now displays the original machinery and exhibits on early settler life. The Clyde Stationary Engine Museum, at the former railway station on Fraser Street (Sun 2–4), shows stationary steam engines.

CROMWELL

⊞ 325 C16 🛈 47 The Mall, tel 03-445 0212 🚌 Services from Queenstown, Christchurch and Invercargill www.cromwell.org.nz

A sculpture of giant pieces of fruit gives a clue to Cromwell's status as 'the fruit bowl of the south'. Its main point of interest is the Old Cromwell Town Precinct, at the end of Melmore Place, where many restored or reconstructed houses are open for viewing (daily 10–4.30). Former gold-mining sites in the area include the Goldfields Mining Centre, 6km (4 miles) west along SH6 (daily 9–5). It lets you explore historic gold workings, a Chinese settlers' village, gold stamper batteries and a sluice gun.

Dunedin

The South Island's second-largest city, with strong Scottish roots.

Flower stall in The Octagon, Dunedin's central square

A photostop on the scenic Taieri Gorge Railway

Dunedin's university was the first in the country

SEEING DUNEDIN

The influence of Scottish architecture is everywhere in this lively and attractive city: grand buildings of stone, built to last and to defy inclement weather. Its streets share the names of Edinburgh's most famous thoroughfares, and presiding over the scene is a statue of one of Scotland's greatest sons, the poet Robert Burns—his nephew Thomas (1796–1871) was one of the city's founding fathers. Princes Street and George Street combine to form the main downtown route, with the open square of the Octagon, surrounded by grand public buildings, at its heart. Dunedin's beautiful backyard, the Otago Peninsula, is where the only mainland breeding colony of albatrosses thrives, along with rare yellow-eyed penguins and Hooker's sealions (▷ 244–245).

HIGHLIGHTS

ARCHITECTURE

During term time, Dunedin's population is boosted by 18,000 students at New Zealand's oldest seat of learning, founded in 1869. The 1906 railway station at the end of Lower Stuart Street is probably the most famous and photographed building in the country, with stained-glass windows, Royal Doulton tiles, mosaics and brass fittings. The New Zealand Sports Hall of Fame, on the first floor (daily 10–4), celebrates the legacy of more than a century of New Zealand champions. Otago University's grand administration building and clock tower on Leith Street (modelled on Glasgow University) is another fine building.

BOTANIC GARDEN

✉ Opoho Road ☎ 03-477 4000 🕐 Daily dawn–dusk 🎟 Free
There are many New Zealand firsts in Dunedin, including the Botanic Garden, first laid out in 1914. The 28ha (69-acre) site is split into upper and lower gardens that straddle Signal Hill and specialise in rhododendrons, plants from Asia, the Americas and Australia, native species and winter and wetland gardens. Access to the Lower Garden is via Cumberland Street; the Upper Garden via Lovelock Lane.

OLVESTON HOUSE

✉ 42 Royal Terrace ☎ 03-477 3320 🕐 Daily guided tours 9.30, 10.45, 12, 1.30, 2.45, 4 💷 Adult NZ$14.50, child (school age) NZ$5 🚌 Moana Pool

This Edwardian time capsule was built in 1906 and bequeathed to the city in 1966 by the last surviving member of the wealthy and much-travelled Theomin family. The Jacobean-style 35-room mansion had been left unaltered since the death of its first owner, David Theomin, in 1933, and its library, oak gallery and billiard room give a vivid glimpse of prosperous family life in the early 20th century. Contents include ceramics, carpets, arms, antiques, silverware and art acquired by the family during their travels in Asia and Europe.

MORE TO SEE

CHURCHES

Dunedin's churches are worth more than a passing glance, particularly the Gothic First Church of Otago (1873), on Moray Place, and St. Paul's Cathedral (1915), in The Octagon, which contains the only stone-vaulted ceiling in the country.

THE SIGHTS

OTAGO MUSEUM

✉ 419 Great King Street ☎ 03-474 7474 🕐 Daily 10–5 💷 Free; donation of NZ$5 suggested. Tours (daily 11.30) from NZ$10 ♿
www.otagomuseum.govt.nz

Established in 1868, this museum is one of the oldest in the country, housing a staggering 1.7 million items. Its primary themes are culture, nature and science. The Southern Land–Southern People exhibit, the museum's centrepiece, is designed to reflect the beauty and diversity of southern New Zealand, and there is a hands-on Discovery World for children (fee payable).

OTAGO SETTLERS MUSEUM

✉ 31 Queens Gardens ☎ 03-477 5052 🕐 Daily 10–5 💷 Adult NZ$4, child (school age) free ♿
www.otago.settlers.museum/

The emphasis here is firmly on people and transport. Among the permanent exhibits are a couple of monstrous steam engines, and the temporary exhibitions cover unexpected topics such as Scotland's second national drink—tea. There is also an extensive archive.

BACKGROUND

The largest Maori *pa* in this area was on the Otago Peninsula. Following on the trail of the whalers and sealers, Dunedin's permanent settlement was begun in 1842 by Scot George Rennie, who planned a Presbyterian colony in a New Edinburgh of the South. With the discovery of gold the population exploded, growing by 500 per cent between 1861 and 1865. Dunedin was the largest city in New Zealand by the late 1860s—and its grandest buildings date from this period.

DUNEDIN PUBLIC ART GALLERY

✉ 30 The Octagon ☎ 03-474 4000 🕐 Daily 10–5 💷 Free
www.dunedin.art.museum

Traditional and contemporary art are shown in the country's oldest gallery, including an interesting collection of New Zealand works from 1860 to the present day.

TAIERI GORGE RAILWAY

✉ Departs from train station, Anzac Avenue ☎ 03-477 4449 🕐 Oct–end Apr daily 2.30, also Fri, Sun 9.30; rest of year daily 12.30 💷 Adult from NZ$67

The four-hour Taieri Gorge Railway journey encompasses the history and superb scenery of Otago's hinterland. Completed in 1891, the line negotiates the Taieri Gorge, with 12 viaducts, and leads to the Otago Central Rail Trail.

Opposite, Robert Burns' statue in The Octagon
Above, the extraordinary Tunnel Beach, southwest of St. Clair

Fiordland National Park

A vast wilderness area of snow-capped mountains, lakes, forests and fiords.

A helicopter flight offers access into remote Doubtful Sound

Visitors sightseeing from the water in Milford Sound

Mountainous terrain makes this one of the least explored parks

SEEING FIORDLAND NATIONAL PARK

Fiordland National Park, in the remote southwest corner of the South Island, covers 1.25 million ha (3,088,750 acres) and is the largest of New Zealand's 14 national parks. Even when this wettest part of the country is under heavy rain (over 7,500mm/ 300 inches are recorded each year), Fiordland has a moody magnificence, with its high mountains, forested hills and deep inlets. Although the vast majority of the park remains inaccessible, there are more than 5,000km (3,100 miles) of walking tracks. The most accessible of the park's 14 fiords and one of the country's biggest visitor attractions is Milford Sound. For cruises see page 208. See also Lake Manapouri (▷ 144) and Te Anau (▷ 147).

HIGHLIGHTS

DOUBTFUL SOUND

➕ 324 A16 🚌 Excursions by boat then bus from Pearl Harbour, Manapouri www.realjourneys.co.nz

Fiordland's mountain topography is generally lower the farther south you go, and its fiords become longer and more indented with coves, arms and islands. Captain Cook named this Doubtful Harbour in 1770, and did not explore beyond the entrance. It was not until 23 years later that Italian explorer Don Alessandro Malaspina, leading a Spanish expedition, sent a small crew into the fiord.

Doubtful Sound, though not as steep as Milford Sound, offers a sense of space and wilderness, and is the deepest of the fiords at 421m (1,381ft). It has three distinct arms and several superb waterfalls, including the 619m (2,031ft) Browne Falls. At the entrance to Hall Arm is an impressive 900m (2,953ft) cliff. Tours take in the dripping beech forests and a hydroelectric plant, and the sound has its own pod of about 60 bottlenose dolphins.

DUSKY TRACK

🚐 Shuttle services from Te Anau to Manapouri and Tuatapere 🚤 Boat access to southern trailhead from Tuatapere and Manapouri ✈ Floatplane and helicopter services to Supper Cove and Lake Hauroko from Te Anau and Tuatapere

Remote Dusky Sound, at the very heart of Fiordland, is a true wilderness that has changed little since Captain Cook first set foot there.

RATINGS	
Outdoor pursuits	●●●
Photo stops	●●●●●
Walkability	●●●●●

BASICS

➕ 324 A17

ℹ Lakefront Drive, Te Anau, tel 03-249 8900; daily 8.30–5.30; DoC, Lakefront Drive, tel 03-249 7924

🚌 Services from Queenstown and Te Anau to Milford Sound

✈ Te Anau airfield between Te Anau and Manapouri; airfield in Milford

www.doc.govt.nz
Basic information on a link from the government's website.

TIPS

● About 30 tour buses regularly make the 12-hour journey to Milford Sound from Queenstown; most run daily in summer from 11am.
● Remember to take insect repellent: the sandflies at Milford are legendary.

Opposite, the regular point of Mitre Peak is Fiordland's most famous landmark

The Dusky Track offers the widest range of experiences of any track in Fiordland, from glacial valleys and densely forested mountains to the possibility of complete immersion in icy water. Both its location and grade of difficulty make it a challenge that should be attempted only by serious walkers and only in summer.

HUMP RIDGE TRACK
🚌 Services to trailhead from Tuatapere

Opened in late 2000 and privately owned, the Hump Ridge Track is a 60km (37-mile), three-day, moderate-grade circuit track at the south-eastern end of Fiordland National Park, reached from the western end of Bluecliffs Beach. Its main attractions are a mix of coastal and podocarp and beech forest landscapes. It also takes in four viaducts, including the 125m (410ft) Percy Burn Viaduct, reputedly the largest wooden viaduct in the world. Wildlife to look for includes keas,

Water tumbles through the Chasm at Milford

Cruise boats make the most of day trips through the fiords

Admiring the view and the reflections at Mirror Lake

bellbirds, fur seals and Hector's dolphins. Boardwalk is laid through the areas most subject to flooding, but always check on track conditions before departure.

KEPLER TRACK
🚌 Services to trailhead (Lake Te Anau outlet control gates) from Te Anau 🚤 Boat services from Brod Bay

This 60km (37-mile), three- to four-day tramp combines lake, mountain and river valley scenery. After skirting the edge of Lake Te Anau the track climbs to the Luxmore Hut, with one of the best views in Fiordland. From here it negotiates the open tops of the Luxmore Range before descending through silver beech and podocarp forest to the Iris Burn Valley, and back to civilisation via Shallow Bay on Lake Manapouri. At night the forest often echoes with the cries of kiwis.

Cruise boats make the remote sounds accessible to visitors

MILFORD SOUND
🔳 324 B15 ℹ️ Boat Terminal, tel 03-249 8110

The approach to majestic Milford Sound is an exciting experience, with the mountains closing in on either side of Milford Road as you enter the Homer Tunnel, an amazing 1,200m (3,937ft) feat of engineering. You emerge in the spectacular Cleddau Canyon, where in heavy rain the water gushes from the steep outcrops in all directions, and where the Cleddau River has, over the millennia, sculpted round shapes and basins in the rock. Presently, Mitre Peak, at 1,683m (5,552ft), and Mount Tutoko, Fiordland's highest peak at 2,723m (8,934ft), are in view. Facing Mitre Peak is The Lion (1,302m/4,272ft), and behind it is Mount Pembroke (2,045m/6,709ft).

The fiord itself is 15km (9 miles) long and about 290m (951ft) at its deepest, and its mouth is only about 120m (394ft) wide. Cruises along the sound take about two hours. In heavy rains the whole sound can seem like one great waterfall, but by far the most impressive at any time are the powerful 160m (525ft) Lady Bowen Falls, a 10-minute walk from the cruiseboat terminal.

The Milford Deep Underwater Observatory (visits as part of cruise packages or by arrangement, tel 0800-326969) opened in 1995 in the sheltered waters of Harrison Cove, about a third of the way out of the sound on its eastern edge. From its interpretive centre you descend 8m (26ft) into a circular viewing chamber, where you can see at close quarters the very rare black coral (which is actually white)—a species that can live for more than 300 years.

MILFORD TRACK

✉ Independent reservations: 03-249 8514. Guided walks: 03-441 1138/0800 659255 ▣ Services to Te Anau Downs from Te Anau ⛴ Boat services from Te Anau and Te Anau Downs to Glade House (south); from Te Anau and Milford Sound to Sandfly Point (north) ✈ Floatplane services from Te Anau **www.doc.govt.nz**

Often spoken of as the world's greatest walk, this four-day, 53km (33-mile) walk must be booked (Apr—end Oct). Numbers are limited to no more than 100 people entering the track each day either as an independent or a guided walker, and everyone goes in the same direction from south to north to maintain the integrity of the environment. Highlights include the awesome vista from the top of the McKinnon Pass at 1,073m (3,520ft), the Sutherland Falls (New Zealand's highest at 580m/1,903ft), and walking through lush rainforest and beside Milford Sound at the end of the track. It rains a lot here—over 6m (235 inches) a year, and winter conditions can be treacherous. Always consult the Department of Conservation (tel 03-249 7924) before setting off. Reservation well in advance is essential.

BACKGROUND

Fiordland was gouged out by glaciers in the last Ice Age. Flora and fauna that once lived on the ancient supercontinent of Gondwana still thrive in this remote terrain. In 1986 its role in evolutionary history, along with its outstanding natural features, earned the park the status of a World Heritage Area. In 1990 Fiordland and three other national parks—Mount Aspiring, Westland and Mount Cook/Aoraki—were linked to form the UNESCO World Heritage Area of Te Wahipounamu—South West New Zealand, its Maori name meaning place of greenstone.

The Fiordland National Park is noted for its rainfall—all the better for spectacular waterfalls

Negotiating a swing bridge over a gorge on the Routeburn Track

Curious natural spheres of rock, formed around 60 million years ago, litter Hampden Beach at Moeraki

THE SIGHTS

GLENORCHY

➕ 324 B16 ℹ️ DoC Visitor Centre, corner of Mill and Oban streets, tel 03-442 9937 🚌 From Queenstown

The tiny former frontier village of Glenorchy lies 48km (30 miles) northwest of Queenstown via the superb Lake Wakatipu scenic drive, and is surrounded by the rugged peaks of the Fiordland and Mount Aspiring national parks, the glacier-fed Rees and Dart rivers and ancient beech forests. A little settlement aptly named Paradise, 20km (12 miles) farther north in the Dart River valley, became a principal filming venue for the *Lord of the Rings* movies as Isengard. Activities available in Glenorchy include jet-boating and horse-trekking, and the village is the main access point for the Routeburn, Greenstone/Caples and Rees-Dart walking tracks (▷ 246).

GORE

➕ 325 C18 ℹ️ Corner of Hokonui Drive and Norfolk Street, tel 03-203 9288 🚌 Services from Dunedin, Invercargill and Queenstown

Gore, on the banks of the Mataura River, is the Southland region's second-largest town and is most famous for its unusual mix of trout-fishing, country music and its once illegal whiskey-distilling. Attractions include the Hokonui Moonshine Museum and the Gore Historical Museum (Oct–May daily 9–5; Jun–Sep Mon–Fri 9–5, Sat, Sun 1–4), both in the Hokonui Heritage Centre and revealing Gore's days of prohibition and boot-legging. The Reservation (daily 10–5.30), at the top of Coutts Road, has a small menagerie including chinchillas and miniature horses.

INVERCARGILL

➕ 324 C18 ℹ️ Gala Street, tel 03-214 6243 🚉 Leven Street station ✈️ 2km (1 mile) south of city; shuttles www.visit.southlandnz.com

Though not much to look at and sandblasted by the worst extremes of the southern weather, Invercargill is the capital of the richest agricultural region in the South Island. Founded by Scots from Dunedin in 1856 on reclaimed swamp, it is the country's southernmost city, serving a wide farming district.

Its main highlight is the Southland Museum and Art Gallery (Mon–Fri 9–5, Sat, Sun 10–5), housed in a large white pyramid on Victoria Avenue, which includes the excellent tuatara display and breeding project. This reptilian species, older than the land on which you stand, can be seen face-to-face in the Tuatarium; its oldest resident, Henry, is more than 120 years old. Beyond the museum is Queen's Park—80ha (198 acres) of trees, flowerbeds and duck ponds. For a fine view over the city head for the 1889 redbrick Water Tower (Sun 1.30–4.30) on the corner of Gala Street and Queen Drive.

The 30km (19-mile) expanse of Oreti Beach lies 10km (6 miles) west of the city past the airport, and nearby Sandy Point, reached from Sandy Point Road, offers a range of short walks and other recreational activities.

🥾 LAKE HAWEA

➕ 325 C15 ℹ️ 100 Ardmore Street, Wanaka, tel 03-443 1233 ✈️ 11km (7 miles) east of Wanaka www.lakewanaka.co.nz

North of Wanaka on SH6 towards the west coast is Lake Hawea and the small resort settlement of Hawea. Lake Hawea—like nearby Lake Wanaka (▷ 147)—occupies an ancient glacial valley, and only a narrow strip of moraine known as the Neck separates the two. Lake Hawea is noted for its fishing and delightful scenery, with mountain reflections that disappear towards its remote upper reaches, 35km (22 miles) north of Hawea. The lake level was raised by 18m (59ft) in 1958 as part of the Clutha River hydropower system. Hawea itself nestles on the southern shore on the former site of an important and strategic Maori *pa*.

LAKE MANAPOURI

➕ 324 B17 ℹ️ Real Journeys, Pearl Harbour, tel 03-249 7416 🚌 Services from Te Anau and Invercargill

Thirty-five islands disguise the boundaries of Lake Manapouri, which is a forbidding 420m (1,378ft) deep. To appreciate its size and complexity you have to get out on the water, which is on the route to Doubtful Sound. Hidden away on the west arm, right in the heart of Fiordland National Park (▷ 140–143), is the country's largest hydroelectric power station, the source of much controversy and around

Advertising big attraction in

Tulips in bloom in Invercargill's Queen's Park

10 per cent of the country's electricity. A 2,040m (6,693ft), 1:10 tunnel carved into the hillside allows access to the underground machine hall, where seven turbines and generators are fed by the water penstocks from 170m (558ft) above. The most impressive part is the 9.2m (30ft) diameter tailrace tunnel that expels used water at the head of Doubtful Sound, 10km (6 miles) away.

MOERAKI BOULDERS

🔲 325 E16 🚹 Corner of Itchen and Thames streets, Oamaru, tel 03-434 1656 🚌 Tours from Oamaru, Dunedin and Invercargill

According to Maori legend, these strange and much-photographed spherical boulders littering the beach at Moeraki, between Oamaru and Dunedin, are *te kai hinaki*, or food baskets and sweet potatoes, washed ashore after a shipwreck. The scientific explanation is that they are septarian concretions—massive rocks left behind from the eroded coastal cliffs. Their formation is described at the Moeraki Boulderpark Visitor Centre, in a building shaped like the boulders themselves, and in an interpretive panel at the parking area, where the path to the boulders starts. Other, smaller boulders can be seen at Katiki Beach and Shag Point, beyond the village of Moeraki.

The small fishing village of Moeraki, 3km (2 miles) from the ̶oulders, can be reached along ̶ beach by foot or via SH1; ̶fers fishing, swimming, ̶fe cruises (to see the rare ̶r's dolphin) and pleasant ̶ walks, as well as a ̶ lighthouse.

̶UNT ASPIRING
̶TIONAL PARK

46.

Yellow-eyed penguins come ashore to their burrows at night

OAMARU

A limestone town of grand architecture, and a haven for rare penguins.

🔲 325 E16

🚹 Corner of Itchen and Thames streets, tel 03-434 1656; Dec–Easter Mon–Fri 9–6, Sat, Sun 10–5; Easter–end Nov Mon–Fri 9–5, Sat, Sun 10–4

🚌 All major east coast services; summer service (Mon, Wed, Fri) from Mount Cook

www.tourismwaitaki.co.nz
Well-designed website that covers the whole Waitaki district.

RATINGS	
Historic interest	●●●○
Outdoor pursuits	●●●○
Specialist shopping	●●○

TIPS
● For local crafts and produce visit Harbour and Tyne Market, 2 Tyne Street (Saturday, Sunday in summer; Sunday in winter).
● The Janet Frame Heritage Trail (▷ 17) starts from the Oamaru i-SITE.

Oamaru is an intriguing town on the east coast shores of Friendly Bay. Thanks to the prosperity of the 1860s to 1890s and the discovery of limestone that could easily be carved and moulded, the early architects of Oamaru created a settlement rich in imposing, classic buildings, earning it the reputation of New Zealand's best-built town. Styles range from Venetian to Victorian, and antiques shops, craft outlets, secondhand book stores and cafés add to the appeal. The Oamaru steam train (Sun), operated by the Oamaru Steam and Rail Restoration Society, is worth a look, too. The shiny engine hisses into action beside the visitor office to the harbour. The North Otago Museum on Thames Street (Mon–Fri 10.30–4.30) has interesting displays about Oamaru stone.

SEEING THE PENGUINS
No visit to Oamaru would be complete without seeing its penguin colonies. The town has two species in residence: the little blue (the smallest in the world) and the larger, yellow-eyed penguin. There are two colonies and observation points—one at Bushy Beach, where you can watch the yellow-eyed penguins from a hide for free; and the official harbourside Oamaru Blue Penguin Colony (tel 03-443 1195), which charges a fee for access. If you know nothing about penguins the best option is to join a tour, or to visit the official colony, before venturing out alone. The only time to view the penguins is from dusk (specific times are posted at the colony reception)—at other times they are at sea. There is a large covered stand from which you are given a brief talk before the penguins come ashore and waddle to their burrows.

Diamond Lake is a highlight of the national park

BASICS

🞣 322 C15

ℹ 100 Ardmore Street, Wanaka, tel 03-443 1233; summer daily 8.30–6.30; winter 9.30–4.30

ℹ DoC office, Upper Ardmore Street, Wanaka, tel 03-443 7660; daily 8–4.45

🚌 Services to Wanaka from Christchurch, Dunedin and Queenstown; Mount Aspiring Express trailhead connections to Raspberry Creek, Mount Roy and Diamond Lake

✈ Wanaka region airfield 11km (7 miles) east of Wanaka

www.doc.govt.nz
Basic information on a link from the government website.

TIPS

● The park's alpine areas are suitable only for experienced trampers and mountaineers.
● Jet-boat trips are available on the park's larger rivers, such as the Dart and the Wilkin (▷ 207).

MOUNT ASPIRING NATIONAL PARK

New Zealand's third-largest national park, with towering peaks, more than 100 glaciers and unique wildlife.

Like most of New Zealand's majestic national parks, Mount Aspiring has an impressive list of vital statistics. Designated in 1964, the park has been extended to cover 355,000ha (877,205 acres), stretching for about 140km (87 miles) from the Haast Pass to the Humbolt Range at the head of Lake Wakatipu. At its widest point it is 40km (25 miles), and it contains five peaks over 2,600m (8,530ft), including Aspiring itself—at 3,027m (9,931ft) the highest outside the Mount Cook Range.

AWESOME TERRAIN

Glaciers include the Bonar, the Therma and the Volta, and among the wildlife are the New Zealand falcon, the kea and the giant weta. The names associated with the area speak volumes about its terrain: Mount Awful, Mount Dreadful, Mount Chaos, The Valley of Darkness, Solitude Creek and Siberia River are just a few. Wanaka is the main base for trips into the park, and the small settlement of Makarora, about 67km (42 miles) away (almost on the border of the Otago and West Coast regions), acts as the portal to its northern trails and activities.

WALKING IN THE PARK

Mount Aspiring National Park offers endless opportunities for walking and tramping. The 33km (20-mile) Routeburn Track crosses Mount Aspiring and Fiordland national parks between the head of Lake Wakatipu and SH94, the Te Anau–Milford Road.

The walk to Rob Roy Glacier takes one day from the Raspberry Creek parking area in the West Matukituki Valley, along the river and up into the Rob Roy Valley. From here the track follows the chaotic Rob Roy River through beautiful rainforest, revealing occasional view of the glacier above. After about an hour and a half it reaches the treeline and enters a hidden valley rimmed with solid rock walls o waterfall and ice.

Farther up this road, past Glendhu and before the entrance to Treble Cone ski field, is the Rocky Mountain and Diamond Lake with grand views of Mount Aspiring and the Matukituki River V Lake Wanaka, and rocks that form unusual mounds and folds the landscape. It is a stiff climb, but the path is marked and i definitely worth the three-hour round trip.

Items preserved in the Skippers Park Museum, Skippers Canyon

Above, a meadow full of Californian poppies, Mount Iron, Wanaka Below, royal albatrosses breed on the Otago Peninsula

OTAGO PENINSULA

⊞ 325 E17 🛈 48 The Octagon, Dunedin, tel 03-474 3300 🚌 Tour buses from Dunedin

The beautiful Otago Peninsula extends 33km (20 miles) northeast from Dunedin into the Pacific Ocean. Its star attraction is the breeding colony of royal albatrosses on Taiaroa Head, at the very tip—the world's only mainland breeding albatross colony. The first egg was laid here in 1920; the colony now numbers almost 100 and can be seen from the Royal Albatross Centre observatory (Oct–end Mar daily 9–dusk; Apr–end Sep Wed–Mon 10–4, Tue 10.30–4). Rare Stewart Island shags also breed on the headland. Watch one of the rarest penguin species in the world from the Yellow-eyed Penguin Conservation Reserve or Penguin Place at Harington Point (Oct–end Apr daily from 10.15; May–end Sep daily 3.15–4.45). You also can visit the Department of Conservation hide at Sandfly Bay at dawn or dusk.

Larnach Castle (daily 9–5), a Scottish-style Baronial mansion perched on the highest point of the peninsula off Castlewood Road, is the former residence of William Larnach (1833–98), a politician and financier known for is personal excesses.

QUEENSTOWN

pages 148–149.

RIVERTON

B18 🛈 127 Palmerston Street, 34 9991 🚌 Services from ill

or Aparima, to use its aori name—is the oldest permanent European settlement in Southland and one of the oldest in the country, established in the 1830s. The Riverton Museum, at 172 Palmerston Street (Nov–Easter daily 10.30–4; Easter–Oct daily 1.30–4), houses displays and photos of the early Maori, whaling and gold-mining days, with more than 500 portraits of the early pioneers. The Riverton Rocks and Howell's Point, at the southern edge of Taramea Bay, provide safe swimming, fishing and fine views across to Stewart Island (▷ 150).

SKIPPERS CANYON

⊞ 324 C16 🛈 Corner of Shotover and Camp streets, Queenstown, tel 03-442 4100

Drivers of rented cars are warned at the entrance to the Skippers Canyon road that their insurance does not cover this route. No wonder, given its rough, pot-holed surface and vertiginous 120m (394ft) drops to the Shotover River below—but it's well worth joining a tour from Queenstown to be driven along this spectacular valley.

The road was funded by taxes raised on gold found in the river, and the remains of the gold-mining town of Skippers can be seen at the head of the canyon. The area's majestic mountains and valleys, terraced by the gold-mining process, were used as backdrops in the *Lord of the Rings* movies.

STEWART ISLAND/RAKIURA

See page 150.

TE ANAU

⊞ 324 B17 🛈 Lakefront Drive, tel 03-249 8900 🚌 Services from Christchurch, Invercargill, Dunedin and Queenstown ✈ Between Te Anau and Manapouri

Every summer the township of Te Anau, on the shores of New Zealand's second-largest lake at the edge of Fiordland National Park (▷ 140–143), is inundated by crowds of trampers eager to visit its magnificent surroundings. Lake Te Anau is 61km (38 miles) long and 10km (6 miles) at its widest point. Along its western edge, between the Middle and South Fiords, are the 200m (656ft) Te Anau Caves, whose rock formations, whirlpools, waterfalls and glow-worms can be accessed only on boat trips from Te Anau wharf, which last around 2 hours (several times daily).

WANAKA

⊞ 325 C15 🛈 100 Ardmore Street, tel 03-443 1233 🚌 Services from Christchurch, Dunedin and Queenstown ✈ 11km (7 miles) east of town www.lakewanaka.co.nz

The quiet service town of Wanaka borders the very pretty Roy's Bay, which opens out beyond Ruby Island into the southern and indented bays of Lake Wanaka. The lake occupies an ancient glacier bed more than 45km (28 miles) long. The town becomes a popular ski venue in winter.

One of the most immediate ways to get acquainted with the Wanaka area is to make the 45-minute ascent up Mount Iron (240m/787ft), along a well-marked track starting shortly before the township on the main road.

On SH6, by Wanaka airfield, is the Wanaka Transport and Toy Museum (daily 8.30–5), with more than 15,000 items on display. The NZ Fighter Pilots Museum (daily 9–4) gives a fascinating insight into general aviation history, with a good collection of World War II fighters and trainers.

Queenstown

More than 150 activities in a year-round, 24-hour-a-day adventure capital set among mountains and lakes.

Aerial view of Lake Wakatipu and Queenstown

Boutiques and restaurants flourish around Steamer Wharf

The Mall is busy even in winter, when the town is a ski destination

RATINGS	
Good for food	● ● ●
Outdoor pursuits	● ● ● ● ●
Walkability	● ● ● ●

BASICS

🗺 324 C16

ℹ Corner of Shotover and Camp streets, tel 03-442 4100; daily 7–7

ℹ DoC, 37 Shotover Street, tel 03-442 7935

🚌 Services from Christchurch, Invercargill, Dunedin, Wanaka, Greymouth, Mount Cook, Te Anau and Franz Josef

✈ 8km (5 miles) east in Frankton

www.queenstown-nz.co.nz
Excellent site with links to activities, wineries and places to stay.

Top, Shotover jet-boat ride
Below, bungy jumping

SEEING QUEENSTOWN

Queenstown is the biggest tourist draw in New Zealand, as one of the top adventure venues in the world. More than a million visitors a year partake in a staggering range of activities, from sedate steamboat cruises to heart-stopping bungy jumps. In winter the walking boots are simply replaced by skis. The town is compact and easily negotiable on foot. The main street for information and activity bookings is Shotover Street; the Mall is the principal shopping and restaurant area.

HIGHLIGHTS

A.J. HACKETT BUNGY AND SHOTOVER JET

✉ The Station, corner of Shotover and Camp streets ☎ Bungy 0800-286 495, jet-boat 0800-SHOTOVER ◷ Summer daily 7am–9pm; winter daily 8am–10pm 💵 Bungy from NZ$125; jet-boat adult NZ$95, child NZ$55 www.AJHackett.com; www.shotoverjet.com

The Station is the main pick-up point for these two longest-established activity operators. A. J. Hackett started professional bungy jumps at Kawarau Bridge, 43m (141ft) over the river east of Queenstown, in 1988. Since then he has created the 102m (335ft) Pipeline Bungy over the Shotover River and the 134m (440ft) Nevis Highwire, among others.

Shotover Jet are the only operators to ply the lower reaches of the Shotover River. A 70kph (43mph) jet down the river includes thrilling 360-degree turns.

QUEENSTOWN GARDENS

✉ Marine Parade 💵 Free

Founded in 1867 on a small promontory pointing out into Lake Wakatipu, the gardens offer some respite from the crowds. There are oaks, sequoias and 1,500 roses planted in 26 named rosebeds. At the entrance is the restored 18. Williams Cottage.

REMARKABLES LOOKOUT

✉ Ski field road off SH6 (1 mile) south of Frank.

Although it takes a rugged drive and a scramble to get there, the view of Lake Wakatipu and Queenstown from the Remarkables Lookout is worth every rut and step. Check that the weather is clear, wear warm clothes and sturdy walking boots and make sure that your car will survive the 1,500m (4,920ft) climb up the unsealed road to the ski fields; in winter you may need chains. If the ski field is open you can take a shuttle from Queenstown, and in winter you can use the Shadow Basin Chair Lift from the parking area. In summer, follow the path up the slopes behind the main building to Mid-Station, and from here continue roughly in line with the chairlift to its terminus. The lookout is about 200m (656ft) behind and farther up from this point.

SKYLINE GONDOLA
✉ Brecon Street ☎ 03-441 0101 🕐 Daily 9–dusk 💲 Adult from NZ$20, child (5–14) NZ$9, under 5s free, family NZ$47 ▤ 🍴 ▢
www.skyline.co.nz
A cable car soars up to Bobs Peak, over 450m (1,476ft) above town, where there's a world-class view and a host of activities, including the Ledge Bungy, the Luge, the Sky-Swing, paragliding and helicopter flightseeing. There are also Maori cultural shows (daily from 5.30).

TSS *EARNSLAW*
✉ Steamer Wharf ☎ 0800-656 501 🕐 Oct–end Apr daily every 2 hours, 10–8; winter 12, 2, 4 💲 Adult from NZ$40, child NZ$15
It won't take you long to spot the delightful twin-screw steamer *Earnslaw* plying the waters of Lake Wakatipu from Queenstown Bay. The steamer is named after the highest peak in the region, Mount Earnslaw (2,819m/9,249ft), and was launched at Kingston in 1912. Options include dinner cruises and trips to Walter Peak Station for an insight into farming life.

Top, thrill-seeking on the Sky-Swing
Above, Queenstown is a good place to catch a Maori cultural performance

BACKGROUND
The first European to visit the area was Scotsman Donald Hay, who explored Lake Wakatipu in 1859. Gold was found in the Shotover River Valley in 1862, and within a year some 2,000 hopefuls were camped here. The Shotover is the richest gold-bearing river of its size in the world, but after a decade the gold was exhausted. By the mid-20th century tourism was already taking hold.

TIP
● Despite the wide range of places to stay it is essential to reserve a room two or three days in advance in mid-summer and during the ski season, particularly in mid-July.

Above, golden sands in Post Office Bay; left, Paterson Inlet

BASICS

✚ 324 A15

ℹ️ DoC Visitor Information and Field Centre, Main Road, Oban, tel 03-219 0009; Mon–Fri 8–5, Sat, Sun 9–4

🚐 Shuttle services from Invercargill to coincide with ferries

⛴ Foveaux Express ferries from Bluff Sep–end Apr 9.30–5; May–end Aug 9.30–4.30; Stewart Island Adventures ferries from Bluff 10am daily

✈️ Flights from Invercargill to Halfmoon Bay, Masons, Doughboy, West Ruggedy and Little Hellfire

www.stewartisland.co.nz
Straightforward site packed with information on walks, activities, shops, eateries and wildlife, including a list of resident birds.

www.doc.govt.nz
Basic information on a link from the government website.

TIP

● Only 15kg (33lb) of personal baggage can be flown to Stewart Island/Rakiura, but additional baggage can be taken on subsequent flights.

STEWART ISLAND/RAKIURA (RAKIURA NATIONAL PARK)

One of the country's most unspoiled and ecologically important areas—and New Zealand's newest national park.

Lying 20km (12 miles) southwest of Bluff, across the Foveaux Strait, is Stewart Island/Rakiura, land of the glowing skies. In 2002, 85 per cent of the island was designated a national park. The island is home to 21 threatened plants, some of which are indigenous or occur only on the island. Thanks to the absence of trout, there are 15 native fish species, and birds include mollymawks (a kind of albatross), petrels and shearwaters (muttonbirds), many of which breed on the offshore islets in vast numbers. Even on the main island (and fighting to survive the ravages of introduced vermin), breeding birds include two of the rarest and most unusual in the world: an odd and enchanting flightless parrot called a kakapo (of which only about 60 remain), and—perhaps most famous of all—*Apteryx australis lawryi*, better known as the Stewart Island brown kiwi, the largest and the only diurnal kiwi in New Zealand. Other inhabitants include the rare yellow-eyed penguins and Hookers sealions.

OBAN AND AROUND

Oban, on Halfmoon Bay, is the island's principal settlement. A short, steady climb to Observation Rock, up Ayr Street at its southern end, gives great views of Paterson Inlet and the impenetrable forests that deck its southern shores. Oban's Rakiura Museum (Mon–Sat 10–12, Sun 12–2) traces a history of Maori occupation, whaling, saw-milling, gold-mining and fishing. The beach on the waterfront (Elgin Terrace) is a fine place to sit and watch the world go by, play industrial-size chess, or contemplate the many water-based trips available.

WALKS

Stewart Island/Rakiura has 245km (152 miles) of walking tracks, ranging from short walks around Oban to the Northwest Circuit, a mammoth 125km (78-mile), 10- to 12-day tramp around the island's northern coast with a side trip to climb Mount Anglem (980m/3,215ft), the island's highest peak. All tramping on Stewart Island/Rakiura presents challenges, as the island is so undeveloped and wet underfoot. Information is available from the Department of Conservation.

This chapter gives information on things to do in New Zealand other than sightseeing. It is divided into six regions, which are identified on the map on the inside front cover. Within each region, towns are listed alphabetically.

What to Do

SHOPPING

WHAT TO DO

Wits used to quip that they had visited New Zealand, but it was closed. Not any more. Liberalised trading hours mean you can shop every day in the cities and major towns. Although in the tourist resorts you might be forgiven for thinking there is little to buy except fluffy sheep or kiwis dressed in rugby jerseys, shopping in New Zealand can be a rewarding experience, and the quality of locally made goods is generally high. In the cities, you'll find everything from chic boutiques and old-fashioned department stores to lively markets, factory outlets, craft co-operatives and supermarkets. In many places, undercover suburban shopping malls are replacing traditional central-city shops.

ARTS AND CRAFTS
New Zealand culture has a strong basis in craft. Wherever you go, you'll probably find a gallery, craft co-operative or community market selling paintings, pottery, wood or stone carving, hand-knits, weaving or the produce of country kitchens. Places such as the Christchurch Arts Centre (▷ 124) enable you to meet the artist and buy direct. Much of the art reflects the vibrant blues and greens of the environment. Native woods, such as kauri and rimu, are fashioned into bowls, ornaments and furniture.

MAORI ART
The Maori carvings on canoes and meeting houses depict ancestors and tell traditional stories. Greenstone (New Zealand jade, or *pounamu*)—traditionally used for weapons and symbolic gifts—is now made into jewellery. Pendants, associated with status and fertility, are carved from bone and greenstone and often depict sacred animals or spirits. If you buy such an object, it is customary to offer it as a gift. Paua (abalone) is harvested naturally under strict controls and the shells are a by-product. You can buy the shells polished and varnished, or as iridescent jewellery.

SHEEP PRODUCTS
In a country with an estimated ten sheep to every person, sheepskin and woollen goods are ubiquitous. Choose from jumpers, hats, coats, gloves, full sheepskins and slippers. The knits are usually home-spun, hand-knitted and high quality. Wool is also made into rugged Swanndri bush jackets and luxuriously soft merino underwear. Lanolin is used in popular skin-care products.

CHAIN STORES

NAME	Menswear	Womenswear	For children	Shoes	Cosmetics and toiletries	Sports equipment and clothes	Accessories	Household items	Books, music and DVDs	Perfume	CONTACT
Canterbury of New Zealand	✔	✔	✔			✔	✔				04-238 4719
The CD and DVD Store									✔		0508-289 223
Country Road	✔	✔	✔								0800-105 655
Esprit	✔	✔	✔	✔			✔				09-271 2472
Farmers	✔	✔	✔	✔	✔		✔			✔	09-272 6996
Glassons	✔										03-366 0784
Hallensteins	✔										09-306 2500
Kimberleys		✔									0800 401 701
Kumfs				✔							09-633 2000
Line 7	✔	✔									09-308 7700
Living and Giving								✔			0800-548 464
Michael Hill Jeweller							✔				09-430 4810
Overland Footwear				✔							0800-OVERLAND
PostiePlus	✔	✔									03-339 5700
Smiths City						✔		✔			03-983 3000
The Warehouse	✔	✔	✔	✔	✔	✔	✔	✔	✔	✔	09-489 7000
Whitcoulls									✔		0800-377 831

CLOTHING

You will see the All Black rugby jerseys, made by Adidas, wherever you go, and the original Canterbury Clothing Company (CCC) jerseys worn by other international sides are excellent quality cotton. The company also makes leisurewear, and has stores up and down the country and a factory shop in Christchurch. Christchurch is a good place for all types of outdoor adventure clothing and high-tech sports gear.

New Zealand fashion designers are making a name for themselves and their designs are often available here at a much better price than overseas. Look out for labels such as Zambesi, Karen Walker and Kate Sylvester. Some designers have their own boutiques, but larger cities also have fashion quarters that are worth exploring—try Newmarket in Auckland, Cuba Street in Wellington and High Street in Christchurch.

WINE AND FOOD

New Zealand is best known for Marlborough Sauvignon blanc, but the country also produces other excellent and distinctive wines, including Pinot noir, Chardonnay, Riesling, red blends and sparkling wines. You can buy wine in supermarkets, but you'll get a better range at specialist stores such as the Glengarry chain in Auckland and Wellington and Vino Fino in Christchurch. Many wines are made in such small quantities that they may be available only at restaurants or from the winery itself.

Most New Zealanders shop for food at the supermarket, but the quality is often better and the produce fresher at specialist stores such as the Auckland Seafood Market and Moore Wilson Fresh in Wellington. In the country, buy from roadside stalls and farms selling local produce. Native flower honeys, such as rata and manuka, make attractive gifts. Kiwifruit (zespri) and other fruits are made into chocolates and preserves.

OPENING HOURS

● Most shops open Monday to Saturday 9 to 5 or 5.30pm and have one late shopping night (usually Friday). In larger places and tourist areas, many open on Sunday.
● Large mall multi-complexes open daily.
● Larger supermarket chains open daily 8am to 9pm at least, some 24 hours, and the small convenience stores known as 'dairies' often open until 10 or 11pm.

PAYMENT

Most city shops accept credit cards and take EFTPOS transactions. You may have to pay cash in rural areas and at markets.

TAX REFUNDS

Goods posted direct to overseas destinations are free of the 12.5 per cent GST tax. Many stores offer mailing and shipping services.

In addition to countless individual boutiques and specialist shops, New Zealand has some chain stores, including well-known American names. The chart below gives details of some of them, stating the number of branches each chain has in the country and the telephone number of the main store or head office.

NUMBER OF SHOPS	DESCRIPTION	WEBSITE
14	Rugby shirts, rugby boots and activewear for men, women and children	www.canterburyofnz.com
25	CDs, DVDs, music accessories	www.thecdanddvdstore.co.nz
6	Classic, elegant clothing for men, women and children	www.countryroad.com.au
8	Smart and sporty casual clothing for men, women and children	www.esprit.com
55	Department store selling clothing, accessories, cosmetics and household items.	www.farmers.co.nz
30	Casual fashion for women	www.glassons.co.nz
52	Reasonably priced clothing for men	www.hallensteins.co.nz
14	Fashion knitwear for women	www.kimberleysfashions.com
17	Shoes and boots for women	www.kumfs.com
15	Nautically inspired casual clothing, accessories, America's Cup gear	www.line7.com
9	Household items and gifts	www.livingandgiving.co.nz
50	Mid-priced jewellery	www.michaelhill.co.nz
28	Fashion shoes and boots for women and men	www.overlandfootwear.co.nz
70	Inexpensive clothing for women and men	www.postieplus.co.nz
17	Department store	www.smithscity.co.nz
88	Discount department store	www.thewarehouse.co.nz
81	Books, magazines, cards, videos, DVDs, stationery, artists' materials	www.whitcoulls.co.nz

ENTERTAINMENT

New Zealand has a strong musical culture, both from its Maori roots and from its Pacific Island and European immigrants. Maori history is told through song and story, with games and dances originally devised to train and support warriors. The culture of Kapa Haka is taught in schools and contested in competitions. You can experience a version of it in concert parties in Rotorua and most large cities. Auckland's Pacific Island cultures are expressed in the Pasifika festival (▷ 171). Choral singing is particularly strong in Christchurch, while Dunedin celebrates its Scottish roots in Burns' Night festivities.

Many New Zealand cities have attractive Victorian theatres and modern venues hosting concerts and shows. Drama, orchestral concerts, ballet, dance, comedy, rock and jazz are all well represented, including tours by international performers. In rural New Zealand, people are used to making their own entertainment through amateur theatrical societies, choirs and local DJs.

Wellington Symphonia, Christchurch Symphony (**www.**christchurchsymphony. co.nz) and Dunedin Symphonia, which give regular performances. Christchurch also has a fine choir, the Christchurch City Choir (**www.**christchurchcitychoir. co.nz), which gives several performances a year. Chamber music concerts by local and visiting groups are arranged by Chamber Music New Zealand (**www.**chambermusic.co.nz), with nationwide tours.

MAORI PERFORMANCES
Maori groups in the main cities

Pipe bands are a tradition introduced by Scottish settlers

James Theatre in Wellington. It presents classical and modern works, and tours the country. Contemporary dance tends to be presented by troupes created for specific events. A wide range of dance styles is incorporated in festivals such as Wellington's Dance Your Socks Off (**www.**feelinggreat.co.nz) in September, Auckland's Tempo (**www.**tempo.co.nz) and Christchurch's The Body (**www.**thebody.co.nz), both in September or October.

Traditional posturing for a haka, with extended tongue

DRAMA
The Auckland Theatre Company lacks a home venue and performs in various places. Wellington has a lively drama scene, with professional companies performing at Downstage, Circa and the alternative Bats, as well as touring shows. Christchurch's Court Theatre and Dunedin's Fortune Theatre are both professional companies presenting repertory seasons.

BALLET AND CONTEMPORARY DANCE
The Royal New Zealand Ballet Company (**www.**nzballet.org.nz) is based at the Westpac St.

OPERA
The NBR New Zealand Opera (**www.**nzopera.com) combines companies in Auckland and Wellington. They present several seasons of classic opera a year, to a high standard.

CLASSICAL MUSIC
The New Zealand Symphony Orchestra (**www.**nzso.co.nz) is based in Wellington at the Michael Fowler Centre. It presents classical and modern works and tours widely. The main cities also support excellent semi-professional orchestras—the Auckland Philharmonia (**www.**akl-phil.co.nz),

organise performances for tourists. Check with the visitor information office for details.

CINEMA
Cinemas range from country halls to multi-venue city complexes where the popcorn is pushed as hard as the movie. Most big cities also have art-house cinemas, and most cinemas show first-release films. Many city complexes have daytime showings for parents and children, with prices to match, and specials early in the week. Typical ticket prices range from NZ$8 to NZ$14, with children around NZ$7.

BOOKING TICKETS AND INFORMATION

Ticketek are the main national administrators for information and ticketing; their website (www.ticketek.co.nz) lists up-and-coming shows and events. Other good sources of information are local newspapers—the *New Zealand Herald* in Auckland, the *Dominion Post* in Wellington, *The Press* in Christchurch and the *Otago Daily Times* in Dunedin.

New Zealand has several excellent orchestras

NIGHTLIFE

By world standards, New Zealand nightlife may be nothing remarkable, but there's still plenty to keep you entertained, especially in the cities. Auckland has a humming club life focusing on Karangahape Road, Wellington's Courtenay Place buzzes with night-time activity, Christchurch has the cafés along the restaurant Strip and Dunedin has hangouts popular with students. Queenstown is the place most dedicated to fun, with bars and clubs regularly open until 5am. There are casinos in Auckland, Christchurch, Hamilton, Queenstown and Dunedin, which are open most of the night. By law you need to be 20 to enter a casino, and dress codes are applied.

PUBS AND BARS

Traditionally, pubs in New Zealand were the preserve of hard-drinking men. Such places still exist, typically in rural areas, but in most places you can now enjoy a good beer and conversation in mixed company by a fire in winter or outside in the summer. Some boutique breweries also have their own bars. Irish pubs have become common, and although some are gimmicky, others try to be authentic and have a good selection of beers to match. Many restaurants and cafés have bars with outdoor seating, which are especially popular in summer.

Pubs and bars are generally open from 11am to 10.30pm. They serve a standard range of food, and many have an extended licence to midnight or 3am on weekends. Many also host gigs, some of which don't start until nearly midnight. You need to be 18 and have proof of age.

GAY AND LESBIAN SCENE

Gay sex was only decriminalised in New Zealand in 1986. Although some homophobia still exists, the larger cities are generally gay- and lesbian-friendly.

Gaytravel New Zealand (www.gaytravel.net.nz) and Go Gay New Zealand (www.gaynewzealand.co.nz) give information on gay and lesbian holidays, accommodation, venues, bars and activities, including events such as the Hero Parade (www.gaynz.com) in Auckland and Gay Ski Week (www.gayskiweeknz.com) in Queenstown.

SPORTS AND ACTIVITIES

New Zealanders are avid followers of spectator sports. Sport takes up a sizeable chunk of daily news coverage on television, radio and in newspapers, and armchair enthusiasts can spend all Saturday afternoon tuned into coverage of their chosen sports. As for activities—New Zealanders love the great outdoors. The vast range of outdoor pursuits available is a big attraction to visitors. The major cities are at or near the sea, and the countryside is never far away. Many Kiwis spend their leisure time at the family *bach* (holiday home) by the sea or in the mountains, tramping (hiking) in the bush (native rainforest), fishing from the family boat or gathering shellfish.

SPECTATOR SPORTS

Rugby is the national game, followed obsessively by young and old alike, who don team jerseys and travel to watch

The Coast to Coast is the ultimate endurance race

their heroes in action. Soccer, by contrast, has never really taken off. In summer, cricket is the major sport, and horse racing, motor sport and netball are all popular, New Zealand having won international events in these disciplines. The country also gets behind the national sailing team during the America's Cup, particularly when the event was held in Auckland. New Zealand also prides itself on mounting some of the world's toughest multi-sport events.

CRICKET

Cricket is popular at both local and national levels. During the summer, city parks and rural domains (parks) are filled with white-clad players and the thwack of bat on ball. New Zealand Cricket (**www.nzcricket.co.nz**) operates the New Zealand cricket team, known as the Black Caps, organising test tours and one-day internationals with other nations. It also organises domestic cricket matches, including the State Championship first-class competition and the State Shield one-day competition. On sunny summer days, crowds of New Zealanders equipped with rugs, food and drinks settle on grassy embankments to watch the game, or tune in to the radio to keep score wherever they are on holiday.

ENDURANCE EVENTS

Held in February, the Coast to Coast (**www.coasttocoast.co.nz**, ▷ 15) across the Southern Alps is one of the most gruelling and well-known multi-sport events in the world.

In March, the Ironman New Zealand Triathlon (**www.ironman.co.nz**) draws crowds in Taupo to cheer on the more than 1,450 competitors from 39 countries who swim 3.8km (2.4 miles) in the lake, cycle 180km (112 miles) and run 42km (26 miles) through the town.

Travel in the vicinity is likely to be slow on competition days, as roads may be partly closed.

GOLF

With 400 golf courses—more per person than anywhere else in the world—New Zealand has a full calendar of events at both amateur and professional levels. New Zealand Golf (**www.nzga.co.nz**) organises a number of competitions, including the New Zealand Open, held at a different links each year in February. Also held in February, the NZPGA championship (**www.pgachampionship.co.nz**), held at Clearwater Golf Club in Christchurch, attracts some of the world's top golfers and an estimated 25,000 spectators.

HORSE RACING

Horse racing, in both thoroughbred (the gallops) and harness (the trots) forms, is so popular that even the smallest towns are likely to have a racecourse, and races are held throughout the year. The main events are a great excuse to dress up and drink up: Cup Week in Christchurch in November, which includes the New Zealand Trotting Cup at Addington Raceway and the New Zealand Cup at Riccarton Park; Derby Day at Ellerslie—Auckland Racing Club on 26 December; and the Auckland Cup in March. Details of events are available through Harness Racing New Zealand (**www.hrnz.co.nz**) and New Zealand Racing (**www.nzracing.co.nz**). Bookmaking is banned; wagers are totalisator-based and the minimum bet is NZ$1.

MOTOR SPORTS

Motor sports in all their forms have a keen following, with New Zealand having produced world champions in Formula

One Grand Prix and motor-cycle racing. Although most spectators watch the races on television, you can catch the sound and smell of live action at raceways such as Manfeild (Manawatu) and Ruapuna (Christchurch), the Rally of New Zealand based in Manukau in April or the Asia Pacific World Rally Championships in Whangarei in May. For details of events, see **www.**nzmotorsport.co.nz and **www.**motorcyclesport. co.nz (V8 Supercars, 2L touring cars and karting).

NETBALL
After rugby, the winter sport with the second-highest player numbers is netball (a game

New Zealand excels at the sport of netball

similar to basketball). It is the number one sport for women and is played extensively in schools. The Southern Sting, based in Invercargill, has been a frequent national champion and the national team, the Silver Ferns, has won the world championship several times. Go to **www.**netballnz.co.nz for details of matches.

RUGBY
Rugby Union is the most popular spectator sport in New Zealand, and the fortunes of New Zealand's national rugby team, the All Blacks—the world's best, according to international ranking—are

followed with much enthusi-asm. When they win, it's a national celebration; when they lose, a time of national soul-searching.

Rugby has three levels of competition. The international Tri-Nations is played between New Zealand, South Africa and Australia. Super 14 Rugby, played in late summer and autumn, has teams from regions in the three countries. The domestic teams—the Highlanders based in Dunedin, Crusaders based in Christchurch, Hurricanes based in Wellington, Chiefs in Hamilton and Blues in Auckland—all command passionate regional followings.

At the next level down is the Air New Zealand Cup, which is played in winter and is divided into two pools. The most coveted provincial trophy is the Ranfurly Shield. In addi-tion, there are occasional test matches between Australia and New Zealand. All the main cities have large stadia that host national matches and international tests. It's worth attending a live game, if you can, to catch the atmosphere; otherwise, find a pub with a big screen, where passions among the crowd run equally high. The New Zealand Rugby Union's website (**www.**allblacks.com) gives details of matches.

Rugby League (**www.**rugby-league.co.nz) has a single professional team, the New Zealand Warriors, who are based in Auckland and play in the Australian National Rugby League.

New Zealand is also part of the IRB Sevens World Series (**www.**sevens.co.nz), the New Zealand leg of which is usually held in Wellington.

SAILING
New Zealand sailors have won more than 60 world titles, and sailing is the country's most successful Olympic sport.

Youngsters start early, and you will see them sailing their P-class yachts in regattas all over the country. The Royal New Zealand Yacht Squadron (**www.**rnzys.co.nz) in Auckland is home to Team New Zealand, the only non-US syndicate to have successfully defended the America's Cup. The Club organises events such as the New Zealand Match Racing Championships, held in November. Yachting New Zealand (**www.**yachtingnz. org.nz), the national body for competitive and recreational sailing, has details of events.

SKIING
Competitors in the New Zealand Speed Ski

Christchurch's Jade Stadium is a venue for rugby matches

Championships (**www.**speed ski.co.nz), held at Turoa in October, hurtle down the mountain at speeds of up to 173kph (107mph). Other events include the Australia New Zealand Cup final at Whakapapa in September, the ANZ FIS (International Ski Federation) series held at Mount Hutt in August, and the New Zealand nationals held at Turoa in September. The Ski Racing New Zealand website (**www.**skiracing.org.nz) lists upcoming events.

SURF LIFE-SAVING
Throughout the summer, the main New Zealand beaches

are patrolled by surf life-savers. Surf Life Saving New Zealand (**www**.slsnz.org.nz) trains children in water safety and also holds contests including swimming, running, paddling a surf ski, board or canoe, rowing a surfboat or racing an inflatable rescue boat. The national championships are held every two years, and a tri-nations series between Australia, South Africa and New Zealand is hosted in alternate years.

TENNIS
One of New Zealand's richest sporting events for women, the ASB Classic international women's tennis tournament is part of the WTA Tour and

The thrill sport of bungy jumping was invented in New Zealand

attracts players among the top 25 in the world. It is played in the first week of January each year at the ASB Bank Tennis Centre in Auckland and is followed by the Heineken Open for men. Tickets start from NZ$32. The website of Auckland Tennis (**www**.aucklandtennis.co.nz) carries details.

The ITF International Women's tournament, held at the Renouf Tennis Centre in Wellington, is the largest international tournament in New Zealand for juniors. The Wellington Tennis website (**www**.wellingtontennis.org.nz) has details.

For visitors, New Zealand has become synonymous with outdoor activities, along with adventure sports such as jet-boating, bungy jumping, kayaking, white-water rafting, sky-diving and ever more daring variations on the theme. Queenstown calls itself the Adventure Capital of New Zealand, but most of these activities are available in other tourist spots as well. Ensure that your insurance covers you to participate in such extreme sports.

BUNGY JUMPING
Diving off a very high bridge with a rubber band attached to your ankles is the best known of New Zealand's thrill-seeking activities (▷ 15).

CAVING
Virtually every part of New Zealand has caves, formed in limestone, marble or volcanic rocks. The most important caving areas are at Waitomo, northwest Nelson and north Westland. The region around Waitomo contains most of the North Island's best-known caves. The New Zealand Speleological Society (**www**.caves.org.nz) and many guided tours operate from there.

In Nelson, the marble mountains at Takaka Hill, Mount Arthur and Mount Owen contain New Zealand's deepest and longest caves: the Bulmer Cavern (39km/ 24 miles), Ellis Basin system (28km/17 miles) and Nettlebed Cave (24km/ 15 miles). Harwoods Hole, one of the world's largest sinkholes, is just off the main Motueka–Takaka road.

On the west coast, Karamea has the 13km (8-mile) Honeycomb Hill Cave, with 70 entrances and New Zealand's largest limestone arches. The Nile River caves also have glow-worm and stalactite displays.

Guided caving trips are listed on **www**.newzealand.com.

FISHING
As well as being one of the best trout-fishing areas in the world, New Zealand provides superb sea- and big-game fishing. The prime trout-fishing spots in the North Island are the lakes around Taupo and Rotorua; in the South Island, around Gore in Southland. Both experienced and novice anglers are well catered for, with numerous boat charters and guides. The warm Pacific waters around the North Island attract dozens of salt-water species from snapper to marlin. Areas particularly well geared up for game- and

Fishing for trout in the glacial waters of Lake Pukaki

sea-fishing include the Bay of Islands, Tutukaka (Northland), Whitianga (Coromandel) and Tauranga/Whakatane (Bay of Plenty). Options range from the three-hour novice trip to the highly organised three-day 'Hemingway' trips to catch that prize marlin. Check the **www**.fishing.net.nz website for information.

FLIGHTSEEING
Almost every provincial airport, airstrip or local flying club in New Zealand offers flights in a small, fixed-wing aircraft or a helicopter. There are several operators on the West Coast and the Southern Lakes

district. If you take only one flight, make it the helicopter flight around the glaciers and summit of Mount Cook/Aoraki. For a more sedate ride consider a hot-air balloon trip, available in a number of locations (see the local visitor information office). Alternatively, you can don goggles and scarf and get strapped into a biplane. The flightseeing section of www.newzealand.com lists many of the operators.

FLY-BY-WIRE
This is claimed to be the world's fastest adventure ride, reaching speeds of 171kph (106mph). Brave souls are strapped to what resembles a metal hospital stretcher with a microlight engine on the back and suspended from a wire. Rides are available only in Queenstown.

GOLF
New Zealand has hundreds of golf courses, from those that require a cute wedge shot to avoid sheep to others with well-manicured greens fit for an open championship. They are frequently set in stunning surroundings, overlooking snowy mountains, lakes, seascapes or forests. World-class courses in New Zealand include Formosa in Auckland, Wairakei in Taupo and Millbrook in Arrowtown. The main season is March to October, both because the winters are relatively mild and because in summer many New Zealanders concentrate on water sports. Most courses have clubs for hire. Green fees start at around NZ$15, and attitudes to golfing etiquette tend to be relaxed. The New Zealand Golf website is www.nzga.co.nz.

HIKING
See Tramping, page 161.

HORSE TREKKING
The New Zealand landscape is ideal for horse trekking, and it can be enjoyed around almost every provincial town. Both the experienced and the novice are well catered for in treks lasting from an hour to several days. The approach tends to be informal, and specialised riding gear is not usually necessary. Helmets are provided. For additional information countrywide contact the International League for the Protection of Horses (ILHNZ), www.horsetalk.co.nz, or the national tour organisation via www.ridenz.com.

JET-BOATING
This usually involves whizzing down a river at high speed in remarkably shallow water, and turning 180 degrees. Although it looks scary, it is actually great fun. A New Zealand invention, the jet-boat was developed by a Canterbury farmer, Bill Hamilton, to navigate the shallow local rivers. Jet-boating is now one of New Zealand's best-known adventure activities. Some of the most exhilarating trips are available near Queenstown, the Buller Gorge, and the Waiau, Whanganui and Waikato rivers, but jet-boating is available on most New Zealand rivers. Not all are adrenalin-pumping trips; some (especially in the North Island) are more scenic affairs. The website www.newzealand.com lists many of the operators.

KAYAKING
New Zealand is a renowned playground for kayaking and canoeing, whether on river, lake, sea or fiord. It is also popular as an eco-sensitive way of interacting with wildlife, such as seals, dolphins and birds. Guided trips are particularly popular in the Abel Tasman National Park, but they are also available throughout New Zealand, and kayak operators can be found in just about every major town. Multi-day trips are available in all the main tourist spots, ranging from family-oriented paddles on calm rivers to the adrenalin rush of white water and rapids. The website www.newzealand.com lists many of the operators.

MOUNTAIN BIKING
New Zealand is a paradise for mountain bikers, with a choice of on- and off-road trails in spectacular locations. Cycling is also a great way to see the country, and many operators offer tours in which your gear is carried from one destination to the next. Some even drive you uphill so you only have to ride the downhill sections. Bicycle hire is available in most towns, and

Jet-boating can now be enjoyed all over the country

you can choose from gentle family expeditions to the multi-day Otago Central Rail Trail or heli-biking from mountain peaks. The New Zealand Mountain Bike website www.mountainbike.co.nz is a comprehensive resource.

MOUNTAINEERING
New Zealand's major peaks, although not especially high, are spectacular, challenging and potentially dangerous. The majority are in the South Island. The Mount Cook Range, Mount Aspiring (Wanaka) and the peaks of the Nelson Lakes National Park are the most accessible. Guides are

available and definitely recommended.

Mount Taranaki/Egmont in the North Island is the country's most-climbed mountain. Other grand peaks in the North Island include Mount Ruapehu and the little-climbed (but superb) Hikurangi in Eastland. If you are a novice, seek advice and above all go well prepared: Check the weather forecast and tell someone of your intentions. Many lives have been lost through lack of common sense and over-confidence. Numerous guided trips are available, especially around Taranaki and Mount Cook/Aoraki (Franz Josef and Fox Glaciers).

There's little margin for error on Lake Taupo's golf course

For specialist enquiries contact the NZ Alpine Club, based in Christchurch, **www.**alpineclub.org.nz. The NZ Mountain Guides Association, **www.**nzmga. org.nz, is also good for further information and contacts.

PARAFLYING AND PARAPENTING

Paraflying (also called parasailing) involves sitting on a seat under a parachute being pulled by a boat. Suitable for all ages, it requires no skill and is available at coastal and lake resorts.

Parapenting (or paragliding) is great fun but is difficult to

master. As with skydiving, the novice is taken in tandem with an expert. There is a limited number of tourist venues: Te Mata Peak in Hawke's Bay is the North Island's top site, while Wanaka is the capital for the South Island.

RAFTING

This is another premier New Zealand activity. The principal locations are the rivers of central and east North Island and throughout the South Island. Rivers and the rapids are graded from I to VI. Although the 45-minute trips are great fun and packed with adrenalin-pumping moments, the real rafting experience only comes with a multi-day expedition. Trips are generally well organised and safe; most will even do the campfire cooking for you. The New Zealand Rafting Association's website is **www.**nz-rafting.co.nz.

RIVER SLEDDING

River sledding involves rafting down a river on a bodyboard with little except a wet suit, flippers and a crash helmet. The prime location for this is the Waingongoro River in Hawera.

ROCK CLIMBING

Many locations offer great rock climbing—but remember, you need tuition and a guide. Many places also have climbing walls for practice. Visitor information offices can give you contacts.

SAILING

For the experienced sailor New Zealand—and in particular the Hauraki Gulf, off Auckland, and the Bay of Islands—provides one of the best sailing playgrounds in the world, and novices are well catered for. Try at least a few hours out on the water and, if you can, go on a multi-day trip. Bare boating gives you a choice of any vessel that matches your

expertise. Skippered yacht charter/rental companies are based in Auckland and the Bay of Islands. Picot's (**www.**charterguide.co.nz) has a comprehensive list of yacht charter operators.

SCUBA DIVING

New Zealand has some world-class dive sites, including the Poor Knights Islands off Tutukaka (**www.**diving.co.nz) in Northland, famed for their geology, marine life and water clarity. In many locations local operators will take you for a full- or half-day basic first dive experience. The main diving locations in the North Island are the Hauraki Gulf (Auckland), Whitianga (Coromandel)

Rock climbing requires expertise as well as fitness

and New Plymouth (Taranaki). In the South Island they are the Marlborough Sounds, Fiordland and Stewart Island/Rakiura. There are also many accessible wrecks on the coast. The prime months are February to June. The website **www.**newzealand.com lists many operators.

SKIING AND SNOWBOARDING

New Zealand is the principal skiing and snowboarding venue in the southern hemisphere. Most of the major commercial ski fields are in the South Island. They include Coronet Peak and

the Remarkables near Queenstown (▷ 148), Treble Cone and Cardrona near Wanaka, Mount Hutt, Mount Potts and Porter Heights west of Christchurch, and the Craigieburn ranges, Arthur's Pass, Hanmer Springs and Nelson regions. The choice is vast. For an authentic Kiwi experience, try skiing the club fields, where the facilities are basic and the skiing is challenging, but the welcome is friendly and the cost is comparatively modest. The Canterbury Snowsports Association (**www.**skisouth. org.nz) has 13 affiliated clubs, from Tukino in the North Island to Fox Peak in the South. In the North Island the commercial fields are on the slopes of Ruapehu (Whakapapa and Turoa) in the Tongariro National Park.

There are a number of packages that include lift pass, equipment hire and one or more lessons. For contacts, see **www.**nzski.com, **www.**snow.co.nz, and **www.**brownbear.co.nz.

SKYDIVING
Tandem skydiving is available in many locations throughout both islands. Jumps range in height from 2,744m (9,000ft) to 4,573m (15,000ft). The latter will give you about 40 seconds free-fall. Prices increase the higher you go, although commercial operators will generally not take first-timers beyond 4,570m (15,000ft).

SURFING
The North Island's west coast locations of Raglan and Piha are perhaps the most famous for surfing, but other great surf spots include Whangamata (Coromandel), the Eastland beaches, and the beaches on Surf Highway 45 around Mount Taranaki/Egmont. To get a taste of surfing, try boogie-boarding or bodysurf-

ing. Boogie-boards, about half the size of a surfboard and made of compressed foam, are readily available and inexpensive to buy or rent. The website **www.**surf.co.nz gives an overview of surfing across New Zealand.

SWIMMING
Rotorua and Taupo are the natural hot-pool capitals but there are many other hot springs throughout the country, including Waiwera north of Auckland, Te Aroha in the Waikato, and Hanmer Springs in Canterbury. You can swim in all the lakes in the Rotorua region, except the Green Lake, which is sacred to Maori.

Coastal swimming can be very dangerous, with notorious riptides, so take care and swim only between the flags on beaches patrolled by surf lifeguards. If in difficulties raise your arm and keep it aloft; lifeguards will come to your rescue.

TRAMPING (HIKING)
Not only is tramping one of the principal pastimes for many New Zealanders, it is also the reason many visitors come to the country. There is a vast network of routes and literally thousands of kilometres of track the length and breadth of the country, from the famous and well-trodden Milford Track to the sporadic trail and markers of the lesser-known Dusky Track (▷ 246).

Under the administration and advocacy of the Department of Conservation (DoC), all advertised tracks are clearly marked, well maintained and have designated campsites and huts offering clean water, basic accommodation, cooking facilities and toilets. Detailed tramping information is available, including route descriptions, with the tracks classified by type and fitness required, and

up-to-date weather forecasts. Guided trips are also offered for those who would like to be accompanied by an expert.

A word of warning: Many of the tracks are very busy, so accommodation must be reserved weeks in advance. Always make sure you are well prepared, properly equipped and at the required level of fitness. Unless you are experienced, tramping alone on the more remote tracks is not advisable.

For detailed information about all the major tramping tracks and Great Walks contact the local DoC Field Centre, **www.**doc.govt.nz. For accommodation reservations and information, visit the office

Walking on the Coromandel Peninsula—it's not all trekking

or send an email to: greatwalksbooking@doc. govt.nz.

WALKING
The opportunities are endless and most visitor information offices or regional DoC offices compile lists of the most notable walks in each region.

For New Zealand walk suggestions, ▷ 214–245 or try **www.**doc.govt.nz; another useful site is **www.**sparc.org.nz.

WHALE- AND DOLPHIN-WATCHING
The Bay of Islands and Whakatane are the dolphin-watching and swimming

capitals of the North Island, while Kaikoura in the South Island is world-famous for both dolphins and whales. The tiny, endangered Hector's dolphin can also be viewed from Curio Bay in the Catlins, Southland, and around Banks Peninsula in Canterbury. Encounter success rates are generally very high in New Zealand, to the extent that many operators offer a refund or another trip if the whales and dolphins do not turn up.

WINDSURFING
New Zealand is very well suited to the experienced windsurfer, with endless locations. The Estuary in Christchurch is particularly popular with novices, as you can travel considerable distances without getting deeper than chest height in water. Windsurfing schools and board hire are available at most of the principal beach resorts. Contact **www.**windsurfingnz.co.nz.

ZORBING
Invented in Rotorua, zorbing (**www.**zorb.co.nz) involves climbing into a clear plastic bubble and rolling down a hill (▷ 177). The hair-raising ride lasts about 10 seconds.

HEALTH AND BEAUTY

WHAT TO DO

New Zealand is located on the active volcanic geothermal belt known as the Pacific Rim of Fire, and is dotted with hot spring mineral water sites, the most famous of which are around Rotorua. Local Maori had long known of the geothermal region's therapeutic powers, and in 1840 gave the new town an area of thermal springs 'for the benefit of the people of the world'. The Government lavished money on making Rotorua 'the spa city of the South Pacific', with a sanitarium, bath houses and landscaped gardens to draw people to 'take the cure'. The famous Blue Baths were one of the first public swimming pools in the world to allow mixed bathing for recreation. Thermal springs in other parts of New Zealand have been developed on a less grand scale.

mud baths, steam rooms, wet and dry massage and beauty therapies are available at the major thermal resorts, including Waiwera, Polynesian Spa and Hell's Gate Wai Ora at Rotorua, Taupo Hot Springs Spa at Lake Taupo, and Hanmer Springs. Spa packages are often available, involving a choice of pampering experiences for both men and women, such as aromatic massage, body wraps, facials, manicures and pedicures. Expect to pay from NZ$40 for a half-hour treatment. Similar massage and beauty therapies are available at day spas attached to luxury hotels and lodges, and in the major cities. Beauty salons tend to offer a more limited range of services, such as facials, make-up and manicures.

PUBLIC POOLS
Most of New Zealand's major hot springs have been developed commercially for recreation, with hot pools of varying temperatures, swimming pools, toddlers' pools, hydroslides, picnic areas and cafés. Towels and swimsuits are often available for hire. The main complexes are at Waiwera, Rotorua, Taupo, Te Aroha and Hanmer Springs.

Swimming complexes in the major towns and cities have a variety of pools and recreational facilities. The most modern also offer fitness classes and are equipped with saunas, steam rooms and a gym. Pool entrance starts at NZ$6 adult, NZ$4 child.

SPA TREATMENTS
Spa treatments involving a combination of thermal pools,

GYMS
City-dwelling New Zealanders are keen users of gyms and fitness facilities, which usually provide a range of workout options, including men's, women's and mixed gyms, aerobics classes, weight training, yoga and personal trainers. Some have crèche facilities and a café.

Casual rates are usually available, starting at around NZ$15. Health and fitness venues should be listed in the Yellow Pages of the telephone directory.

FOR CHILDREN

New Zealand is a generally child-friendly destination. Families can happily spend the day at a beach patrolled by lifeguards, take well-marked bush walks, or visit parks and playgrounds for free. During the summer holidays, from mid-December to the end of January, many local councils organise free concerts and family activities. Shopping malls in the big cities have children's play areas, and most public gardens have well-equipped playgrounds for young children. There are swimming pool complexes with hydroslides in most large towns, cinemas have special rates for children, and many attractions such as zoos and theme parks have reasonable family combo prices.

ACTIVITIES AND ATTRACTIONS

In New Zealand, children can do things which may be more expensive in other countries, such as horse-riding, skiing, farm experiences and water sports. Tame versions of jet-boating and rafting are available for families in many places, and although age restrictions apply to activities such as bungy jumping and paragliding, they may be open to children as young as 10.

Many cities and holiday areas have themed attractions that are popular with children.

In Wellington, the national museum, Te Papa, has a range of activities, including Story-Place, a haven for small children.

Visitor information offices are a good source of information about facilities and activities. There are also useful websites:

● Kidz Go! (**www.kidzgo.co.nz**) website and free magazine focuses on Christchurch and Queenstown, Wanaka and Fiordland, with sections on accommodation, activities, free things to do, age limits for adventure activities, and child-minding services.
● Kidsport (**www.**kidspot.com) is an online magazine.
● KidsNewzealand.com (**www.**KidsNewzealand.com) is a shopping and information site for families with children.

FESTIVALS AND EVENTS

From wild foods in Hokitika to art deco in Napier, Kiwis enjoy any excuse for a festival. Whether the official reason is fruit trees in blossom in Hastings, autumn foliage in Arrowtown, or the pohutukawas in the Coromandel, communities celebrate with everything from parades and concerts to art exhibitions, races, shop window competitions, flea markets and balls. In summer many councils sponsor free or low-cost entertainment, with buskers in the street, lunchtime concerts, family picnics and children's activities. Highlights are the free evening concerts in local parks, which draw huge crowds to join in Christmas carols or listen to opera, classical music or popular singers. For many, the most significant national event is Waitangi Day (6 February), when the founding treaty of the nation is celebrated at Waitangi and in *marae* all over the country.

WINE AND FOOD

Almost every city holds a wine and food festival. One of the oldest and best known is Wine Marlborough (February). Held under marquees in a vineyard, it has tastings from local wineries, food stalls, entertainment and seminars on wine-related subjects. At Toast Martinborough (November), the approach is different: You go from vineyard to vineyard, where tastings are matched with food prepared by local chefs, and the music ranges from jazz to string quartets. The focus is on local bounty of a different sort in Kaikoura's Seafest (October) and the Bluff Oyster and Southland Seafood Festival (April).

ARTS

The largest cities hold biennial arts festivals, those in Auckland and Christchurch alternating with the month-long International Festival of the Arts, held in February and March in even years in Wellington. Literary, dance and jazz festivals are held annually in the main cities.

AGRICULTURAL SHOWS

Agricultural and pastoral shows are important events in each region of New Zealand—even in the cities, when the country comes to town. Competitions for prize cattle, sheep-shearing and wood-chopping are held alongside food stalls and funfairs. The most popular are Auckland's Royal Easter Show and Showtime Canterbury, held in Christchurch in November.
● Tourism New Zealand's website has more details (**www.newzealand.com**).

AUCKLAND, NORTHLAND AND COROMANDEL

Auckland is not called 'the City of Sails' for nothing. One in every four Aucklanders is reckoned to have a boat, and a glance at the map gives one reason: The city sprawls around such a narrow strip of land that everywhere the view is of water, beaches, harbours and islands. The same is true in the Coromandel Peninsula and Bay of Islands. Water-based activities are a popular leisure pursuit in the whole northern region—sailing, surfing, windsurfing, water-skiing, kayaking, canoeing, fishing, snorkelling, diving and collecting seafood. The Bay of Islands has an international reputation for game-fishing.

A sophisticated, fashion-conscious city, Auckland has plenty of smart bars and restaurants, a casino complex that dominates the skyline, and a humming club scene based on Karangahape Road. The main focus of performance is the Edge complex in Aotea Square. The city has the excellent Auckland Philharmonia orchestra, and the Auckland Theatre Company produces drama of a high standard. The 'Time Out' section in Saturday's *New Zealand Herald* is a good place to see what's on.

The city's downtown shopping area, Queen Street, is an odd mix of smart and tawdry. While you'll find some of New Zealand's leading fashion designers—such as Kate Sylvester, Trelise Cooper, Zambesi and Karen Walker—in the central city, many also have stores in the chic suburb of Newmarket, where locals prefer to shop. Suburban shopping malls such as St. Lukes are popular for day-to-day shopping, and a wander around the Otara market on a Saturday morning reminds you that Auckland is the largest Pacific Island city.

KEY TO SYMBOLS

⊕	**Shopping**
🎭	**Entertainment**
▽	**Nightlife**
⚽	**Sports**
✪	**Activities**
♡	**Health and Beauty**
✿	**For Children**

AUCKLAND

⊕ AOTEA SQUARE MARKET
Aotea Square, Queen Street, Auckland
Tel 09-307 5493
In the heart of downtown Auckland, this market sets up under sun umbrellas in Aotea Square on Fridays and Saturdays. The stalls are a mix of arts and crafts, Pacific culture, funky fashion and ethnic food, with the added fun of street entertainers.
🎭 Fri–Sat 10–6

⊕ ELEPHANT HOUSE
237 Parnell Road, Parnell, Auckland
Tel 09-309 8740
www.nzcrafts.co.nz
A co-operative owned and operated by local craftspeople, Elephant House sells direct to the public. It carries only items handmade in New Zealand and the range is huge: wood, mobiles, leather, greenstone, clothing, honey and kiwifruit products, ceramics, Maori carving, paua and other jewellery, glass, souvenirs and gifts.
🎭 Mon–Fri 9.30–5.30, Sat, Sun 10–5
🚌 On the Link bus route

⊕ KATE SYLVESTER
47 High Street, Auckland
Tel 09-307 3282
www.katesylvester.com
One of New Zealand's leading fashion designers, Kate Sylvester has a minimalist approach to tailoring and a

quirky sense of humour. Also at 1 Teed Street, Newmarket.
🕐 Mon–Thu 9.30–6, Fri 9.30–7.30, Sat 10–5, Sun 11–4

🏬 OTARA MARKET
Newbury Street, Otara, Auckland
Tel 09-274 0830
On Saturday mornings the Otara shopping centre car park is crammed with stalls serving Auckland's Pacific Island communities, with fruit and vegetables, ethnic ingredients, clothing, Island music, crafts and prepared foods.
🕐 Sat 6–noon 🚍 Bus 487,497
🚗 20km (12 miles) south of Auckland CBD. Take the East Tamaki off-ramp (exit 444) from the Southern Motorway (SH1)

🏬 SMITH AND CAUGHEY'S
253–261 Queen Street, Auckland
Tel 09-377 4770
www.smithandcaughey.co.nz
This elegant, 1880s department store sells classy accessories, clothing, cosmetics, household items, perfume, shoes, stationery and food. Also at 225 Broadway, Newmarket.
🕐 Mon–Thu 9.30–6.30, Fri 9.30–7, Sat 10–5, Sun 10.30–5

🏬 TWO DOUBLE SEVEN
277 Broadway, Newmarket, Auckland
Tel 09-978 9400
www.twodoubleseven.co.nz
Shopping complex with smart international and local fashion boutiques such as Oroton, Polo Ralph Lauren, Esprit, Country Road, Scarpa, Barkers, Max and Keith Matheson. Also food, accessories, CDs, leisure and household items.
🕐 Mon–Wed, Thu, Fri 9–6, Sat 9–6, Sun 10–5 🚌 On the Link bus route
🚗 From downtown Auckland, exit SH1 at Gillies Avenue (exit 431), turn left then first right into Mortimer Pass

🏬 VICTORIA PARK MARKET
210 Victoria Street, West Auckland
Tel 09-309 6911
www.victoria-park-market.co.nz
Recognisable by its tall brick chimney, this shopping mall is housed in the former work-

shops and stables of the furnace that burnt the city's rubbish in the early 1900s. Shops around a cobbled court-yard sell crafts, clothing and souvenirs. Also a food court.
🕐 Daily 9–6 🚌 On the Link bus route
☕ Several cafés

🏬 WESTFIELD DOWNTOWN SHOPPING
11–19 Customs Street West, Auckland
Tel 09-978 5265
Centrally located between Queen Street and the water-front, this brings together more than 60 speciality and service stores under one roof, including fashion, books, handcrafts and souvenirs,

Auckland's Victoria Park Market is a mall with an unusual setting

America's Cup clothing and accessories, sheepskins, jewellery and an international food court.
🕐 Mon–Fri 8–6, Sat 10–6, Sun 10–4

🏬 ZAMBESI
Corner of Vulcan Lane and O'Connell Street, Auckland
Tel 09-303 1701
www.zambesi.co.nz
Zambesi is one of New Zealand's leading fashion labels, that of designer Elisabeth Findlay. Also found at 2 Teed Street, Newmarket (tel 09–523 1000), the shops carry other designer fashion, including Nom D., Martin Margiela, Dirk Bikkemberg

shoes, Comme Des Garçons and Bisonte. Zambesi Man carries leading international and local men's fashion (10 O'Connell Street).
🕐 Mon–Thu 9–6, Fri 9–8, Sat 9–5, Sun 11–4

🎭 AUCKLAND THEATRE COMPANY
Level 2, 108 Quay Street, Auckland
Tel 09-309 0390
www.atc.co.nz
Performs at various venues. Shows are listed on the website.

🎭 THE EDGE
Aotea Square, Queen Street, Auckland
Tel 09-309 2677
www.the-edge.co.nz
Several venues make up The Edge: the multipurpose Aotea Centre, built in 1990 and adjoining Aotea Square; the Auckland Town Hall, built in 1911 and favoured as a concert hall; and the opulent Civic Theatre, built in 1929 as a cinema, and now popular for music theatre.

🎭 MAIDMENT THEATRE
8 Alfred Street, Auckland
Tel 09-308 2383
www.maidment.auckland.ac.nz
Twin theatre complex on the University of Auckland city campus. Events are listed on the website.

🎭 SKYCITY METRO
291–297 Queen Street, Auckland
Tel 09-369 2411
This futuristic building bordering Aotea Square has a six-level atrium and houses an entertainment complex including a 13-screen cinema, Time Out games, Borders bookstore and a food hall.
🕐 Cinema: Mon–Thu, Sun 10–9.30, Fri, Sat 10am–11.30pm 💵 Adult NZ$9–NZ$14, child (3–15) NZ$7–NZ$8.50

🎭 SKYCITY THEATRE
Corner of Federal and Victoria streets, Auckland
Tel 09-363 6010
www.skycity.co.nz
Part of the SKYCITY complex. Hosts live shows and concerts.

🍸 CLASSIC COMEDY AND BAR
321 Queen Street, Auckland
Tel 09-373 4321
www.comedy.co.nz
Professional comedians and new faces entertain from Wednesday to Saturday. The venue also hosts cabaret, films and music. Events are listed on the website.
🕐 Daily 7–late 💷 NZ$10–NZ$20
🍷 Two bars

🍸 DOGS BOLLIX IRISH BAR
2 Newton Road, Auckland
Tel 09-376 4600
www.dogsbollix.co.nz
As well as having all the usual mock-Irish paraphernalia, this bar pulls in the crowds with gigs featuring New Zealand bands, jam sessions and Irish music nights.
🕐 Mon–Wed 3–late, Thu–Sun noon–late 💷 NZ$5 cover charge for some performances

🍸 THE LOADED HOG
204 Quay Street, Viaduct Basin
Tel 09-366 6491
www.theloadedhog.co.nz
A combination of its prime location on the Viaduct Basin, beer brewed on site and good food ensure this is always a popular place. Part of a chain, it serves its own tap lager, draught, wheat beer and dark ale. Paintings of famous New Zealanders adorn the walls.
🕐 Daily 11am–late

🍸 SKYCITY CASINO
Corner of Federal and Victoria streets, Auckland
Tel 09-363 6010
www.skycity.co.nz
Part of the SKYCITY complex, the casino has table games and 1,200 gaming machines.
🕐 Daily 24 hours

🍸 STAIRCASE NIGHTCLUB AND BAR
340 Karangahape Road, Auckland
Tel 09-374 4278
A gay-friendly nightclub and venue on Auckland's nightlife strip, the Staircase has resident DJs, a bar, pool tables and a dance auditorium. It also hosts concerts and events.
🕐 Tue–Sat 4–late

🍸 SURRENDER DOROTHY
175 Ponsonby Road, Ponsonby, Auckland
Tel 09-376 4460
A small gay, lesbian and trans-sexual bar, Surrender Dorothy has a friendly neighbourhood atmosphere with couches

Labelling at the vineyards makes sense for visitors

inside, tables outside, and a ceiling decorated with high-heeled shoes.
🕐 Tue–Sat 5pm–12.30am

🏇 ELLERSLIE RACECOURSE
80–100 Ascot Avenue, Greenlane East, Auckland
Tel 09-524 4069
www.ellerslie.co.nz
Ellerslie is the home of the Auckland Racing Club, which hosts 26 horse-racing events a year. Details of dates are listed on the website. A highlight is the Auckland Cup, held in March. It is also the venue for other major events.
🚆 Take Greenlane off-ramp (exit 433) from SH1

🚢 FULLERS
Fullers Cruise Centre, Ferry Building, 99 Quay Street, Auckland
Tel 09-367 9111
www.fullers.co.nz
Fullers operates ferry services to destinations such as Devonport, Rangitoto and Waiheke Island, and cruises including a 90-minute Harbour Cruise. The day trip to Tiritiri Matangi (▷ 71) is particularly recommended.
🕐 Harbour cruise daily 10.30, 1.30
💷 Harbour cruise adult NZ$30, child NZ$15, family NZ$76

🏟 MOUNT SMART STADIUM
Beasley Avenue, Penrose, Auckland
Tel 09–571 1603
www.mountsmartstadium.co.nz
The main venue for rugby league matches and other sports events, the stadium also hosts celebrity concerts.
🚆 Take Mount Wellington off-ramp (exit 438) from SH1

⭐ AUCKLAND BRIDGE CLIMB
Westhaven Reserve, Westhaven Marina, Auckland
Tel 09-361 2000
www.ajhackett.co.nz
Specially designed walkways provide a safe and not-too-demanding experience with great views over the harbour and city. The experience lasts 1.5 hours and can be combined with bungy jumping. No children under 7, and children 7 to 15 must have written parental consent. Night trips are available on Saturday in summer on request.
🕐 Daily 9, 11.30, 2.30 💷 NZ$65

⭐ DOLPHIN AND WHALE SAFARI
PO Box 105-337, Auckland
Tel 09-357 6032
www.dolphinsafari.com
Trips lasting 4 to 5 hours with a marine research team in the Hauraki Gulf Marine Park viewing dolphins, whales and a variety of seabirds. You can also swim with the dolphins (conditions apply).

WHAT TO DO

⊙ Daily 9.30am (weather permitting) from Pier 3 on the waterfront
▣ Adult NZ$140, child (5–15) NZ$100, family NZ$380

✪ FORMOSA COUNTRY CLUB
110 Jack Lachland Drive, Beachlands, South Auckland
Tel 09–536 5895
www.formosa.co.nz
Best known for its 160ha (395-acre), 18-hole golf course designed by Bob Charles with views over the Hauraki Gulf. Also villa accommodation, fine dining, sports stadium including heated pool.
⊙ From 7am ▣ Green fees with cart from NZ$77

✪ HOWICK HISTORICAL VILLAGE
Bells Road, Lloyd Elsmore Park, Pakuranga, Auckland
Tel 09–576 9506
www.fencible.org.nz
Life in Auckland's colonial past is re-created in this museum of living history, where characters in 19th-century costume inhabit authentic buildings, including a store, church, forge and settlers' houses.
⊙ Daily 10–4 ▣ Adult NZ$13, child NZ$7 (under 5 free), family NZ$35

✪ LIONZONE
Lion Breweries, 380 Khyber Pass Road, Auckland
Tel 09-358 8366
www.lionzone.co.nz
Interactive tour of New Zealand's largest brewery, home of Steinlager and Lion Red, with tastings.
⊙ Wed–Mon 9.30, 12.15, 3 ▣ Adult NZ$15, child (5–15) NZ$7.50, family NZ$40 ▣ On the Link bus route

✪ SAILNZ
Tel 09-359 5987
www.sailnz.co.nz
Experience life on America's Cup racer NZL40 or NZL41. You can become the crew and take the helm, pump the grinders or sit back and enjoy the action.
⊙ Daily, usually 2pm ▣ Adult from NZ$135, child NZ$110

✪ SKY JUMP
SKYCITY, corner of Victoria and Federal streets, Auckland
Tel 0800-SKYJUMP
www.skyjump.co.nz
A harness jump from just above the restaurant of the Sky Tower (▷ 65); maximum weight 120kg (265lbs). No children under 10; written parental consent is required for children aged 10 to 13.
⊙ Daily 10–5.15 ▣ NZ$195

✪ AUCKLAND ZOO (▷ 62)

✪ KELLY TARLTON'S ANTARCTIC ENCOUNTER AND UNDERWATER WORLD (▷ 63–64)

Auckland's Harbour Bridge is a landmark with fabulous views

✪ RAINBOW'S END
Corner of Great South and Wiri Station roads, Manukau City, Auckland
Tel 09-262 2030
www.rainbowsend.co.nz
This theme park has a mix of entertainment, with wild rides like the corkscrew roller coaster and tame rides for the little ones, as well as dodgems, go-karts, bumper boats, mini golf, a pirate ship and interactive games. Refreshments and free parking are available.
⊙ Daily 10–5 ▣ Adult NZ$40, child (4–13) NZ$33, (2–3) NZ$31, under 2 free. Family discounts ▣ Bus 471 or 472 from 55 Customs Street East ▣ Take Manukau off ramp (exit 448) from SH1

CLEVEDON

✪ CLEVEDON COAST OYSTERS
914 Clevedon–Kawakawa Bay Road, Clevedon
Tel 09-292 8017
www.clevedonoysters.co.nz
Buy live oysters direct from the farm and watch them being processed. You can also buy live and smoked mussels and wines from the owner's Pakihi Island vineyard.
⊙ Mon–Fri 7–4.30, Sat 9–2

✪ CLEVEDON GALLERY
9 North Road, Clevedon
Tel 09-292 8660
www.countryknits.co.nz
In this gallery you'll find local arts and crafts, especially knitwear, sheepskins and mohair rugs made from wool, mohair and possum/merino blend yarns. The local information centre is also here.
⊙ Daily 10–5

✪ VIN ALTO
424 Creightons Road, Clevedon
Tel 09-292 8845
www.vinalto.com
A high hillside vineyard inland from Clevedon specialising in Italian grape varieties and traditional Italian wine-making methods, including Retico, made from grapes dried in the Amarone style. Cellar-door tastings, wine museum, shop and wine-tasting lunches of antipasto, tasting of four wines, dessert and liqueur (NZ$50).
⊙ Sep–end Jul Sat, Sun 11–4.30

COROMANDEL TOWN

✪ THE COROMANDEL SMOKING COMPANY
70 Tiki Road, Coromandel Town
Tel 07-866 8793
www.corosmoke.co.nz
Coromandel seafood is smoked daily over native manuka sawdust at this smokehouse and deli. Specialities include mussels, oysters, kingfish, trevally, tarakihi and kahawai. They'll also smoke the fish you catch.
⊙ Daily 9–5.30

WHAT TO DO

WHAT TO DO

✪ COROMANDEL ARGO ADVENTURE TOURS
PO Box 132, Coromandel
Tel 07-866 7667
The Coromandel's mussel farms are a popular recreational fishing ground. Mussel Barge Snapper Safaris take you there on a traditional flat-bottomed wooden scow. Rods are available for hire. If you prefer to stay on land, the same operator takes tours of old gold-mine workings on eight-wheel-drive all-terrain vehicles.
🕐 Daily 🖐 From NZ$35

HAHEI

✪ CATHEDRAL COVE KAYAKS
88 Hahei Beach Road, Hahei
Tel 07-866 3877
www.seakayaktours.co.nz
Explore the dramatic volcanic coastline of the Coromandel Peninsula by kayak in half- or full-day tours, with all equipment provided. The scenery is spectacular and cappuccino is served on the beach to revive you.
🕐 Daily Oct–end May, otherwise on demand 🖐 From NZ$75

KAITAIA

✪ HARRISONS CAPE RUNNER
123 North Road, Kaitaia
Tel 09-408 1033
www.ahipara.co.nz/caperunner
These bus tours to Cape Reinga via Ninety Mile Beach include a break for some exciting sand-dune tobogganing, and a picnic lunch is included in the cost. Harrisons also offer a more personalised 4x4 Reef Runner tour, which includes sand tobogganing.
🕐 Daily 9am 🖐 Adult NZ$45, child NZ$25

KAWAKAWA

✪ ✪ BAY OF ISLANDS ADVENTURE COMPANY
Tirohanga Road, Kawakawa
Tel 09-404 1142
www.bushnbike.co.nz
Guided tours of a 62ha (153-acre) cattle farm on either horseback or quad bikes

explore farmland, native bush and the Tirohanga River. No experience is necessary, and the horse treks are suitable for beginners or advanced riders. Families can opt for a 4x4 safari, and the children can meet the farm animals.
🕐 Daily 🖐 Adult from NZ$55, child NZ$25 🚗 3km (2 miles) north of Kawakawa

KERIKERI

⊞ MAHOE FARMHOUSE CHEESE
SH10, Oromahoe, Kerikeri
Tel 09-405 9681
Bob and Anna Rosevear make Dutch-style cheese out of milk from the cows that line the

Macadamia chocolate by Makana Confections

driveway to the factory on their dairy farm. You can buy the cheeses from the rustic shop.
🕐 Mon–Sat 8.30–5, Sun 10–5
🚗 12km (7 miles) south of Kerikeri on SH1

⊞ MAKANA CONFECTIONS
Kerikeri Road, Kerikeri
Tel 09-407 6800
www.makana.co.nz
A viewing window allows you to watch chocolates being made by hand, often using local ingredients such as macadamia nuts. The shop is elegant, the quality of the chocolates excellent, and you can taste before you buy.
🕐 Daily 9–5.30

MATAKANA

⊞ MORRIS AND JAMES
Tongue Farm Road, Matakana
Tel 09-422 7116
www.morrisandjames.co.nz
Clay dug from the banks of the Matakana River is the inspiration for Morris and James pottery. The showroom, filled with their vibrant ware, has become a popular attraction on the Matakana wine trail. The restaurant is an added draw, serving food on their ceramic ware with local wines.
🕐 Mon–Fri 8–4.30, Sat, Sun 10–5
🍽 Mon, Tue 9–3, Wed–Sun 9–3, 6–9

MATAURI BAY

✪ KAURI CLIFFS GOLF COURSE
Kauri Cliffs, Matauri Bay Road, Matauri Bay
Tel 09-407 0010
www.kauricliffs.com
Aimed at the luxury market, this spectacularly sited golf course overlooks the ocean and is designed to use the natural features of the site. You can stay in beautifully appointed, secluded cottages and dine at the lodge, which also has tennis courts, a swimming pool and fitness centre.
🖐 From NZ$300 a round 🚗 Turn off SH10 at Matauri Bay Road

MERCER

⊞ MERCER CHEESE
Old Great South Road, Mercer
Tel 09-232 6778
You can drive past Mercer without blinking, but it's worth slowing down to stop at the cheese shop. The shelves inside are stacked with fine Dutch-style cheeses, made at the nearby farm, which can be cut to order.
🕐 Daily 10–5

MIRANDA

✪ MIRANDA SHOREBIRD CENTRE
283 East Coast Road, Miranda
Tel 09-232 2781
www.miranda-shorebird.org.nz
More than 60 species of shore-birds congregate here, including the rare wrybill and the New Zealand dotterel, which flock on the tidal flats at the Firth of Thames. Some species fly 12,000km (7,455 miles) from Arctic breeding grounds to over-winter from October to March. The centre has displays, information, birdwatching and accommodation.
🕐 Daily 9–5 💷 Donation 🏠 20km (12 miles) off SH2

⊙ MIRANDA HOT SPRINGS
East Coast Road, Miranda
Tel 07-867 3055
www.mirandahotspring.co.nz
Don't miss a visit to what is reputedly the largest naturally heated mineral pool in the southern hemisphere. The hot springs complex also has a toddlers' pool, private spa, barbecue area and a holiday park next door.
🕐 Daily 8am–9.30pm 💷 Adult NZ$14, child (5–13) NZ$7, (1–4) NZ$4.50 🏠 12km (7 miles) off SH2

MURIWAI

⊛ MURIWAI GOLF CLUB
Coast Road, Muriwai
Tel 09-411 8454
www.muriwaigolfclub.co.nz
This links course is located in a bird sanctuary, on naturally rolling fairways with views of the sea and forests. Book well in advance. ▷ 72
🕐 Daily 7am–4pm 💷 From NZ$35 🏠 Take Muriwai Road off SH16

PAIHIA

⊕ THE CABBAGE TREE
Williams Road and the Maritime Building, Paihia
Tel 09-402 7318
www.thecabbagetree.co.nz
With three outlets in Paihia, the Cabbage Tree has a com-prehensive range of New

Zealand-made products, including men's and women's fashion clothing, All Black merchandise, possum-fur products, knitwear, bone and jade carving, wood, jewellery and paintings.
🕐 Mon–Sat 9–6, Sun 9.30–6

✪ FULLERS BAY OF ISLANDS
Maritime Building, Waterfront, Paihia
Tel 09-402 7421
www.fullers-bay-of-islands.co.nz
Fullers runs ferry services between Paihia and Russell, Opua and Okiato, and catamaran tours around the islands, including the famous Hole in the Rock at Cape Brett, making them the major sight-

Galloping on the sands at Paihia Beach

seeing operator in the region. Choose from lunch cruises, swimming with the dolphins, an island stopover, or land tours to Cape Reinga, Russell and Kerikeri.
🕐 Daily 💷 Adult from NZ$45, child from NZ$25

✪ THE ROCK
Corner of Marsden and Williams roads, Paihia
Tel 09-402 7796
www.rocktheboat.co.nz
Dubbed "the backpackers' cruise ship", this 24-hour trip combines sightseeing with activities such as snorkelling and mussel diving, fishing for your dinner, night kayaking,

dolphin- and penguin-watching, and island walks. You sleep in dormitories or double cabins on a purpose-built craft. Meals are included.
💷 From NZ$148

✪ SALT AIR
PO Box 293, Paihia
Tel 09-402 8338
www.saltair.co.nz
If you want to see a lot in a short time, Salt Air's half-day trip to Cape Reinga combines scenic flights with a 4X4 driv-ing tour. You can also choose from a number of scenic flights around the Bay of Islands by Cessna aircraft or helicopter.
🕐 Daily from 8am 💷 From NZ$115

PAKIRI BEACH

✪ PAKIRI BEACH HORSE RIDES
Rahuikiri Road, Pakiri Beach
Tel 09-422 6275
www.horseride-nz.co.nz
Horseback-riding on the beach is the speciality here. Choose from a one-hour ride to a seven-day trek, taking in the beach, pine forest and native bush. There are horses to suit all ages and skill levels, with tuition available. Overnight accommodation is in cabins with farmhouse cooking.
🕐 Daily 💷 From NZ$40 🏠 SH1 to Warkworth, turn right, follow signs to Leigh and Goat Island Marine Reserve. Continue over the hill to Pakiri. At the village turn 2nd right into Rahuikiri Rd

RUSSELL

✪ CAPE BRETT WALKWAYS
PO Box 149, Russell, Bay of Islands
Tel 09-403 8823
www.capebrettwalks.co.nz
This gives access to walking tracks on the Cape Brett penin-sula on both DoC and Maori Trust land, with spectacular seascapes and forested ridges. Walks take from two hours to two days over easy to moder-ate terrain, and are suitable for people of all ages as long as you are fit.
💷 From NZ$30 independent, NZ$250 guided

WHAT TO DO

TUTUKAKA

✪ DIVE TUTUKAKA
Poor Knights Dive Centre, Marina Road, Tutukaka
Tel 09-434 3867
www.diving.co.nz
Diving around the Poor Knights Islands is the main attraction here, with underwater caves, tunnels and archways, and shipwrecks to explore. You can also go snorkelling, kayaking or whale- and dolphin-watching.
🖐 From NZ$119

WAIHEKE ISLAND

⊞ GREENHILLS WINES AND SPIRITS
153 Ocean View Road, Oneroa, Waiheke Island
Tel 09-372 6139
This impressive wine store in Oneroa specialises in Waiheke wines. For NZ$15 you can taste four local wines and sample Waiheke olive oil.
🖐 NZ$15

✪ ANANDA TOURS
20 Seaview Road, Ostend, Waiheke Island
Tel 09-372 7530
www.ananda.co.nz
Visit Waiheke artists in their studios, tour the island's vineyards, do coastal walks (moderate fitness required), or take an eco-tour in Whakanewha Regional Park. Other options include garden tours and overnight stays.
🕐 Daily 🖐 From NZ$85

✪ STONYRIDGE VINEYARDS
80 Onetangi Road, Waiheke Island
Tel 09-372 8822
www.stonyridge.co.nz
Stephen White aims to make the highest quality Cabernet blend in the world. His flagship Larose is one of New Zealand's most sought-after wines, with a price tag to match. Vineyard tours and tastings are held at 11.30am on weekends. Olives are also grown on the estate, and the café serves Mediterranean food.
🕐 Sat, Sun 11.30–5, daily in high summer 🖐 Tours NZ$10 ▢

WAIMAUKU

⊞ BEESONLINE HONEY CENTRE AND CAFÉ
791 State Highway 16, Waimauku
Tel 09-411 7953
www.beesOnline.co.nz
A working honey centre with a bee theatre, a range of honey products, tastings, a retail outlet and a café serving indigenous and organic food.
🕐 Mon–Fri 9–4, Sat, Sun 9–5 ⊞ ▢

⊞ CORBAN ESTATE ARTS CENTRE
426 Great North Road, Henderson
Tel 09-838 4488/4455
www.ceac.org.nz
Former winery buildings on the original Corban's Wine Estate

Birdwatching from Whangamata with Kiwi Dundee Adventures

have been turned into studios for artists and artisans. The Pacific Island community holds regular markets and events.
🕐 Daily 10–4.30 🖐 Free ▤ Near the intersection of Lincoln Road and Mount Lebanon Lane

✪ BUSH AND BEACH
Tel 09-837 4130
www.bushandbeach.co.nz
Coach tours tailored to age and fitness explore the black-sand beaches and lush native bush within 30km (18 miles) of Auckland. Half-day, full-day and overnight tours are available.
🕐 Daily 🖐 From NZ$110

WAITANGI

🎵 CULTURE NORTH SOUND AND LIGHT SHOW
Waitangi
Tel 09-402 5990
www.culturenorth.co.nz
This informative, entertaining show gives a Maori perspective on events right through from the story of Kupe, the first Maori chief to discover New Zealand, to the signing of New Zealand's founding document and the present day.
🕐 Oct–end Apr, Mon, Wed, Thu, Sat 7.30pm–9.30pm 🖐 NZ$50

✪ COASTAL KAYAKERS
Te Karuwha Parade, Ti Bay, Waitangi
Tel 09-402 8105
www.coastalkayakers.co.nz
Choose to explore the outer islands, lagoons, natural rock caves and beaches, or challenge the Haruru Falls on these guided kayaking and canoeing trips, which last from half a day to several days. All equipment and refreshments provided.
🕐 Daily 🖐 From NZ$55

WAIWERA

✪♡ WAIWERA INFINITY SPA
21 Main Road, Waiwera
Tel 09-427 8800
www.waiwera.co.nz
This complex of 26 indoor and outdoor naturally heated thermal pools is popular with families. There are waterslides for the children, facial and body treatments for adults, spa packages and a fitness centre.
🕐 Sun–Thu 9am–10pm, Fri, Sat 9am–10.30pm 🖐 Adult NZ$22, child NZ$11, family NZ$53 ⊞ ▢

WHANGAMATA

✪ KIWI DUNDEE ADVENTURES
PO Box 198, Whangamata
Tel 07-865 8809
www.kiwidundee.co.nz
Personalised walks and nature tours, from relatively easy day walks to challenging hikes, taking in native bush, beaches and former gold mines.
🖐 From NZ$190

FESTIVALS AND EVENTS

JANUARY

ASB CLASSIC AND HEINEKEN OPEN
ASB Tennis Centre, 1 Tennis Lane, Parnell, Auckland
Tel 09-373 3623
www.asbbankclassic.co.nz
www.heinekenopen.co.nz
These annual international tennis tournaments are held consecutively over two weeks.

FEBRUARY

DEVONPORT FOOD AND WINE FESTIVAL
Winsor Reserve, Devonport
Tel 09-378 9031
www.devonportwinefestival.co.nz
This beachside food, wine and music festival in the picturesque village of Devonport has two stages, with non-stop entertainment and 30 stalls of New Zealand's wine and food.
NZ$25 via www.ticketmaster.co.nz and door sales From the Auckland ferry terminal

WAIHEKE ISLAND WINE FESTIVAL
Isola Estate, Onetangi Road, Waiheke Island
Tel 09-372 7676
www.waihekewinefestival.co.nz
Wines from the island's vineyards are showcased in a one-day festival, which also includes food and live music at several vineyards. Tickets are limited, so book early.
Tickets NZ$65 (NZ$89 including return ferry trip). Bookings at Ticketek, tel 09-307 5000, www.ticketek.co.nz
From the Auckland ferry terminal

FEBRUARY–MARCH

AUCKLAND FESTIVAL
PO Box 3787, Shortland Street, Auckland
Tel 09-309 0101
www.ak05.co.nz
This biennial arts festival is held over three weeks in venues all over the city. Book through Ticketek, tel 09-307 5000.

MARCH

PASIFIKA
Western Springs Lakeside and Stadium, Great North Road, Auckland
Tel 09-379 2020
www.aucklandcity.govt.nz
This annual one-day festival is New Zealand's largest Pacific Island celebration, with contemporary arts and music, traditional food, craft and cultural performances. Parking is limited, but public transport goes to the venue.
Free Bus 045 from Downtown

EASTER

ROYAL EASTER SHOW
ASB Showgrounds, 217 Greenlane West, Epsom, Auckland
Tel 09-623 7728
www.royaleastershow.co.nz
As well as the traditional agricultural competitions such as shearing, dog trials and equestrian events, the show puts on family entertainment with carnival rides, children's stage shows and Farmworld 'petting pens'. At the same venue are artworks from the Royal Easter Show Art Awards.
Adult NZ$15, child (2–12) NZ$5, family NZ$30 Buses 302–312, 327–359 from Midtown Exit Southern Motorway at Greenlane (exit 433)

WAIHEKE ISLAND OF JAZZ
PO Box 170, Oneroa, Waiheke Island
Tel 09-372 5301
www.waihekejazz.co.nz
Concerts featuring local and international performers are

held over five days at pubs, cafés and vineyards around Waiheke Island, linked by a shuttle bus. Book your accommodation well ahead.
From the Auckland ferry terminal

SEPTEMBER

AIR NEW ZEALAND FASHION WEEK 2004
PO Box 147240, Auckland
Tel 09-377 8033
www.nzfashionweek.com
This is aimed at fashion buyers and media, but the public can get close with shows such as ANZFW 4 U public access day (tickets through Ticketek, tel 09-307 5000), and big-screen coverage at Viaduct bars.

NOVEMBER

ELLERSLIE INTERNATIONAL FLOWER SHOW
Auckland Regional Botanic Gardens, Manukau City
Tel 09-579 6260
www.ellerslieflowershow.co.nz
The largest flower show in the southern hemisphere, Ellerslie showcases New Zealand horticulture, landscape design and garden art, with food, wine and entertainment.
Adult NZ$35, child (5–14) NZ$5
Manukau Station and shuttle bus
Exit the Southern Motorway (SH1) at Manukau (exit 433) and follow signs

NOVEMBER–DECEMBER

POHUTUKAWA FESTIVAL
PO Box 592, Thames, Coromandel Peninsula
Tel 07867 9077
www.pohutukawafest.com
Timed to coincide with the flowering of the 'New Zealand Christmas tree', this 17-day festival is an umbrella for many different events in the area, including swimming and diving competitions, an adventure run, outdoor expo, food and wine festival and jazz brunch.
Bookings at Ticketek, tel 09-307 5000, www.ticketek.co.nz

WHAT TO DO

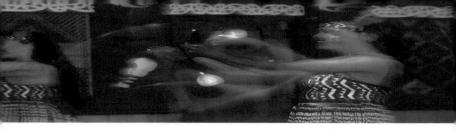

CENTRAL NORTH ISLAND

Maori culture and geothermal wonders are what bring most visitors to the central North Island, but Rotorua and Taupo also vie with each other in catering for thrill seekers, whether it's bungy jumping, water sports, off-road adventures, throwing yourself out of aeroplanes or hurtling downhill at high speed. Children are offered tamer versions of many activities, and those who get their thrills in more sedate ways find the fishing and golf world class. After so much exertion, you'll want to soak in the hot pools or be pampered in a spa, of which there are plenty. After that, you may well be too tired to do much other than have a good meal—which is as well, since the nightlife is limited. The most interesting shopping tends to be souvenirs of Maori culture, such as greenstone, carved bone and woven flax.

The North Island's only commercial ski fields are on Mount Ruapehu, one of several volcanoes in the region, not all of them extinct—which adds an extra frisson to the experience. The landscape of the Central Plateau is also well worth exploring in summer, either on short treks from Whakapapa or on the famous Tongariro Crossing. To the west, the lone, almost perfect cone of another volcano, Taranaki/Mount Egmont, is also a magnet for hikers, and surfers love the nearby beaches on Surf Highway 45. Catch a concert if you can at one of New Zealand's prettiest venues, the TSB Bowl of Brooklands at New Plymouth. On the eastern coast, Gisborne and Hawke's Bay are traditional fruit-growing areas, which also produce some of New Zealand's best wine. Hawke's Bay leads the country in wine and food tourism, with many producers open to the public. Napier also makes the most of its art deco heritage with guided tours and a not-too-serious festival.

KEY TO SYMBOLS	
⊕	Shopping
♪	Entertainment
▽	Nightlife
⚡	Sports
✪	Activities
♡	Health and Beauty
✪	For Children

CAMBRIDGE

✪ CAMBRIDGE THOROUGHBRED LODGE
SH1, Karapiro, Cambridge
Tel 07-827 8118
www.cambridgethoroughbredlodge.co.nz
An hour-long New Zealand

Horse Magic Show on a 40ha (100-acre) farm show-cases various horse breeds, which perform with audience participation. Afternoon tea and a horse ride are included.
🕐 Daily 10–3, shows at 10.30 or 11.30. Check for times and dates. Bookings are essential 🎫 Adult NZ$12, child NZ$5
🚌 6km (4 miles) south of Cambridge

GISBORNE

⊕ BULMER HARVEST CIDER
Customhouse Street, Gisborne
Tel 06-868 8300
You can taste and buy a range of ciders made on site by

New Zealand's largest cider producer. They also make honey mead and a liqueur.
🕐 Mon–Fri 10–4

▽ SMASH PALACE
24 Banks Street, Gisborne
Tel 06-867 7769
A bar, barbecue and museum of eccentricities in the heart of Gisborne's industrial area, Smash Palace hosts DJs and live bands, particularly in summer. It also has a reputation for its flaming pizza.
🕐 Mon–Thu 3pm–late, Fri, Sat 12pm–3am, Sun 3pm–late

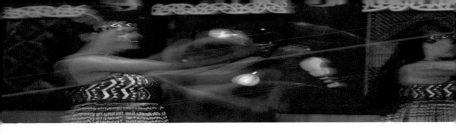

CHALET SURF LODGE
62 Moana Road,
Wainui
Tel 06-868 9612
www.chaletsurf.co.nz
Surfing is the theme of this lodge, 8km (5 miles) north of Gisborne, which combines with a local surf retailer, The Boardroom, to provide an experience of the region's surf beaches. Surf coaching, accommodation and board rental are also available.
From NZ$22

MILLTON VINEYARDS
119 Papatu Road, Manuluke,
Gisborne
Tel 06 862 8680
www.millton.co.nz
The Millton vineyards were the first in New Zealand to have full organic certification. Wines here are grown biodynamically, mixing organics with the theories of Rudolf Steiner. The flagship Clos de Ste. Anne Pinot noir and Chardonnay from Naboth's Vineyard are particularly highly regarded.
Dec daily 10–5; Oct, Nov, Jan–end Apr Mon–Sat daily 10–5; otherwise by appointment Off SH2

NEW ZEALAND SAFARI ADVENTURES
Tangihau Station Enterprise,
Rere
Tel 06-867 0872
www.tangihau.com
Hunting is the focus of this operation, spread over 6,667ha (16,474 acres) at Tangihau Station, where you can pursue big game such as red stag and fallow buck, or water fowl, turkeys and ducks in season. Non-hunters can experience station life with farm tours, rock sliding, swimming at the Rere Falls, golf and wine trails.
NZ$75–NZ$800 44km (27 miles) from Gisborne

ANIMAL KRACKERS PET PARK
Oakland Truffière, Ferry Road,
Waerenga-a-hika, Gisborne
Tel 06-862 5597
www.oaklandtruffles.co.nz
Children can cuddle and feed the rabbits, miniature horses, deer, llama and kunekune pigs at this little pet park. Their parents may also be interested in visiting the *truffière*, New Zealand's first commercial producers of prized Périgord black truffles. A trained dog sniffs out the delicacies from May to the end of August.
Daily 1–4; *truffière* visits by appointment Adult NZ$5, child NZ$2
Turn off SH2 at the Bushmere Arms

An Italianate building forms a backdrop at Hamilton Gardens

HAMILTON

DONOVANS CHOCOLATES
137 Maui Street, Hamilton
Tel 07-847 5771
www.donovanschocolates.co.nz
A family firm specialising in European-style chocolates, Donovans has a factory shop selling 40 kinds of confectionery, including truffles, fudges and liqueur chocolates.
Mon–Sat 9.30–5, Sun 10–4
Serves espresso and snacks

THE GOUDA CHEESE SHOP
245 Cambridge Road, Hillcrest, Hamilton
Tel 07-856 6633
www.meyer-cheese.co.nz
Ben and Fieke Meyer make Dutch-style cheeses using the milk from their farm outside Hamilton. You can buy the cheeses cut to order at this retail outlet in the suburb of Hillcrest, which also carries a selection of Dutch foods.
Mon–Fri 9.30–5.30, Sat 9.30–1

FOUNDERS THEATRE
221 Tristram Street, Hamilton
Tel 07-838 6600
Hamilton's major performance venue, this 1,250-seat auditorium is located in Boyes Park and hosts international acts, musicals and concerts, opera, dance and cultural events. More intimate concerts and plays are staged at the Clarence Street Theatre (59 Clarence Street), and alternative theatre and dance at The Meteor (1 Victoria Street).

RIVERSIDE ENTERTAINMENT CENTRE
346 Victoria Street, Hamilton
Tel 07-834 4900 (Sky City)
www.skycityhamilton.co.nz
This complex houses SKYCITY Hamilton Casino, with 23 gaming tables and 339 gaming machines. On level two, The Bowlevard has 10-pin bowling, laser games, a sports bar and nightclub. Minimum age 20, smart casual dress required.
Sky City: Sun–Wed 9am–3am, Thu–Sat 9am–5am. The Bowlevard: Mon 4pm–10pm, Tue, Wed 10am–11pm, Thu–Sat 10am–2am, Sun 10am–11pm

HAMILTON GARDENS
Cobham Drive, State Highway 1, Hamilton
Tel 07-856 6782
www.hamiltongardens.co.nz
Hamilton's most famous attraction, this is a collection of themed gardens with river walks, lakes and exotic pavilions. Guided tours are available. The Gardens Pavilion hosts a full schedule of shows and other events.
Oct–end Apr daily 7.30am–8pm; May–end Sep 7.30–6

❂ MV *WAIPA DELTA*

Memorial Park Jetty, Memorial Drive, Hamilton
Tel 07-854 7813
www.waipadelta.co.nz
Replica 'paddleboat' cruises explore the Waikato River, with lunch, afternoon tea or a buffet dinner. There is a bar on board.
🕐 Thu–Sun 12, 2.45, 6.30 💰 From NZ$20 adult, child (under 15) half price

♡ WATERS DAY SPA

1226a Victoria Street, Hamilton
Tel 07-838 2202
www.waters.net.nz
Spa treatments including facials, massage, pedicures and a range of body treatments are offered in premises overlooking the Waikato River. There is also an infrared sauna.
🕐 Tue–Sat 9–5 💰 From NZ$45

❂ EXSCITE

1 Grantham Street, Hamilton
Tel 07-838 6553
www.exscite.org.nz
With a name that stands for Explorations in Science and Technology, Exscite is an interactive science exhibit aimed at children, attached to the Waikato Museum (▷ 77).
🕐 Daily 10–4.30 💰 Adult NZ$6, child NZ$5, under 3s free, family NZ$20

HASTINGS

⊞ HAWKE'S BAY FARMERS' MARKET

Hawke's Bay Showgrounds, Kenilworth Road, Hastings
Tel 06-974 8931
Local growers and artisan food producers sell their wares from market stalls, and local people come here to buy fresh food direct from the grower. Stalls include fruit and vegetables, meat, poultry, small goods, eggs, herbs, coffee, ice cream, preserves, confectionery and flowers.
🕐 Sun 8.30–12.30

⊞ RUSH MUNRO'S ICE CREAM GARDENS

704 Heretaunga Street West, Hastings
Tel 06-878 9634
www.rushmunro.co.nz
Rush Munro's have been making delicious handcrafted natural ice creams to their own traditional recipes since 1926. They use no colourings or additives, and their fruit ice creams contain real fruit. The choice of flavours offered is huge, ranging from passionfruit to cappuccino or hokey pokey.
🕐 Dec–end Feb Mon–Fri 11–8, Sat, Sun 10–9; Mar–end Nov Mon–Fri 12–5, Sat, Sun 11–5

Fun in the sunshine at Splash Planet water park

❂ EARLY MORNING BALLOONS

71 Rosser Road, RD4, Hastings
Tel 07-879 4229
www.early-am-balloons.co.nz
Hot-air balloon flights over Hawke's Bay last approximately an hour, but allow four hours' total excursion time as balloons are launched from the best sites according to the conditions. The flight fee includes a picnic. Minimum four people, maximum six, and not recommended for children under 10.
💰 Adult NZ$290, child (under 12) NZ$240

❂ ON YER BIKE WINERY TOURS

129 Rosser Road, RD4, Hastings
Tel 06-879 8735
www.onyerbikehb.co.nz
Visit the wineries of the Ngatarawa area on these self-guided bicycle tours. Comfortable mountain bikes, maps and a picnic lunch are provided, as well as a mobile phone for back-up (such as arranging to have your wine purchases collected). Routes up to 28km (18 miles) long cater to various levels of fitness. Minimum age 18.
🕐 Oct–end Apr daily 10–5.30; May–end Sep daily 11–4 💰 From NZ$50

❂ SPLASH PLANET

Grove Road, Hastings
Tel 06-873 8033
www.splashplanet.co.nz
There's something for the whole family to enjoy at this themed water park, with 15 rides and attractions including the Sky Castle Screamer, Master Blaster and Never-Ending River ride. For the less adventurous there are land-based activities such as mini-golf and a toddlers' pool.
🕐 Mid-Nov to Feb daily 10–6
💰 Adult NZ$25, child (15 and under) NZ$19.50

HAVELOCK NORTH

⊞ VILLAGE GROWERS' MARKET

Black Barn Vineyards, Black Barn Road, Havelock North
Tel 06-877 7985
www.blackbarn.com
This delightful small market takes place on Saturday mornings in the summer months under a ring of trees in the heart of the vineyard. Local growers and producers sell their seasonal wares, along with artisan breads, coffee, flowers, meat, pickles, olive oil and lavender products.
🕐 Late Oct to end Apr Sat 9–12

AIRPLAY
Te Mata Peak,
Havelock North
Tel 0274 512 886
www.airplay.co.nz
Specialists in foot-launched
paragliding, Airplay fly from a
variety of graded sites. Tandem
paragliding flights range from
15 minutes over the cliffs of
Te Mata Peak to cross-country
flights lasting up to four hours.
Courses are also available.
From NZ$140

ARATAKI HONEY
66 Arataki Road,
Havelock North
Tel 06-877 7300
www.aratakihoneyhb.co.nz
A honey factory and shop
with a bee wall and tours on
weekdays at 1.30pm (▷ 78).
Daily 9–5

HAWERA

DAM DROPPING
Kaitiaki Adventures, Surf Highway,
Hawera
Tel 021-461 110/0800 DAMDROP
www.damdrop.com
This three-hour trip on water
sledges on the Waingongoro
River includes an 8m (26ft)
drop over a dam. It differs
from white-water rafting as
you are in control of your
individual sledge.
Oct–end Mar daily 9, 12, 3.30
From NZ$100

HAWERA WATER TOWER
55 High Street, Hawera
Tel 06-278 8599
Climb to the top of the 54m
(177ft) tower, built in 1914 for
fire-fighting, for views over the
whole of South Taranaki, and
to the mountain.
Mon–Fri 8.30–5, Sat, Sun 10–2
Adult NZ$2

NAPIER

ART DECO SHOP
Deco Centre, 163 Tennyson Street,
Napier
Tel 06-835 0022
www.artdeconapier.com
The shop stocks a wide range
of art deco products, including

books, posters, clothing,
writing paper, needlepoint,
place mats, coasters and
table napkins.
Daily 9–5

NAPIER MUNICIPAL
THEATRE
119 Tennyson Street,
Napier
Tel 06-835 1087
www.venues.co.nz
An art deco building that has
been sensitively extended to
create a modern performing
space, this theatre seats 970
and is regularly used for
concerts, drama, dance and
international acts. The website
gives performance details.

*The gannet colony is the big
draw on Cape Kidnappers tours*

ART DECO TOURS
Art Deco Trust, 163 Tennyson Street,
Napier
Tel 06-835 0022
www.artdeconapier.com
Enjoy a guided or self-guided
art deco tour of the city, by car
or on foot. A 2.5-hour tour,
starting at 2pm at the Art Deco
shop (▷ this page), includes a
two-hour guided walk and
video screening with refreshments. Shorter morning walks
start at 10am from the visitor
information office, or you can
pick up an *Art Deco Walk*
booklet (NZ$4) for a self-
guided tour. Self-drive touring
maps (NZ$4) are also avail-
able, or you can tour in a

vintage Buick (NZ$99 for up to
three people).
Daily From NZ$10, children free

CHURCH ROAD WINERY
150 Church Road, Taradale,
Napier
Tel 06-844 2053
www.churchroad.co.nz
Founded in 1897, the Church
Road winery is one of the
oldest in New Zealand and is
known particularly for the
work of pioneering wine-
maker Tom McDonald, after
whom the winery's top red
wine and cellar are named.
The winery also houses New
Zealand's only wine museum.
Daily 9–5; tours daily at 10, 11, 2
and 3, NZ$10

GANNET BEACH
ADVENTURES
PO Box 1463,
Hastings
Tel 06-875 0898
www.gannets.com
Tours leave from Clifton Beach
on trailers pulled by vintage
tractors, following the Cape
Kidnappers coastline to the
gannet colonies. Stopping for
90 minutes allows time to
swim or see the displays at the
shelter and get a close view of
the birds. Departure times
depend on the tides.
Oct–early May daily Adult from
NZ$33, child NZ$19

OCEAN SPA
Marine Parade,
Napier
Tel 06-835 8553
Built on the site of the original
Hot Sea Water Baths, the
complex has pools of differing
depths and temperatures,
spas, sauna, steam room,
massage and beauty therapies.
The stylish Soak café is
licensed and has good food.
Mon–Sat 6am–10pm, Sun
8am–10pm Admission adult NZ$6,
child (2–14) NZ$4, private spa NZ$8,
massage from NZ$35

NEW PLYMOUTH

⊕ KINA
101 Devon Street West, New Plymouth
Tel 07-759 1201
www.kina.co.nz
Kina is located in the 1894 Exchange Chambers and specialises in New Zealand-made arts and crafts, including jewellery, pottery, glass, prints, turned wood, flax weaving and paua. Monthly local exhibitions are held in the adjacent art space.
🕐 Mon–Thu 9.30–5.30, Fri 9.30–7, Sat 9.30–4, Sun 11–4

✪ TSB BOWL OF BROOKLANDS
Pukekura Park, New Plymouth
Tel 07-759 6080
www.bowl.co.nz
Attractively set in parkland, with a lake in front of the stage, this natural amphitheatre seating up to 15,000 is a popular summer venue for Christmas in the Bowl, ballet, concerts, international acts and events such as the WOMAD world music festival.
🕐 Events listed on the www.newplymouthnz.com website

✪ YARROW STADIUM
Maratahu Street, New Plymouth
Tel 07-759 6060
Major local and national sporting events are held in the 25,000-seater stadium, including rugby, cricket and soccer.
🕐 Events listed on the www.newplymouthnz.com website

♡ TARANAKI MINERAL POOLS
8 Bonithon Avenue, New Plymouth
Tel 06-759 1666
www.windwand.co.nz/mineralpools
Incorporating the original Tarawhata Mineral Baths, the Bonithon Spa Health company has reopened the artesian mineral well and transformed it into a modern healing facility. Communal and private pools are available. Advance booking essential.
🕐 Mon, Wed–Fri 9am–8pm, Tue 9–5, Sat, Sun 12–9 💷 From NZ$6

✪ FUN HO! NATIONAL TOY MUSEUM
25 Rata Street, Inglewood (Inglewood is around 20km/12 miles southeast of New Plymouth)
Tel 07-756 7030
www.funho.com
For more than 50 years Fun Ho! miniature vehicles and other toys could be found in every New Zealand playground and sandpit. This collection contains more than 3,000 of them, made between the 1930s and 1980s, as well as other New Zealand-made toys. Replica toys are also made at the museum.
🕐 Daily 10–4 💷 Adult NZ$6, child NZ$3, family NZ$15

A guided river trip with Canoe Safaris of Ohakune

OHAKUNE

✪ TUROA SKIFIELD
Ohakune
Tel 07-385 8456
www.mtruapeu.com
On the Ohakune side of Mount Ruapehu, with reputedly the biggest vertical drop of all ski fields in Australasia, Turoa is popular with both skiers and snowboarders. It covers 500ha (1,200 acres) and has 11 lifts, equipment hire and cafés. Ski passes are also valid at Whakapapa on the other side of Mount Ruapehu.
🕐 Usually mid-Jun to end Oct 💷 From NZ$60, youth NZ$29

✪ CANOE SAFARIS
Tay Street, Ohakune
Tel 06-385 9237
www.canoesafaris.co.nz
Guided canoeing trips lasting from one to five days can be taken on the Whanganui and Rangitikei rivers. Rafting trips are also available on the Mohaka River. Most trips are suitable for families with children aged five upwards, with guides going ahead to set up campsites and lunches.
🕐 Oct–end Apr 💷 From NZ$95, child NZ$65

ORAKEI KORAKO THERMAL RESERVE

✪ NZ RIVERJET
Vaile Road, Reporoa
Tel 07-333 7111
www.riverjet.co.nz
Jet-boat trips take in lovely scenery on the Waikato River for one hour, or head to the hidden valley of Orakei Korako Thermal Reserve.
🕐 Daily 10.30 💷 From NZ$125, child NZ$50, family NZ$300 🚌 37km (23 miles) north of Taupo, off SH5

RAGLAN

✪ RAGLAN SURFING SCHOOL
5 Whaanga Road, Whale Bay, Raglan
Tel 07-825 7873
www.raglansurfingschool.co.nz
You can learn to ride Raglan's famed 'Endless Summer' breaks at the Raglan Surf School, which offers three-hour lessons and two- to five-day surf adventure packages, including equipment and accommodation.
🕐 Daily 10am 💷 From NZ$89

ROTORUA

⊕ JADE FACTORY
1288 Fenton Street, Rotorua
Tel 07-349 3968
www.jadefactory.com
Visit the workshop to watch jade carvers create pendants and sculptures in traditional and contemporary designs, many of which have symbolic associations—as the carvers will explain. The adjacent gift

WHAT TO DO

centre sells their works as well as souvenirs, woollen products, clothing, jewellery and items made from native wood.
🎫 Daily 9–6

🏛 TE PUIA MAORI ARTS AND CRAFTS INSTITUTE

Hemo Road, Whakarewarewa, Rotorua
Tel 07-348 9047
www.tepuia.com
Part of the Whakarewarewa complex (▷ 87), the institute preserves the arts of wood carving (*whakairo*) and weaving (*raranga*). You can walk around the carving school, visit a greenstone jeweller's studio and watch women weaving flax to make clothing, baskets and mats. Many products are for sale.
🎫 Daily 8–5 💵 General admission adult NZ$28, child (5–15) NZ$14

👪 TAMAKI MAORI VILLAGE

1220 Hinemaru Street, Rotorua
Tel 07-349 2999
www.maoriculture.co.nz
Maori life in pre-European times is re-created at this village, which gives an insight into *marae* protocol with demonstrations of culture and crafts, a concert party and a *hangi* (food cooked in an earth oven, ▷ 251). You can also buy carvings, flax weaving, foods, Maori medicines and clothing.
🎫 Oct–end Apr daily 5.30, 6.30, 7.30; May–end Sep 5.30, 7.30 💵 Adult NZ$90, child (5–15) NZ$50

🍺 THE PIG AND WHISTLE

1182 Tutanekai Street, Rotorua
Tel 07-347 3025
www.pigandwhistle.co.nz
Housed in a former police station (which gives rise to plenty of jokes), this lively bar sells micro-brewed beers with names like Swine Lager. Live bands play on Thursday, Friday and Saturday nights, and a guitarist on Wednesday and Sunday. There's also a big screen in the garden bar with Sky Sport.
🎫 Daily 11.30am–late

⭐ MOKOIA ISLAND TOURS

Memorial Drive, Lakefront, Rotorua
Tel 07-348 6634
www.mokoiaisland.com
Paddleboat cruises on the lake are combined with breakfast, lunch, afternoon tea or dinner and dancing. A trip to Mokoia Island Nature Reserve includes a Maori cultural experience related to the history of Hinemoa and Tutanekai.
🎫 Daily 10, 12, 2, 4 💵 Adult from NZ$85, child NZ$49

⭐ MOUNT TARAWERA NZ LTD

171 Fairy Springs Road, Rotorua
Tel 07-349 3714/0274 963083
www.mt-tarawera.co.nz

Traditionally carved greenstone (pounamu), New Zealand jade

A choice of six tours is available from one of the few operators licensed to take visitors to the crater left by the eruption of 1886. You can travel by 4X4 or helicopter, walk the crater rim or scree slide, and combine Tarawera visits with other Rotorua attractions.
🎫 Daily 8, 1 💵 From NZ$121, child (under 12) NZ$71.50

⭐ MV *REREMOANA*

The Landing, Lake Tarawera
Tel 07-362 8595
A morning cruise on Lake Tarawera retraces the route of Maori canoes that visited the famed Pink and White Terraces before the 1886 Mount Tarawera eruption, with a stop to walk to Lake Rotomahana. Afternoon scenic cruises are also available. Advance booking essential.
🎫 Daily 11, 1.30, 2.30 💵 From NZ$27, child NZ$15.50

⭐ WET 'N' WILD

2 White Street, Rotorua
Tel 07-348 3191
www.wetnwildrafting.co.nz
Depending on the level of adrenalin rush desired, you can choose from white-water rafting at various grades on five rivers. Trips last anything from 45 minutes to a highly recommended multi-day trip down the remote Motu River.
💵 From NZ$85

⭐ ZORB ROTORUA

Agrodome Adventure Park, Western Road, Ngongotaha, Rotorua
Tel 07-357 5100
www.zorb.co.nz
Zorbing is a local invention: rolling downhill in an inflated ball at up to 50kph (30mph). You can choose to go harnessed in a dry Zorb, or loose in a Hydro Zorb (known as the 'wash cycle'), or try the zigzag track. The Hydro Zorb can be done alone or with friends, which reduces the cost. There's also a children's Zorb for playing on flat ground.
🎫 Nov to mid-Feb daily 9–8.30; mid-Feb to end Oct 9–5 💵 NZ$45

🔵 BLUE BATHS (▷ 86)

🔵 HELL'S GATE AND WAI ORA SPA (▷ 84)

🔵 POLYNESIAN SPA (▷ 86)

⭐ AGRODOME (▷ 86)

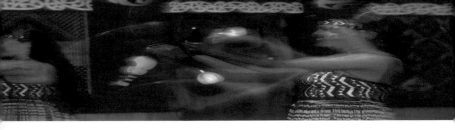

😊 RAINBOW SPRINGS

Fairy Springs Road,
Rotorua
Tel 07 350 0440
www.rainbowsprings.co.nz
This nature park sets out to be family friendly, with bush walks, kiwi and other native birds, and trout that can be fed. An entertaining farm show also gives an insight into life on a New Zealand farm.
🕐 Daily 8–5 💲 Adult NZ$23.50, child (5–15) NZ$13.50, under 5s free, family NZ$69 🔲 🏛

TAUPO

🏛 KURA GALLERY

47A Heu Heu Street,
Taupo
Tel 07-377 4068
www.kura.co.nz
This small gallery specialises in contemporary New Zealand ethnic art and craft, including jewellery, carving, wood turning, paintings and flax weaving.
🕐 Mon–Fri 10–6, Sat, Sun 10–4

🏛 THE MERCHANT OF TAUPO

14 Spa Road, Taupo
Tel 07-378 4626
www.themerchant.co.nz
The Merchant provides all the ingredients for a slap-up picnic: cheese, pâté, olives and cured meats, salmon, sauces, biscuits and chocolates, wines, beers and spirits. He also does glassware and gifts.
🕐 Daily 9–6

😊 CHRIS JOLLY OUTDOORS

Taupo Boat Harbour,
Taupo
Tel 07-378 0623
www.chrisjolly.co.nz
A wide-ranging tour operation, Chris Jolly offers scenic cruises, lake fishing, fly fishing, hunting, water skiing, jet skiing, self-drive boats, guided walks and scenic flights. One option is to take a two-hour guided bush walk, be met by boat, and fish and cruise back to Taupo (NZ$1,040 for 2–4 people).
💲 From NZ$30, child NZ$16

😊 ECO EXPLORER

PO Box 1725, Taupo
Tel 07-378 7902
www.ecoexplorer.co.nz
Aimed at people seeking gentle eco-adventure experiences rather than an adrenalin rush, these tours include a half-day guided kayak trip to the Maori carvings on Lake Taupo, a half-day kayak and launch cruise combo, guided forest walks.
💲 From NZ$95

😊 WAIRAKEI INTERNATIONAL GOLF COURSE

State Highway 1, Taupo
Tel 07-374 8152
www.wairakeigolfcourse.co.nz

Kiwifruit provides the theme at Kiwi360's theme park

Designed as a green-fee course rather than a club, this internationally recognised golf course welcomes visitors and has a driving range, pro shop, bar and restaurant.
💲 From NZ$135 🚗 9km (6 miles) north of Taupo on SH1

💗 😊 TAUPO HOT SPRINGS SPA

Tel 07-377 6502, SH5, Taupo
www.taupohotsprings.com
Beauty treatments and family fun are combined at this thermal complex, which has hot pools, private spas and an interactive warm-water children's playground with hydroslide. Spa treatments include therapeutic massage, skin care, beauty treatments and features such as wet massage, acupressure jets and air massage seats.
🕐 Daily 7.30am–9.30pm 💲 From NZ$12, child (3–12) NZ$4; treatments from NZ$65

TAURANGA

🎭 BAYCOURT ENTERTAINMENT CENTRE

Durham Street, Tauranga
Tel 07-577 7198
www.baycourt.co.nz
Baycourt supports Tauranga's lively performing arts scene, with a modern 590-seat theatre hosting local and touring shows, and a 1926 Wurlitzer theatre organ.

😊 BUTLER'S SWIMMING WITH DOLPHINS

Tel 0508 BUTLER
www.swimwithdolphins.co.nz
Gemini Galaxsea, an eco-friendly 20m (65ft) sailing boat, takes you on a leisurely trip to watch and swim with dolphins. It leaves from either Tauranga or Mount Maunganui. The boat has a swim bar for hanging onto when the dolphins swim faster than you can. Whales, seals and seabirds are also plentiful.
🕐 Daily 9am Tauranga Marina, 9.30 Salisbury Wharf, Mount Maunganui 💲 Adult NZ$110, child (under 13) NZ$85

TE AROHA

💗 😊 TE AROHA MINERAL POOLS

Te Aroha Hot Springs Domain, Te Aroha
Tel 07-884 4498
www.tearohapools.co.nz
Established in 1883 to take advantage of the health-giving properties of the mineral soda hot springs, the complex is in a landscaped domain (park) and retains many Edwardian buildings. You can choose from modern or Edwardian private bath houses or outdoor spas.
🕐 Spa daily 10–10; pool Mon–Fri 10–6, Sat, Sun 10–7 💲 From NZ$6, child NZ$4

WHAT TO DO

TE PUKE

✪ KIWI360
State Highway 2, Te Puke
Tel 07-573 6340
www.kiwi360.com
Kiwifruit orchard tours and
horticultural theme park (▷ 92).
🕐 Daily 9–5 💲 Tours adult NZ$23,
child (5–12) NZ$10, family NZ$60
🚌 36km (22 miles) south of Tauranga

WAIPUKURAU

✪ AIRLIE MOUNT WALKS
PO Box 368, Waipukurau
Tel 06-858 7601
Itineraries lasting from half a
day to three days combine
walks on private farms with
visiting grand 1800s home-
steads not otherwise open to
the public. The walks take in
native bush, bird and marine
life, beaches and *pa* sites.
🕐 Daily 💲 From NZ$90

WAITOMO

✪ THE LEGENDARY BLACK
WATER RAFTING COMPANY
PO Box 13, Waitomo Caves
Tel 07-878 6219
www.blackwaterrafting.co.nz
Best known for its underground
cave-tubing experience, Black
Labyrinth, this company also
offers Black Abyss abseiling
(rappelling). Reasonable fitness
is required. Minimum age 13.
🕐 Black Labyrinth daily 9, 10.30, 12,
1.30, 3; Black Abyss daily 9.30, 2.30
💲 Black Labyrinth NZ$90; Black Abyss
NZ$175

✪ WAITOMO GLOW-WORM
CAVES (▷ 90)

WHITE ISLAND

✪ PEEJAY WHITE ISLAND
TOURS
15 The Strand East, Whakatane
Tel 07-308 9588
www.whiteisland.co.nz
Enjoy an 80-minute launch trip
to White Island's active volcano,
and a guided walk (with hard
hat and gas mask) through the
remains of a sulphur factory to
the rim of the volcano.
🕐 Daily 9.15 (more trips Dec–end Feb)
💲 From NZ$150, child (1–13) NZ$110
(child rates not available Nov–end Mar)

FESTIVALS AND EVENTS

FEBRUARY

BREBNER PRINT ART DECO
WEEKEND
Deco Centre, 163 Tennyson Street,
Napier
Tel 06-835 11911
www.artdeconapier.com
This not-too-serious celebration of Napier's art deco
heritage has become so
popular it now runs into
several days, with walks and
tours, events on stage and
screen, a vintage car cruise,
street jazz and a seaside ball.

HARVEST HAWKE'S BAY
Hawke's Bay Wine Country
Tel 0800-442 946
www.harvesthawkesbay.co.nz
Around 30 Hawke's Bay
vineyards open their doors to
show off their wines in this
festival of tastings, tours,
concerts, art exhibitions
and workshops.
💲 Adult NZ$15

MARCH

WOMAD NEW ZEALAND
TSB Bowl of Brooklands,
New Plymouth
Tel 06-759 8412
www.womad.co.nz
This three-day biennial
celebration of world music,
arts and dance is held in odd
years, with concerts, workshops, storytellers, crafts and
Kidzone for children.

EASTER

MONTANA NATIONAL
JAZZ FESTIVAL
Baycourt, corner of Durham and
Wharf streets, Tauranga
Tel 07-577 7188
www.jazz.org.nz
Concerts at Baycourt span the
decades from New Orleans,
Chicago and Latin America,
with a New Zealand spin,
while downtown Tauranga
holds a Mardi Gras celebration
of wine, food and music.

JUNE

MATARIKI
Hawkes Bay Showgrounds
Tel 06-873 3526
www.matarikifestival.co.nz
This celebrates the Maori New
Year, the first new moon after
the rising of Pleiades star cluster in the eastern sky at dawn.
There are feasting and fun
activities here, and in other
parts of the country.

NEW ZEALAND NATIONAL
AGRICULTURAL FIELDAYS
Mystery Creek, Mystery Creek Road,
Hamilton
Tel 07-843 4499
www.fieldays.co.nz
The biggest agricultural trade
show in the southern hemisphere, Mystery Creek attracts
1,000 exhibitors and more
than 115,000 visitors. It is also
famous for its Rural Bachelor
of the Year contest.
💲 Adult NZ$15, child (5–14) NZ$6

SEPTEMBER

HASTINGS BLOSSOM
FESTIVAL
106 Russell Street South, Hastings
Tel 06-878 9447
www.blossomfestival.co.nz
The apple orchards are in full
bloom for this celebration
of spring in one of New
Zealand's leading fruit-
growing regions. The 10 days
of concerts and events include
a blossom parade.

NOVEMBER

TASTE GISBORNE
Showgrounds Events Centre
Tel 06-868 4123
www.gisbornenz.com
Taste Gisborne is a day-long
festival held in the events
centre at the showgrounds. It
involves many of the region's
top wineries, food and beverage producers, craftspeople
and chefs, with continuous
live entertainment.
💲 Adult NZ$30, child (under 12) free

SOUTHERN NORTH ISLAND

New Zealand's most cosmopolitan and lively city, Wellington is the country's arts capital as well as the seat of government. The politics may be on the dull side, but the arts are definitely not, particularly during the biennial month-long International Festival of the Arts and concurrent Fringe Festival, when the city barely sleeps. Wellington is the home of the New Zealand Symphony Orchestra, the Royal New Zealand Ballet, some excellent professional theatre companies, Te Papa (the national museum), interesting art galleries, the child-focused Capital E, and a humming jazz and alternative arts scene, so even outside festival time, there is always something going on. See the *Dominion Post* newspaper for listings.

The city also has the advantage of being compact, making walking the easiest way to get around. It has resisted other New Zealand cities' drift towards suburban shopping malls, so the locals shop, eat and are entertained downtown. For nightlife, head for Courtenay Place; for quirky shops and alternative boutiques, stroll down Cuba Street; for smart shopping browse Lambton Quay. You'll find great coffee in cafés on almost every corner. Also downtown, or very close, is the Basin Reserve, one of New Zealand's oldest and certainly most characterful sports grounds.

Its location on the harbour makes Wellington popular for water sports, especially sailing. The inner-city beach is more suitable for sunbathing than swimming, but it does have good indoor baths. Lyall Bay is popular with surfers. For a family excursion, take the ferry to Days Bay, where there is a beach with kayaks and small boats for rent.

Over the Rimutaka hills to the northeast of Wellington, about an hour's drive away, is the highly regarded Martinborough wine region, one of the few places in New Zealand where the vineyards are so close together that you can walk between many of them—a particular advantage during the popular Martinborough Wine Festival.

KEY TO SYMBOLS	
⊕	Shopping
🎭	Entertainment
🍷	Nightlife
🏀	Sports
✪	Activities
♡	Health and Beauty
✪	For Children

CARTERTON

⊕ PAUA WORLD
54 Kent Street, Carterton
Tel 06 379 6777
www.pauashell.co.nz
The iridescent bluey-green shell of the paua (abalone) is turned into all sorts of distinctive New Zealand souvenirs at this factory and outlet. Boggle at the paua hallway, watch a video about the life of this curious mollusc, and take the free factory tour for an insight into the processing of the shells. There's also a children's playground and a salt-water aquarium.
🕐 Daily 9–5 🎟 Free

✪ BALLOONING NEW ZEALAND
54B Kent Street, Carterton
Tel 06-379 8223
Early-morning flights complete with a café 'champagne

breakfast' are a speciality. Flights last an hour.

⏰ Oct–end Apr daily 6am; May–end Sep daily 7am 🎫 NZ$260 including breakfast

GREYTOWN

🏛 THE FRENCH BAKER MOÏSE CERSON

81 Main Street,
Greytown
Tel 06-304 8873
www.frenchbaker.co.nz
Croissants, palmiers, *religieuse, pissaladière*—artisan baker Moïse Cerson bakes wonderful authentic French breads, savouries and pâtisserie at his bakery and espresso bar.

⏰ Tue–Sun 8.30–4

✪ THE ADVENTURE CENTRE

76 Main Street,
Greytown
Tel 06-304 8565
www.ecoadventure.co.nz
Interactive ecology tours on the Waiohine Gorge involve rafting the gentle Grade II river, studying flora and birdlife as part of a conservation project. Night rafting is also available, finishing with a barbecue, roaring fire and mulled wine. Half-day rafting trips are suitable for all ages, with 'river bugging' for the more adventurous, caving and a full-day 'extreme' trip including bridge swing and 'rap jumping', which finishes with a winery tour.

🎫 From NZ$70

MANAKAU

🏛 SOO'S BROWN ACRES

Main Road,
Manakau, Levin
Tel 06-362 6029
Home-grown vegetables, fruit and berries ripened on the property are sold at Soo's stall on the main road near Levin. Tree-ripened apples of many varieties are a speciality. They also sell confectionery and ice cream.

⏰ Daily 9–5.30

MANGATAINOKA

🏛 TUI BREWERY

State Highway 2, Mangatainoka
Tel 06-376 0615
www.tui.co.nz
Tui beer has been associated with the Tararua region since it was first brewed on this site in the 1880s. The building is known by some as the local equivalent of the Taj Mahal! Brewery tours are available (advance booking essential), and there is promotional clothing for those so inclined.

⏰ Tours Mon–Fri 10.30, 1, Sat, Sun 1, 2 🎫 NZ$10, under 16s free 📅 Mon–Fri 10–4 🚌 On SH2, 24km (15 miles) east of Palmerston North

Local delicacies are brought together in Martinborough

MARTINBOROUGH

🏛 MARTINBOROUGH WINE CENTRE

6 Kitchener Street,
Martinborough
Tel 06-306 9040
www.martinboroughwinecentre.co.nz
A good starting point for the Wairarapa wine trail, the centre has information about local wineries and an excellent selection of wines to taste and buy. They also stock wine books and local products such as olive oil.

⏰ Daily 10–5

🏛 MARTINBOROUGH BEER AND ALES

Corner of New York and Princess streets, Martinborough
Tel 06-306 8310
Martinborough may be best known for its wine, but it also produces some fine craft beers. Martinborough Beer and Ales makes wheat beer, lager, ale and stout, which you can taste while you watch the beer being made.

⏰ Late Oct to end Mar Wed–Sun 11–7; Apr–late Oct Fri, Sat 11–7

🏛 SUNDAY MARKET

6 Kitchener Street, Martinborough
Tel 06-306 9040
www.martinboroughwinecentre.co.nz
Wairarapa food producers and craftspeople sell their wares at the weekly Sunday market. It's held in a rustic workshop at the back of the Martinborough Wine Centre.

⏰ Sun 10–2

🏛 TASTE OF MARTINBOROUGH WINE AND CHEESE SHOP

8 Kitchener Street, Martinborough
Tel 06-306 8383
www.tasteofmartinborough.co.nz
Fine boutique cheeses can be cut to order at this shop, which also stocks local wines and gourmet items. The store has a café selling coffee, snacks, drinks and wine by the glass.

⏰ Daily 9–5 🖥

✪ ATA RANGI

Puruatanga Road, Martinborough
Tel 06-306 9570
www.atarangi.co.nz
Wines of international stature are made at Ata Rangi, known particularly for its Pinot noir, which is regarded as one of New Zealand's top wines. The Paton and Masters families who make the wines live on site, and you're likely to meet them if you visit their rustic cellar door.

⏰ Oct to mid-Apr Mon–Fri 1–3, Sat, Sun 12–4

✪ MCLEODS QUAD ADVENTURES

White Rock Road, Martinborough
Tel 06-306 8846
www.mcleodsadventures.co.nz
If you've ever wanted to experience the thrill of exploring by quad bike, then this could be your chance. Tours across farmland take in river crossings and fabulous views. No experience required, but advance booking is essential.
🖐 From NZ$100

✪ OLIVO

Hinakura Road, RD4, Martinborough
Tel 06-306 9074
www.olivo.co.nz
Wander through the Wairarapa's first commercial olive grove, which is located in beautiful gardens. You can also taste and buy the oil and learn about its production.
🕐 Sat, Sun 🚗 3km (2 miles) from Martinborough Town Square

✪ TORA COASTAL WALK

Wairewa Farm, RD2 Martinborough
Tel 06-307 8115
www.toracoastalwalk.co.nz
This three-day, circular, 40km (25-mile) walk crosses the southern Wairarapa hills and drops down to the coast. The hosts are farmers who give you a warm welcome—you dine at their homes. You stay in well-equipped farm cottages and can opt for provisions or take your own food. Your baggage can also be carried.
🕐 Oct–end Apr 🖐 Adult NZ$330

✪ AU SPA BELGE

41 Strasbourge Street,
Martinborough
Tel 06-306 8188
Yvette Françoise Bonfond brings European techniques to this women's day spa, offering facials, massage therapy, mud treatments, full body treatments, detoxification and hydrotherapy spa baths.
🕐 Wed–Sun 9.30–5 🖐 From NZ$50

MASTERTON

🏛 KINGSMEADE CHEESE

8b First Street,
Masterton
Tel 06-378 7178
www.kingsmeadecheese.co.nz
Kingsmeade specialises in sheep cheeses made from milk from its own flock. You can buy the cheeses, as well as jams, chutneys, crafts and local products, at their retail outlet. To find out more about how the cheese begins life, join a farm tour to watch the sheep-milking take place.
🕐 Mon–Fri 9–5, Sat 10–1

✪ PUKAHA MOUNT BRUCE WILDLIFE CENTRE (▷ 95)

Olive oil products are for sale at Olivo, in Martinborough

✪ WAIRAPAPA GOURMET WINE ESCAPES

Tranzit Coachlines,
Masterton
Tel 06-377 1227
www.tranzit.co.nz
Wine tours depart daily from Wellington (by train to Featherston), Masterton, Carterton, Greytown, Featherston and Martinborough, visiting four Martinborough wineries and the Martinborough Wine Centre, with lunch in a vineyard café.
🕐 Daily 🖐 From NZ$76

PALMERSTON NORTH

🏛 EZIBUY

170–178 John F Kennedy Drive,
Palmerston North
Tel 06-952 2112
www.ezibuy.co.nz
The retail outlet of a well-known Palmerston North mail-order company, Ezibuy has shopping areas for women, men and children, and stocks clothing, footwear, homeware and gift lines. There is also a four-screen video wall and a children's play area.
🕐 Mon–Wed, Fri 8.30–5.30, Thu 8.30am–8pm, Sat 9–5, Sun 10–5
💻

🎭 CENTREPOINT THEATRE

Corner of Pitt and Church streets,
Palmerston North
Tel 06-354 5740
www.centrepoint.co.nz
One of the few theatres to have its own full-time professional theatre company, Centrepoint stages regular shows, from comedy to classic drama, with an emphasis on local New Zealand plays.
🕐 Tue 6.30, Wed–Sat 8, Sun 5
🖐 NZ$35

🎭 REGENT THEATRE

Broadway Avenue, Palmerston North
Tel 06-350 2100
www.regent.co.nz
Opened in 1930, the original picture palace of Palmerston North was restored in 1998. With a seating capacity of almost 1,400, it hosts events such as ballet, musicals, orchestra concerts and comedy.

✪ GO 4 WHEELS

Horne Road, Ballance, Pahiatua
Tel 06-376 7043
Two-hour trips to the Tararua Wind Farm are the main attraction on these rides—from the hilltops you can see both sides of the North Island. Expect it to be windy! One-hour trips are also available (NZ$65). Advance booking is essential.
🖐 NZ$95

PARAPARAUMU

🏛 LINDALE CENTRE
State Highway 1, Paraparaumu
Tel 04-297 0916
A complex of agricultural
speciality shops, this is well
worth stopping at for local
Kapiti cheeses, honey, olive
products, sheepskins, and a
farm-kitchen restaurant.
🕐 Daily 9–5 🍴

★ PARAPARAUMU BEACH GOLF CLUB
376 Kapiti Road, Paraparaumu
Tel 04-902 8200
www.paraparaumubeachgolfclub.co.nz
An international-standard golf
links ranked 73rd in the world,
graced by Tiger Woods at the
NZ Open in 2001, and the
venue for 12 New Zealand
golf opens.
🎫 NZ$90

PIPIRIKI

★ BRIDGE TO NOWHERE TOURS
Pipiriki, RD6 Wanganui
Tel 06-348 7122
www.bridgetonowhere-lodge.co.nz
You can hunt deer, pigs, goats
or possums from this remote
lodge, but it is also accessible
to daytrippers with a four-hour
jet-boat ride along the
Whanganui River and a
guided walk to the Bridge
to Nowhere. Overnight
accommodation can be
arranged. Also trips to the
Matemateaonga Track, and
Tieke Marae, for an experience
of Maori river culture.
🎫 From NZ$75

TAIHAPE

★ MOKAI GRAVITY CANYON
Mokai Bridge, Taihape
Tel 06-388 9109
www.gravitycanyon.co.nz
This company offers the North
Island's highest bungy
(80m/262ft) and New
Zealand's longest Flying Fox
(aerial cableway), stretching
1km (0.6 miles), on which
you can reach 160kph
(107mph)—not for the faint-
hearted! If you still have the

nerve, a Giant Swing swoops
into the Mokai Canyon.
🎫 From NZ$99 🚗 Off SH1, south
of Taihape

UPPER HUTT

★ EFIL DOOG GARDEN OF ART
1995 Akatarawa Road, RD 2,
Upper Hutt
Tel 04-526 7924
www.efildoog-nz.com
Explore 4ha (10 acres) of
beautiful gardens full of quirky
sculpture. There's also a small
art gallery, which specialises in
early New Zealand paintings.
Guided tours are available.
🕐 Oct–end Mar Wed–Sun 10–4.30
🎫 Adult NZ$14, child (5–16) NZ$6

Lilac-hued irises by a pool at Efil Doog Garden of Art

★ SILVER STREAM RAILWAY
Silverstream,
Upper Hutt
Tel 04-563 7348
www.silverstreamrailway.org.nz
Take a Sunday afternoon ride
on a vintage steam train,
leaving from the site of the
country's biggest collection of
historic railway engines.
🕐 Trains operate Sun 11–4
🎫 Adult NZ$10, child (5–15) NZ$5,
family NZ$25

WAIKANAE

★ KAPITI ISLAND (▷ 94)

WANGANUI

🎭 ROYAL WANGANUI OPERA HOUSE
Saint Hill Street, Wanganui
Tel 06 349 0511
www.royaloperahouse.co.nz
Small but very grand, the
opera house was built in 1899.
It seats 800 and is used for
touring shows, opera and
rock bands.

★ WANGANUI RIVERCITY TOURS
PO Box 4224, Wanganui
Tel 06-344 2554
www.rivercitytours.co.nz
No experience is needed
for these escorted canoe
adventures over four days in
Whanganui National Park. The
service includes hotel pick-up,
safe vehicle storage, fresh food
supplies and informed guides.
Sleeping bags and mats are
available for hire.
🕐 Nov to mid-Apr 🎫 Adult NZ$545,
child (under 16) NZ$272

★ WHANGANUI RIVER CRUISES
Whanganui Riverboat Centre
1A Taupo Quay, Wanganui
Tel 06-347 1863
www.riverboat.co.nz
New Zealand's last operating
coal-fired passenger paddle
steamer, PS *Waimarie*, was
built in 1899 and restored
in 2000, and now runs
scheduled cruises on the
Whanganui River.
🕐 Late Oct–end Apr daily 2pm;
May–end Jul, Sep–late Oct Sat, Sun
1pm 🎫 Adult NZ$30, child (5–15)
NZ$12, family NZ$84

WELLINGTON

🏛 FRUTTI
166 Cuba Street, Wellington
Tel 04-384 6965
One of Cuba Street's many
funky designer shops, Frutti
has a lively mix of streetwear
and party gear. Many items are
made out of vintage fabrics,
including one-off designs, bags
and accessories.
🕐 Mon–Thu 10.30–6, Fri 10–9, Sat
10–6, Sun 11–5

WHAT TO DO

KIRKCALDIE AND STAINS

165–177 Lambton Quay, Wellington
Tel 04-472 5899
www.kirkcaldies.co.nz
Wellington's grand department store, founded in 1863, retains an elegant air, with a commissionaire still present. Originally a draper's store, it still specialises in fashion for men and women, but also carries cosmetics, stationery, lingerie, children's wear, household items, gifts and food.
🕐 Mon–Thu 9–5.30, Fri 9–6, Sat 10–5, Sun 11–4

MOORE WILSON FRESH

Corner of College and Tory streets, Wellington
Tel 04-384 9906
www.moorewilson.co.nz
A must for food lovers, Moore Wilson Fresh is the leading fresh produce store in New Zealand, selling artisan breads, fresh meat, fresh chicken, fresh fish, a huge cheese selection and deli range, coffee and flowers. (Also at Porirua Masterton.)
🕐 Mon–Fri 7.30–7, Sat 7.30–6, Sun 9–5.30

OLD BANK SHOPPING ARCADE

223–237 Lambton Quay, Wellington
Tel 04-922 0600
www.oldbank.co.nz
The arcade contains 27 shops, many of them exclusive to the Wellington region, including fashion, food and cosmetics. It occupies the former banking chamber of the heritage BNZ bank building, with the buried remains of the ship *Inconstant* on display in the basement.
🕐 Mon–Thu 9–6, Fri 9–7, Sat 10–4, Sun 11–3

SCOTTIES

4 Blair Street, Wellington
Tel 04-384 3805
www.fashionz.co.nz/scotties
Scotties sells high fashion womenswear by New Zealand designers such as Marilyn Sainty, Julia Fong and Beth

Ellery. You'll also find international labels, including Issey Miyake, Lanvin and Comme des Garçons.
🕐 Mon–Fri 9.30–6, Sat 10–5

SOMMERFIELDS

296 Lambton Quay, Wellington
Tel 04-499 4847
www.sommerfields.net
Specialising in New Zealand-made gifts and souvenirs, this store carries many items made exclusively for them. The range includes Maori carvings, greenstone, native timber products, hand-blown glass and paua shell.
🕐 Mon–Thu 9–5.30, Fri 9–6, Sat 10–5, Sun 11–3

You'll find a top-class range of souvenirs at Sommerfields

STARFISH

128 Willis Street, Wellington
Tel 04-385 3722
www.starfish.co.nz
Wellington designers Laurie Foon and Carleen Schollum create innovative clothing for men and women reflecting the New Zealand lifestyle and environment. The shop also stocks the luxury Laurie Foon range and other New Zealand designer labels, including Doris De Pont, Fix, Din and Sabatini. You can also buy national and international accessories. Samples, seconds and sale items are available

at Star X (213 Left Bank, Cuba Mall, tel 04-384 7827).
🕐 Mon–Thu 9.30–6, Fri 9.30–8, Sat 10–5, Sun 11–4

TAMARILLO

102–108 Wakefield Street, Wellington
Tel 04-473 6095
www.tamarillonz.com
A dealer gallery and craft shop, Tamarillo holds monthly exhibitions and carries contemporary New Zealand works of art by established and emerging artists, including glass, ceramics, wood, sculpture and jewellery. Worldwide shipping is available.
🕐 Mon–Fri 9.30–6, Sat 10–4, Sun 12–4

UNITY BOOKS

57 Willis Street, Wellington
Tel 0800-486 489
www.unitybooks.co.nz
An excellent bookshop committed to New Zealand publishing, Unity is strong on fiction, politics, history and cookery. It has useful review boards and a knowledgeable staff.
🕐 Mon–Thu 9–6, Fri 9–7, Sat 10–5, Sun 11–4

BATS THEATRE

1 Kent Terrace, Wellington
Tel 04-802 4176
www.bats.co.nz
Alternative and experimental theatre and dance are regularly performed in this casual and intimate theatre, which specialises in New Zealand works. It is also a venue for the annual Fringe Festival (▷ 187).

CIRCA THEATRE

1 Taranaki Street, Wellington
Tel 04-801 7992
www.circa.co.nz
Located next to Te Papa (▷ 96–99), Circa is a professional theatre which presents international drama and comedy as well as New Zealand works on two stages. The atmosphere is casual but

WHAT TO DO

the standard of productions is high.
🕐 Usually Tue–Wed 6.30, Thu–Sat 8, Sun 4 🎭 From NZ$35 📺

🎭 DOWNSTAGE THEATRE
12 Cambridge Terrace, Wellington
Tel 04-801 6946
www.downstage.co.nz
Downstage, New Zealand's longest-running professional theatre, is an intimate venue which presents classic and contemporary drama, dance and comedy, as well as touring shows.
🕐 Mon–Thu 6.30, Fri, Sat 8 🎭

🎭 EMBASSY THEATRE
10 Kent Terrace, Wellington
Tel 04-384 7657
www.deluxe.co.nz
A restored cinema with a giant screen, this is a popular venue during film festivals and hosted the world première of *Lord of the Rings—Return of the King.* The first-floor café, Blondini's, is also a venue for live jazz. Details of films and jazz concerts are carried on the website.
🎬 From NZ$9

🎭 THE OPERA HOUSE
111 Manners Street, Wellington
Tel 04-802 4060
www.stjames.co.nz
The Opera House is the grand old lady of Wellington theatres—typical of lavish early 1900s architecture, and with a large stage. It is a popular venue for concerts, musicals and touring shows.

🎭 READING CINEMAS COURTENAY CENTRAL
100 Courtenay Place, Wellington
Tel 04-801 4601
www.readingcinemas.co.nz
A 10-screen complex located on level 3 of a shopping and entertainment complex, Reading Cinemas shows popular films and has good parking. Details of films are listed on the website.
🎬 From NZ$9.50, child NZ$8.50

🎭 WELLINGTON CONVENTION CENTRE
111 Wakefield Street, Wellington
Tel 04-801 4231
www.wellingtonconventioncentre.com
An umbrella for 19 venues around Wellington, this includes the modern Michael Fowler Centre (111 Wakefield Street), which stages opera and concerts and is home to the New Zealand Symphony Orchestra; the beautifully restored 1904 Wellington Town Hall next door, which is also a concert hall; and the modern TSB Bank Arena (Queens Wharf), used for sports and pop concerts, accommodating up to 5,000.

Wellington's best-known cinema, the Embassy Theatre

🎫 Tickets available through Ticketek, tel 04-384 3840, www.ticketek.co.nz

🎭 WESTPAC ST. JAMES THEATRE
Courtenay Place, Wellington
Tel 04-802 4060
www.stjames.co.nz
The St. James was built in 1912 as a vaudeville and picture theatre, and extended and refurbished in 1998. Today it has one of the best stages in New Zealand. The ornate interior has been retained and a spacious foyer with a café added. It hosts musicals, dance and touring shows and is home to the Royal New Zealand Ballet.

🍸 BAR BODEGA
101 Ghuznee Street, Wellington
Tel 04-384 8212
www.bodega.co.nz
Bar Bodega hosts local and occasional international music events, and is dedicated to real ale and good music.
🕐 Daily 4pm–3am

🍸 THE ESTABLISHMENT
Corner of Courtenay Place and Blair Street, Wellington
Tel 04-382 8654
www.theestablishment.co.nz
You can dance until late at this popular hangout on Courtenay Place, listen to jazz or watch the weekend's big match. The Establishment serves Southwest American food and tapas in its restaurant, and there's also a lounge bar.
🕐 Mon–Fri 11–late, Sat, Sun 10–late

🍸 HAPPY
Corner of Vivian and Tory streets, Wellington
Tel 04-384 1965
www.happy.net.nz
A relaxed basement venue, Happy has nightly gigs featuring alternative live music and jazz. It is one of the venues in the Wellington Jazz Festival.
🕐 Gigs 8pm and/or 10pm

🍸 SPICEHAMMER
71 Cuba Street, Wellington
Tel 04-389 2120
www.pound.co.nz
A gay nightclub, Spicehammer has resident and guest DJs and weekly drag shows.
🕐 Tue–Sat 5–late

🏏 BASIN RESERVE
Rugby Street, Wellington
Tel 04-384 3171
www.westpacstadium.co.nz
Arguably New Zealand's most famous sports ground, and the only one with heritage status, the Basin Reserve is maintained largely for regional and national cricket fixtures. It is also home to the New Zealand Cricket Museum (▷ 104). During the winter it is used for club rugby.

WHAT TO DO

⊕ WESTPAC STADIUM
Waterloo Quay, Wellington
Tel 04-473 3881
www.westpacstadium.co.nz
Seating 34,500, with seven food and beverage outlets, this is the main venue for national and international rugby fixtures, international rugby sevens tournaments and cricket. It also hosts big popular events, such as Carols by Candlelight and rock concerts.

⊕ FERGS ROCK 'N' KAYAK
Shed 6, Queens Wharf, Wellington
Tel 04-499 8898
www.fergskayaks.co.nz
Owned by Olympic champion Ian Ferguson, Fergs guides and coaches kayaking, climbing and in-line skating on the waterfront. You can have a paddle along the shore or a full guided tour, and the indoor rock wall caters to all levels of climbing.
🕐 Mon–Fri 10–8, Sat, Sun 9–6
💰 From NZ$9

⊕ HELIPRO
Queens Wharf, Wellington
Tel 04-472 1550
www.helipro.co.nz
Scenic helicopter flights give views over the city and harbour, or can take you farther afield on a wine tour to the Marlborough Sounds or lunch at Wharekauhau.
💰 From NZ$45

⊕ MUD CYCLES
338 Karori Road, Wellington
Tel 04-476 4961
www.mudcycles.co.nz
Close to Makara Peak Mountain Bike Park, standard mountain bikes and 24-speed cycles are available for hire, with the option of central city drop-off and collection. Mud Cycles also offer instruction classes and tours, which range from easy sightseeing to advanced technical trails for eager thrill seekers.
💰 From NZ$25

⊕ SEAL COAST SAFARI
32 Salamanca Road, Wellington
Tel 0800-732 527
www.sealcoast.com
Tours of Wellington's wild south coast take in the Red Rocks and the wind turbine, as well as the fur seal colony at Tongue Point and Sinclair Head. There is time to meet the seals, learn about their life cycle and have refreshments. Tours leave from the visitor information office.
🕐 Daily 10.30, 1.30 💰 NZ$74, child (under 14) NZ$40

⊕ WALK WELLINGTON
Tel 04-472 8280
www.wellingtonnz.com/Walk-Wellington/

Seal Coast Safaris get you close to these intriguing creatures

Knowledgeable locals take guided walks around the city, which can be personalised to suit your interests or focus on arts, heritage, shopping or nature. Book at least three days ahead. Scheduled Essential Wellington walks give a general introduction to the city. They leave from the visitor information office and you can book them there (tel 04-802 4860).
🕐 Essential Wellington: Nov–end Mar daily at 10am; Apr–end Oct call ahead to find out times and days 💰 From NZ$20, child (5–16) NZ$10, under 5s free

⊕ WELLINGTON ROVER TOURS
PO Box 11167, Wellington
Tel 021-426211
www.wellingtonrover.co.nz
With these coach tours you can visit *Lord of the Rings* locations (including lunch at Rivendell), take a 'hop on hop off' day pass or search for glow-worms on a sunset drive around the south coast.
💰 From NZ$40, child NZ$25

⊕ CAPITAL E
Civic Square, Wellington
Tel 04-913 3720
www.capitale.org.nz
A creative technology and performance facility for children, located in Civic Square, Capital E has professional theatrical shows, including puppets, masks and music. There are also events, exhibitions, activities, and workshops, which include a TV studio.
🕐 Daily 10–5

⊕ CARTER OBSERVATORY AND PLANETARIUM
40 Salamanca Road, Wellington
Tel 04-472 8167
www.carterobservatory.org.
The observatory is located in the Botanic Garden, close to the top terminal of the Cable Car (▷ 101), and includes a planetarium, several telescopes and a giftshop. Choose from two shows at the planetarium (one of which is always the current night sky), and enjoy solar viewing or night sky telescope viewing.
🕐 Nov–end Feb Sun–Tue 10–5, open late Wed–Sat; Mar–end Oct Mon–Thu 11–4, open late Fri, Sat 🎫

⊕ KARORI WILDLIFE SANCTUARY (▷ 104)

⊕ WELLINGTON CABLE CAR (▷ 101)

⊕ WELLINGTON ZOO (▷ 105)

FESTIVALS AND EVENTS

JANUARY

WELLINGTON CUP WEEK
Trentham Racecourse, Upper Hutt
www.trentham.co.nz
The highlight of the Wellington race calendar also marks Wellington's Anniversary Weekend. And high fashion is all part of the race-day fun.

WINGS OVER WAIRARAPA
Hood Aerodrome, Masterton
Tel 027-477 417
www.wings.org.nz
Organised by the New Zealand Sport and Vintage Aviation Society, this biennial show (odd years) commemorates milestones in aviation, with displays of World War I and II warbirds and many other famous and interesting vintage aircraft.

FEBRUARY–MARCH

FRINGE FESTIVAL
61 Abel Smith Street, Wellington
Tel 04-382 8015
www.fringe.org.nz
The Fringe started as an offshoot of the International Festival to cater for people with smaller pockets and alternative tastes. It has now become an annual festival in its own right, with comedy, dance, new media, parties, spoken word, music and free performances.

MARTINBOROUGH FAIR
The Square, Martinborough
Tel 06-304 9933
www.martinboroughfair.org.nz
This country fair—the largest event of its type in New Zealand—is held on two days, one month apart, and includes arts, crafts and food from all over the country. It attracts around 480 stallholders and more than 40,000 visitors each year.
🌐 Free

NEW ZEALAND INTERNATIONAL ARTS FESTIVAL
PO Box 10113,
Wellington
Tel 04-473 0149
www.nzfestival.telecom.co.nz
The city barely sleeps during this month-long biennial festival (held in even years) as Wellington hums with top international acts that would not normally come to New Zealand—cabaret, jazz, circus, classical music and avant garde theatre—along with fresh, commissioned local work.

MARCH

GOLDEN SHEARS
12 Dixon Street,
Masterton
Tel 06-378 8008
www.goldenshears.co.nz
Reckoned to be the world's premier shearing and wool-handling championship, this three-day event gives a unique insight into New Zealand's rural community as sheep are shorn at lightning speed.

SEPTEMBER

MONTANA WORLD OF WEARABLE ART
TSB Bank Arena,
Wellington
Tel 03-548 9299
www.worldofwearableart.com
Art is taken off the wall to adorn the body in wildly wonderful ways in this annual show, which started in Nelson and has spread to the extent that it has had to make a home in Wellington. The WOW exhibition remains in Nelson (▷ 115).

OCTOBER–NOVEMBER

WELLINGTON INTERNATIONAL JAZZ FESTIVAL
PO Box 11981, Manners Street,
Wellington
Tel 04-385 9602
www.jazzfestival.co.nz
From jazz standards to avant cabaret, free jazz to funky dance grooves, there is jazz for every taste in cafés, bars and venues all over the city during this annual two-week festival of international and local talent.
🌐 From NZ$10, tickets from Ticketek

NOVEMBER

SCARECROW'S BIG DAY OUT
Gladstone School, Gladstone
Tel 06-372 7601
www.gladstone.org.nz
Scarecrows are scattered throughout the Gladstone district in this lighthearted fair, which includes a 'Scarecrow Scamper' 10km (6-mile) walk and fun run.

TOAST MARTINBOROUGH
Kitchener Street, Martinborough
Tel 06-306 9183
www.toastmartinborough.co.nz
A highlight of the New Zealand wine calendar, this festival is so popular that the 10,500 tickets sell out fast. Festival-goers move from vineyard to vineyard, where local and Wellington chefs match food to the winemaker's selection, and there is top live entertainment. You also get the chance to sample vintages that have been saved for the festival, but have otherwise sold out. There is a free shuttle bus.
🌐 NZ$60

WHAT TO DO

NELSON AND MARLBOROUGH

Nelson is reckoned to be New Zealand's sunniest region; it is also one of the prettiest, with acres of golden-sand beaches, rolling hills and lush farmland, orchards and vineyards. Nelson also has one of the country's most popular walks, the Abel Tasman Coast Track. Every settlement is crowded with craft studios, and Nelson city has an astonishing number of restaurants. Eco-tourism on both land and sea is especially popular here.

The same is true of the Marlborough Sounds, an intricate network of bays and inlets, many of them reachable only by boat. A cruise on the Sounds is a must; better still, stay at one of the isolated resorts, where you can spend the day doing bush walks such as the Queen Charlotte Track, swim, cycle, kayak or sail, then pamper yourself with spa treatments, and eat and sleep in comfort. (Note: Outdoors you'll need to protect yourself against biting sandflies.)

Marlborough is also New Zealand's largest wine region, famous for its Sauvignon blanc but also producing a wide range of styles. A comprehensive wine trail map is available from visitor information offices, or you can choose from several tours. Don't expect great shopping, entertainment or nightlife, however.

Whale-watching made Kaikoura's name as a destination. Because of the marine geography, whales come close to the coast, and the environment attracts rare seabirds and other marine life. You can view them from a boat, a plane, a helicopter or a kayak, and swim with some of them. Landlubbers can get close to the seal colony by driving along the Kaikoura Peninsula. The road south from Kaikoura hugs the precipitous coast and is particularly scenic, as is the train journey from Picton to Christchurch, stopping at Kaikoura. The township itself comes alive during the annual Seafest.

KEY TO SYMBOLS	
⊕	Shopping
♪	Entertainment
♈	Nightlife
⊗	Sports
✪	Activities
♡	Health and Beauty
✿	For Children

ABEL TASMAN NATIONAL PARK

✪ ABEL TASMAN WILSON'S EXPERIENCES
265 High Street, Motueka
Tel 03-528 2027
www.abeltasman.co.nz
Depending on your budget and the time you have available, you can choose from half-day to five-day experiences of the Abel Tasman Coast Track (▷ 109–110), cruising, walking and/or kayaking, with or without a guide. There's also the opportunity to stay overnight in beachfront accommodation, with food provided.
🚣 Adult from NZ$53, child NZ$26

✪ KAITERITERI KAYAKS
Sandy Bay Road, Kaiteriteri
Tel 03-527 8383
www.seakayak.co.nz
As well as kayaking trips lasting from two hours to five days, this company offers the option

of swimming with the seals at the Tonga Island Marine Reserve. Swimming is combined with kayaking, water taxi trips or walking the Abel Tasman Coast Track.

🔘 Adult from NZ$55, child NZ$40

BLENHEIM

⊕ MARLBOROUGH FARMERS' MARKET

A&P Showgrounds, Maxwell Road, Blenheim

Tel 03-579 3599

www.mfm.co.nz

Fresh local produce is sold direct to the community at this summer market, where more than 30 producers supply wild game, organic salmon and koura, preserves and pickles, roasted coffee, potato plates, fresh vegetables, heirloom potatoes, half-baked baguettes and other natural products.

🔘 Nov–end Mar Sun 9–12

⊕ THE VILLAGE

193 Rapaura Road, Blenheim

Tel 03-579 3520

Several speciality stores are found under one roof here, including coffee, olive products, giftware, Mud House and Le Grys wines, Prenzel fruit liqueurs and schnapps (▷ 119).

🔘 Daily 10–5

⊙ CLOUDY BAY

Jacksons Road, Blenheim

Tel 03-520 9140

www.cloudybay.co.nz

New Zealand's most internationally acclaimed Sauvignon blanc is made here, and so are some other less well known but equally interesting wines, including barrel-fermented Chardonnay, Pinot noir, Pelorus *méthode traditionelle* and Te Koko, an oak-aged Sauvignon blanc fermented with wild yeasts.

🔘 Daily 10–5

⊙ DANIEL LE BRUN

Terrace Road, Renwick (west of Blenheim)

Tel 03-572 8859

www.lebrun.co.nz

With its courtyard café and cellars tunnelled into the hillside, Daniel Le Brun is a romantic spot for a bite to eat or a winery tour. The company makes a range of wines, and is best known for its *méthode traditionelle* sparkling wine—it's well worth taking a winery tour, which explains the specialist techniques involved

🔘 Daily 10–4.30 📷

⊙ HUNTERS WINES (▷ 232–233)

Searching for bargains at a Marlborough farmers' market

⊙ MARLBOROUGH OLIVES NEW ZEALAND

Fell Street, Grovetown, Blenheim

Tel 03-577 8834

www.marlborough-olives.co.nz

New Zealand's first commercial olive grove was established here in 1986 by the late Gidon Blumenfeld, and the oil they press here is named after him. The grove is part of a world-wide trial based on the olive collection at Córdoba, Spain, and the research centre of Israel. Phone before you visit.

🔘 Mon–Fri 8.30–4.30

⊙ MARLBOROUGH RIVER QUEEN

Riverside Park, Horton Street, Blenheim

Tel 03-577 5510/0800-266 322

www.riverqueencruise.co.nz

Gentle Cruises along the Opawa River in a replica paddle steamer, Mississippi-style. Lunch cruises take two leisurely hours, afternoon ones last an hour, and dinner cruises three.

🔘 Thu–Sat 12, 3.15, 6.30, Sun 12, 3.15

🔘 From NZ$12.50

⊙ MARLBOROUGH TRAVEL

PO Box 1000, Blenheim

Tel 03-577 9997

www.marlboroughtravel.co.nz

Insights into many aspects of Marlborough life are offered in these land- and sea-based tours. The signature Greenshell Mussel Cruise visits a mussel farm in the Sounds, and serves mussels cooked on board with a glass of locally made Sauvignon blanc. A gourmet tour focuses on wine and food matching. Other tours visit gardens, olive groves, vineyards and craftspeople. Tours can be personalised to your interests.

🔘 From NZ$95

⊙ MONTANA BRANCOTT WINERY (▷ 119)

⊙ PRENZEL DISTILLING COMPANY (▷ 119)

⊙ WINE TOURS BY BIKE

191 Bells Road, Blenheim

Tel 03-577 6954

www.winetoursbybike.co.nz

Cycling is a popular way to see the vineyards in this flat countryside. This service, operated by Argrove Lodge, allows you to join a guided tour or hire a bicycle and have it delivered to your door. Trailer bicycles cater for young children.

🔘 From NZ$40

WHAT TO DO

COLLINGWOOD

✪ CAPE FAREWELL HORSE TREKS

McGowan Street, Puponga, Collingwood
Tel 03-524 8031
www.horsetreksnz.com
Horse treks in this beautiful countryside take in stunning views over farmland and beach, with river crossings, caves and the option of a gallop along the sands. Trips can last from 1.5 hours to four days.
From NZ$35

✪ FAREWELL SPIT TOURS

Tasman Street, Collingwood
Tel 03-524 8257
www.farewellspit.com
This company has more than 50 years experience of taking people out onto Farewell Spit. The tours go to the lighthouse, the gannet colony, Cape Farewell, and to see the wading birds (▷ 111). Trips last from 3 to 6.5 hours.
Adult from NZ$80, child (under 16) NZ$45

KAIKOURA

◉ DONEGAL HOUSE

Schoolhouse Road, RD1, Kaikoura
Tel 03-319 5083
www.donegalhouse.co.nz
Donegal House is a lively Irish pub, restaurant and B&B surrounded by beautiful gardens and run by Murray Boyd, whose ancestors arrived from Donegal, Ireland, in 1865. The bar is a popular place to meet the Kaikoura locals and there is often live music, as well as Guinness and Kilkenny on tap and a choice of 140 whiskeys.
Daily 7am–midnight 🚗 4km (2.5 miles) north of Kaikoura on SH1; turn left into Schoolhouse Road

✪ DOLPHIN ENCOUNTER AND ALBATROSS ENCOUNTER

96 Esplanade, Kaikoura
Tel 03-319 6777
www.dolphin.co.nz
www.oceanwings.co.nz
You can swim with dolphins or watch rare seabirds on launch trips by these sister companies. Wetsuits and snorkelling equipment are provided for swimmers, and there are hot showers on board.
Adult from NZ$60, child NZ$40
Oct–end May daily 5.30, 8.30, 12.30; Jun–end Sep 8.30, 12.30

✪ KAIKOURA HELICOPTERS

PO Box 5, Kaikoura
Tel 03-319 6609

A traditional Maori greeting (hongi), Maori Tours Kaikoura

www.worldofwhales.co.nz
In a helicopter you don't get as close to the wildlife as you can on a boat, but you do get a bird's-eye view of the whole whale on these World of Whales flights. Other scenic flights are also available.
Daily on demand (weather permitting) From NZ$195, family NZ$680

✪ KAIKOURA KAYAK

Tel 021-462 889
www.seakayakkaikoura.co.nz
Kayaking is a good way to encounter seals and watch ocean-going birds such as albatrosses, while keeping the impact on the environment to

a minimum. You can freedom-hire or take a half-day guided tour, combined with optional diving and snorkelling. Kayak training is also available.
Oct–end Apr daily 8.30, 12.30, 4.30; May–end Sep daily 9, 1 Adult from NZ$70, child (under 12) NZ$50. Freedom hire from NZ$55

✪ MAORI TOURS KAIKOURA

10 Churchill Street, Kaikoura
Tel 03-319 5567
www.maoritours.co.nz
A good introduction to local culture and protocol, these tours visit local pa sites and a Maori home, and explore native bush to see how the Maori used plants. Tours leave from the Kaikoura Information Office.
Daily 9, 1.30 Adult NZ$85, child (under 15) NZ$45

✪ WHALEWATCH KAIKOURA

Whaleway Station, off Beach Road (SH1), Kaikoura
Tel 03-319 6767
www.whalewatch.co.nz
You need to book well in advance for these boat trips. As well as whales, you can expect to see dolphins, seals, albatrosses and other seabirds (there is an 80 per cent refund if no whales appear). An on-board computer animation explains the marine geography of the Kaikoura Canyon. Trips are weather-dependent. Children under 3 are not permitted.
Mar–end Oct daily 7.15, 10, 12.45; Nov–end Feb 7.15, 10, 12.45, 3.30
Adult NZ$130, child NZ$60

✪ WINGS OVER WHALES

Kaikoura Airfield, 6km (4 miles) south of Kaikoura
Tel 03-319 6580/0800-226629
www.whales.co.nz
Sightseeing flights give you a bird's-eye view of whales, dolphins and seals, as well as the spectacular Kaikoura scenery.
Daily 9–4 Adult from NZ$135, child (4–13) NZ$75

MAPUA

🏛 COOL STORE GALLERY
7 Aranui Road, Mapua
Tel 03-540 5778
www.coolstoregallery.co.nz
The works of more than 70 artists and craftspeople from the Nelson and West Coast regions are displayed here.
🕙 Daily 10–5

🏛 THE NAKED BUN
66 Aranui Road, Mapua
Tel 03-540 3656
Grab a croissant or Danish pastry for breakfast, stock up for a picnic with speciality breads, quiches and pastries at this village bakery, or have a coffee and eat in the café.
🕙 Wed–Sun 7–5 🔲

✪ MAPUA ADVENTURES
8 Aranui Road, Mapua
Tel 03-540 3833
www.mapuaadventures.co.nz
Jet-boating, mountain biking, birdwatching and kayaking are among the diversions available, with options for individuals, families and children. Trips explore the Mapua estuary, coastline and forests.
🚣 From NZ$35

MOTUEKA

🏛 MOTUEKA SUNDAY MARKET
Decks Reserve Carpark, Motueka
Tel 03-540 2709
This eclectic market mixes food, New Zealand crafts, Asian and Peruvian clothing, collectables, second-hand items, plants, seasonal fruits and vegetables with live music and street drama.
🕙 Sun 8–1

✪ ABEL TASMAN AIR
PO Box 125, Motueka
Tel 03 528 8290
www.abeltasmanair.co.nz
If you are short of time and want to see a lot, this may be the way to go. Tours fly to Abel Tasman National Park for lunch at Awaroa Lodge, to the West Coast for part of the Heaphy Track, or head to Kaikoura for whale-watching and a crayfish lunch. The company also operates scenic flights and connecting flights for trampers.
🚣 From NZ$65

✪ BUSH AND BEYOND
35 School Road, RD3 Motueka
Tel 03-528 9054
www.naturetreks.co.nz
Bush and Beyond is a conservation-based guiding business specialising in flora and birds. Treks last from one to eight days in Kahurangi National Park. Itineraries cater for all ages and fitness levels and can be personalised. You can stay in comfortable lodges,

Checking out the coffee roaster at Pomeroy's, Nelson

walk the Heaphy Track or go off-track wilderness backpacking.
🚣 From NZ$115, family NZ$350

MURCHISON

✪ RUSSELL FROST'S TICKLISH TROUT TOURS
PO Box 30, Murchison
Tel 03-523 9868
www.guidedflyfishingnz.com
Russell Frost specialises in 'New Zealand-style stalking' of wild brown trout in high country streams, braided rivers and glacial lakes. Trips can last from half a day to an overnight camp-out.
🚣 From NZ$450 for two people

✪ ULTIMATE DESCENTS
51 Fairfax Street, Murchison
Tel 03-523 9899
www.rivers.co.nz
Despite the name, this company arranges family-friendly rafting trips on the Buller River, as well as adrenaline-pumping whitewater kayaking and rafting, camp-outs, and one-to five-day heli-journeys. Minimum ages apply to all trips.
🕙 Adult from NZ$95, child NZ$75
🏛 🔲

NELSON

🏛 NELSON MARKET
Montgomery Square, Nelson
Tel 027-270 2600
www.nelsonmarket.com
On Saturday mornings a dreary car park in central Nelson is transformed into a marketplace, with a flea market mix of clothes and crafts and a fine selection of food. Look for local organic fruit and vegetables, speciality breads, local sheep's cheese, bratwurst made from local pork, and Blackbird Valley Forge's knives made from recycled materials.
🕙 Sat 8–1

🏛 POMEROY'S COFFEE AND TEA CO.
80 Hardy Street, Nelson
Tel 03-546 6944
www.pomeroys.co.nz
An old-fashioned boutique coffee roaster, Pomeroy's sells 25 blends of coffee and a huge variety of speciality teas. It also serves excellent coffee to drink on the spot, and stocks Nelson olive oils and deli items.
🕙 Mon–Fri 9–5, Sat 9.30–12.30

🎭 THEATRE ROYAL
Rutherford Street, Nelson
Tel 03-548 3840
New Zealand's oldest wooden theatre, built in 1878, the Royal is in need of restoration but it still hosts the Nelson Repertory and other local and visiting shows.

PHAT CLUB
137 Bridge Street, Nelson
Tel 03-548 3311
www.phatclub.co.nz
A mix of dance music and live acts makes this a popular late-night dance club and venue. Whether your taste runs to techno, dub, rock, hip-hop, indie or punk reggae, you can find it here.
Thu–Sat 10pm–late

VICTORIAN ROSE
281 Trafalgar Street, Nelson
Tel 03-548 7631
www.victorianrose.co.nz
A firm supporter of local music, the Victorian Rose pub has regular Tuesday night gigs with the Nelson Jazz Club, Wednesday and Thursday nights devoted to freewheeling jazz, and weekends get feet dancing with jazz-rock blends of local and imported bands. There's a blackboard menu, Mac's beers and local wines.
Daily 11am–late

HAPPY VALLEY ADVENTURES
194 Cable Bay Road, Nelson
Tel 03-545 0304
www.happyvalleyadventures.co.nz
This 650ha (1,600-acre) farm offers eco-tours on 4X4 motor-cycles, taking in an extensive native forest valley with a 2000-year-old matai tree. Other attractions include bush-walks, Skywire rides reaching up to 100kph (60mph), and rides on an eight-wheel drive amphibious all-terrain vehicle.
From NZ$70, child (under 16) NZ$1 per year of age

JJ'S QUALITY TOURS
31a Stansell Avenue, Nelson
Tel 03-546 5470/0800-568 568
www.jjs.co.nz
As well as wine tours of the region that made their name, JJ's now offer a tour of five Nelson breweries, and sight-seeing and craft tours. You may be able to mix and match, according to your interests.
From NZ$50

NELSON GOLF CLUB
38 Bolt Road, Nelson
Tel 03-548 5029
www.nelsongolf.co.nz
This championship-standard, 18-hole course is near the air-port on the shores of Tasman Bay—a short drive from the city. It has fine views over the sea and mountains, a fully stocked pro-shop and clubs, trundlers and carts for hire.
Daily 7–7 NZ$40

VERTICAL LIMITS
34 Vanguard Street, Nelson
Tel 03-545 7511
www.verticallimits.co.nz
Even if you have no previous experience you can join a

Strapped in for the Skywire ride at Happy Valley Adventures

rock-climbing expedition, or learn the principles indoors on a climbing wall.
Mon–Thu 12–9, Fri–Sun 10–6 From NZ$40

FOUNDERS HISTORIC PARK
87 Atawhai Drive, Nelson
Tel 03-548 2649
www.founderspark.co.nz
This collection of buildings from the late 1800s houses several businesses, including a bone carver and a café. There are also displays of vintage transport, and train rides daily between 26 December and 10 January. Children can enjoy the

playground and 3-D maze, and their parents can sample the excellent organic brews produced on-site by Founders craft brewery.
Daily 10–4.30 Adult NZ$5, child NZ$2, family NZ$13

NATURELAND
Tahunanui Beach, Tahunanui (southwest of downtown Nelson)
Tel 03-548 6166
www.naturelandzoo.co.nz
This little family-oriented zoo has exotic, domestic and native wildlife, a walk-through aviary and an aquarium. Families can feed the animals and enjoy a picnic by the playground.
Daily 9–4 Adult NZ$5, child (2–14) NZ$2

NELSON FUN PARK
Tahunanui Beach, Tahunanui (southwest of downtown Nelson)
Tel 03-548 6267
A hydroslide, bumper boats and mini-golf are the attractions at this beachside family fun park. The hydroslide is closed from May to the end of September.
Sat, Sun 11.30–5, plus school holidays Adult from NZ$4, child NZ$2.50

PICTON

THE COUGAR LINE
The Waterfront, Picton
Tel 03-573 7925
www.cougarlinecruises.co.nz
Scheduled trips around the Marlborough Sounds visit various bays to drop off and take on passengers. Short cruises are also available, taking in up to 80km (50 miles) of coastline in three hours, with a commentary on the way. A popular option is the day trip to Ship Cove, with the opportunity to walk for five hours on the Queen Charlotte Track to Furneaux Lodge.
From NZ$50

DOLPHIN WATCH ECOTOURS

The Waterfront, Picton
Tel 03-573 8040
www.dolphinwatchmarlborough.co.nz
As well as the popular swimming with dolphins, this company takes trips to Motuara Island bird sanctuary, to walk a section of the Queen Charlotte Track, and do some birdwatching for king shags (found only in the Sounds), New Zealand robins, little blue penguins and saddlebacks.
From NZ$80

MARLBOROUGH SOUNDS ADVENTURE COMPANY

London Quay, Picton
Tel 0800-283283
www.marlboroughsounds.com
Adventures of all kinds are on offer in trips that combine kayaking, mountain biking and walking on the Queen Charlotte Track. One of the most popular is the Ultimate Sounds Adventure, a guided one-day hiking, one-day sea kayaking, one-day mountain biking adventure. There is an overnight stay at Portage Resort Hotel, either backpacker-style or in twin-share ensuite accommodation.
From NZ$50

SOUNDS CONNECTION

10 London Quay, Picton
Tel 03-573 8843
www.soundsconnection.co.nz
Choose from launch and coach tours, or fishing or wine tasting on scheduled and private half- to full-day tours.
From NZ$55

RICHMOND

CRAFT HABITAT

Champion Road, Richmond
Tel 03-544 1488
www.crafthabitat.co.nz
Watch the makers at work at Nelson's arts and crafts village, buy their work or commission them to make something for you. There is also a specialist food shop.
Daily 9–5 ☐ Courtyard café

THE GRAPE ESCAPE

Corner of McShane Road and Coastal Highway, Richmond
Tel 03-544 4341
www.grapeescape.co.nz
Organic vineyard Richmond Plains and Te Mania Estate share an outlet for their wines in this rustic complex, which also sells arts and crafts, the Prenzel range of liqueurs and schnapps (▷ 119), and chocolate.
Daily 10.30–4.30 ☐

HÖGLUND ART GLASS

Landsdowne Road, Richmond
Tel 03-544 6500
www.hoglund.co.nz

Watching the glass-blowing at Höglund Art Glass

Ola Höglund and Marie Simberg-Höglund have an international reputation as hot-glass blowers and their gallery is a candy store of brilliant hues and design. Their International Glass Centre includes a glass-blowing studio, exhibition hall, engraving studio, and cold-work studio for cutting, sandblasting and polishing. Guided tours show you the artists at work.
Daily 9–5; tours 10.30, 1.30, 3
Tours: adult NZ$15, child (under 14) free

STOKE

MAC'S BREWERY

660 Main Road, Stoke
Tel 03-547 0526
www.macs.co.nz
Nelson's local brewery, Mac's makes naturally brewed lagers, ales and innovative limited-release beers. You can tour, sample the beers and browse in the shop.
Daily 10–5.30; tours daily 11, 2

TAKAKA

ANATOKI SALMON

McCallums Road, Takaka
Tel 03-525 7251
www.anatokisalmon.co.nz
Catch your own salmon here and tour the salmon farm on the banks of the Anatoki River. Fishing rods and tackle are supplied, and you can hire a barbecue to cook your fish.
Daily 9–5

BENCARRI NATURE PARK

McCallums Road, Takaka
Tel 03-525 8261
Feeding the Anatoki eels has been a popular holiday pastime here since 1914, and Bencarri has plenty of other friendly farm animals to feed, touch and interact with. Horse-riding and mini-golf are among the other attractions, and the gallery sells knitwear and alpaca/llama yarns.
Sep–end Apr daily 10–6 ☐

WAIRAU VALLEY

LEIGHVANDER

RD1 Wairau Valley
Tel 03-572 2851
www.leighvandercottage.co.nz
A collection of 140 varieties of lavender grows in this lovely garden, which surrounds a restored 1859 cob cottage. Handmade soaps and body products made from lavender are among the products sold in the studio, which also offers gifts, including ribboned lace, candle wicking and furniture.
Nov–end Mar by appointment

WHAT TO DO

WHAT TO DO

JANUARY

NELSON JAZZFEST

Nelson Jazz Club, PO Box 7188, Nelson

Tel 03-546 9269

www.nelsonjazz.co.nz

A wide variety of jazz bands from the Nelson region and around the country perform in this week-long festival, with events on the streets and at various venues around the town. There's a grand finale on New Year's Day at Fairfield Park.

🎟 Tickets from Everyman Records, 249 Hardy Street, Nelson

NELSON SUMMER KITE FESTIVAL

Neale Park, Nelson

Tel 03-548 8707

http://nkc.nayland.school.nz

This two-day festival, hosted by Nelson Kite Club, fills the Nelson sky with kites in every conceivable shape and form. Don't be surprised to see a flying cat or a giant lizard.

JANUARY–FEBRUARY

MARLBOROUGH 4 FUN SUMMER CONCERTS

Various locations

Tel 03-577 8935

www.marlborough4fun.co.nz

Free outdoor concerts are held during the summer holiday season.

FEBRUARY

BLUES BREWS AND BBQS

A&P Park, Maxwell Road, Blenheim

www.bluesbrews.co.nz

Held on the first Saturday in February, this festival combines tastings of local ales, alcoholic lemonades, ciders and beers, with a variety of barbecue food, live bands and children's entertainment.

🕐 Noon–7.30 🎟 NZ$35 from Ticket Direct, tel 0800-224 224

WINE MARLBOROUGH FESTIVAL

Brancott Vineyard, Brancott Road, Blenheim

Tel 03-577 9299

www.wine-marlborough-festival.co.nz

This showcase for Marlborough wines, held in a vineyard on the second Saturday and Sunday in February, provides an opportunity to sample over 150 wines from more than 40 wineries. The event also includes wine workshops, wine and food matches, entertainment and music.

🕐 10–6 🎟 NZ$35 from Ticket Direct, tel 0800-224 224 🚌 Shuttle buses from Blenheim

EASTER

CLASSIC FIGHTERS MARLBOROUGH

Tel 03-578 8227

Omaka Aerodrome, Blenheim

www.classicfighters.co.nz

Aircraft are displayed as part of a theatrical spectacle, where battle scenes from both world wars are re-enacted on the ground as well as in the air.

🕐 From 7.30am 🎟 Gate sales: adult from NZ$15, child (6–12) NZ$5

JULY

NELSON SCHOOL OF MUSIC WINTER FESTIVAL

Nelson School of Music, 48 Nile Street, Nelson

Tel 03-548 9477

www.nsom.ac.nz

This annual two-week festival of music, comedy, dance and drama features local, national and international artists.

OCTOBER

KAIKOURA SEAFEST

Takahanga Domain, Kaikoura

Tel 03-319 5641

www.kaikoura.co.nz/seafest

Held on the first Saturday of October, Seafest is an annual celebration of the abundance of the ocean and all it represents for the Kaikoura region. It combines continuous live entertainment with cooking demonstrations and food, wines and beverages from the Kaikoura, Marlborough and North Canterbury regions. Beforehand, you can dance at the Big Top Bash.

🕐 10–5 🎟 Adult NZ$20, child (5–17) NZ$5

NELSON ARTS FESTIVAL

Nelson City Council, 110 Trafalgar Street, Nelson

Tel 03-546 0212

www.nelsonfestivals.co.nz

Entertainment of all kinds is provided in this annual two-week festival, which includes a mask carnival, sculpture symposium, street fun and other cultural events.

NOVEMBER

HUNTER'S GARDEN MARLBOROUGH

PO Box 1180, Blenheim

Tel 03-577 5500

www.garden-marlborough.co.nz

Green-fingered enthusiasts from all over New Zealand gather in Blenheim for this annual six-day celebration of gardening, which includes garden tours, seminars, workshops and a market day with 200 stalls in Seymour Square.

DECEMBER

KAHURANGI ENDURANCE TRIATHLON AND MOUNTAIN CLASSIC RUN

Golden Bay

www.nelsontriclub.co.nz

One-day multi-sport events in New Zealand started here in 1984, and this is still one of the best, combined with a classic off-road run. An endurance test strictly for the super fit, combining cycling, kayaking and running.

CANTERBURY AND THE WEST COAST

The 'English' city of Christchurch may lack the sophistication of Auckland or the liveliness of Wellington, but it makes up for it in ease of access to a wide range of facilities and activities. You can visit beautiful gardens or an interactive Antarctic exhibit, find trendy fashions in the High Street or see craftspeople at work in the Arts Centre, attend a concert by the Christchurch Symphony or play golf on one of many courses, take a gondola up the Port Hills or find some of the country's best windsurfing on the Estuary. *The Press* newspaper carries entertainment listings.

Christchurch's main shopping area is a pleasant network of pedestrian malls intersecting Colombo Street and fringing Cathedral Square, in which you can find speciality shops, international fashion and lifestyle chains, food courts, cafés and bookshops. The heart of New Zealand's high-tech sports and leisurewear industry, Christchurch is the home of labels such as Fairydown and Macpac. Locals tend to shop at look-alike suburban malls such as Eastgate, Westfield Riccarton and The Palms.

Shops are few and far between on the West Coast, where 'wild' sums up the scenery, the weather and the folks. You can sample the atmosphere of the place at the Mahinapua pub, south of Hokitika, and get it in spades at the annual Hokitika Wildfood Festival. Farther south, the Fox and Franz Josef glaciers are amazingly easily accessible.

An hour's drive north of Christchurch, Waipara is the region's main wine-growing area, with a number of vineyards open to the public, some with restaurants. In the same area, Hanmer Springs is noted for its thermal pools.

Less than two hours driving west from Christchurch gives you a great choice of skiing, from commercial fields such as Mount Hutt to the club fields of the Craigieburn Range, which offer a particularly New Zealand experience with primitive facilities, friendly people and ungroomed slopes.

KEY TO SYMBOLS	
🏬	Shopping
🎭	Entertainment
🍸	Nightlife
🏃	Sports
⭐	Activities
♥	Health and Beauty
✹	For Children

AKAROA

🏬 **AKAROA BLUE PEARLS**
Main Wharf, Akaroa
Tel 03-304 7877
www.akaroabluepearls.com
Iridescent blue mabe (hemi-spherical) pearls are cultured in paua in Akaroa Harbour and Tory Channel. The Eyris Blue Pearl Centre tells the story of their creation and sells them.
🕐 Oct–end Mar daily 10.30–5.30; Apr–end Sep 11–4.30

🏬 **BARRYS BAY CHEESE**
Main Road, Barrys Bay, Akaroa Harbour
Tel 03-304 5809
At Barrys Bay, Don and Jeanette Walker are carrying on a cheese-making tradition going back more than 150 years. They are the only people in New Zealand still making traditional cloth-bound rinded cheddar, and also make a range of European cheeses. You can watch the cheese

being made on alternate days during the season, and taste it in the shop, which also sells local wine and deli items.

⏰ Aug–end May Mon–Fri 8.30–5, Sat, Sun 9.30–5; Jun, Jul Mon–Fri 9–5, Sat 9.30–1, Sun 9.30–4.30

🏢 NATURALLY JADE
57 rue Lavaud, Akaroa
Tel 03-304 7781
www.naturallyjade.co.nz
You can watch the craftsman at work here, carving items from greenstone (*pounamu*, or New Zealand jade). The gallery has a superb collection of greenstone works, from large sculptures to jewellery—many show designs with symbolic associations, which he will explain. The shop also stocks gold, silver, paua and bone jewellery by other artists.

⏰ Mon–Fri 9–5, Sat, Sun 10–5

⭐ AKAROA HARBOUR CRUISES
Main Wharf, Akaroa
Tel 03-304 7641
www.blackcat.co.nz
Two-hour scenic wildlife cruises at 11am and 1.30pm are on offer here. Although the highlight is the likely sighting of Hector's dolphins, you may also see little blue penguins, spotted shags and fur seals. You can also swim with dolphins and take a guided kayak trip.

⏰ Nov–end Apr 11, 1.30; May–end Oct 1.30 💲 Adult from NZ$52, child (5–15) NZ$20

⭐ AKAROA SEAL COLONY SAFARI
PO Box 4, Akaroa
Tel 03-304 7255
www.sealtours.co.nz
The four-wheel-drive safari takes a crater-rim road and goes through sheep and cattle paddocks to the seal colony on the eastern bays of Banks Peninsula. You can observe the colony from a distance, or walk around the rocky coastline to see it at close quarters.

⏰ Daily 9.30am, 1pm 💲 Adult NZ$70, child NZ$50, family NZ$190

⭐ BANKS PENINSULA TRACK
PO Box 54, Akaroa
Tel 03-304 7612
www.bankstrack.co.nz
Leaving from Akaroa, the track takes in 35km (22 miles) of spectacular coastline, native bush, waterfalls and beaches. It can be done in two or four days, staying in farm cottages with hot showers and well-equipped kitchens. You can take your own food and some supplies are available on route. Pack cartage is available (at extra cost) for parts of the track.

⏰ Oct–end Apr 💲 2 days NZ$125, 4 days NZ$225

A stunning greenstone carving at Naturally Jade, Akaroa

⭐ LINTON ARTIST'S GARDEN VISITS
68 rue Balguerie, Akaroa
Tel 03-304 7501
www.linton.co.nz
Surprises are everywhere in Josie Martin's enchantingly eccentric artist's garden, dotted with sculptures and mosaics, including an extraordinary sculptural wall mosaic. The house is a showcase for her paintings, and the venue for art workshops and concerts. You can also stay on a bed-and-breakfast basis.

⏰ Oct to mid-Jun daily 2–4 💲 House NZ$10; garden NZ$12

⭐ POHATU PENGUINS
Pohatu Flea Bay, Akaroa
Tel 03-304 8552
www.pohatu.co.nz
Pohatu is home to the largest white-flippered penguin colony on the South Island. The best time to come is during the breeding season, from September to January. Guided evening walks are available through the colony; as the road is only accessible to four-wheel-drive vehicles or mountain bikes, the recommended option is to join the tour at Akaroa. Scenic day tours and kayak rental are also available.

💲 Adult from NZ$55, child (under 12) NZ$40

🌿 LUMIÈRE
8 rue Balguerie, Akaroa
Tel 03-304 7404
www.lumieremassage.co.nz
Therapeutic massage, exfoliation, body wraps, outdoor hot tubs and reflexology are among the services offered at this 'private outdoor wilderness'.

⏰ Daily 10–5 💲 From NZ$25

CHRISTCHURCH

🏢 ARTS CENTRE
Worcester Boulevard, Christchurch
Tel 03-366 0989
www.artscentre.org.nz
Take a guided retail therapy tour or browse around the 40 art and craft outlets, many of which are working studios (▷ 124). Try to catch the weekend market, when up to 70 stalls put up their awnings and the smell of cooking from many countries fills the air.

⏰ Daily 9.30–5

🏢 BALLANTYNES
City Mall, Christchurch
Tel 03-379 7400
www.ballantynes.co.nz
A Christchurch institution, this traditional, family-run department store stocks everything from perfume to household items, bed linen to toys, and furniture to fashions

for men, women and children. Branches at Christchurch Airport and Timaru.
🕐 Mon–Thu 9–6, Fri 9–8, Sat 9–5, Sun 10–5

🏢 BIVOUAC OUTDOOR
Corner of Lichfield and Colombo streets, Christchurch
Tel 03-366 3197
www.bivouac.co.nz
Bivouac specialises in mountaineering and alpine sports equipment, including clothing, tents and packs, sleeping bags, ski gear and climbing equipment.
🕐 Mon, Wed, Thu 9–5.30, Tue 9.30–5.30, Fri 9–8, Sat, Sun 10–4

🏢 MAPWORLD
Corner of Manchester and Gloucester streets, Christchurch
Tel 03-374 5399
www.mapworld.co.nz
Mapworld has a wide range of digital and topographical city, town, provincial and national maps; also atlases and accessories such as binoculars.
🕐 Mon–Thu 8–6, Fri 8–8, Sat, Sun 9–5

🏢 MERIVALE MALL
189 Papanui Road, Christchurch
Tel 03-355 9692
www.merivalemall.co.nz
Serving a smart residential suburb, Merivale Mall has more than 40 speciality shops, many of them devoted to New Zealand and international fashion labels. It also houses several stylish restaurants and wine bars and a particularly good supermarket.
🕐 Mon–Wed, Fri 9–6, Thu 9–8, Sat 10–5, Sun 10–4

🏢 RICCARTON ROTARY MARKET
Riccarton Park Racecourse, Racecourse Road, Christchurch
Tel 03-339 0011
A community project operated by the local Rotary Clubs, this popular weekly market has more than 300 stalls selling crafts, food, clothing, jewellery, bric-à-brac and produce.
🕐 Sun 9–2

🏢 SWANNDRI CONCEPT STORE
132 Gloucester Street, Christchurch
Tel 03-379 8674
www.swanniestore.com
Best known for its famous bush shirts of checked wool—much loved by hunters, farmers and trampers needing rugged protection from the elements—Swanndri also produces a range of more fashion-conscious lightweight merino garments for men, women and children.
🕐 Mon–Fri 9–5.30, Sat 10–5

🏢 UNTOUCHED WORLD
155 Roydvale Avenue, Christchurch
Tel 03-357 9399

Stylish outdoor gear from the Untouched World collection

www.untouchedworld.co.nz
Located not far from the airport, Untouched World is a stylish modern store specialising in high-quality New Zealand lifestyle products, including its own-label merino-opossum blend knitwear, leisure and fashion clothing, skincare, art and food. A courtesy bus is available.
🕐 Daily 9–5 🍴 Restaurant and wine bar

🎭 ARTS CENTRE
Worcester Boulevard, Christchurch
Tel 03-366 0989
www.artscentre.org.nz
Several performance venues are clustered on the Arts

Centre site (▷ 124), including the Court Theatre (tel 03-963 0870, www.courttheatre.org.nz), one of New Zealand's leading professional theatre companies, which presents local and international drama, musicals and comedy. Occasional performances are also given at the University Theatre (tel 03-374 5483) and the Southern Ballet and Dance Theatre (tel 03-379 7219). The Academy Cinema and Cloisters Cinemas (tel 03-366 0167) screen art-house films. Plays and concerts, including Friday lunchtime concerts, are performed in the Great Hall.

🎭 CHRISTCHURCH TOWN HALL
95 Kilmore Street, Christchurch
Tel 03-366 8899
www.convention.co.nz
The 2,000-seat auditorium, noted for its acoustics, is a regular venue for concerts by the Christchurch Symphony Orchestra and Christchurch City Choir, as well as touring orchestras and performers. The smaller proscenium-arch James Hay Theatre hosts chamber music, opera and theatrical productions.

🎭 ISAAC THEATRE ROYAL
145 Gloucester Street, Christchurch
Tel 03-366 6326
www.isaactheatreroyal.co.nz
The grand old lady of Christchurch theatres, the Theatre Royal opened in 1908. It retains its ornate interior, and refurbishments backstage in 2005 brought it up to international standards. It hosts ballet, drama and musicals.

🎲 CHRISTCHURCH CASINO
30 Victoria Street, Christchurch
Tel 03-365 9999
www.chchcasino.co.nz
The casino has 350 gaming machines as well as blackjack, baccarat, Caribbean stud poker, American roulette, keno and *tai sai*. The dress code is smart casual and the

minimum age is 20. There are several restaurants and bars.
🕐 Daily 24 hours

🍷 CRUZ
90 Lichfield Street, Christchurch
Tel 03-379 2910
www.cruz.co.nz
A gay bar and nightclub upstairs in the Ministry nightclub, Cruz provides a relaxed lounge environment with a free pool table early weeknights, before becoming a nightclub at 11pm.
🕐 Wed–Sun 7–late

🍷 DUX DE LUX
41 Hereford Street, Christchurch
Tel 03-366 6919
www.thedux.co.nz
A restaurant and pub in the Arts Centre, the Dux hosts regular gigs by local and visiting performers. The venue is tiny and noisy, but the large outdoor courtyard acts as a popular meeting place. The attached restaurant serves vegetarian dishes and seafood, but the pub is most highly regarded for its boutique brewery. The beers are available only on tap, and are given quirky local names such as Nor'Wester (after Canterbury's famous wind). Ginger Tom ginger ale is recommended.
🕐 Daily 11am–late

🍷 ILLUSIONS
Corner of Chancery Lane and Gloucester Street, Christchurch
Tel 03-379 0572
A popular dance hangout, Illusions plays 1960s and '80s disco classics to a young crowd, with live performers on Friday and Saturday nights.
🕐 Wed–Sat 10–late

🍷 SAMMY'S JAZZ REVIEW
14 Bedford Row, Christchurch
Tel 03-377 8618
www.sammys.co.nz
Sammy's has live jazz seven nights a week, and supports local musicians with regular weekly gigs, as well as hosting

visiting groups. There's also a good à la carte menu, so you can dine while you listen.
🕐 Mon–Sat 5–late, Sun 10.30–1.30, 5–late

🍷 THE TWISTED HOP
6 Poplar Street, Lichfield Lanes, Christchurch
Tel 03-962 3688
http://thetwistedhop.co.nz
The Twisted Hop brews its own English-style cask-conditioned Golding, Challenger and Twisted Ankle ales year-round, and India Pale Ale in summer. There's a quiz night every other Sunday, and live jazz on Wednesday and Thursday.
🕐 Daily noon–late

Celebrating a win at Christchurch's Addington Raceway

🏇 ADDINGTON RACEWAY
Jack Hinton Drive, Christchurch
Tel 03-338 9094
www.addington.co.nz
The New Zealand Metropolitan Trotting Club offers harness racing all year round, including the popular Christchurch Casino and New Zealand Trotting Cup. Advance booking is required.

🏇 CENTENNIAL LEISURE CENTRE
Armagh Street, Christchurch
Tel 03-941 6853
www.centennial.org.nz
Less than 10 minutes' walk from Cathedral Square in the heart of the city, Centennial

has both a leisure pool and a lap pool, sauna, steam and spa facilities, and a fitness centre.
🕐 Mon–Thu 6am–9pm, Fri 6am–7pm, Sat, Sun 7–7 🎫 Fitness centre NZ$8, pool NZ$5, child (under 16) NZ$2.50

🏇 JADE STADIUM
Wilsons Road, Christchurch
Tel 03-379 1765
www.jadestadium.co.nz
Major rugby fixtures and test cricket attract huge crowds here. Check events on the website and book tickets through Ticketek (tel 03-377 8899).

🏇 RICCARTON PARK RACECOURSE
Racecourse Road, Christchurch
Tel 03-342 0000
www.riccartonpark.co.nz
The Canterbury Jockey Club holds 20 race days through the year, including the New Zealand Cup, New Zealand Grand National and Easter Racing Carnival.

⭐ ADVENTURE CANTERBURY
PO Box 1259, Christchurch
Tel 03-358 5991
www.adventurecanterbury.com
Whether it's golf or skiing, Akaroa or Mount Cook/Aoraki, rafting or horse-trekking, farm visits, a wine trail or fishing, this company has a tour on offer.
🎫 From NZ$45

⭐ CHRISTCHURCH BIKE TOURS
4A Ramahana Road, Huntsbury, Christchurch
Tel 03 366 0337
www.chchbiketours.co.nz
Billed as the country's only guided city bike tours, the two-hour route takes you through Hagley Park to Riccarton Bush and Mona Vale, taking advantage of the city's flatness and its good cycle facilities. Bikes are provided.
🕐 Nov–end Mar daily 2pm 🎫 NZ$25

✪ CHRISTCHURCH PERSONAL GUIDING SERVICE
1/28 Packe Street, Christchurch
Tel 03-365 8480
Daily two-hour walks leave from a kiosk in Cathedral Square, with trained guides providing informative commentary about historic and modern buildings.
🕐 Oct–end Apr daily 10am, 1pm; May–end Sep 1pm 🖐 NZ$10

✪ EXPLORE NEW ZEALAND BY BICYCLE
Tel 03-339 4020
www.cyclehire-tours.co.nz
You can go bicycling almost anywhere in the South Island with this company, from short-term hire of family bikes for an excursion in Hagley Park to taking the gondola up the Port Hills and mountain biking down, or touring farther afield.
🖐 From NZ$25

✪ HAGLEY GOLF CLUB
Hagley Park, Christchurch
Tel 03-379 8279
www.hagley.nzgolf.net
Located in Hagley Park, in the heart of Christchurch, the golf course caters for players of all abilities. The regular Friday morning 12-hole tee-off is a feature, and non-members are welcome.
🕐 Daily, open to green-fee players after 10.30am 🖐 NZ$20 for 18 holes

✪ NIMBUS PARAGLIDING
PO Box 17712, Sumner, Christchurch
Tel 03-389 1999
www.nimbusparagliding.co.nz
The Port Hills above Christchurch make a good take-off spot for paragliders. You can do a tandem paraglide without training, or Nimbus will instruct you until you are able to do a solo flight. Flying at Taylors Mistake, Scarborough Cliffs or Castle Rock, you get great views over the Canterbury Plains.
🖐 From NZ$140

✪ TASTE CANTERBURY
3 Scarborough Road, Christchurch
Tel 03-326 6753
www.goodthings.co.nz
Tailor-made food and wine tours take you to meet the makers, see them at work, and taste their wares. Half-day and full-day tours explore Christchurch city and plains, Akaroa and Banks Peninsula, West Melton, Ellesmere and Waipara.
🖐 From NZ$100

✪ TRANZALPINE HIGH COUNTRY EXPLORER TOUR
6 Fraser Place, Rangiora
(north of Christchurch)
Tel 03-377 1391

Panoramic windows make a ride on the TranzAlpine a treat

www.high-country.co.nz
Enjoy a variety of Canterbury attractions on this tour, with a coach trip across the Canterbury Plains, morning tea, a jet-boat trip, a four-wheel-drive safari, lunch and then a scenic rail trip back to Christchurch from Arthur's Pass on the TranzAlpine train.
🖐 Adult NZ$330, child (4–14) half price

✪ TRANZALPINE RAILWAY
Christchurch Railway Station, Troup Drive, Addington
Tel 0800 872467
www.tranzscenic.co.nz
This 4.5-hour rail trip from Christchurch to Greymouth takes in spectacular mountain, farm and rainforest scenery, including areas not seen from the road, such as the Waimakariri Gorge. An open-air viewing deck adds to the experience, and there is a buffet car. You can do the return trip in a day.
🕐 Daily 8.15am 🖐 Adult day return NZ$182, child NZ$101

✪ UP UP AND AWAY
PO Box 36308, Merivale, Christchurch
Tel 03-381 4600
www.hallooning.co.nz
Early-morning balloon flights over the Canterbury plains give spectacular views of the Southern Alps. You can help with preparations for take-off and, after landing in a farmer's field, celebrate with a glass of bubbly.
🖐 Adult NZ$260, child (5–11) NZ$199

✪ QEII PARK
Travis Road, New Brighton
Tel 03-941 6849
www.qeiipark.co.nz
Built for the 1974 Common-wealth Games, QEII is a multi-sport and leisure complex. The aquatic facility includes a 40m (131ft) wave pool, lazy river and children's play zone with interactive water toy features. Spa, sauna and café facilities are available poolside. QEII also has a modern fitness centre and aerobic studio, squash courts, Olympic weight-lifting gym, athletic stadium and cricket wicket.
🕐 Mon–Fri 6am–9pm, Sat, Sun 7am–8pm 🖐 Adult from NZ$5, child NZ$2.50

✪ SCIENCE ALIVE!
392 Moorhouse Avenue, Christchurch
Tel 03-365 5199
www.sciencealive.co.nz
The whole family can be entertained while learning about science through hands-on experiences and shows in this interactive exhibit. There is also a well-stocked science shop.
🕐 Mon–Thu 10–5, Fri–Sun 10–6 🖐 NZ$12 📷

WHAT TO DO

FOX GLACIER

✪ ALPINE GUIDES
Main Road, Fox Glacier
Tel 03-751 0825
www.foxguides.co.nz
Trips leave throughout the day
to suit various fitness levels,
from a gentle walk to the
glacier terminal or a half-day
hike on the lower reaches
of the glacier to heli-hikes,
ice climbing or multi-day
mountaineering. Ice-climbing
instruction days are a speciality.
Some equipment is provided,
including crampons.
🏔 Adult from NZ$79, child NZ$46

FRANZ JOSEF

✪ AIR SAFARIS
Main Road, Franz Josef
Tel 03-752 0716
www.airsafaris.co.nz
A 30-minute scenic flight gives
overviews of the Franz Josef
and Fox glaciers, rainforest
and Westland Tai Poutini
National Park. The popular
50-minute Grand Traverse
also takes in the Southern
Alps, Aoraki/Mount Cook and
the Tasman and Murchison
glaciers.
🏔 Adult from NZ$260, child NZ$180

✪ FRANZ JOSEF GLACIER GUIDES
Main Road, Franz Josef
Tel 03-752 0763
www.franzjosefglacier.com
A choice of trips is available,
ranging from an easy 2km
(1.2-mile) walk to the glacier
terminal or a half-day hike on
pre-cut steps, to a full-day
climb on spectacular icefalls
and overnight trips staying in
alpine huts. Popular heli-hikes
combine a scenic flight with a
two-hour guided trip around
the ice pinnacles of the middle
glacier. Some equipment is
provided, including strap-on
crampons. Minimum ages
and numbers apply.
🏔 Adult from NZ$90, child (6–16)
NZ$45

GERALDINE

⊕ BARKER'S BERRY BARN
Te Moana Road, Geraldine
Tel 03-693 8969
www.barkers.co.nz
Barker's fruit processors make
juices, jams, toppings, spiced
fruit sauces and condiments
from local and Central Otago
fruit. You can taste before you
buy at this retail outlet, which
also sells gift baskets, fruit
smoothies and sundaes.
🕐 Daily 9–5.30

⊕ TALBOT FOREST CHEESE
16 Talbot Street, Geraldine
Tel 03-693 1111
A remarkable range of cheeses
is produced at this little factory

A rich variety of preserves is sold at Barker's Berry Barn

in the heart of Geraldine's
shopping complex. You can
watch the cheeses being made
and sample them at the
attached retail outlet, which
also sells a variety of food-
related gift items.
🕐 Daily 9–5.30

GREYMOUTH

⊕ LEFT BANK ART GALLERY
(▷ 121)

✪ ECO-RAFTING
108 Mawhera Quay, Greymouth
Tel 03-768 4005
www.ecorafting.co.nz
Relaxing river excursions,
fly-fishing trips and extreme
white-water adventures are

offered in half-day to multi-day
trips on the Arnold, Grey
and Buller rivers.
🏔 From NZ$100

✪ MONTEITH'S BREWING COMPANY
Corner of Turumaha and Herbert
streets, Greymouth
Tel 03-768 4149
www.monteiths.co.nz
The Monteiths name has been
associated with brewing on
the West Coast since the
1850s, and this is the only
brewery in New Zealand
where the beer is made in
open fermenters by coal-fired
boilers. Tours fill you in on the
history, show the brewing
process, explain the different
beer styles and include a
formal tasting. Advance
booking is essential.
🕐 Tours Mon–Fri 10, 11.30, 2, Sat, Sun
11.30, 2 🏷 NZ$10

✖ SHANTYTOWN (▷ 121)

HANMER SPRINGS

✪ HANMER FOREST CONSERVATION PARK
Hanmer Springs
Tel 03-315 7128
www.doc.govt.nz
Some of New Zealand's oldest
exotic forest can be accessed
in self-guided walks, ranging
from easy trails taking less
than an hour to hill climbs
taking between one and five
hours. Trail maps from the
visitor information office.

✪ HANMER SPRINGS ADVENTURE CENTRE
20 Conical Hill Road, Hanmer Springs
Tel 03-315 7233
www.hanmeradventure.co.nz
You can rent mountain bikes of
all kinds from this store, as well
as in-line skates, motorised
scooters, skis and snowboards,
and fishing rods—with local fishing information and licences.
Transport to the Hanmer
Springs Ski Area is also available. The shop sells outdoor
clothing, swimwear, camping,
fishing, mountain biking and ski

gear. Quad-bike trips are available (minimum age 12), plus rental of mountain bikes (one hour NZ$14, full day NZ$28), scooters, motorbikes, ATVs, fishing tackle and ski equipment.
◷ Daily 8.30–5.30 🚵 Mountain bike hire from NZ$14

✪ THRILLSEEKERS CANYON ADVENTURE CENTRE
Waiau Ferry Bridge, Main Road, Hanmer Springs
Tel 03-315 7046
www.thrillseeker.co.nz
Bungy jumping off the 135 year-old Waiau Ferry Bridge, jet-boat rides and rafting are organised on this spectacular stretch of the Waiau River gorge near the Hanmer turn-off from SH7. You can recover from your exertions at the on-site café.
🚵 Adult from NZ$85, child NZ$50
🚌 9km (6 miles) south of Hanmer 💺

✪ ✪ HANMER SPRINGS THERMAL RESERVE (▷ 123)

HAWARDEN

✪ ALPINE HORSE SAFARIS
Waitohi Downs, Hawarden
Tel 03-314 4293
www.alpinehorse.co.nz
Lawrie and Jenny O'Carroll are best known for their high-country trail rides lasting up to 11 days. They also offer two-hour and half-day treks, and the opportunity to take part in farm life by joining a sheep or cattle round-up.
🚵 From NZ$50

HOKITIKA

✪ JUST JADE EXPERIENCE
197 Revell Street, Hokitika
Tel 03-755 7612
www.jadeexperience.co.nz
Gordon Wells combines jade carving with a backpacker's stop in Hokitika. Spend a day learning how to carve and polish greenstone, then create a piece of your own.
🚵 From NZ$20

✪ SCENIC WATERWAYS PADDLE BOAT CRUISES
Main South Road, Hokitika
Tel 03-755 7239
www.paddleboatcruises.com
Takutai Belle, a stern-drive paddleboat, takes trips through rainforest up the Mahinapua Creek to Lake Mahinapua, on the old Gold Trail Waterway route. Tours can be arranged to suit—ask for a refreshment stop at the Mahinapua pub, an authentic West Coast tavern.
◷ Daily 2pm 🚵 Adult NZ$25, child NZ$15

✪ NATIONAL KIWI CENTRE
Sewell Street, Hokitika
Tel 03-755 5251

Riding out on an Alpine Horse Safari from Hawarden

This is a kiwi house and indoor marine aquarium on the outskirts of Hokitika, which displays sea life unique to the West Coast. Watch sharks being fed by divers, as well as giant eels, crayfish, seahorses and octopuses. You can also catch a salmon in the lake and have it cooked in the restaurant.
◷ Daily 9–5 🚵 Adult NZ$12, child NZ$6, family NZ$30

LAKE TEKAPO

✪ EARTH AND SKY
PO Box 112, Lake Tekapo
Tel 03-670 6960
www.earthandsky.co.nz
Day and evening tours to Mount John Observatory.

◷ Daily 11–3. Also 10pm in summer and 8pm in winter 🚵 Adult from NZ$42, child NZ$5

✪ LAKE TEKAPO ADVENTURES AND CRUISES
PO Box 129, Lake Tekapo
Tel 03-680 6629
www.laketekapo.co.nz
An attractive combination tour includes a cruise around Motuariki Island on Lake Tekapo with optional fishing plus a 4X4 trip up Mount John, giving spectacular views over the Mackenzie Basin and Southern Alps. Another option is a day's fly fishing with lessons and lunch.
🚵 Combination NZ$120 with fishing, NZ$70 without; fly fishing NZ$600, for up to 3 people

✪ MOUNT COOK ALPINE SALMON
Tekapo-Pukaki Canal Road, Lake Tekapo
Tel 03-435 0085
www.mtcooksalmon.com
At 677m (2,221ft) above sea level, with a stunning view of the mountain after which it is named, Mount Cook Alpine Salmon is reckoned to be the highest salmon farm in the world. The farm makes use of the hydro canal, growing 70,000 salmon in cages. You can take a self-guided tour and feed the fish, catch your own fish (rod supplied), or buy one at the shop and barbecue it on the spot.
◷ Daily, daylight hours 🚵 Tour: 2 adults NZ$5, child free 🚌 From SH8, take Hayman Road at Lake Pukaki, or the Heritage Trail at Irishman Creek

LITTLE RIVER

⊞ LITTLE RIVER GALLERY
Main Road, Little River, Banks Peninsula
Tel 03-325 1944
www.littlerivergallery.com
A popular stop halfway between Christchurch and Akaroa, this gallery shows the work of local artists in sculpture, painting and jewellery. The adjacent café and general store sells excellent country food.
◷ Daily 9.30–5.30

LYTTELTON

✪ SEA CRUISES
B Jetty, Lyttelton
Tel 03-328 7720
www.sea-cruises.co.nz
Combine city sightseeing with dolphin-watching on the Scenic Lyttelton Tour, which includes pick-up, a scenic coach tour and dolphin cruise. Other cruises go to Ripapa and Quail islands.
🕐 Daily 🖐 Adult NZ$50, child (5–15) NZ$17.50, family NZ$117.50

METHVEN

✪ BLACK DIAMOND SAFARIS
PO Box 60, Methven
Tel 0274-508 283
www.blackdiamondsafaris.co.nz
These skiing enthusiasts take people to Canterbury's club fields for a special New Zealand skiing or boarding experience on ungroomed slopes, with rope tows and no tow queues. Tours include one-day and multi-day trips, safety equipment included.
🖐 From NZ$150

✪ MOUNT HUTT SKI AREA
Mount Hutt, Methven
Tel 03-302 8811
www.nzski.com
Canterbury's largest commercial ski area, Mount Hutt has nine lifts and a vertical drop of 675m (2,214ft), with snow-making equipment, and slopes suitable for everyone from beginners to advanced skiers. It has a ski shop, gear for rent, and a restaurant with a deck.
🕐 Jun–end Oct 🖐 Adult from NZ$79, child NZ$42

MOUNT COOK

✪ ALPINE GUIDES
Bowen Drive, Mount Cook
Tel 03-435 1834
www.alpineguides.co.nz
The only resident guiding company in the national park, they can take you on anything from half- and full-day walks to mountaineering trips and heli-skiing on the Tasman Glacier.
🖐 From NZ$130, child NZ$60

✪ HELICOPTER LINE
Tel 03-435 1801
www.helicopter.co.nz
Three flights are offered in the park: a 20-minute trip landing on the Ben Ohau Range, a 30-minute trip to the Richardson Glacier, and a 45-minute Mountains High adventure which takes you over the Tasman Glacier, makes a snow landing and flies across the Main Divide and the Franz Josef and Fox glaciers.
🖐 From NZ$195

OKARITO

✪ OKARITO NATURE TOURS
PO Box 89, Franz Josef
Tel 03-753 4014

Safety gear is part of the scene when rafting on the Buller River

www.okarito.co.nz
Kayaking is a good way to explore Okarito Lagoon, New Zealand's largest unmodified wetland (3,240ha/8,000 acres). It's the main feeding ground for kotuku (white herons), and visited by more than 70 other bird species.
🖐 From NZ$35

PUKEKURA

✪ PUKEKURA BUSHMAN'S CENTRE LODGE
Pukekura, Lake Ianthe, South Westland
Tel 03-755 4144
www.pukekura.co.nz
While staying in this tiny settlement, you can browse in the museum, try gold panning, or

fish in a Canadian canoe, then revive yourself with a plate of possum pie at the Puke Pub and soak in the hot pools before retiring to the Lodge.
🕐 When it suits

STAVELEY

✪ TUSSOCK AND BEECH ECOTOURS
Staveley, RD1, Ashburton
Tel 03-303 0880
www.nature.net.nz
The 'In the Hobbits' Footsteps' tour includes a visit to Mount Sunday, site of Edoras in *The Lord of the Rings: The Two Towers*. The trip includes lodging in a heritage-registered cottage, meals, a tour through the spectacular glaciated landscape, a beech forest walk along a mountain stream, and lunch beside a lake. You can also join nature tours.
🖐 From NZ$275

WAIPARA

✪ ATHENA OLIVE GROVES AND MILL HOUSE
164 Mackenzies Road, Waipara
Tel 03-314 6774
www.athenaolives.co.nz
Producers of Canterbury's first olive oil, Athena presses its olives on a traditional Tuscan press within hours of picking them, producing extra virgin olive oil of high quality. You can watch the process in season or see a video, and taste the olive products in the shop.
🕐 Daily 9–4

WESTPORT

✪ BULLER ADVENTURES
Buller Gorge Road, Westport
Tel 03-789 7286
www.adventuretours.co.nz
You can choose from several adventures in and around the spectacular Buller Gorge, with rafting graded from family to white-water and heli-rafting, as well as jet-boating, horse-trekking and eight-wheel-drive Argo tours.
🖐 From NZ$75, child NZ$55

WHAT TO DO

FESTIVALS AND EVENTS

JANUARY–FEBRUARY

WORLD BUSKERS FESTIVAL
PO Box 845, Christchurch
Tel 03-377 2365
www.worldbuskersfestival.com
Street performers from around
the world converge on
Christchurch for 10 days in
the summer. They come
in many forms—acrobats,
comedians, contortionists,
escapologists, fire-eaters,
jugglers, 'living statues',
magicians, mime artists,
sword swallowers and street
artists. Performances
are generally free.

FEBRUARY

**CANTERBURY WINE AND
FOOD FESTIVAL**
North Hagley Park, Christchurch
Tel 03-343 5953
Around 40 local wine
producers, food producers
and restaurants set up stalls
under the trees in Hagley Park,
and families gather on the
grass to listen to live music.

MARCH

**HOKITIKA WILDFOODS
FESTIVAL**
Cass Square,
Hokitika
Tel 03-756 9048
www.wildfoods.co.nz
Hokitika has become famous
for its annual Wildfoods
Festival, on the second
weekend of March, which
attracts 18,000 visitors eager
to sample 'bushtucker' such
as huhu grubs, worms,
grasshoppers, eels, mussels,
snails, and the famous West
Coast whitebait, washed
down with local beer. There's
a dance in the evening.
Reserve accommodation well
in advance.
🕐 11–5 💲 Adult NZ$30, child (5–18)
NZ$5

**WAIPARA WINE AND FOOD
CELEBRATION**
Glenmark Church, Waipara
Tel 03-314 6962
Started as a European-style
church and community
celebration of grape-gathering
and wine-making, the Waipara
festival remains an appealingly
small community event, which
includes organ concerts in the
church, and food and wine
stalls and music outdoors.
💲 NZ$25

JULY–AUGUST

**CHRISTCHURCH ARTS
FESTIVAL**
PO Box 705, Christchurch
Tel 03-365 2223
www.artsfestival.co.nz
This two-week biennial winter
festival is held in odd years,
with live performances including opera, classical music, jazz,
cabaret, drama and dance.

OCTOBER

HERITAGE WEEK
Tel 03-941 8688
www.heritageweek.co.nz
Plenty of heritage-related
activities in the Christchurch
area, including events, tours,
quizzes and fairs.

REEFTON WILD WEST HUNT
Visitor Centre, 67 Broadway, Reefton
Tel 03-732 8391
The quality and variety of local
wild foods are celebrated in
this weekend hunt for the
heaviest deer, pig and trout.
There's a special section for
children, too.

NOVEMBER

CANTERBURY A&P SHOW
Canterbury Agricultural Park,
Christchurch
Tel 03-343 3033
www.theshow.co.nz
The country comes to town in
New Zealand's largest agricul-
tural and pastoral show,
attended by more than
100,000 people each year. In

addition to livestock competitions, showjumping, dressage,
dog trials and wood-chopping,
there are 350 trade exhibitors
and a Canterbury food pavilion. Look for local 'A&P' shows
all over the country, too.

TIMARU FESTIVAL OF ROSES
Caroline Bay, Timaru
Tel 03-688 5531
www.festivalofroses.co.nz
The largest annual community
event in the central South
Island, this three-day festival
attracts around 15,000 gardening enthusiasts and others
with seminars, workshops,
displays, competitions, shows,
demonstrations, tours and 150
stalls and exhibits from across
New Zealand. There are also
children's activities.

DECEMBER

**WAIMATE STRAWBERRY
FARE**
Seddon Square, Waimate
Tel 03-689 7771
Waimate celebrates its
berryfruit-growing tradition on
the first or second Saturday in
December—timed to coincide
with the peak of the strawberry
season. The festival is a mix
of stalls, strawberry-picking
competitions, free all-day
family entertainment—and of
course, lots of strawberries
and ice cream.

DECEMBER–MARCH

SUMMERTIMES
Christchurch City Council Leisure
Tel 03-941 8999
www.summertimes.org.nz
Organised annually by the City
Council, this festival of free
outdoor entertainment
includes musical, sporting,
children's and community
events, including the Classical
Sparks orchestral concert with
fireworks. The festival takes
place for two months some
time between December
and March.

OTAGO AND THE FAR SOUTH

Queenstown dominates this region, with its spectacular location and a reputation as New Zealand's adventure capital. You can do almost anything here, with companies vying to offer the most extreme experience—from flying like a rocket to bungy jumping from a parachute. It's a very tourist-oriented town, with service and prices to match, but compensatingly long shop-opening hours (daily 9–9) and a nightlife that goes on until 5am. Queenstown is also the site of two contrasting ski slopes: the lower, more sophisticated Coronet Peak, and the higher Remarkables. Wanaka is less frenetic and more popular with locals, who enjoy sailing and fishing on the lake and skiing at Treble Cone, one of New Zealand's top ski slopes.

The Central Otago wine region has pockets of vineyards producing remarkable wines in good years. A wine trail map is available from visitor information offices.

By contrast with Queenstown, Invercargill, Dunedin and Oamaru are redolent of their past, with grand Victorian buildings and a quieter pace of life. Expect to visit fine gardens, view penguins or albatrosses at close quarters, and meet locals speaking with a distinctive burr. Dunedin celebrates its Scottish heritage with Burns' Night celebrations. The site of New Zealand's first university, it is still very much a university city, and a large student population makes for a humming café and pub scene. It also has lively performing arts and music, with a professional theatre and local orchestra.

In the interior, the region's gold-mining past has left its mark on the land and its people: one good way to experience this is by taking the Otago Central Rail Trail by bicycle, on horseback or on foot, stopping at the conveniently located old pubs on the way. Central Otago also has more than 100 rivers, streams, lakes and dams, where you can fish for brown and rainbow trout.

Southland is the heart of one of New Zealand's most prosperous dairy regions, and is also famous for its fishing and wild game. For a wilderness experience, take a slow journey through the Catlins or cross Foveaux Strait to Stewart Island/Rakiura, which is still largely undeveloped.

KEY TO SYMBOLS	
⊞	Shopping
🎭	Entertainment
▽	Nightlife
⚽	Sports
✪	Activities
♡	Health and Beauty
⊛	For Children

ALEXANDRA

🍷 BLACK RIDGE VINEYARD AND WINERY

Conroys Road, Alexandra
Tel 03-449 2059
www.blackridge.co.nz

A wild, rocky ravine makes a dramatic and unusual location for this vineyard, where bulldozers had to reshape the schist to allow pockets of vines to be planted. The resulting wines are distinctive, in particular a highly regarded, flinty Gewürztraminer. You can purchase cheese and cured meats to go with wine tastings. Cheeseboard and nibbles are available alfresco from 27 December to mid-January,

and there is often live music on weekends.
⊙ Daily 10–5

ARROWTOWN

⊞ THE GOLD SHOP
29 Buckingham Street, Arrowtown
Tel 03-442 1319
www.thegoldshop.co.nz
The Gold Shop reflects Arrowtown's gold-mining heritage in jewellery fashioned from gold bought from local miners. Gold flakes are shown off in lockets, and nuggets fashioned into pendants and bracelets.
⊙ Daily 8.30 5.30

⊞ OUT THERE CLOTHING
18 Buckingham Street, Arrowtown
Tel 03-442 1500
www.otclothing.co.nz
Two local sisters design this relaxed, easy-to-wear but trendy clothing for men and women who want to be 'out there' doing things (also at 27 Beach Street, Queenstown).
⊙ Daily 10–5

✪ AMISFIELD
Lake Hayes Winery, 10 Lake Hayes Road, Arrowtown
Tel 03-442 0556
www.amisfield.co.nz
Just outside Arrowtown, Amisfield is the closest winery to Queenstown. It has vineyards at picturesque Lake Hayes, and extensive plantings on the shores of Lake Dunstan. Specialists in Pinot noir and *méthode traditionelle*, it also produces Pinot gris, Sauvignon blanc, Riesling and an excellent rosé. The attractive stone winery has a spacious cellar door facility, which hosts art exhibitions, and an underground barrel hall.
⊙ Daily 10–8

✪✪ MILLBROOK
Malaghans Road, Arrowtown
Tel 03-441 7000
www.millbrook.co.nz
The resort is based around one of New Zealand's most

beautiful and well-appointed golf courses, designed by Sir Bob Charles. Casual players can pay green fees and rent clubs, and packages are available (from NZ$200) that include green fees, golf clubs and shoes, golf cart, balls, tees, and a taxi to and from your accommodation. You can also stay on site. Millbrook has extensive facilities, including tennis courts, a swimming pool, a gymnasium, spa pools and sauna. It also has an associated day spa (tel 03-441 7017) offering massage, hydrotherapy, facials and body treatments.
▯ Green fees from NZ$75

Trackers Ecotours take you to the heart of the Catlins

THE CATLINS

✪ CATLINS WILDLIFE TRACKERS ECOTOURS
Papatowai, RD2, Owaka
Tel 03-415 8613
www.catlins-ecotours.co.nz
These very informative two- and four-day tours give an in-depth look at the area's flora and fauna, geology, history and conservation. Small groups are taken to remote places to walk and appreciate rare wildlife, such as Hooker's sealions and yellow-eyed penguins. Accommodation is provided, and connections from Balclutha can be made.
▯ From NZ$345

CROMWELL

✪ THE BIG PICTURE
Corner of Sandflat Road and SH6, Cromwell
Tel 0800 wineadventure
www.wineadventures.co.nz
The Big Picture offers 'the essential wine adventure', combining an interactive wine and film experience with an adjoining restaurant where you can sample Central Otago wines as you dine. There's an 'aroma room' featuring up to 60 aromas associated with wine, and an auditorium where you are taken on a virtual flight over the region while wine-makers from various vineyards lead you through a tutored tasting.
⊙ Dec–end Feb 9am–11pm; Mar–end Nov 9–6 ▯ NZ$15

DUNEDIN

⊞ MERIDIAN SHOPPING MALL
267–287 George Street, Dunedin
Tel 03-474 7500
Meridian Mall is a multi-level shopping precinct housing 40 speciality stores, including Arthur Barnett's department store, K-Mart, fashion chains, food outlets, books, sporting goods and computer games.
⊙ Mon–Thu 9–6, Fri 9–9, Sat 9–5, Sun 10–5

⊞ OTAGO FARMERS' MARKET
Dunedin Railway Station, Anzac Square, Dunedin
Tel 03-477 6701
www.otagofarmersmarket.org.nz
Up to 4,000 people visit this Saturday market on a fine day, to buy fruit and vegetables, venison, free-range eggs, free-range pork, fresh fish, organic lamb and beef direct from the growers. Artisan producers also bring speciality breads, pies, pastries and chocolates. In season you can also find wild mushrooms, quinces, artichokes, hazelnuts and chestnuts.
⊙ Sat 8–1.30

⊕ PLUME

310 George Street, Dunedin
Tel 03-477 9358

One of the country's leading fashion designers, Margi Robertson exports her Nom D. label worldwide but remains in Dunedin, where she started in 1986. She reinvents stylistic conventions on how a garment is cut, assembled and worn, using New Zealand wool.

🕓 Mon–Thu 9–5.30, Fri 9–7.30, Sat 10–4

⊕ THE SCOTTISH SHOP

17 George Street, Dunedin
Tel 03-477 9965
www.scottishshop.co.nz

Trading on Dunedin's Scottish heritage, this shop sells products made in Scotland alongside New Zealand-made items in a Scottish style. From tartan kilts, ties and stockings to oatcakes and shortbread—if it's Scottish, they'll have it.

🕓 Mon–Fri 9–5.30, Sat 10–3

🎭 DUNEDIN TOWN HALL

1 Harrop Street, Dunedin
Tel 03-474 3614
www.cityofdunedin.com

Excellent acoustics make Dunedin Town Hall a popular venue for chamber music, symphony and choral concerts.

🎭 FORTUNE THEATRE

Corner of Moray Place and Stuart Street, Dunedin
Tel 03-477 8323
www.fortunetheatre.co.nz

Dunedin's professional theatre operates from a converted 1870 church, staging regular productions of local and international drama in two venues: the Mainstage and Studio. Bookings can be made at the theatre or via the website.

🕓 Tue 6, Wed–Sat 8, Sun 4

🎭 REGENT THEATRE

17 The Octagon, Dunedin
Tel 03-477 6481
www.regenttheatre.co.nz

The beautifully restored Regent Theatre combines the spacious elegance of a 1920s movie palace with state-of-the-art projection and sound. It hosts live theatre, cinema, musicals and special events, including the annual film festival.

🕓 Booking office Mon–Fri 9–5, Sat 10.30–1

☯ ARC CAFÉ

135 High Street, Dunedin
Tel 03-474 1135
www.arc.org.nz

The Arc is a combination of arts venue, recording studio and vegan/vegetarian café, and is popular with local artists, musicians and students. It's run by a non-profit trust, and holds regular live gigs.

🕓 Mon–Sat noon–late

Preparing to sample the ales at Speight's Brewery

⚽ CARISBROOK SPORTING COMPLEX

Burns Street, Dunedin
Tel 03-466 4010
www.orfu.co.nz

Carisbrook, home of the Otago Rugby Football Union and the venue for international rugby and cricket matches, is known locally as 'the house of pain'—because visiting teams find it so hard to succeed here.

⚽ EDGAR SPORTS CENTRE

Portsmouth Drive, Dunedin
Tel 03-456 1200
www.edgarcentre.co.nz

Non-members are welcome and you can rent equipment at this sports centre, which includes 21 tennis courts.

🕓 Mon–Thu 9am–10pm, Fri 9–8, Sat, Sun 9–6

✴ DUNEDIN CASINO

Southern Cross Hotel, 118 High Street, Dunedin
Tel 0800-477 4545
www.dunedincasino.co.nz

This boutique casino in the boutique Southern Cross Hotel aims for a sophisticated atmosphere, with a dress code of smart attire. Play blackjack, roulette, baccarat, *tai sai*, poker, or gaming machines. There is also a restaurant. Minimum age 20.

🕓 Daily 10am–3am

✴ NEW ZEALAND SPORTS HALL OF FAME

Dunedin Railway Station, Anzac Square, Dunedin
Tel 03-477 7775
www.nzhalloffame.co.nz

New Zealand's great sporting moments are relived in this exhibit, in the splendidly grandiose heritage Railway Station. A shop sells sporting paraphernalia.

🕓 Daily 10–4 🏛

✴ SPEIGHT'S BREWERY

200 Rattray Street, Dunedin
Tel 03-477 7697
www.speights.co.nz

Still on the site it has occupied since 1876, Speight's Brewery has become synonymous with the 'Southern Man' image of rural Otago and Southland. The Heritage Centre takes tours through the gravity-fed working brewery and museum, ending with a tasting session. You can also bottle, label and cap your own beer to take away in a wooden gift pack. The Ale House Bar and Restaurant (tel 03-471 9050) is a popular meeting place and open until late.

🕓 Alehouse: Mon–Thu, Sat 11.30am–1am, Sun 11.30am–midnight; Heritage Centre tours: Mon–Thu 10, 12, 2, 7; Fri, Sun 10, 12, 2, 4 🎟 Tours: adult NZ$17, child (5–15) NZ$6

❸ CADBURY WORLD

280 Cumberland Street, Dunedin
Tel 03-467 7967
www.cadbury.co.nz
Cadbury World combines a visitor centre with heritage and interactive displays, a theatre presentation and a guided tour of the factory showing how various products are made. Reduced tours are available when the factory is not operating. A shop sells chocolates, clothing, hats, bags, toys, novelty items and souvenirs.

🕐 Jan–end Apr daily 9am–7pm; May–end Dec daily 9–3.30 💲 Mon–Sat adult NZ$16, child (under 15) NZ$10, family NZ$42; Sun, public holidays adult NZ$10, child NZ$5 ▥

GLENORCHY

❖ DART RIVER SAFARIS

Mull Street, Glenorchy
Tel 03-442 9992
www.dartriver.co.nz
The safaris focus on the Dart River, involving a bus ride from Queenstown to Glenorchy, 4X4 drive through Paradise (taking in *Lord of the Rings* film locations on the way), walks through beech forest and a jet-boat trip back to Glenorchy. Horseback riding and kayaking options are also available.

💲 Adult from NZ$209, child NZ$104.50

GIBBSTON

❖ GIBBSTON VALLEY WINES AND GIBBSTON VALLEY CHEESERY

State Highway 6, Gibbston, RD1 Queenstown
Tel 03-442 6910 (winery); 03-441 1388 (cheesery)
www.gvwines.co.nz
www.gvcheese.co.nz
Gibbston Valley is a popular spot with visitors, not just because of the fine wines—notably its flagship Pinot noir and Chardonnay—but also for the educational tours it offers of the vineyard, winery and barrel cave; the food, featuring local produce in its restaurant; and the adjacent cheesery, where you can learn how the handcrafted cow, goat and sheep cheeses are made.

🕐 Daily 10–5; tours: 10–4 on the hour 💲 NZ$9.50

INVERCARGILL

❖ THE SERIOUSLY GOOD CHOCOLATE COMPANY

20 Windsor Street, Invercargill
Tel 03-217 5107
www.seriouslygoodchocolate.com
Jane Stanton specialises in handmade chocolates with special fillings, such as branded wines, and is best known for her truffles made with local produce, such as Bluff oyster cinnamon truffles

Splash Palace offers swimming and leisure facilities

and tuatara chocolate eggs. Buy them direct from her shop or in stores in Invercargill and nationwide.

🕐 Mon–Wed, Thu 9–6.30, Fri–Sun 9–5.30

❼ CIVIC THEATRE

Tay Street, Invercargill
Tel 03-211 1777
A fine Renaissance-style Victorian theatre, the 1,000-seat Civic was built in 1906 as a cinema and to host opera, musicals, comedies and ballets. It is now home of the Invercargill Repertory Society, and is used by professional touring companies.

❼ EMBASSY THEATRE

112 Dee Street,
Invercargill
Tel 03-214 0050
www.bdlhire.co.nz
Originally a cinema, the Embassy was revamped and reopened in 1999 as a performance and production venue with high-tech facilities. It is operated by an audio, lighting and DJ company and hosts functions and rock concerts.

❼ READING CINEMA

29 Dee Street,
Invercargill
Tel 03-211 1555
This five-screen cinema complex shows first-release movies. The phone line gives information on the movies currently showing.
💲 From NZ$7

❸ STADIUM SOUTHLAND

Surrey Park, Isabella Street,
Invercargill
Tel 03-217 1200
www.stadiumsouth.co.nz
This modern stadium has four squash courts and doubles as a concert venue. Home to one of the country's top netball teams, Southern Sting, it also has international-standard indoor courts.

🕐 Mon–Fri 8.30am–10pm, Sat, Sun 9–5

❖ SPLASH PALACE

Southland Aquatic Centre, Elles Road,
Invercargill
Tel 03-217 7506
www.splashpalace.co.nz
A modern indoor complex, Splash Palace has a main pool, diving pool, whirlpool and steam room and leisure pool. It is used for national swimming championships and other sports.

🕐 Mon–Fri 6am–9pm, Sat 6am–8pm, Sun 8am–8pm 💲 Adult NZ$4.40, child NZ$2.20 ▣

KINGSTON

⚙ KINGSTON FLYER
Kingston Railway Station, Kingston
Tel 03-248 8848
www.kingstonflyer.co.nz
The Kingston Flyer was originally a passenger service that operated between Kingston and the main railway line at Gore, from 1878 through to the mid-1950s. It provided a passage to Queenstown and the surrounding areas by meeting the lake steamers at Kingston Wharf. Today it puffs along a 14km (9-mile) track while passengers listen to 1920s music.
🕐 Oct–end Apr daily 10, 1.30 🎫 Adult NZ$40, child NZ$20, family NZ$99
🚌 47km (29 miles) south of Queenstown

MANAPOURI AND DOUBTFUL SOUND

⚙ REAL JOURNEYS
Pearl Harbour, Manapouri
Tel 03-249 7416
www.realjourneys.co.nz
High tech and wild nature are combined in these trips to the Manapouri Power Station and Doubtful Sound. The Wilderness Day Cruise crosses Lake Manapouri by launch, takes a bus over the Wilmot Pass, and then a launch cruise on Doubtful Sound. You visit the hydro station on the way back. An overnight option lets you stay in Doubtful Sound on the *Fiordland Navigator*, designed along the lines of a trading scow. A shorter option visits only the power station.
🕐 Daily 9.30 (Te Anau 8.30) 🎫 Adult from NZ$230, child NZ$55

MILFORD SOUND

⚙ MILFORD SOUND RED BOAT CRUISES
Milford Wharf Visitor Centre, Milford Sound
Tel 0800-264536
www.redboats.co.nz
Cruises explore the Sound to the Tasman Sea, taking in the majestic scenery, waterfalls, seal colonies and an optional underwater observatory (additional charge, ▷ 142).
🕐 Daily 🎫 Adult from NZ$55, child NZ$15

⚙ ROSCO'S MILFORD SOUND SEA KAYAKS
Deep Water Basin, Milford Sound
Tel 03-249 8500
www.kayakmilford.co.nz
Choose from a variety of day, twilight or full-moon trips, as well as fly/kayak combinations, or paddle and walk part of the Milford Track.
🎫 From NZ$98

OAMARU

⚙ BLUE PENGUIN COLONY (▷ 145)

Relive the glory days of steam travel on the Kingston Flyer

⚙ WHITESTONE CHEESE
3 Torridge Street, Oamaru
Tel 03-434 8098
www.whitestonecheese.co.nz
Whitestone cheeses are named after local landmarks, because handmade cheeses reflect the local geography, pastures and climate. All the cheeses are on display and can be tasted and bought in the adjoining licensed café, which has a cheese-influenced blackboard menu and Central Otago wines. You can see the Make Room from an exterior platform.
🕐 Daily 9–5

OTAGO PENINSULA

⚙ ELM WILDLIFE TOURS
Elm Backpackers Lodge, 19 Irvine Road, The Cove, Dunedin
Tel 03-454 4121
www.elmwildlifetours.co.nz
These informative guided nature tours of the Otago Peninsula include Hooker's sea lions, fur seals, albatrosses and yellow-eyed penguins. The five- to six-hour trip takes in the Albatross Centre, a New Zealand fur seal colony and their own yellow-eyed penguin-breeding beach at the remote Cape Saunders. Other options include kayaking, a cruise around the heads, and the Catlins. You can stay at the backpackers' lodge or be picked up from elsewhere.
🎫 From NZ$75

⚙ E-TOURS
67 Stuart Street, Dunedin
Tel 03-476 1960
www.inmark.co.nz/e-tours
Packages for doing the Otago Central Rail Trail at your own pace, including accommodation, transport, maps and gear.
🎫 From NZ$75

QUEENSTOWN

⊕ O'CONNELLS SHOPPING CENTRE
Corner of Camp and Beach streets, Queenstown
Tel 03-442 7760
This shopping mall has 25 stores selling everything from food to fashion.
🕐 Daily 9–9

⊕ OUTSIDE SPORTS
Shotover Street, Queenstown
Tel 03-491 0074
www.outsidesports.co.nz
Every kind of outdoor sport is catered for here, with clothing, footwear and equipment. They specialise in trekking, camping, rock climbing, mountain and road bikes, and performance multisport clothing. Their sister shop, Outdoor Adventure, is farther down the Mall.
🕐 Summer daily 8.30am–9pm; winter daily 7.30am–9.30pm

WINEDELI
40 Shotover Street,
Queenstown
Tel 03-442 4482
www.winedeli.com
As the name suggests, this
shop specialises in Otago and
other New Zealand wines,
deli items, cheese and
preserves.
Daily 10–10

EMBASSY CINEMA
11 The Mall, Queenstown
Tel 03-442 9994
www.readingcinemas.co.nz
Three screens show first-
release movies and host the
International Film Festival.
Details of screenings are
carried on the movie line,
tel 03-442 9990.
Adult from NZ$9.50, child NZ$8.50

HAKA PA MAORI VILLAGE
Waterfall Park, 345 Lake Hayes Road,
Queenstown
Tel 03-442 1534
www.hakapa.com
The cultural experience starts
with a traditional welcome
and viewing of the Maori
village, followed by a
performance of traditional
action songs and dances, *haka*
(warrior dance) and *poi*
(performed by the women).
Dinner is a four-course feast,
or *hangi,* based around meat
and vegetables steamed in
an earth oven. Pick-ups and
drop-offs in Queenstown can
be arranged.
Pa daily 9–5; dinner 7–10
Cultural experience: adult NZ$89,
child (5–15) NZ$40

QUEENSTOWN EVENTS CENTRE
Joe O'Connell Drive, Frankton
Tel 03-442 3664
www.qtevents.co.nz
The Events Centre hosts local
and touring shows and indoor
sporting fixtures. There is also
a climbing wall. Outdoor
concerts are held in the
adjoining Oval.

SKYCITY QUEENSTOWN CASINO
16–24 Beach Street, Queenstown
Tel 03-441 0400
www.skycityqueenstown.co.nz
Located above the Hard Rock
Café, the casino offers live
entertainment, table games,
more than 70 gaming
machines and a restaurant
and bar. You need to be
age 20 or over, and a dress
code applies.
Daily noon–4am

SURREAL
7 Rees Street, Queenstown
Tel 03-441 8492
One of Queenstown's popular
nightspots, this nightclub is

Spoilt for choice amid the wines
at Queenstown's WineDeli shop

gay-friendly and has great DJs
and sounds. It starts getting
busy around 10.30pm. When
the party swings, it's open
until 5am.
Daily 11am–late

A.J. HACKETT BUNGY AND SHOTOVER JET (▷ 148)

APPELLATION CENTRAL WINE TOURS
Queenstown
Tel 03-442 0246
www.appellationcentral.co.nz
Philip Green has a Diploma
of Wine and has been a wine
collector for 15 years. He
organises small group tours
(up to nine people) which

depart daily, and customises
tours for wine enthusiasts.
Afternoon tours visit four
wineries in the Gibbston and
Bannockburn areas and
Cromwell, and include lunch.
Full-day tours include a wine
cave tour, cheese tasting, lunch
and a wine experience at The
Big Picture.
Daily 9.30, noon From NZ$135

CORONET PEAK/ REMARKABLES SKI AREAS
Queenstown Snow Centre, corner
of Camp and Shotover streets,
Queenstown
Tel 03-442 4640
www.nzski.com
The original commercial
ski-field—and still one of the
best when it gets a good
covering of snow—Coronet
Peak (1,649m/5,410ft) has
excellent facilities and the
added advantage of being
an easy drive (18km/11
miles of sealed road) from
Queenstown. Not surprisingly,
it gets very busy. Its sister
field across the valley, the
Remarkables, is reached by
a longer and more tortuous
road (28km/17 miles of gravel
road) but often has more
snow as it goes higher
(1,935m/6,348ft).
Late Jun to mid-Oct Lift passes
from NZ$72

EXTREME GREEN RAFTING
39 Camp Street,
Queenstown
Tel 03-442 8517
www.nzraft.com
White-water rafting on the
spectacular and action-packed
Shotover and Kawarau rivers
can be combined with jet-
boating, helicopter flights,
skydiving or bungy jumping,
and the combinations can be
done on different days.
From NZ$149

🟠 FLY-BY-WIRE
Corner of Shotover and Rees streets, Queenstown
Tel 03-442 2116
www.flybywire.co.nz
The closest you'll get to flying a rocket, Fly-by-Wire is an adventure flight in a high-speed plane suspended from an overhead tether, which allows you to pilot it anywhere within the spectacular canyon. You will experience exhilarating speeds, a huge adrenalin rush, total weight-lessness and, finally, serenity as the plane glides gently to the end—all in six minutes. Minimum age 15.
🖐 NZ$139

🟠 FLYFISHING NEW ZEALAND
Queenstown Bay, Queenstown
Tel 03-442 5363
www.wakatipu.co.nz
Queenstown and the surrounding area offers great opportunities for fly fishing, lake trolling, drift-boat fishing and heli-fishing. The high-country stream fishing season opens on 1 October and runs to 30 May. Lake Wakatipu and the Kawarau River are open all year round.
🖐 From NZ$85, plus NZ$18 fishing licence

🟠 GLENORCHY AIR
Queenstown Airport, Queenstown
Tel 03-442 2207
www.glenorchy.net.nz
www.trilogytrail.com
Capitalising on its experience of flying the *Lord of the Rings* cast and crew, this company does Trilogy trips to the loca-tions used to represent Lothlorien, Amon Hen, Nen Hithoel, Amon Lhaw, Parth Galen, Ford of Bruinen, The Pillars of the King on the River Anduin, and the site of Gandalf's ride to Isengard. There is also a road trip to local filming sites (NZ$125 adult, NZ$62.50 child).
🖐 From NZ$325, child NZ$162.50

🟠 MILFORD SOUND SCENIC FLIGHTS
Tel 03-442 3065
www.milfordflights.co.nz
The quickest and easiest way to see Milford Sound, this flight is also spectacular. You can choose from a combination of tours, including a launch trip on the Sound and the option of going one way by coach or helicopter.
🖐 Adult from NZ$295, child NZ$175

🟢 TSS *EARNSLAW* (▷ 149)

🟢 BODY SANCTUM
50 Stanley Street, Queenstown
Tel 03-442 8006

The Fly-by-Wire is a unique adrenalin-pumping experience

www.bodysanctum.co.nz
A soothing place to recover from the rigours of the day's activities, Body Sanctum is in a new building, with fine views from the treatment rooms. There is an outdoor spa, steam room and sauna, and treatments include skier's, snowboarder's or tramper's foot revival, aromatic body wraps, massage, reflexology, facials and water therapies.
🕐 Daily 9–9 🖐 From NZ$20

STEWART ISLAND/ RAKIURA

🟠 RUGGEDY RANGE WILDERNESS EXPERIENCE
170 Horseshoe Bay Road, Stewart Island
Tel 03-219 1066
www.ruggedyrange.com
Former Department of Conservation guide Furhana Ahmad organises a comprehensive itinerary of day and overnight guided walks, sea kayaking, kiwi-spotting and birdwatching trips on Stewart and Ulva islands. Packages are available and she assists with travel and accom-modation bookings. Outdoor clothing and equipment is available for rent or sale. Some trips are suitable for children.
🖐 Adult from NZ$85, child NZ$60

TE ANAU

🟠 FIORDLAND BIKE AND HIKE
Sinclair Road, Te Anau
Tel 03-249 7098
www.bikefiordland.co.nz
Offering an appealing way of making the journey from Te Anau to Milford Sound, these trips combine mountain biking on the downhill sections of the Milford Road with nature walks and a cruise on the sound, and the option of hiking part of the Routeburn Track. All equipment is provided, including wet weather gear. Suitable for children 14 and over.
🕐 Oct–end Apr daily 7.30am 🖐 From NZ$99

🟠 KIWI REEL-RIFLE
175 Aparima Drive, Te Anau
Tel 03-249 9071
www.kiwireelrifle.com
Hunting, fishing and kayaking trips can be arranged to suit your level of experience and the time available. Overnight fishing trips run from October to the end of April, but one-day fishing and kayaking excursions are available all year. Hunting for small game or red deer and chamois can be combined with flying,

WHAT TO DO

walking and/or kayaking. Fishing instruction is available. From NZ$140

✪ SINBAD CRUISES
15 Fergus Square, Te Anau
Tel 03-249 7106
www.sinbadcruises.co.nz
Help sail the 11m (36ft) gaff ketch *Little Ship Manuska*, or just sit back and enjoy the scenery. Trip options include day, afternoon, evening and overnight cruises, or you can combine cruising with a helicopter trip and/or walking at Mount Luxmore. From NZ$20

WANAKA

ⓕ PARADISO CINEMA AND CAFÉ
3 Ardmore Street, Wanaka
Tel 03-443 1505
www.paradiso.net.nz
A one-of-a-kind cinema, Paradiso shows first-release and art-house movies, but is best known for its quirky style. Seating includes a motley collection of old sofas and three seats in an old Morris Minor. A café and bar serves meals before, during or after the movie, and home-made ice cream and hot cookies at intermission.
Mon–Wed 5pm, Thu, Fri 2.30pm, Sat, Sun 11am NZ$12

✪ ALPINE AND HELI MOUNTAIN BIKING
Tel 03-443 8943
www.mountainbiking.co.nz
These folk put the mountain back into biking, with a choice of seven trips to some of the country's highest and most scenic track trailheads, including Mount Pisa, Mount Alpha and the Treble Cone. You can go by four-wheel drive or helicopter. The biggest range of options is available in summer, but some winter rides are also available. You can also do multi-day rides, staying overnight in old gold-miners' cabins.
From NZ$150

✪ LAKELAND ADVENTURES
The Log Cabin, Waterfront, Wanaka
Tel 03-443 7495
www.lakelandadventures.co.nz
From their lakeside log cabin, Lakeland Adventures organise jet-boat trips on the Clutha River, guided fishing trips on Lake Wanaka, and cruises to the islands. They also rent aqua bikes, kayaks, mountain bikes, fishing rods and boats.
Adult from NZ$50, child NZ$25

✪ RIPPON VINEYARD
246 Mount Aspiring Road, Wanaka
Tel 03-443 8084
www.rippon.co.nz
One of the most stunningly located vineyards in New

The bizarre Leaning Tower at Puzzling World

Zealand, Rippon was planted in 1981. Known for its Pinot noir, it also makes other wines, including a *méthode traditionelle*, Riesling, Gamay rosé and a Merlot Syrah blend. Picnic lunches are served in summer, and a rock festival is held on Waitangi weekend in even years.
Dec–end Apr daily 11–5; Jul–end Nov daily 1.30–4.30

✪ TREBLE CONE SKI AREA
Wanaka
Tel 03-443 7443
www.treblecone.co.nz
Treble Cone is one of the top ski and snowboarding areas in New Zealand, with more

skiable terrain than anywhere else, plus great views of Lake Wanaka and Mount Aspiring. Equipment rental and tuition are available, and there is a childcare facility. The area is open in high summer for walking and mountain biking.
Late Jun to early Oct for skiing; 30 Dec to mid-Jan for summer activities Lift passes from NZ$89, child NZ$37, family NZ$217
20km (12 miles) northwest of Wanaka via Matukituki Valley Road

✪ WANAKA PARAGLIDING
PO Box 118, Wanaka
Tel 03-443 9193
www.wanakaparagliding.co.nz
Paragliders like the conditions in Wanaka so much they come here for the New Zealand championships. You can tandem paraglide from Treble Cone all year round, for magnificent views over Wanaka and the mountains. Short summer Eco Flights are also available from Mount Iron (but you walk up first).
From NZ$170

♡ ASPECTS BEAUTY AND HEALTH
61 Browston Street, Wanaka
Tel 03-443 5051
www.aspectsofbeauty.co.nz
Men and women can get a full range of therapies and beauty treatments at this salon, including massage, body wraps, pedicures and facials.
Mon–Sat 9–8, Sun by appointment From NZ$60

✪ PUZZLING WORLD
State Highway 84, Wanaka
Tel 03-443 7489
www.puzzlingworld.co.nz
You can't miss the crazily angled towers of Stuart Landsborough's Puzzling World, on the road into Wanaka. Within is a modern maze and a variety of eccentric or puzzling attractions, including illusion rooms.
Nov–end Apr 8.30–5.30; May–end Oct 8.30–5 Adult NZ$10, child (5–15) NZ$7

FESTIVALS AND EVENTS

WHAT TO DO

JANUARY–FEBRUARY

CENTRAL OTAGO WINE AND FOOD FESTIVAL
Queenstown Visitor Centre,
PO Box 253, Queenstown
Tel 03-442 4100
The Central Otago Wine and Food Festival is held annually in the lovely setting of Queenstown Gardens, on the shores of Lake Wakatipu. It's a small but high-quality event. Foods of the region, prepared by members of the local Chefs Association, are matched with wines from 18 local wineries, and there is a farmers' market for small producers.
🕐 11–5 💰 NZ$25

APRIL

BLUFF OYSTER AND SOUTHLAND SEAFOOD FESTIVAL
Bluff Events Centre, Gore Street, Bluff
Tel 03-211 1400
www.bluffoysterfest.co.nz
Bluff's famous oysters are celebrated at the annual Bluff Oyster and Southland Seafood Festival, where restaurants and community groups from Invercargill and Bluff have stalls featuring fresh local seafood, and chefs create dishes matching wines from a regional winery. A formal Southern Seas Ball is held the night before.
🕐 11–5 💰 Adult NZ$20, child NZ$10

APRIL–MAY

ARROWTOWN AUTUMN FESTIVAL
PO Box 148, Arrowtown
Tel 03-442 0809
Arrowtown celebrates its brilliant autumn hues in a 10-day community festival of arts and crafts, talks and tours, with tournaments, markets and a street parade.

JUNE

COUNTRY MUSIC FESTIVAL GORE
PO Box 382, Gore
Tel 03-208 1978
www.goldguitars.co.nz
Gore has established itself as the country music capital of New Zealand, hosting a 10-day country music festival each June, which culminates in the Gold Guitar Awards.

JUNE–JULY

LINDAUER QUEENSTOWN WINTER CARNIVAL
Destination Queenstown, PO Box 353, Queenstown
Tel 03-441 2453
www.winterfestival.co.nz
This annual 10-day celebration of the mountains takes place at three venues—Coronet Peak, Earnslaw Park and Queenstown Bay—and is a great excuse to party. As well as concerts, music and arts events, it includes the Classic Challenge of wild and wacky events. Some events are ticketed, others—such as the opening party, the parade and Mardi Gras—are free.

SEPTEMBER

GAY SKI WEEK
Queenstown
www.gayskiweeknz.com
A national gay and lesbian event, the ski week takes advantage of Queenstown's proximity to four major ski resorts. For those who are neither skiers nor boarders, the adventure capital of New Zealand still has plenty of off-piste activities.

SEPTEMBER–OCTOBER

ALEXANDRA BLOSSOM FESTIVAL
PO Box 370, Alexandra
Tel 03-440 2097
www.blossom.co.nz
The fruit-growing district of Alexandra has been celebrating spring with this festival since the 1950s. Now held over two weeks, it includes crowning the Blossom Queen, a shearing competition, vintage car rally, motocross, boat races, a charity ball and the Grand Festival Parade with floats, bands, classic cars, floral princesses and animals. There is also a fair with arts and crafts, entertainment, wine and food (adult NZ$15, child (5–15) NZ$5, family NZ$30).

OCTOBER

DUNEDIN RHODODENDRON FESTIVAL
PO Box 980, Dunedin
Tel 03-474 5162
www.rhododunedin.com
Dunedin's famous Botanic Garden's planting of 3,500 rhododendrons is regarded as one of the most significant in the world. The annual four-day celebration involves events for families and visitors as well as gardening enthusiasts, including garden tours, golf and a fête.

NOVEMBER

BANNOCKBURN GUTBUSTER MOUNTAIN BIKE RACE
www.cromwell.org.nz
The Gutbuster is a marathon pub-to-pub cycle race over a distance of 75km (47 miles) across the precipitous heights of the Nevis Pass. It starts from the Garston Hotel and finishes at the Bannockburn Hotel, with many participants raising money for charity.
🕐 Entry from NZ$20

OAMARU VICTORIAN HERITAGE CELEBRATIONS
Visitor Information Office, Oamaru
Tel 03-434 1406
Oamaru celebrates its Victorian heritage in five days of festivities, when local people dress in period costume and take part in a fair, street parade, Penny Farthing races, a ball and other activities.

Get out and about in New Zealand with these eight driving tours and eight walks. They explore the varied attractions of both the North and the South islands. The locations of the walks and tours are marked on the map on page 214. It is advisable to buy a detailed map of the area before you set out.

Out and About

OUT AND ABOUT

KEY TO THIS MAP
- **1** Drive
- **2** Walk
- ■ Capital City
- ■ City / Town

KEY TO ROUTE MAPS IN THIS CHAPTER
- ★ Start point
- ▬ Route
- ▬▬ Alternative route
- ▶ Route direction
- **5** Walk start point on drive
- **6** Featured sight along route
- ● Place of interest in Sights section
- ● Other place of interest
- ☀ Viewpoint
- 621▲ Height in metres

Cape Reinga
Kaitaia
Paihia
Whangarei
Dargaville
Auckland
Thames
Hamilton
Tauranga
Hicks Bay
Rotorua
New Plymouth
Taumarunui
Taupo
Gisborne
Waiouru
Napier
Hastings
Wanganui
Palmerston North
Collingwood
Masterton
Nelson
Picton
WELLINGTON
Westport
Blenheim
St Arnaud
Reefton
Kaikoura
Greymouth
Hokitika
Arthur's Pass
Cheviot
Franz Josef Glacier
Rangiora
Christchurch
Mount Cook/ Aoraki
Haast
Geraldine
Milford Sound
Timaru
Wanaka
Queenstown
Oamaru
Te Anau
Alexandra
Riverton
Gore
Milton
Dunedin
Invercargill

1. Drive
West Coast Beaches and the Waitakere Ranges (▷ 215–217)

2. Walk
Devonport and North Head (▷ 218–219)

3. Drive
Coromandel Countryside and Coast (▷ 220–221)

4. Drive
Around Lake Rotorua (▷ 222–223)

5. Walk
The Rotorua Walkway (▷ 224–225)

6. Drive
A Circuit of Tongariro National Park (▷ 226–227)

7. Walk
Hahei and Cathedral Cove (▷ 228)

8. Walk
The Waitomo Walkway (▷ 229)

9. Walk
A Taste of the Abel Tasman (▷ 230–231)

10. Drive
Queen Charlotte Drive (▷ 232–233)

11. Walk
Cliffs of Kaikoura (▷ 234–235)

12. Drive
Lake Kaniere and Hokitika Gorge (▷ 236–237)

13. Drive
Over the Port Hills (▷ 238–239)

14. Walk
First Steps to Mount Cook/ Aoraki (▷ 240–241)

15. Walk
Diamond Lake and Wanaka Views (▷ 242–243)

16. Drive
Otago Peninsula's Secret Side (▷ 244–245)

WEST COAST BEACHES AND THE WAITAKERE RANGES

This circular tour explores Auckland's wild west-coast beaches and the Waitakere Ranges, with their memorable city views.

THE DRIVE

Distance: 95km (59 miles)
Allow: 6–8 hours
Start/end: Sky Tower, SKYCITY, Auckland

★ From SKYCITY take Hobson Street south to the motorway on-ramps. Take the Northwestern motorway, SH16 (signposted). After 3km (2 miles) take the Great North Road exit (exit 8) onto urban route 11, then 19 southwest to Titirangi Road (urban route 24).

❶ The suburban village of Titirangi is considered the gateway to the Waitakeres and has a number of laid-back cafés, interesting shops and a good art gallery, Lopdell House (daily 10–4.30), on the corner of Titirangi and South Titirangi roads. Titirangi is part of Waitakere City, known for its liberal attitudes, art, vineyards and orchards, and its spectacularly wild unspoiled bush and beaches. As a result, it has attracted many seeking an alternative lifestyle, and is home to artists and craftspeople. On the last Sunday of the month the village market is held in the Memorial Hall (10–2).

From the middle of Titirangi continue west to the roundabout (traffic circle) and turn onto Scenic Drive, signposted to Piha (urban route 24). Take care on this road as it has many blind corners and connecting residential driveways. Follow Scenic Drive for another 5km (3 miles) to the Arataki Information Centre, which is on the left.

❷ The information centre is an impressive modern building with a vast amount of information and interesting interpretive and audiovisual displays, which provide the perfect introduction to the region and its natural history. There is also a short nature trail from here with spectacular views south over the Nihotupu Reservoir and Manukau Harbour. An impressive Maori *pou* (guardian post) dominates the entrance to the centre. It lost its not insignificant 'manhood' a few years ago through vandalism, but thankfully for this great warrior another was duly carved, and the glint in his little paua-shell eye restored.

From the information centre continue north along Scenic Drive for 4km (2.5 miles), then turn left onto Piha Road to Piha (11km/7 miles).

❸ Piha has been luring dreamers and surfers for years, and is one of the west coast's most popular beaches and coastal enclaves. If you swim at Piha you can do so in relative safety, but always stay

Titirangi's arts centre, at the heart of a thriving community

between the flags and under the vigil of the lifesavers. When you are weary of sunbathing, swimming or trying to hold on to your surfboard in the fierce surf, there are two things you must do. The first is to climb Lion Rock, the guardian of the beach, via the steep track (allow 30 minutes to reach the top). The second, especially when the surf is high, is to take the Tasman Lookout Track at the south end of the beach to The Gap, where breakers crash into the narrow rock crevice.

There is also an interesting, if less dramatic, walk at the northern end of Piha Beach, which leads to the isolated and beautiful Whites Beach. If you have time, also try to see the Kitekite Falls—they're reached via the Kitekite Track, up Glenesk Road behind the main camping ground in the middle of the village.

From Piha drive back up the hill and look for Karekare Road to Karekare Beach (right). Descend to the parking area.

❹ Karekare is another fine west coast beach and was used as a backdrop to the hugely successful New Zealand film *The Piano* (1993). There are a number of short walks and tracks around Karekare, some of which head inland or south to join the network of

tracks in the Waitakeres. The short walk up the Taraire Track to Karekare Falls is worthwhile, especially if you intend to swim in the pool beneath it. Another is the Colmans Track from the end of Watchmans Road (signposted on the right before the parking area), where the path creeps up the hill at the northern point of Karekare Beach and terminates with a magnificent view. Looking south you can see well past Karekare Beach to the huge expanse of Whatipu Beach beyond, as well as the tiny, inaccessible Mercer Bay, immediately below and north.

Return to Piha Road and the junction with Scenic Drive (urban route 24). Turn left towards the TV mast. After 1km (0.6 miles) look for signs to Rose Hellaby House (right).

❺ The Scenic Drive (28km/ 17 miles long) winds along the eastern fringe of the Waitakeres, offering stunning views across Auckland, but one of the best viewpoints is the garden of Rose Hellaby House. Its owner, Rose, who loved these hills with a passion, donated the property to the city.

Continue north along Scenic Drive, taking care on blind corners. There are a number of other viewpoints across the city along the way. Descend back to the fringe of the city and the junction with Swanson Road. Turn right along Swanson Road (urban route 24) to the roundabout, and then continue straight across onto Universal Drive. At the end of Universal Drive turn left onto Lincoln Road to rejoin SH16 Northwestern Motorway (signposted) back into the city centre and SKYCITY (exit 4B).

Top, on Scenic Drive
Below, Piha Beach, with its high surf and black sands

Rose Hellaby loved this view of the Waitakere hills from her house

A café spills out onto the street in the village suburb of Titirangi

WHERE TO EAT

Hardware Café
✉ 404 Titirangi Road (in the heart of Titirangi)
☎ 09-817 5059
Light, healthy meals with a traditional Kiwi edge–and good coffee.
🕐 Mon–Tue 9–5, Wed–Sun 7–10

BASICS

Tourist Information
✉ Auckland Visitor Centre, Atrium, Sky City, corner of Victoria and Federal streets, Auckland
☎ 09-363 7184
www.aucklandnz.com
🕐 Daily 9–5

Arataki Information Centre
✉ 333 Scenic Drive, Titirangi
☎ 09-366 2000
www.arc.govt.nz
🕐 Sep–end Apr daily 9–5; May–end Aug Mon–Fri 10–4, Sat, Sun 9–5

Rose Hellaby House
✉ 515 Scenic Drive
☎ 09-366 2000
🕐 Gardens: daily 8–5. House: Sat, Sun 1–4 🆓 Free

DEVONPORT AND NORTH HEAD

Escape the city bustle by ferry to experience the history and village feel of Devonport, and the views from North Head, one of Auckland's most iconic (extinct) volcanoes.

THE WALK

Distance: 5km (3 miles)
Allow: 3 hours
Start/end: Devonport Wharf, Devonport

Located at the southernmost tip of the North Shore and named after the naval base in Plymouth, England, the suburb of Devonport was one of the first areas to be settled in Auckland and is home to the Royal New Zealand Navy.

Long before the first Europeans dropped anchor there in the early 1800s, the Maori used the two small but distinct volcanic mountains as *pa* (fortified settlements). They would almost certainly have witnessed the dramatic eruption of Rangitoto (▷ 71), the most recent and least modified volcano of the Auckland volcanic field and an unmistakable natural feature that dominates the view from North Head.

★ From the Devonport Wharf and ferry terminal, facing towards the middle of Devonport, turn right and walk along the waterfront (King Edward Parade), then turn left into Cheltenham Road. Turn right off Cheltenham Road onto Takarunga Road and climb to the summit of North Head.

❶ North Head (Maungauika) is one of about 50 dormant volcanoes within Greater Auckland, and at 65m (213ft) offers some of the most memorable views of the city and Waitemata Harbour. From here it is easy to see why Auckland is dubbed the City of Sails and is renowned as one of the most desirable sailing venues in the world. During international yachting events, including the Whitbread Round the World in 1993 and America's Cup campaigns in 2000 and 2003, this was a prime viewpoint for locals cheering on the New Zealand crews. Today huge cargo ships

and cruise liners are also a common sight.

In the days when tall ships brought the first European settlers to New Zealand, a small gun was sited on North Head to signal the much-anticipated arrival of mail ships.

The activity on North Head has not always been so celebratory in its mood. In response to the fear of a Russian invasion in the 1880s and of a possible Japanese invasion in World War II, the mound was heavily fortified and a maze of tunnels, bunkers and gun emplacements were constructed. Convicts built tunnels with nothing more than a pick, a shovel and their bare hands. The remnants of these tunnels, along with gun emplacements and lookouts, can be explored today (torch/flashlight recommended).

Take time to explore and walk around North Head. Then, from the northern slope, descend the steps onto Cheltenham Beach, the first of the northern beaches and considered by many to be the best on the North Shore. Walk to the top end of the beach onto Vauxhall Road. Head south along Vauxhall Road back towards Mount Victoria, looking for signs on the right for the Mount Cambria Reserve.

❷ The Mount Cambria Reserve was once a volcanic mount in its own right, and named Takaroro by Maori. Quarried for scoria in the late 1800s, it is now an attractive landscaped garden and home to the Devonport Museum. A relatively low-key affair, the museum showcases the early days of the historic suburb with artefacts and photographs.

Walk through Mount Cambria Reserve onto Church Street, turning left past the old power station to the Mount Victoria

Walkway steps (signposted right). Climb round the mount on the spiral walkway to the summit.

❸ At 881m (2,890ft), Mount Victoria (Takarunga) commands superb views across the harbour, city and surrounding suburban streets. From here you can see the wooden villas and colonial architecture that characterises the suburb.

Steeped in history and intrigue, Mount Victoria still has remnants of the Maori Kawerau tribe fortifications. At its foot, on the northern edge, there is an old cemetery where some of the North Shore's first settlers are buried.

From the Mount Victoria summit parking area follow the summit road onto Flagstaff Lane, then Victoria Road, Devonport's main thoroughfare.

❹ Victoria Street is the commercial and social heart of Devonport. Here you will find a range of tourist-oriented shops selling everything from secondhand books or antiques to local art. Alternatively, relax and enjoy a cappuccino in one of several streetside cafés. If you have an interest in naval tradition and antiquity you may also want to visit the Devonport Navy Museum in the dockyard, which forms the principal base for the Royal New Zealand Navy (▷ 63). Opened in 1888, its Calliope dry dock was once the largest dry dock in the southern hemisphere. Although often seconded for peacekeeping missions overseas, some vessels from the nation's limited fleet may be in evidence.

Walk down Victoria Street past the visitor information centre and Esplanade Hotel back to the Devonport Wharf and ferry terminal.

OUT AND ABOUT

Masts top the volcanic peak of Mount Victoria, left

The ferry terminal at Devonport

WHERE TO EAT

There is plenty of choice in Devonport, from streetside cafés for coffee or light snacks to à la carte restaurants. For a good coffee, healthy light meals and great atmosphere try Manuka, 49 Victoria Road. For a buffet dinner or Sunday brunch (from NZ$16), try the Watermark on the waterfront (33 King Edward Parade). For fish and chips it's hard to resist the Cod Piece, 26 Victoria Road, or the more traditional Catch 22, 19 Victoria Road.

HOW TO GET THERE

Fullers ferry from the Ferry Building, Quay Street, Auckland. Every 30 minutes, from NZ$9 return. Crossing: 15 minutes.

TIP

● Take binoculars, and a torch if you plan to explore the tunnels on North Head.

BASICS

Tourist Information
www.tourismnorthshore.org.nz
✉ 3 Victoria Road, Devonport
☎ 09-4460677

Devonport Museum
www.devonportmuseum.org.nz
✉ Mount Cambria Reserve
☎ 09-445 2661
⏰ Sat, Sun 2–4 or by arrangement

Navy Museum
www.navymuseum.mil.nz
✉ Spring Street
☎ 09-445 5186
⏰ Daily 10–4.30

The view of central Auckland from Mount Victoria

COROMANDEL COUNTRYSIDE AND COAST

A circular tour exploring the rugged hills, townships and spectacular coastal scenery of the Coromandel Peninsula.

THE DRIVE

Distance: 135km (84 miles)
Allow: 8 hours (or two days)
Start/end: Coromandel Township

★ From the old gold-mining township of Coromandel (▷ 66) take SH25 south for 3km (2 miles), then turn left onto The 309 Road. This is unsealed in places, but manageable with care. The first stop on The 309 Road is the Waiau Waterworks.

❶ Waiau Waterworks is a garden full of fascinating, whimsical water sculptures and gadgets. You are greeted by a metal stick figure who operates a waterwheel hung, not with wooden boards, but with pots, pans and other kitchenware. Within the gardens are many more unusual interactive water-powered inventions, including an old bicycle that you peddle furiously to squirt a hose of water across a lily pond.

Continue south on The 309 Road, keeping an eye open (left) for the aptly named Castle Rock (526m/1,725ft), a knobbly volcanic plug that can be seen from many points on the peninsula.

❷ The stiff climb to the top of Castle Rock takes up to two hours. To reach the summit track (signed) take the forest road left 2km (1mile) south of the Waiau Waterworks. The track is more like a stream for much of the year, but the view is well worth the effort.

Just over 7km (4 miles) south from the Coromandel end of The 309 are the Waiau Falls, with a drop of 6m (20ft). View them from a lookout by the road, or via an access track.

Less than a kilometre (0.6 miles) south of the falls is Kauri Grove.

❸ Kauri Grove is a small stand of ancient kauri trees that survived the rapacious logging at the end of the 19th century. Now fully protected, they offer a glimpse of what much of the upper North Island must once have looked like. The walk (signed) takes 20 minutes.

From Kauri Grove continue southeast on The 309 to the junction with SH25. Turn right and drive through the settlement of Coroglen. Eight kilometres (5 miles) beyond Coroglen turn left, signed to Hahei and Hot Water Beach. Turn right to the beach.

❹ At Hot Water Beach, about two hours each side of low tide you can dig a hole in the sand to access natural hot water (the local store hires out spades for NZ$5). The beach is very pleasant, but it is also very dangerous for swimming, with notorious rips. Once suitably boiled in your own hot spa, pop your head into the Moko Artspace at 24 Pye Place, just opposite the main car park.

About 10km (6 miles) north of Hot Water Beach is Hahei, signposted right.

❺ Hahei is an unspoiled coastal settlement surrounded by some of the best coastal scenery on the peninsula. Dramatic Cathedral Cove is the highlight (▷ 228).

From Hahei return to SH25 and head back north to Whitianga.

❻ The peninsula's most popular holiday spot, Whitianga (▷ 67) presents the perfect opportunity for a lunch stop, or an overnight stay (book ahead October–March). There's plenty of accommodation in the town, with Villa Toscana one of the top bed-and-breakfasts in the region (▷ 275).

North from Whitianga, SH25 straddles bush-clad hills before descending towards the coast again at Kuaotunu.

❼ The small beachside hamlet of Kuaotunu is a lovely spot, especially for swimming, but it also acts as the gateway to Otama and Opito bays via the scenic Black Jack Road (this is unsealed but manageable for standard vehicles). Both bays have lovely beaches and magnificent views across to the Mercury Islands. This is a great spot to escape the crowds.

Back on SH25 and a little farther west (signposted 1km off SH25) is the sterile real-estate settlement of Matarangi. Although it's usually bypassed by visitors, you may like to spend time enjoying its 5km (3-mile) sweep of beach, or perhaps book a tee time at its well groomed golf course (tel 07-866 5394). From Matarangi continue west on SH25 to Te Rerenga. On a clear day you will see Castle Rock straight ahead. At Te Rerenga turn right, following signs to Whangapoua.

❽ Whangapoua is little more than a conglomeration of *baches* (holiday homes) that come alive in summer. The village is the gateway to one of

Sunset bathes the bay at Coromandel township in gold

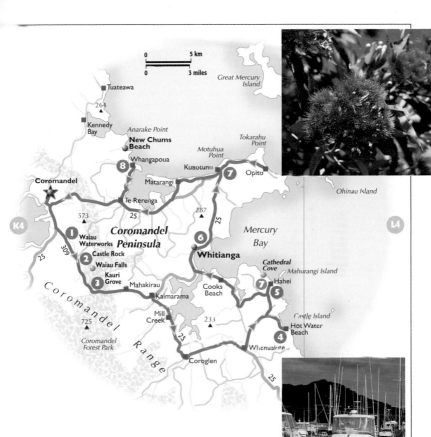

the most idyllic beaches on the peninsula—New Chums Beach (▷ 67), which can be reached only by foot. From the northern end of Whangapoua, cross the small river (at low tide) and follow the edge of the beach, where you will find a track. Follow this to the headland, where it ducks left through the bush, soon revealing the beach. The slopes surrounding the headland are noted for their pohutukawa trees, which flower crimson in December, earning it the label New Zealand's Christmas tree.

From Whangapoua return to SH25 at Te Rerenga then turn right. From here SH25 winds its way over the ranges, offering fine views of the Hauraki Gulf before descending steeply to the west coast and Coromandel township. On a clear day, with binoculars, you should be able to see the needle-sharp Sky Tower in Auckland (▷ 65), just beyond the volcanic cone of Rangitoto.

Digging on Hot Water Beach

WHERE TO EAT

Café Nina
✉ 20 Victoria Street, Whitianga
☎ 07-866 5440
Café Nina offers an imaginative black-board menu and a fine cup of coffee.
🕐 Daily 8–4.30

Top, pohutukawa blossom
Above, boats at Whitianga

WHERE TO STAY

Villa Toscana
✉ Ohuka Park, Whitianga
☎ 07-866 2293
www.villatoscana.co.nz
A grand villa offering memorable views.

BASICS

Tourist Information
✉ Coromandel Visitor Centre, 355 Kapanga Road, Coromandel
☎ 07-866 8598
www.coromandeltown.co.nz

Waiau Waterworks
✉ The 309 Road, Coromandel
☎ 07-866 7191
🕐 Oct–end Mar daily 9–dusk; Apr–end Sep daily 9–5
💰 Adult NZ$10, child NZ$5

AROUND LAKE ROTORUA

Drive around Lake Rotorua to sample just a few of the natural and manmade features that first spawned tourism in New Zealand and made the region the tourism capital of the North Island.

THE DRIVE

Distance: 85km (53 miles)
Allow: 8 hours
Start/end: Rotorua Visitor Information Centre

Rotorua is where tourism began in New Zealand. The Government's Department of Tourist and Health Resorts took over the spa in 1901, and in 1902 appointed the first official balneologist. For over a century the diverse volcanic and geothermal features of the region have lured visitors with the hope of both drama and cure: Drama in the form of gushing geysers, bubbling mud, or the former pink silica terraces (▷ 87), and cure in the form of therapeutic pools and curative treatments. From its inception in 1908, the town's world-famous Bath House was the main focus for many making the journey to the Bay of Plenty. The Bath House now forms part of the Rotorua Museum of Art and History (▷ 86).

★ From Fenton Street head south, following signs for the airport (east) and SH30. After 2km (1.5 miles) turn right onto Tarawera Road. On the right is the northern fringe of the Whakarewarewa Forest Park.

❶ Whakarewarewa Forest Park has a good network of tracks that are mostly used for mountain biking. The park is said to be one of the best venues in the country, and if you have never tried the sport this presents a perfect opportunity. A small visitor centre and gift shop on Long Mile Road provides all the details, including advice on bicycle hire and organised tours.

❷ At the eastern fringe of the park (8km/5 miles along Tawarewa Road) are Lake Rotokakihi (the Green Lake) and Lake Tikitapu (the Blue Lake; ▷ 86). The difference in colour between the two lakes is a result of the effects of subterranean minerals.

From Lake Tikitapu the road veers east towards Lake Tarawera and the partly excavated Maori Buried Village. Here you can gain a fascinating insight into the eruption of Mount Tarawera in 1886. Tarawera Landing is just a little farther east, from where boat trips are available on MV *Reremoana* (▷ 177).

From Tarawera Landing return to SH30 and head east (right) around the lake, past the airport to the junction between SH30 (Whakatane) and SH33 (Tauranga). Remain on SH30 as it heads east away from the lake, following signs to Hell's Gate ❸ (3km/2 miles, ▷ 84).

After your thermal experience at Hell's Gate, return to the lake and turn right onto the Tauranga Road (SH33). Cross over the Ouau Channel (that connects Lake Rotorua with Lake Rotoiti) and continue north to Okere (2km/1 mile). At Okere turn left, following signs to the Okere Falls Scenic Reserve, just before the river bridge.

❹ The Okere Falls Scenic Reserve offers an excellent opportunity for a short bush walk and to watch the rafting and white-water action on the tempestuous Kaituna River. It is one of the best venues for the sport in the North Island, and the 7m (23ft) drop from the Tutea Falls is a dramatic highlight. There is a viewing platform just a short distance from the main track (signposted) where you can watch the rafters plummeting over the edge with trepidation, or glee. If you are tempted, trips can be arranged through the visitor centre in Rotorua (from NZ$85).

From Okere return south and turn right just before the lake and Ohau Channel. This road hugs the northern fringe of Lake Rotorua and offers pleasant views back towards Rotorua. Take a brief stop at the crystal-clear Hamurana Springs. (Look for the golf course on the right and park your car in the golf course parking area.)

❺ Hamurana Springs are the largest in the North Island, and erupt at a volume of over one million gallons per hour, creating a beautifully clear river that flows the short distance into Lake Rotorua. The head of the springs can be reached via a 10-minute walk through a glade of giant redwood trees that fringe the river. Access is from the former Hamurana Gardens parking area (which doubles as the Hamurana Golf Course parking area) beside the main road. Cross the bridge at the car park and follow the path upstream.

From Hamurana Springs continue west through Ngongotaha to join SH5 towards Rotorua. Continue south for 3km (2 miles), stopping at the Skyline Skyrides (▷ 87) on the left. Rainbow Springs (▷ 178) is opposite.

From Skyline Skyrides continue south on SH5, bearing left on Lake Road into the city to return to the visitor information centre on Fenton Street. Alternatively, a perfect end to your tour would be a soak in the thermal pools at the Polynesian Spa (▷ 86) at the southern end of Government Gardens, off Fenton Street. The best bet is to go at lunchtime, when the tour buses are elsewhere.

WHERE TO EAT

Skyline Skyrides complex
✉ On the slopes of Mount Ngongotaha, SH5
☎ 07-347 0027
Enjoy traditional Kiwi fare with views across the city and lake.
◎ Jan–end Mar daily 9–8.30; Apr–end Dec daily 9–6. Entry fee applies for gondola: adult NZ$18, child (5–14) NZ$8 (▷ 87)

Mist hangs above Waimangu
volcanic valley

TIP

● Before leaving the rather grand and well-stocked visitor information centre, gather any detailed information you may require about the sights on this drive that take your fancy.

BASICS

Tourist Information

✉ Rotorua Visitor Centre, 1167 Fenton Street, Rotorua

☎ 07-348 5179

www.rotoruaNZ.com

🕐 Daily 8–5.30

Whakarewarewa Forest Park visitor information centre

✉ Long Mile Road, off Tarawera Road

☎ 07-346 2082

🕐 Mon–Fri 8.30–5, Sat–Sun 10–4

The Green Lake, or Rotokakihi, is
sacred to the Maori

OUT AND ABOUT

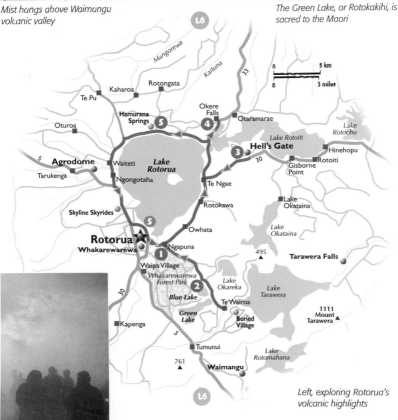

Left, exploring Rotorua's
volcanic highlights

AROUND LAKE ROTOR

THE ROTORUA WALKWAY

This easy circular walk through the heart of the city and around the lakefront offers a great introduction to Rotorua's intriguing natural and human history.

THE WALK

Distance: 2km (1 mile)
Allow: 2–3 hours
Start/end: Polynesian Spa car park, lake end of Hinemoa Street

As the North Island's most popular tourist destination, and host to almost 2 million visitors a year, there is no doubting Rotorua's commercialism, or its ability to entertain. But amid all the hype and adrenalin-pumping activities, one of the best ways to get a feel for the place (if not to escape the crowds) is to explore part of the 26km (16-mile) Rotorua Walkway. The short section described below concentrates on the heart of the city and the lakefront and offers a mix of local history, architecture and—of course—a sample of the region's celebrated and unpredictable geothermal features.

★ From the Polynesian Spa (▷ 86) car park head west through the heart of the city along Hinemoa Street to the junction with Ranolf Street. Turn right and enter Kuirau Park at the junction of Pukuatua and Ranolf streets. Head north through the park.

❶ With your nose assailed by the pungent smell of sulphur, you quickly realise that Kuirau Park is not your average town park. It is pock-marked with fenced-off craters and steaming hot pools, and you could be forgiven for thinking you were on another planet. Once a dangerous swamp, the 30ha (74-acre) Kuirau Park was endowed as a reserve by the local Maori, Ngati Whakaue, and first developed during the Depression of the 1930s.
  Although all the pools in Kuirau Park are now out of bounds to the public, for many decades locals and visitors used the more temperate among them for bathing and relaxation. Maori legend has it that a local girl, Kuiarau, who

used to bathe in the biggest lake (originally known as Taokahu), was seized by a despicable *taniwha* (spirit) who inhabited a lair beneath the waters. This was noticed by the gods, who decided to boil the lake in order to destroy the *taniwha*. From that time on the lake was known as Kuiarau, or Kuirau, in memory of the unlucky girl.

From the northern fringe of Kuirau Park head right up Pukeroa Hill on Lake Road.

❷ Pukeroa Hill (also known as Hospital Hill) was a *pa* site used by the local Maori, Ngati Whakaue, who adapted the small hilltop for their defences. There are still some burial sites (*urupa*) present on the hill. In 1961 the hill became the site for a military hospital, which later developed into the King George V Hospital.

From Lake Road turn left down Haukotuku Street, then right along Tunohopu Street to the historic Maori settlement of Ohinemutu, home to St. Faith's Church and the magnificent Tamatekapua Meeting House ❸ (▷ 85).
  Continue round the lakefront, which then forms the fringe of Government Gardens. A short distance from the Rotorua Museum of Art and History is another Rotorua icon, the Blue Baths ❹ (▷ 86).
  From the museum, return to the lakefront and head east

to the Motutara Point and Sulphur Bay.

❺ From beyond Motutara Point Lake, Rotorua (▷ 84) is laid out before you, with Mokoia Island dominating the horizon. Among the waterbirds you may see here are brown teal, along with black swans and a colony of pied shags.

From Motutara Point continue south on the marked walkway to Sulphur Point.

❻ The view of Sulphur Bay, the southernmost bay on Lake Rotorua, is dominated by a steaming, sulphurous crust that sits above an active geothermal field. Although a hostile and unproductive habitat for wildlife, it still provides sanctuary for both roosting and nesting birds, including the omnipresent and handsome red-billed gulls. It was officially designated as a wildlife refuge in 1967.
  Local Maori also made use of the thermal features and the small islands of Sulphur Bay, particularly Moturere Island—which before lake levels rose had a thermal pool known for its therapeutic properties. The soft rock and warm waters also made it a perfect site to sharpen greenstone tools and weapons.

From Sulphur Point continue south to return to the Polynesian Spa car park.

Bathing outdoors in the thermal luxury of Rotorua's Polynesian Spa

Hoping for titbits: black swans beside the walkway

Above, the half-timbered former Bath House of 1908, now the city's museum, looms on the skyline

Right, natural steam vents at the Tamatekapua Marae

Left, relaxing in the sunshine on the lakeside

WHERE TO EAT

The Fat Dog Café
✉ 1161 Arawa Street, Rotorua
☎ 07-347 7586
Something of a local institution, with an imaginative blackboard menu and plenty of character.

BASICS

Tourist Information
✉ Rotorua Visitor Centre, 1167 Fenton Street, Rotorua
☎ 07-348 5179
www.rotoruanz.com

A CIRCUIT OF TONGARIRO NATIONAL PARK

Throughout this tour you'll have the company of two large and unpredictable landmarks—Ruapehu and Ngauruhoe—the North Island's most celebrated volcanoes.

THE DRIVE

Distance: 328km (203 miles)
Allow: 8 hours
Start/end: Taupo

★ From Taupo (▷ 92) follow SH1 south along the eastern shore of Lake Taupo.

❶ Given the sheer expanse of water and its apparent serenity, it is hard to imagine that Lake Taupo is a massive volcanic crater. It was formed after a massive eruption that occurred around AD230.

At the southeastern edge of the lake, near the mouth of the Tongariro River, is the small resort of Turangi ❷ (▷ 92). The Tongariro is renowned for its excellent trout-fishing, and is also popular for white-water rafting and canoeing.

At the southern fringe of Turangi turn right onto SH41. Follow this for 3km (2 miles), and then turn left onto SH47.

SH47 climbs to a viewpoint looking back towards Lake Taupo before straddling a pass between Pihanga (1,325m/4,347ft) on the left and Kakaramea (1,301m/4,268ft) on the right. If you feel like a break, you might consider the relatively easy two-hour walk around Lake Rotopounamu, which is hidden in the bush on the western flank of Pihanga. The car park and track are signposted.

❸ Just south of the Lake Rotopounamu car park, Lake Rotoaira comes in to view. Beyond this you will see the northern slopes of Mount Tongariro (1,967m/6,455ft) and the volcanic cone of Ngauruhoe (2,287m/7,501ft). Lake Rotoaira is another good place for trout-fishing, and is frequented by hundreds of black swans. If you look carefully, about two-thirds of the way up the slopes of Mount Tongariro (to the south), you may be able to see the Ketetahi Hut. This 'sanctuary in the clouds' has been a

welcome sight to many a tired soul undertaking the Tongariro Crossing (▷ 89), considered one of the best day hikes in New Zealand.

Continue south on SH47 and enjoy the spectacular views on the left over the Tongariro National Park (▷ 88–89). The dominant features are Mount Ngauruhoe, with its classic volcano shape, and Mount Ruapehu, also a volcano and at 2,797m (9,176ft) the highest mountain in the North Island.

At the foot of Mount Ruapehu you will see the historic Chateau Tongariro hotel (▷ 278), another icon of the national park.

Turn left onto SH48 following signs to the Chateau and Whakapapa Village (7km/4 miles).

❹ Park in the middle of Whakapapa Village (▷ 89) to explore, then continue up the main road (Bruce Road) to reach the Whakapapa Ski Field (Top o' the Bruce). The dramatic rocky outcrops around the main skiing complex were used in the *Lord of the Rings* movies as Mount Doom in Mordor.

From Whakapapa, return via SH48 to SH47 and continue left (west) to the village of National Park (9km/6 miles).

❺ A drab-looking place, National Park is an accommodation base for the ski fields.

Turn left again onto SH4 and continue south for 26km (16 miles) before turning left onto SH49 to Ohakune (▷ 89), the halfway point on the tour.

East of the heart of the village and signposted off SH49, the 17km (11-mile) drive up Mountain Road to the Turoa ski fields is well worth the journey in good weather, providing fine views to the west. If it is a

particularly clear day you may be able to see the snow-capped volcanic peak of Mount Taranaki/Mount Egmont (▷ 80).

According to Maori legend, there was a feud between the mountains of Tongariro and Taranaki after both fell in love with the beautiful Pihanga. A mighty battle ensued. Taranaki lost the fight and, wild with grief and anger, ripped himself from his roots and tore a path towards the coast, where he now stands alone. Perhaps through indifference or appeasement, Tongariro created the waters that filled Taranaki's path of destruction, and the Whanganui River was born.

From Ohakune follow SH49 east as it circles the southern fringe of Ruapehu. Twelve kilometres (7 miles) beyond Ohakune on the left are two lakes collectively known as Lake Rotokura (signposted). Access is on foot only.

❻ The tranquil upper lake reflects the peak of Ruapehu, and can be reached with an easy 30-minute walk from the car park, just off SH49.

A little farther east on SH49 is the Whangaehu River, straddled by a new road bridge. Alongside it is the Tangiwai Memorial.

On Christmas Eve 1953, the walls of the crater lake of Ruapehu collapsed without warning and a mighty lahar rushed down the Whangaehu River, wiping out the rail bridge at Tangiwai. The night train to Auckland arrived moments later—151 lives were lost.

A further 7km (4 miles) brings you to Waiouru and a junction. Turn left, heading north on SH1.

❼ Just north of Waiouru, SH1 cuts through a barren, flat expanse of grassland known as the Rangipo Desert, in the rain shadow of Ruapehu.

OUT AND ABOUT

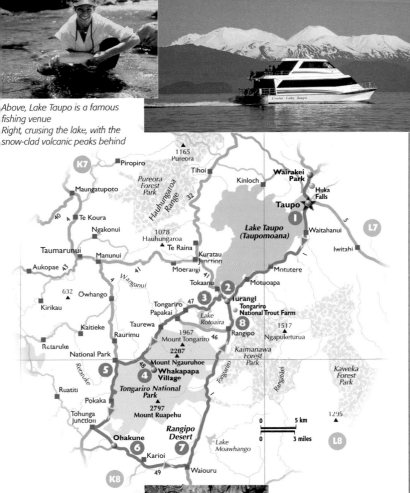

Above, Lake Taupo is a famous fishing venue

Right, cruising the lake, with the snow-clad volcanic peaks behind

OUT AND ABOUT

This stretch, dubbed the Desert Road, is often temporarily closed in winter due to snow.

Continue on SH1 back to Turangi. Three kilometres (2 miles) south of Turangi, pass the Tongariro National Trout Centre.

8 At this trout hatchery you can observe wild trout in the Waihukahuka stream through a viewing window. The visitor centre showcases the history of fishing in the region, and how to catch your own fish on Lake Taupo.

From Turangi return on SH1 to Taupo, where you can enjoy a dip at the Taupo Hot Springs.

Maori carvings in the cliffs above Lake Taupo

WHERE TO EAT/STAY
The Chateau Tongariro (▷ 278)

WHEN TO GO
Snow sometimes causes road closures.

BASICS

Tourist Information
✉ Taupo Visitor Centre, 30 Tongariro Street, Taupo
☎ 07-376 0027
www.LakeTaupoNZ.com
🕐 Daily 8.30–5

DoC Whakapapa Visitor Information Centre
✉ Whakapapa Village
☎ 07-892 3729
www.doc.govt.nz
🕐 Daily 8–6

Tongariro National Trout Centre
✉ Turangi
☎ 07-386 9254
🕐 Dec–Apr daily 10–4; rest of year 10–3
💵 Free, but donations appreciated

HAHEI AND CATHEDRAL COVE

The highlight of this walk is Cathedral Cove, where secluded beaches are connected by a natural arch and guarded by bizarre rocky stacks.

THE WALK

Distance: 6km (4 miles)
Allow: 3 hours
Start/end: Kotare Domain car park, Pa Road, Hahei

★ On entering Hahei village turn right onto Pa Road. Park in the Kotare Domain car park on the left, 200m (220 yards) from the end of Pa Road. Walk to the end of Pa Road, to Te Pare Point.

❶ The Te Pare Point Historic Reserve, which dominates the southern end of Hahei Beach, is the site of a *pa* occupied by the Ngati Hei people. This local tribe (and the settlement itself) is named after the Maori chief Hei, a *tohunga* (priest) who arrived at the time of the great Polynesian migration to New Zealand, around 1350. He settled his people here in Mercury Bay mainly because of its plentiful resources—but there is little doubt the stunning beauty of the area also influenced his decision. Hei's descendants, as *tangata whenua*, retain a strong ancestral and spiritual attachment to the site, and proudly continue their role as guardians, or *kaitiaki*, of the resources within it. Information panels at the Cathedral Cove Lookout (see below) give a brief history of the Ngati Hei and the influence of the first European settlers.

From Te Pare Point descend the steps to the beach—this is only possible at low tide. At high tide, walk back along Pa Road for 100m (110 yards) to the grass walkway on the right (marked) and cross the bridge. Steps onto the beach are signposted at the end of the road.
   Walk to the northern end of the beach and look for the steps and walkway up the hill to the Cathedral Cove Lookout (signposted). From the lookout take the Cathedral Cove track (signposted). The track ducks

Strolling through the natural rock arch of Cathedral Cove

through tracts of native bush and pine before descending to the first of the two beaches collectively known as Cathedral Cove.

❷ The scenic jewel in the region's crown, Cathedral Cove guards the Te Whanganui-A-Hei (Cathedral Cove) Marine Reserve. This reserve covers 9sq km (3.5sq miles) and became New Zealand's sixth marine reserve in 1992. Cathedral Cove is actually two coves and two beaches connected by a natural limestone arch, which is negotiable at low tide. There are sandstone pinnacles on both beaches, with the highest, Sail Rock, on the western beach. Although the beach can get very busy, it offers great sunbathing and swimming and unforgettable scenery. By far the best time to go is at dawn, when you can sometimes—if only for a short while—have the beach all to yourself.
   The snorkelling opportunities in Te Whanganui-A-Hei Marine Reserve are also outstanding, especially at Gemstone Bay and the western side of Mahurangi Island. In early 2004 a snorkel trail was installed at Gemstone Bay. Four marker buoys with information panels depicting which species inhabit each area are anchored from 50m (55 yards) to 165m (180 yards) offshore. For information contact the Department of Conservation in Thames, tel 07-867 9180.

Return to the lookout and take Grange Road back into Hahei

and the small shopping centre. From here, turn right onto the main road. Head south back to Pa Road and return to the Kotare Domain car park. If you wish you can take a short cut through the Domain itself, 100m (110 yards) south of the shopping centre on the left (signposted).

WHERE TO EAT

Luna Café
✉ 1 Grange Road (in the main shopping centre)
☎ 07-866 3016
Come here for a bite to eat during the day or a well-deserved cup of coffee.
🕐 Daily in summer from 9am until late, with reduced hours in winter

The Church
✉ 87 Beach Road, Hahei
☎ 07-866 3797
www.thechurchhahei.co.nz
This is the best-known and most characterful option in Hahei.
🕐 Wed–Sun

HOW TO GET THERE

Hahei is 35km (22 miles) by road from Whitianga. Go Kiwi offers regular shuttle services from Ferry Landing, Whitianga (book at Whitianga information centre). In summer, the five-minute, passenger-only ferry crossing to Ferry Landing operates continuously 7.30am–6.30pm, 7.30pm–8.30pm, 9.30pm–10.30pm. In winter hours may be reduced.

BASICS

Tourist Information
✉ Whitianga i-SITE, 66 Albert Street, Whitianga
☎ 07-866 5555
www.whitianga.co.nz

OUT AND ABOUT

THE WAITOMO WALKWAY

Often described as one of the finest short walks in the North Island, the Waitomo Walkway follows the meandering course of the Waitomo Stream, culminating in a 40-minute loop to take in the major limestone features within the Ruakuri Scenic Reserve.

THE WALK

Distance: 12km (7 miles)
Allow: 3 hours
Start/end: Waitomo Glow-worm Caves car park

The limestone around Waitomo was once the sea-bed, and formed about 30 million years ago from the layered remains of countless marine animals. Over millennia these layers have been raised by the action of the earth's plates, and in some places the limestone is more than 200m (656ft) thick.

Through its gradual uprising the limestone bends and buckles, creating a network of cracks and joints. As rainwater drains in to these cracks it mixes with small amounts of carbon dioxide in the air and soil, forming a weak acid. Over thousands of years this acid slowly dissolves the limestone and the cracks and joints widen. Yet more time sees small streams flow through converging cracks, to create the features we see within the Ruakuri Scenic Reserve. Eventually these streams disappear underground, where they can scour out dramatic underground caves such as Waitomo and Aranui.

Within these caves the acidic water continues to seep from the walls or drips from the roof, leaving a minute deposit of limestone crystal. Gradually these deposits form stalactites, stalagmites and other features. The size and rate of their formation depends on the rate of flow. In time, the caves collapse, forming gorges, holes or arches.

★ From the Waitomo Glow-worm Caves (▷ 90) car park follow the signposted walking track (Waitomo Walkway) southwest to the Ruakuri

Scenic Reserve and Aranui Cave car park.

❶ According to local tradition, the Aranui Cave was inhabited by a pack of wild dogs—hence its name, 'rua', which means cave and 'kuri', the name for a Maori dog. There are burial caves in the cliffs along the track, making this a place of special significance for Maori. The entrance to Ruakuri Cave, marked by karaka trees with a burial cave above, is *waahi tapu* (sacred).

From the car park begin your circuit of the Scenic Reserve.

❷ The Ruakuri Scenic Reserve encompasses typical karst landscape, characterised by caves, natural arches, tunnels, gorges, depressions and sculpted rock outcrops, the presence and formation of which are explained and outlined on information boards along the way.

The first 50m (55 yards) of the walk are fringed with damp walls and small over-hangs that are inhabited by glow-worms (obviously best seen if you return after dark, but take a torch/flashlight).

One of the highlights of the walk is the Ruakuri natural bridge tunnel, which is home to a colony of native long tailed bats. They are an endangered species and one of only two land mammals native to New Zealand (both of which are species of bats).

After completing the Ruakuri circuit return via the Waitomo Walkway to the Waitomo Glow-worm Caves car park.

WHERE TO EAT

Morepork Café
✉ Kiwipaka Hostel, School Road, Waitomo Caves Village
☎ 07 878 3395
A congenial pizza café with spacious deck.
🕐 Daily 8am–9pm

HOW TO GET THERE

The Waitomo turn-off is 16km (10 miles) south from Otorohanga on SH3, and Waitomo is 7km (4 miles) west of SH3 on SH37.

BASICS

Tourist Information
✉ Waitomo Museum of Caves Visitor Information Centre, 21 Waitomo Caves Road, Waitomo
☎ 0800-474839/07-878 7640
www.waitomo-museum.co.nz

TIP

● Take a tour to the Waitomo Glow-worm Caves (▷ 90) before or after your walk.

Top, blackwater rafting on inner tubes through the caves
Above, stalactites and stalagmites fused into columns

OUT AND ABOUT

THE WAITOMO WALKWAY 229

A TASTE OF THE ABEL TASMAN

**This section of the Abel Tasman Coast Track, from Bark Bay to Anchorage,
includes dense native bush, turquoise bays, golden beaches and idyllic swimming spots.**

OUT AND ABOUT

THE WALK

Distance: 12km (7 miles)
Allow: 7 hours; 4 hours of walking
Start/end: Marahau, 67km
(42 miles) northwest of Nelson

It takes up to five days to walk the entire Abel Tasman Coast Track (▷ 109–110), but water taxis make it easy to walk this delicious one-day taster. The walking track is in excellent condition, the climbs are gentle and there's plenty of time to relax and enjoy the beauty.

Abel Tasman is New Zealand's smallest and most popular national park. It was named after Dutch explorer Abel Janszoon Tasman (1603–c1659), who managed to upset the Maori without actually setting foot on land. His two ships moored off the northern coast of the South Island in 1642, watched warily by the Ngati Tumatakokiri tribe. A small boat, ferrying sailors between the ships, was rammed by one of eight Maori canoes. A skirmish erupted and four of Tasman's crew were killed. Tasman heatedly named the beach Murderers' Bay; it was later renamed Golden Bay.

★ Meet the water taxi at its Marahau base for the 9am departure to Bark Bay.

❶ The hour-long trip takes you past Split Apple Rock, a huge ball of porous granite from Separation Point that, at some unknown time, broke clean in half. It is stained red by the iron oxide that gives the beaches their golden tone and the oysters an interesting tang.

As you step off the boat at Bark Bay, the track is at the south (left-hand) end of the beach. There are toilets here: it's 8km (5 miles) to the next ones, and the Department of Conservation does not encourage bushland emergencies.
❷ Bark Bay was home to a family of European settlers—Timothy Huffam and his sons, who arrived in 1870. One of

their money-earning activities was to gather beech and rimu bark to sell in Nelson for the tanning process. They stayed until 1904. The DoC hut at the north end of Bark Bay beach is built on the site of their homestead, and the redwoods they planted are still there.

Follow the well-formed track as it gradually meanders away from the coast and through native bush, which includes tree ferns, kanuka and beech. After 1km (0.6 miles), a signposted track on the left points to South Head. The short track gives views over the sea and Pinnacle Island. Once back on the main track, take your time crossing the Falls River swingbridge—seals often cruise for fish here at high tide.

Descend into Torrent Bay ❸ and walk down the two sandy 'streets' of holiday *baches*. At the south end of the beach a picturesque jetty gives a superb view of the bay and is a good spot for lunch. Toilets are another 500m (550 yards). Stay on the main track. (It is also possible to get to Anchorage across the bay at low tide; this route is 3km/2 miles shorter, but be sure of the tides.)

❹ The bush in this section of the walk is lush compared to other areas. From Bark Bay to Onetahuti Beach, the next beach to the north, there is a lot of scrubby manuka and kanuka, while visitors to the park's northwestern entrance

at Wainui Bay pass a stretch of invasive, prickly gorse. It's all part of a massive experiment in land recovery. This land was leased to European settlers on the condition that it was cleared for productive use, and sawmills, granite quarries, boatyards and farms appeared. None were sustainable: Farmland was quickly drained of nutrients and stock failed to thrive. Through the 1930s Nelson conservationist Perrine Moncrieff led a vigorous campaign to have 15,000ha (37,000 acres) of the land made into a national park, and in 1942 the park formally opened.

The track follows a series of picturesque coves. Birdlife is prolific and seals often come up the rivers to play and forage. The seals that frequent these coves are New Zealand fur seals. Sealers decimated the population in the 19th century, but now they are fully protected, numbers are crawling back by around 2 per cent a year. The marine reserve around Tonga Island, north of Bark Bay, attracts them with a plentiful supply of squid and fish. Pups are born in early summer, and learn to swim at about four weeks old. As teenagers, they are playful and curious, and even climb aboard the odd sea kayak. As adults they can be fierce if disturbed.

In 2km (1 mile) look for a sign to Cleopatra's Pool, 1km (0.6 miles) inland from the main track. This detour follows a stream to a delightful freshwater swimming hole and picnic area ❺.

Return to the main track and continue south towards Anchorage. After 1.5km (1 mile) the path rises up; at the brow of the hill there's a signpost. Turn left down the hill and it's 500m (550 yards) to the broad curve of Anchorage Beach. Relax here until 4pm, when the water taxi will pick you up and take you back to Marahau.

A watchful cormorant

Tourist Information
✉ Wallace Street, Motueka
☎ 03-528 6543
www.AbelTasmanGreenRush.co.nz

Department of Conservation
✉ Corner of King Edward and High
streets, Motueka
☎ 03-528 1810
www.doc.govt.nz

WHEN TO GO

Spring and autumn are more
peaceful in the Abel Tasman,
though the weather can be
cool. December and January
are very busy, while Christmas/
New Year is plain crazy.

*A combination of native bush
and scenic coastline make the
Abel Tasman Coast Track
popular with trampers*

*Mind the gap—standing between the neat halves of Split Apple Rock
provides a popular photo opportunity*

Water taxis, booked ahead, enable you to walk sections of the track

OUT AND ABOUT

WHERE TO EAT

Have a picnic at Torrent Bay.
Supplies can be ordered the
day before from Hooked
on Marahau at the Marahau
Beach Camp (tel 03-527 8576,
daily 8am–9pm, summer; 8–6,
winter). Take ample drinking
water with you, and a spare
bag for rubbish.

TIP

● For a water taxi, book with
Aqua Taxi at least one day
ahead, tel 0800-278 282. The
Beaches and Bays trip costs
around NZ$48.

QUEEN CHARLOTTE DRIVE

This route combines the Queen Charlotte scenic drive between Havelock and Picton with exploring the wine-making region of Marlborough.

THE DRIVE

Distance: 100km (62 miles)
Allow: 2.5 hours
Start/end: Picton Visitor Centre, near the ferry terminal

Beyond the towns of Blenheim and Picton, Marlborough is one of the country's least populated regions. Even the gorgeous coastline is under-whelmed by human inhabitants, and holiday homes far outnumber perma-nent residences. It could have been so different—in the 1860s Picton had high hopes of becoming New Zealand's capital city. Now it is most famous for being the South Island port for the interisland ferries (▷ 52–53), and more than a million travellers pass through every year.

★ From the visitor centre in Picton (▷ 117), drive south down Auckland Street to the intersec-tion with Broadway. Continue on the southeast fork, Wairau Road. The road goes around Nelson Square and continues out of Picton as SH1 towards Blenheim. This road wiggles comfortably south past the Para Wetlands ❶, a signposted area frequented by duck-shooters in season. Mount Richmond Forest Park rises up 4km (2.5 miles) to the west.

❷ **The Wairau Plains**—the flat area north of Blenheim—is superb farmland. The river valley soil is fertile, the sun-shine hours are long, and it's all sheltered by the Richmond Ranges. Grapes grow marvel-lously well, but so do apples, cherries and berries.

After 21km (13 miles) reach the small township of Spring Creek. At Spring Creek, turn right into Rapaura Road and within 1km (0.6 miles) you are deep in vineyard country. Rows and rows of vines make up the vista on both sides of the road, while mountains rise up to the north.

In 7km (4 miles) reach the acclaimed Hunter's Estate.

❸ **Hunter's**, with its pleasant winery, garden, restaurant and resident artist's studio, is well worth a stop. The estate has one of the highest international profiles of any in New Zealand. Its founder, Ernie Hunter, was a pioneer of Marlborough wine-making, putting grapes down in 1983 and winning major UK awards just three years later. The estate is now run by his wife, Jane Hunter, herself a viti-culturalist. In 2004 she won the inaugural Women in Wine award at the International Wine and Spirits Awards, held in London.

In another 4km (2.5 miles) reach the Mud House.

❹ **The Mud House** offers regional specialities such as olive oil, gifts and Prenzel liqueurs, as well as Mud House boutique wines.

Two kilometres (1 mile) after the Mud House, take SH6 to Havelock. The highway crosses the mighty Wairau River after 2km (1 mile), then follows the Kaituna River. After 25km (16 miles) there is a clearly sign-posted turn-off for Queen Charlotte Drive.

If you would like to buy fresh green-shell mussels, continue ahead for a detour into Havelock (▷ 112, try the Four Square supermarket or Mussel Boys Restaurant on the main street).

From Queen Charlotte Drive there's a view of Havelock's marina to the north, then the road starts winding upwards through Mahakipawa Scenic

Reserve. For 8km (5 miles) the road tracks the Mahakipawa Arm of Mahau Sound. The picnic area at the end of this stretch, developed by Linkwater locals, is the best place to stop and absorb the views. The next 6km (4 miles) are relatively straight with farmland on both sides, but it gives access onto Kenepuru Road, which leads to the Queen Charlotte Track.

❺ **The Queen Charlotte Track** is notable among New Zealand walking tracks for its accessibil-ity. The long sliver of land offers 55km (34 miles) of ridge and coastal walking and mountain biking. Apart from the beautiful bays and bush sections, the joy is the number of points connecting with boats or cars, so walkers can do as much or as little as they fancy. The other bonus is the amount of accommodation en route, from campsites to luxury rooms, so heavy packs aren't required.

The final 17km (11 miles) of Queen Charlotte Drive are the most rewarding. This tight stretch of road passes pretty marinas at Momorangi and Ngakuta bays, enclaves of secluded housing, cool tracts of native bush and views of the jagged inlets of Queen Charlotte Sound. Governor's Bay is a good place to stop, with safe parking and a look-out a couple of metres from the road, and a sandy swim-ming beach 1km (0.6 miles) down the hill.

Port Shakespeare's logging wharf is the first sign of Picton, 5km (3 miles) away. Before your final descent, there's a large roadside car park overlooking the ferry terminal and Picton township. In 1km (0.6 miles) reach a major roundabout (traffic circle), and turn east into Dublin Street. The next left (northward) turn is Auckland Street, which leads back to the visitor centre.

Roadside fern fronds

OUT AND ABOUT

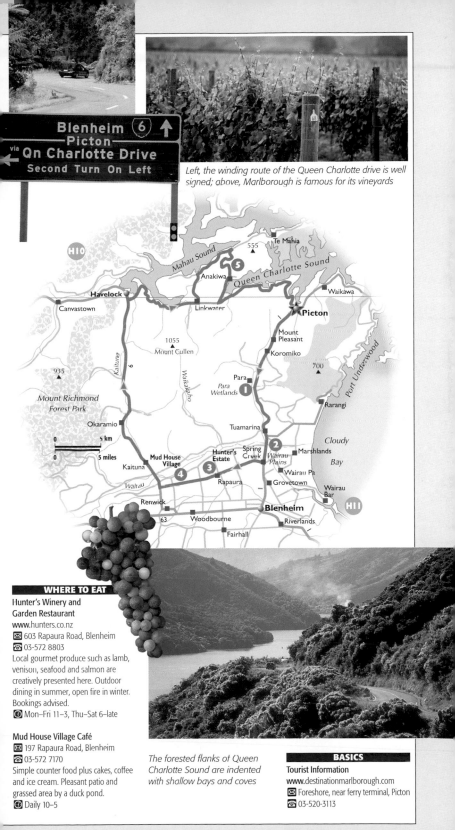

Left, the winding route of the Queen Charlotte drive is well signed; above, Marlborough is famous for its vineyards

The forested flanks of Queen Charlotte Sound are indented with shallow bays and coves

WHERE TO EAT

Hunter's Winery and Garden Restaurant
www.hunters.co.nz
✉ 603 Rapaura Road, Blenheim
☎ 03-572 8803
Local gourmet produce such as lamb, venison, seafood and salmon are creatively presented here. Outdoor dining in summer, open fire in winter. Bookings advised.
🕐 Mon–Fri 11–3, Thu–Sat 6–late

Mud House Village Café
✉ 197 Rapaura Road, Blenheim
☎ 03-572 7170
Simple counter food plus cakes, coffee and ice cream. Pleasant patio and grassed area by a duck pond.
🕐 Daily 10–5

BASICS

Tourist Information
www.destinationmarlborough.com
✉ Foreshore, near ferry terminal, Picton
☎ 03-520-3113

CLIFFS OF KAIKOURA

This way-marked walk takes you from the seal colony to the cliff-tops, where you can look over colonies of birds to the same ocean vista as the early whalers.

THE WALK

Distance: 8.5km (5.5 miles)
Allow: 2 hours
Start/end: Peninsula car park at the northeast end of the Kaikoura Peninsula

★ The Peninsula car park overlooks a large (and pungent) fur seal colony and tidal rock pools. Start at the eastern end, following a sign to the Cliff-Top Walk. A 200m (220-yard) climb is rewarded with a fantastic view of the Seaward Kaikoura Ranges, the shoreline and ocean. Take the southwest path over the stile and past the squat, yellow lighthouse. After 500m (550 yards), the fence line turns at a right-angle. Walk right to the corner.

❶ In spring, you'll see the busy comings and goings of a red-billed seagull colony below this point—but don't lean on the fence, it may be electrified. Around 12,000 of these gulls nest on the peninsula, which is also popular with black-backed gulls, white-fronted terns and shags. The tidal platforms along the shoreline attract wading birds such as turnstones, oystercatchers and herons.

After another 200m (220 yards), a stile leads you onto the cliff-side of the fence, but the track is still clear and secure. In another kilometre (0.6 miles), you reach Whalers' Bay Lookout. There's a bench here, or in another 300m (330 yards) you can take a seat above the rocky white hump known as Sugar Loaf.

❷ These points are where whalers sat in the 1840s, looking out to sea for spouting whales. Once they were spotted, a signal was sent to boats on the shore below and the oarsmen set to work. The preferred quarry was the southern right whale, which would rise to the surface when dead and usually yielded vast quantities of oil. The animal was hauled back to shore and butchered on the beach. The oil was generally sent to England for lamp fuel and as a lubricant, while the pliable bone of the whale's jaw was used in corsets, stays and horsewhips. Demand dropped with the increased use of electricity. The last whale commercially killed in New Zealand was caught off Kaikoura in 1964.

Shortly, green signposts turn you inland towards South Bay, and soon you have a view of the wharves. White posts with orange triangles lead you down the hill, heading northwest. At the stile before Atia Point, turn north and follow the fence line straight down the hill. After a cliff-edge walk along a wider dirt track, pass through a double gate and walk beside pine trees, then along a stony beach until you enter South Bay Recreation Reserve.

❸ The name Atia Point alludes to one of the Cook Islands. Such names are thought to be very old, as they hark back to the Maori homelands. Oral tradition testifies that Kaikoura's first Maori settlers, the Waitaha, arrived a thousand years ago with Chief Rakaihautu.

At the end of the grassy area, turn west onto Kaka Road to reach Moa Point, site of a whale-processing factory that closed in 1922. Now it shelters the boats of today's commercial whaling industry—Whalewatch Kaikoura (▷ 190).

Shortly turn inland up Tui Drive, then eastwards along South Bay Parade for 1km (0.6 miles). Houses on the seaward side give way to reserve land; beyond this, white fences mark a stream bed and a green sign points inland to Kaikoura township (▷ 113). Follow this route across the grassy reserve towards a stile. Follow the white marker post to a steep climb heading north, with pine trees to the east. This brings you to a viewpoint overlooking South Bay. Continue north and cross two stiles onto Scarborough Street.

❹ Across Scarborough Street is the site of Nga Niho *pa*. This terrace-edged village was fortified with defensive earthworks that still stand over 2m (7ft) tall. It was probably built in the 1820s, one of 15 *pa* known to have stood on the peninsula. Its position was ideal—easy to defend with a plentiful food source nearby.

Walk eastwards up Scarborough Street, turn north up Austin Terrace, then east onto Cromer Terrace at the corner. Where Cromer Terrace meets Ward Street there's a green signpost for Fyffe Quay. Cross the stile and follow the southern fence line until you see a track winding down the hill. In the northeast corner, a yellow triangle sign and stile lead onto a back road. Walk westwards and descend onto Jimmy Armer's Beach on Fyffe Quay. Continue east along the road for 1km (0.6 miles) to return to the car park.

Fur seal pups drying out on the rocky wave-cut platforms are a familiar sight along this route

OUT AND ABOUT

The Kaikoura peninsula, with good bays on each side, proved a good defensive site in the past for Maori pa; inset, dolphins off the coast

Below, the Department of Conservation administers the Coastal Walkway

Right, Fyffe Quay, with the Kaikoura mountains behind

WHERE TO EAT

Pipi's Restaurant and Café
✉ 80 Beach Road, Kaikoura
☎ 03 319 7160
Here you'll find fresh Marlborough mussels cooked innovatively. Mussel fritters and spicy paella are popular. Relaxed atmosphere; counter meals and cakes during the day.
🕐 Daily 10.30–10

BASICS

Tourist Information
✉ West End, Kaikoura
☎ 03-319 5641
www.kaikoura.co.nz

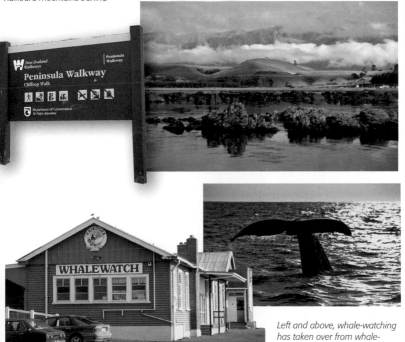

Left and above, whale-watching has taken over from whale-catching as Kaikoura's mainstay

OUT AND ABOUT

LAKE KANIERE AND HOKITIKA GORGE

Easy walking detours enable you to explore the bush and a tumbling waterfall around the lake, then it's a short trek across farmland to the swingbridge across the Hokitika Gorge.

THE DRIVE

Distance: 95km (60 miles)
Allow: 3 hours
Start/end: Junction of Stafford Street and SH6, Hokitika, West Coast

★ Stafford Street is the more southerly of two roads heading inland from Hokitika (▷ 123). After 5km (3 miles) it forks; take the left arm signposted Lake Kaniere Road. In another 8km (5 miles) enter Lake Kaniere Scenic Reserve. The surroundings become markedly more lush and the Southern Alps dominate the horizon. In another 4km (2.5 miles) pass the Hokitika Angling Club. About 500m (550 yards) after this the road forks. In the middle is the start of a water-race known as The Landing, and your first view of Lake Kaniere.

❶ The Landing was built in 1875 to bring water to the Kaniere goldfield. By 1907 it had been reconstructed to feed the powerhouse 7km (4 miles) west on Lake Kaniere Road. This is now the smallest hydro-power station in Westland, supplying about 40 houses in Hokitika. The lake also provides Hokitika's drinking water.

Lake Kaniere was gouged out by glaciers some 12,000 years ago. It is 195m (640ft) deep and home to trout, eels and freshwater mussels, and attracts birds such as teal, scaup and crested and little grebes.

Turn south into Sunny Bight Road and drive for 1km (0.6 miles), passing a row of holiday *baches*. Park the car at Sunny Bight picnic area and take the Kahikatea Forest Walk.

❷ This 1km (0.6-mile) loop track begins on a boardwalk over wetland for 200m (220 yards) and continues on a wide, well-formed path. Kahikatea trees grow up to 60m (197ft) high, distinctively straight with branches that start high on the trunk. These

characteristics make it ideal for milling, so thick stands of mature trees like this are few and far between. Kahikatea are great hosts to epiphytes—mosses, lichens and ferns.

Drive back up Sunny Bight Road and turn east into Dorothy Falls Road. In 1km (0.6 miles) there's a small parking area for Canoe Cove walk. Take your picnic and stroll through podocarp forest to a secluded beach. It's a great spot to enjoy the lake, the mountains and perhaps a quick dip.

Continue north on Dorothy Falls Road. In 1.5km (1 mile) you'll pass through Hans Bay, a quiet holiday village. The road then becomes unsealed and narrow in places. After 4.5km (2.5 miles) there's a car park for Dorothy Falls.

❸ You can see Dorothy Falls from the road, but for the full impact walk down and stand on the rocks near the bottom. The waterfalls are most dramatic from autumn to spring. If you didn't swim at Canoe Cove, now's your chance.

The gravel road continues for another 5km (3 miles), most of it on fair surface through farmland. After 3km (2 miles), pass the western end of Lake Kaniere

walkway, a 13km (8-mile) path through bush and lakeside that emerges near the Kahikatea loop. At the Mark Wallace Bridge over Styx River the road becomes sealed again. This marks the edge of the Kaniere Reserve and you continue through open farmland. Mount Lathrop, at 1,905m (6,250ft), is the highest of the ranges to the east.

Thirteen kilometres (8 miles) from Mark Wallace Bridge reach Kokatahi. At the eastern end is the Hokitika junction. Continue straight on towards Hokitika Gorge. After 1km (0.6 miles) the road turns southeast, so you have excellent views of the Southern Alps. The road takes five right-angle turns, all well signposted. Sixteen kilometres (10 miles) beyond Kokatahi, the road is unsealed again and you enter the Hokitika Gorge Scenic Reserve. The car park is in another 1.5km (1 mile).

❹ To see the gorge, walk from the car park down steep, rough steps. Once over the bridge, the track on your left (upriver) takes you down a difficult track to a view of the bridge. The original was built in the late 19th century, and marked the start of the Westland farmers' long journey across the Southern Alps into Canterbury, to the nearest sale yards. In 2004, the bridge became the focus of new controversy. An Australian company planned to surround it with an 'airwalk'—platforms enabling visitors to walk a loop around the tree tops, up to 21m (69ft) above ground. The 'pro' crowd said it would bring road improvements and economic spin-offs; the 'anti' group said the tranquillity and views would be disturbed.

Return to your car and retrace your path to Kokatahi. At the junction, turn north for the road back to Hokitika. It's 10km (6 miles) to the Stafford Street/Lake Kaniere Road junction, and another 5.5km (3 miles) to SH6.

OUT AND ABOUT

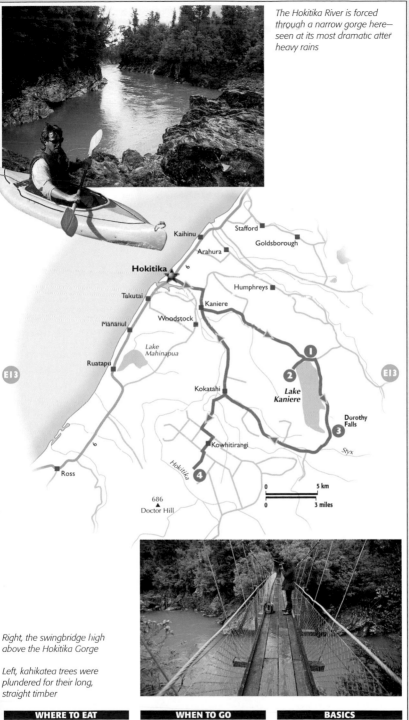

The Hokitika River is forced through a narrow gorge here—seen at its most dramatic after heavy rains

Stafford
Kaihinu
Goldsborough
Arahura
Hokitika
Humphreys
Takutai
Kaniere
Woodstock
Mananui
Lake Mahinapua
Ruatapu
Kokatahi
Lake Kaniere
Dorothy Falls
Kowhitirangi
Styx
Hokitika
Ross
686
Doctor Hill

0   5 km
0   3 miles

Right, the swingbridge high above the Hokitika Gorge

Left, kahikatea trees were plundered for their long, straight timber

WHERE TO EAT

Have a picnic at Canoe Cove. Supplies can be bought from Café de Paris, 19 Tancred Street, Hokitika (tel 03-755 8933, daily 7.30am–11pm).

WHEN TO GO

On damp days with low cloud you won't see the mountains, but the lake and bushwalks are still magical.

BASICS

Tourist Information
✉ Carnegie Building, corner of Hamilton and Tancred streets, Hokitika
☎ 03-755 6166

LAKE KANIERE AND HOKITIKA GORGE 237

OVER THE PORT HILLS

This route climbs into the Port Hills and follows an impressive course along the historic Summit Road. The hilltop lookouts contrast the ragged inlets of Lyttelton Harbour with Christchurch's rambling flatness, while the dramatic Southern Alps rise up in the distance.

THE DRIVE

Distance: 40km (25 miles)
Allow: 2.5 hours
Start/end: Ferrymead Heritage Park, Christchurch

In 1849, Sumner, a beach town southeast of Christchurch, was expected to become a bustling business hub, buoyed by Evans Pass traffic between Lyttelton and Christchurch. It only happened on paper—the Lyttelton rail tunnel was built in 1867 and by the 1870s there was little more to Sumner than a hotel. Then, in 1888, a tramline opened between Sumner and the city. It started the trend for day-trippers.

★ From Ferrymead Heritage Park, drive east to the end of Ferrymead Park Drive and turn left (north) along Bridle Path Road. At the T-junction opposite the estuary, turn right onto Main Road. It's an easy drive past Mount Pleasant, Balmoral Hill, Redcliffs and Moncks Bay. After 4km (2.5 miles), Shag Rock marks the western end of Sumner Beach. Once you pass the Clifton turn-off (south) and the surf club (north), turn left (northeast) into the Esplanade.

❶ On the seaward side of the Esplanade, Cave Rock can be climbed for a lifeguard's lookout, or walk right through it at low tide. Opposite Cave Rock is the broad entrance to a cave where moa bones were found.

Drive 1km (0.6 miles) to the playground at the end of the Esplanade. Turn right (south) up Heberden Avenue and cross the speed bump at the Nayland Street intersection. After 1km (0.6 miles), turn left (south) onto Evans Pass Road and begin your climb into the Port Hills countryside. After 2km (1 mile), a viewing area looks over Sumner. Straight after this, turn west, following yellow signs for The Sign of the Kiwi and Summit Road.

❷ Summit Road is linked with the life of Harry G. Ell (1863–1934), maverick MP and conservationist. Ell envisaged a continuous network of paths along the Port Hills and across Banks Peninsula to Akaroa with 14 rest stations. By the time he died only four had been built—but even this was a feat. He had a knack of upsetting authorities from the Prime Minister down, and repeatedly brought his Summit Road trust to the brink of bankruptcy, only to be bailed out by friends.

The next 12km (7 miles) follow the winding Summit Road. At regular intervals on either side there are parking bays to enjoy the fabulous views over Christchurch, Lyttelton Harbour and Banks Peninsula. Good spots to stop are the Memorial to Pioneer Women, 1km (0.6 miles) after you pass under the Christchurch Gondola cables, and the Sugar Loaf Scenic Reserve car park, 7km (4 miles) after the memorial. By this point you will also have a good view of the 120m (394ft) television transmitter.

Summit Road is crisscrossed with walking tracks. For a break, stop at Tihiokahukura (Castle Rock), 1km (0.6 miles) after the memorial. It's a 500m (550-yard) track with unhindered views across the Canterbury Plains. In 2km (1 mile) you'll reach The Sign of the Kiwi restaurant.

❸ Compared to Ell's fanciful masterpiece, The Sign of the Takahe (finished 1939, ▷ 265), The Sign of the Kiwi is modest—a stone cottage with a warm, wooden interior and pleasant views towards Christchurch. It was opened in 1916 but, true to Ell's form, did not operate without controversy. When the Summit Road and Reserves Association publicly disowned Ell in 1920 (due to a NZ$5,000 debt), Ell moved into the Kiwi and refused to leave. His wife, Ada, came to the rescue by running the tearooms at a profit each year until 1926, when she suffered a nervous breakdown.

As you leave the Kiwi car park, turn south onto Dyers Pass Road, signposted Lyttelton. After 3km (2 miles) and some nerve-racking switchbacks, turn east to skirt Governor's Bay and follow the road to Lyttelton. Drive through the scenic hamlets of Rapaki and Cass Bay. As you leave Corsair Bay you will see the yachts of Lyttelton Harbour. At the T-junction of Simeon Quay, turn right (east). About 300m (330 yards) farther is the SH74 Lyttelton Tunnel roundabout.

❹ Governors Bay Road gives clear views of Quail Island. Now an attractive destination for walkers and daytrippers, it held a leper colony from 1907 to 1925, when the remaining sufferers were moved to Fiji. There are scant remnants of its huts, nurses' quarters and small hospital.

For a jaunt through Lyttelton, continue east towards the heart of town. After 500m (550 yards), turn left (north) into Oxford Street. Pass the visitor office, then turn left (west) into London Street. After 250m (275 yards), turn left (south) into Dublin Street and arrive back at the roundabout. Turn north through the tunnel on SH74. Exit SH74 immediately after the tunnel, following signs for the gondola and Ferrymead.

Right, Banks Peninsula is named after botanist Joseph Banks (1744–1820)
Below, the precipitous Summit Road

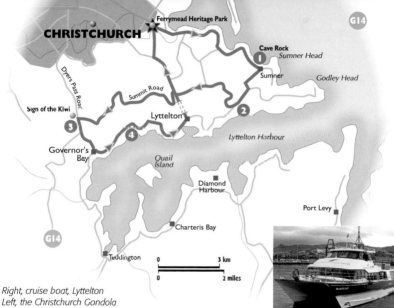

CHRISTCHURCH

Ferrymead Heritage Park

Cave Rock
Sumner Head
Sumner
Godley Head

Dyers Pass Road

Summit Road

Sign of the Kiwi

Lyttelton

Governor's Bay

Quail Island

Lyttelton Harbour

Diamond Harbour

Port Levy

Charteris Bay

Teddington

0   3 km

0   2 miles

G14

Right, cruise boat, Lyttelton
Left, the Christchurch Gondola in the Port Hills

G14

WHERE TO EAT

Sign of the Kiwi
✉ Corner of Dyers Pass and Summit roads
☎ 03-329 9966
Friendly arts and crafts-style bungalow with an all-day menu designed for walkers and sightseers. Three-course set-lunch menu NZ$20; morning and afternoon teas a speciality.
🕐 Jan–end Mar daily 10–6; Apr–end Dec daily 10–4

BASICS

Tourist Information
www.christchurchnz.net
✉ Old Chief Post Office, Cathedral Square (West), Christchurch
☎ 03-379 9629

Ferrymead Heritage Park
www.ferrymead.org.nz
✉ Ferrymead Park Drive, off Bridle Path Road, Christchurch
☎ 03-384 1970 🕐 Daily 10–4.30

WHEN TO GO

This is a popular Sunday drive route for all Christchurch, so go during the week if possible.

Below left and right, Lyttelton was the arrival port for early settlers, who had to haul everything over the steep hill (now cut through by two tunnels) to Christchurch

OUT AND ABOUT

FIRST STEPS TO MOUNT COOK/AORAKI

The Hooker Valley Track is Mount Cook/Aoraki National Park's most popular route, offering perfect views of Mount Cook and the smaller giants around it. The linear track takes you past a glacier terminal lake via two dramatic swingbridges and ends at Hooker Lake.

THE WALK

Distance: 12km (8 miles) return; ascent 140m (460ft)
Allow: 4 hours
Start/end: Visitor information centre, Mount Cook Village

★ From the visitor centre in the village (▷ 131), 760m (2,493ft) above sea level, take the cobblestone path by the Hermitage Hotel, heading north. Cross the road to a green Department of Conservation sign for White Horse Hill Campground and Kea Point Track.

❶ The gravel track is fairly flat for this section (1.5km/1 mile) and winds through scrub and scree. The landscape was formed in 1913, when heavy rains caused the outwash stream of the Mueller Glacier to burst through the moraine wall, pushing a mass of boulders before it and destroying the original Hermitage. West is the Mueller range, 1,200m (3,936ft) above the track. North are the Footstool (2,764m/9,066ft), Mount Sefton (3,158m/10,358ft) and a glimpse of Mount Cook/Aoraki.

Forty per cent of the national park's area (70,000ha/172,970 acres) is covered by glacial ice. Five glaciers fill the upper reaches of the main valleys, including the Tasman Glacier, which at 29km (18 miles) is the longest in New Zealand. The mountains are being forced up by the Alpine Fault at the same pace their tops erode—about 1cm (0.3 inches) a year.

Turn east, following a sign for the campground and the Hooker Valley Track. Just south of the campground is the old Hermitage's fireplace. In the northeast corner of the campground is the track's official start. In 200m (220 yards) you come across a 3m (10ft)-high stone pyramid just north of the track, a memorial to lives claimed by Mount Cook/Aoraki. Shortly after, the track climbs to a stone wall

lookout over Mueller Glacier lake, Mount Sefton and the Footstool. In another 600m (656 yards) it zigzags downhill to the first swingbridge across the Hooker River. The milky-blue of the water is due to fine particles of rock crushed by the Hooker Glacier.

❷ The Mount Cook lily—actually the world's largest buttercup—is symbolic of this region, but hundreds of other alpine plants thrive, too. After the white buttercups in spring come the mountain daisies of early summer and the gentians of early autumn. Many other plants put on more subtle displays, so it's worth taking a patient look on hands and knees. Ninety-three per cent of New Zealand's alpine species are endemic and many have no close relatives anywhere else in the world.

Once across the first swingbridge, the track skirts the eastern side of Mueller Glacier terminal lake. Uphill sections are made easier by stone steps. The trickiest part occurs at the bluff just before the second swingbridge, where the path is cut out of a rock face by

the river. It may challenge the nerves, but a railing on the riverside means there is little real danger. Take special care in winter, when it may be icy.

❸ The dark green keas are the park's resident clowns. These protected alpine parrots are curious, sociable and intelligent. They are notorious for roughing up climbing gear and windscreen wipers, but often engage in harmless fun—sliding down hut roofs, skidding across snow fields, gliding in storm winds and tumbling on the Hermitage lawn. They are easily identified by a flash of red under the wing.

After the bridge, the track narrows but it's easier underfoot. Here you find the most magnificent views of Mount Cook/Aoraki, its south face framed by the rocky valley and underlined by the river. In summer there can be a profusion of Mount Cook lilies. After 1.2km (0.7 miles) you arrive at Stocking Stream ❹, which has a shelter and toilets.

Despite serious attempts from 1882, Mount Cook/Aoraki remained unconquered until 1894, when the imminent attempt of an English climber and his Swiss guide spurred three young Kiwis—Tom Fyfe, George Graham and Jack Clarke—to have a go. They made it to the top on Christmas day, much to the pride and relief of New Zealanders, although they had no flag and had to fly an old sugar bag instead.

The final kilometre (0.6 miles) begins with a flat section and some boardwalks. It then rises slightly and as you reach the top, you see Hooker Lake in front of you. It's often sunny and sheltered, a good place to lunch before you retrace your steps to the village.

Mount Cook lily, Hooker Valley

Picnic at Hooker Lake. Supplies from The Hermitage Hotel, Mount Cook Village (tel 03-435 1809, ▷ 287). Hampers (from NZ$21) can be provided at two hours' notice.

Peak seasons are October to April and July to September. There's a quiet window between April and June. This popular track is often busy, so start bright and early if you can.

Above, crossing a swingbridge in the Hooker Valley

Left, the Old Mountaineers' Café at Mount Cook Village reflects the mountain peaks

Below, lupins are among the wildflowers here

Tourist Information
🖾 1 Larch Drive, Mount Cook Village
☎ 03-435 1186
www.doc.govt.nz

Stopping for a breather on the magnificent Hooker Valley Track

DIAMOND LAKE AND WANAKA VIEWS

A clear track takes you through bush and tussock farmland to the summit of Rocky Mountain (775m/2,542ft), where a 360-degree view reveals Lake Wanaka and surrounding mountain ranges in full splendour.

THE WALK

Distance: 7km (4 miles); ascent 400m (1,312ft)
Allow: 2.5 hours
Start/end: Diamond Lake Walking Track car park, near Wanaka, Central Otago

★ From the car park, cross the cattle grid and follow the gravel farm road up the hill. As you arrive at the top, there's a toilet eastwards (right) and a wooden sign marked 'track' on the left. Walk to this and you will see a sign for the start of the track proper, and a donation box—NZ$2 per adult is asked for track maintenance. The next 300m (330 yards) follow the edge of Diamond Lake.

❶ Diamond Lake, surrounded by willows and raupo rushes, is an alpine tarn. It was formed some 10,000 years ago by the same receding glaciers that carved out Lake Wanaka. Minerals leaching out of the soil cause its dark appearance. It often freezes over in winter and was popular for ice-skating in the days before health and safety regulations took hold.

The track narrows and the ascent begins. The next kilometre (0.6 miles) takes you through bush, climbing on a series of flat rocks and wooden staircases before you emerge into open farmland. After 500m (550 yards) a hand-painted sign shows your place on the route, at the bottom of the figure-of-eight. For the first emergency exit, take the eastern branch. A signposted view of Lake Wanaka is 1km (0.6 miles) up this track. For Rocky Mountain, continue on the western branch.

❷ Like much farmland in Central Otago, this area is speckled with wiry brown bracken, which prohibits sheep from grazing and sticks in their wool, depreciating its quality. To combat this, sections of the hillside are burned between August and October. A specialist makes sure the fire is hot enough to burn bracken but not grasses or native flora.

After a glimpse of Lake Wanaka, the path turns west towards Mount Aspiring and returns to bush. In another 800m (875 yards), a stile leads you back into farmland. Soon you reach a large flat rock on which to sit and admire the lake. If you've had enough, the next emergency exit is only 300m (310 yards) farther, at the middle of the figure-of-eight.

For both routes, turn west towards the hills and follow two marker poles for 200m (220 yards). Shortly after a wooden bridge, you'll find another hand-painted sign. Continue uphill if you want the second emergency exit, or turn westwards to push for Rocky Mountain.

❸ You are approaching large schist rock-faces that are part of the area's attraction for climbers. The land on the opposite side of Wanaka Mount Aspiring Road is also popular. Its name—Hospital Flat—relates to its historic use as a recuperation spot for horses, rather than any association with climbing accidents.

The next 2km (1 mile) are a hard slog through tussocky farmland. The path zigzags steeply beneath large rocky overhangs, then turns east so you walk above them. After a tantalising glimpse of the lake, you burst over the brow of the hill to a wonderful view of Lake Wanaka, its islands and peninsulas, the Matukituki River and bridge **❹**. At the western end of the valley is Mount Aspiring (▷ 146).

Much of this vista could have been lost but for a chance meeting in 1968. Plans were afoot to dam the outlet, at the east side of Lake Wanaka, for hydro-electricity; the community had been assured the water level would not rise significantly. Marion Borrie, a minister's wife, was walking up Mount Iron one day when she met a couple and stopped to commiserate over the plans. It turned out she was talking to the manager of the New Zealand Electricity Department, who quietly admitted the plan would raise the lake by 6m (20ft), drowning much of the land between Cromwell and Wanaka and parts of Wanaka township (▷ 147). Mrs Borrie raised the alarm, and after intense political furore the plans were shelved.

The descent starts north of the viewpoint—look for two red metal poles. The path becomes very steep and rocky; it can be slippy, so take care. The distinctive Piggyback Rock marks the end of this section. After 400m (440 yards) the path flattens to a dirt track. In another 100m (110 yards), there's an option to turn east and walk 500m (550 yards) for another view over the lake. Another 1,500m (1,640 yards) takes you back to the first painted signpost and you retrace your steps to Diamond Lake.

Lake Wanaka, surrounded by hills

The beauty spot of Diamond Lake, in the hills above Wanaka

Left, a profusion of California poppies on the mountainside

WHERE TO EAT

The lake viewpoints are perfect for a picnic. Supplies can be bought from Kai Whaka Pai, at the corner of Helwick and Ardmore streets (tel 03-443 7795, daily 7am–late).

HOW TO GET THERE

From the information centre on the Wanaka lakefront, drive 18.5km (11 miles) west along Mount Aspiring Road. The car park is 6km (4 miles) after Glendhu Bay motor camp.

WHEN TO GO

Intense summer heat can make the walk more challenging—an early morning start is recommended. The track may be closed in winter if conditions are not suitable—check with the DoC office (tel 03-443 7660).

BASICS

Tourist Information
✉ 100 Ardmore Street, Wanaka
☎ 03-443 1233

TIP

● For a half-day's effort, this walk offers exceptional rewards. Be prepared—the route is steep and a good level of fitness is required. However, its figure-of-eight structure provides two 'emergency exits' if it gets too tough, both affording excellent lake views.

Walkers near the start of the scenic Diamond Lake-Rocky Mountain track

OTAGO PENINSULA'S SECRET SIDE

Discover the inlets and beaches of the southeastern corner of the Otago Peninsula. The steeply rolling hills and sandy beaches belong to sheep, seals and wading birds. It's utterly remote, but just a short drive away from the friendly attractions of the northern side.

THE DRIVE

Distance: 32km (20 miles)
Allow: 2.5 hours
Start/end: The parking bay at the southern end of Portsmouth Drive, 3km (2 miles) from The Octagon, in the heart of Dunedin. It's marked by an information board and signposts to the peninsula.

Before you set off, look south to the opposite side of Portsmouth Drive, where Shore Street meets Portobello Road. There you will see a huge rock with 'Rongo' carved into it. This is a memorial to the Taranaki Maori prisoners of war held in Dunedin from 1869 to 1872 and from 1879 to 1881. They—and fellow European prisoners–built the seawall that runs all the way to Portobello. Rongo is the Maori god of peace.

★ From the car park turn east and cross Portobello Road's causeway. Continue straight on, following a blue sign for the peninsula. On your seaward side, pass Vauxhall yacht club. Take the first inland turn up Doon Street, which takes you behind a once grand private home. Stay on Doon Street as it turns abruptly left. At the end of Doon Street, turn right into Connell Street, then left into Larnach Road (a main road). This turns into McKerrow Street after 500m (550 yards). When you reach the T-junction, turn left onto Highcliff Road.

About 200m (220 yards) down Highcliff Road, Rotary Park

lookout gives a dramatic glimpse of Dunedin city and harbour. From here, the road narrows and enters countryside. After 1.5km (1 mile) pass a parking bay; just beyond is a well-marked track to the Soldier's Memorial, a 700m (765-yard) climb. Continue for another 5km (3 miles) and you come to Pukehiki, with its white, rectangular church tower and tiny public library on the north. The next intersection signposts Larnach Castle (▷ 147) to the north, but stay on Highcliff Road.

❶ Peninsula farms are distinctive for their use of drystone walls, rather than the typical No. 8 fencing wire (▷ 12). It shows skill and thrift on behalf of the early Scottish farmers—while neatly divvying up their paddocks, they cleaned up the volcanic stones that littered the ground. Look for the skewed macrocarpa trees, which tell tales about the southerly wind. Sandfly Bay did not get its name from the insects, but the gales.

After 2km (1 mile) pass the modern stone wall of Gatesheath bed-and-breakfast. At this corner, turn south down Sandymount Road. This marks the end of the tourist trail and after 600m (656 yards) the road is unsealed. To the north there are good views of Harbour Cone; to the south, the Pacific Ocean, beaches and rolling sheep country.

After 2km (1 mile) reach a triangular intersection. For a detour, continue up the steep road to Sandymount Recreational Reserve.

❷ From the reserve, well-marked tracks lead to the cliff known as Lovers Leap (2km/ 1 mile), and the high dunes of Sandfly Bay (5km/3 miles). Note that they are closed during the lambing season, from August to October.

To continue the tour, turn north onto Hoopers Inlet Road. After 1km (0.6 miles), the inlet is before you.

❸ The tidal mudflats of Hoopers Inlet (and Papanui Inlet to the northeast) offer good feeding for wading birds. Pied stilts, godwits, black and variable oystercatchers and spur-winged plovers are regular visitors, and spoonbills occasionally drop by.

Turn west and drive 2km (1 mile) around the inlet to a yellow signpost for Portobello. Follow this sign left (northwards) along Allan's Beach Road for 1.5km (1 mile), which brings you over the hill and into Portobello. From here, the Royal Albatross Centre (▷ 147) is a farther 11km (7 miles) out from the city, while Westpac Aquarium is 1.5km (1 mile) down Hatchery Road. Turn left (west) onto Portobello Road and take the 'low road' 14km (9 miles) back to Portsmouth Drive. The Portobello Coffee Shop is on Highcliff Road, which is to the south, opposite the inlet.

❹ Thematically painted bus shelters punctuate the drive back to Dunedin. These concrete caves were brightened up in 1989 by Broad Bay artist John Noakes. There are 12 of them on the route, often with designs relating to local names—a flock of chooks (chickens) are near the Happy Hens shop, four-leaf clovers enliven Dublin Bay, while comic characters Wallace and Grommit appear for good measure.

The road is tightly snaking, with excellent views towards the city and north across the harbour towards Port Chalmers. It passes a number of well-signposted and worthwhile attractions such as the 1909 Fletcher House, Macandrew Bay beach and Glenfalloch Gardens. Take your time, especially as you go around Burns Point, 11km (7 miles) from Portobello. Despite the railings, cars end up in the harbour about once a year.

Black oystercatchers are among the waders in Hooper's Inlet

OUT AND ABOUT

The grand mansion of Larnach Castle makes for a worthy detour from the main route

BASICS

Tourist Information
✉ 48 The Octagon, Dunedin
☎ 03-474 3300
www.cityofdunedin.com

Fletcher House
✉ 727 Portobello Road
☎ 03-478 0180
🕐 Daily 11–4, Boxing Day–Easter
💵 Adult NZ$3, child free

Glenfalloch Woodland Gardens
✉ 430 Portobello Road
☎ 03-476 1775
🕐 Daily dawn–dusk
💵 Adult NZ$3, child NZ$1

NZ Marine Studies Centre and Westpac Aquarium
☎ 03-479 5826
🕐 Daily noon–4.30; guided tours 10.30am
💵 NZ$9; guided tour NZ$18

Drystone walls—field dividers skilfully built without mortar—are typical of this area

Above right, a royal albatross colony is the big attraction at the eastern tip of the peninsula

WHERE TO EAT
Portobello Coffee Shop
✉ 699 Highcliff Road, Portobello
☎ 03-478 1055
You'll get homestyle fare here, including traditional kiwi slices. Highlights are the craft gallery at the back featuring local knitting and pottery, and outdoor seating overlooking the bay.
🕐 Daily 9–5

LONG-DISTANCE WALKS

Tramping, trekking, hiking, walking—whatever you call it, New Zealanders like to do it, and manage a network that includes some of the finest walking tracks in the world. Most are equipped with simple hut accommodation or campsites, some require reservation ahead, and all offer a chance to get closer to native plants, wildlife and spectacular scenery. Some of the most popular are listed below, but there are many shorter options—just ask at any DoC or visitor information centre. More information on all these may be found on www.doc.govt.nz.

ABEL TASMAN COAST TRACK

Where: Marahau–Wainui
Distance: 51km (32 miles)
Time: 2–5 days
This easy-to-moderate walking track passes through a picturesque landscape of coastal forests and golden sandy beaches at the top of the South Island. While all the streams are bridged, some sections are tide-dependent. Water taxis give access to shorter sections (▷ 109–110).

DUSKY TRACK

Where: Lake Hauroko–West Arm, Lake Manapouri, via Supper Cove
Distance: 84km (52 miles)
Time: 8–11 days
One of the country's most remote walking trails, in the fiordlands of the southwest South Island, provides a challenge for dedicated trampers, with the promise of 21 three-wire bridge crossings, and access in summer only (▷ 141–142).

GREENSTONE AND CAPLES TRACKS

Where: End of Greenstone Road–Elfin Bay, western Lake Wakatipu
Time: 4–5 days
A round-trip through the open tussock valley of the Greenstone River and the wooded vale of the Caples River, which both flow into Lake Wakatipu, the South Island's second biggest lake. The valleys are linked by the McKellar Saddle, a high sub-alpine pass.

HEAPHY TRACK

Where: Aorere Valley, near Collingwood–near Karamea
Distance: 82km (51 miles)
Time: 4–6 days
A challenging trail in Kahurangi National Park, the Heaphy crosses various landscapes, from the junction of the Brown and Aorere rivers, over tussock grassland to the lush forests and roaring sea of the South Island's West Coast (▷ 112).

KEPLER TRACK

Where: Circuit from Te Anau
Distance: 60km (37 miles)
Time: 3–4 days
A moderately difficult circuit in Fiordland takes in alpine meadows, beech forest and glacial valleys. You're recommended to tackle it in an anti-clockwise direction (▷ 142).

MILFORD TRACK

Where: Glade Wharf, Lake Te Anau–Sandfly Point, Milford Sound
Distance: 53.5km (33 miles)
Time: 4 days
Numbers are strictly controlled on this, New Zealand's most famous tramp, and advance booking is essential. It can be wet and muddy, but—weather permitting—the waterfalls, alpine flowers and viewpoints are spectacular (▷ 143).

QUEEN CHARLOTTE TRACK

Where: Ship Cove–Anakiwa
Distance: 71km (44 miles)
Time: 4 days
www.queencharlottetrack.co.nz
Easy access by water taxis means you can send luggage ahead by boat each day on this stunning walkway, which passes through ancient

forest and beside the coast, with fabulous Sounds views (▷ 116).

RAKIURA TRACK

Where: Stewart Island/Rakiura circuit from Halfmoon Bay
Distance: 36km (22 miles)
Time: 3 days
Stewart Island/Rakiura is a natural paradise, known for its plants and wildlife. This circular route around the coast and through forest is described as suitable for anyone with moderate fitness (▷ 150).

ROUTEBURN TRACK

Where: Routeburn Shelter, Mount Aspiring National Park–The Divide, Fiordland National Park
Distance: 33km (20 miles)
Time: 3–4 days
A high track through spectacular lake and mountain scenery, the ever-popular Routeburn links Mount Aspiring and Fiordland national parks via the Harris Saddle (▷ 140–143, 146).

ST. JAMES WALKWAY

Where: Lewis Pass
Distance: 66km (41 miles)
Time: 5 days
Through varied mountain, forest, open farmland and sub-alpine landscapes (▷ 130).

TONGARIRO NORTHERN CIRCUIT

Where: Circuit from Whakapapa village
Time: 3–4 days
The Tongariro Northern Circuit, in the central North Island, winds over the volcanic peak of Mount Tongariro and around Mount Ngauruhoe, with volcanic craters and glacial valleys to admire. In winter, you'll need alpine equipment and a guide (▷ 88).

Footpaths are well maintained across New Zealand, with detailed guide books readily available and touring options

OUT AND ABOUT

This chapter lists places to eat and stay, broken down by region, then alphabetically by town.

Eating and Staying

EATING OUT IN NEW ZEALAND

You can eat almost any kind of food in New Zealand. The country's European heritage is largely British, with a tradition of roast meat, 'three veg' and hearty breakfasts, which can still be widely found. Good home baking still characterises many cafés. A typical family meal is likely to be a barbecue of sausages, chops or seafood that folk have caught or gathered themselves, usually washed down with beer or wine.

Eating out in New Zealand is getting more sophisticated, as Kiwis embrace the café society and bring back a taste for international cuisines from their overseas travels. Modern New Zealand chefs draw inspiration from Asia, the Mediterranean and the Pacific, developing a style of cooking that reflects New Zealand's position in the world. Often called Pacific Rim cuisine, it aims to enhance the tastes of fresh local produce. Indigenous ingredients, traditionally used by Maori, are increasingly being incorporated, with exciting results. With a climate ranging from subtropical to temperate, New Zealand can grow anything from oranges to avocados, saffron to swede, and sheep and cattle are fed year round on pasture. The quality of ingredients is superb.

Immigrants from many countries have opened restaurants, too, so it's easy to find Indian, Chinese, Malaysian, Thai, Japanese, Korean, Italian, Greek and Mexican food. Sometimes they modify their cooking to what they perceive as New Zealand tastes—so in a Chinese restaurant, for example, you may need to ask for the Chinese menu to get authentic dishes. Although New Zealand is still largely a nation of meat eaters, most restaurants offer vegetarian options.

WHAT TO EAT
New Zealand lamb is arguably the best in the world. Farm-raised venison, known as Cervena, is also a speciality (▷ 19). Farmed green-lip mussels, oysters and salmon are also of high quality, thanks to the pristine waters in which they are grown. Despite New Zealand's reputation as perhaps the best trout-fishing country in the world, buying and selling trout is illegal. However, if you

catch your own, many restaurants will be happy to cook it for you.

When you can get wild seafood, seize the chance. As an island nation, New Zealand's seafood resources are vast, but more than 80 per cent is exported, so chefs in New York, Tokyo or Sydney have a better chance of getting a regular supply than the locals. Look for snapper, monkfish, blue cod, hapuka, turbot, flounder (cooked on the bone is best) and swordfish. For an authentic experience, catch the fish yourself and barbecue it. Other seafood treats include crayfish (spiny lobster), Bluff oysters, paua (abalone), pipi, tuatua, cockles, scampi, koura (freshwater crayfish) and scallops.

Below ground, the kumara (sweet potato) is prized by Maori and used in many ways. Kiwifruit or 'zespri' are deservedly celebrated and most often appear sliced on top of New Zealand's most famous dessert, the pavlova—a concoction of meringue, whipped cream and fresh fruit. Other locally grown fruits worth trying are the feijoa and tamarillo.

WHERE TO EAT
Throughout New Zealand there are eateries to suit every taste and budget, from international fast-food joints to world-class restaurants. The main cities are rich in choice (reputedly, Wellington has more cafés and restaurants per capita than New York) with cafés, café-bars, brasseries, traditional and specialist restaurants flying the flags of many countries. Generally, there is little to distinguish between cafés and restaurants, although cafés tend to be more informal during the day and serve more substantial dishes at night. They also almost always serve coffee, breakfast or brunch, are often licensed (or at least

welcome BYO) and often provide outdoor seating. You can get good coffee almost everywhere.

Kiwis are a casual lot and few restaurants expect formal attire. The restaurants of many of the top hotels, motels and lodges are open to non-residents and can be a good option. If what you want is a hearty feed, you can generally find good pub grub in the cities and most major towns, particularly in popular Irish- and English-style pubs. Fish and chips is New Zealanders' most popular takeaway—with a menu so you can choose what fish you want.

OPENING HOURS

Hours vary and are often seasonal. Most cafés open for breakfast between 7 and 9am, often remaining open until 5pm. Some also stay open late into the evening on the early hours. This usually applies seven days a week, with special Sunday brunch hours. Most mid-range restaurants open daily for lunch (often 11–2) and dinner (from 6). The more exclusive establishments usually open for dinner from about 6, with some (especially in winter) opening selected weekday evenings only and on weekends.

BRING YOUR OWN (BYO)

BYO restaurants or cafés are licensed for the consumption of (but not the sale of) alcohol and allow you to bring your own wine or bottled beers, sometimes charging a corkage fee (typically NZ$2–NZ$10). Some restaurants are both licensed and BYO wine.

FOODSTORES

The main supermarket chains are Foodtown, Woolworths and New World, with Pak 'n Save and Countdown being marginally less expensive. Try to buy fresh vegetables and fruit from the roadside stalls or wholesale fruit markets, where the prices are lower and the quality fresher than the supermarkets.

BEER

Steinlager may be internationally famous, but the most interesting New Zealand beers are the boutique brews. Try Galbraith's in Auckland (Mount Eden Road), Dux de Lux in Christchurch and Emerson's in Dunedin. More widely produced beers worth trying are Speight's (the tipple of the Southern Man), Monteith's (especially lauded on the West Coast of the South Island) and Mac's, originally brewed in Nelson. All the main international brands and some specialist ones are available, and you can also get New Zealand-brewed Guinness. Beer and lager is usually sold by the 'handle' (pint) or the 'jug' (up to three pints). Half-pints come in a 12fl oz (350ml) glass. Rarely is a pint a full imperial pint; it's usually just under. Drinks generally cost from NZ$6 to NZ$7 for a pint, about NZ$4 to NZ$5 for a jug of Lion Red and up to NZ$7 for a double shot. Drinks cost much less in rural pubs and RSAs (Returned Services Association clubs), where you can usually get yourself signed in. The minimum drinking age is 18. Liquor shops are everywhere and in most places you can buy alcohol seven days a week.

For further information on Kiwi beer visit the websites **www.Realbeer.co.nz** or **www.**brewing.co.nz.

WINE

New Zealand's diversity of climates and soil types has produced a distinctive array of wines. Wine is made the length and breadth of the country, but the Hawke's Bay and Nelson/Marlborough areas are the principal wine-producing regions. Sauvignon blanc from Marlborough is New Zealand's most internationally acclaimed wine, but there is growing recognition for its Chardonnay, Pinot noir, *méthode traditionelle* sparkling wine, Riesling, Cabernet Sauvignon and Merlot. Striking contemporary architecture and Pacific Rim cuisine combine to make vineyard restaurants exciting places to dine. Fruit wines, including kiwifruit, are also produced. Many vineyards offer tastings and cellar-door sales.

NON-ALCOHLIC DRINKS

All the major international soft-drink brands are available. New Zealand has its own soft drink, a brand called L&P, which stands for Lemon and Paeroa. The 'Lemon' speaks for itself and Paeroa relates to a town in the Waikato where the drink was founded and made famous by the use of the local mineral-rich spring water. Although it is not made there now, the traditional recipe is still used. Bright green spirulea drinks contain a mineral-rich seaweed.

Given New Zealand's colonial roots, tea is popular and widely available. Increasingly, the standard Bell teabag is being joined by green and herbal teas, often served in specialist shops. New Zealanders expect a high standard from their coffee, and support a number of local roasteries. Expect to ask for a flat white, latte, cappuccino, ristretto, long or short black, or any number of permutations.

TIPPING

Tipping is not normal in New Zealand, and most New Zealanders don't tip, but a service charge of 10 to 15 per cent may be included at some smarter restaurants.

SMOKING

New Zealand has banned smoking in the workplace—which includes restaurants, bars, pubs, clubs and casinos.

RESTAURANT CHAINS

	Price per meal (NZ$)	Alcohol	Child Menu	Takeout	Phone Number	Website
RESTAURANTS, FAST FOOD AND CAFÉS						
Cobb and Co	20–30	✔	✔		09-377 0595	www.cobb.co.nz
Domino's Pizza	12–15			✔	0800-304 050	www.dominospizza.co.nz
KFC	8–10		✔	✔	0800-KFC KFC	www.kfc.co.nz
McDonald's	3–8		✔	✔	09-306 5600	www.mcdonalds.co.nz
Pizza Hut	15–20			✔	0800-838383	www.pizzahut.co.nz
Valentines	20			✔	09-444 4819	www.valentines.co.nz

MENU READER

aubergine: eggplant
BBQ: barbecue
cervena: New Zealand venison
BYO: restaurants or cafés that allow you to bring your own wine or beer
capsicum: bell pepper
entrée: appetizer or hors d'oeuvre
feijoa: an aromatic fruit, also known as the pineapple guava
fritter: as in whitebait or crab fritters (also known as patties)—seafood or fish cakes
hokey pokey: aerated toffee, usually in vanilla ice cream
jug: as in jug of beer (about 4 pints)
hangi: traditional Maori feast cooked on hot stones underground (see opposite)
kai: Maori word for food (*kai moana*—seafood)
kumara: sweet potato. Originally from Peru, the kumara came to New Zealand via Samoa and was a staple food of Maori. Very popular because of its sweet taste and versatility, it may be steamed, boiled, baked or eaten raw
kina: sea eggs with a prickly shell
and edible roe, usually eaten raw and an acquired taste
lollies: sweets or confectionery
manuka honey: honey with a distinctive taste from the flowers of the manuka (tea tree, known for its medicinal properties)
muttonbird: the young of the sooty petrel, with a strong, fishy taste
paua: abalone (a mollusc)
Pavlova: also known as 'Pav'. A traditional pudding made of cream and meringue. Though hotly debated and claimed on both sides of the Tasman Sea, it was thought to have originated in the 1930s to celebrate a visit to New Zealand by Russian ballerina Anna Pavlova
schooner: large glass of beer, usually 0.4L (0.75 pint)
stubby: a small bottle of beer
tamarillo: egg-shaped, deep-red or gold-skinned fruit with tart flesh and edible seeds

EATING

EATING OUT IN NEW ZEALAND

Outlets	Location	Description
16	Nationwide	Family dining, reasonably priced home-style fare
61	Nationwide	Dial-out pizzas
103	Nationwide	Chicken meals
104	Nationwide	Burgers and salads
106	Nationwide	Family dining
11	North Island	Buffet family meals

HANGI

Pronounced 'hungi', this is the traditional Maori and Pacific Island method of cooking. It's a great social occasion as much as anything else.

Traditionally, the men would light a large fire and place river stones in the embers. While the stones were heating, a pit was dug in the earth (in active thermal areas, such as around Rotorua, the stones and pit might be naturally heated).

The stones were then placed in the pit with sacking or plant material onto which the meat was laid. Nowadays this includes chicken, wild pig and lamb, but formerly it would have been moa, pigeon, seafood and vegetables, including kumara and watercress. Smaller items were wrapped in leaves or in foil and placed in a basket covered with earth. The steam slowly cooked the food, sealing in the wonderful tastes.

Although—due to modern health and safety requirements—it is not possible to sample an authentic *hangi*, the feasts produced for visitors are a good second-best.

EATING OUT IN NEW ZEALAND

AUCKLAND, NORTHLAND AND COROMANDEL

While most of New Zealand has a temperate climate, the 'winterless north' is generally regarded as subtropical. Oranges, kiwifruit and avocados grow in abundance, and are sold at roadside stalls around Kerikeri. The Bay of Islands is renowned for big-game fishing so you will find snapper, giant hapuka and marlin on many restaurant menus, as well as the locally farmed Orongo Bay oysters. Grapevines were introduced to New Zealand in Kerikeri and a number of boutique vineyards make up the Northland wine trail. Farther south, Puhoi is a cheese-making heartland. Boutique cheeses from Mahoe, Matatoki and Mercer are also a speciality of the region. The developing wine region of Matakana, with its attractive vineyard cafés, is well worth a detour off the main highway between Whangarei and Auckland. Some of the country's finest wines and olive oils are produced on Waiheke Island, and the Auckland wine regions of Henderson and Kumeu are both within easy reach of the city. Shellfish are farmed in Clevedon and around the Coromandel Peninsula—or you can gather them yourself from the beach.

EATING

AUCKLAND

KERMADEC
Viaduct Quay, Auckland
Tel 09-309 0412
www.kermadec.co.nz
This seafood complex in the Viaduct Basin is a clever combination of the owner's fishing business, a casual brasserie and bar with a balcony, and a classy restaurant. The restaurant carries the sea theme into

its décor, with tapa-cloth sails slung from the ceiling and water-walled *tatami* rooms. You can order traditional Japanese or modern New Zealand dishes such as seared snapper on corn risotto and chervil beurre blanc.
🅖 Brasserie daily 10–late; restaurant Mon–Fri 6–late
🍴 Brasserie L NZ$40, D NZ$50, W NZ$29; restaurant, D NZ$60, W NZ$29

LAVA
425 Tamaki Drive, St. Heliers, Auckland
Tel 09-575 9969
www.lavanz.co.nz
Opposite the beach, with great views over the harbour, Lava has become known for its modern New Zealand food, such as oven-baked veal roulade wrapped with prosciutto with bell peppers, polenta cake, ratatouille and rocket pesto. The décor is elegantly subdued: grey walls, brown leather chairs and white tablecloths, with artworks complementing the beachfront location.
🅖 Daily 9am–late
🍴 L NZ$25, D NZ$60, W NZ$40

OH CALCUTTA
151 Parnell Road, Parnell, Auckland
Tel 09-377 9090
www.ohcalcutta.co.nz
Oh Calcutta ranks highly in all departments, from food quality to ambience and service. The dishes are a mixture of northern and southern Indian. Whole snapper marinated, skewered and smoke-roasted in the tandoor is a speciality. A large, bustling place popular with expatriate Indians and families, it has indoor and outdoor seating.
🅖 Daily 5.30–11.30, also Wed–Fri 12–2
🍴 L NZ$25, D NZ$35, W NZ$25

ORBIT AND THE OBSERVATORY
Sky Tower, corner of Victoria and Federal streets, Auckland
Tel 09-363 6000
www.skycityauckland.co.nz
Up the Sky Tower, with views over the city, the Orbit à la carte restaurant revolves sedately while serving modern New Zealand brasserie food, such as *wakame*-seared tuna loin on a tabouleh salsa with

avocado aioli. Reservations are required. The Observatory, above the main level, serves buffets at a fixed price, with children charged according to age.

🅖 Daily 5.30–9.30; also Orbit Mon–Fri 11.30–2.30, Sat, Sun 10–3; Observatory Fri–Sun 12–2
🍴 Orbit L NZ$25, D NZ$57, W NZ$29.50; Observatory L NZ$37.50, D NZ$52.50, W NZ$29.50

SPECIAL IN AUCKLAND
PONSONBY FRESH FISH AND CHIP CO
127 Ponsonby Road, Ponsonby, Auckland
Tel 09-378 7885
Fish and chips are New Zealanders' takeaway food of choice, and this is one of Auckland's most popular places to get them. An institution in Ponsonby for many years, it may have reduced its portions over time, but the quality has stayed generally good. Try the local Pacific fish. If you don't want fish, the vegetarian burgers are also good. There is always a crowd but there's no place sit, so plan to place an order and return about 20 minutes later.
🅖 Daily 11–9.30
🍴 From NZ$6

WHITE

Hilton Hotel, Princes Wharf, 147 Quay Street, Auckland
Tel 09-978 2000
www.whiterestaurant.co.nz
For a combination of views across the water, classy atmosphere, food and service, White is hard to beat. Surrounded on three sides by the sea, it has the style of a cruise ship. The restaurant is split-level, with a long table at the entrance for single diners or couples who want to mix. It serves the best of local seafood and regional produce in a modern cooking style. The wine list is vast. It is within the Hilton Hotel, ▷ 273.
🕐 Mon–Fri 6.30am–10.30am, 12–3, 6pm–11pm, Sat, Sun 11–3
🍽 L NZ$39, D NZ$80, W NZ$70

SOUL BAR AND BISTRO

Viaduct Harbour, Auckland
Tel 09-356 7249
www.soulsearch.co.nz
With open-air decks over-looking the harbour, this stylish restaurant has award-winning chef Mark Wylie. The food blends influences from the Mediterranean, North Africa and the Middle East, as in quail stuffed with Moroccan sausage roasted in vine leaves. The seafood is excellent: you can choose to have the day's choices grilled, pan-fried, roasted or blackened and served with accompaniments appropriate to the cooking style.
🕐 Mon–Fri 11am–late, Sat, Sun 10am–late
🍽 L NZ$55, D NZ$70, W NZ$38

COLVILLE

COLVILLE GENERAL STORE AND CAFF

Main Road, Colville, Coromandel Peninsula
Tel 07-866 6805
Take a photograph here, as places like this are disappearing fast. A classic Kiwi rural store, it is the last place to get provisions and fuel before continuing on a journey farther north. Like the store, the attached café is the day-time hub of social contact in these parts. It has the usual café fare, including cakes, pastries, pies and coffee,

but the real delight is listening to the local gossip.
🕐 Daily 9.30–4, also Fri–Sun 6–8pm
🍽 From NZ$6

COROMANDEL TOWN

PEPPER TREE RESTAURANT AND BAR

31 Kapanga Road, Coromandel Town
Tel 07-866 8211
www.coromandeltown.co.nz
In the heart of Coromandel Town, the Pepper Tree is a community meeting place, with a big-screen TV and weekly music club jam sessions. The buffets and à la carte menus focus on local seafood such as oysters, mussels, snapper, smoked fish and crayfish. You can also get hearty country fare like

steak, chips and eggs. Special children's dishes, such as spare ribs, are available. On summer evenings book in advance.
🕐 Daily 10–9
🍽 L NZ$25, D NZ$50, W NZ$25

KERIKERI

MARSDEN ESTATE

Wiroa Road, Kerikeri
Tel 09-407 9398
www.marsdenestate.co.nz
This winery and restaurant are named after Samuel Marsden, who planted New Zealand's first grapevines close by in 1819. The restaurant is charmingly located beside a lake among the vines. There is seating indoors, where wine-tasting takes place, or outdoors on the terrace. The menu includes dishes such as black pudding with blue cheese, pear and blueberry sauce, designed to complement the wines from the 4ha (10-acre) vineyard.
🕐 Aug–end May daily 10–5; Jun, Jul Sun–Thu 10–4, Fri, Sat 10–4, 6–late
🍽 L NZ$25, W NZ$19.50

ROCKET CAFÉ AND DELI

Kerikeri Road, Kerikeri
Tel 09-407 3100
Surrounded by gardens and orchards, this is a good place to stop for refreshments or lunch. It has excellent coffee, a small menu of hot dishes, and a tempting deli counter of cakes, muffins and quiches. You can sit inside or under a canopy among the fruit trees. Children have their own menu and playground.
🕐 Tue–Fri 8.30–3.30, Sat, Sun 9–4
🍽 L NZ$20, W NZ$26

MATAKANA

ASCENSION VINEYARD RESTAURANT

480 Matakana Road, Matakana
Tel 09-422 9601
www.ascensionvineyard.co.nz
An eye-catching building next to the Ascension winery, this popular restaurant on the Matakana wine trail serves a comprehensive menu of New Zealand cuisine with a Mediterranean twist. Ascension wines are served, and the gift shop in the wine-tasting room sells their own preserves, jellies, oils and relishes. The restaurant is open for dinner during summer and regularly hosts live music and gigs.
🕐 Mon–Fri 11–4, Sat, Sun 11–5

PAIHIA

ONLY SEAFOOD

40 Marsden Road, Paihia
Tel 09-402 6066
While in Paihia, the capital of game fishing in New Zealand, chances are you'll want to try the local speciality. At Only Seafood, located on the waterfront above its companion restaurant Bistro 40, you get a fine view across the bay as well. Game fish is typically served seared in a light soy sauce. Other dishes include char-grilled hapuka, scallops and local Orongo Bay oysters. It's an informal place where you can feel comfortable coming straight from the beach. Eat indoors or out on the deck. The restaurant doesn't take reservations, but you can have a drink in the bar while you wait.
🕐 Daily from 5pm
🍽 Main and veg NZ$30

EATING

HOTEL DU VIN

Lyons Road, Mangatawhiri Valley, Pokeno
Tel 09-233 6314
www.hotelduvin.co.nz
Just off the main road to the Coromandel Peninsula, this restaurant is part of a luxury retreat amid the vines of Firstland Vineyard. The food is modern New Zealand, with a focus on seafood and game in dishes such as venison fillet with tomato, mozzarella, basil and macadamia-nut ravioli. On Sundays you can combine a fixed-price three-course lunch (NZ$45) with use of the hotel's leisure facilities. Reserve in advance.
🕐 Mon–Sat 12–2.30, 6–9.30, Sun 11.30–2.30, 6–9.30
🍴 L NZ$48, D NZ$65, W NZ$49

RAWENE

BOATSHED CAFÉ

Clendon Esplanade, Rawene
Tel 09-405 7728
A welcome refreshment stop before or after the ferry crossing, the Boatshed Café serves a surprisingly varied selection of light snacks and good coffee, with views across the Hokianga Harbour. Bright works by local artists are displayed and may be purchased.
🕐 Daily 8.30–4, closed mid-Sep to mid-Oct
🍴 L from NZ$10

RUSSELL

DUKE OF MARLBOROUGH

Duke of Marlborough Hotel, The Waterfront, Russell
Tel 09-403 7829
www.theduke.co.nz
It's hard to think of a more romantic place to dine than this old waterfront hotel, particularly if you can sit outdoors on the veranda and look out over the water while boats bob in the bay. Indoors, the grand dining room is more formal. You can order local fish and seafood, including Orongo Bay oysters, but the menu is also strong on char-grills and game.
🕐 Daily 7.30am–9pm
🍴 L NZ$25, D NZ$55, W NZ$30

KAMAKURA

The Strand, Russell
Tel 09-403 7771
www.kamakura.co.nz
A stylish restaurant on Russell's waterfront, Kamakura has a reputation for superb food and interesting wine. The menu is Pacific Rim, with an emphasis on fresh local produce including Orongo Bay oysters, and everything—including bread—is made on site. Advance booking is recommended.
🕐 Mon, Thu–Sat 12–2, 6–9, Sun 11–3
🍴 L NZ$45, D NZ$70, W NZ$45

WAIHEKE ISLAND

MUDBRICK RESTAURANT

Church Bay Road, Oneroa, Waiheke Island
Tel 09-372 9050
www.mudbrick.co.nz
Named after the earth bricks from which it is built, Mudbrick Restaurant is in a spectacular location, surrounded by vines, with expansive views over the Hauraki Gulf. The restaurant and winery blend in with the landscaped gardens, and are designed in a French provincial style. The food has a rural and Mediterranean theme, with Waiheke Pacific oysters, home-baked foccacia, and dishes such as saffron and spinach ravioli, set off by local wines. Advance booking is essential.
🕐 Daily 11–5, 6–late
🍴 L NZ$47, D NZ$70, W NZ$38

WAITANGI

WAIKOKOPU CAFÉ

Treaty Grounds, Waitangi
Tel 09-402 6275
www.waitangi.net.nz
A good place for coffee or lunch after exploring the Treaty Grounds (▷ 74), this attractive café has indoor and outdoor dining areas overlooking a bush walk and pond, the *waka* (Maori canoe) and the coastline. You can choose from snacks and cakes or a blackboard menu of substantial dishes such as corn and coriander fritters served with guacamole, sour cream and tomato salsa. There is also plenty of food on the menu that appeals to children.
🕐 Daily 9–5
🍴 L NZ$20, W NZ$22

WHANGAREI

A DECO

70 Kamo Road, Kensington, Whangarei
Tel 09-459 4957
Art deco décor, original combinations of tastes and good service make this place worth a detour off the main road between Auckland and the Bay of Islands. Chef Brenton Low's signature dish is a braised oxtail and wild mushroom tart with porcini polenta and Parmesan crumble, but the menu ranges widely, from chilled mushroom soup to pina colada crème brulée.
🕐 Tue, Sat 6–late, Wed–Fri 11–2.30, 6–late
🍴 L NZ$25, D NZ$50, W NZ$28

WHENUAKITE

COLENSO COUNTRY CAFÉ & SHOP

Main Road, Whenuakite, Coromandel Peninsula
Tel 07-866 3725
Surrounded by old-fashioned herb gardens, the Colenso Café is a pleasant place to stop for a snack or lunch on the road between Whitianga and Tairua. You can sit on a shady veranda or indoors, where local crafts are displayed for sale. The food is simple but good home baking. Although it's licensed for the sale of alcohol, the real treat here is freshly squeezed juice from the café's organic orchard. You can also buy orchard products from the roadside stall.
🕐 Sep–end Jul daily 10–5
🍴 L NZ$30, W NZ$25

WHITIANGA

THE FIRE PLACE

9 The Esplanade, Whitianga, Coromandel Peninsula
Tel 07-866 4828
www.thefireplace-restaurant.com
There is no escaping the motif of this rustic restaurant on the Whitianga waterfront—you are greeted by a giant fireplace and there are others inside. The food continues the theme, with pizza from the wood-fired oven, but there are many other dishes including pasta, salads and seafood. There's a good selection of coffees and teas, too, and wines are reasonably priced. Reservations are recommended.
🕐 Daily 5pm–9.30pm (also 11am–2pm in summer)
🍴 L NZ$30, D NZ$50, W NZ$25

EATING

CENTRAL NORTH ISLAND

The lush dairy country of Taranaki is the heart of the North Island's cheese industry, producing some excellent European-style cheeses like Raclette and St. Paulin, as well as New Zealand creations such as Shades of Blue, mainly under the Ferndale label. Fine boutique cheeses are also made in the Dutch style at Meyer Gouda near Hamilton. In Gisborne, look for the local Waimata cheeses. Paeroa has a national reputation thanks to L&P (lemon and Paeroa) mineral waters, originally from the town. Orchards surround Tauranga, producing citrus, tamarillos, feijoas and kiwifruit—nearby Te Puke calls itself the kiwifruit capital. Gisborne and Hawke's Bay are also traditional fruit- and vegetable-growing areas, producing citrus and stonefruit, berries, avocados, peas, beans, corn and many other crops. Both regions have a reputation for producing top-class wine—Gisborne is noted particularly for its Chardonnay and Hawke's Bay for its reds. More than 40 wineries are open to the public on the Hawke's Bay wine trail (▷ 79).

CAMBRIDGE

SOUTER HOUSE
19 Victoria Street, Cambridge
Tel 07-827 3610
www.souterhouse.co.nz
Deep red carpeting, chandeliers and Royal Doulton china grace the dining room at Souter House, an 1870s Victorian mansion with a licensed restaurant and accommodation. The food is traditional European and beautifully presented. Starters include shrimp cocktail, scallops and bacon and deep-fried Camembert; main courses are strong on roasts and grills, including lamb, venison, ostrich and salmon; and desserts include dishes such as lemon meringue pie.
🕐 Tue–Sat from 6pm
🍴 D NZ$50, W NZ$25

GISBORNE

THE COLOSSEUM CAFÉ & WINE BAR
4 Riverpoint Road, Matawhero, Gisborne
Tel 06-867 4733
Matawhero is regarded as the cradle of Gewürztraminer in New Zealand, and its winemaker Denis Irwin is one of the wine industry's great characters, producing fine and sometimes unusual wines since 1970. You can taste his

wines and have brunch, lunch, evening meals and casual snacks at his vineyard café, the grandly named Colosseum, 10km (6 miles) south of Gisborne, off SH2. The antipasto platter (NZ$35) is a generous introduction to the menu.
🕐 Sep–end May daily 10.30–7
🍴 L NZ$25, D NZ$38, W NZ$20

THE WHARF CAFÉ
The Wharf, 60 The Esplanade, Gisborne
Tel 06-868 4876
www.wharfbar.co.nz
Set in a former wharf building, the café has big windows looking out over the marina. Inside the styling is simple, with sails stretched across the ceiling, and the outdoor tables are understandably popular. The food is mainly modern New Zealand, such as fresh crayfish with salad greens, roast gourmet potatoes, smoked salmon and roquette butter.
🕐 Daily 9am–late
🍴 L NZ$25, D NZ$60, W NZ$35

THE WORKS
The Wharf, 60 The Esplanade, Gisborne
Tel 06-863 1285
This harbourside winery and café houses the cellar door for the Gisborne Wine Company and several other local wineries. The brick building is a former freezing works, cleverly converted into a casual restaurant with indoor and outdoor dining, where you can have anything from coffee and a snack to lunch or dinner. The food has a regional focus; seafood and paua (abalone) are among the specialities.
🕐 Daily 10–10
🍴 L NZ$25, D NZ$45, W NZ$18

HAMILTON

IGUANA
Victoria Street, Hamilton
Tel 07-834 2280
www.iguana.net.nz
Spacious and popular, Iguana serves a mainly Pacific Rim menu, including steak, chicken

and lamb, and pizzas. Cook-your-own hot rocks are a speciality—a mini barbecue of heated granite with your choice of ingredients. Sit on the street or in a booth.
🕐 Mon–Wed 10am–late, Thu, Fri 10am–3am, Sat, Sun 9am–3am
🍴 L NZ$23, D NZ$55, W NZ$29

SPECIAL IN HAMILTON

CANVAS
Grantham Street, Hamilton
Tel 07-839 2535
www.canvas.net.nz
Modern art on the walls, lots of plants, muted lighting and jazz on the sound system give Canvas a sophisticated atmosphere, and the food and service are both highly regarded. The menu is modern New Zealand, with dishes such as twice-baked duck on kumara blinis with sweet soy, or salt and pepper squid with coriander (cilantro) and palm sugar dip.
🕐 Mon–Fri 11.30–2.30, 6–late, Sat 6–late
🍴 L NZ$25, D NZ$55, W NZ$31

TERRÔIR

Craggy Range Vineyards, 253
Waimarama Road, Havelock North
Tel 06-873 0143
www.craggyrange.com

This stunning modern stone-built winery restaurant looks out over vines to Te Mata Peak. There is seating indoors by a log fire or on the lakeside terrace. The restaurant has a French country theme, specializing in rôtisserie and wood-fired oven cooking, and showcasing Craggy Range wines. There is an outstanding international wine list. For a specifically New Zealand experience, try the paua sausage with potatoes and fern fronds.

ⓒ Late Oct to mid-Apr Mon–Sat 11–3, 6–late, Sun 11–3; mid-Apr to late Oct Tue–Sat 11–3, 6–late, Sun 11–3
🍴 L NZ$44, D NZ$57, W NZ$35

HASTINGS

SILENI ESTATES RESTAURANT

Sileni Estates, 2016 Maraekakaho Road (SH 50), Bridge Pa, Hastings
Tel 06-879 4831,
www.sileni.co.nz

This striking modern winery complex is a landmark on the outskirts of Hastings. In addition to a stylish restaurant, it has a gourmet food store, cheese larder and wine-tasting room. You can dine indoors or out, overlooking the vineyard. The food is Mediterranean with global additions.

ⓒ Dec to mid-Apr Sun–Wed 11–2, Thu–Sat 11–2, 6–late
🍴 L NZ$40, D NZ$60, W NZ$30

LAKE TARAWERA

THE LANDING CAFÉ

Spencer Road, The Landing, Lake Tarawera
Tel 07-362 8595
www.purerotorua.com

It would be hard to find a more idyllic spot than this café beside Lake Tarawera. Have a drink in the Old Trout Bar or take a veranda table overlooking the lake. The only trouble is, the sandflies love it too— so protect yourself. The menu includes open sandwiches, salads and pasta.

ⓒ Daily 9.30–4.30, evenings by arrangement
🍴 L NZ$30, D NZ$45, W NZ$30

MOUNT MAUNGANUI

ASTROLABE

82 Maunganui Road, Mount Maunganui
Tel 07-574 8155
www.astrolabe.co.nz

A stylish restaurant and bar with modern minimalist décor, Astrolabe is laid out in separate but interrelated areas with a bar, café, courtyard and formal dining room, giving a range of options depending on your mood. It's popular for brunch/lunch, casual drinks or more serious meals, with standards like scrambled eggs and smoked salmon or Pacific Rim dishes such as coconut-fried prawns with saffron and vanilla risotto.

ⓒ Daily 9am–10pm
🍴 L NZ$30, D NZ$45, W NZ$30

NAPIER

CAUTION AND SHED 2

West Quay, Ahuriri, Napier
Tel 06-835 2202
www.shed2.com

Cleverly converted from a 19th-century wool store, Shed 2 makes the most of its waterfront location, with large quayside decks overlooking the harbour. On cold days there's a welcome open fire. The international menu includes wood-fired pizzas— tandoori spiced chicken with onion, avocado and banana is popular—pasta, wok-cooked dishes and local seafood. The nextdoor Caution dining lounge provides a retreat from the big-screen TVs with a more formal menu, local wine list and brunch at weekends.

ⓒ Mon–Fri 11.30am–late, Sat, Sun 9am–late
🍴 L NZ$25, D NZ$40, W NZ$33

CHAMBERS RESTAURANT

County Hotel, 12 Browning Street, Napier
Tel 06-835 7800
www.countyhotel.co.nz

Located on the Napier waterfront in the gracious Edwardian County Hotel (▷ 277), Chambers is one of the few silver-service restaurants in the city. It is noted for its elegant décor, attentive service and extensive wine lists. The menu is international, with dishes such as tiger prawns Thai style with saffron rice and sweet and sour sauce, and herb-crusted lamb rack on minted potatoes, caramelized shallots, capsicums and a balsamic jus; and cranberry and frangipane tart.

ⓒ Daily 6.30pm–late
🍴 D NZ$54, W NZ$28

MISSION ESTATE

198 Church Road, Taradale, Napier
Tel 06-845 9354
www.missionestate.co.nz

New Zealand's oldest winery, Mission Estate is located on a hillside overlooking Napier. The restaurant is in a restored seminary building, and offers a modern, seasonally focused, European-influenced menu— using Hawke's Bay produce when possible. Specialities are Aoraki salmon fillet panfried medium rare, in puff pastry with smoked salmon, spinach and summer greens and drizzled with salmon caviar butter sauce; and roast rack of venison encrusted with horopito spice, with roast potato, kumara and black pudding. There are only Mission Estate wines on the list, and the waiters are well briefed to advise on wine matches.

ⓒ Daily 10am–late
🍴 L NZ$30, D NZ$50, W NZ$25

NEW PLYMOUTH

ANDRÉ L'ESCARGOT

37–43 Brougham Street, New Plymouth
Tel 06-758 4812
www.andres.co.nz

L'Escargot has been part of the New Plymouth restaurant scene since 1976. Its 1870s premises give the place a timeless quality, with dark wood furniture and crisp white linen. The menu is unashamedly French, with classics such as steak au poivre, goat's cheese soufflé and tarte tatin. A popular option is the platter of seasonal dishes for two (NZ$39.50 per person). The wine list includes French as well as New Zealand and Australian wines.

ⓒ Mon–Sat from 5pm
🍴 D NZ$65, W NZ$40

SIMPLY READ

2 Dawson Street, New Plymouth
Tel 06-757 8667

A small, sunny café overlooking the sea, Simply Read has the added appeal of having a bookshop attached. The library-like atmosphere is peaceful, the coffee is good, and there's a choice of light,

EATING

healthy snacks, including plenty of vegetarian options.
◐ Daily 9–5
🍴 L from NZ$8

OHAKUNE

FAT PIGEON GARDEN CAFÉ
Mountain Road, Ohakune
Tel 06-385 9423
This bright café is ideally located for skiers, at the bottom of the Mountain Road. There's a wood fire to snuggle up to in winter, and tables in the garden for warm weather. The coffee is good and the deli cabinet is full of snacks, such as filled panini. They also do a good line in pizzas, frittatas and pancakes. An à la carte menu is available in the evening.
◐ Jul–end Oct daily 9am–10pm; Nov–end Jun Thu–Sun 9am–10pm
🍴 L NZ$20, D NZ$50, W NZ$22

RAGLAN

AQUA VELVET KITCHEN AND BALLROOM
17 Bow Street, Raglan
Tel 07-825 8588
www.aquavelvet.net.nz
Everything is prepared from scratch at this restaurant, including bread, cakes, pasta and desserts. The emphasis is on seasonal produce, much of which is organic. The coffee is organic and there's a choice of leaf teas. Brunches are particu-

larly good, with choices such as brioche French toast, and porridge with honeyed walnuts. The evening menu offers dishes like chicken on almond rice with saffron cauliflower. This is also a lively music venue.
◐ Sun–Thu 8–3, Fri, Sat 8–3, 6–9
🍴 L NZ$14, D NZ$40, W NZ$28

ROTORUA

BISTRO 1284
1284 Eruera Street, Rotorua
Tel 07-346 1284
www.bistro1284.co.nz
An intimate restaurant in a 1930s wooden house, Bistro

SPECIAL IN ROTORUA

AORANGI PEAK
Top of Mountain Road, Rotorua
Tel 07-347 0036
www.aorangipeak.co.nz
Both the food and the view are worth experiencing at Aorangi Peak. Chefs with French and Japanese experience produce dishes such as sautéed spinach and smoked salmon in a sushi roll served with an aioli dressing, followed by chicken breast wrapped with prosciutto and flaky puff pastry, served with a melting prawn and escargot butter.
◐ Daily 12–late
🍴 L NZ$30, D NZ$65, W NZ$33

1284 has frequently been voted Rotorua's best. The décor is stylishly minimalist, with cream walls and polished floors. The menu is also minimalist, but carefully considered, and the dishes are beautifully presented. A specialty is slow-roasted chicken with fried rice cake, shang-hi and mild red curry. Reservations essential.
◐ Tue–Sat 6–9
🍴 D NZ$60, W NZ$34

FAT DOG
1161 Arawa Street, Rotorua
Tel 07-347 7586
One of Rotorua's most popular cafés, Fat Dog combines quirky décor with a casual atmosphere, a wide-ranging menu and good coffee. Choose from a blackboard menu of snacks or light meals, such as panini and steak sandwiches. In the evening there are additional main dishes such as venison

and sirloin steaks. Portions are generous. The café is always busy but the wait is worth it.
◐ Sun–Wed 8am–9pm, Thu–Sat 8am–9.30pm
🍴 L NZ$15, D NZ$30, W NZ$25

TAUPO

THE BACH
2 Patuka Road, Lake Terrace, Taupo
Tel 07-378 7856
www.thebach.co.nz
The Bach offers a complete dining experience. A former fishing lodge with a view over Lake Taupo to Tongariro National Park, it combines innovative food with a remarkable wine list. The owner is a wine merchant, and the reserve list includes many rare labels. The cooking is modern New Zealand, with dishes such as crispy skinned quail tossed with spinach and shredded prosciutto served in a pastry tart case.
◐ Nov to mid-Apr daily 6–late; mid-Apr to end Oct Tue–Sun 6–late; also Dec, Jan daily 12–2
🍴 L NZ$30, D NZ$55, W NZ$38

TAURANGA

HARBOURSIDE BRASSERIE AND BAR
The Strand, Tauranga
Tel 07-571 0520
www.harbourside-tga.co.nz
The former home of the local yacht club, the Harbourside has a prime waterfront location. Its vast menu is a mix of classical and modern Pacific Rim dishes with plenty of seafood.

Choices include sushi and sashimi, with Asian pickled vegetables, wasabi and ponzu; Asian-style mussels, infused with ginger, garlic, coriander (cilantro) and soy; and Whangamata scallops, pan seared with a potato blini, citrus salad and turmeric broth.
◐ 11.30am–late
🍴 L NZ$30, D NZ$60, W NZ$23

EATING

SOUTHERN NORTH ISLAND

The Wairarapa region has become noted internationally for its wines, particularly Pinot noir, and many of the vineyards around the town of Martinborough are open to visitors. The region also produces some excellent cheese, including the boutique Gladstone Chèvre (goat), Kingsmead (sheep), Rangiuru (Dutch-style) and Zany Zeus (Mediterranean). Kapiti, one of New Zealand's largest speciality cheesemakers, is based at Paraparaumu on the Kapiti Coast. Crabs from nearby Waikanae are highly prized.

GREYTOWN

MAIN STREET DELI
88 Main Street,
Greytown
Tel 06-304 9022
A charming little café, snug inside and with a large outdoor eating area, the Main Street Deli serves breakfasts and lunches, along with excellent home-cooked slices, quiches and cakes. The coffee is good, too. The café is fully licensed and BYO.
⊙ Daily 8–6
✴ L NZ$30, W NZ$15

SALUTÉ
83 Main Street,
Greytown
Tel 06-304 9825
www.salute.greytown.co.nz
Modern Mediterranean cuisine is the inspiration for this restaurant, which has an enthusiastic following. The menu is eclectic, with Spanish *chorizo*, Italian pizzas, Turkish *pide* (flat bread) and Moroccan *harira* (soup). Dinners can start with mezze and finish with baklava or lemon fritters rolled in cinnamon sugar with pomegranate molasses and lemon ice cream. If such things are unfamiliar, the staff are ready with explanations. There's an attractive outside seating area with trees and a fountain; indoors there's a fire in winter.
⊙ Tue–Sat 12–10.30, Sun 11–3
✴ L NZ$25, D NZ$50, W NZ$27

THE WHITE SWAN
Main Street,
Greytown
Tel 06-304 8894
www.thewhiteswan.co.nz
Created from a former Railways building, the White Swan cleverly combines old and new. The hotel has a bar with pub food, and you can have a drink by the fire, in the library or on the veranda. The Lilac Dining Room also opens out onto the veranda and serves modern country food, such as chicken encrusted with basil pesto and pinenuts. Children's meals are also available.
⊙ Daily 10–4, 7.30–9.30
✴ L NZ$17, D NZ$50, W NZ$27

MARTINBOROUGH

RIVERVIEW CAFÉ
Murdoch James, Dry River Road,
Martinborough
Tel 06-306 9165
www.murdochjames.co.nz
A beautiful location, good food and highly regarded wines combine to make a memorable lunch at this scenic vineyard 8km (5 miles) south of Martinborough. The grounds have been landscaped with a picnic area, walks, gardens and ponds. The 25ha (62-acre) vineyard produces Pinot noir, Syrah, Chardonnay, Sauvignon blanc, Cabernet Sauvignon, Cabernet Franc and Riesling, and the Mediterranean-themed lunches are designed to match them with dishes such as risotto or South Island smoked salmon. Reservations are essential.
⊙ Nov–end Feb daily 11.30–3.30; Mar–end Oct Fri–Sun 11.30–3.30
✴ L NZ$23, W NZ$25

THE VILLAGE CAFÉ
6 Kitchener Street,
Martinborough
Tel 06-306 8814
www.martinboroughwinecentre.co.nz
Centrally located next to the Martinborough Wine Centre, the café serves breakfast, brunch, lunch and snacks. The focus is on local products, such as manuka-smoked bacon, and they make their own sausages, bread, cakes and biscuits. A lunchtime menu of blackboard specials includes soups, pasta and meat dishes. You can also get local wines, locally brewed beer, organic coffee and speciality teas.
⊙ Daily 9–5
✴ L NZ$20, W NZ$20

OTAKI

BROWN SUGAR CAFÉ
Corner of SH1 and Riverbank Road,
Otaki
Tel 04-364 6359
The Brown Sugar Café is a popular refreshment stop in a heritage building with an attractive garden on SH1, north of Wellington. The quality of the coffee may depend on the person making it, but the food tastes like home cooking, and the garden setting makes up for any deficiencies. There's a tasty breakfast menu.
⊙ Daily 9–5
✴ From NZ$10

SPECIAL IN MASTERTON

CAFÉ CECILLE
Queen Elizabeth Park,
Masterton
Tel 06-370 1166
www.cafececille.co.nz
Café Cecille is set in the pretty Queen Elizabeth Park near the heart of Masterton, and its menu uses local ingredients such as Gladstone ham, Kilrae olive oil and Parkvale mushrooms. It's a café by day, serving brunch and lunch, and a restaurant and wine bar in the evenings.
⊙ Tue 10–3, Wed–Fri 10–9, Sat 9–9, Sun 9–3
✴ L NZ$20, D NZ$60, W NZ$35

EATING

PAHIATUA

BLACK STUMP CAFÉ AND HARROWS RESTAURANT

106 Main Street,
Pahiatua
Tel 06-376 7123
www.blackstump.tripod.com
On the road between Palmerston North and Masterton, in the heart of a little-known scenic area, this is worth a stop for its rustic barn setting, with 'wool press' tables, native wood flooring and exposed-beam ceilings. You can warm yourself by the fire, play pool and eat bar snacks or stay for dinner in the 1900s-themed dining room. The food is unexpectedly modern and interesting, with choices such as bacon, potato and roast pear salad with blue-cheese dressing, or seared beef with caramelized red onions and Parmesan.
⊙ Tue–Sun 11.30–late
🖤 L NZ$??, D NZ$45, W NZ$22

PALMERSTON NORTH

BELLA'S CAFÉ

2 The Square,
Palmerston North
Tel 06-357 8616
www.bellas.co.nz

A popular café, Bella's mixes Italian with Thai and Pacific Rim dishes. For lunch, choose from tapas, home-made breads, salads or pasta. For dinner, Thai chicken curry is popular, but you can also get a range of grills and interesting vegetarian dishes. Desserts are good, too: Bella's Blitz of confectionery, fresh fruit and nuts, bound with chocolate cream and coulis, is made for sharing.
⊙ Tue–Sat 11.30–3, 6–10
🖤 L NZ$30, D NZ$50, W NZ$28

DÉJEUNER

159 Broadway Avenue,
Palmerston North
Tel 06-952 5581
www.dejeuner.co.nz

Déjeuner has a formal mood, knowledgeable service and a seasonally changing menu. The food is a fusion of European, Asian and Pacific cuisines. Twice-roasted lamb shanks are a speciality, but you can also get more adventurous dishes such as ostrich or tandoori beef salad. If you don't want to linger over your meal, the pre-theatre 'Eat and Out by 8' option on Thursday to Saturday nights is good value at NZ$45 for two courses.
⊙ Mon–Sat 6–late
🖤 D NZ$60, W NZ$29

WANGANUI

AMADEUS RIVERBANK CAFÉ

69 Taupo Quay, Wanganui
Tel 06-345 1538
In a prime position overlooking

the river, a short stroll from Victoria Avenue, the Amadeus is a good place for a relaxing, casual breakfast, light lunch or good coffee. 'The Works' (NZ$12) is their signature breakfast, guaranteed to fill you up with eggs, bacon and all the trimmings. There's an all-day menu, with blackboard specials and snacks such as samosas, bagels and nachos, along with cakes and tarts made on site.
⊙ Daily 8.30–4
🖤 L NZ$20, W NZ$17

WELLINGTON

THE BACKBENCHER

34 Molesworth Street, Wellington
Tel 04-472 3065
In the heart of the Parliamentary district, the Backbencher assures you of a good pub lunch and a fair assortment of tap ales, plus the entertainment of political satire on the walls in the form of cartoons and three-dimensional caricatures. Centre stage, of course, are the current and former New

Zealand prime ministers and noted parliamentarians, none of them very flattering portraits.
⊙ Daily 11–late
🖤 L NZ$15, D NZ$25

BOULCOTT STREET BISTRO AND WINE BAR

99 Boulcott Street, Wellington
Tel 04-499 4199
www.boulcottstreetbistro.co.nz
This is one of Wellington's top restaurants, occupying a charming Victorian house and headed by a celebrated chef, Chris Green. The menu mixes classics such as fillet béarnaise and crème brûlée with innovative dishes like shallot tarte tatin with lamb's brains and salsa verde, or five-spice pannacotta. The wine list showcases boutique wines, many available by the glass to

facilitate food matching. Bookings are accepted only for lunch.
⊙ Mon–Fri 12–2 (wine bar all day), 6–late, Sat 6–late
🖤 L NZ$40, D NZ$60, W NZ$30

CAFFE L'AFFARE

27 College Street, Wellington
Tel 04-385 9748
www.laffare.co.nz
Credited with introducing Wellingtonians to espresso, L'Affare is a thriving coffee business as well as a relaxed

café. Tucked down a side street off Tory Street, it is away from the main shopping area but worth searching out. It's a

CHOCOLATE FISH CAFÉ AND CONES

497a Karaka Bay Road, Seatoun, Wellington
Tel 04-388 2808

The Chocolate Fish—Wellington's most relaxed waterfront café—is hugely popular, especially since the cast and crew of *The Lord of the Rings* chose it as their preferred hangout. On sunny summer afternoons you'll have to queue, but it's worth trying to sit outside and soak up the atmosphere and the view over Scorching Bay. The ice cream is excellent, and there is a blackboard menu as well as counter snacks and cakes. The service is variable, but the place is child-friendly.

🕒 Daily 8.30am–5pm
🖐 From NZ$8

popular meeting place, with a children's play area, and serves filled paninis, counter snacks and all-day breakfast. Seafood chowder is a speciality, and as you might expect, the coffee is excellent.

🕒 Mon–Fri 7am–4.30, Sat 8am–4
🖐 L NZ$20, W NZ$35

THE DUBLINER

134 Courtenay Place, Wellington
Tel 04-384 2896

Located above the popular Molly Malone's pub, the Dubliner restaurant carries on the Irish theme in giving its dishes pseudo-Irish names, but the food is fairly standard hotel fare: soup of the day, salads and pasta, grills and apple crumble. Value for money and hearty portions are the main attractions, as well as its convenient location near Te Papa (▷ 96–99). Beware, however: lunch may become extended thanks to some fine ales and a good head on the Guinness.

🕒 Daily 12–late
🖐 L NZ$20, D NZ$35

KAI IN THE CITY

21 Majoribanks Street, Wellington
Tel 04-801 5006
www.kaicity.co.nz

This *whare kai* (restaurant) in the heart of the city is based on traditional Maori culture. The décor is of Maori design,

Maori names are given for all the foods (with an English glossary) and indigenous seasonings, such as piko piko ferns and miro berries, give a unique taste to the dishes. *Kaimoana* (seafood) is prominent. You are encouraged to ask the staff questions and there is entertainment on Saturday night. Reservations are essential.

🕒 Mon–Sat 5pm–late
🖐 D NZ$50, W NZ$26

LEUVEN

135 Featherston Street, Wellington
Tel 04-499 2939
www.leuven.co.nz

Leuven brings a touch of Belgium to central Wellington, with Belgian beers—Stella Artois, Leffe Blonde, Leffe Brune, Hoegaarden are all on tap—and Belgian food. The signature dish is a kilo of mussels served with frites and mayonnaise. You can sit outside and watch Wellington's world go by.

🕒 Mon–Fri 7am–late, Sat, Sun 10am–late
🖐 L NZ$25, D NZ$45, W NZ$32

LOGAN BROWN

192 Cuba Street, Wellington
Tel 04-801 5114
www.loganbrown.co.nz

Wellington's most elegant restaurant, Logan Brown is located in grand premises in a neo-Grecian 1920s banking chamber. Although it's large, booth seating gives diners some privacy and allows for conversation. The food is modern New Zealand, including dishes like duck with kumara (sweet potato) confit, or mango tarte tatin. A three-course bistro menu is available at lunch and pre-theatre. Reservations are essential.

🕒 Mon–Fri 12–2, 6–late, Sat, Sun 6–late
🖐 L NZ$38, D NZ$60, W NZ$39

MONSOON POON

12 Blair Street, Wellington
Tel 04-803 3555

Monsoon Poon brings the tastes of India, South China, Vietnam, Thailand, the Philippines, Malaysia and Indonesia together under one roof. This makes for a lively setting, as the chefs cook in full view of the dining room. The menu is designed so that

you can sample different cooking styles by sharing dishes. There are no reservations.

🕒 Mon–Thu 11–11, Fri 11am–midnight, Sat 5pm–midnight, Sun 5–11
🖐 L NZ$20, D NZ$40, W NZ$28

SHED 5

Queens Wharf, Wellington
Tel 04-499 9069
www.shed5.co.nz

Built in 1888 as a wool store, Shed 5 has been cleverly transformed into an elegant restaurant and bar. Indoors can get crowded and noisy, so take a table outdoors and watch

the boats come and go. The menu is modern New Zealand with a focus on seafood, with entrées such as crayfish risotto. Main courses include seafood, lamb, venison and poultry.

🕒 Daily 11am–late
🖐 L NZ$40, D NZ$60, W NZ$39

TULSI

135 Cuba Street, Wellington
Tel 04-802 4144
www.tulsirestaurant.co.nz

Deservedly popular in lively Cuba Mall, Tulsi serves contemporary Indian cuisine at affordable prices. Butter chicken is a speciality, voted best in Wellington on a local radio station. There are also Tulsi restaurants in Petone and Christchurch.

🕒 Daily 11.30am–late
🖐 L NZ$12.50, D NZ$35, W NZ$30

EATING

NELSON AND MARLBOROUGH

Marlborough is the largest wine-growing region in New Zealand, renowned internationally for its Sauvignon blanc—Cloudy Bay is probably the best known—but it also produces fine Chardonnay, Pinot noir and other varieties. Nearby Nelson also produces notable wines, outstanding among them Neudorf Chardonnay and Pinot noir. Many wineries welcome visitors and a number have vineyard restaurants attached. New Zealand's fledgling olive industry began in Marlborough, and small amounts of high-quality extra virgin oils are made by boutique producers across the region. You will find them on restaurant tables and at the farmers' market. Also look out for boutique sheep's milk cheeses produced by River Terrace Farm.

Nelson and Marlborough are known for fruit growing, especially berries and pip- and stone-fruit, which can be bought from roadside stalls in season. Surplus fruit is made into preserves. Nelson is also known for its hops, prized by the brewing industry. The Marlborough Sounds support mussel, oyster and salmon farms, and koura (native crayfish) are also farmed in the region. Nelson is the fishing capital of New Zealand, with the largest fishing port in Australasia—hoki is the main catch. Nelson scallops and Golden Bay crabs are highly regarded. Crayfish (lobster) is a speciality in Kaikoura, which is named after the Maori words for food and crayfish.

APPLEBY

SEIFRIEDS VINEYARD RESTAURANT

Corner of SH60 and Redwood Road, Appleby
Tel 03-544 1555
www.seifried.co.nz

The Seifried family pioneered wine-making in Nelson, starting in 1976, and remain one of the largest producers in the area. They are particularly noted for their Riesling, Chardonnay and dessert wines. The restaurant is surrounded by vineyards, with indoor and outdoor dining allowing families to sit by the playground. They serve seasonal local produce, including popular antipasto platters, and homemade breads and desserts.
🕐 Daily 10–5, and evenings in summer
🍴 L NZ$20, W NZ$15

BLENHEIM

BELLAFICO CAFFE AND WINE BAR

17 Maxwell Road, Blenheim
Tel 03-577 6072
www.bellafico.co.nz

A casual café by day and serious restaurant at night, Bellafico has excellent coffee,

a German chef enthusiastic about local produce, and an outstanding list of local and international wines. Havelock mussels may come steamed either in a coconut cream and ginger broth, or battered in Marlborough Moa Noir beer.

SPECIAL IN BLENHEIM

HERZOG'S WINERY AND RESTAURANT

81 Jeffries Road, Blenheim
Tel 03-572 8770
www.herzog.co.nz

One of the top restaurants in the country, Herzog's has been created as a gourmet destination in the style of the celebrated restaurant Hans and Therese Herzog had in Switzerland. When they came to Marlborough to establish a vineyard they brought their chef and their superb collection of wines with them. The restaurant is furnished with Limoges china, Riedel crystal and French silverware. The food focuses on seasonal produce.

🕐 Mid-Oct to end Apr Tue–Sun 7–late; Dec–end Feb Tue–Sun 12–4,
🍴 L NZ$75, D NZ$98, W NZ$50

Wild venison cutlet is served on a home-made corn cake with a pomegranate jus.
🕐 Mon–Fri 10am–late, Sat 6pm–late
🍴 L NZ$25, D NZ$60, W NZ$29

TWELVE TREES RESTAURANT

Allan Scott Wines and Estates,
Jacksons Road, Blenheim
Tel 03-572 7123
www.allanscott.com

This indoor-outdoor garden restaurant, named after the walnut trees that line the entrance to the winery, is constructed from rammed earth, with a walled courtyard and picnic area. The menu is simple and fresh, reflecting local seasonal specialities such as mussels and strawberries. There is usually a pasta dish and a salad, and the vineyard platter is always popular. Allan Scott is a pioneer of viticulture in Marlborough and noted for his wines, so it's a good place to try them, too.
🕐 Daily 9–4.30
🍴 L NZ$25, W NZ$20

COLLINGWOOD

COURTHOUSE CAFÉ

Corner of Gibbs Road and Elizabeth Street, Collingwood
Tel 03-5248 572

This is a great place to be found guilty of gluttony with intent to demolish three-fruit smoothies. The old colonial building, which was once the district courthouse, is a remnant of far busier times, when Collingwood was the focus of a gold boom. Alas m'lud, now the only case in session revolves around the levels of relaxation, the black-board menu (with some criminally good vegetarian

EATING

options) and the quality of the coffee bean.

🕐 Dec–end Jun daily 8am–late; Jul–end Nov 11–4
🍴 L NZ$20, D NZ$40, W NZ$22

MUSSEL INN
Onekaka, Golden Bay
Tel 03-525 9241
www.musselinn.co.nz
Between Takaka and Collingwood on SH60, the Mussel Inn serves good pub grub, but the mussels, the beer and the atmosphere are what you come for. Local mussels are served simply steamed with bread. The beer is brewed

EATING

on site, using home-grown hops. The range includes lager, stout, bitter and pale ale, the most unusual being Captain Cooker manuka beer. In the evening, it hosts regular gigs.
🕐 Sep–end Jul daily from 11
🍴 L NZ$12, D NZ$35, W NZ$20

HAVELOCK
MUSSEL BOYS RESTAURANT
73 Main Road, Havelock
Tel 03-574 2824
www.musselboys.co.nz
Mussel Boys has done its best to put Havelock on the map as the green-lipped mussel capital of New Zealand. The distinctive restaurant, with out-size mussels on the roof, has spawned a franchise, and it would be hard to find fresher or tastier mussels. Choose from chowder, steamers or flats grilled with a choice of

toppings (and there are meats and salads for diehard non-mussel eaters).
🕐 Mid-Apr to end Oct daily 11.30–7; Nov, Feb, Mar daily 11–9; Dec, Jan daily 10.30–9.30
🍴 L NZ$20, D NZ$43, W NZ$28

KAIKOURA
FINZ OF SOUTH BAY RESTAURANT AND BAR
103 South Bay Parade, Kaikoura
Tel 03-319 6688
An intimate, family-run restaurant overlooking the sea, Finz is outstanding in Kaikoura. Many of the dishes are simple, relying on the superb taste of really fresh fish: crayfish grilled with butter and lemon zest, *sashimi* with Japanese accompaniments, or a succulent slab of citrus-dusted bluenose. Other dishes use contrasting accompaniments to highlight the seafood, such as scallops tossed with zucchini ribbons in pernod. The wine list showcases Marlborough vineyards. With only eight tables, Finz soon fills up, so book ahead.
🕐 Oct–end May daily 6pm–late; Jun–end Sep Wed–Sun 6pm–late
🍴 D NZ$55, W NZ$30

HISLOPS CAFÉ
33 Beach Road, Kaikoura
Tel 03-319 6971
www.hislops-wholefoods.co.nz
A renovated villa with dining on the veranda and in the garden, Hislop's is a pleasant place to stop for refreshments or lunch. The café specialises in wholefoods, using organically grown ingredients where possible. Most vegetables come from the family farm, which has a long history of using organic methods. The beverage list also includes organic wines and beers. The cakes are a treat, notably the apricot and chocolate cream cheese slice.
🕐 Summer daily 10–9; winter Tue, Wed 10–4, Thu–Mon 10–9
🍴 L NZ$25, D NZ$50, W NZ$26

KEKERENGU
THE STORE AT KEKERENGU
State Highway 1, Kekerengu
Tel 03-575 8600
Dramatically located on the coast halfway between Blenheim and Kaikoura, the Store is a must-stop for refreshments or lunch. The café has indoor seating around

a double-sided fireplace, and tables on the deck outdoors with spectacular views over the thundering surf. The décor is modishly rustic with massive wharf piles supporting the hessian-draped roof. The food is all made on site, with light meals including pizza, filled focaccia and venison pies through to sophisticated dishes of crayfish and blue cod.
🕐 Oct to mid-Apr daily 7.30–7; mid-Apr to end Sep 8–6.30
🍴 L NZ$23, D NZ$45, W NZ$33

MAPUA
FLAX RESTAURANT AND BAR
Mapua Wharf, Mapua
Tel 03-540 2028
Looking out over the Mapua estuary, Flax is one of the Nelson region's finest restaurants. A family affair, run by chef Tim Greenhough and *maître d'* Karen Hannan, it has an extensive wine list that also features Greenhough wines made by brother Andrew. The style of food is modern New Zealand, with interesting combinations such as lambs' brains with balsamic roast cherry tomatoes, ricotta pesto and bacon. The pork belly is also a popular choice. Service is friendly and informative.
🕐 Daily 10.30–3.30, 5–9
🍴 L NZ$25, D NZ$45, W NZ$30

SPECIAL IN MAPUA
THE SMOKEHOUSE RESTAURANT
Shed 2, Mapua Wharf, Mapua
Tel 03-540 2280
www.smokehouse.co.nz
You can buy smoked fish to take away or eat in the restaurant overlooking the water at the Smokehouse. The menu is based on locally supplied fish, mussels and vegetables hot-smoked on site, using a traditional brick kiln, manuka wood shavings and no artificial additives. Some of the less-prized fish smoke best, so try the warehou, hake or trevally, as well as the snapper and salmon. Smoked mushrooms and smoked tomato soup are also good.
🕐 Daily 11–late
🍴 L NZ$28, D NZ$50, W NZ$32

MARAHAU

PARK CAFÉ
Harveys Road, Marahau
Tel 03-527 8270
www.parkcafe.co.nz
Hikers finishing the Abel
Tasman Coast Track can't
believe their luck when they
stumble on this café, with its
blackboard menu, bar, good
coffee and internet access. It's
popular with daytrippers and
hikers starting from Marahau,
too. The café has indoor and
outdoor tables and a children's
playground. You can get
anything from breakfast to
evening meals or snacks and
cakes, from burgers, soups and
salads to steaks, pasta, fish and
vegetarian dishes.

🕐 Oct–end May daily 8am–9pm
🖐 L NZ$20, D NZ$40, W NZ$28

MOTUEKA

HOT MAMAS CAFÉ
105 High Street, Motueka
Tel 03-528 7039
A bright and relaxed café
with comfy sofas and lively
murals, Hot Mamas has live
music on Fridays and
Saturdays. You can dine by the
fire in winter, or out in the
garden in summer. The blackboard menu has an Italian
theme, with bruschetta,
antipasto, pizza, pasta and
Tuscan salads.

🕐 Daily 8.30am–late
🖐 L NZ$18, D NZ$32, W NZ$18

NELSON

THE BOAT SHED
350 Wakefield Quay, Nelson
Tel 03-546 9783
www.boatshedcafe.co.nz
You can't get much closer to
the water than this converted

scallops, Golden Bay crabs
and locally farmed salmon,
oysters and green-lipped
mussels. Non-seafood eaters
are also well catered for.

🕐 Daily 9am–10.30pm
🖐 L NZ$30, D NZ$70, W NZ$36

THE OYSTER BAR
115 Hardy Street, Nelson
Tel 03-545 8955
The emphasis is on fresh
seafood at this New York-
inspired oyster bar. An
intimate, narrow space with
bar stools, it encourages you
to chat with the chef as you
watch him at work. As well as
oysters every which way,
there's a Californian sushi
menu including smoked eel,
blackened scallop, smoked
salmon and vegetarian options.

🕐 Summer Tue–Sat 5.30pm–late;
winter Thu–Sun 5.30pm–late
🖐 D NZ$40, W NZ$30

WATERFRONT CAFÉ AND BAR
341 Wakefield Quay, Nelson
Tel 03-546 6685
www.waterfrontcafenelson.co.nz

LAMBRETTA'S CAFÉ-BAR
204 Hardy Street,
Nelson
Tel 03-545 8555
www.lambrettascafe.co.nz
Devoted to all things Italian,
this café behind the grand
Greco-Roman pillars of a
former insurance office has
the popular scooters bolted
to the walls, along with a
selection of Lambretta
paraphernalia. The theme is
carried on in the décor and
the food, with pizza, pastas
and antipasto to challenge

True to its name, Waterfront
has views of the harbour and
Tasman Bay from its upstairs
restaurant, and a café and bar
on the street frontage. Local
seafood, venison and duck
are on the menu, and the
signature dish is a 650g
Chateaubriand roast prime
fillet steak for two, rolled in
fresh herbs and spices, and
served with a truffle potato
purée, roast garlic bulbs, roast
vegetables and a red wine jus.

🕐 Daily 11am–late
🖐 L NZ$25, D NZ$50, W NZ$30

RICHMOND

CAFÉ IN THE VINEYARD AT WAIMEA ESTATES
Appleby Highway, Hope, Richmond
Tel 03-544 4963
www.waimeaestates.co.nz
Just outside Richmond, Café in
the Vineyard is the cellar door
and café for Waimea Estates.
You can sample and purchase
the wines, including Sauvignon
blanc, Riesling, Chardonnay
and Merlot, and lunch in the
extensive dining area, which
flows out to the vines. Fresh,
local ingredients are used in
dishes like char-grilled ribeye.

🕐 Sep–end Mar daily 11–5; Apr–end
Aug Wed–Sun 11–4
🖐 L NZ$24, W NZ$20

TAKAKA

WHOLEMEAL CAFÉ
Commercial Street, Takaka
Tel 03-525 9426
www.wholemealcafe.co.nz
In the old Takaka Theatre, the
café has become an institution
since it opened in 1977. The
mood is bohemian, with
modern art on the walls and
visitors in bare feet and beads.

boatshed, with water lapping
at the piles. The view over the
harbour is stunning, particularly if you brave the breeze
and take a table on the deck.
Seafood is a speciality, particularly Nelson white fish and

the heartiest appetite.
Children are welcome, with a
special menu and play area.

🕐 Daily 9am–late
🖐 L NZ$20, D NZ$40, W NZ$22

It has good coffee, fresh juices
and organic beers, and a daytime menu of free-range egg
dishes, salads, sandwiches
and cakes.

🕐 Daily 7.30am–9.30pm
🖐 L NZ$15, D NZ$35, W NZ$25

EATING

CANTERBURY AND THE WEST COAST

Canterbury is traditionally famous for its lamb, which is found on most restaurant menus, as is locally farmed deer, marketed as Cervena. Locally farmed ostrich can also be found. Salmon fishing is popular in the major rivers, and salmon is also farmed in Akaroa and in the high country lake district. Although vineyards are scattered through the region, the most successful wine-growing area is Waipara, known for its Riesling, Chardonnay and Pinot noir. A number of wineries are open to the public, some with restaurants attached. Several olive groves produce small quantities of extra virgin olive oil, which appears on menus along with locally produced hazelnut and walnut oils. Canterbury is also known for its pipfruit and berryfruit, and produces much of the country's asparagus. Boutique Dutch-style cheeses are made at Karikaas in Loburn; Barry's Bay Cheese on Banks Peninsula is most famous for its rinded cheddar; and boutique cheeses are made under the Talbot Forest label in Geraldine. Geraldine and Waimate are known for berry fruit, particularly blackcurrants and strawberries. Native honeys such as rata, kamahi and manuka are collected from the mountain beech forest. The West Coast is noted for its game and seafood, especially whitebait.

PRICES AND SYMBOLS

The prices given are for a two-course lunch (L) and a three-course dinner (D) for one person, without drinks. Many restaurants add a 15 per cent charge on public holidays. The wine price (W) is for the least expensive bottle. Restaurants are listed alphabetically by town. For a key to the symbols, ▷ 2.

AKAROA

HARBOUR 71

71 Beach Road, Akaroa
Tel 03-304 7656
Harbour 71 has great views over the water, and is set in one of Akaroa's character waterfront buildings, a former drapery, grocery and hardware business. It serves casual food during the day and has a more formal menu at night. Pizzas are the daytime speciality. The evening menu turns Pacific Rim, with dishes like coconut, lime and coriander-infused mussels.
🕐 Daily 10–late
🍴 L NZ$20, D NZ$65, W NZ$32

CHRISTCHURCH

ANNIE'S WINE BAR AND RESTAURANT

Arts Centre, Christchurch
Tel 03-365 0566
www.annieswinebar.co.nz
Annie's, in the heart of the Arts Centre, has outdoor dining in the cloisters or indoors where the brick walls are exposed and the furniture is recycled wood. The atmosphere is casual, with a menu of modern New Zealand food. The platter of breads and spreads is particularly popular. Annie's is

SPECIAL IN AKAROA

C'EST LA VIE

33 Rue Lavaud,
Akaroa
Tel 03-304 7314
With only eight tables at this intimate, highly regarded restaurant, you may be expected to share: once people get used to the idea, the owners say, it adds to the enjoyment, as you get to meet people from all over the world. The menu is French, changing seasonally with dishes such as duck à l'orange, venison with wild mushrooms and lamb provençal.
🕐 Mid-Sep to end Jun daily 6pm–late
🍴 D NZ$65, W NZ$30

well known for its wine list, served by knowledgeable staff. Reservation recommended.
🕐 Daily 11–late
🍴 L NZ$25, D NZ$60, W NZ$30

CAFFE ROMA

176 Oxford Terrace, Christchurch
Tel 03-379 3879
www.caffe-roma.co.nz
This European-styled coffee house with views over the river is a popular place for breakfast, brunch and lunch. As well as the usual egg dishes, breakfast specialities include home-

baked bagels and porridge cooked with apple juice, apples, honey, walnuts and sultanas, served with cream or milk. The lunch choices include pasta, risotto and salads.
🕐 Daily 7–4
🍴 L NZ$25, W NZ$34

COOK'N' WITH GAS

23 Worcester Boulevard,
Christchurch
Tel 03-377 9166
www.cooknwithgas.co.nz
A quirky restaurant in a converted villa opposite the Arts Centre, Cook'n' with Gas has walls covered in old photos, and a garden courtyard. The restaurant concentrates on New Zealand cuisine, serving, for example, baked *warehou* (fish) with a basil and karengo crust topped with garlic prawns, on a smoked tomato risotto, with a squid, lime and cucumber salad. They have a wide selection of local beers.
🕐 Mon–Sat 6pm–late
🍴 D NZ$55, W NZ$35

HAY'S

63 Victoria Street, Christchurch
Tel 03-379 7501
www.foodandwine.co.nz
Located opposite the Casino, this restaurant specialises in serving lamb grown on the Hay family's Banks Peninsula farm. The menu is modern New Zealand, with dishes such as lamb rack with Dijon mustard, parsley and tarragon crust, redcurrant and red wine jus and dauphinoise potatoes. The wine list focuses on top New Zealand wines.
🕐 Nov to mid-Apr daily from 5pm; mid-Apr to end Oct Tue–Sat from 5pm
🍴 D NZ$47, W NZ$31

EATING

MAINSTREET VEGETARIAN RESTAURANT

840 Colombo Street,
Christchurch
Tel 03-365 0421

Mainstreet is one of Christchurch's few vegetarian restaurants—a relaxed, informal place where you queue at the counter and point to what you want. The dishes are imaginative, substantial and well priced. Try the pumpkin and kumara (sweet potato) balls in spicy peanut and sesame seed sauce.

🕐 Tue–Thu 8am–9.30pm, Fri 8am–10pm, Sat 9am–10pm, Sun 9am–4pm

🍴 L NZ$12, D NZ$26, W NZ$20

OXFORD ON AVON

794 Colombo Street,
Christchurch
Tel 03-379 7148
www.oxfordonavon.co.nz

This popular carvery and buffet is the place to go when you're ravenously hungry. The restaurant operates on two floors, with a courtyard overlooking the Avon River. The Old English Breakfast (NZ$13.50) is available until 11am, when the queues start building for the set-price carvery lunch and all-you-can-eat buffet of European, Asian and Indian dishes. Children under 12 are charged NZ$1 for each year of their age.

🕐 Daily 6.30am–10.30pm

🍴 L N7$16, D NZ$21, W NZ$19

PESCATORE

The George Hotel, 50 Park Terrace,
Christchurch
Tel 03-371 0257
www.thegeorge.com

The George Hotel's (▷ 285) classy restaurant triumphs in seafood. The style is Pacific Rim executed in exquisitely presented dishes, either à la carte or in dégustation menus showcasing

regional specialities matched with local wines. Typical dishes include crayfish bisque with cumin and fennel, or big eye tuna with red onion confit, kumara and ginger dauphinoise and spiced consommé. Fang au Chocolat is the signature dessert.

🕐 Oct–end Apr daily from 6pm; May–end Sep Thu–Sun from 6pm

🍴 D NZ$77, W NZ$45

THE SIGN OF THE TAKAHE

200 Hackthorne Road, Cashmere,
Christchurch
Tel 03-332 4052
www.signofthetakahe.co.nz

A 1908 neo-Gothic castle on the Port Hills overlooking Christchurch, the Sign of the Takahe provides à la carte dining and bar facilities, with a lunchtime buffet. The menu tends towards fusion, with dishes such as venison rack served with soft truffle polenta, broad beans, mushrooms and crispy parsnips topped with a spicy rice crust; oven-baked chicken breast with sweet pomegranate, eggplant two ways and a soft herb, Persian feta and lemon salad; and jasmine rice pudding.

🕐 Daily 10–4, 6–10

🍴 L NZ$25, D NZ$70, W N7$30

DUNSANDEL

DUNSANDEL STORE

Main South Road,
Dunsandel
Tel 03-325 4037

On the main road south of Christchurch, the Dunsandel Store is an appealing combination of rustic café, deli, country store and shop selling local produce. You can buy anything from soap powder to local wines, there's a pretty courtyard planted with herbs, and the food is fresh and interesting. Typical dishes include old-fashioned pork pie, and rabbit and prune terrine. Apples feature strongly, as the owner makes juices and cider.

🕐 Daily 7am–8pm

🍴 L NZ$17, D NZ$27, W NZ$26

FOX GLACIER

CAFÉ NEVÉ

Main Road, Fox Glacier
Tel 03-751 0110

Café Nevé is small and friendly, with the feeling of being at home rather than in a restaurant. You can have breakfast,

SPECIAL IN FAIRLIE

THE OLD LIBRARY CAFÉ

7 Allandale Road, Fairlie
Tel 03-685 8999

The Old Library Café has made the small town of Fairlie a must-stop for visitors on the road to Mount Cook/Aoraki and the Southern Lakes. The 1912 building has been converted into a sophisticated restaurant and friendly café, retaining the character of the building. There's an attractive outdoor dining area, and the menu caters both for people in a hurry and diners wanting to relax. Local Mackenzie Country lamb and beef are specialities.

🕐 Daily 10am–late

🍴 L NZ$27, D NZ$51, W NZ$20

lunch or an evening meal. Pizzas are served from 11am in various sizes, to eat in or take away, or choose from West Coast treats such as whitebait, venison, salmon and fresh

seafood. Espresso coffee is the speciality; hot chocolate and herbal teas are available too.

🕐 Daily 8am–late

🍴 L NZ$20, D NZ$40, W NZ$25

FRANZ JOSEF

BLUE ICE CAFÉ

Main Road (SH6),
Franz Josef
Tel 03-752 0707

Downstairs an à la carte restaurant serves local specialities such as whitebait patties and venison. Upstairs is a bar with a pool table, Sky TV, pizza, snacks and a well-stocked bar—the late-night party venue with regular DJs.

🕐 Oct–end Apr daily 2–10; May–end Sep daily 4–10

🍴 D NZ$45, W NZ$29

EATING

GREYMOUTH

THE SMELTING HOUSE CAFÉ

102 Mackay Street, Greymouth
Tel 03-768 0012

In a former bank building, this café is run by a dietitian, who cooks home-style food and serves good coffee. Enjoy a full

Farmer's Breakfast, and lunch dishes such as pasta.

🕐 Daily 8.30–4.30
✋ L NZ$15, W NZ$26

HANMER SPRINGS

THE OLD POST OFFICE

2 Jacks Pass Road, Hanmer Springs
Tel 03-315 7461

The former post office retains much of its character in this country restaurant, with its flowery décor, lush drapes, deep-pastel walls and heavy linen. The menu is strong on beef, lamb and game, and portions are generous.

🕐 Daily 6–9pm
✋ D NZ$60, W NZ$32

HOKITIKA

CAFÉ DE PARIS

19 Tancred Street, Hokitika
Tel 03-755 8933

Owners Joy (from New Zealand) and Pierre (from France) Esquilat have been in Hokitika for 20 years and bring a distinctive style to this West Coast café—French cuisine with a Kiwi accent. An airy café during the day, it serves coffee, pastries and blackboard lunches. In the evening enjoy classics like French onion soup

KOHAN JAPANESE RESTAURANT

State Highway 8, Lake Tekapo
Tel 03-680 6688
www.laketekapo.cc/kohan

This restaurant has views over the lake and mountains and serves Japanese food of a high standard. The bento lunch boxes and combination menus are a good way of sampling several dishes, as they include appetizers, miso, rice, *sashimi*, pickles and a hot dish such as grilled fish.

🕐 Mon–Sat 11–2, 6–9, Sun 11–2
✋ L NZ$18, D NZ$30, W NZ$25

and profiteroles, or more unusual dishes such as wild boar baked in pastry with mushrooms and red wine.

🕐 Daily from 7.30am
✋ L NZ$15, D NZ$30

METHVEN

STEEL-WORX RESTAURANT AND BAR

36 Forest Drive, Methven
Tel 03-302 9900
www.steel-worx.co.nz

Steel is the principal material used in this 1910 building, which has been converted into a bar with a city feel, a restaurant and a beer garden. It's popular in the ski season, when the bar hosts party nights with DJs and dancing. The restaurant is warmed by a log-burning stove and serves après-ski dishes like venison on mushroom risotto.

🕐 May–end Nov daily 5pm–late
✋ D NZ$46, W NZ$28

MOUNT COOK VILLAGE

OLD MOUNTAINEERS' CAFÉ AND BAR

Mount Cook Village
Tel 03-435 1890
www.mtcook.com

Opened in 2003, the Old Mountaineer is a welcome addition to the dining options in the village, with a casual atmosphere, great views, an open fire and a wide-ranging menu. You can have the usual breakfast items until 12.30, then lunch on paninis or fill up on a selection of steaks, curries and pizzas.

🕐 Nov–end Mar daily 9am–late;
Apr–end Oct 11am–late
✋ L NZ$25, D NZ$43, W NZ$22

OMARAMA

CLAY CLIFFS ESTATE VINEYARD AND CAFÉ

Pinot Noir Court, Omarama
Tel 03-438 9654

This Tuscan-style vineyard café south of the village overlooks a pond and vine-covered hills. The 4ha (10-acre) vineyard is New Zealand's highest, at 440m (1,445ft) above sea level. The restaurant serves lunchtime snacks, as well as substantial meals such as rack of lamb.

🕐 Jul–end May daily 11am–late
✋ L NZ$30, D NZ$60, W NZ$18

WAIPARA

PEGASUS BAY WINERY

Stockgrove Road, Waipara
Tel 03-314 6869
www.pegasusbay.com

A grand vineyard restaurant in landscaped gardens with outstanding wine and food, Pegasus Bay is a place for leisurely dining. The vineyard specialises in Riesling, Chardonnay, Pinot noir, late-harvest wines and reserve red blends. The menu is seasonal and created around the wine list, with suggested matches.

🕐 Daily 12–4
✋ L NZ$45, W NZ$37

WESTPORT

THE BAY HOUSE CAFÉ RESTAURANT GALLERY

Tauranga Bay, Cape Foulwind
Tel 03-789 7133
www.thebayhouse.co.nz

The waves roll into the ruggedly beautiful Tauranga Bay by this café, where you can have excellent coffee, admire the art exhibitions and dine on distinctly Aotearoa fare. A typical dish is the Bay

House Platter, which changes to reflect West Coast produce such as green-lip mussels in manuka honey and soy.

🕐 Daily 9am–late
✋ L NZ$30, D NZ$55, W NZ$30

EATING

OTAGO AND THE FAR SOUTH

Central Otago is famous for its stone fruit, especially apricots, nectarines and cherries, which can be bought from roadside stalls in season. The region is also successful with wine, and Gibbston Valley Winery is next to a cheese-making facility. Dairy farming is increasingly dominating local agriculture, with one of the world's largest cheese factories at Clandeboye, and highly regarded speciality cheeses made at Evansdale and Whitestone in Oamaru. The Oamaru region is also noted for its gourmet potatoes. Gore calls itself the capital of brown-trout fishing and although restaurants cannot put trout on their menus, they may be prepared to cook what you catch. Bluff is famous for its oysters and Stewart Island/Rakiura for its blue cod and crayfish. Paua (abalone) is also farmed on the island.

PRICES AND SYMBOLS

The prices given are for a two-course lunch (L) and a three-course dinner (D) for one person, without drinks. Many restaurants add a 15 per cent charge on public holidays. The wine price (W) is for the least expensive bottle. Restaurants are listed alphabetically by town. For a key to the symbols, ▷ 2.

CLYDE

OLIVER'S RESTAURANT
34 Sunderland Street, Clyde
Tel 03-449 2860
www.olivers.co.nz
Oliver's, part of a boutique historic lodge, was established in 1977 in an 1863 stone building, and features schist walls and two large stone fireplaces. Typical dishes on the menu are king salmon with

SPECIAL IN ARROWTOWN
SAFFRON
16 Buckingham Street, Arrowtown
Tel 03-442 0131
www.saffronrestaurant.co.nz
A quality restaurant in Arrowtown's heritage precinct, Saffron uses wild local ingredients whenever possible: Lindis Pass hare, West Coast boar, porcini and rosehips. The menu shows Mediterranean and Asian influences. Croutons come with creamy lambs' brains, and mussels are cooked with pernod. Central Otago wines head the wine list. The more casual Pesto restaurant next door is run by the same people, and serves a simple menu of pasta, pizza and salads. Their Blue Door Bar is a tiny, comfy cellar.
⊙ Daily 11–4, 6.30–late
L NZ$30, D NZ$90, W NZ$35

wasabi-infused mash, wilted bok choi, rich honey mustard glaze and fresh coriander tomato confit; and glazed lamb shoulder rack served with warm lentil casserole and roast seasonal vegetables.
⊙ Tue–Sun 9–1, 6.30–8.30
L NZ$20, D NZ$50, W NZ$34

THE POST OFFICE CAFÉ AND BAR
2 Blyth Street,
Clyde
Tel 03-449 2488
Housed in Clyde's original post office (established in 1862), the restaurant retains much of the building's character, with stone walls and a dark wood interior. It's a pleasant place to have lunch, particularly on a sunny day when you can sit out in the garden. The food is simple but tasty, with a blackboard menu featuring anything from venison to blue cod. The pies are a speciality.
⊙ Daily 10am–late
L NZ$15, D NZ$30, W NZ$25

CROMWELL

LAZYDOG CAFÉ AND WINE BAR
Akarua Winery, Cairnmuir Road, Bannockburn
Tel 03-445 3211
www.akarua.com
You can eat indoors or out at this attractive restaurant attached to Akarua Vineyard, 8km (5 miles) from Cromwell. Lamb and beef dishes are a strength, along with the produce of local orchards and Stewart Island salmon. Lamb backstrap with roasted tomato is a signature dish, served with kumara (sweet potato) and butternut squash, fettucine and a Pinot noir reduction.
⊙ Summer daily 11–3, 6–late; winter Wed–Sun 11–3, 6–late
L NZ$25, D NZ$50, W NZ$34

DUNEDIN

BELL PEPPER BLUES AND THE CHILE CLUB
474 Princes Street, Dunedin
Tel 03-474 0973
www.bellpepperblues.co.nz
The names of chef Michael Coughlin's restaurant and bar are tributes to his passion for the cooking of the south-western US, although he now takes inspiration from many cuisines. Cervena venison is a signature dish, which may be served as a grilled Denver leg cut with smoked venison sausage, kumara and leek hash cake. Both the service and presentation show meticulous attention to detail. The Chile Club offers a lunch menu.
⊙ Mon–Sat 6.30pm–late; also Wed–Fri 12–3
D NZ$60, W NZ$32

YELLOW TRAIN BISTRO
4 Dowling Street, Dunedin
Tel 03-477 1657
www.yellowtrain.co.nz
Yellow Train is in a historic building looking out onto the Queens Gardens, offering New Zealand food in a friendly atmosphere. Specialities are deep dish home-style pie, served with potato, and Lebanese vegetarian sambousik filo parcel.
⊙ Daily 5.30pm–late
D NZ$60, W NZ$32

INVERCARGILL

THE CABBAGE TREE
379 Dunns Road, Otatara, Invercargill
Tel 03-213 1443
www.thecabbagetree.com
On the way to the beach from Invercargill, The Cabbage Tree has been rebuilt from the old Beach Store using Central Otago schist and recycled timber, with lots of native planting outside. The menu includes giant sandwiches, all-day breakfast and high tea: a

EATING

speciality is the 'Chatter Platter' of blue cheese, salami, brie, pâté, smoked salmon, squid rings, ham strips, stuffed mushrooms, olives, guacamole, basil pesto, gherkins, sun-dried tomatoes, marinated vegetables with bread and crackers.

🕐 Tue–Sun 11am–late
🖐 L NZ$25, D NZ$55, W NZ$35

HMS KING'S
80 Tay Street, Invercargill
Tel 03-218 3443
A traditional New Zealand fish restaurant decked out like a ship, King's is popular with

families and serves fresh, locally caught seafood such as Bluff oysters, crayfish and whitebait. The cooking style is simple, and many of the dishes are fried. Seafood chowder is a speciality and there is a children's menu.

🕐 Mon–Fri 11.30–3, Sat–Sun 5–10
🖐 L NZ$16, D NZ$40, W NZ$20

ZOOKEEPER'S CAFÉ
50 Tay Street, Invercargill
Tel 03-218 3373
A funky café and bar with 'wild' décor and a laid-back atmosphere, Zookeeper's has

excellent coffee, and is a good place for a casual lunch.

🕐 Daily 10am–late
🖐 L NZ$20, D NZ$35, W NZ$30

MANDEVILLE

THE MOTH RESTAURANT AND BAR
Old Mandeville Airfield, SH94, Mandeville
Tel 03-208 9662
www.themoth.co.nz
On the Gore to Milford highway, and next to an air museum, The Moth is adorned with aviation memorabilia. The food is fresh and simply presented, with home-made bread, and the menu includes roast chicken breast, lamb rump seared in mint oil, spicy BBQ pork loin and poached blue cod. Leave space for desserts such as dessert pizza of the day (at the chef's whim) and berry jelly pannacotta.

🕐 Nov–end Apr daily 10am–late; May–end Oct Tue–Sun 10am–late
🖐 L NZ$30, D NZ$50, W NZ$25

MOERAKI

FLEURS PLACE
The Old Jetty, Moeraki
Tel 03-439 4480
www.fleursplace.com
This quirky restaurant on the waterfront is built from demolition materials and specialises in fresh fish straight from Moeraki Bay fishing boats. The blackboard menu offers blue cod, dory, moki, blue nose, gurnard, sole, flounder, grouper, crayfish, mussels and other delicacies such as titi (muttonbird). Reservations are essential.

🕐 Daily 9am–late
🖐 L NZ$25, D NZ$47, W NZ$25

OAMARU

CRITERION HOTEL
Corner of Tyne and Harbour streets, Oamaru
Tel 03-434 6247
www.criterion.net.nz
In the heart of the town's Harbour and Tyne Historic Precinct, this restored Victorian pub has hand-pumped ales, boutique beers and lots of atmosphere. The food is suitably traditional, with beef hotpot, pies, roasts and 'bangers and mash' (sausage and mashed potato). You can also stay overnight in Victorian-themed rooms. If you are inspired to join your hosts in Victorian dress, costumes are available.

🕐 Mon–Wed 12–9.30, Thu 12–11, Fri, Sat 12–12, Sun 12–8
🖐 L NZ$15, D NZ$50, W NZ$18

QUEENSTOWN

THE BATHHOUSE CAFÉ AND RESTAURANT
15 Marine Parade, Queenstown
Tel 03-442 5625
www.bathhouse.co.nz
This was the original Victorian bath house on the beach, and it retains its period charm. You can come for breakfast, lunch, afternoon tea or dinner. The menu is small. You can eat simply with an omelette, miso soup or waffles. For lunch there are crispy duck dumplings, roast lamb rump and chocolate truffles. By dinner time it's dishes like roulade of local wild rabbit with spinach, red rice risotto and Canterbury goat's cheese.

🕐 Tue–Sun 10am–late
🖐 L NZ$30, D NZ$80, W NZ$26

THE COW
Cow Lane, Queenstown
Tel 03-442 8588
The Cow—formerly a milking shed—is cramped but full of character. A Queenstown institution, it specialises in pizza and pasta, and serves up simple, hearty fare at reasonable prices. It's the place to go after a hard day's skiing when you need some tasty fuel to replenish your energy. You can expect to wait for a table, and may be seated at a large table with people you don't know.

🕐 Daily 12–late
🖐 L NZ$25, D NZ$35, W NZ$25

DUX DE LUX
14 Church Street, Queenstown
Tel 03-442 9688
In a heritage stone cottage in central Queenstown, this atmospheric pub and café was formerly McNeills Cottage Brewery. It still offers a range of boutique beers, plus vegetarian and seafood dishes.

🕐 Daily from 11am
🖐 L NZ$20, D NZ$60, W NZ$27

GANTLEY'S
Arthur's Point Road, Queenstown
Tel 03-442 8999
www.gantleys.co.nz
Gantley's is 7km (4 miles) on the road to Arrowtown, and was a wayside inn during the 1860s gold rushes. The rough stone walls of the building contrast romantically with deep red curtains, leather sofas, white tablecloths and

candle-light. The restaurant is known for both its food and its wine, with an international list of about 300 vintages. The food is simple but can be exciting: pears are poached in Pinot gris and saffron and served with a chai jelly and lemongrass and ginger ice cream.

🕐 Daily 6.30–9pm
🍽 D NZ$75, W NZ$38

RANFURLY

DANSEYS PASS INN
781 Kyeburn Diggings Road, Danseys Pass, Ranfurly
Tel 03-444 9048
www.danseyspass.co.nz
Built in 1862, during the height of the Otago gold rush, the inn is now quite isolated but retains much of its character. You can stay overnight, or stop for breakfast, lunch or dinner. Lunches tend to be from a blackboard menu; dinners are à la carte, with a wine list promoting Central Otago wines. Typical dishes include beef fillet with avocado béarnaise, salmon poached in vodka, and venison with morello cherries.

🕐 Daily 8am–9pm
🍽 L NZ$22, D NZ$45, W NZ$32

ST. BATHANS

THE VULCAN HOTEL
1670 Loop Road, St. Bathans, Oturehua
Tel 03-447 3629
When gold fever was at its height, there were 14 hotels in St. Bathans. Now there is only one: the Vulcan, a mud-brick building dating from 1882. The walls are thick and the place is full of charm. As well as visitors, you're likely to meet some characterful locals propping up the bar. You can get bar snacks here and 'Devonshire' teas, and the hotel bistro serves a blend of traditional New Zealand with Polynesian, French, Italian and local ingredients. If you don't

mind basic accommodation, you can also stay the night.

🕐 Daily 8am–11pm
🍽 L NZ$15, D NZ$35, W NZ$28

STEWART ISLAND

SOUTH SEA HOTEL
Half Moon Bay, Oban, Stewart Island
Tel 03-219 1059
www.stewart-island.co.nz
Right on the Oban waterfront, this is a typical country hotel and a popular meeting place for the locals. Don't expect sophistication, but you can get a good taste of the island from the restaurant, which serves

locally sourced oysters, mussels, salmon and scampi. The chowder is a speciality and the titi (mutton bird) is baked to order.

🕐 Daily 7am–9pm
🍽 L NZ$20, D NZ$35, W NZ$18

TE ANAU

REDCLIFF CAFÉ AND BAR
12 Mokonui Street, Te Anau
Tel 03-249 7431
The Redcliff is a casual and intimate café with inside-outside dining and a convivial bar, set in a rustic cottage a block from the lake. It's also a popular venue for live entertainment. The menu focuses on fresh produce, with as much attention paid to the vegetables as the meat dishes. You can eat as simply as breads with spreads and pasta to hearty lamb and venison dishes, and finish with crème brûlée.

🕐 Daily 5–9.30pm
🍽 D NZ$45, W NZ$25

WANAKA

MISSY'S KITCHEN
Level 1, 80 Ardmore Street, Wanaka
Tel 03-443 5099
www.missyskitchen.co.nz
Missy's has expansive views over the lake and mountains and a sophisticated city

CARDRONA HOTEL
Crown Range Road, Wanaka
Tel 03-443 8153
www.cardronahotel.co.nz
Today it's hard to imagine Cardrona as the thriving gold-rush town it was in 1870, with four hotels, European and Chinese stores, butcheries, a blacksmith and a baker. The Cardrona Hotel and the adjoining buildings are all that remain. The pub is full of atmosphere and you can stay in the modernised units. It's a great place to stop for an après-ski mulled wine, and in summer there's a garden with a children's playground. The restaurant serves an à la carte menu and regional and local wines.

🕐 Daily 11.30am–late
🍽 L NZ$25, D NZ$45, W NZ$25

atmosphere. The food is modern Pacific Rim, with dishes such as Marlborough mussels fried with chilli jam, pickled carrot, coriander and mung bean salad; red braised pork belly, hot and sour Savoy cabbage salad, crispy shallots and garlic and steamed rice; round off the meal with Belgian chocolate soufflé with vanilla bean ice cream. The beverage list includes a good range of wines, beers, whisky and speciality teas, and the sommelier is knowledgeable.

🕐 Daily 4pm–late
🍽 D NZ$46, W NZ$30

SARGOODS RESTAURANT
Edgewater Resort, Sargood Drive, Wanaka
Tel 03-443 8311
www.edgewater.co.nz
You can dine in the restaurant or outdoors with spectacular Wanaka views. The menu includes merino lamb, seared wild goat loin, three-tomato risotto and house-smoked Akaroa salmon pasta—but since chef Andrew Spiegel focuses on seasonal New Zealand ingredients, this can change.

🕐 Daily 7am–late
🍽 L NZ$25, D NZ$60, W NZ$35

EATING

STAYING IN NEW ZEALAND

New Zealand offers a wide choice of accommodation, from
backpackers' hostels to luxury lodges in stunning locations.
Whichever part of the country you are in, you will rarely end up
without a bed for the night, but book ahead in the high season
(November to end February). To encounter real Kiwi hospitality,
try to stay in a home or farmhouse. Visitor information
offices can reserve all kinds of accommodation.

HOTELS
The hotels in New Zealand usually fall into
one of four categories:

Large luxury hotels: There are a number of
large, modern, luxury (four- or five-star) hotels
in the main cities. Most are part of major
international or trans-Tasman chains (▷ 272)
and prices range from about NZ$250 to
NZ$500 per night. All rooms are equipped
with the latest technology, including laptop
plug-in ports and satellite TV. Restaurants and
leisure facilities such as swimming pools, spas
and gyms are standard.

Standard chain hotels: Available in all the
major cities and most of the larger provincial
towns, they charge rates between about
NZ$175 to NZ$300, but they have regular
weekend or off-season deals. Again, most
have in-house restaurants and additional
facilities such as a heated pool.

Boutique hotels: Often used to enhance
marketing, the 'boutique' label should still
ensure that the hotel is small, luxurious and
offers something a little different, be it in
décor, location or service. The owners may
live on site and extend a personal welcome.
Very often the rooms or suites are themed.
Although most boutique hotels are urban,
you will find the boutique label applied to
anything from a modern country home to a
heritage building in a city suburb. Dinner is
often available by arrangement. On average,
double rooms cost from NZ$175 to NZ$400.

Traditional pubs and budget hotels: Many
rural towns have retained their traditional
old wooden hotels. Some of these may
look grand from the outside, but invariably

the interior doesn't match up. A basic,
comfortable room can often be found, but
there may be late-night noise from the bar.
Prices are usually pitched somewhere
between a standard backpackers' hostel
and a basic motel unit (from NZ$20 to
NZ$60).

LODGES
From heritage buildings furnished with
antiques to purpose-built sporting retreats
with fishing, hunting or golf, lodges are usually
highly luxurious and often in outstanding rural
locations. They may have up to 20 suites,
often in self-contained units in secluded, park-
like grounds, with opulent reception rooms in
the main building. The price usually includes
dinner, bed and breakfast, and extras such
as pre-dinner drinks. Personal guiding,
individuality and good food are assured. Prices
range from NZ$200 to NZ$2,600 per night.
● www.lodgesofnz.co.nz.

BED-AND-BREAKFAST (B&B)
This covers a wide variety of hosted accommodation, from guesthouses to rooms in
private homes, and can consist of anything
from a basic double room with shared
bathroom and cereal for breakfast to a
luxurious room with private bathroom and full
breakfast. Again prices vary, with the standard
cost being around NZ$100 to NZ$150 for a
double room. When looking at prices bear in
mind a full breakfast costs at least NZ$12 in a
café or restaurant. Many B&Bs also offer
evening meals at extra cost, but advance
notice is usually required.

HOMESTAYS AND FARMSTAYS
These give you the chance to stay in a family
home and mix with your hosts. Breakfast is

usually included, and an optional evening meal may be available on request.

Farmstays offer the additional attraction of a taste of rural life. You are welcome to help around the farm, and children are particularly welcome. Rates for both homestays and farmstays are comparable with B&B prices.

● New Zealand Farm Holidays, based near Auckland, produce a free catalogue listing about 300 establishments, tel 09-412 9649, **www.**nzfarmholidays.co.nz.

● For farmstay options in Southland contact Western Southland Farm Hosting Group, tel 03-225 8608, **www.**farmhost.co.nz.

● Visitor information offices can help you find homestays or farmstays, and the Tourism New Zealand website (**www.**newzealand.com) also has a detailed listing of nationwide farmstays.

HOSTELS AND BACKPACKER ORGANISATIONS

As a popular destination for the independent traveller or backpacker, New Zealand is well served with hostels and budget accommodation.

The Youth Hostels Association NZ (part of the international YHA network) runs 64 hostels, from modern, purpose-built establishments in the cities to ex-churches. Many have double rooms, some with private bathroom. You can expect free linen, bedding and pillows, adequately equipped kitchens, laundry facilities, games room or TV room, secure storage facilities, phones and the internet. Prices vary from NZ$12 to NZ$20 for a dormitory bed, depending on season, and NZ$22 to NZ$30 per adult for doubles. Membership is available from **www.**yha.org.nz. The annual fee is NZ$40 (NZ$30 for renewals). YHA membership cards also entitle you to a number of discounts, including up to 30 per cent off air and bus travel. Other organisations include:

● VIP group, PO Box 60177, Titirangi, Auckland, tel 09-816 8903, **www.**vip.co.nz.

● Budget Backpacker Hostels Ltd (BBH), Foley Towers, 208 Kilmore Street, Christchurch, tel 03-379 3014, **www.**bbh.co.nz.

● Nomads, Travellers' Contact Point, 87 Queen Street, Auckland, tel 09-300 7197, **www.**travellersnz.com.

MOTORCAMPS AND CABINS

New Zealand is very well served with motorcamps (also known as holiday parks), where there are both powered sites for motor vehicles and tent pitches for campers. Camps are usually equipped with laundry facilities, hot showers and kitchens. Larger parks may also have a pool, games and sports facilities, a general store and café.

Motorcamps often also have a range of cabins, units or tourist apartments for rent. Cabins are the most basic, with little except a bed, sink and electric supply, but some also have a small kitchen. They cost between NZ$35 and NZ$60 for two. Units and apartments are similar to motels, being fully self-contained, some with multiple rooms. They vary in price but rarely exceed NZ$100 per night (for two people), with an additional charge of NZ$12 to NZ$15 per extra person.

● The Top Ten chain of motorcamps has a good reputation and a 'Club Card' scheme offering a 10 per cent discount, tel 03-377 9900, **www.**topparks.co.nz.

CAMPSITES

The Department of Conservation (DoC; **www.**doc.govt.nz) manages more than 200 vehicle-accessible campsites all over the country, many in prime locations. They are typically basic, provide clean running water, toilet facilities and barbecue areas, but rarely allow open fires. Sites in the national parks have well-equipped huts. The camping fee is NZ$2 to NZ$10 a night. Fees for huts are anything from NZ$5 to NZ$40 per night, depending on category and location. If you plan to use DoC campsites and huts, book well in advance.

SELF-CATERING

Holiday homes of all kinds, including tiny country cottages known as *baches*, are available for rent. *Bach* is pronounced 'batch', and is a shortened version of 'bachelor pad'. Most self-catering accommodation operates on a minimum weekend or week-long stay basis. Look in the travel or house-rental sections of national newspapers. Regional visitor offices may also be able to help. Motels are the choice of most New Zealanders. They range from the utilitarian to luxurious condos with a spa pool, but have at least a shower, kitchen facilities and a TV, and are usually clean and comfortable. Studio units cost about NZ$80 to NZ$100, one-bedroom units NZ$90 to NZ$120 and suites are available for an additional charge for each adult. Many of the larger motel complexes have a restaurant and a swimming pool, plus spas. Most motels offer breakfast, delivered to the door at extra charge.

RESERVATIONS AND PAYING

It is advisable to reserve at least three days in advance during the high season (November to March) and further ahead during New Zealand's summer holidays (from Christmas to the end of January). Payment is generally straightforward, with most establishments taking all major credit cards through EFTPOS (Electronic Funds Transfer at Point of Sale). Cash is also readily accepted, and recommended at B&Bs and homestays.

QUALMARK

Qualmark is New Zealand tourism's official symbol of quality, instigated to encourage high standards of hospitality and service. Lists of Qualmark-rated places to stay, graded from two to five stars, are available from visitor information offices and AA Travel Centres.

HOTEL CHAINS

Name of Hotel Chain	Description	Website	Telephone Numbers
Accor	The world's largest hotel group, encompassing the All Seasons, Ibis, Mercure, Novotel and Sofitel brand names. Full online search and booking service. 24 properties.	www.accorhotels.com.au	0800 444 422
Golden Chain	New Zealand-based, mid-range chain with hotels, motels and resorts nationwide. Offers two pre-booked or open-dated pass schemes or with a B&B 'mix and match'. 90 properties.	www.goldenchain.co.nz	0800-80 GOLDEN
Grand Hotels International	Asia-based chain with hotels in Auckland, Christchurch and Wellington. Full range of options including units, studios and apartments. 4 properties.	www.ghihotels.com	
Heritage	New Zealand-based group with luxury standard and apartment properties available in all major places. Online booking service. 9 properties.	www.heritagehotels.co.nz	0800 368 888
Intercontinental	Expensive international group including the Centra, Holiday Inn, Crowne Plaza and Park Royal brands. Properties in Auckland and Queenstown. 7 properties.	www.ichotelsgroup.com	0800 154 181
Langham	Expensive resort-style international hotel group with one hotel in Auckland. 1 property.	www.langhamhotels.com	09-379 5132
Mainstay	New Zealand-based, independently owned hotel chain. Wide variety of 3- to 4-star properties nationwide offering standard room types and self-contained apartments. 41 properties.	www.mainstay.co.nz	03-358 7900 0800 624 646
Millennium/ Copthorne/ Kingsgate	Chain with properties in all the main places around New Zealand. Regular special deals and weekend packages. 21 properties.	www.millenniumhotels.com	09-309 4420
Scenic Circle	New Zealand-based group with a diverse range of properties throughout the main places. Online booking service. 15 properties.	www.scenic-circle.co.nz	03-357 1919 0800 696 963

AUCKLAND, NORTHLAND AND COROMANDEL

AUCKLAND

AACHEN HOUSE BOUTIQUE HOTEL
39 Market Road, Remuera, Auckland
Tel 09-520 2329
www.aachenhouse.co.nz
Aachen House is a five-star luxury B&B hotel in the chic suburb of Remuera. The grand 1904 house is superbly furnished with antiques and porcelain. Guest rooms look out over tranquil gardens and are decorated in period style, with king-size or twin beds.

🍷 NZ$345–NZ$590, inc pre-dinner drinks and gourmet breakfast
ℹ️ 5 rooms, 3 suites
Ⓢ Ⓟ Off-street 🚗 Take Market Road exit (exit 432) signposted from SH1 Southern Motorway

CITY CENTRAL HOTEL
Corner of Wellesley and Albert streets, Auckland
Tel 09-307 3388
www.citycentralhotel.co.nz
A no-nonsense hotel, the City Central is well placed, clean and comfortable. There is a choice of rooms, some

sleeping up to five people, but all have TV, tea-making facilities and telephone, and some have air-conditioning. The standard rooms are very small. Continental and cooked breakfasts are extra.

🍷 NZ$99–NZ$160
ℹ️ 104 rooms (25 non-smoking)
Ⓢ Except standard rooms
Ⓟ Parking available in Crowne Plaza

ESPLANADE HOTEL
1 Victoria Road, Devonport, Auckland
Tel 09-445 1291
www.esplanadehotel.co.nz
Ten minutes by ferry from the Central Business District (CBD), this boutique hotel is one of Auckland's oldest, built in 1903. It dominates Devonport's promenade and has fine harbour views. Rooms are spacious, with satellite TV and tea-making facilities. A

penthouse apartment has two bedrooms, two bathrooms, a lounge and fully equipped kitchen. The smart Esplanade restaurant and the more relaxed Mecca café both serve meals throughout the day.

🍷 NZ$210–NZ$560, inc breakfast
ℹ️ 15 rooms, 2 suites, 1 apartment
Ⓢ
🚌 On main bus route from Takapuna
⛴ Ferries half-hourly from Auckland

GREAT PONSONBY BED AND BREAKFAST
30 Ponsonby Terrace, Ponsonby, Auckland
Tel 09-376 5989
www.ponsonbybnb.co.nz
The Great Ponsonby is a stylish, century-old villa in a quiet cul-de-sac, a short stroll away from 'funky' Ponsonby Road. Brightly decorated rooms and self-contained studios are equipped with direct-dial phones and modems, coffee plungers, wine glasses, satellite TV, CD players, irons and de-mist mirrors—among other thoughtful touches. Bicycles, laundry facilities and beach towels are available on request. There's even a friendly dog and cat.

🍷 NZ$180–NZ$330, inc breakfast
ℹ️ 5 rooms, 6 studios, 1 penthouse
Ⓢ Ⓟ Off-street
🚌 Near main bus route from CBD

HILTON HOTEL
Princes Wharf, 147 Quay Street, Auckland
Tel 09-978 2000
www.hilton.com
Completed in 2002, the Hilton sits in an enviable position, occupying a wharf in the harbour close to the heart of the city. The accommodation is first class, with custom woven carpets, contemporary furniture and spacious bathrooms.

Rooms have king-size or twin beds, private decks and internet access. Luxury suites have 180-degree views. There are also serviced apartments, a stylish restaurant, White (▷ 253), a cocktail bar, fitness facility and shops. Breakfast costs NZ$25–NZ$35.

🍷 NZ$461–NZ$1,142
ℹ️ 160 rooms, 6 suites, 35 apartments
Ⓢ 🏊 Outdoor 🏋️ Ⓟ Valet

COROMANDEL TOWN

COROMANDEL HOLIDAY PARK
636 Rings Road, Coromandel
Tel 07-866 8830
www.coromandelholidaypark.co.nz
Coromandel Holiday Park is set in 1.4ha (3.5 acres) of parkland just five minutes' walk from Coromandel town. You can be a traditional camper in a tent or caravan, or stay in a fairly basic cabin or more upmarket motel room. Facilities include barbecues, a playground, trampolines and a games room, and fish-cleaning facilities for when you catch your own supper.

🏕️ Tent sites from NZ$20, powered sites NZ$24, cabins NZ$50, motel units NZ$75
ℹ️ 40 tent sites, 26 powered sites, 10 cabins, 6 motel units.
🏊 Outdoor
Ⓢ

STAYING

KARAMANA HOMESTEAD
84 Whangapoua Road,
Coromandel Town
Tel 07-866 7138
www.karamanahomestead.com
One of the oldest homes on the Coromandel Peninsula, dating from 1872, Karamana has three guest rooms, named French, Victorian and Colonial and furnished accordingly.

There is also a two-bedroom cottage. Devonshire teas are a speciality. Breakfast includes fresh fruit and pancakes.

🛏 NZ$150–NZ$170
ℹ 3 rooms, 1 cottage
🚭 🅿 Off-street

POTTERY LANE COTTAGE
15 Pottery Lane, Coromandel Town
Tel 07-866 7171
www.geocities.com/potterylanecottage
These two cottages, plus a self-contained loft in the main house, are in a peaceful garden, a short stroll from the village. One cottage has two bedrooms (a twin and a double); the other is smaller and open-plan with a queen-size bed and a single bed. The wooden, single-storey buildings are simply furnished. Breakfast on request (NZ$5).

🛏 NZ$100–NZ$140
ℹ 2 cottages
🚭 🅿 Off-street

GREAT BARRIER ISLAND
OASIS LODGE
Tryphena, Great Barrier Island
Tel 09-429 0021
www.barrieroasis.co.nz
Set in a vineyard, this large homestead offers spacious, open-plan rooms with modern décor, TV and video, a bar and fridge, and outdoor decks overlooking the garden. There is also a self-contained chalet sleeping up to six. Diving, fishing, kayaking and horse-riding are available close by. A small restaurant serves international dishes.

STAYING

THE CHURCH ACCOMMODATION
87 Beach Road, Hahei,
Coromandel Peninsula
Tel 07-866 3533
www.thechurchhahei.co.nz

Lovely gardens surround this former village church, which has been turned into a restaurant. Accommodation is in separate studio units or self-contained cottages, all with french doors leading onto verandas. Studios and cottages have a queen-size bed and window-seat bed, refrigerator and tea-making facilities. Self-contained cottages also have a separate living area, kitchen and TV; two have an open fire.

🕐 Closed Aug
🛏 NZ$95–NZ$150, inc breakfast; additional adults NZ$20 extra
ℹ 4 studio units, 11 cottages
🚭 🅿 Off-street
🚗 37km (23 miles) southeast of Whitianga: turn off SH 25 at Whenuakite. No public transport

🛏 NZ$250, inc breakfast
ℹ 3 rooms, 1 chalet
🚭 🅿 Off-street
⛴ Ferry (4.5 hours) from Auckland or by air

KERIKERI
THE SUMMER HOUSE BED AND BREAKFAST
424 Kerikeri Road, Kerikeri
Tel 09-407 4294
www.thesummerhouse.co.nz
Subtropical gardens and a citrus orchard add to the appeal of this popular B&B, only two minutes' walk from Kerikeri. The two rooms have antique beds, while the self-contained suite is contemporary in style, with a South Pacific theme, including Maori weavings. Excellent breakfasts might include home-made bread and fruit from the orchard.

🛏 NZ$225–NZ$295, inc breakfast
ℹ 2 rooms, 1 suite
🅿 Off-street 🚭
🚗 2km (1 mile) off State Highway 10 on Kerikeri Rd. Airport pick-up available

MANGONUI
CARNEVAL
360 State Highway 10, Cable Bay,
Mangonui
Tel 09-406 1012
www.carneval.co.nz
This modern B&B, on a hill overlooking Doubtless Bay, provides a fine base to relax, or explore the Aupori Peninsula. The rooms, with king-size beds, refrigerators, ironing, tea-making facilities and private bathrooms, have either garden or ocean views. The Swiss-German owners have created a fine marriage of European and Kiwi hospitality and, as a former chef, Roly can ensure some memorable cooking. A sauna and log-burning fire add to the appeal.

🛏 NZ$140–NZ$170
ℹ 2 suites
🚭
🚗 Just after Mangonui on SH10

MATAURI BAY
HUNTAWAY LODGE
Wainui Road, Te Ngaere Bay, Matauri Bay
Tel 09-405 1611
www.huntawaylodge.com
You'll need your own transport or a helicopter to reach this exclusive lodge, in a superb setting overlooking the ocean and three secluded beaches. The three stylish guest rooms are named after them, and each has its own deck. Food is a speciality, with a three-course dinner available for NZ$90 per person. Activities include fishing, diving and golf.

🛏 NZ$375–NZ$425, inc breakfast
ℹ 3 rooms
🚭 🅿 Off-street
🚗 Take the Matauri Bay turnoff SH10 and follow the signs to Te Ngaere Bay. Veer left at the letter boxes

OHAEAWAI
LUDBROOK HOUSE
State Highway 1, Ohaeawai
Tel 09-405 9846
www.ludbrook.co.nz
The Ludbrook family have been farming their 420ha (1,037-acre) sheep and cattle property halfway between Paihia and the Kauri Coast since 1860. They welcome visitors for dinner, B&B at the

1920s homestead. Decorated in period style, Ludbrook House has four simple but comfortable guest rooms with private bathrooms. Chris Ludbrook makes preserves and cakes commercially, and many guests gravitate to the kitchen to chat as meals are prepared.

🍽 From NZ$760 per person, inc breakfast and dinner
🛏 4 rooms
🅿 Off-street
🚗 On SH1 near the junction with SH12

PAIHIA
ALLEGRA HOUSE
39 Bayview Road, Paihia
Tel 09-402 7932
www.allegra.co.nz
In the heart of Paihia, with fine views across the bay to Russell and beyond, this modern home offers two B&B rooms or a spacious apartment. Both rooms have TV, tea-making facilities and a fridge, and Internet access is available. The owners are fluent in German and French. Minimum two-night stay required.

🍽 NZ$105–NZ$220
🛏 2 rooms, 1 apartment
🚭 ♿ 🅿 Off-street
🚗 Turn left after the wharf and off Marsden Road onto Bayview Road. Follow Bayview to its terminus

COPTHORNE HOTEL AND RESORT BAY OF ISLANDS
Tau Henare Drive, Paihia
Tel 09-402 7411
www.copthornebayofislands.co.nz
Right on the waterfront, set in spacious grounds within the Waitangi National Reserve, this hotel has modern rooms with standard facilities. There is an in-house café restaurant serving Pacific Rim food. The hotel is well set up for children.

🍽 NZ$139–NZ$515
🛏 102 rooms (88 non-smoking), 7 suites
🅿 Off-street
🚗 2km (1 mile) past Paihia town centre. Follow signs on Marsden Road to the Waitangi Reserve; hotel is immediately right after the bridge

PUKENUI
PUKENUI LODGE
Corner of Main Highway North and Wharf Road, Pukenui
Tel 09-409 8837
www.pukenuilodge.co.nz
Close to Cape Reinga and Ninety Mile Beach, overlooking Houhora Harbour, Pukenui

SPECIAL IN RUSSELL
PUKEMATU LODGE
Flagstaff Hill, Russell
Tel 09-403 8500
www.pukematulodge.co.nz
Perched high on the hill, this modern B&B has spectacular views to Waitangi and Paihia. The hosts go the extra mile to make sure your stay is memorable. The stylish suites are furnished in recycled native wood, with a sofa, fresh flowers, robes, fruit and organic bathroom products. Breakfast is served on the deck. Evening meals, including a Maori *hangi* barbecue, are available on request.

🍽 NZ$295, inc breakfast
🛏 2 suites
🚭 🅿 Off-street
🚗 10km (6 miles) from Opua vehicle ferry and 1km (0.5 miles) from the middle of Russell

Lodge has tidy, self-contained queen, family and studio motel units with their own kitchen and bathroom, satellite TV, in-house video, telephone and electric blankets. Breakfast is available (from NZ$8.50).

🍽 NZ$89–NZ$119
🛏 9 motel units, hostel
🏊 Outdoor 🅿 Off-street

RUSSELL
DUKE OF MARLBOROUGH
Waterfront, Russell
Tel 09-403 7829
www.theduke.co.nz
The 'Duke', right on the water-front, holds New Zealand's oldest pub licence, granted in 1840. The bay views are stunning. Downstairs is a lounge with a log fire, the bar and an à la carte restaurant specialising in local seafood. The price includes Continental breakfast.

🍽 NZ$195–NZ$550, inc breakfast
🛏 25 rooms, 6 waterfront suites
🚭 🅿 Off-street
🚢 2km (1 mile) from Paihia by passenger ferry, or 20km (13 miles) by car and vehicle ferry via Opua

WAIHEKE ISLAND
ONETANGI BEACH APARTMENTS
27 The Strand, Onetangi
09-372 0003/0800-663 826
www.onetangi.co.nz
On the 2km-long (1-mile) Onetangi Beach, close to all facilities. The complex has

spa pools and a sauna, and kayaks are available. There are studios and beachfront and courtyard options.

🍽 NZ$100–NZ$350
🛏 8 units
🚭
🚢 Ferry from Auckland

POUHUTUKAWA RETREAT
40 Tiri Road, Oneroa
Tel 09-372 8219
www.pohutukawaretreat.com
The Pouhutukawa Retreat offers four modern self-contained chalets with sea and rural views, close to the ferry and walking distance from beaches, shops and restaurants.

🍽 From NZ$180
🛏 4 chalets
🚭
🚢 Ferry from Auckland

WHITIANGA
VILLA TOSCANA
Ohuka Park, Whitianga, Coromandel Peninsula
Tel 07 866 2293
www.villatoscana.co.nz
Villa Toscana is a grand villa high on a hill 4km (2.5 miles) north of Whitianga, surrounded by native bush. Lavishly furnished with Carrara marble and antique furniture, the suite has its own entrance,

two bedrooms, a granite kitchen, a large bathroom, an outdoor spa pool and a deck with views across the bay. Breakfast is provided. Gourmet Italian cuisine (dinner NZ$120) and an extensive wine cellar add to the appeal.

🍽 NZ$440–NZ$640
🛏 1 suite
🚭 🚭
🅿 Off-street
🚗 Take the main road past the airfield, turn left at the beach, left onto Centennial Drive, left onto Rimu Street and straight into Ohuka Park. The entrance is 1km (0.5 miles) on the right

STAYING

CENTRAL NORTH ISLAND

CAMBRIDGE

MAUNGATAUTARI LODGE

844 Maungatautari Road, Lake Karapiro, Cambridge
Tel 07-827 2220
www.malodge.com
Purpose built in 2002, this

luxury boutique hotel is on a 16ha (40-acre) stud farm. The spacious, sumptuously furnished suites in the main building and three villas next door all have super-king beds, double spa baths and private balconies or terraces with views of the gardens and Lake Karapiro. The four-course dinner features home-grown and organic produce. Mini-golf, horseback-riding, massage and beauty therapies are available.
🖐 NZ$630–NZ$1,030, inc breakfast, pre-dinner drinks and dinner
🛏 5 suites, 3 villas
Ⓢ Ⓕ 🏊 Outdoor Ⓟ
🚗 9km (6 miles) south of Cambridge

DAWSON FALLS

DAWSON FALLS TOURIST LODGE

Manaia Road, Dawson Falls
Tel 06-765 5457
www.dawson-falls.co.nz
The Alpine-Swiss style lodge is set in native bush on the slopes of Mount Taranaki/Egmont, in the heart of Egmont National Park. Rooms are furnished with hand-crafted furniture. A bar, with a log fire and a restaurant are added attractions.

🖐 NZ$150
🛏 11
Ⓢ 🖥 Ⓟ
🚗 Accessed from the north via Opunake (SH45) or Stratford (SH3), or from the south via Manaia (SH45)

GISBORNE

ONE ORANGE

98 Wairere Road, Wainui Beach, Gisborne
Tel 06-868 8062
www.oneorange.co.nz
This self-contained 'designer apartment' right next to the beach in Wainui encompasses a studio apartment and king-size bedroom that can be booked separately or in combination. Both are fresh, modern and minimalist in design, with leather furniture and a well-equipped kitchen. Food-and-wine-matching dinners and trout-fishing trips are a speciality. Two nights minimum.
🖐 NZ$225, inc breakfast
🛏 1 room, 1 studio apartment
Ⓢ Ⓕ Ⓟ
🚗 On the right just past Wainui, 8km (5 miles) north of Gisborne

HAMILTON

NOVOTEL TAINUI HOTEL

7 Alma Street, Hamilton
Tel 07-838 1366
www.accorhotels.co.nz
Centrally located in the Central Business District (CBD), on the banks of the Waikato River, the four-star Tainui is Hamilton's premier hotel. Some rooms have river views, and all have internet access, a safe and ironing facilities. The restaurant has indoor and outdoor dining,

and the hotel offers a special package in conjunction with SKYCITY Hamilton Casino.
🖐 NZ$135–NZ$334
🛏 177 rooms (130 non-smoking), including 4 suites
Ⓢ Ⓕ Ⓟ Valet

HAVELOCK NORTH

MANGAPAPA PETIT HOTEL

466 Napier Road, Havelock North
Tel 06-878 3234
www.mangapapa.co.nz
Mangapapa Petit Hotel, a luxury hotel in a grand country home 3km (2 miles) from Havelock North, is surrounded by 9ha (22 acres) of orchards and manicured gardens. The rooms are opulently furnished in a blend of traditional and contemporary, with meticulous attention to detail. Guests can indulge in a four-course dinner matched with local wines, play tennis and rent bicycles.

🖐 NZ$306–NZ$2,300, inc breakfast
🛏 12 rooms, 5 suites
Ⓢ Ⓕ 🏊 Outdoor Ⓟ Off-road

OLEA COTTAGES

101 Ru Collin Road, Havelock North
Tel 06-879 7674
www.oleacottages.co.nz
These two functional, modern cottages occupy a peaceful rural setting in the heart of Hawke's Bay wine country. One cottage has two bedrooms and a pull-out couch; the other has one double bedroom. Both have well-equipped kitchens with dishwasher, satellite TVs and CD player. Complimentary breakfast supplies are provided the first two mornings, as are fresh flowers, local wine and fruit.
🖐 NZ$220–NZ$230 inc breakfast (surcharge of NZ$30 for single-night stays)
🛏 2 cottages
Ⓢ Ⓟ

KATIKATI

FANTAIL LODGE

117 Rea Road, Katikati
Tel 07-549 1581
www.fantaillodge.co.nz
This popular country lodge estate offers a fine base from which to explore the Bay of

STAYING

Plenty and the Coromandel Peninsula. Set in beautiful rural surroundings, it has luxury suite accommodation with lounge, bedroom, dressing room and bathroom, and self-contained two-bedroom villas. Additional attractions are the restaurant, in-house spa complex and informative eco-tours of the region.

🖐 NZ$356–NZ$394, inc breakfast
ℹ️ 6 suites, 2 villas
🔲 🏊 Outdoor 🅿️
🚗 35km (22 miles) north of Tauranga

NAPIER

COUNTY HOTEL
Browning Street, Napier
Tel 06-835 7800
www.countyhotel.co.nz

This Edwardian hotel in the middle of town was one of the few buildings to survive the 1931 earthquake. Restored in 1995, it has 18 spacious suites named after New Zealand birds, ranging from standard double to two bedrooms with private lounge, spa bath and balcony. All rooms have satellite TV and internet connection. The hotel also has a popular restaurant, Chambers (▷ 256) and bar. Parking is available across the road.

🖐 NZ$286–NZ$900
ℹ️ 18 suites (all non-smoking)
🔲 🔲

MCHARDY HOUSE
11 Bracken Street, Napier
Tel 06-835 0605
www.mchardyhouse.com
High on a hill above Napier, McHardy House has been made into a luxury boutique hotel, with restored ornate stained glass, plasterwork ceilings and billiard room of the former grand residence, and each suite and deluxe room is furnished with a different theme, using fine fabrics and antiques. The

owner is a chef, and a speciality is his four-course menu using local produce.

🖐 NZ$615–NZ$695, inc breakfast, aperitifs and dinner
ℹ️ 6 rooms
🔲 🏊 Outdoor 🅿️ Off-street
🚗 From the city centre turn right off Tennyson into Carlyle Street, then right into Chaucer Road S. Continue up hill, turn left onto Napier Terrace, right onto Chaucer Road N., right into George Street and right again into Bracken Street

NEW PLYMOUTH

THE NICE HOTEL
71 Brougham Street, New Plymouth
Tel 06-758 6423,
www.nicehotel.co.nz
Art and history are the themes of this offbeat boutique hotel in the 1850s former Redcoats Hospital building. Each room is named after a local landmark, such as Len Lye's Wind Wand on the waterfront. In addition to stylish design and contemporary artworks, the rooms include luxuries such as double spa baths and comfy armchairs. The award-winning Table restaurant is spacious and airy, with good Pacific Rim cuisine. Complimentary airport transfers are available.

🖐 NZ$225–NZ$280
ℹ️ / rooms, 1 suite
🔲 🅿️ Off-street

OHAKUNE

POWDERHORN CHATEAU
Corner of Mangawhero Terrace and Thames Street, Ohakune
Tel 06-385 8888
www.powderhorn.co.nz
The Alpine-style Powderhorn Chateau is a popular base for skiing in winter. Each of the 30 suites has a queen-size bed, a double sofa bed, a lounge suite and satellite TV. The Mansion apartment can sleep up to eight. There is babysitting, a small casino and internet access. Two restaurants—the ski chalet-style Matterhorn and more informal Powderkeg—are lively après-ski venues. The Lord of the Rings cast stayed here during filming.

🖐 NZ$165–NZ$215
ℹ️ 30 suites, 1 apartment
🔲 🏊 Indoor 🔲
🚗 At the northern end of the village, at the start of Mountain Road

SOLSCAPE
611 Wainui Road,
Raglan
Tel 07-825 8268
www.solscape.co.nz
If you are looking for something completely different, this really is the place to stay in Raglan. The owners have renovated an array of railway guard's vans with native rimu floors and ceilings as bright lodgings, arranged as dormitories or self-contained units. Two self-contained cottages with open fires are also available. The property enjoys fabulous views across the Tasman Sea and there is also a menagerie of animals.

🖐 NZ$58–NZ$135
ℹ️ 17 cabooses, 2 cottages
🔲
🚗 From Raglan follow the Wainui Road for 5.5km (3.5 miles)

ROTORUA

MILLENNIUM HOTEL ROTORUA
Corner of Eruera and Hinemaru streets, Rotorua
Tel 07-347 1234
www.millenniumhotels.co.nz
This popular chain hotel is located close to the Polynesian Spa. The modern rooms and suites have marble-floored bathrooms, direct-dial phones, ironing facilities, satellite TV and modem points. The nightly Maori cultural performance and hangi (feast) illustrates traditional myth and legend through song and dance. The restaurant has a wood-fired oven and is considered one of the city's best.

🖐 NZ$220–NZ$375
ℹ️ 227 rooms (120 non-smoking)
🔲 🔲 🔲 🏊 Indoor 🅿️

REGAL PALMS MOTOR LODGE
350 Fenton Street, Rotorua
Tel 07-350 3232
www.regalpalmsml.co.nz
Of the dozens of motels in Rotorua, the Regal Palms is one of the newest and best. Its classy décor and attention to detail have helped earn it a five-star rating. It has one- and two-bedroom suites and three serviced apartments, all with kitchen facilities and a spa

pool. Facilities also include a sauna, internet access, a bar, mini-golf, children's playground and barbecue area.

Ⓦ NZ$185–NZ$255
① 41 suites, 3 apartments
Ⓢ Ⓢ Ⓦ Ⓢ Outdoor Ⓟ
🚌 On the main bus route
🚗 2km (1 mile) south of the CBD

SOLITAIRE LODGE
Lake Tarawera, Rotorua
Tel 07-362 8208
www.solitairelodge.co.nz
The staff know how to look after their guests at this celebrated hideaway on the shores of Lake Tarawera. There are nine spacious, luxurious suites, some with spa, private deck and lake views. Adding to the appeal is a fine art collection and the innovative New Zealand cuisine.

Ⓦ NZ$1,280–NZ$1,990, inc breakfast and dinner
① 9 suites
Ⓢ Ⓢ
Ⓧ Helicopter access
🚗 20km (13 miles) south of the CBD

TAUPO

CABOOSE LODGE
100–102 Lake Terrace, Taupo
Tel 07-376 0116
www.taupocaboose.co.nz
In case something completely different takes your fancy, this hotel has an African rail safari theme. Built in a log-cabin style on the waterfront, it has standard double rooms with shower called Caboose Sleepers, larger Sleepers with full bathrooms, and three executive suites sleeping up to six. In-house facilities include spas, internet access, a lounge/bar with an open fire and a restaurant with ostrich on the menu. Fishing safaris are a speciality.

Ⓦ NZ$119–NZ$199
① 22 compartments, 28 sleepers, 1 suite
Ⓢ Ⓢ Outdoor Ⓟ
🚗 1km (0.5 mile) from Taupo CBD

SPECIAL IN TAUPO
HUKA LODGE
Huka Falls Road, Taupo
Tel 07-378 5791
www.hukalodge.com
Huka Lodge remains New Zealand's most popular luxury lodge. Hidden in parkland beside the Waikato River, it regularly hosts royalty and rock stars seeking privacy. The complex has a classic lodge feel with wood predominating, a library, roaring fire and deep armchairs. The suites offer every comfort, and cuisine is first-class.

Ⓦ NZ$1,790–NZ$4,250, inc breakfast, cocktails, dinner, airport transfer
① 20 suites
Ⓢ Ⓢ
Ⓧ Helicopter access
🚗 3km (2 miles) from Taupo CBD

WAIRAKEI RESORT
State Highway 1, Wairakei
Tel 07-374 8021/0800 RESORT
www.wairakei.co.nz
The resort, in the Wairakei Thermal Park, has a range of good facilities for sporty guests, with tennis, golf, squash and a gym, plus a spa, pool and sauna in which to relax afterwards. There is a wide variety of accommodation available, from standard rooms with a double and single bed to family villas, and air-conditioned executive suites with a separate lounge. All rooms have satellite TV, mini bar, hair dryer and tea-making facilities.

Ⓦ NZ$146–NZ$225
① 157 rooms, 9 suites and 15 villas (most non-smoking)
Ⓢ Ⓢ Ⓦ Ⓢ Outdoor
🚗 7km (4 miles) north of Taupo

TAURANGA

HARBOUR CITY MOTEL
50 Wharf Street, Tauranga
Tel 07-571 1435
www.taurangaharbourcity.co.nz

This classy motel is ideally located in the heart of Tauranga's shopping and café district. What strikes you most is its stylish design and the attention to detail. Modern furnishings and a minimalist décor make it seem like a chic boutique hotel. All rooms have spa baths. Harbour City also caters for children, with cots and high chairs provided free.

Ⓦ NZ$120–NZ$240
① 16 studios, 4 one-bedroom units
Ⓢ Ⓢ Ⓟ
🚗 4km (3 miles) southwest of the airport

WHAKAPAPA

THE CHATEAU TONGARIRO
Whakapapa Village, State Highway 48, Mount Ruapehu
Tel 07-892 3809
www.chateau.co.nz
Perhaps the most famous hotel on the North Island, the Chateau Tongariro provides traditional luxury in a grand location—Tongariro National Park. Whether for relaxing or as a base for skiing or trekking the Tongariro Crossing, it offers elegance in keeping with its age (built in 1929), including a restaurant, bar, café, pool and golf course. It's worth paying extra for a guaranteed mountain view.

Ⓦ NZ$180–NZ$1,000
① 95 rooms, 5 suites. Family units available in a separate building
Ⓢ Ⓢ Indoor Ⓟ
🚗 45km (28 miles) south of Turangi on SH48

SKOTEL ALPINE RESORT
Whakapapa Village, State Highway 48, Mount Ruapehu
Tel 07-892 3719
www.skotel.com
A low mountain chalet, with extensive views over Tongariro National Park, Skotel will appeal to budget-conscious visitors. With a restaurant and bar, lounge, games room, spa pools, drying room, ski shop and tramping gear rental, it provides a comfortable base for all activities in the park. Hostel accommodation and family chalets are also available.

Ⓦ NZ$130–NZ$160
① 22 deluxe, 7 standard rooms
Ⓢ Ⓟ
🚗 46km (28 miles) south of Turangi

STAYING

SOUTHERN NORTH ISLAND

CARTERTON

DORNEYWOOD HOMESTAY BED AND BREAKFAST
170 Park Road, RD2, Carterton
Tel 06-379 5099
Two private self-contained suites on a 7ha (17-acre) small farm, with a lake for kayaking. The farm is 3km (2 miles) from Carterton. One room is wheel-chair accessible.
🦽 NZ$95, inc breakfast supplies
ⓘ 2 units
🅢

FEATHERSTON

LONGWOOD
Longwood Road East, Featherston
Tel 06 308 8289
www.longwood.co.nz
Longwood, built in 1920 and reputedly New Zealand's largest private home, is surrounded by park-like grounds in the heart of the Wairarapa wine country. The lodge has magnificent reception rooms and four spacious bedrooms with canopied beds, antique furnishings, private bathrooms and fireplaces. The tariff includes breakfast, afternoon tea on arrival and a four-course dinner. There is also a choice of self-contained accommodation in the 1850s former game-keeper's cottage, coach house and groom's quarters.
🦽 Cottages NZ$150–NZ$250, inc breakfast; lodge NZ$495 per person, inc breakfast and dinner
ⓘ 4 rooms, 3 cottages
🅢 🅟

MANGAWEKA

MOUNT HUIA
906 Ruahine Road, RD 54 Kimbolton
Tel 06-382 5726
www.mthuia.co.nz
You can join in farm activities, walk through pastureland and native bush, or enjoy river sports at Mount Huia, a 351ha (867-acre) sheep and cattle

top luxury lodges. Part of its appeal is its location on a 2,000ha (5,000-acre) working sheep station overlooking the ocean, where you can relish getting away from it all. Lodging is in self-contained cottages dotted round the estate, with four-poster beds, open fireplaces and a naturalistic décor of cotton, clay, hemp and wool. TV, newspapers, internet and activities are available. Dinner in the lodge features French/Italian cuisine matched with top local wines.
🦽 NZ$1,220–NZ$3,050 per person, inc breakfast, cocktails and dinner
ⓘ 12 cottage suites, 2 houses
🅢 🅢 🅣 🐾 🅟

farm in the Rangitikei hill country. Self-contained Hodd Cottage has three bedrooms, two bathrooms, a kitchen, and an open fire. Breakfast ingredients can be provided. Bed-and-breakfast accommodation in the 1920s farmhouse has private access, and a private bathroom and spa pool on the deck. Dinner is available (from NZ$20).
🦽 Farmstay NZ$180, inc breakfast; cottage NZ$50 per adult (breakfast provisions NZ$10)
ⓘ 1 room, 1 cottage
🅢 🅟
🚌 9km (6 miles) from SH1

MARTINBOROUGH

AYLSTONE WINE COUNTRY RETREAT
Huangarua Road, Martinborough
Tel 06-306 9505
www.aylstone.co.nz
A spacious homestead, built in the early 1900s, Aylstone is surrounded by vineyards. The guest rooms are individually designed, in keeping with the house's colonial heritage, with a choice of super-king, queen or twin beds. All rooms have telephones, TV and internet facilities. Leisurely, seasonal breakfasts are a speciality, and there is a restaurant in the summer. Bicycles are provided free of charge.
🦽 NZ$230, inc breakfast
ⓘ 6 rooms
🅢 🅟

PEPPERS MARTINBOROUGH HOTEL
The Square, Martinborough
Tel 06-306 9350
www.peppers.co.nz
Dating from 1882, the hotel is a focal point of this Wairarapa village, in an area becoming internationally known for its wines. The 16 luxury rooms are individually designed and named after early European settlers. Attractive features include claw-foot baths and french doors opening onto either a private veranda or the garden. The bar has an open fire and serves pub food, while the Dining Room is noted for its wine list and more sophisticated fare.
🦽 NZ$275–NZ$355, inc breakfast
ⓘ 16 rooms
🅢 🅢 2 rooms 🅟

PALMERSTON NORTH

AVENUE MOTEL
116 Fitzherbert Avenue, Palmerston North
Tel 06-356 3330/0888-116 333
www.avenuemotel.co.nz
This modern motel in a quiet location is just a few minutes' walk from the heart of the city. There are private spa pools and the standard, family and two-bedroom units are all on the ground floor. A studio unit is wheelchair-accessible.
🦽 NZ$88–$118
ⓘ 13 units 🅢
🅟 Off-street parking

STAYING

BENTLEYS MOTOR INN

Corner of Linton and Chaytor streets,
Palmerston North
Tel 06-358 7074/0800 BENTLEYS
www.bentleysmotorinn.co.nz
Refurbished in 2003, Bentleys
has 22 modern, ground-floor,
smoke-free units, including
studios, one- and two-
bedroom suites and a three-
bedroom apartment with full
kitchen and laundry. All suites
have spa pools or spa baths,
satellite TV, CD players,
business amenities and
cooking facilities. The inn is
quiet and within walking
distance of shops and cafés,
and there are on-site squash
courts, a sauna and a gym.
Breakfast is available.

🏨 NZ$135–NZ$280
🛏 22 rooms
🚭 🛁
🅿 Secure
🚗 Close to the main square, off
Fitzherbert Avenue

PARAPARAUMU

COPPERFIELD
SEASIDE MOTEL

7–13 Seaview Road,
Paraparaumu Beach
Tel 04-902 6414
www.seasidemotel.com
This modern Best Western
motel offers a convenient stop
on the Kapiti Coast. Close to
the beach and golf course, it
has studio units and one- and
two-bedroom apartments with
full kitchen facilities and
balconies. Many have sea
views and some have double
spa baths. Other facilities

include Sky and cable TV,
internet connection, hair dryers
and in-room ironing. A buffet
restaurant, vegetarian café,
wine bar and Italian restaurant
are on site.

🏨 NZ$95–NZ$135
🛏 15 units, studios and apartments
(9 non-smoking)
🚭 🅿
🚗 3km (2 miles) west of SH1

GREENMANTLE ESTATE

214 Main North Road,
Paraparaumu
Tel 04-298 5555
www.greenmantle.co.nz
Close to the site of the New
Zealand Open, this was where
champion golfer Tiger Woods
chose to stay in 2001. A
spacious, rambling 1940s
mansion set in gardens full of
native birds, it offers six beautifully appointed private rooms
and suites, with romantically
draped king beds, oak furniture and double showers.
Guests also have use of a gym,
heated pool and hot tub
hidden away in native bush.
A *table d'hote* dinner can be
booked in advance.

🏨 NZ$525–NZ$595, inc breakfast
🛏 6 rooms
🚭 🛁 ⛱ Outdoor
🅿
🚗 3km (2 miles) north of
Paraparaumu

WANGANUI

BRAEMAR HOUSE

2 Plymouth Street, Wanganui
Tel 06-348 2301
www.braemarhouse.co.nz
Braemar House is an
Edwardian villa which retains
its period charm as a guest
house, in a quiet location close
to the Whanganui River.
Backpacker accommodation is
also available. The house has
attractive formal dining and
living rooms, a well-equipped
kitchen and simply but
appropriately furnished,
centrally heated single, double
and twin rooms, with shared
bathroom.

🏨 NZ$95
🛏 8 rooms
🚭 🅿 Off-street
🚗 1km (0.5 miles) from Wanganui
CBD

RUTLAND ARMS INN

Corner of Victoria Avenue and Ridgway
Street, Wanganui
Tel 06-347 7677
www.rutland-arms.co.nz
A heritage hotel centrally
located in downtown
Wanganui, the Rutland Arms
has individually designed
double, triple and twin suites
in the old English style.
Some have spa baths and all
have satellite TV, phone, fax,
hair dryers and ironing
facilities. The first floor is non-
smoking. A guest lounge is

available for relaxing, with
large screen TV and reading
material. A bar, restaurant,
courtyard café and shops
are attached.

🏨 NZ$145–NZ$175
🛏 8 suites
🚭 First-floor rooms
🅿 Off-street
🚗 5km (3 miles) from the airport

WELLINGTON

COPTHORNE HOTEL
ORIENTAL BAY

73 Roxburgh Street,
Wellington
Tel 04-385 0279/0800-404 010
www.millenniumhotels.co.nz
Visitors who revel in having a
five-star view without having
to pay for five-star accommodation are happy to walk
into the CBD from this hotel,
which clings to the hillside at
Oriental Bay. Located on the
waterfront, it has 113 rooms,
as well as an indoor swimming
pool, a restaurant and a bar.
Ask for a room with a harbour
view and a balcony. The
rooms are comfortable and
have direct dial telephone,
satellite TV, a hair dryer and
ironing facilities.

🏨 NZ$140–NZ$170
🛏 113 rooms, 3 suites
🚭 ⛱ Indoor
🅿 Off-street
🚗 2km (1 mile) from the CBD

EIGHT PARLIAMENT
STREET

8 Parliament Street,
Wellington
Tel 04-499 0808
www.boutique-BB.co.nz
This stylish, artistic wooden
villa is typical of Wellington's
traditional colonial houses,
offering three rooms (one with
private bathroom, two with
shared bathrooms) with
bright decoration and modern
style. A courtyard offers outdoor relaxation and privacy
and there is a modern kitchen

and living area. The house can be rented for NZ$270–NZ$370, which does not include breakfast.

 NZ$120–NZ$185
 3 rooms

 2km (1 mile) from the CBD

HOTEL INTERCONTINENTAL

Grey Street,
Wellington
Tel 04 472 2722
www.wellington.intercontinental.com
A stone's throw from the waterfront, this striking, bronze-hued building is a city landmark, near the Lambton Quay shops, Parliament and the major sports stadium. The ambience is set as you are welcomed by the doorman, and the lobby gleams with marble. Rooms include luxury suites—queen, twin and standard—with the extras you

SPECIAL IN WELLINGTON
THE LIGHTHOUSE

326 The Esplanade, Island Bay,
Wellington
Tel 04-472 4177
www.thelighthouse.net.nz
If you have ever wanted to stay in a lighthouse, this is your chance. This replica offers impressive views across the harbour entrance and oozes character. All that is missing is the flashing light and pounding waves. There is a small kitchen and bathroom on one floor—the living and sleeping areas (two rooms, one main bedroom with spa) are above. Breakfast is included. For a different experience, the owners also offer bed-and-breakfast in a stone keep in Houghton Bay.

 NZ$180–NZ$200
 2 rooms

 6km (4 miles) south of the CBD

would expect: direct-dial telephone, internet, ironing facilities, hair dryer and bathrobes. There is a fitness centre, and restaurants and bars include the Western-themed Arizona Bar and Grill.

 NZ$245–NZ$1,824
 231 rooms, 7 suites (187 non-smoking)
 Indoor
 Valet
 In the CBD

MUSEUM HOTEL—HOTEL DE WHEELS

90 Cable Street
Wellington
Tel 04-802 8900, 0800 994 335
www.museumhotel.co.nz
The Museum Hotel is subtitled 'Hotel de Wheels' because the entire building was shifted 120m (395ft) on railway bogies from the other side of Cable Street to allow for the building of Te Papa. As a result it is very conveniently located for Te Papa, and also the rejuvenated waterfront and the Courtenay Place entertainment district. There are a lobby café and wine bar, a licensed restaurant and bar, and a fitness facility.

 Mon–Fri NZ$149–NZ$269, Sat, Sun NZ$197–NZ$276
 65 rooms, 5 suites, 100 studio, one- and two-bedroom apartments
 Some
 Limited on-site parking, valet parking

SHEPHERD'S ARMS HOTEL

285 Tinakori Road, Thorndon,
Wellington
Tel 04-472 1320
www.shepherds.co.nz
Located near Parliament, the Shepherd's Arms was established in 1870. Refurbished in 2001, it is still full of character. The 14 individually appointed rooms are decorated in keeping with their Victorian origins, some with four-poster king or queen beds. Most double rooms have hair dryers, coffee plungers and satellite TV, and all have private bathrooms. There is a popular bar and dining room with an open fire.

 NZ$149–NZ$169
 14 rooms

 2km (1 mile) from the CBD

THE TERRACE VILLAS

202 The Terrace,
Wellington
Tel 04-920 2020
www.terracevillas.co.nz
A collection of historic houses on The Terrace, close to the Cable Car and the Lambton Quay shopping district, the Terrace Villas are divided into 50 self-contained serviced apartments, from studios to three-bedroom units. Although furnished in keeping with their age, all have modern facilities, cable TV, laundry and full kitchens. Breakfast is also available (NZ$9).

 NZ$111–NZ$433
 50 apartments
 Off-street
 In heart of the CBD

THE WELLESLEY HOTEL

2–0 Maginnity Street,
Wellington
Tel 04 474 1308,
www.thewellesley.co.nz
If you are fed up with flashy, modern, high-rise hotels, the 1920s neo-Georgian Wellesley is a splendidly restored heritage building offering furnished suites with character in the heart of the Lambton Quarter. Rooms have queen-size beds, spacious bathrooms with dual basins and claw-foot baths, air-conditioning, satellite TV, tea-making and ironing facilities, a hair dryer and bathrobes. Facilities include a gymnasium,

sauna, guest lounge and a popular English-style restaurant, which features an open fire and regular live music and entertainment (mainly jazz).

 NZ$282–NZ$326
 Luxury guest and executive suites and rooms

 Near the Parliamentary district

STAYING

NELSON AND MARLBOROUGH

ABEL TASMAN NATIONAL PARK

AWAROA LODGE

Awaroa Bay, Abel Tasman National Park
Tel 03-528 8758
www.awaroalodge.co.nz
Inaccessible by road, Awaroa Lodge combines a wilderness experience with sophisticated accommodation and dining. The lodge is set in native bush, close to the beach and the Abel Tasman Track, and offers a choice of suites with a private deck, deluxe rooms and family rooms. All units are designed with natural materials, and have tea-making facilities and a fridge. Local seafood and organic garden produce are staples on the café menu.

🖐 NZ$235–400
ℹ️ 12 suites, 10 deluxe, 4 family
🅂
❌ Tasman Helicopters, Abel Tasman Air and Flightcorp fly to Awaroa airstrip from Nelson, Motueka and Wellington
🚗 No road access. On foot from the Abel Tasman Track or 1.5 hours by water taxi from Marahau

BLENHEIM

ANTRIA BOUTIQUE LODGE

276 Old Renwick Road, Blenheim
Tel 03-579 2191
www.antria.co.nz
Described as a modern European castle, Antria is certainly different—but don't

expect ramparts or moats. Mediterranean meets

Antipodes in this cultural explosion, with massive neo-Gothic copper front doors, timber ceilings, Greek-inspired lime-washed walls, Italian ceramics and contemporary New Zealand artwork. Rooms are decorated with furnishings from around the world. It's built around a courtyard.

🖐 NZ$335, inc breakfast
ℹ️ 2 rooms
🅂 ♨️ Outdoor 🅿️ Covered
🚗 6km (4 miles) from Blenheim. Take Bells Road north off SH6 onto Old Renwick Road

HOTEL D'URVILLE

52 Queen Street, Blenheim
Tel 03-577 9945
www.durville.com
A boutique hotel full of character has been created in the old bank vaults of the grand Public Trust Building in downtown Blenheim. The individually themed suites have lofty ceilings, native wood floors scattered with rugs, and an eclectic mix of four-poster beds, exotic fabrics and antiques—from African textiles to a Javanese daybed. The central vault has been converted into a lounge. The hotel is also known for its lively bar and restaurant.

🖐 NZ$362
ℹ️ 11 suites
🅂 🍴 🅿️ Limited off-street
❌ 7km (4 miles) from the airport

OLD SAINT MARY'S CONVENT

Rapaura Road, Blenheim
Tel 03-570 5700
www.convent.co.nz
This century-old two-storey convent has been transformed into an intimate retreat, surrounded by vineyards and olive groves. Seven spacious, airy rooms have expansive views, satellite TV and access to the balcony or garden. The original character of the building has been retained, with heating and air-conditioning hidden behind the native wood panelling and timbered floors. There is a billiard room, and a chapel in the garden.

🖐 NZ$550–NZ$650, inc breakfast
ℹ️ 5 rooms, 2 suites
🅂 🍴
🚗 15km (9 miles) from Blenheim

COLLINGWOOD HOMESTEAD

Elizabeth Street, Collingwood
Tel 03-524 8079
www.collingwoodhomestead.co.nz
A colonial-style home, Collingwood Homestead is beautifully decorated and maintained, with polished wooden floors and antiques mixed harmoniously with modern facilities to offer comfort and a homey setting. The lounge has a piano, open fire and veranda. The guest rooms are charmingly furnished, with private bathrooms. Breakfasts are gourmet and a four-course dinner is available (NZ$50, including pre-dinner drinks and wine).

🖐 NZ$265, inc breakfast
ℹ️ 4 rooms
🅂 🅿️ Off-street
🚗 27km (16 miles) from Takaka

COLLINGWOOD

THE INNLET

Main Road, Pakawau
Tel 03-524 8040
www.goldenbayindex.co.nz
A good base for bush walks, kayaking, horseback-riding, cycling and trips to Farewell Spit, this backpackers' hostel has double and twin rooms (with shared bathroom), a rustic hut and a self-contained cottage in a lovely bush setting. The simply furnished cottage sleeps up to seven, with a downstairs double and loft bedrooms reached by ladder. Guests have access to a streamside barbecue and hot tub, and can gather shellfish at the sandy swimming beach 200m (219 yards) away.

🖐 NZ$60–NZ$146
ℹ️ 2 cottages, backpacker rooms
🅂 🅿️
🚗 11km (7 miles) north of Collingwood

KAIKOURA

ANCHOR INN MOTEL

208 The Esplanade, Kaikoura
Tel 03-319 5426/0800-720 033
www.anchorinn.co.nz
One of the best motels in New Zealand, the five-star Anchor Inn is located right on the

STAYING

THE OLD CONVENT

Mount Fyffe Road, Kaikoura
Tel 03-319 6603/0800-365 603
www.theoldconvent.co.nz
In a quiet setting, this former
convent, built for French nuns
in 1911, has become an
unusual B&B with loads of
character. The cells and
schoolrooms are now
bedrooms with private bathrooms, and the former chapel
is the guest lounge. An added
attraction is the four-course
French-style dinner (NZ$50
or NZ$75 with Kaikoura's
famous crayfish). Guests also
have access to bicycles,
pétanque, croquet and
tennis.

NZ$120–NZ$175
16 rooms
Outdoor Off-street
Signposted 5km (3 miles) north
of Kaikoura

Kaikoura waterfront, with most
rooms enjoying magnificent
sea and mountain views. The
complex includes executive,
luxury and standard studios, as
well as one- and two-bedroom
apartments. All units are self-
contained, with fully equipped
kitchens, satellite TV, individual
air-conditioning and double
glazing. There is also a barbecue area. Breakfast is available.

NZ$125–NZ$245
15 units

FYFFE COUNTRY LODGE

State Highway 1, Kaikoura
Tel 03-319 6869
www.fyffecountrylodge.com
A striking building made of
rammed earth and native
timber, Fyffe Country Lodge is
surrounded by English-style
gardens. All rooms have tea

and coffee, a hair dryer, robes
and TV. Seafood chowder is a

speciality of the in-house
restaurant, which has an open
fire, and the bar leads onto a
pretty courtyard. Courtesy
mountain bikes are available.

NZ$189–NZ$750, inc breakfast
6 studios, 1 suite

6km (4 miles) south of Kaikoura
on SH1

MARAHAU

ABEL TASMAN
MARAHAU LODGE

Marahau Beach, RD2 Motueka
Tel 03-527 8250
www.abeltasmanmarahaulodge.co.nz
Built close to the start of the
Abel Tasman Coast Track, this
attractive accommodation
offers self-contained, two-
room units and studio. Rooms
are provided with fold-out
desks, coffee plunger and local
wine in the fridge. There is a
communal kitchen for the six
studio units that do not have
kitchens, and the complex also
includes a pool, sauna and
spa. Room service breakfast
and evening meals available.

NZ$130–NZ$185
8 suites, 4 self-contained units

16km (10 miles) north of Motueka

MARLBOROUGH
SOUNDS

HOPEWELL

Kenepuru Sound
Tel 03-573 4341
www.hopewell.co.nz
You get an ideal blend of
isolation, relaxation, value and
comfort at this waterfront
accommodation. Arriving by
water taxi is recommended,
as the road is tortuous. Five
cottages provide shared rooms
and doubles with bathrooms.
A self-contained, two-bedroom
cottage sleeps up to six. Linen
is supplied, but not food. The
well-equipped kitchen and
lounge has a wood fire, TV,
stereo and library. Other attractions include an outdoor spa,
bush walks, kayaking, mountain biking, fishing, golf, water
skiing and gathering shellfish.

NZ$64–NZ$84
8 double/twin rooms, 1 cottage

Soundsair flies from Wellington to
the local airfield

85km (53 miles) from Picton, via
Linkwater and Te Mahia. Water taxi from
Picton or Havelock recommended

RAETIHI LODGE

Kenepuru Sound, RD2 Picton
Tel 03-573 4300
www.raetihi.co.nz
This modern, luxury lodge
overlooking Double Bay is
noted for its architecture,
secluded location and stunning views. Superior sea view,
garden and hillside rooms are
individually themed to reflect
aspects of the Sounds or exotic
locations. The licensed restaurant offers cooked breakfasts
(NZ$30), bar lunches and
three-course dinners (NZ$70).
The lodge has a helipad and is
accessible, if required, by road,
but is best approached by sea.
Guests can enjoy walking and
water-based activities, and
aromatherapy massage.

NZ$125–NZ$250
13 rooms

85km (53 miles) from Picton, via
Linkwater and Te Mahia. Water taxi from
Picton or Havelock North recommended

MOTUEKA

MOTUEKA RIVER LODGE

Motueka Valley Highway, Ngatimoti,
Motueka
Tel 03-526 8668
www.motuekalodge.co.nz
This luxury fishing lodge in the
picturesque Motueka Valley is
designed in French provincial
style. It has an elegant,
country-style interior with
spectacular views in every
direction. Anglers get guided
trout-fishing in local rivers and
streams, and even non-anglers
will find plenty to enjoy. Guests
tend to congregate in the
farmhouse kitchen, where the
chef uses local produce to
offer a 'taste of Kiwi' with a
touch of class. They can also
sample Chardonnay from the
lodge's own vineyard.
Minimum two-night stay.

NZ$1,025–NZ$1,462, inc breakfast
and dinner
5 rooms

30km (19 miles) southwest of
Motueka

NELSON

THE HONEST LAWYER
COUNTRY PUB

1 Point Road, Monaco, Nelson
Tel 03-547 8850/0800-921 192
www.honestlawyer.co.nz
Located near the airport on a
peninsula in the Waimea
estuary, the Honest Lawyer is

a popular English-style pub, complete with exposed beams hung with memorabilia and a blazing open fire. It also has good food and accommodation, with king and twin rooms, a honeymoon suite, and a self-contained cottage. All rooms have internet connections, and a guest pantry has complimentary drinks and snacks.

🛏 NZ$170–NZ$230
ℹ 8 rooms, 1 suite, 1 cottage
🚫 🅿 Off-street
🚌 6km (4 miles) from Nelson CBD. Turn right off Nayland Road into Songer Street which leads to Monaco

RUTHERFORD HOTEL
Trafalgar Square, Nelson
Tel 03-548 2299/0800-437 227
www.rutherfordhotel.co.nz

The principal hotel in the city, the Rutherford is centrally placed with a view of the cathedral gardens. It has spacious double rooms and two executive suites, all supplied with a hair dryer, bathrobes, an iron, tea-making facilities and a minibar. Executive rooms have a connection for laptops. The Japanese Miyazu restaurant is highly regarded.

🛏 NZ$159–NZ$199
ℹ 113 rooms
🚫 🅵 🛜 🏊 Outdoor 🅿

TE PUNA WAI LODGE
24 Richardson Street, Nelson
Tel 03-548 7621
www.tepunawai.co.nz

A restored early Victorian villa on the Port Hills, Te Puna Wai commands extensive views over Haulashore Island and the bay. One suite occupies the entire top floor and can sleep four, but the ground floor apartment is the most desirable, with french doors opening onto the veranda and garden, antique furniture, fresh flowers, a marble tiled bathroom with underfloor heating

and a designer kitchen stocked with local produce for breakfast. Another double with private bathroom can be booked with it.

🛏 NZ$145–NZ$325, inc breakfast
ℹ 3 rooms
🚫 🅿 Limited off-street
🚌 Richardson Road is off the waterfront. Follow it uphill and through a sharp left-hand turn; Te Puna Wai is on the right

PICTON
BROADWAY MOTEL
113 High Street, Picton
Tel 03-573 6563/0800 101 919
www.broadwaymotel.co.nz

The four-star Broadway is on the edge of town and handy for the ferry terminal. Its top-range units have a private

balcony or courtyard, super-king and queen beds, and kitchens with microwaves. Some rooms also have spa baths. Continental or cooked breakfasts can be ordered.

🛏 NZ$105–NZ$185
ℹ 18 units
🚫 😊
🅿 Off-street
🚌 1km (0.5 miles) from the Interislander Ferry Terminal

ST. ARNAUD
ALPINE LODGE
Main Road, St. Arnaud
Tel 03-521 1869/0800-367 377
www.alpinelodge.co.nz

The Alpine Lodge offers a wide choice of accommodation, from self-contained two-bedroom apartments and spa bath suites to standard and superior double rooms, family units sleeping up to six, and a chalet for budget-conscious visitors which has double and shared rooms. Superior rooms have underfloor heating and double glazing. The Lodge has a house bar with an open fire, a café and a licensed restaurant specialising in fish and game dishes.

CRANBROOK COTTAGE
Giffords Road, Rapaura RD3, Blenheim
Tel 03-572 8606
www.cranbrook.co.nz

Surrounded by vines and fruit trees, this 135-year-old cottage is private and romantic, with breakfast delivered to your door on a tray with fresh flowers. The cottage is self-contained, with queen and twin bedrooms decorated in white linen and nets, cooking facilities, lounge and dining area and private bathroom. Breakfast is likely to include home-grown produce and preserves. The hosts specialise in culinary tours.

🛏 NZ$180, inc breakfast
ℹ 1 cottage
🚫
🚌 Giffords Road is off Rapaura Road, reached from SH6 or SH1

🛏 NZ$135–NZ$160
ℹ 28 rooms (8 non-smoking), 4 studios and 4 apartments in the lodge
🚫

TAKAKA
SANS SOUCI INN
Richmond Road, Pohara, Takaka
Tel 03-525 8663
www.sanssouciinn.co.nz

Environmentally friendly accommodation is the theme of this inn, with rustic adobe-brick bungalows in a garden setting and an ecological sanitation system. Single, twin, double and family rooms are furnished with king-size futons and cane furniture. The popular licensed restaurant

serves home-style meals, with a set menu changing daily.

🛏 NZ$95
ℹ Single, twin, double and family bungalow rooms
🚫
🚌 8km (5 miles) northeast of Takaka

STAYING

CANTERBURY AND THE WEST COAST

SPECIAL IN AKAROA

WILDERNESS HOUSE

42 rue Grehan, Akaroa
Tel 03-304 7517
www.wildernesshouse.co.nz
This charming 1878 villa, on a quiet street a short stroll from the village, is surrounded by old-fashioned gardens and has a small vineyard. Bedrooms, furnished with antiques, are thoughtfully appointed with wool duvets, fresh flowers and New Zealand-made toiletries. A lounge has TV and complimentary refreshments. Dinner is available by arrangement. No children under 14.
🛏 NZ$240, inc breakfast
🚪 4 rooms
🅢 🅟 Off-street
🚌 Rue Grehan is on the left as you enter Akaroa

AMBERLEY

BREDON DOWNS HOMESTAY

233 Carters Road (SH1), Amberley
Tel 03-314 9356
www.bredondownshomestay.co.nz
Bredon Downs is an old farmhouse in English gardens with a pool and tennis court, and makes a good base for exploring the Waipara wine trail. You can choose between queen, twin or single rooms, all with private spa bathroom. The owners breed ostriches and are happy to show them to you. Dinner by arrangement.
🛏 NZ$110–NZ$130, inc breakfast
🚪 3 rooms
🅢 🏊 Outdoor 🅟 Off-street
🚌 1km (0.5 miles) south of Amberley

ARTHUR'S PASS

THE TRANS ALPINE LODGE

Main Road, Arthur's Pass
Tel 03-318 9236
www.arthurspass.co.nz
Designed to look like a Swiss lodge, the Chalet combines alpine lodge accommodation with a European-influenced restaurant. Rooms are simply furnished, with en suite or shared bathrooms, and satellite TV. There is an outdoor spa pool. Cooked breakfasts, coffee and lunches are served in the bistro; at night there's fireside dining in the restaurant.
🛏 NZ$120, inc breakfast
🚪 14 rooms (2 with shared bathroom)
🅢

CHRISTCHURCH

CROWNE PLAZA

Corner of Kilmore and Durham streets, Christchurch
Tel 03-365 7799/0800-154 181
www.crowneplaza.co.nz
A stylish building beside the Avon River, the Crowne Plaza is by the Town Hall, Convention Centre and Casino. It has a choice of standard rooms and suites, with views over Victoria Square or the city and Alps. The hotel has a sports bar, a café, a highly regarded restaurant and an authentic Japanese restaurant with traditional and *teppan-yaki* areas.
🛏 NZ$176–NZ$475
🚪 298 rooms (177 non-smoking), 19 suites
🅢 🅢 🛎 🏊 🅟

THE GEORGE HOTEL

50 Park Terrace, Christchurch
Tel 03-379 4560
www.thegeorge.com
Facing the Avon River and Hagley Park, the George combines an attractive location with attention to detail. It has 57 deluxe rooms and suites, some with balconies, spas and butler service, and a self-contained Residence wing. The emphasis is on understated elegance and good service. The Pescatore restaurant (▷ 265) specialises in seafood, and the brasserie has some of the best breakfasts in town.
🛏 NZ$422
🚪 57 rooms and suites
🅟 Off-street
🚌 1.5km (1 mile) from Cathedral Square

STONEHURST ACCOMMODATION

241 Gloucester Street, Christchurch
Tel 03-379 4620
www.stonehurst.com
Stonehurst—best known as a top-end backpackers'—has expanded to include a modern motel annex with one- to three-

bedroom units and apartments. These are well appointed, with super-king beds and fully equipped kitchens; some also have spa baths, CD players and garages. The backpackers' also has single and double/twin rooms, some en suite. Facilities include a pool, pizza bar, internet access and travel shop.
🛏 NZ$115–NZ$180
🚪 19 motel units, 9 apartments, 22 double/twin en suites
🅢 🏊 Outdoor 🅟 Off-street
🚌 1km (0.5 miles) from Cathedral Square

SUMNER BAY MOTEL AND APARTMENTS

26 Marriner Street, Sumner, Christchurch
Tel 03-326 5969, 0800 496 949
www.sumnermotel.co.nz
Every unit at the modern Sumner Motel has a private balcony or courtyard, and two have spa baths. The motel is only metres from Sumner Beach, with surfboards and bikes available for hire. Sumner has a village atmosphere, just 15 minutes' drive from the heart of Christchurch.
🛏 NZ$145–NZ$195
🚪 12 units

FOX GLACIER

TE WEHEKA INN

Main Road, Fox Glacier
Tel 03-751 0730
www.weheka.co.nz
Te Weheka Inn is a modern, purpose-built, two-storey small hotel, four-star rated, with spacious modern bedrooms, a choice of en suite bath or shower, fluffy towels, hair dryer and ironing facilities. The lounge has a balcony, a small

STAYING

library and internet connection, and there is a laundry. Full or continental breakfast is included, and dinner is served during summer months.

🏨 NZ$236–NZ$348, inc breakfast
🛏 20 rooms
🚭 Ⓟ Covered
🚌 Opposite Visitor Information Office

FRANZ JOSEF

RAINFOREST RETREAT

Cron Street, Franz Josef
Tel 03-752 0220
www.rainforestretreat.co.nz
Log cabins nestle among the trees in this quiet bush setting. Some accommodation is on the forest floor, some up in the canopy. Standard tree houses have queen and single beds, en suites, satellite TV, electric blankets and heating. Tree

lodges upgrade to a full kitchen, air-conditioning and central heating. The complex also has motel and en suite accommodation, a spa, sauna, internet access, bar, café and restaurant.

🏨 NZ$129–NZ$199
🛏 6 tree lodges, 2 tree houses, 9 tree hut motel units
🚭 🍴
🚌 One block from the shopping centre

SCENIC CIRCLE FRANZ JOSEF GLACIER HOTELS

Main Road (SH6), Franz Josef
Tel 03-752 0729
www.scenic-circle.co.nz
The hotel has two wings, 1km (0.5 miles) apart, in the village and on the outskirts. All

rooms have satellite TV, telephones, tea-making facilities and hair dryers. Rooms in the Douglas and Graham wings also have fridges and in-house video. Between them the

hotels have three restaurants, four bars, two spa pools and guest laundries.

🏨 NZ$298–NZ$360
🛏 177 rooms
🚭 🍴
🚌 On SH6, 1km (0.5 miles) north of Visitor Information Office

GREYMOUTH

THE BREAKERS SEASIDE BED AND BREAKFAST

Nine Mile Creek, State Highway 6
Tel 03-762 7743
www.breakers.co.nz
Stunning ocean views and beach access add to the friendly welcome at this four-star seaside B&B lodge and homestay on the coast road between Greymouth and Westport. The rooms, inspired by the traditional Kiwi *bach* (holiday home), are close to the sea and have a large bedroom and lounge area, as well as en suite and a balcony. Dinner is available with 24 hours notice.

🏨 NZ$180–NZ$250, inc breakfast
🛏 4 rooms
🚭
🚌 14km (8 miles) north of Greymouth

HAAST

MCGUIRES LODGE

State Highway 6, Haast Junction
Tel 03-750 0020/0800-624847
www.mcguireslodge.co.nz
Modern McGuires Lodge is on a 3.5ha (8.5-acre) deer farm. The 19-unit complex comprises standard, studio and family rooms. There is also a spa pool, barbecue and laundry. The restaurant serves local specialities such as crayfish from the house tank, venison, Hereford steak and blue cod. The bar is finished in recycled

native woods. Continental and cooked breakfasts are available.

🏨 NZ$95–NZ$190
🛏 19 rooms
🚭 Ⓟ
🚌 700m (760 yards) southeast of Haast River Bridge on SH6, by the DoC office at the Haast junction

HANMER SPRINGS

HERITAGE HOTEL AND RESORT

1 Conical Hill Road, Hanmer Springs
Tel 03-315 0060/0800-368 888
www.heritagehotels.co.nz
A local landmark, the former Hanmer Lodge was elegantly refurbished in 2000, retaining the Spanish design of its heyday in the 1930s, with Moorish arches, a bell tower and a Grand Dining Room to seat 120. Accommodation is a combination of rooms, garden suites and self-contained three-bedroom villas among mature trees. The restaurant serves Pacific Rim cuisine, such as local salmon on a *sushi nori* cake. In summer, take breakfast or dine more casually on the sunny patio.

🏨 NZ$150–NZ$361
🛏 36 rooms (31 non-smoking), 15 suites, 11 villas (non-smoking)
🚭 In restaurant 🏊 Outdoor
🚌 500m (545 yards) from the Visitor Information Office

HOKITIKA

BUSHLINE RETREAT BED AND BREAKFAST

Bluespur Road, RD2, Hokitika
Tel 03-755 8557/03-755 6603
www.bushline.co.nz
This bed-and-breakfast is ten minutes' drive from Hokitika, in a bush setting, with views of the sea. Three of the rooms have private facilities, and families are welcome.

🏨 NZ$95–NZ$180
🛏 5 rooms 🚭

SHINING STAR BEACHFRONT ACCOMMODATION

11 Richards Drive, Hokitika
Tel 03-755 8921/0800-744 646
www.accommodationwestcoast.co.nz
Sea views are a speciality at this beachfront motel with log cabin lodging, studios and family chalets. Double (queen) and triple (queen and single bed) chalets have a kitchen and bathroom; two-bedroom apartments sleep four to six. Executive spa chalets have

STAYING

mezzanine floors, satellite TV, DVD and CD players. Breakfast (Continental) can be delivered.

🏨 NZ$55–NZ$145
🛏 20 rooms
🚭 🅿
🚌 Turn onto Richards Drive off SH6 at the northern end of town; 1km (0.5 miles) from downtown

KARAMEA

KARAMEA HOLIDAY PARK
Maori Point Road, Karamea
03-782 6758
www.karamea.com
This campground, beside an estuary and surrounded by native bush, offers anything from tent sites to motel units. It's 3km (1.8 miles) south of Karamea, with transport to the Heaphy and Wangapeka tracks.

🏨 Tent sites NZ$20, power sites NZ$22, cabins NZ$25–NZ$35, motel NZ$60–NZ$65, all excluding breakfast
🛏 70 tent sites, 32 power sites, 20 cabins, 3 motel units

SPECIAL IN KARAMEA
LAST RESORT
71 Waverley Street, Karamea
Tel 03-782 6617
www.lastresort.co.nz
The Last Resort offers an opportunity to get back in tune with nature. This modern and imaginatively designed complex has lodge-style accommodation blocks interconnected by a walkway, with a large bar/café and restaurant. You can choose from two-bedroom cottages, studio en suites and shared accommodation. Room service and internet access are available.

🏨 NZ$65–NZ$140
🛏 Cottages, 13 studio en suites, 12 double lodge rooms (6 with en suite)
🚭
✈ Charter flights available from Karamea to Nelson and Takaka. Helicopter access
🚌 On SH67

LAKE MOERAKI

WILDERNESS LODGE LAKE MOERAKI
State Highway 6, Lake Moeraki
Tel 03-750 0881
www.wildernesslodge.co.nz
This eco-lodge in a remote West Coast location offers a high level of comfort in double lodge rooms and larger garden rooms. The restaurant overlooking the Moeraki rapids serves wilderness food, such as whitebait from the river, seafood from the coast and game from the forest. There are canoes for you to explore the lake and river, and guided nature walks. Minimum two-night stay in the busy season.

🏨 NZ$290–NZ$490, inc breakfast, dinner and some activities
🛏 22 rooms
🚭 🅿
🚌 On SH6 at the Moeraki River outlet 30km (19 miles) north of Haast

LAKE TEKAPO

LAKE TEKAPO LUXURY LODGE
Aorangi Crescent, Lake Tekapo
Tel 03-680 6566/0800 LAKE TEKAPO
www.laketekapolodge.co.nz
Built in 1998, this spacious, earth-block lodge overlooks Lake Tekapo, a short stroll from the heart of the village. The four rooms have super-king or queen/single beds with en suites, one with spa bath. Most have lake and mountain views. Bathrobes and slippers are provided. The lounge has an open fire, and internet access and satellite TV are available.

🏨 NZ$200–NZ$395, inc breakfast
🛏 4 rooms
🚭 🅿
🚌 1km (0.5 miles) from Tekapo village

MOUNT COOK VILLAGE

THE HERMITAGE
Mount Cook Village
Tel 03-435 1635
www.mount-cook.com
Spectacularly situated at the foot of the Alps, The Hermitage is one of New Zealand's most famous hotels, its isolation being part of the mystique. The complex includes rather tired traditional hotel rooms, a luxury wing, self-contained motels and chalets. There is a shop, sauna, tennis courts and a choice of bars and restaurants, including a buffet and the fine-dining Panorama Room in summer.

🅖 Chalets closed May–end Sep
🏨 Motel units NZ$235–NZ$275, inc breakfast; chalets NZ$240, inc breakfast; hotel rooms NZ$520–NZ$770, inc breakfast and dinner
🛏 221 rooms, 32 motels, 19 chalets
🚭 🚭 🅿
✈ 3km (2 miles) from Mount Cook airstrip
🚌 56km (35 miles) north of SH8

PUNAKAIKI

PUNAKAIKI ROCKS HOTEL AND VILLAS
State Highway 6, Punakaiki
Tel 03-731 1168/0800-786 2524
www.punakaiki-resort.co.nz
Only 400m (435 yards) from the Pancake Rocks and Blowholes, the resort has studio units with private decks facing the ocean or eco, solar-powered rooms set farther back from the highway, in bush. Rooms have cooking facilities, private outdoor seating and satellite TV. The villas are linked by suspended boardwalks, and a walk-through underpass gives easy beach access.

🏨 NZ$236–NZ$292
🛏 35 rooms
🚭 🅿
🚌 400m (435 yards) south of Paparoa National Park Visitor Information Office

WAIPARA

CLAREMONT COUNTRY ESTATE
828 Ram Paddock Road, Waipara Gorge
Tel 03-314 7559
www.claremont-estate.com
Claremont blends five-star accommodation in a heritage building on a 980ha (2,400-acre) sheep station with stunning scenery. The suites and rooms have spacious bathrooms and are furnished with antiques, but also have central heating, satellite TV and internet access. There is a tennis court, and a spa and sauna. Families are accommodated in a separate self-contained cottage. Claremont is also a good base for exploring the Waipara wine region. Note that it is closed from July to September.

🏨 NZ$696–NZ$996, inc dinner and refreshments
🛏 5 suites, 1 cottage
🚭 🅿
✈ Private airstrip
🚌 55km (34 miles) north of Christchurch. Turn off SH1 at Georges Road opposite Waipara Hills Winery and follow the road for 12km (7 miles)

STAYING

OTAGO AND THE FAR SOUTH

PRICES AND SYMBOLS

Prices are for a double room for one night. All the hotels listed accept credit cards unless otherwise stated. Note that rates vary widely throughout the year.
For a key to the symbols, ▷ 2.

CLYDE

OLIVERS LODGE

34 Sunderland Street, Clyde
Tel 03-449 2860
www.olivers.co.nz

Equally lauded for the quality of its accommodation and its restaurant, Olivers offers a classic mix of old-world character and fine cuisine. Rooms are individually styled and range from the Stable and Homestead rooms to the individual Smokehouse room with its charming old shower and

sunken bath. The restaurant, which also exudes character with its cobblestone fireplace and red-brick floor, has been a focus for quality dining in the region for years.

🖐 NZ$140–NZ$300, inc breakfast
ⓘ 12 rooms
Ⓢ
🚗 1km (0.5 miles) off SH8

CROMWELL

GOLDEN GATE LODGE

Barry Avenue, Cromwell
Tel 03-445 1777
www.goldengate.co.nz

Smart and spacious, the lodge is designed to reflect the region's gold-mining heritage. Accommodation is in twin, double and king studios, suites (some with spa) and units, all with tea-making facilities. There are also a sauna and spa, licensed restaurant, café and wine bar. The Lodge is located at the entrance to the

town, opposite the shopping mall and by the golf course.

🖐 NZ$115
ⓘ 47 rooms
Ⓢ Ⓟ
🚗 500m (550 yards) from Cromwell Visitor Information Office

DUNEDIN

HULMES COURT

52 Tennyson Street, Dunedin
Tel 03-477 5319
www.hulmes.co.nz

Hulmes Court B&B is in a turreted 1860s Victorian mansion located two blocks from the Octagon. It is quiet, comfortable and friendly. Together with Hulmes Too, an Edwardian house next door, it has 14 bedrooms decorated in keeping with the period, with harbour and garden views, some with shared bath.

🖐 NZ$100–NZ$160, inc breakfast
ⓘ 14 rooms
Ⓢ Ⓟ Off-street
🚗 1km (0.5 miles) from Dunedin Visitor Information Office

MOTEL MORAY PLACE

97 Moray Place, Dunedin
Tel 03-477 2050

This modern, centrally located motel has quiet standard and executive units with comfortable beds and tiled bathrooms. Executive units come with spa baths. The units do not have full cooking facilities, but continental breakfast is available and each unit has a TV, a microwave, tea-making facilities, a toaster, a fridge and an iron.

🖐 NZ$97–NZ$150
ⓘ 40 unit
Ⓢ Ⓟ Off-street
🚗 200m (220 yards) from the Octagon and Dunedin Visitor Information Office

SOUTHERN CROSS

Corner of Princes and High streets, Dunedin
Tel 03-477 0752
www.scenic-circle.co.nz

Dunedin's premier hotel, located in the heart of the city, the Southern Cross dates back to 1883 when it was the original Grand Hotel. It has three in-house restaurants and two bars. The boutique casino is an added attraction for some guests. Rooms all have satellite TV, ironing facilities, hair dryers, tea-making facilities and internet access.

🖐 NZ$230–NZ$360
ⓘ 170 rooms, 8 suites
Ⓢ 🐾 Ⓟ Off-street
🚗 1km (0.5 miles) from the Octagon and Dunedin Visitor Information Office

SPECIAL IN DUNEDIN

CORSTORPHINE HOUSE PRIVATE HOTEL

23A Milburn Street, Corstorphine, Dunedin
Tel 03-487 6676/6672
www.corstorphine.co.nz

A listed 1863 heritage building, this five-star Edwardian-style private hotel sits in a 5ha (12-acre) estate and

commands fine views across the city. The house is beautifully appointed throughout, with stylish themed suites, from Scottish to art deco or a French boudoir. The estate produces flowers, vegetables, herbs, fruits, nuts and eggs for the house restaurant.

🖐 NZ$395–NZ$595, inc breakfast
ⓘ 7 rooms
Ⓢ Ⓟ
🚗 6km (4 miles) south of downtown

STAYING

INVERCARGILL

ASCOT PARK HOTEL

Corner of Tay Street and Racecourse Road, Invercargill
Tel 03-217 6195/0800-272 687
www.mainstay.co.nz
Ascot Park is in peaceful, park-like surroundings on the outskirts of Invercargill, and is the city's top hotel. Large and modern, it has a mix of deluxe,

superior and standard rooms and motel units. It also has a restaurant, bar and tavern complex.
🛏 NZ$109–NZ$185
🛌 72 rooms, 24 motel units
🚭 ♿ 🐕 🅿 Off-street
🚌 4km (2.5 miles) from the CBD

KAKA POINT

NUGGET VIEW, KAKA POINT AND CATLINS COAST MOTELS

11 Rata Street, Kaka Point
Tel 03 412 8602/0800-525 278
www.catlins.co.nz
As the name suggests, this complex has a variety of accommodation options, from economy to five-star luxury, all with ocean views. Open-plan studios have double beds; two-room apartments are suitable for families; superior spa units have a king bed and double spa bath. Kayaks and body boards are provided. The owners also operate fishing trips and eco-tours to The Nuggets.
🛏 NZ$75–NZ$280
🛌 14 rooms
🚭 🅿
🚌 23km (14 miles) from Balclutha and SH1 via Highway 92. Turn off Highway 92 at Romahapa

MANAPOURI

BEECHWOOD LODGE

40 Cathedral Drive, Manapouri
Tel 03-249 6993
www.beechwoodlodge.com
A modern, deservingly popular boutique B&B that overlooks the lake and mountains, Beechwood accommodates

guests in two spacious en suites, which have their own private entrance and kitchen The entire floor can also be booked as a suite. The real drawcard is the lounge, from which you can sit and muse upon the ever-changing moods of the lake. Not suitable for children.
🛏 NZ$300–NZ$400
🛌 2 rooms
🚭 🅿 Off-street
🚌 20km (13 miles) south of Te Anau

MILFORD SOUND

MILFORD SOUND LODGE

Milford Road, Milford Sound
Tel 03-249 8071
www.milfordlodge.com
For the independent visitor, this backpackers' lodge is a great choice in Milford Sound. It can be very cosmopolitan and in midsummer, outside the local pub's opening hours, forms the hub of Milford's leisure activity. Single, double/twin and shared rooms are available, with shared bathrooms. The restaurant serves breakfast and pub meals. There's a kitchen, a large lounge and a store.
🛏 NZ$78
🛌 8 double/twin units
🚭
🚌 On Milford Road, 1km (0.5 miles) east of Milford Sound airfield

OAMARU

KINGSGATE HOTEL BRYDONE

115 Thames Street, Oamaru
Tel 03-434 0011
www.millenniumhotels.co.nz
Oamaru's oldest and largest hotel, in the heart of town, the Brydone has an elegant Historic Wing, built in 1881 and furnished in period style, and a Pacific Wing, built in the 1970s. Despite the odd creaking floorboard, it's worth trying to book the former and soak up the atmosphere. The hotel has doubles or suites, some with spa baths, and there is a popular bar and restaurant.
🛏 NZ$140–NZ$248
🛌 50 rooms
🚭 🅿
🚌 1km (0.5 miles) from Oamaru Visitor Information Office

QUEENSTOWN

EICHARDT'S PRIVATE HOTEL

Marine Parade, Queenstown
Tel 03-441 0450
www.eichardtshotel.co.nz

LARNACH LODGE

145 Camp Road, Otago Peninsula
Tel 03-476 1616
www.larnachcastle.co.nz
Larnach Lodge has beautifully appointed themed rooms, from the tartan Scottish Room to the Goldrush Room, with a king-size bed made

from an old cart found on the property. The views across the harbour and peninsula are superb. Breakfast is served in the former stables. Dinner is optional (NZ$50) in the castle. Less expensive rooms with shared bathrooms in the former coach house are also available. It's essential to book ahead.
🛏 NZ$270–NZ$240
🛌 12 rooms
🚭
🚌 12km (8 miles) from Dunedin CBD via Highcliff and Camp roads

This centrally located, historic hotel was founded in 1866. Refurbished since the 1990s Queenstown floods, it now caters to the luxury boutique market. It has elegantly appointed suites with antiques and an open fire, and a guest parlour with overstuffed chairs and sofas against a backdrop of exquisite antiques.
🛏 NZ$1,375–NZ$1,595, inc breakfast
🛌 5 suites
🚭
🚌 200m (220 yards) from Queenstown Visitor Information Office

HERITAGE QUEENSTOWN

91 Fernhill Road, Queenstown
Tel 03-442 4988/0800-368 888
www.heritagehotels.co.nz
The Heritage is on the western edge of town in a quiet position, with great views. Bedrooms include luxury suites, some self-contained

with kitchen and laundry facilities, dishwasher and a full complement of crockery and glassware. There is an in-house restaurant with open fire.

💷 NZ$140–NZ$618
ⓘ 197 rooms
🚫 🚫 💷 🚭 🅿
🚌 2km (1 mile) west of Queenstown Visitor Information Office

MATAKAURI LODGE
Glenorchy Road, Queenstown
Tel 03-441 1008
www.matakauri.co.nz
This is a magnificent place, set in private bush with uninterrupted views across Lake Wakatipu. Accommodation is in modern villas and fully self-contained suites. The spacious lodge has a library and four fireplaces, and the spa pavilion in the grounds is perfect for après-ski. Dinner is served with top local wines.

SPECIAL IN QUEENSTOWN

QUEENSTOWN HOUSE
69 Hallenstein Street, Queenstown
Tel 03-442 9043
www.queenstownhouse.co.nz
Refurbished in 2002, this well-established modern upper-range B&B is in a central location overlooking the town. Accommodation

comprises elegant en suites and new villa suites with fireside sitting rooms. The pre-dinner hospitality hour is a speciality—you can sample NZ wine, cheeses and seasonal treats, while exchanging experiences and sharing restaurant recommendations. The full cooked or Continental breakfasts are excellent. Internet access.

💷 NZ$225–NZ$895, inc breakfast
ⓘ 13 rooms
🚫 🅿 Off-street
🚌 500m (550 yards) from Queenstown Visitor Information Office

💷 NZ$1,164–NZ$1,991, inc dinner
ⓘ 6 suites and villa suites
🚫 🚫 💷
🚌 5km (3 miles) west of Queenstown

STEWART ISLAND/ RAKIURA
PORT OF CALL BOUTIQUE ACCOMMODATION
Jensen Bay, Stewart Island
Tel 03-219 1394
www.portofcall.co.nz
In an idyllic spot overlooking the entrance to Halfmoon Bay, surrounded by 8ha (20 acres) of native bush and abundant

bird life, this B&B has a charming double en suite, with great breakfasts and views from the deck. There are also the Bush and Tree cottages, both self-contained. The friendly hosts also have an eco-guiding operation.

💷 NZ$285, inc breakfast, cottage NZ$160–NZ$250
ⓘ 1 guest room, 2 cottages
🚫
🚌 1km (0.5 miles) east of the village

SOUTH SEA HOTEL
Main Road, Oban
Tel 03-219 1059
www.stewart-island.co.nz
This is a great place to stay if you wish to mix with the locals and experience Stewart Island life. There are traditional hotel rooms (some with sea views) and self-contained motel units on a nearby property. There is a bar, and a restaurant where you can sample the local delicacy—muttonbird.

💷 NZ$80–NZ$135
ⓘ 30 rooms, 9 motel units
🚫
🚌 100m (110 yards) from the ferry

TE ANAU
FIORDLAND LODGE
472 Te Anau–Milford Highway
Tel 03-249 7832
www.fiordlandlodge.co.nz
A purpose-built luxury lodge in the classic style, this has

stunning views across the lake and mountains. Facilities include smart guest rooms, two self-contained log cabins and a restaurant. The high

ceilings, full tree-trunk pillars and huge windows add to the appeal and sense of space.

💷 Cabins NZ$300–NZ$420, inc breakfast; suites NZ$520–NZ$1,040, inc breakfast and dinner
ⓘ 10 rooms, 2 cabins
🚫
🚌 5km (3 miles) north of Te Anau

WANAKA
CARDRONA HOTEL
Crown Range Road (SH89), Cardrona
Tel 03-443 8153,
www.cardronahotel.co.nz
The Cardrona may be a little out of the way, but is well worth the journey. The hotel is over 140 years old and retains much of its character. Double rooms in the old stables look out over a beautiful garden and courtyard. There is a great rustic restaurant and bar. Advance booking essential.

💷 NZ$185
ⓘ 16 rooms
🚫
🚌 On the Crown Range Road 26km (16 miles) south of Wanaka

THE MOORINGS
17 Lakeside Road, Wanaka
Tel 03-443 8479
www.themoorings.co.nz
This modern, classy boutique apartment and motel block overlooks the lake, and is only metres from the lakeshore and the heart of town. Stylish motel rooms have underfloor heating and balcony views, and the spacious apartments have log burners and individual carports. Satellite TV and ski-drying room are available.

💷 NZ$160–NZ$345
ⓘ 14 motel units, 8 apartments
🚫
🚌 100m (110 yards) from Wanaka Visitor Information Office

STAYING

Planning

TIME ZONES		
CITY	TIME DIFFERENCE IN HOURS	TIME AT 12 NOON IN NZ
Amsterdam	-11	1am
Berlin	-11	1am
Brussels	-11	1am
Cairo	-10	2am
Chicago	-18	6pm (previous day)
Dublin	-12	midnight
Johannesburg	-10	2am
London	-12	midnight
Madrid	-10	2am
Montréal	-17	7pm (previous day)
New York	-17	7pm (previous day)
Paris	-11	1am
Perth, Australia	-4	8am
San Francisco	-20	4pm (previous day)
Sydney	-2	10am
Tokyo	-3	9am

New Zealand is one of the first countries in the world to see the dawn. Standard time is 12 hours ahead of Greenwich Mean Time, and New Zealand Daylight Saving Time (summer time) runs from 2am on the first Sunday in October to 2am on the third Sunday in March. During this period clocks go forward one hour.

CLIMATE

New Zealand has what is called an ocean temperate climate—that is, generally agreeable. As the country is fairly elongated and lies at a north-to-south angle, the weather varies considerably. The north is consistently a few degrees warmer than the south; the warmest region is usually Northland and the coldest Southland. However, especially in recent years, uncommon weather patterns have seen the reverse to be true, sometimes for days on end.

● In Auckland average temperatures for winter (June–August) are 8°C to 15°C (46°F to 59°F) and for summer (December–March) 14°C to 23°C (57°F to 74°F).

● In Dunedin winter temperatures average at 4°C to 12°C (39°F to 53°F) and summer temperatures at 9°C to 19°C (48°F to 66°F). But this can be misleading. Inland from

Snow on the central volcanic peaks of the North Island

Dunedin, Alexandra is often the hottest spot in the country.
● Nelson and Marlborough, in the South Island, have won the competition for sunniest place for several years running. Next year, though, it could just as easily be Napier, on the relatively dry and sunny east coast of the North Island, or even Whakatane in the Bay of Plenty.
● Wellington and Auckland also boast a lot of sunshine, Auckland being far more humid and Wellington notoriously windier.
● The west coast and Fiordland also have extremes of wind and rain, but even in winter the rain in New Zealand doesn't last for long periods.

WHEN TO GO

The summer, or high season, lasts from November to March and is the busiest time, when New Zealanders are themselves taking a break. At these times, especially over Christmas and

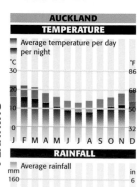

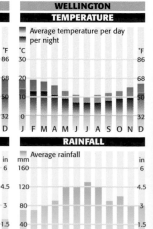

WEATHER STATIONS

Auckland
6m
20ft

WELLINGTON
128m
420ft

Christchurch
34m
112ft

AUCKLAND
TEMPERATURE
■ Average temperature per day
■ per night

CHRISTCHURCH
TEMPERATURE
■ Average temperature per day
■ per night

WELLINGTON
TEMPERATURE
■ Average temperature per day
■ per night

RAINFALL
■ Average rainfall

RAINFALL
■ Average rainfall

RAINFALL
■ Average rainfall

PLANNING

the whole of January, almost the entire country shuts up shop and heads for the beach or the mountains. Accommodation is at a premium and the roads to major resorts can be busy— though in some areas, particularly the remoter parts of the South Island, 'busy' can mean a car passing every five or ten minutes.

● The months of late spring (September–October) or early autumn (March–April) are good alternatives. At these times the weather is still pleasant, accommodation easier to find and prices lower. The winter, or low season, sits between April/May and August/ September.

● Some places close in winter but generally New Zealand serves its visitors year-round. Places such as Queenstown, where skiing is a major activity, can be busier in winter than they are in summer.

NATURAL HAZARDS

Be aware that the sun in New Zealand is dangerous. Ozone depletion is heavy in the southern latitudes and the incidence of melanoma and other skin cancers is above average. Burn times, especially in summer, are greatly reduced: always wear a hat and appropriate sun block.

● If you are climbing, tramping or going into the bush, note that the weather is particularly changeable at higher elevations and can sometimes be deadly. Make sure you are properly clothed and shod and take maps, a first-aid kit and a compass. Above all, inform someone of your intentions.

● Major volcanic eruptions and earthquakes are rare but they do happen and can prove fatal. In

the event of an earthquake stand in a doorway, get under a table or, if you are in the open, get indoors or keep away from loose rock formations and trees.

● Advance weather reports and safety information can be found on the Department of Conservation's website, www.doc.govt.nz.

PASSPORTS AND VISAS

All visitors must be in possession of a passport that is valid for three months beyond the date of intended departure. Australian citizens or holders of an Australian returning resident visa do not need a visitor's visa and can stay in New Zealand indefinitely. Citizens of some countries, including the UK and the US, do not need visas for stays of up to three months (six months for UK citizens).

● For detailed visa information consult the Visiting section of the Immigration New Zealand (INZ) website, www.immigration.govt.nz or contact them at NZIS, Private Bag, Wellesley Street, Auckland (tel 09-914 4100/0508-558 855).

● Entry requirements can change: Always check before you travel.

LONGER STAYS/WORK VISAS

It is illegal to work on a visitor's permit. Non-residents (with the exception of Australian citizens)

New Zealand's exceptionally clear air makes for great photos but also certain health risks

must obtain a work visa, which allows entry to the country, and then a work permit, which allows the holder to work on arrival. Applications for both should be made well before arrival. The INZ website has details and application forms that can be downloaded.

● One exception to the rule is the working holiday visa, which is available for those aged 18 to 30 from countries including Argentina, Canada, Chile, Denmark, France, Germany, Hong Kong, Ireland, Italy, Japan, Korea, Malaysia, Netherlands, Singapore, Sweden, Taiwan, UK and Uruguay. This allows holders to work for 12 months.

● Student visas are needed for anyone (other than Australian citizens) planning to study a course of more than three months; anyone studying shorter courses will need a valid visitor's permit.

TRAVEL INSURANCE

Full travel insurance is recom- mended, covering at least medical care and personal effects.

● The New Zealand accident compensation scheme (ACC) covers visitors to New Zealand for personal injury by accident. Benefits include some emergency medical expenses, but do not include loss of earnings.

● Healthline gives free 24-hour health advice and tells you how best to access the New Zealand health system, tel 0800 611 116.

● There is a wide variety of policies from which to choose, so shop around. Always read the small print carefully and check

NEW ZEALAND EMBASSIES ABROAD		
COUNTRY	**ADDRESS**	**WEBSITE**
Australia	High Commission: Commonwealth Avenue, Canberra, ACT 2600, tel 02-6270 4211	www.nzembassy.com
Canada	High Commission: Suite 727, Metropolitan House, 99 Bank Street, Ottowa, Ont K1P 6G3, tel 613/238-5991	www.nzembassy.com
France	7ter, rue Leonard de Vinci, 75116 Paris, tel 01 45 01 43 43	www.nzembassy.com
Germany	Atrium, Friedrichstrasse 60, 10117, Berlin, tel 30 206 210	www.nzembassy.com
Ireland	Consulate, PO Box 999, Dublin 6, tel 01 660 4233	www.nzembassy.com
Netherlands	Carnegielaan 10, 2517 KH, Den Haag, tel 703 469324	www.nzembassy.com
UK	High Commission: New Zealand House, Haymarket, London SW1Y 4TQ, tel 020 7930 8422	www.nzembassy.com
USA	37 Observatory Circle NW, Washington DC 20008, tel 202/328-4800	www.nzembassy.com

that the policy covers any activities you may intend to pursue, such as white-water rafting or bungy jumping. Also check exactly what the medical cover includes—for example, ambulance, helicopter rescue or emergency flights home. You may have to pay before being reimbursed by the insurance company, so check the payment protocol.

WHAT TO TAKE
New Zealand is a well-developed nation and all you are likely to need, from pharmaceuticals to camping equipment, is readily available throughout the country.
● If you are backpacking, bring a good sleeping bag and a bed sheet, items which are not always provided in hostels and which are certainly not available in backcountry tramping huts.
● Other items to remember are a compatible electrical adaptor plug, binoculars, a sun hat, sunscreen, insect repellent and sunglasses.

CUSTOMS AND DUTY-FREE ALLOWANCES
New Zealand's environment and unique biodiversity have been decimated by non-native flora and fauna. Not surprisingly, therefore, the country has strict bio-security laws. You must not bring with you any fruit, animal or plant matter of any kind without prior permission. Heavy fines are imposed on those breaking the rules. Comprehensive advice for visitors is available on the New Zealand Customs Service website, **www.**customs.govt.nz.

If you are over 17 years of age you may import the following:

* **200 cigarettes or 250g of tobacco or 50 cigars or a combination of all three weighing no more than 250g**
* **4.5 litres of wine or beer and one 1.125l bottle of spirits, liqueur or other alcoholic drink**

Goods of value up to NZ$700 are duty- and tax-free.

PRACTICALITIES

ELECTRICITY
The New Zealand supply is 230/240 volts (50 hertz).
● Plugs are either two- or three-pronged with flat pins.
● North American appliances require both an adaptor and a transformer.
● UK appliances need an adaptor only, and Australian appliances are the same.
● Adaptors and transformers are available at local hardware stores or at the airport.

Laundromats are convenient if you're travelling widely

LAUNDRY
Most towns, villages and places to stay have laundry services.
● Washing and drying machines tend to operate with NZ$1 or NZ$2 coins.
● A full wash and dry costs about NZ$6.

MEASUREMENTS
New Zealand uses the metric system. Distances are measured and signed in kilometres and fuel is sold in litres. However, if you ask for a pint in a pub you will be understood.

PUBLIC TOILETS
Public toilets are readily available in towns and large villages and at major visitor attractions, urban parks and fuel stations. They are usually clean and well maintained. You may also be able to use conveniences at libraries or visitor offices.

CONVERSION CHART

FROM	TO	MULTIPLY BY
Inches	Centimetres	2.54
Centimetres	Inches	0.3937
Feet	Metres	0.3048
Metres	Feet	3.2810
Yards	Metres	0.9144
Metres	Yards	1.0940
Miles	Kilometres	1.6090
Kilometres	Miles	0.6214
Acres	Hectares	0.4047
Hectares	Acres	2.4710
Gallons	Litres	4.5460
Litres	Gallons	0.2200
Ounces	Grams	28.35
Grams	Ounces	0.0353
Pounds	Grams	453.6
Grams	Pounds	0.0022
Pounds	Kilograms	0.4536
Kilograms	Pounds	2.205
Tons	Tonnes	1.0160
Tonnes	Tons	0.9842

CLOTHING SIZES
The chart below shows how British, European and US clothing sizes differ.

UK	Europe	US	
36	46	36	SUITS
38	48	38	
40	50	40	
42	52	42	
44	54	44	
46	56	46	
48	58	48	
7	41	8	SHOES
7.5	42	8.5	
8.5	43	9.5	
9.5	44	10.5	
10.5	45	11.5	
11	46	12	
14.5	37	14.5	SHIRTS
15	38	15	
15.5	39/40	15.5	
16	41	16	
16.5	42	16.5	
17	43	17	
8	36	6	DRESSES
10	38	8	
12	40	10	
14	42	12	
16	44	14	
18	46	16	
20	46	18	
4.5	37.5	6	SHOES
5	38	6.5	
5.5	38.5	7	
6	39	7.5	
6.5	40	8	
7	41	8.5	

PLANNING

- Public toilets are usually free of charge and are run by local councils. Find out where they are located and when they open on **www.govt.nz**.
- Many toilets have two press-button flushes: one (usually marked with a circle) gives a full flush and the other (marked with a semi-circle) gives a half-flush to save water.

SMOKING REGULATIONS
New Zealand is increasingly smoke-free, and since December 2004, all bars, clubs, restaurants, cafés, casinos and gaming machine venues have been required to be entirely smoke-free indoors if they are work-places, serve alcohol or have a gambling licence.
- Budget Rent-a-Car have declared themselves a smoke-free company (0800-283 438, www.budget.co.nz).

VISITING WITH CHILDREN
Smelly springs, steaming vents, sandy beaches and a bewildering range of activities make New Zealand an excellent destination for children—not to speak of the set locations to be tracked down from the *Lord of the Rings* movies.
- There are discounts for children on public transport and at most attractions, and many offer family tickets as well. Most major attractions allow very young children free admission.
- Several companies specialise in organising trips and tours tailored for families: try www.familytravel.co.nz.
- A good source of information on family-based activities throughout New Zealand is www.familystophere.com.

Discounts for children are usually available

- Most hotels offer or can recommend a babysitting service, but don't be afraid to ask about the qualifications of the babysitter or the conditions applied to the service.
- Make sure children are well protected against the New Zealand sun, as their skin is more vulnerable than adult skin. Hats, sun-screen and long sleeved shirts can all help to avoid painful sunburn.
- Baby-on-the-Move is a company renting out and selling baby products to overseas visitors. Products include lightweight frames for prams or pushchairs (strollers), newborn and toddler seats for cars, detachable cots and child-carrying backpacks (tel 0800 222 966, www.babyonthemove.co.nz).

VISITORS WITH A DISABILITY
For visitors with disabilities New Zealand can be a frustrating place. While most public amenities are well equipped for wheelchair use, older hotels and some public transport systems (particularly rural buses) are not well adapted. However, it is now a requirement by law to have adequate facilities in new buildings.
- Larger airlines such as Air New Zealand and Qantas are well equipped and this applies both to international and to domestic flights.
- Visitors with disabilities usually receive discounts on travel and some admission charges, and parking concessions are also available, with temporary cards issued on receipt of a mobility card or medical certificate.
- Full details on local services are available from regional Disability Information Centres; a list of contacts can be obtained from the head office at PO Box 24-042, Royal Oak, Auckland (tel 09-625 8069/0800 693 342, www.weka.net.nz).
- Some tour operators specialise in providing itineraries and equipment for visitors with disabilities ▷ 54, On the Move: Visitors with a Disability.

PLACES OF WORSHIP
Most large urban centres in New Zealand have Anglican,

The oldest church in the country is at Russell and dates from 1835

Presbyterian, Baptist, Methodist and Catholic places of worship.
- Some useful websites are: www.baptist.org.nz www.rcnz.org.nz www.methodist.org.nz www.presbyterian.org.nz www.anglican.org.nz www.catholic.org.nz
- There are several mosques in Auckland, Hamilton, Palmerston North, Wellington, Christchurch and Dunedin. Full addresses are available on www.nzmuslim.net.
- There are synagogues in Auckland, Hamilton, Christchurch, Wellington and Dunedin; details of addresses are listed on the website www.haruth.com.
- The Auckland Buddhist Centre is run by the Western Buddhist Order and has a shrine room at 381 Richmond Road, Grey Lynn, Auckland (tel 09-378 1120, www.aucklandbuddhistcentre.org).
- The largest Maori religious movements are Ringatu and Ratana, now both regarded as Maori Christian churches. Ratana has more than 49,000 members and Ringatu over 8,000. The Ratana Church is based at Ratana, Taranaki province, in the North Island, and Ringatu membership is largely concentrated in the northern half of the island.

MONEY

BANKNOTES AND COINS

● The New Zealand currency is the dollar (NZ$), which is divided into 100 cents (c). Coins are in denominations of 10c, 20c, 50c, NZ$1 and NZ$2. Notes come in NZ$5, NZ$10, NZ$20, NZ$50 and NZ$100 denominations.

● Banknotes feature people important to New Zealand: Sir Edmund Hillary, conqueror of Everest (NZ$5); Kate Sheppard, pioneer of female emancipation (NZ$10); The Queen (NZ$20); Sir Apirana Ngata, Maori statesman (NZ$50); and Lord Rutherford, who split the atom (NZ$100).

CREDIT CARDS, ATMS AND EFTPOS

● All major credit cards (Visa, MasterCard, Amex, JCB, Diners)

ATMs are widely available

are widely accepted. New Zealand operates an EFTPOS (Electronic Funds Transfer at Point of Sale) system, which effectively means that there are mini-ATMs at points of sale

throughout the country. Most hotels, shops, retail outlets and fuel stations have EFTPOS. Debit and credit cards may be used with the relevant PIN numbers.

● Standard ATMs are available in almost all towns and accept non-host bank cards, though there may be hidden fees. Some banks are linked internationally via such networks as Cirrus and Plus.

● New Zealand's banks include the ANZ National Bank, ASB Bank, Bank of New Zealand, Kiwibank, TSB Bank and Westpac. Most are represented in all main towns, and branches or ATMs operated by one or more of the banks can be found in smaller places. Internet banking facilities are also popular. For a full list see www.rbnz.govt.nz/nzbanks/.

● Bank opening hours are

CASH

The New Zealand currency is the dollar (NZ$), which is divided into 100 cents (c). Coins are in denominations of 10c, 20c, 50c, NZ$1 and NZ$2. Notes come in NZ$5, NZ$10, NZ$20, NZ$50 and NZ$100 denominations.

For further information on New Zealand currency, and how to tell whether a New Zealand note is genuine, please go to

www.rbnz.govt.nz/currency/money/index.html.

All images shown are not to scale.

Relaxed café society has become a regular part of New Zealand life

10 EVERYDAY ITEMS AND HOW MUCH THEY COST	
Sandwich	NZ$4
50cl bottle of water	NZ$2
Cup of tea or coffee	NZ$3
Pint of beer	NZ$6–NZ$7
Glass of wine	NZ$5
Daily newspaper	NZ$1.20
Roll of camera film	NZ$7–NZ$14
20 cigarettes	NZ$10
Ice cream	NZ$2.50
Litre of fuel	NZ$1.50

LOST OR STOLEN CREDIT CARDS

Visa International
0800-443 019

MasterCard International
0800-449 140
or any bank displaying the VISA
or MasterCard trademark

American Express
0800-656 660
or any American Express
Travel Service Office

Monday to Friday 9–4.30; some city branches also open on Saturday until 12.30.

● Exchange offices such as Travelex and American Express sometimes stay open until 9pm in the cities.

TRAVELLERS' CHEQUES

The safest way to carry money is in travellers' cheques. These are available for a small commission from all major banks. American Express (Amex), Visa and Thomas Cook cheques are widely accepted.

● Most banks do not charge for changing travellers' cheques and they usually offer the best exchange rates.

● Be sure to keep a record of your cheque numbers and keep the cheques you have cashed separate from the cheques themselves, so that you can get a full refund of all uncashed cheques should you lose them.

● It is best to bring NZ$ cheques to avoid exchange costs.

WIRING MONEY

If you need money quickly or in an emergency, you can have it wired to you via any major bank with Western Union (through New Zealand Post, tel 0800-005 253) or via Travelex and moneygram (tel 0800-200 232, www.travelex.co.nz). This transfer can be completed in less than an hour or may take up to a week depending on how much is being wired and how much you are willing to pay (about NZ$30–NZ$80).

TAXES

A 12.5 per cent GST (Goods and Services Tax) is placed on almost every bought item in New Zealand. Prices quoted almost always include GST, but on bigger items or services it pays to check. On leaving New Zealand there is a departure charge of NZ$20–NZ$25, depending on which airport you use. This is not included in your ticket price.

TIPPING

Tipping is at the customer's discretion and is not generally expected in New Zealand.

Visitors can reclaim GST on more expensive items

HEALTH

VACCINATIONS

No vaccinations are officially required for entry into New Zealand. You are, however, advised to get a tetanus shot or ensure that your booster is up to date.

TREATMENT COSTS

If you are injured in an accident while in New Zealand you are covered for treatment, regardless of fault, under the national personal injury insurance scheme, run by the Accident Rehabilitation and Compensation Insurance Corporation (ACC): PO Box 242, Wellington (tel 04-918 7700/0800 101 996, www.acc.co.nz); there are also 31 branch offices spread all over the country—details are available on the website. The provider of your treatment will help you complete the appropriate form.
- If you see a doctor or another healthcare professional for treatment for a personal injury, you may be asked to pay part of the cost.
- ACC does not cover illness, so health insurance is highly recommended, as standard visits to the doctor cost about NZ$40 excluding prescription charges, and dental and hospital services are expensive. See also Before You Go, pages 292–294.

WHAT TO TAKE

- It's advisable to take photocopies of your insurance documents and to keep these separately from the originals, or scan them onto an e-mail address that can be reached from abroad, in case they are lost in an accident or stolen.
- If you are on unusual medication take supplies with you in case they are not easily available locally, and bring your prescription certificate in case of difficulties at customs.
- New Zealand's sun is dangerous due to ozone depletion, so be sure to bring a hat, sunglassess and the strongest possible sunblock to protect against the damage caused by ultraviolet rays. Be prepared to cover up, and be sure to wear this protection even on overcast days.
- Bring an insect repellent, especially to ward off the common and very annoying

HEALTHY FLYING

- Visitors to New Zealand from as far as the US, UK and other parts of Europe may be concerned about the effect of long-haul flights on their health. The most widely publicised concern is Deep Vein Thrombosis, or DVT. Misleadingly called 'economy class syndrome', DVT is the forming of a blood clot in the body's deep veins, particularly in the legs. The clot can move around the bloodstream and could be fatal.
- Those most at risk include the elderly, pregnant women, those using the contraceptive pill, smokers and the overweight. If you are at increased risk of DVT see your doctor before departing. Flying increases the likelihood of DVT because passengers are often seated in a cramped position for long periods of time and may become dehydrated.

To minimise risk:
Drink water (not alcohol)
Don't stay immobile for hours at a time
Stretch and exercise your legs periodically
Do wear elastic flight socks, which support veins and reduce the chances of a clot forming

EXERCISES

1 ANKLE ROTATIONS   **2 CALF STRETCHES**   **3 KNEE LIFTS**

Lift feet off the floor. Draw a circle with the toes, moving one foot clockwise and the other counterclockwise

Start with heel on the floor and point foot upward as high as you can. Then lift heels high, keeping balls of feet on the floor

Lift leg with knee bent while contracting your thigh muscle. Then straighten leg, pressing foot flat to the floor

Other health hazards for flyers are airborne diseases and bugs spread by the plane's air-conditioning system. These are largely unavoidable but if you have a serious medical condition seek advice from a doctor before flying.

Sun hats are essential wear, even on hazy days

sandflies. The size of a pinhead, they are found in some coastal and wetter inland areas, and their bite can produce unpleasant spots on the skin that may itch for weeks. Repellents come in two forms: chemical-based—which are toxic and should be used only in the lowest concentrations (5–10 per cent)—and natural. If you are unable to find natural repellent at home, New Zealand manufacturers offer a wide range of natural creams and oils using ingredients such as eucalyptus or citronella.

HAZARDS
● New Zealand is a great outdoors destination for visitors. Make sure you match your chosen activities to your level of fitness and skill, and that you are fully equipped for sudden changes in the weather.
● When tramping (hiking) be aware that water levels in streams and rivers can change swiftly. On coastal walks such as the Abel Tasman (▷ 108–110) be aware of local tides and their likely impact on your route and schedule.
● If you are planning a serious hike or an overnight trip, make sure someone knows your intentions and when to raise the alarm if you are missing. You can sign in at the start of your trip at a Department of Conservation (DoC) visitor centre—but make sure you remember to sign out again on your safe return. Unless you are very experienced, tramping alone on the more remote and quieter tracks is not advisable.
● There are very few dangerous creatures in New Zealand. One exception is the katipo spider, about 25mm (0.9in) from leg tip to leg tip and found on beaches, under stones and in driftwood throughout the North Island and

Watch out for falling rocks

in parts of the South. Its bite inflicts agonising localised pain and can be fatal. Antivenom is readily available in hospitals.
● Sharks are a common sight around New Zealand shores, but shark attacks on humans are rare. The last fatal attack occurred in Eastland in 1976.
● Giardia is a water-borne parasite which, if it enters your system, causes severe vomiting and diarrhoea and rapid weight loss. The best safeguard is not to drink water from lakes, ponds or rivers without boiling it first.
● Tap water is safe to drink throughout New Zealand; city supplies are chlorinated and most are also fluoridated.

HOSPITALS
● There are public hospitals throughout the North and South Islands of New Zealand. Most, but not all, of these have emergency facilities—details are in the front of every white pages telephone directory.

AMBULANCES
● In an emergency dial 111 anywhere in the country for an ambulance.
● Ambulances in most of the country are provided by organisations like St. John Ambulance, which charge patients for their use—this cost should be covered by medical insurance.
● The exception is Wellington, where the Wellington Free Ambulance makes no charge for its services, and is supported by public donations.
● In remoter areas and offshore islands, rescue helicopters and fixed-wing air ambulances are used where necessary.

DOCTORS
● There are about 10,000 doctors in New Zealand. The Medical Council of New Zealand supplies a list of registered doctors and updates it weekly: The Medical Council of New Zealand, Level 13, Mid City Tower, 139–143 Willis Street, PO Box 11 649, Wellington (tel 04-384 7635, www.mcnz.org.nz).
● Many cities and towns have private after-hours clinics and pharmacies, which treat non-emergency cases for a fee. Details are in the white pages telephone directory.

DENTISTS
● Emergency dentists can be found in the telephone directory Yellow Pages.

PHARMACIES
● New Zealand pharmacists are known as chemists, and their shops sell a selection of cosmetics and other products, as well as drugs.
● Chemist shops open during normal shopping hours, and in most large towns and cities

emergency dispensaries are open outside these hours as well. These are listed in the front of the phone book, under Hospitals.
● Some drugs sold over the counter in other countries may be available in New Zealand only with a prescription.

ALTERNATIVE MEDICINE
● The New Zealand Charter of Health Practitioners is the biggest organisation representing complementary and alternative health (CAM) practitioners in New Zealand. Members of its signatories must meet a set level of competence and are entitled to advertise as chartered health practitioners:
New Zealand Charter of Health Practitioners, Private Box 302 305, North Harbour, Auckland, tel 09-414 5501, www.healthcharter.org.nz.
● The New Zealand Register of Complementary Health Professionals (NZRCHP) provides a directory of practitioners who have trained and qualified in their discipline and who abide by their field's code of ethics: NZRCHP, PO Box 337, Christchurch.

EMERGENCIES
● Contact details for hospital Accident and Emergency departments are listed in the front of the white pages telephone directory.
● In an emergency, dial 111 for an ambulance.

COMMUNICATION

USEFUL NUMBERS

National directory assistance
018
International directory assistance
0172
International operator
0170
Toll help desk
123

TELEPHONES
Payphones are readily available throughout the country and are colour-coded. Both coin (blue) and credit card (yellow) booths are available.

● Phone cards come in NZ$5, NZ$10, NZ$20 and NZ$50 denominations and can be bought from many retail outlets, post and visitor information offices, fuel stations and hostels. Do not use these cards for anything other than domestic calls within New Zealand.

● Coin phones take 10c, 20c, 50c, NZ$1 and NZ$2 coins.

● If you dial 013 (instead of 0) before the number the operator will call back after you have finished to let you know the cost of your call, but this service adds NZ$2.80 to the overall cost.

● Local non-business calls cost 50c from public telephones, but are free from residential telephones in New Zealand, so it should not cause offence if you

COUNTRY CODES FROM NEW ZEALAND	
Australia	00 61
Belgium	00 32
Canada	00 1
France	00 33
Germany	00 49
Greece	00 30
Ireland	00 353
Italy	00 39
Netherlands	00 31
Spain	00 34
Sweden	00 46
UK	00 44
USA	00 1
New Zealand international code: 00 64	

AREA CODES WITHIN NEW ZEALAND	
Auckland	09
Northland	09
Bay of Plenty	07
Coromandel	07
Taupo	07
Ruapehu	07
Waikato	07
Eastland	06
Hawkes Bay	06
Wanganui	06
Taranaki	06
Wellington	04
South Island	03

Internet cafés offer swift communication (top); public phone boxes (right) accept a variety of payment methods

POST SHOPS WITH POST RESTANTE PICK-UP POINTS		
CITY	**ADDRESS AND TELEPHONE**	**OPEN**
Auckland	24 Wellesley Street, Bledisloe Street, tel 09-379 6710	Mon–Fri 7.30–5.30
Christchurch	3 Cathedral Square, tel 03-377 5411	Mon–Fri 8–6, Sat 10–4
Dunedin	243 Princes Street, tel 03-477 3518	Mon–Fri 8.30–5.30
Nelson	Corner of Trafalgar and Halifax streets, tel 03-546 7818	Mon–Fri 7.45–5, Sat 9.30–12.30
Queenstown	15–19 Camp Street, tel 03-422 7670	Mon–Fri 8.30am–10pm, Sat 9–4
Wellington	43 Manners Street, tel 04-473 5922	Mon–Fri 8–5.30, Sat 10–1.30

ask to use a host's or a friend's domestic (non-business) telephone for that purpose.

● Toll-free numbers start with 0508 or 0800. 0900 numbers are usually very expensive.

● Cell phone numbers usually start with 027 (Telecom) or 021 (Vodafone).

INTERNATIONAL CALLS

There are now numerous inexpensive international calling cards and call centres, one of the best being E Phone, www.telstraclear.co.nz, a calling card that accesses the net through an 0800 number. The cards, which vary from NZ$10 to NZ$50, can be bought from shops displaying the E Phone flag sign. Cards come with simple instructions and can be used from any landline telephone. Voice instructions guide you through the process and tell you how much credit you have available before you make each call.

● Credit cards can be used directly in many public phones.

INTERNET AND E-MAIL

Internet cafés and terminals are everywhere in New Zealand and it is fairly easy to get email access. The major cities are well served with internet outlets and most towns have cafés or terminals, often in visitor information offices or libraries. These charge the standard rates of NZ$2–NZ$5 per hour.

● Speed of access varies considerably.

POSTAL SERVICES

Post offices, called Post Shops, typically open Monday to Friday 9–5, Saturday 9–12.30.

● Mail can also be sent to Post Restante, CPO (Chief Post Office) in the main cities, where it will be held for up to 30 days.

● If you are being sent mail make sure the sender marks your surname in capitals and underlines it.

● Within New Zealand standard post costs 45c for medium letters and postcards (two to three days); 80c for Fastpost (airmail) to domestic centres (one to two days); NZ$1.50 for airmail letters to Australia and NZ$2 for standard overseas airmail letters to Europe, North America and East Asia.

● When sending cards and letters overseas be sure to use the free blue 'air economy' stickers. Books of stamps are available in Post Shops, as are pre-paid envelopes and a range of purpose-made cardboard boxes. Stamps can also be bought in bookstores, fuel stations and supermarkets.

● Average international delivery times depend on the day of the week the item is posted, and can take anywhere from four to twelve days to the UK or North America.

INTERNET ACCESS POINTS		
CITY	**ADDRESS**	**TELEPHONE**
NORTH ISLAND		
Auckland	City Library, 44–46 Lorne Street	09-377 0209
	Cyberdate2, 320 Queen Street	09-377 0320
	Login 1, 1/12 Rialto Centre, 163 Broadway, Newmarket	09-522 9303
	Net Central Cybercafé, 5 Lorne Street	09-373 5186
	Net Zone, 4 Fort Street	09-377 3906
	Email access: Travellers Contact Point, 87 Queen Street	09-300 7197
Napier	Cybers, 98 Dickens Street	06-835 0125
Palmerston North	icafé, corner of the Square and Fitzherbert Avenue	06-353 7899
Rotorua	E-Funz, 1174 Huapapa Street	07-349 3789
	Cybershed, 1176 Pukuatua Street	07-349 4965
	Heavenley's Internet Bar and Café, 1195 Fenton Street	07-348 3288
Wellington	Cyber City, 99 Courtenay Place	04-384 3717
	Cyber Spot, Lambton Square, 180 Lambton Quay	04-473 0098
	Library, Victoria Street, Civic Square	04-801 4040
SOUTH ISLAND		
Christchurch	E Blah Blah, 53–57 Cathedral Square	03-377 2381
	Cyber Pass Internet Café, 27 Chancery Lane	03-365 9000
	Dungeon and Dragon, 705 Colombo Street	03-372 3450
Dunedin	Dunedin Cue Club and Cyber Café, 65 St. Andrew Street	03-477 3064
	Webrunner, 237 Moray Place	03-471 8182
Greymouth	Grey District Library, Mackay Street	03-768 5597
Nelson	Aurora Tech, 161 Trafalgar Street	03-546 6867
	Café Affair, 295 Trafalgar Street	03-548 8295
Queenstown	Internet Output, 27 Shotover Street	03-441 3018
	E Café, 50 Shotover Street	03-442 9888
	Internet Depot, 26 Shotover Street	03-442 8581

FINDING HELP

PERSONAL SECURITY

New Zealand has its fair share of crime, and while visitors are rarely targeted for anything other than petty crime, it pays to be careful.

● Theft is rife, especially in Auckland, and tourist hotels, hostels and other accommodation are not exempt.

● Cars and campervans and their contents are regularly targeted, and are especially vulnerable when left at isolated but well-known beauty spots. Carry all money and valuables with you, and lock anything else safe and out of sight in the boot (trunk). Keep your vehicle locked at all times, and make sure your insurance covers theft.

● Hitching is still quite heavily practised in New Zealand but is not entirely safe, and is inadvisable for those travelling alone. If you do decide to hitch, keep to the main highways and restrict your hitching to the daylight hours; and never take off a rucksack and put that or a bag in the car first.

EMERGENCY PHONE NUMBER
Police, Fire or Ambulance **111**

LOST PROPERTY

Report any lost property to the local police station; www.police.govt.nz has a list of all station addresses.

● See page 297 for numbers to contact regarding lost or stolen credit cards.

POLICE

The New Zealand police force is a national service responsible for enforcing criminal and traffic laws.

● Police wear light blue shirts with epaulettes and insignia on the arms; darker blue tie and trousers; and dark blue peaked caps with a chequerboard design around the band.

● The police organisation is divided into 12 districts, each of which has a central station. Contact details for some of the major stations are listed in the table below. For a list of all police stations, see www.police.govt.nz

WHAT TO DO IF YOU'RE ARRESTED

If you are taken to a police station because the police suspect you might have committed a crime, give your name, address, occupation and date and place of birth.

● The police have the right to search, fingerprint and photograph you, and you are

Police in New Zealand do not routinely carry firearms

entitled to see a lawyer privately without delay. There should be a list of lawyers at the station; ask for the list and pick one. If you use a lawyer from the roster it will not cost anything.

● For legal advice contact the local Citizens Advice Bureau. A full list of branches is available on www.cab.org.nz.

CITY	ADDRESS	TELEPHONE
Auckland	Corner of Cook and Vincent streets	09-302 6400
Christchurch	Corner of Hereford Street and Cambridge Terrace	03-363 7400
Dunedin	25 Great King Street	03-471 4800
Palmerston North	400 Church Street	06-351 3600
Wellington	Corner of Victoria and Harris streets	04-381 2000

COUNTRY	ADDRESS	TELEPHONE
EMBASSIES AND CONSULATES IN NEW ZEALAND		
Australia	72–78 Hobson Street, Wellington	04-473 6411
	7th Floor, 188 Quay Street, Auckland	09-921 8800
Canada	Level 11, 125 The Terrace, Wellington	04-473 9577
France	34–42 Manners Street, Wellington	04-384 2555
Germany	Private Bag 92-093, Auckland	09-375 8709
	90 Hobson Street, Wellington	04-473 6063
Ireland	7th Floor, Citibank Building, 23 Customs Street West, Auckland	09-977 2252
UK	IAG House, 151 Queen Street, Auckland	09-303 2973
	44 Hill Street, Wellington	04-924 2888
US	Level 3, Citibank Centre, 23 Customs Street East, Auckland	09-303 2724
	29 Fitzherbert Terrace, Thorndon, Wellington	04-462 6000

PLANNING

OPENING TIMES AND TICKETS

BANKS
Bank opening hours are Monday to Friday 9–4.30. Some branches in cities open Saturday until 12.30.

CHURCHES
City churches are generally open to visitors Monday to Saturday 9 or 10–5 and to worshippers during church services.

DOCTORS AND CHEMISTS
Pharmacies open Monday to Friday 9–5. Emergency services are provided outside these hours; dispensaries are listed under Hospitals in the front of the phone book.

Typical doctors' surgery hours are Monday to Friday 7.30–6.30, and Saturday 8–noon; each clinic will supply details and contact numbers for after-hours arrangements.

FUEL STATIONS
Fuel stations in more populous areas open until about 11pm, and some open 24 hours a day; expect earlier closure in rural areas. Many sell a substantial range of supermarket-type items.

MUSEUMS AND GALLERIES
Opening hours for museums and galleries vary widely according to their size and location. In major cities and resorts they may open any time between 8am and 10am and close some time between 4.30pm and 7pm during weekdays, and some have restricted hours during weekends or on Sunday. In remoter areas museums may open on a seasonal basis or by previous arrangement only; others close during weekends or for part of the week. See individual entries for details, and check ahead with the local visitor information

centre if you are planning a special trip.

RESTAURANTS, CAFÉS, BARS
Opening hours vary and are often seasonal. Most cafés open for breakfast between 7am and 9am and remain open until at least 5pm. Many also remain open until late into the evening or into the small hours. This usually applies seven days a week, with special Sunday brunch hours.

Most mid-range restaurants open their doors daily for lunch (11–2) and dinner (from 6pm). The more exclusive establishments usually open for dinner at about 6pm and some have restricted days or hours, especially in winter.

Pubs and bars are generally open 11am–11.30pm. Many have extended licences and stay open until midnight or even 3am during weekends.

SHOPS AND OFFICES
Most shops and businesses open Monday to Friday 9–5. Many shops also open on Saturday and Sunday. Large malls open daily and have at least one late shopping night a week. Larger supermarket chains open most

evenings, and New Zealand dairies—convenience stores, found on almost every main street—are often open until 10 or 11pm.

DISCOUNTS AND CONCESSIONS
Virtually all visitor attractions and transportation systems offer discounted entrance fees and fares to children, usually of school age, and many give free admission or travel to under 5s.

● Senior citizens are also offered discounts at most major attractions and on trains and buses. Savings can range from 30 per cent to 50 per cent of the full price.

● Many, though not all, attractions offer family tickets; the definition of 'family' varies from place to place. See individual attractions for details.

● Student discounts are not as widespread, but holders of YHA or VIP cards can save on accommodation and travel, and there are plenty of budget options for anyone backpacking around the country.

National museums, such as Te Papa in Wellington (▷ 96) have the longest opening times

TOURIST INFORMATION

'Flightseeing' tours are just one of the adventures you can book at i-SITES

VISITOR OFFICES

The official New Zealand Visitor Information Network is made up of around 100 accredited visitor information centres, nationally known as i-Sites.

● National i-Sites are based in Auckland and Christchurch and main visitor resorts such as Rotorua and Queenstown. They open seven days a week and provide a comprehensive information service, including advance hotel reservation and domestic airline, bus and train tickets. Souvenir shops and occasionally other retail outlets, currency exchange and cafés may be attached.

● Regional i-Sites are found throughout the country; there may be more than one in each region. They provide a general information and reservation service, usually seven days a week, and there is also a huge amount of free material available.

● Local i-Sites can be found almost anywhere, providing local information as well as assistance in lodging and transport reservations. They open at least five days a week, but are subject to varying hours during weekends and in low season.

NATIONAL I-SITES
Auckland
Princes Wharf,
137 Quay Street,
tel 09-307 0612/
0800 AUCKLAND,
www.aucklandnz.com

Christchurch
Old Chief Post Office,
Cathedral Square, PO Box 2600,
tel 03-379 9629,
www.christchurchnz.net

Queenstown
Corner of Shotover and Camp streets,
tel 03-442 4100,
www.queenstown-vacation.com

Rotorua
1167 Fenton Street, tel 07-348 5179, www.rotoruanz.com

SELECTED REGIONAL AND LOCAL INFORMATION
North Island
Auckland
International Terminal,
Arrivals Lounge,
Auckland Airport,
tel 09-275 6467,
www.aucklandnz.com

SKYCITY, tel 09-363 7182,
www.aucklandnz.com

Bay of Islands
Marsden Road, Pahia, tel 09-402 7345, www.fndc.govt.nz/infocentre

Coromandel
355 Kapanga Road,
tel 07-866 8598,
www.coromandeltown.co.nz

Hamilton
Corner of Bryce and Anglesea streets, tel 07-839 3580,
www.waikatonz.com

Hastings
Russell Street North, tel 06-873 0080/ 0800 HASTINGS,
www.hastings.co.nz

Mount Maunganui
Salisbury Avenue, tel 07-575 5099,
www.bayofplentynz.com

Napier
100 Marine Parade, tel 06-834 1911, www.isitehawkesbaynz.co.nz

Palmerston North
The Square, tel 06-354 6593,
www.manawatunz.co.nz

Taupo
30 Tongariro Street, tel 07-376 0027, www.laketauponz

Thames
206 Pollen Street, tel 07-868 7284, www.thames-info.co.nz

Wanganui
101 Guyton Street, tel 06-349 0508, www.wanganui.com

Wellington
101 Wakefield Street, Civic Square, tel 04-802 4860,
www.wellingtonnz.com

Whakatane
Quay Street, tel 07-308 6058,
www.whakatane.com

Whangarei
Tarewa Park, 92 Otaika Road,
tel 09-438 1079,
www.whangareinz.org.nz

MAIN TOURISM NEW ZEALAND OFFICES OVERSEAS		
www.newzealand.com		
COUNTRY	**ADDRESS**	**TELEPHONE**
Australia	Suite 3, Level 24, 1 Albert Street, Sydney, NSW 2000	02-8220 9000
Canada	Suite 1200, 888 Dunsmuir Street, Vancouver BC V6C 3K4	604/634-2117
UK	New Zealand House, Haymarket, London SW1Y 4QT	020 7930 1662
US	Suite 2510, 221 East 41st Street, New York, NY 10017	212/661-7088
	Suite 300, 501 Santa Monica Boulevard, Los Angeles, CA 90401	310/395-7480

PLANNING

South Island

Arthur's Pass
Main Road, tel 03-318 9211,
www.doc.govt.nz

Christchurch
Domestic Terminal, Christchurch
Airport, tel 03-353 7774,
www.travelinfo.co.nzz

Dunedin
48 The Octagon, tel 03-474
3300, www.cityofdunedin.com

Franz Josef
Main Road, tel 03-752 0796,
www.doc.govt.nz

Greymouth
Corner of Mackay and Herbert
streets, tel 03-768 5101,
www.greydistrict.co.nz

Haast
Main Road, tel 03 750 0809,
www.doc.govt.nz

Hanmer Springs
42 Amuri Avenue, tel 03-315
7128, www.hurunui.com

Hokitika
The Carnegie Building, tel 03-
755 6166, www.hokitika.org

Invercargill
Queens Park, 108 Gala Street,
tel 03-214 6243,
www.invercargill.org.nz

Kaikoura
Westend, tel 03-319 5641,
www.kaikoura.co.nz

Mount Cook
Bowen Drive, tel 03-435 1186,
www.doc.govt.nz

Nelson
Corner of Trafalgar and Halifax
streets, tel 03-548 2304,
www.nelsonnz.com

Picton
The Foreshore, tel 03-520 3113,
www.destinationmarlborough.com

Stewart Island/Rakiura
Halfmoon Bay, tel 03-219
0009, www.doc.govt.nz

Te Anau
Lakefront Drive, tel 03-249 8900,
www.fiordland.org.nz

Wanaka
Ardmore Street, tel 03-443
1233, www.lakewanaka.co.nz

Westport
1 Brougham Street, tel 03-789
6658, www.westport.org.nz

USEFUL WEBSITES

VISITOR INFORMATION
www.newzealand.com
Official New Zealand visitor
information website

ACCOMMODATION
www.purenz.com
National farmstay information

www.stayyha.com
Youth Hostals Association website

www.vip.co.nz
Backpacker organisation

www.backpack.co.nz
Budget Backpacker Hostels Ltd
website

www.doc.govt.nz
Information on Department of
Conservation (DoC) campsites
and huts

RESTAURANTS
www.vegsoc.wellington.net.nz
National list of vegetarian
restaurants

www.time2dine.co.nz
Online guide and reservation
facility

MAJOR SIGHTS
www.doc.govt.nz
Department of Conservation
(DoC) site with information on
national parks and walks

www.nzmuseums.co.nz
Guide to museums nationwide

www.tepapa.govt.nz
Te Papa-Museum of New Zealand

www.rotoruanz.com
Rotorua website

www.skycity.co.nz
Sky Tower, Auckland

www.mtcooknz.com
Mount Cook/Aoraki National Park

www.abeltasmangreenrush.co.nz
Motueka visitor office website,
with information on Abel Tasman
National Park

HISTORY
www.enzed.com
Links to history, from the arrival
of Maori

www.nzhistory.net.nz
National history resource

www.teara.govt.nz
The encyclopedia of New
Zealand

ENTERTAINMENT
www.nz-events.co.nz
NZ AA's online guide to New
Zealand

www.ticketek.co.nz
Listings of shows and events and
ticketing information

WEATHER AND CLIMATE
www.metservice.co.nz
Weather information and analysis

www.nzcity.co.nz
Regional news and weather
satellite picture

CULTURE AND SOCIETY
www.gaytravelnet.com/nz
www.gaynewzealand.com
Information for gay and
lesbian visitors

www.tpk.govt.nz
Maori life and culture

www.wwoof.co.nz
Organic farm work in return for
bed and board

**NEWS AND GENERAL
INTEREST**
http://tvnz.co.nz
National site with regional
news links

www.stuff.co.nz
Website of the *Dominion Post*,
The Press and sister newspapers

www.nzherald.co.nz
New Zealand's largest daily
newspaper; national and
international news

**INFORMATION ON
MAORI LIFE**

Te Puni Kokiri
(Ministry of Maori Development)
143 Lambton Quay, PO Box 3943,
Wellington, tel 04-819 6000,
www.tpk.govt.nz

PLANNING

MEDIA

MAGAZINES

Several national New Zealand magazines are particularly worth a look for visitors: *The Listener*, covering national issues, politics and the arts; *North and South*, a magazine covering a wide range of traditional and contemporary issues; *New Zealand Geographic*, the quality New Zealand equivalent of the American icon; and two glossy outdoor activity publications, *New Zealand Wilderness* and *New Zealand Outside*. All are widely available at bookshops or Post Shops.

Most mainstream international magazines and newspapers can be found at specialist outlets such as Magazzino in Auckland.

Major Magazine Retailers:
Auckland
Magascene
33 Hurstmere Road, Takapuna
tel 09-489 5953

Magazzino
123 Ponsonby Road
tel 09-376 6933

Maggazino
Extreme on Broadway
Newmarket
tel 09-524 0604

Magazine City
Westfield Shoppingtown
West City, Henderson
tel 09-978 6752,
www.nzmagazineshop.co.nz

Christchurch
Canterbury Magazines
246 High Street
tel 03-377 0991

Hamilton
Accent on Magazines
113 Alexandra Street
tel 07-838 0269

Nelson
Page & Blackmore Booksellers
254 Trafalgar Street
tel 03-548 9992
www.pageandblackmore.co.nz

New Plymouth
Wadsworth's Bookcentre Ltd
Shop 9, Centre City, Gill Street
tel 06-759 4350

Wellington
City Cards and Mags
112 Lambton Quay
tel 04-472 7448

Magnetix, Midland Park
Lambton Quay
tel 04-472 2820

Village Newsagent
6/142 Willis Street
tel 04-385 1230

NEWSPAPERS
The principal daily newspapers (except Sundays) are the *New Zealand Herald* (Auckland and upper North Island), the *Dominion Post* (Wellington and lower North Island), *The Press* (Christchurch and central South Island) and the *Otago Daily Times* (South Island).

Smaller local newspapers can be accessed online from **www.stuff.co.nz** and include the *Waikato Times*, the *Manawatu Standard*, *The Daily News*, *The Nelson Mail*, *The Marlborough Express*, *The Timaru Herald* and *The Southland Times*.

TELEVISION
The four terrestrial TV channels have very little to offer except news and current affairs programmes. The rest of the output chiefly consists of UK or US soaps, reality and quiz shows.

All four channels carry advertising, which is heavily repetitive, sometimes featuring the same commercial every 10 minutes for several days. TV One shows news, sports and current affairs; Channel Two mainly drama and light entertainment; both are state-owned. TV3 and TV4 combine news and entertainment and are privately owned. Maori Television broadcasts bilingually in Maori and English, with 90 per cent New Zealand content.

Many New Zealanders (and most hotels and bed-and-breakfasts) subscribe to Sky TV.

There are local TV stations in some cities and towns.

RADIO
State-owned radio stations include Radio New Zealand Concert (classical music) and Radio New Zealand National (news, drama, light entertainment, talk shows). These broadcast on medium wave and VHF nationwide. There are also several stations broadcasting to Maori audiences. Some areas outside the large centres of population receive only medium wave.
● Tourist Information FM broadcasts 24 hours a day and features items on New Zealand's history and culture, news for visitors and commercials for places to stay and eat. It transmits in English (88.2MHz), Japanese (100.8MHz) and German (100.4MHz).

Newspapers are well read, and contain a high proportion of local news

BOOKS, MAPS AND FILMS

BACKGROUND READING

Despite its forbidding extent (some 570 pages) *The Penguin History of New Zealand*, by Michael King (2003), is a very readable account of New Zealand's history. King has contributed other history books, including *Nga Iwi O Te Motu: 1,000 Years of Maori History*. *The Oxford Illustrated History of New Zealand*, by Keith Sinclair (1997), does it with pictures.

There are various anthologies of Maori mythology available—the *Reed Book of Maori Mythology*, by AW Reed (2004) is an update of an old favourite.

Old New Zealand Houses 1800–1940, by Jeremy Salmond (1986) is a beautifully illustrated account of the country's vernacular architecture, from early Maori dwellings to gingerbread villas, which also acts as a fascinating record of social history.

Two natural history guides are particularly recommended to make the most of what you see: Geoff Moon's *Reed Field Guide to New Zealand Birds* (2000), and the Collins *Field Guide to New Zealand Wildlife*, by Rod Morris and Terence Linsey.

GUIDES AND MAPS

If you're planning a tramping (trekking) holiday, the Moirs Guides, published by the New Zealand Alpine Club, are recommended, as is *New Zealand's Great Walks*, by Pearl Hewson. Bruce Ringer's *New Zealand by Bike* is a useful guide for cyclists, while skiers will want to obtain a copy of the annual *Ski and Snowboard* guide, which is available free from Brown Bear Publications, PO Box 31–207, Christchurch, tel 03-388 5331, www.brownbear.co.nz.

The NZ AA produces a road atlas, and an extensive listing guide to accommodation, updated annually. Wises and Minimaps are the major city and provincial town map companies, producing a range of handbooks and foldout city maps. Visitor information centres also stock free leaflet maps.

NEW ZEALAND IN FICTION

New Zealand literature is flourishing, with a wealth of new talent writing across all genres. A selective cross-section is suggested in the panel here, and you can find out more about the authors and their works on www.bookcouncil.org.nz.

The genre which New Zealand authors have made their own is the short story. Katherine Mansfield started it in 1906, writing in London but drawing on her Wellington childhood (▷ 33)—and her short stories are still widely available. Other names to look for are Frank Sargeson, Maurice Shadbolt and Owen Marshall. Witi Ihimaera's collection of short stories, *Pounamu, Pounamu* (1972), was the first fiction to be published by a Maori—he came to wider world attention when his novel *The Whale Rider* (1987) was filmed.

English artist and writer Samuel Butler, who farmed in Canterbury around 1860, was one of the first to describe the landscape of the high country in his famous satire *Erewhon* (1872). A better picture of New Zealand appears in his letters to his father, published as *A First Year in Canterbury Settlement* (1863).

Novelists flourished in the second half of the 20th century—look for authors such as Janet Frame, Maurice Gee, Maurice Shadbolt, C.K. Stead, Alan Duff and Dame Ngaio Marsh—the country's best known writer of detective fiction.

James K. Baxter is New Zealand's most celebrated poet, but a wealth of other names includes Fleur Adcock and Alan Curnow.

FILMS

The movie scene has been dominated in recent years by the success of Peter Jackson's filming of the *Lord of the Rings* trilogy against a New Zealand backdrop. Check out the locations with Ian Brodie's comprehensive *The Lord of the Rings Location Guide* (2000), complete with GPS references. The 13-year-old actress at the heart of *Whale Rider,* Keisha Castle-Hughes, was another New Zealand star in the Oscars firmament of 2004.

Jackson's earlier film *Heavenly Creatures*, based on the story of two schoolgirl murderers in Christchurch in the 1950s, was a popular success. Jane Campion's *The Piano* (1993) was the award-winning tale of a mute immigrant. Lee Tamahori's *Once Were Warriors* (1995) is the shockingly violent and highly praised film of Alan Duff's novel about a Maori family struggling with poverty in inner-city Auckland.

PLANNING

SPEAKING 'KIWI'

English is the common language of New Zealand, and in its written form generally follows British rather than US spelling conventions. There is little difference in pronunciation from one part of the country to another, although you may detect a burr in the southern half of the South Island and other locations where localised settlement was particularly strong. New Zealand has developed its own slang words and phrases, a selection of which are listed below.

bach holiday cottage (pronounced 'batch', originates from a shortened form of 'bachelor', referring to a dwelling fit for a single man)
Beehive the main government building in Wellington
bludge scrounge, borrow
bush forest, native woodland
BYO a café or restaurant that allows you to take your own beer or wine

chook chicken
cocky farmer (usually 'cow cocky')

chilly-bin portable cooler box for a picnic
crib holiday cottage (South Island)
crook sick, ill
cuppa cup of tea

dag a character, or entertaining person
dairy general grocery store

good as gold fine, OK

handle beer glass with a handle

jandals flip-flops, thongs
judder bars speed bumps in the road

morning tea mid-morning tea or coffee break
mozzie mosquito

Pakeha person of European descent

smoko tea or coffee break
she'll be right that's OK
shout a round pay for a round of drinks

togs swimwear

wopwops the back of beyond
wowser killjoy

MAORI WORDS AND PHRASES

Maori words and phrases are used throughout New Zealand and the Maori language is generally encouraged and spoken with pride within the *whanau* and *iwi* (Maori family and tribes). It is wise to be aware of a few basic rules before arriving in the country. The easiest way to say Maori words is to pronounce each syllable phonetically. Perhaps the most important feature is the pronunciation of 'wh' as the English 'f'. For example, *whanau* is pronounced 'fha-now' and Whangarei 'Fhongarei'. Vowels are pronounced openly, as in Italian, and all words end in a vowel.

ana cave
Aotearoa New Zealand
ara path, road
ariki tribal leader
atua spiritual being
au rain
awa river, valley

haere mai welcome
haera ra farewell
hangi Maori feast
hau wind
harakeke flax plant, leaves
Hawaiiki ancestral Polynesian homeland
hapu sub-tribe/to be pregnant
he ao a land or a world
he tangata the people
hei tiki carved figure worn round the neck, usually shortened to tiki
hoe paddle
hongi traditional greeting (pressing noses)
huka spray, snow

iti small
iwi tribe, bone

kahu blue
kai eat
Kaikaiawaro a dolphin (also known as Pelorus Jack) who cruised the Marlborough Sounds and became a guardian to *iwi*
kaitiaki protector, caretaker
kainga village
kapa haka group of Maori performers
kia ora welcome
kaumatua elders
kawa protocols
kete basket
kohu mist, fog
kowhaiwhai rafter patterns

ma stream, white
mana integrity, prestige, control
manawhenua people with tribal affiliations with the area
manu bird

Maori ordinary people
Maoritanga Maoriness
marae sacred courtyard or plaza
maunga mountain
mauri life essence
moana lake, sea
moko tattoo
motu island, or anything isolated
muka flax fibre

namu sandfly
Ngati people of
nui big, plenty

o of, the place of
one sand, beach, mud

pa fortified village
Pakeha foreigner, white person, European
papa broad, flat
poi ball attached to flax string
pounamu sacred greenstone
puke hill
puna spring of water

rangatira tribal leader
rangi sky
roa long
roto lake

taiaha a fighting staff
tangata people/person
tangihanga death ritual
taonga treasure, prized object
(often passed down by
ancestors)
tapu sacred, out of bounds

te the
Te Ika-a-Maui North Island
tiki see hei tiki
tipuna ancestor
tukutuku wall panels

utu cost, retribution

wahakatauki proverb or saying
wai water
waiata song, flute music
wairua soul

waka canoe
whakairo carvings
whakapapa origins or
genealogy
whanau extended family/to
give birth
whanga bay, inlet
whare house
whare runanga meeting
house
whenua land
whero red

GLOSSARY FOR US VISITORS

A&E	emergency room (hospital department)	**lorry**	truck
anticlockwise	counterclockwise	**licensed**	a café or restaurant that has a license to serve alcohol
aubergine	eggplant	**lift**	elevator
bill	check (at restaurant)	**nappy**	diaper
biscuit	cookie	**note**	bill (when referring to money)
bonnet	hood (car)		
boot	trunk (car)	**pants**	underpants (men's)
busker	street musician	**pavement**	sidewalk
		petrol	gas
caravan	house trailer or RV	**plaster**	Band-Aid or bandage
car park	parking lot	**post**	mail
carriage	car (on a train)	**pudding**	dessert
chemist	pharmacy	**purse**	change purse
chips	french fries	**pushchair**	stroller
coach	long-distance bus		
corridor	hall	**return ticket**	roundtrip ticket
courgette	zucchini	**rocket**	arugula
crèche	day care	**roundabout**	traffic circle or rotary
dual carriageway	two-lane highway	**self-catering**	accommodation including a kitchen
en suite	a bedroom with its own private bathroom; may also just refer to the bathroom	**single ticket**	one-way ticket
		stalls	(in theatre) orchestra seats
		subway	underpass
		surgery	doctor's office
football	Rugby (sometimes soccer)	**tailback**	stalled line of traffic
full board	a hotel tariff that includes all meals	**takeaway**	takeout
		taxi rank	taxi stand
		ten-pin bowling	bowling
garden	yard (residential)	**T-junction**	an intersection where one road meets another at right angles (making a T shape)
GP	doctor		
half board	hotel tariff that includes breakfast and either lunch or dinner		
		toilets	restrooms
handbag	purse	**torch**	flashlight
high street	main street	**trolley**	cart
hire	rent	**trousers**	pants
jelly	Jello™	**way out**	exit
junction	intersection		
layby	rest stop; *also* payment of a deposit to secure an article		
level crossing	grade crossing		
loo	rest room		

TIMELINE

AD 800 Polynesian navigator Kupe lands at Hokianga, in Northland.

1000 Polynesians move southeast to Pacific Islands from Asia.

1300 Polynesian colonies established on North Island and some tribes are clearing bush and hunting in the South Island.

1642 Dutch explorer Abel Tasman, commissioned by East India Company, sights the land he calls Staten Landt, later renamed Nieuw Zeeland.

1769 British explorer Captain James Cook makes the first of three voyages to New Zealand on the *Endeavour*, claiming the country for King George III.

1773 Cook lands at Dusky Cove on the *Resolution* and returns to Ship Cove via the South Island's west coast.

1776 Cook returns to Ship Cove and the Sounds before sailing to Hawaii, where he is killed.

1791 The *William and Ann*, the first whaling vessel, anchors at Doubtless Bay, heralding a period of intensive whaling, sealing and timber- and flax-trading.

1814 British missionary Samuel Marsden establishes an Anglican mission station in the Bay of Islands.

1820–35 Maori Musket Wars: fierce inter-tribal warfare.

1833 Official British Resident James Busby arrives in Waitangi and encourages adoption of United Tribes flag.

1835 Declaration of Independence by United Tribes of New Zealand signed by 34 northern chiefs.

1839 Captain William Hobson appointed Lieutenant Governor with remit to transfer sovereignty of land from Maori Chiefs to British Crown.

1840 Treaty of Waitangi signed in the Bay of Islands, proclaiming British sovereignty. French settlers land at Akaroa.

1844 Chief Hone Heke cuts down British flagpole and instigates two-year War of the North.

1848 Dunedin founded as a Scottish Presbyterian colony.

1850 Christchurch founded as an Anglican colony.

1852 Constitution Act creates General Assembly and six provinces. Discovery of gold in the Coromandel.

1855 Earthquake changes the face of Wellington.

1858 Te Wherowhero installed as first Maori king, taking the name Potatau I.

1860s Gold boom attracts thousands of prospectors.

1865 Wellington becomes capital of New Zealand. Native Lands Act investigates Maori land ownership and distributes land titles.

1867 First Maori Members of Parliament elected.

1882 First refrigerator ship sails to London with a cargo of frozen lamb, heralding a new economic era.

1893 New Zealand is the first country in the world to give women the vote.

1907 New Zealand constituted as a British Dominion.

1914–18 New Zealand suffers the greatest casualties per head of population of any combat nation in World War I.

1931 Earthquake destroys Napier.

1938 Government lays basis of welfare state.

1939–45 New Zealand fights on the Allied side in World War II.

1945 New Zealand is one of the founding member states of the United Nations.

1947 New Zealand is declared an independent nation.

1952 Population tops 2 million.

1953 New Zealander Edmund Hillary conquers Mount Everest.

1966 International airport opens at Auckland.

1973 Preferential trade with Britain ends when the UK joins the Common Market, and a new economic era starts.

1980s Anti-nuclear policy is adopted. Deregulation of economy.

1985 Greenpeace vessel *Rainbow Warrior* is bombed by French Secret Service in Auckland harbour.

1987 Maori Language Act gives Maori language official status. The All Blacks win the first Rugby World Cup title.

1988 Unemployment exceeds 100,000.

1990 Dame Catherine Tizard becomes the first woman Governor-General.

1993 Referendum votes in favour of mixed-member proportional representation, giving each elector two votes and Maori retaining the choice of voting in a general or a Maori electorate.

1995 Peter Blake's *Black Magic* crew wins the hugely prestigious America's Cup, heralding a yachting revival based in Auckland.

1997 Jenny Shipley of the National Party becomes New Zealand's first woman prime minister.

1999 Peter Jackson, from Wellington, begins filming *The Lord of the Rings* trilogy by J. R. R. Tolkien, mainly around Queenstown, Otago.

2004 *The Return of the King*, last in the *Rings* trilogy, scoops 11 Oscars at the Academy Awards.

2008 New Zealand voters go to the polls once again to elect the government that will take them through the next three years.

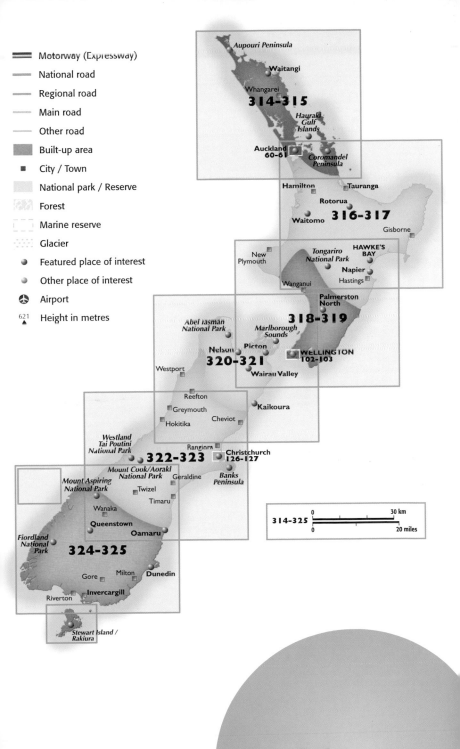

Motorway (Expressway)

National road

Regional road

Main road

Other road

Built-up area

■ City / Town

National park / Reserve

Forest

Marine reserve

Glacier

● Featured place of interest

● Other place of interest

✈ Airport

621 ▲ Height in metres

Aupouri Peninsula

Waitangi

Whangarei
314–315

Hauraki
Gulf
Islands

Auckland
60–61

Coromandel
Peninsula

Hamilton   Tauranga

Rotorua
316–317
Waitomo

Gisborne

New
Plymouth

Tongariro
National Park   HAWKE'S
BAY

Napier
Wanganui   Hastings

Palmerston
North
318–319

Abel Tasman
National Park   Marlborough
Sounds
Nelson   Picton
320–321   WELLINGTON
102–103
Westport
Wairau Valley

Reefton

Greymouth
Kaikoura
Hokitika   Cheviot

Westland
Tai Poutini   Rangiora
National Park   Christchurch
322–323   126–127
Mount Cook/Aoraki
National Park   Geraldine   Banks
Mount Aspiring   Peninsula
National Park   Twizel
Wanaka   Timaru

Queenstown
Oamaru
Fiordland
National
Park   **324–325**

Gore   Milton   Dunedin

Riverton   Invercargill

Stewart Island /
Rakiura

314–325 | 0   30 km |
| 0   20 miles |

Maps

I

2

3

4

5

of Islands
time and
oric Park

pe Brett

iri Bay

Whangaruru
Harbour
Helena Bay
ananaki
Mohitara Point
Matapouri
Tutukaka
gunguru
Ngunguru
Bay
Pataua North
arua
Bay
Awarua Rock
ngarei
bour
Ocean Beach
Bream Head
Marsden
Bay
Ruakaka
Hen and Chickens
Islands
Bream Bay
Waipu
Bream Tail

Brynderwyn
Mangawhai
Kaiwaka
Te Arai
Port
Albert
Wellsford
iri
Leigh
Matakana
Warkworth
oa

Woodcocks
Araparera
Puhoi
Tahekeroa
Orewa
Kaukapakapa
arepapa
Dairy Flat
mauku
Albany
Kumeu
iwai
each
Swanson
Henga
Waiatarua
iha
akere Ranges
Regional Park
Cornwallis
hatipu
Awhitu

Jellicoe Channel
Little
Barrier
Island

Goat Island
Goat Island Marine Reserve
Cape Rodney
Omaha Bay
Takatu Point

Kawau
Island

Hauraki Gulf
Marine Park

Tiritiri Matangi
Island
Whangaparaoa

Whangaparaoa
Bay
108

Motutapu
Island
Rakino
Island

Haraki Gulf
Islands

Cradock Channel
Motairehe
Port Fitzroy
Whangaparapara
Claris

Aiguilles Island
Rakitu Island
Whakatautuna Point
Awana Bay

Great Barrier
Island

Tryphena
Cape Barrier

Colville
Channel

Cape
Colville
Port
Jackson
Port Charles
Coromandel
Forest Park
Waiaro
375
Colville
Waikawa
Waikawau Bay

Great Mercury
Island
Red Mercury
Island

The Aldermen
Islands

Hauraki Gulf
Papaaroha
Coromandel
Coromandel
Harbour
Coromandel
Peninsula
Kereta
Coroglen
725
New Churns
Beach

Te Rerenga
Kuaotunu
Tokarahu
Point

Mercury Bay
Whitianga
Cooks
Beach
Hot Water Beach
Te Ororoa Point
Pauanui

Slipper Island

AUCKLAND
Rangitoto
Island
Oneroa
Waiheke
Island
220
Rotoroa
Island
Maraetai
Ponui
Island
Whitford
Clevedon
Kawakawa
Bay
Papakura
Hunua
477

Orere Point
Tapu

Firth of

Hikuai
Coromandel
Forest Park

Clarks Beach
Te Hihi
Runciman
Kaiaua
Wharekawa Harbour
Opoutere
Bombay
Miranda
Thames
Wahakaruru
Kopu
664

Whangamata Harbour
Whangamata
Pukekohe
Tuakau
Pokeno
Mangatawhiri
Maramarua
2
25
Ngatea
Waiuku
Otaua
Meremere
Okaeria
Omahu
Coromandel
Forest Park
Whiritoa
Mataora Bay

Mayor Island

Tauranganui
Pukekawa
Te Kauwhata
Kaihere
390
Netherton
Paeroa
Waihi

J **Waikato**
Wairamarama
Glen Murray
Lake
Waikato
Lake
K
K
Piako
Waihou
Range
Waihi Beach

L
315

316

Tasman Sea

Turakina

Koitiata
Marton
Santoft
Bulls
Sanson

Tangimoana
9
Glen Oroua
Ka
Himatangi Beach
Bainesse
Foxton

Hokio Beach
Levin
Manakau
Mo

Kapiti Island
Nature Reserve
and Marine Reserve
Te Horo
Otaki
Otaki
Tararua
Forest Park
Kapiti Island
364
Waikanae
Otaki
Forks
10
Carring
924
Cloustonville
Carte

Paraparaumu

Paekakariki
Plimmerton
Pakuratahi
Greytown
Mana Island
Porirua
Upper Hutt
2
Tawa
Featherston
53

318

Cape Jackson
*Marlborough
Sounds*

Stephens
Island
Cape Stephens
Patuki
D'Urville Island
Rangitoto Islands
Haukawakawa
French Pass
Admiralty Bay
Sauvage Point
*Forsyth
Island*

Tasman Bay

Cape Soucis
Okiwi Bay
*Delaware
Bay*
Tennyson
Inlet
1203
Mount
Stokes
Endeavour
Inlet
Pepin Island
Pelorus Sound
Manaroa
Pakapuaka
Rai Valley
Kenepuru Head
*Cape
Koamaru*
Te Rewarewa Point
Arapawa Island
Lower Hutt
Wainuiomata
Lake
Wairarapa
Martinborough
Tuhitarata

Nelson
Pelorus
Bridge
Havelock
Queen Charlotte Sound
Picton
Perano Head
*Oharui
Bay*
Makara
*Somes/
Matiu Island*
Ruakokoputuna
*Haurangi
Forest
Park*

chmond
1330
Okaramio
Tuamarina
Robertson Point
WELLINGTON
Orongorongo
Lake
Ferry
Aorangi Ridges

t Richmond
orest Park
Te Rou
Renwick
Blenheim
Cloudy Bay
Cook Strait
*Turakirae
Head*
*Palliser
Bay*
**Putangirua
Pinnacles**
*Haurangi
Forest
Park*
Te

Wairau Valley
Hillersden
Seddon
Lake
Grassmere
Clifford Bay
Te Humenga Pt
Ngawihi
Cape Palliser
11
63
Wairau
Altimarloch
Cape Campbell

1579
Mount Horrible
Peggioh
Ward

09
Gladstone
Wharanui

Langridge
Awatere
2621
Mitre Peak
Kekerengu

Molesworth
Inland Kaikoura Range
Clarence
Clarence
12

2610
Manakau
Rakautara

Seaward
Kaikoura
Range
Kowhai
Kaikoura
Kaikoura Peninsula

wk Hills
Oaro

ehurst
Claverley
594
Parnassus
amington
13
Cheviot

Hurunui Mouth

ACKNOWLEDGMENTS

Abbreviations for the picture credits are as follows:
AA = AA World Travel Library, **t** (top), **b** (bottom), **c** (centre), **l** (left), **r** (right), **bg** (background)

UNDERSTANDING NEW ZEALAND

4 New Zealand Tourist Board; **5cl** Destination Lake Taupo/Marcel Tromp; **5c, 5cr, 5b** AA/P Kenward; **6tl** Destination Lake Taupo/Marcel Tromp; **6tr, 6bl, 6bc, 7** AA/P Kenward; **6ctl, 6cbl, 6br** AA/M Langford; **8tl, 8ctr, 8c, 8cb, 8b, 9tctl, 9tcl** AA/P Kenward; **8tr** Collingwood Homestead Lodge; **8tctr** SkyCity Auckland; **9tl** AA/A Belcher; **9tr** Hilton Hotel Auckland; **9bcl** International Antarctic Centre; **9bcbl** Te Papa, Wellington; **9b** Te Papa, Wellington; **10l, 10trt, 10cbr** AA/P Kenward; **10trbg, 10ctr** AA/M Langford; **10cr** AA/M Langford; **10br** Destination Lake Taupo

LIVING NEW ZEALAND

11 AA/M Langford; **12/13bg, 13tl, 13clt** AA/A Belcher; **12tl** Photo by Simon Runting/Rex Features; **12tr, 12cl, 12b, 13tr** AA/M Langford; **12cr** Mountain Buggy; **13tc** Office of the Governor General of New Zealand; **13clb** Wingnut Productions; **13c** Office of the Prime Minister of New Zealand; **13cr** Oxford University Press; **14/15bg** AA/A Belcher; **14tl** Speight's Coast to Coast Race; **14tr, 15tl, 15cl** AA/A Reisinger & V Meduna; **14cl** Speight's Coast to Coast Race; **14clt, 14/15c, 15tr** AA/M Langford; **14b** © Simon Baker/Reuters/Corbis; **15lcl, 15cr** AA/P Kenward; **15rcr** Burton Silver/Golf Cross; **16/17bg, 16tl, 16tc, 17tl** AA/A Belcher; **16tr, 16cr, 16cb, 16b, 17tr, 17cr** AA/M Langford; **16cl** New Zealand Film Commission/The Kobal Collection; **17cl** Brian Rasic/Rex Features; **17c** World of WearableArt; **18/19bg, 18tr** AA/P Kenward; **18tl, 18tc, 18c, 18b, 19tl, 19cl, 19c, 19cr** AA/M Langford; **19tr** AA/A Belcher; **20/21bg, 20tr, 20c, 20r, 21r, 21ii, 21iii** AA/M Langford; **20tl, 20cl, 21tc, 21i** AA/A Belcher; **20b, 21tl, 21iv** AA/P Kenward; **21tr** Latitude Nelson; **21cl** New Zealand Tourist Board; **21c** Kiwi Experience; **22bg** AA/P Kenward; **22tl, 22cl** AA/A Belcher; **22tr** Charles Royal/Kinaki Wild Herbs; **22c** AA/A Belcher; **22cr** Charles Royal/Kinaki Wild Herbs

THE STORY OF NEW ZEALAND

23 AA; **24/25bg, 24bl** AA/P Kenward; **24c** AA/M Langford; **24/25b** AA; **25c** © The Natural History Museum, London; **25cb** AA; **25bc** Mary Evans Picture Library; **25br** AA; **26/27bg** AA; **26cl** AA; **26cr** AA; **26cb** AA; **26bl** National Library of Australia, Canberra, Australia/Bridgeman Art Library; **26bc** AA/M Langford; **26/27b** The Signing of the Treaty of Waitangi, February 6th 1840. 1938, by Marcus King (library reference G-821-2)/Alexander Turnbull Library, Wellington, New Zealand/Bridgeman Art Library; **27c** AA; **27cr** AA; **27b** © The Natural History Museum, London; **28/29bg, 28cl** AA/P Kenward; **28c** Illustrated London News Picture Library; **28cr** AA; **28bl** Mary Evans Picture Library; **28/29** © Corbis; **29cl** Illustrated London News Picture Library; **29cr** AA/A Belcher; **29b** Mary Evans Picture Library; **30/31bg, 31b** AA/P Kenward; **30c** AA; **30bl** National Library of Australia, Canberra, Australia/Bridgeman Art Library; **30bc** AA; **30/31** Mary Evans Picture Library; **31cl, 31cb** AA/M Langford; **31cr** Mary Evans Picture Library; **32/33bg, 33cl, 33br** AA/P Kenward; **32c** Private Collection, Barbara Singer/Bridgeman Art Library. *We have been unable to trace the copyright holder of 'Together' by English School and would be grateful to receive any information as to their identity.* **32cr** Getty Images; **32bl** Illustrated London News Picture Library; **32/33b** Getty Images; **33c** Getty Images; **33bl** AA/M Langford; **34/35bg, 35cl** AA/P Kenward; **34c** ©Amos Nachoum/Corbis; **34bcl** Getty Images;

34bl © Kevin Fleming/Corbis; **34/35** © Neil Rabinowitz/Corbis; **35cr** AA/P Aithie; **35bl** Rex Features; **35br** Getty Images; **35bg** AA/M Langford; **36c** Office of the Governor General of New Zealand; **36bl** © Guido Cantini/ACM; **36br** © Paul Hanna/Reuters/Corbis

ON THE MOVE

37 AA/M Langford; **38t** Digital Vision; **38b** AA/A Belcher; **39t** Digital Vision; **39b** AA/P Kenward; **39c** Auckland International Airport; **40t** Digital Vision; **40c** Air New Zealand; **40b** Britz New Zealand; **41** Britz New Zealand; **42t** Christchurch Tram; **42c** AA/M Langford; **43t** Christchurch Tram; **43c** Christchurch Tram; **44t** Digital Vision; **44c, 45c** AA/M Langford; **45t** Digital Vision; **46t** Digital Vision; **46c, 46b, 47cl, 47c, 47bcl** AA/M Langford; **47t** Digital Vision; **47cr** AA/P Kenward; **47bcr** AA/N Hanna; **48t** Digital Vision; **48c** AA/P Kenward; **48b, 49c,** AA/M Langford; **49b** Magic Travellers Network; **49t** Digital Vision; **50t** Digital Vision; **50c, 50b** AA/M Langford; **51** Digital Vision; **52t, 53t, 53b** AA/A Belcher; **52c** Sounds Air New Zealand; **52b** AA/A Belcher; **53c** AA/M Langford; **54t** AA/N Sumner; **54c** AA/C Jones

THE SIGHTS

55 AA/P Kenward; **Sights background picture** AA/M Langford; **57t** Destination Northland (courtesy of Fullers BOI); **57cr** Destination Northland; **58c** SkyCity Auckland; **58c** AA/A Belcher; **59tr** SkyCity Auckland; **59br** AA/P Kenward; **62cl, 62c, 63cr** AA/A Belcher; **62cr** AA/M Langford; **63tl** SkyCity Auckland; **64tl** AA/P Kenward; **64/65cr, 64bl, 65br** AA/M Langford; **65cr** SkyCity Auckland; **66tc, 66cl, 66c, 66cr, 66bl, 67cl, 67cr** AA/M Langford; **68tl, 68b, 69tl** AA/A Belcher; **68tc** Destination Northland; **68tr** Destination Northland; **69tr** AA/P Kenward; **70t, 70cl, 70cr, 71c** AA/M Langford; **70c, 70b** AA/A Belcher; **71tr** AA/P Kenward; **72tl** Destination Northland; **72tr** Destination Northland; **73tl, 73b** AA/P Kenward; **73tr** AA/M Langford; **74t** AA/A Belcher; **74cl** AA/P Kenward; **75tl, 75tr** AA/M Langford; **77tl, 77tr** AA/M Langford; **78tl, 78tc, 78tr, 78br, 79cr** AA/M Langford; **79t** Hawkes Bay Tourism; **80tl, 80tr, 80b** AA/P Kenward; **81tl, 81tc, 81tr** AA/M Langford; **82t, 83cl** AA/P Kenward; **82cl, 82c, 82c, 82cr, 82b, 83cr, 83b** AA/M Langford; **84t, 84cl, 84cr** AA/A Belcher; **84c, 85t, 85cr** AA/M Langford; **86/87t, 87cr, 87br** AA/M Langford; **86cl** AA/A Belcher; **88t** AA/P Kenward; **88cl** AA/A Belcher; **88cr** Destination Lake Taupo; **88b** Destination Lake Taupo/Marcel Tromp; **89cl** AA/M Langford; **89c** Destination Lake Taupo; **89cr** Destination Lake Taupo; **90t, 90cr, 91bl** AA/M Langford; **90cl** AA; **90c** Waitomo Caves (Tourism Holdings Limited); **91br** Jean-Paul Ferrero/Auscape; **92tl** AA/A Belcher; **92c** AA/A Reisinger & V Meduna; **92tr** AA/M Langford; **94tl** Martinborough Wine Centre; **94tr** Steam Inc; **95tl** AA/M Langford; **95tr** Pukaha Mount Bruce National Wildlife Centre; **95b** Southward Car Museum; **96/97** Te Papa, Wellington; **96c** Te Papa, Wellington; **98cl** Te Papa, Wellington; **98c** Te Papa, Wellington; **98b** Te Papa, Wellington; **98/99t** Te Papa, Wellington; **98/99b** Worldwide Picture Library/Alamy; **99cl** Te Papa, Wellington; **100** AA/P Kenward; **101t, 101cl, 101c, 101cr** AA/A Belcher; **104cl** AA/P Kenward; **104c, 104cr** AA/A Belcher; **105** AA/M Langford; **106tl** Wairarapa Tourism; **106tr** AA/P Kenward; **106b** Paua Shell Factory, Carterton; **108, 109t, 109cl, 109c, 109cr, 109b** AA/M Langford; **110cr, 111tl, 111c** AA/M Langford; **110br** AA/P Kenward; **111tr** Nelson Tourism;

111b Nelson Tourism; 112tl, 112b AA/M Langford; 112tr, 113t, 113cr AA/P Kenward; 114t, 114lcl, 114cl, 114cr, 114rcr, 114b, 115t, 115b AA/M Langford; 116t, 116cl, 117tr AA/M Langford; 117tl Nelson Tourism; 118tl, 118tr, 118b AA/M Langford; 119t Centrestage New Zealand; 119cr Centrestage New Zealand; 121tl, 121tr AA/A Belcher; 122t, 122cl, 122b AA/A Belcher; 123tl AA/P Kenward; 123tr, 123c AA/M Langford; 124t AA/M Birkitt; 124cl, 124c, 124cr, 124b, 125 AA/M Langford; 128cl, 128c, 128cr, 129t, 129b AA/M Langford; 130tl World Pictures; 130tr, 130b AA/P Kenward; 131t, 131tr, 131b AA/M Langford; 132tl, 132tr, 133tr, 133b AA/M Langford; 133tl AA/P Kenward; 134t, 134c, 134cr, 134b, 135 AA/A Belcher; 134cl AA/M Langford; 137tl AA/P Kenward; 137tc, 137tr, 137b AA/M Langford; 138t, 138cl, 138c, 138cr, 138b, 139 AA/A Belcher; 140, 141t, 141c AA/A Belcher; 141cl AA; 141cr AA/P Kenward; 142cl AA/A Belcher; 142c, 142cr, 142b, 143 AA/P Kenward; 144tl, 144tr AA/P Kenward; 144b, 145tl AA/M Langford; 145tr Nature Photographers; 146 AA/P Kenward; 147tl AA/A Reisinger & V Meduna; 147tr AA/M Langford; 147c Royal Albatross Centre; 148t, 148c, 149c AA/P Kenward; 148cl, 148cr AA/A Belcher; 148b AJ Hackett Bungy; 149t AJ Hackett Bungy; 150t, 150c AA/M Langford

WHAT TO DO

151 AA/M Langford; 152, 153 AA/M Langford, 154t, 155t AA/M Langford; 154cl AA/C Coe; 154cr AA/P Kenward; 155c Digital Vision; 155b AA/K Paterson; 156t, 157t, 157cl, 157cr AA/M Langford, 156c Speight's Coast to Coast Race; 158t, 158cr, 159t AA/M Langford; 158cl AA/A Reisinger & V Meduna; 159c Destination Lake Taupo; 160t, 161t, 161c AA/M Langford; 160cl Destination Lake Taupo/Marcel Tromp; 160cr AA/A Reisinger & V Meduna; 162t, 162c, 163 AA/M Langford; 164t Matana Confections; 164c AA/M Langford; 165t Matana Confections; 165c AA/A Belcher; 166t Matana Confections; 166c Auckland Fine Wine Tours; 167t Matana Confections; 167c AJ Hackett Bungy; 168t Matana Confections; 168c Matana Confections; 169t Matana Confections; 169c Pakiri Beach Horse Riding; 170t Matana Confections; 170c Kiwi Dundee Adventures; 171t Matana Confections; 171c Auckland Festival; 172t, 173t AA/A Belcher; 172c Destination Lake Taupo; 173c Hamilton Gardens; 174t, 175t AA/A Belcher; 174c Splash Planet; 175c AA/P Kenward; 176t, 177t, 177c AA/A Belcher; 176c Canoe Safari; 178t, 179 AA/A Belcher; 178c Kiwi360; 180t, 181t AA/C Sawyer; 180c Centrestage New Zealand; 181c Martinborough Wine Centre; 182t, 183t AA/C Sawyer; 182c Olivo; 183c Efil Doog Garden of Art; 184t, 185t AA/C Sawyer; 184c Sommerfields; 185c Embassy Theatre; 186t, 187 AA/C Sawyer; 186c Seal Coast Safari; 188t, 189t AA/P Kenward; 188c Latitude Nelson; 189c Marlborough Farmer's Markets; 190t, 191t AA/P Kenward; 190c Maori Tours; 191c Pomeroys Coffee and Tea Company; 192t, 193t AA/P Kenward; 192c Happy Valley Adventures; 193c Höglund Art Glass; 194 AA/P Kenward; 195t Addington Raceway; 195c Addington Raceway; 196t Addington Raceway; 196c Naturally Jade; 197t Addington Raceway; 197c Untouched World; 198t Addington Raceway; 198c Addington Raceway; 199t Addington Raceway; 199c AA/A Belcher; 200t Addington Raceway; 200c Barker's Berry Barn; 201t Addington Raceway; 201c Alpine Horse Safaris; 202t Addington Raceway; 202c AA/M Langford; 203 Addington Raceway; 204t Catlins Wildlife Trackers; 204c AA/M Langford; 205t Catlins Wildlife Trackers; 205c Catlins Wildlife Trackers; 206t Catlins Wildlife Trackers; 206c Speight's Brewery; 207t Catlins Wildlife Trackers; 207c Photodisc; 208t Catlins Wildlife Trackers; 208c Kingston Flyer; 209t Catlins Wildlife Trackers; 209c Wine Deli; 210t Catlins Wildlife Trackers; 210c Fly by Wire; 211t Catlins Wildlife Trackers; 211c Puzzling World; 212 Catlins Wildlife Trackers

OUT AND ABOUT

213 Destination Lake Taupo; 215 AA/M Langford; 216t, 216c, 216b, 217b AA/M Langford; 217c AA/P Kenward; 219t AA/P Kenward; 219ct, 219b AA/M Langford; 220, 221c AA/M Langford; 221t, 221b AA/P Kenward; 223tl, 223tr, 223b AA/M Langford; 224, 225tr, 225c, 225b AA/M Langford; 225tl AA/P Kenward; 227tl Destination Lake Taupo; 227tr Destination Lake Taupo; 227b Destination Lake Taupo; 228b AA/M Langford; 229t AA/P Kenward; 229b Waitomo Caves (Tourism Holdings Limited); 230, 231b AA/M Langford; 231t Latitude Nelson; 231c Apex News and Pictures Agency/Alamy; 232, 233tl, 233tr, 233ct, 233b AA/M Langford; 233cb AA/P Kenward; 234 Kaikoura Information and Tourism Inc.; 235tc D Parer & E Parer-Cook/Auscape; 235tr Kaikoura Information and Tourism Inc.; 235cl Ann Stonehouse; 235cr, 235bl AA/P Kenward; 235br Kaikoura Information and Tourism Inc.; 236 AA/A Belcher; 237t, 237c, 237b AA/M Langford; 238 AA/P Kenward; 239tl AA/M Langford; 239tr, 239c, 239bl, 239br AA/A Belcher; 240, 241t, 241ct, 241cb, 241b AA/M Langford; 242, 243c AA/M Langford; 243t, 243b AA/P Kenward; 244 AA/M Langford; 245t AA/P Kenward; 245c Royal Albatross Centre; 245b AA/A Belcher; 246 AA/A Reisinger & V Meduna

EATING AND STAYING

247 AA/M Langford ; 248cl, 248cr, 249 AA/M Langford; 248c Matana Confections, 250cl Destination Lake Taupo; 250c Charles Royal/Kinaki Wild Herbs; 250cr AA/A Belcher; 250b, 251cl, 251c, 251cr AA/M Langford; 251b Destination Lake Taupo; 252c, 252cr, 253 AA/M Langford; 255 AA/M Langford; 257bl, 257bc, 257br AA/M Langford; 259c, 259cr, 259bl, 259br AA/M Langford; 260c, 260cr, 260br, 261 AA/M Langford; 262t, 263bl, 263bc, 263br AA/M Langford; 263b Mussel Inn; 264, 265cl, 265cr AA/M Langford; 266tl, 266bl, 266br, 267t, 267b AA/M Langford; 268c Gantleys; 268cr AA/M Langford; 270cl, 270cr AA/C Sawyer; 270c AA/M Langford; 273c, 273bl, 273br AA/M Langford; 273cr Hilton Hotel Auckland; 274 AA/M Langford; 275 Villa Toscana; 276cl Maungatautari Lodge; 276cr, 276b, 277 AA/M Langford; 278tl, 278b AA/M Langford; 279 Wharekauhau Country Estate; 200tr, 200bl, 201tl, 201r AA/M Langford; 282 AA/M Langford; 283 Fyffe Country Lodge; 284ct, 284c, 284b, 285t AA/M Langford; 286tl, 286tc, 286cl, AA/M Langford; 288t, 288bl, 289tl AA/M Langford; 288bc Corstorphine House Private Hotel; 289tr Larnach Lodge; 290c AA/M Langford; 290tr Fiordland Lodge; 290b Queenstown House

PLANNING

291 AA/M Langford; 292 Destination Lake Taupo/Craig Wilson; 293 Destination Lake Taupo; 294 AA/M Langford; 295t AA/P Kenward; 295b AA/A Belcher; 296t, 297b AA/M Langford; 296b courtesy of RBNZ; 297t AA/A Belcher; 298b AA/M Langford; 299bl AA/P Kenward; 299tr AA/C Sawyer; 300ct AA/A Belcher; 300b AA/M Langford; 301 AA/P Kenward; 302, 303c AA/A Belcher; 303b AA/P Kenward; 304 AA/P Kenward; 306 AA/M Langford

Project editor
Ann F Stonehouse

Interior design
Kate Harling

Picture research
Vivien Little

Cover design
Tigist Getachew

Internal repro work
Susan Crowhurst, Ian Little, Michael Moody

Production
Helen Brown, Lyn Kirby

Mapping
Maps produced by the Cartography Department of AA Publishing

Main contributors
Mavis Airey, Jane Bellerby, Darroch Donald, Kathryn Fitzpatrick, Michael Mellor

Copy editors
Rebecca Snelling, Nia Williams

Updater
Michael Mellor

Revision management
Bookwork Creative Associates Ltd

See It New Zealand
ISBN 978-1-4000-1847-5
Second Edition

Color separation by Keenes
Printed and bound by Leo, China
10 9 8 7 6 5 4 3 2 1

A03163
Maps in this title produced from map data:
© New Holland Publishing (South Africa) (PTY) Limited 2007
and © Footprint Handbooks Limited 2004

Administrative regions map © Crown copyright, Government of New Zealand
Relief map images supplied by Mountain High Maps® Copyright © 1993 Digital Wisdom, Inc
Weather chart statistics supplied by Weatherbase © Copyright 2004 Canty and Associates, LLC
Communicarta assistance with time chart gratefully acknowledged

Important note: Time inevitably brings changes, so always confirm prices, travel facts,
and other perishable information when it matters. Although Fodor's cannot accept
responsibility for errors, you can use this guide in the confidence that we have taken
every care to ensure its accuracy.

Fodor's Key to the Guides

AMERICA'S **GUIDEBOOK LEADER** PUBLISHES GUIDES FOR **EVERY KIND OF TRAVELER**. CHECK OUT OUR MANY SERIES AND FIND YOUR **PERFECT MATCH**.

GOLD GUIDES
Built for today's travelers with unique graphics and maps for easy planning and advice on quintessential local experiences, along with Fodor's Choice rated hotels, restaurants, and sights to guarantee an exceptional vacation.

EXPLORING GUIDES
Splendid color photography paired with exquisitely written articles on history, culture, art, and architecture; suggested walks and excursions; and full-color maps allow you to experience a destination like a well-informed local.

COMPASS AMERICAN GUIDES
Long-time resident writers and photographers reveal the culture and character of American cities, states, and regions through intelligently written essays, literary excerpts, and stunning color imagery.

AROUND THE CITY WITH KIDS
68 great ideas for family fun in and around the city, hand-picked by resident parents, with age-appropriate ratings, entertaining trivia, and nearby kid-friendly snack spots.

SEE IT GUIDES
Colorful and practical, these illustrated guides feature smart writing on history and culture, rich photography, *and* practical travel information. Complete dining and restaurant reviews, exact admission fees, kid-friendly ratings, and everything from sightseeing and shopping, to nightlife, performing arts, and outdoor activities.

25 BEST
Compact city guides of must-see sights and the best dining, shopping, and activities; with a detailed, full-size street map conveniently built-in so you can confidently navigate the city.

FLASHMAPS
Easy-to-follow maps perfect for residents or visitors who want to quickly locate restaurants, shops, museums, movie theaters, subway and bus routes, and more.

LANGUAGES FOR TRAVELERS
All the words and phrases you need for greeting locals, dining out, and getting around in a handy phrasebook along with two CDs for pronunciation practice.

Available at bookstores everywhere.
For a complete list of more than 300 guidebooks,
visit **Fodors.com/shop**.